PENGUIN BOOKS

THE MARGERY ALLINGHAM OMNIBUS

Margery Allingham took to writing naturally; indeed in her family no other occupation was considered natural or indeed sane. Educated at the Perse School and Regent Street Polytechnic, she wrote her first novel while still in her teens. She began to leave a lasting mark on modern fiction in 1928 when, at the age of twenty-three, she wrote the first of her Albert Campion detective novels. Her early books, such as *The Crime at Black Dudley*, *Mystery Mile* and *Look to the Lady* (collected in this omnibus edition), had to be written in spare time hard won from her film work. At that time her books were beloved by the few advanced spirits who enjoyed her gay and distinctive approach to the problems and pleasures of post-war youth. Since then her gentle detective and his strong-arm colleagues have become known and loved by readers of all ages all over the world. She also acquired a reputation as a more serious writer. In an *Observer* review of *The Fashion in Shrouds* Torquemada remarked that 'to Albert Campion has fallen the honour of being the first detective to feature in a story which is also by any standard a distinguished novel'. Her novels cover a broad field. They vary in treatment from the grave to the frankly satirical, yet each example contrives to conform to the basic rules of the good detective tale.

Margery Allingham was married to Philip Youngman Carter and lived for many years on the edge of the Essex Marshes. She died in 1966.

The
Margery Allingham
Omnibus

The Crime at Black Dudley

Mystery Mile

Look to the Lady

Penguin Books

Penguin Books Ltd, Harmondsworth, Middlesex, England
Penguin Books, 625 Madison Avenue, New York, New York 10022, USA
Penguin Books Australia Ltd, Ringwood, Victoria, Australia
Penguin Books Canada Ltd, 2801 John Street, Markham, Ontario, Canada L3R1B4
Penguin Books (NZ) Ltd, 182–190 Wairau Road, Auckland 10, New Zealand

–

The Crime at Black Dudley first published 1929
Published in Penguin Books 1950
Copyright © P. & M. Youngman Carter Ltd, 1929

–

Mystery Mile first published by William Heinemann Ltd 1930
Published in Penguin Books 1950
Revised edition 1968
Copyright © P. & M. Youngman Carter Ltd, 1930, 1968

–

Look to the Lady first published 1931
Published in Penguin Books 1950
Copyright © P. & M. Youngman Carter Ltd, 1931

–

This collection published as *The Margery Allingham Omnibus* 1982
Copyright © P. & M. Youngman Carter Ltd, 1982
All rights reserved

–

Reproduced, printed and bound in Great Britain by
Hazell Watson & Viney Ltd, Aylesbury, Bucks
Set in Baskerville by
Rowland Phototypesetting Ltd, Bury St Edmunds, Suffolk
Maps drawn by Reg Piggott

Contents

The Crime at Black Dudley   7

Mystery Mile   197

Look to the Lady   385

The Crime at Black Dudley

To 'The Gang'

Chapter 1

Candle-Light

The view from the narrow window was dreary and inexpressibly
lonely. Miles of neglected park-land stretched in an unbroken plain to
the horizon and the sea beyond. On all sides it was the same.

The grey-green stretches were hayed once a year, perhaps, but
otherwise uncropped save by the herd of heavy-shouldered black
cattle who wandered about them, their huge forms immense and
grotesque in the fast-thickening twilight.

In the centre of this desolation, standing in a thousand acres of its
own land, was the mansion, Black Dudley; a great grey building, bare
and ugly as a fortress. No creepers hid its nakedness, and the long
narrow windows were dark-curtained and uninviting.

The man in the old-fashioned bedroom turned away from the
window and went on with his dressing.

'Gloomy old place,' he remarked to his reflection in the mirror.
'Thank God it's not mine.'

He tweaked his black tie deftly as he spoke, and stood back to
survey the effect.

George Abbershaw, although his appearance did not indicate it,
was a minor celebrity.

He was a smallish man, chubby and solemn, with a choir-boy
expression and a head of ridiculous bright-red curls which gave him a
somewhat fantastic appearance. He was fastidiously tidy in his dress
and there was an air of precision in everything he did or said which
betrayed an amazingly orderly mind. Apart from this, however, there
was nothing about him to suggest that he was particularly distinguished or even mildly interesting, yet in a small and exclusive circle of
learned men Dr George Abbershaw was an important person.

His book on pathology, treated with special reference to fatal
wounds and the means of ascertaining their probable causes, was a
standard work, and in view of his many services to the police in the
past his name was well known and his opinion respected at the Yard.

At the moment he was on holiday, and the unusual care which he took over his toilet suggested that he had not come down to Black Dudley solely for the sake of recuperating in the Suffolk air.

Much to his own secret surprise and perplexity, he had fallen in love.

He recognized the symptoms at once and made no attempt at self-deception, but with his usual methodical thoroughness set himself to remove the disturbing emotion by one or other of the only two methods known to mankind – disillusionment or marriage. For that reason, therefore, when Wyatt Petrie had begged him to join a week-end party at his uncle's house in the country, he had been persuaded to accept by the promise that Margaret Oliphant should also be of the party.

Wyatt had managed it, and she was in the house.

George Abbershaw sighed, and let his thoughts run on idly about his young host. A queer chap, Wyatt: Oxford turned out a lot of interesting young men with bees in their bonnets. Wyatt was a good lad, one of the best. He was profoundly grateful to Wyatt. Good Lord, what a profile she had, and there was brain there too, not empty prettiness. If only . . . ! He pulled himself together and mentally rebuked himself.

This problem must be attacked like any other, decently and in order.

He must talk to her; get to know her better, find out what she liked, what she thought about. With his mind still on these things the booming of the dinner gong surprised him, and he hurried down the low-stepped Tudor staircase as nearly flurried as he had ever been in his life.

However bleak and forbidding was Black Dudley's exterior, the rooms within were none the less magnificent. Even here there were the same signs of neglect that were so evident in the Park, but there was a certain dusty majesty about the dark-panelled walls with the oil-paintings hanging in their fast-blackening frames, and in the heavy, dark-oak furniture, elaborately carved and utterly devoid of polish, that was very impressive and pleasing.

The place had not been modernized at all. There were still candles in the iron sconces in the hall, and the soft light sent great shadows, like enormous ghostly hands, creeping up to the oak-beamed ceiling.

George sniffed as he ran down the staircase. The air was faintly clammy and the tallow smelt a little.

'Damp!' said he to himself. 'These old places need a lot of looking after . . . shouldn't think the sanitary system was any too good. Very nice, but I'm glad it's not mine.'

The dining-hall might have made him change his mind. All down one side of the long, low room was a row of stained-glass windows. In a great open fireplace a couple of faggots blazed whole, and on the long refectory table, which ran nearly the entire length of the flagged floor, eight seven-branched candlesticks held the only light. There were portraits on the walls, strangely differing in style, as the artists of the varying periods followed the fashions set by the masters of their time, but each face bearing a curious likeness to the next – the same straight noses, the same long thin lips, and above all, the same slightly rebellious expression.

Most of the party had already assembled when Abbershaw came in, and it struck him as incongruous to hear the babble of bright young conversation in this great tomb of a house with its faintly musty air and curiously archaic atmosphere.

As he caught sight of a gleam of copper-coloured hair on the other side of the table, however, he instantly forgot any sinister dampness or anything at all mysterious or unpleasant about the house.

Meggie Oliphant was one of those modern young women who manage to be fashionable without being ordinary in any way. She was a tall, slender youngster with a clean-cut white face, which was more interesting than pretty, and dark-brown eyes, slightly almond-shaped, which turned into slits of brilliance when she laughed. Her hair was her chief beauty, copper-coloured and very sleek; she wore it cut in a severe 'John' bob, a straight thick fringe across her forehead.

George Abbershaw's prosaic mind quivered on the verge of poetry when he looked at her. To him she was exquisite. He found they were seated next to each other at table, and he blessed Wyatt for his thoughtfulness.

He glanced up the table at him now and thought what a good fellow he was.

The candle-light caught his clever, thoughtful face for an instant, and immediately the young scientist was struck by the resemblance to the portraits on the wall. There was the same straight nose, the same wide thin-lipped mouth.

Wyatt Petrie looked what he was, a scholar of the new type. There was a little careful disarrangement in his dress, his brown hair was not quite so sleek as his guests', but he was obviously a cultured, fastidious man: every shadow on his face, every line and crease of his clothes indicated as much in a subtle and elusive way.

Abbershaw regarded him thoughtfully and, to a certain degree, affectionately. He had the admiration for him that one first-rate scholar always has for another out of his own line. Idly he reviewed the other man's record. Head of a great public school, a First in Classics at Oxford, a recognized position as a minor poet, and above all a good fellow. He was a rich man, Abbershaw knew, but his tastes were simple and his charities many. He was a man with an urge, a man who took life, with its problems and its pleasures, very seriously. So far as the other man knew he had never betrayed the least interest in women in general or in one woman in particular. A month ago Abbershaw would have admired him for this attribute as much as for any other. Today, with Meggie at his side, he was not so sure that he did not pity him.

From the nephew, his glance passed slowly round to the uncle, Colonel Gordon Coombe, host of the week-end.

He sat at the head of the table, and Abbershaw glanced curiously at this old invalid who liked the society of young people so much that he persuaded his nephew to bring a houseful of young folk down to the gloomy old mansion at least half a dozen times a year.

He was a little man who sat huddled in his high-backed chair as if his backbone was not strong enough to support his frame upright. His crop of faded yellow hair was now almost white, and stood up like a hedge above a narrow forehead. But by far the most striking thing about him was the flesh-coloured plate with which clever doctors had repaired a war-mutilated face which must otherwise have been a horror too terrible to think upon. From where he sat, perhaps some fourteen feet away, Abbershaw could only just detect it, so skilfully was it fashioned. It was shaped roughly like a one-sided half-mask and covered almost all the top right-hand side of his face, and through it the Colonel's grey-green eyes peered out shrewd and interested at the tableful of chattering young people.

George looked away hastily. For a moment his curiosity had overcome his sense of delicacy, and a wave of embarrassment passed over him as he realized that the little grey-green eyes had rested upon him for an instant and had found him eyeing the plate.

He turned to Meggie with a faint twinge of unwanted colour in his round cherubic face, and was a little disconcerted to find her looking at him, a hint of a smile on her lips and a curious brightness in her intelligent, dark-brown eyes. Just for a moment he had the uncomfortable impression that she was laughing at him.

He looked at her suspiciously, but she was no longer smiling, and when she spoke there was no amusement or superiority in her tone.

'Isn't it a marvellous house?' she said.

He nodded.

'Wonderful,' he agreed. 'Very old, I should say. But it's very lonely,' he added, his practical nature coming out in spite of himself. 'Probably most inconvenient . . . I'm glad it's not mine.'

The girl laughed softly.

'Unromantic soul,' she said.

Abbershaw looked at her and reddened and coughed and changed the conversation.

'I say,' he said, under the cover of the general prittle-prattle all around them, 'do you know who everyone is? I only recognize Wyatt and young Michael Prenderby over there. Who are the others? I arrived too late to be introduced.'

The girl shook her head.

'I don't know many myself,' she murmured. 'That's Anne Edgeware sitting next to Wyatt – she's rather pretty, don't you think? She's a Stage-cum-Society person; you must have heard of her.'

Abbershaw glanced across the table, where a striking young woman in a pseudo-Victorian frock and side curls sat talking vivaciously to the young man at her side. Some of her conversation floated across the table to him. He turned away again.

'I don't think she's particularly pretty,' he said with cheerful inconsequentialness. 'Who's the lad?'

'That boy with black hair talking to her? That's Martin. I don't know his other name, he was only introduced to me in the hall. He's just a stray young man, I think.' She paused and looked round the table.

'You know Michael, you say. The little round shy girl next to him Jeanne, his fiancée; perhaps you've met her.'

George shook his head.

'No,' he said, 'but I've wanted to; I take a personal interest in Michael' – he glanced at the fair, sharp-featured young man as he spoke – 'he's only just qualified as an MD, you know, but he'll go far. Nice chap, too . . . Who is the young prize-fighter on the girl's left?'

Meggie shook her sleek bronze head at him reprovingly as she followed his glance to the young giant a little higher up the table. 'You mustn't say that,' she whispered. 'He's our star turn this party. That's Chris Kennedy, the Cambridge rugger blue.'

'Is it?' said Abbershaw with growing respect. 'Fine-looking man.'

Meggie glanced at him sharply, and again the faint smile appeared on her lips and the brightness in her dark eyes. For all his psychology, his theorizing, and the seriousness with which he took himself, there was very little of George Abbershaw's mind that was not apparent to her, but for all that the light in her eyes was a happy one and the smile on her lips unusually tender.

'That,' she said suddenly, following the direction of his gaze and answering his unspoken thought, 'that's a lunatic.'

George turned to her gravely.

'Really?' he said.

She had the grace to become a little confused.

'His name is Albert Campion,' she said. 'He came down in Anne Edgeware's car, and the first thing he did when he was introduced to me was to show me a conjuring trick with a two-headed penny – he's quite inoffensive, just a silly ass.'

Abbershaw nodded and stared covertly at the fresh-faced young man with the tow-coloured hair and the foolish, pale-blue eyes behind tortoiseshell-rimmed spectacles, and wondered where he had seen him before.

The slightly receding chin and mouth so unnecessarily full of teeth was distinctly familiar. 'Albert Campion?' he repeated under his breath. 'Albert Campion? Campion? Campion?' But still his memory would not serve him, and he gave up calling on it and once more his inquisitive glance flickered round the table.

Since the uncomfortable little moment ten minutes ago when the Colonel had observed him scrutinizing his face, he had been careful to avoid the head of the table, but now his attention was caught by a man who sat next to his host, and for an instant he stared unashamedly.

The man was a foreigner, so much was evident at a glance; but that in itself was not sufficient to interest him so particularly.

The man was an arresting type. He was white-haired, very small and delicately made, with long graceful hands which he used a great deal in his conversation, making gestures, swaying his long, pale fingers gracefully, easily.

Under the sleek white hair which waved straight back from a high forehead his face was grey, vivacious, and peculiarly wicked.

George could think of no other word to describe the thin-lipped mouth that became one-sided and O-shaped in speech, the long thin nose, and more particularly the deep-set, round, black eyes which glistened and twinkled under enormous shaggy grey brows.

George touched Meggie's arm.

'Who is that?' he said.

The girl looked up and then dropped her eyes hurriedly.

'I don't know,' she murmured, 'save that his name is Gideon or something, and he is a guest of the Colonel's – nothing to do with our crowd.'

'Weird-looking man,' said Abbershaw.

'Terrible!' she said, so softly and with such earnestness that he glanced at her sharply and found her face quite grave.

She laughed as she saw his expression.

'I'm a fool,' she said. 'I didn't realize what an impression the man had made on me until I spoke. But he looks a wicked type, doesn't he? His friend, too, is rather startling, don't you think – the man sitting opposite to him?'

The repetition of the word 'wicked', the epithet which had arisen in his own mind, surprised Abbershaw, and he glanced covertly up the table again.

The man seated opposite Gideon, on the other side of the Colonel, was striking enough indeed.

He was a foreigner, grossly fat, and heavily jowled, and there was something absurdly familiar about him. Suddenly it dawned upon George what it was. The man was the living image of the little busts of Beethoven which are sold at music shops. There were the same heavy-lidded eyes, the same broad nose, and to cap it all the same shock of hair, worn long and brushed straight back from the amazingly high forehead.

'Isn't it queer?' murmured Meggie's voice at his side. 'See – he has no expression at all.'

As soon as she had spoken George realized that it was true. Although he had been watching the man for the last few minutes he had not seen the least change in the heavy red face; not a muscle seemed to have moved, nor the eyelids to have flickered; and although he had been talking to the Colonel at the time, his lips seemed to have moved independently of the rest of his features. It was as if one watched a statue speak.

'I think his name is Dawlish – Benjamin Dawlish,' said the girl. 'We were introduced just before dinner.'

Abbershaw nodded, and the conversation drifted on to other things, but all the time he was conscious of something faintly disturbing in the back of his mind, something which hung over his thoughts like a black shadow vaguely ugly and uncomfortable.

It was a new experience for him, but he recognized it immediately.

For the first time in his life he had a presentiment – a vague, unaccountable apprehension of trouble ahead.

He glanced at Meggie dubiously.

Love played all sorts of tricks with a man's brains. It was very bewildering.

The next moment he had pulled himself together, telling himself soberly not to be a fool. But wriggle and twist as he might, always the black shadow sat behind his thoughts, and he was glad of the candle-light and the bright conversation and the laughter of the dinner-table.

Chapter 2
The Ritual of the Dagger

After dinner, Abbershaw was one of the first to enter the great hall or drawing-room which, with the dining-room, took up the best part of the ground floor of the magnificent old mansion. It was an amazing room, vast as a barn and heavily panelled, with a magnificently carved fire-place at each end wherein two huge fires blazed. The floor was old oak and highly polished, and there was no covering save for two or three beautiful Shiraz rugs.

The furniture here was the same as in the other parts of the house, heavy, unpolished oak, carved and very old; and here, too, the faint atmosphere of mystery and dankness, with which the whole house was redolent, was apparent also.

Abbershaw noticed it immediately, and put it down to the fact that the light of the place came from a huge iron candle-ring which held some twenty or thirty thick wax candles suspended by an iron chain from the centre beam of the ceiling, so that there were heavy shadows round the panelled walls and in the deep corners behind the great fire-places.

By far the most striking thing in the whole room was an enormous trophy which hung over the fire-place farthest from the door. It was a vast affair composed of some twenty or thirty lances arranged in a circle, heads to the centre, and surmounted by a feathered helm and a banner resplendent with the arms of the Petries.

Yet it was the actual centre-piece which commanded immediate interest. Mounted on a crimson plaque, at the point where the lance-heads made a narrow circle, was a long, fifteenth-century Italian dagger. The hilt was an exquisite piece of workmanship, beautifully chased and encrusted at the upper end with uncut jewels, but it was not this that first struck the onlooker. The blade of the Black Dudley Dagger was its most remarkable feature. Under a foot long, it was very slender and exquisitely graceful, fashioned from steel that had in it a curious greenish tinge which lent the whole weapon an unmistakably sinister appearance. It seemed to shine out of the dark background like a living and malignant thing.

No one entering the room for the first time could fail to remark upon it; in spite of its comparatively insignificant size it dominated the whole room like an idol in a temple.

George Abbershaw was struck by it as soon as he came in, and instantly the feeling of apprehension which had annoyed his prosaic soul so much in the other room returned, and he glanced round him sharply, seeking either reassurance or confirmation, he hardly knew which.

The house-party which had seemed so large round the dinner-table now looked amazingly small in this cathedral of a room.

Colonel Coombe had been wheeled into a corner just out of the firelight by a man-servant, and the old invalid now sat smiling benignly on the group of young people in the body of the room. Gideon and the man with the expressionless face sat one on either side of him, while a grey-haired, sallow-faced man whom Abbershaw understood was a Dr White Whitby, the Colonel's private attendant, hovered about them in nervous solicitude for his patient.

On closer inspection Gideon and the man who looked like Beethoven proved to be even more unattractive than Abbershaw had supposed from his first somewhat cursory glance.

The rest of the party was in high spirits. Anne Edgeware was illustrating the striking contrast between Victorian clothes and modern manners, and her vivacious air and somewhat outrageous conversation made her the centre of a laughing group. Wyatt Petrie stood amongst his guests, a graceful, lazy figure, and his well-modulated voice and slow laugh sounded pleasant and reassuring in the forbidding room.

It was Anne who first brought up the subject of the dagger, as someone was bound to do.

'What a perfectly revolting thing, Wyatt,' she said, pointing at it. 'I've been trying not to mention it ever since I came in here. I should toast your muffins with something else, my dear.'

'Ssh!' Wyatt turned to her with mock solemnity. 'You mustn't speak disrespectfully of the Black Dudley Dagger. The ghosts of a hundred dead Petries will haunt you out of sheer outraged family pride if you do.'

The words were spoken lightly, and his voice had lost none of its quiet suavity, but whether it was the effect of the dagger itself or that of the ghostly old house upon the guests none could tell, but the girl's flippancy died away and she laughed nervously.

'I'm sorry,' she said. 'I should just loathe to be haunted. But quite seriously, then, if we mustn't laugh, what an incredible thing that dagger is.'

The others had gathered round her, and she and Wyatt now stood in the centre of a group looking up at the trophy. Wyatt turned round to Abbershaw. 'What do you think of it, George?' he said.

'Very interesting – very interesting indeed. It is very old, of course? I don't think I've ever seen one like it in my life.' The little man spoke with genuine enthusiasm. 'It's a curio, some old family relic, I suppose?'

Wyatt nodded, and his lazy grey eyes flickered with faint amusement.

'Well, yes, it is,' he said. 'My ancestors seem to have had high old times with it if family legends are true.'

'Ah!' said Meggie, coming forward. 'A ghost story?'

Wyatt glanced at her.

'Not a ghost,' he said, 'but a story.'

'Let's have it.' It was Chris Kennedy who spoke; the young rugger blue had more resignation than enthusiasm in his tone. Old family stories were not in his line. The rest of the party was considerably more keen, however, and Wyatt was pestered for the story.

'It's only a yarn, of course,' he began. 'I don't think I've ever told it to anyone else before. I don't think even my uncle knows it.' He turned questioningly as he spoke, and the old man shook his head.

'I know nothing about it,' he said. 'My late wife brought me to this house,' he explained. 'It had been in the family for hundreds of years. She was a Petrie – Wyatt's aunt. He naturally knows more about the history of the house than I. I should like to hear it, Wyatt.'

Wyatt smiled and shrugged his shoulders, then, moving forward, he climbed on to one of the high oak chairs by the fire-place, stepped up from one hidden foothold in the panelling to another, and stretching out his hand lifted the shimmering dagger off its plaque and carried it back to the group who pressed round to see it more closely.

The Black Dudley Dagger lost none of its sinister appearance by being removed from its setting. It lay there in Wyatt Petrie's long, cultured hands, the green shade in the steel blade more apparent than ever, and a red jewel in the hilt glowing in the candle-light.

'This,' said Wyatt, displaying it to its full advantage, 'is properly called the "Black Dudley Ritual Dagger". In the time of Quentin Petrie, somewhere about 1500, a distinguished guest was found murdered with this dagger sticking in his heart.' He paused, and glanced round the circle of faces. From the corner by the fire-place Gideon was listening intently, his grey face livid with interest, and his little black eyes wide and unblinking. The man who looked like Beethoven had turned towards the speaker also, but there was no expression on his heavy red face.

Wyatt continued in his quiet voice, choosing his words carefully and speaking with a certain scholastic precision.

'I don't know if you know it,' he said, 'but earlier than that date there had been a superstition which persisted in outlying places like this that a body touched by the hands of the murderer would bleed afresh from the mortal wound; or, failing that, if the weapon with which the murder was committed were placed into the hand which struck the blow, it would become covered with blood as it had been at the time of the crime. You've heard of that, haven't you, Abbershaw?' he said, turning towards the scientist, and George Abbershaw nodded.

'Go on,' he said briefly.

Wyatt returned to the dagger in his hand.

'Quentin Petrie believed in this superstition, it appears,' he said, 'for anyway it is recorded that on this occasion he closed the gates and summoned the entire household, the family, servants, labourers, herdsmen, and hangers-on, and the dagger was solemnly passed around. That was the beginning of it all. The ritual sprang up later – in the next generation, I think.'

'But did it happen? Did the dagger spout blood and all that?' Anne Edgeware spoke eagerly, her round face alive with interest.

Wyatt smiled. 'I'm afraid one of the family was beheaded for the murder,' he said; 'and the chronicles have it that the dagger betrayed him, but I fancy that there was a good deal of juggling in affairs of justice in those days.'

'Yes, but where does the ritual come in?' said Albert Campion, in his absurd falsetto drawl. 'It sounds most intriguing. I knew a fellow once who, when he went to bed, made a point of taking off everything else first before he removed his topper. He called that a ritual.'

'It sounds more like a conjuring trick,' said Abbershaw.

'It does, doesn't it?' agreed the irrepressible Albert. 'But I don't suppose your family ritual was anything like that, was it, Petrie? Something more lurid, I expect.'

'It was, a little, but nearly as absurd,' said Wyatt, laughing. 'Apparently it became a custom after that for the whole ceremony of the dagger to be repeated once a year – a sort of family rite as far as I can ascertain. That was only in the beginning, of course. In later years it degenerated into a sort of mixed hide-and-seek and relay race, played all over the house. I believe it was done at Christmas as late as my grandfather's time. The procedure was very simple. All the lights in the house were put out, and the head of the family, a Petrie by name and blood, handed the dagger to the first person he met in the darkness. Acceptance was of course compulsory, and that person had to hunt out someone else to pass the dagger on to, and the game continued in that fashion – each person striving to get rid of the dagger as soon as it was handed to him – for twenty minutes. Then the head of the house rang the dinner gong in the hall, the servants relit the lights, and the person discovered with the dagger lost the game and paid a forfeit which varied, I believe, from kisses to silver coins all round.'

He stopped abruptly.

'That's all there is,' he said, swinging the dagger in his fingers.

'What a perfectly wonderful story!'

Anne Edgeware turned to the others as she spoke. 'Isn't it?' she continued. 'It just sort of fits in with this house!'

'Let's play it.' It was the bright young man with the teeth again, and he beamed round fatuously at the company as he spoke. 'For sixpences if you like,' he ventured as an added inducement, as no one enthused immediately.

Anne looked at Wyatt. 'Could we?' she said.

'It wouldn't be a bad idea,' remarked Chris Kennedy, who was willing to back up Anne in anything she chose to suggest. The rest of the party had also taken kindly to the idea, and Wyatt hesitated.

'There's no reason why we shouldn't,' he said, and paused. Abbershaw was suddenly seized with a violent objection to the whole scheme. The story of the dagger ritual had impressed him strangely. He had seen the eyes of Gideon fixed upon the speaker with curious intensity, and had noticed the little huddled old man with the plate over his face harking to the barbarous story with avid enjoyment. Whether it was the great dank gloomy house or the disturbing effects of love upon his nervous system he did not know, but the idea of groping round in the dark with the malignant-looking dagger filled him with a distaste more vigorous than anything he had ever felt before. He had an impression, also, that Wyatt was not too attracted by the idea, but in the face of the unanimous enthusiasm of the rest of the party he could do nothing but fall in with the scheme.

Wyatt looked at his uncle.

'But certainly, my dear boy, why should I?' The old man seemed to be replying to an unspoken question. 'Let us consider it a blessing that so innocent and pleasing an entertainment can arise from something that must at one time have been very terrible.'

Abbershaw glanced at him sharply. There had been a touch of something in the voice that did not ring quite true, something hypocritical – insincere. Colonel Coombe glanced at the men on either side of him.

'I don't know . . .' he began dubiously.

Gideon spoke at once: it was the first time Abbershaw had heard his voice, and it struck him unpleasantly. It was deep, liquid, and curiously caressing, like the purring of a cat.

'To take part in such an ancient ceremony would be a privilege,' he said.

The man who had no expression bowed his head.

'I too,' he said, a trace of foreign accent in his voice, 'would be delighted.'

Once the ritual had been decided upon, preparations went forward with all ceremony and youthful enthusiasm. The man-servant was called in, and his part in the proceedings explained carefully. He was to let down the great iron candle-ring, extinguish the lights, and haul it up to the ceiling again. The lights in the hall were to be put out also, and he was then to retire to the servants' quarters and wait there until the dinner-gong sounded, at which time he was to return with some of the other servants and relight the candles with all speed.

He was a big man with a chest like a prize-fighter and a heavy florid face with enormous pale-blue eyes which had in them an innately sullen expression. A man who could become very unpleasant if the occasion arose, Abbershaw reflected inconsequentially.

As head of the family, Wyatt the last of the Petries took command of the proceedings. He had the manner, Abbershaw considered, of one who did not altogether relish his position. There was a faintly unwilling air about everything he did, a certain over-deliberation in all his instructions which betrayed, the other thought, a distaste for his task.

At length the signal was given. With a melodramatic rattle of chains the great iron candle-ring was let down and the lights put out, so that the vast hall was in darkness save for the glowing fires at each end of the room. Gideon and the man with the face like Beethoven had joined the circle round the doorway to the corridors, and the last thing George Abbershaw saw before the candles were extinguished was the little wizened figure of Colonel Coombe sitting in the chair in the shadow of the fire-place smiling out upon the scene from behind the hideous flesh-coloured plate. Then he followed the others into the dim halls and corridors of the great eerie house, and the Black Dudley Ritual began.

Chapter 3

In the Garage

The weirdness of the great stone staircases and unlit recesses was even more disquieting than Abbershaw had imagined it would be. There were flutterings in the dark, whisperings, and hurried footsteps. He was by no means a nervous man, and in the ordinary way an experience of this sort would probably have amused him faintly, had it not bored him. But on this particular night and in this house, which had impressed him with such a curious sense of foreboding ever since he had first seen it from the drive, he was distinctly uneasy.

To make matters worse, he had entirely lost sight of Meggie. He had missed her in the first blinding rush of darkness, and so, when by chance he found himself up against a door leading into the garden, he went out, shutting it softly behind him.

It was a fine night, and although there was no moon, the starlight made it possible for him to see his way about; he did not feel like wandering about the eerie grounds alone, and suddenly it occurred to him that he would go and inspect his AC two-seater which he had left in the big garage beside the drive.

He was a tidy man, and since he had no clear recollection of turning off the petrol before he left her, it struck him that now was a convenient opportunity to make sure.

He located the garage without much difficulty, and made his way to it, crossing over the broad, flagged drive to where the erstwhile barn loomed up against the starlit sky. The doors were still open and there was a certain amount of light from two hurricane lanterns hanging from a low beam in the roof. There were more than half a dozen cars lined up inside, and he reflected how very typical each was of its owner. The Rover coupé with the cream body and the black wings was obviously Anne Edgeware's; even had he not seen her smart black-and-white motoring kit he would have known it. The Salmson with the ridiculous mascot was patently Chris Kennedy's property; the magnificent Lanchester must be Gideon's, and the rest were simple also; a Bentley, a Buick, and a Swift proclaimed their owners.

As his eye passed from one to another, a smile flickered for an instant on his lips. There, in the corner, derelict and dignified as a maiden aunt, was one of the pioneers of motor traffic.

This must be the house car, he reflected, as he walked over to it, Colonel Coombe's own vehicle. It was extraordinary how well it matched the house, he thought as he reached it.

Made in the very beginning of the century, it belonged to the time when, as some brilliant American has said, cars were built, like cathedrals, with prayer. It was a brougham; coach-built and leathery, with a seating capacity in the back for six at least, and a tiny cab only in front for the driver. Abbershaw was interested in cars, and since he felt he had time to spare and there was nothing better to do, he lifted up the extraordinarily ponderous bonnet of the 'museum-piece' and looked in.

For some moments he stood staring at the engine within, and then, drawing a torch from his pocket, he examined it more closely.

Suddenly a smothered exclamation broke from his lips and he bent down and flashed the light on the underside of the car, peering under the ridiculously heavy running-boards and glancing at the axles and shaft. At last he stood up and shut down the bonnet, an expression of mingled amazement and curiosity on his cherubic face.

The absurd old body, which looked as if it belonged to a car which would be capable of twenty miles all out at most, was set upon the chassis and the engine of the latest 'Phantom' type Rolls-Royce.

He had no time to reflect upon the possible motives of the owner of the strange hybrid for this inexplicable piece of eccentricity, for at that moment he was disturbed by the sounds of footsteps coming up the flagged drive. Instinctively he moved over to his own car, and was bending over it when a figure appeared in the doorway.

'Oh – er – hullo! Having a little potter – what?'

The words, uttered in an inoffensively idiotic voice, made Abbershaw glance up to find Albert Campion smiling fatuously in upon him.

'Hullo!' said Abbershaw, a little nettled to have his occupation so accurately described. 'How's the Ritual going?'

Mr Campion looked a trifle embarrassed.

'Oh, jogging along, I believe. Two hours' clean fun, don't you know.'

'You seem to be missing yours,' said Abbershaw pointedly.

The young man appeared to break out into a sort of Charleston, apparently to hide further embarrassment.

'Well, yes, as a matter of fact I got fed up with it in there,' he said, still hopping up and down in a way Abbershaw found peculiarly irritating. 'All this running about in the dark with daggers doesn't seem to me healthy. I don't like knives, you know – people getting excited and all that. I came out to get away from it all.'

For the first time Abbershaw began to feel a faint sympathy for him.

'Your car here?' he remarked casually.

This perfectly obvious question seemed to place Mr Campion still less at ease.

'Well – er – no. As a matter of fact, it isn't. To be exact,' he added in a sudden burst of confidence, 'I haven't got one at all. I've always liked them, though,' he continued hastily, 'nice, useful things. I've always thought that. Get you where you want to go, you know. Better than a horse.'

Abbershaw stared at him. He considered that the man was either a lunatic or drunk, and as he disliked both alternatives he suggested stiffly that they should return to the house. The young man did not greet the proposal with enthusiasm, but Abbershaw, who was a determined little man when roused, dragged him back to the side door through which he had come, without further ado.

As soon as they entered the great grey corridor and the faintly dank musty breath of the house came to meet them, it became evident that something had happened. There was a sound of many feet, echoing voices, and at the far end of the passage a light flickered and passed.

'Someone kicking up a row over the forfeit, what!' The idiotic voice of Albert Campion at his ear jarred upon Abbershaw strangely.

'We'll see,' he said, and there was an underlying note of anxiety in his voice which he could not hide.

A light step sounded close at hand and there was a gleam of silk in the darkness ahead of them.

'Who's there?' said a voice he recognized as Meggie's.

'Oh, thank God, it's you!' she exclaimed, as he spoke to her.

Mr Albert Campion then did the first intelligent thing Abbershaw had observed in him. He obliterated himself and faded away up the passage, leaving them together.

'What's happened?' Abbershaw spoke apprehensively, as he felt her hand quiver as she caught his arm.

'Where have you been?' she said breathlessly. 'Haven't you heard?

Colonel Coombe had a heart attack right in the middle of the game. Dr Whitby and Mr Gideon have taken him up to his room. It was all very awkward for them, though. There weren't any lights. When they sounded the gong the servants didn't come. Apparently there's only one door leading from their quarters to the rest of the house and that seems to have been locked. They've got the candles alight now, though,' she added, and he noticed that she was oddly breathless.

Abbershaw looked down at her; he wished he could see her face.

'What's happening in there now?' he said. 'Anything we can do?'

The girl shook her head. 'I don't think so. They're just standing about talking. I heard Wyatt say that the news had come down that it was nothing serious, and he asked us all to go on as if nothing had happened. Apparently the Colonel often gets these attacks . . .' She hesitated and made no attempt to move.

Abbershaw felt her trembling by his side, and once again the curious fear which had been lurking at the back of his mind all the evening showed itself to him.

'Tell me,' he said, with a sudden intuition that made his voice gentle and comforting in the darkness. 'What is it?'

She started, and her voice sounded high and out of control.

'Not – not here. Can't we get outside? I'm frightened of this house.' The admission in her tone made his heart leap painfully.

Something had happened, then.

He drew her arm through his.

'Why, yes, of course we can,' he said. 'It's a fine starlit night; we'll go on to the grass.'

He led her out on to the roughly cut turf that had once been smooth lawns, and they walked together out of the shadows of the house into a little shrubbery where they were completely hidden from the windows.

'Now,' he said, and his voice had unconsciously assumed a protective tone; 'what is it?'

The girl looked up at him, and he could see her keen, clever face and narrow brown eyes in the faint light.

'It was horrible in there,' she whispered. 'When Colonel Coombe had his attack, I mean. I think Dr Whitby found him. He and Mr Gideon carried him up while the other man – the man with no expression on his face – rang the gong. No one knew what had happened, and there were no lights. Then Mr Gideon came down and said that the Colonel had had a heart attack . . .' She stopped and looked steadily at him, and he was horrified to see that she was livid with terror.

'George,' she said suddenly, 'if I told you something would you think I – I was mad?'

'No, of course not,' he assured her steadily. 'What else happened?'

The girl swallowed hard. He saw she was striving to compose herself, and obeying a sudden impulse he slid his arm round her waist, so that she was encircled and supported by it.

'In the game,' she said, speaking clearly and steadily as if it were an effort, 'about five minutes before the gong rang, someone gave me the dagger. I don't know who it was – I think it was a woman, but I'm not sure. I was standing at the foot of the stone flight of stairs which leads down into the lower hall, when someone brushed past me in the dark and pushed the dagger into my hand. I suddenly felt frightened of it, and I ran down the corridor to find someone I could give it to.'

She paused, and he felt her shudder in his arm.

'There is a window in the passage,' she said, 'and as I passed under it the faint light fell upon the dagger and – don't think I'm crazy, or dreaming, or imagining something – but I saw the blade was covered with something dark. I touched it, it was sticky. I knew it at once, it was blood!'

'Blood!' The full meaning of her words dawned slowly on the man and he stared at her, half-fascinated, half-incredulous.

'Yes. You must believe me.' Her voice was agonized and he felt her eyes on his face. 'I stood there staring at it,' she went on. 'At first I thought I was going to faint. I knew I should scream in another moment, and then – quite suddenly and noiselessly – a hand came out of the shadows and took the knife. I was so frightened I felt I was going mad. Then, just when I felt my head was bursting, the gong rang.'

Her voice died away in the silence, and she thrust something into his hand.

'Look,' she said, 'if you don't believe me. I wiped my hand with it.'

Abbershaw flashed his torch upon the little crumpled scrap in his hand. It was a handkerchief, a little filmy wisp of a thing of lawn and lace, and on it, clear and unmistakable, was a dull red smear – dry blood.

Chapter 4

Murder

They went slowly back to the house.

Meggie went straight up to her room, and Abbershaw joined the others in the hall.

The invalid's corner was empty, chair and all had disappeared.

Wyatt was doing his best to relieve any feeling of constraint amongst his guests, assuring them that his uncle's heart attacks were by no means infrequent and asking them to forget the incident if they could.

Nobody thought of the dagger. It seemed to have vanished completely. Abbershaw hesitated, wondering if he should mention it, but finally decided not to, and he joined in the half-hearted, fitful conversation.

By common consent everyone went to bed early. A depression had settled over the spirits of the company, and it was well before midnight when once again the great candle-ring was let down from the ceiling and the hall left again in darkness.

Up in his room Abbershaw removed his coat and waist-coat, and, attiring himself in a modestly luxurious dressing-gown, settled down in the armchair before the fire to smoke a last cigarette before going to bed. The apprehension he had felt all along had been by no means lessened by the events of the last hour or so.

He believed Meggie's story implicitly: she was not the kind of girl to fabricate a story of that sort in any circumstances, and besides the whole atmosphere of the building after he had returned from the garage had been vaguely suggestive and mysterious.

There was something going on in the house that was not ordinary, something that as yet he did not understand, and once again the face of the absurd young man with the horn-rimmed spectacles flashed into his mind and he strove vainly to remember where he had seen it before.

His meditations were cut short by the sound of footsteps in the passage outside, and the next moment there was a discreet tap at his door.

Abbershaw rose and opened it, to discover Michael Prenderby, the young, newly qualified MD, standing fully dressed in the doorway.

The boy looked worried, and came into the room quickly, shutting the door behind him after he had glanced up and down the corridor outside as if to make certain that he had not been followed.

'Forgive the melodrama,' he said, 'but there's something darn queer going on in this place. Have a cigarette?'

Abbershaw looked at him shrewdly. The hand that held the cigarette-case out to him was not too steady, and the facetiousness of the tone was belied by the expression of anxiety in his eyes.

Michael Prenderby was a fair, slight young man, with a sense of humour entirely unexpected.

To the casual observer he was an inoffensive, colourless individual, and his extraordinary spirit and strength of character were known only to his friends.

Abbershaw took a cigarette and indicated a chair.

'Let's have it,' he said. 'What's up?'

Prenderby lit a cigarette and pulled at it vigorously, then he spoke abruptly.

'In the first place,' he said, 'the old bird upstairs is dead.'

Abbershaw's blue-grey eyes flickered, and the thought which had lurked at the back of his mind ever since Meggie's story in the garden suddenly grew into a certainty.

'Dead?' he said. 'How do you know?'

'They told me.' Prenderby's pale face flushed slightly. 'The private medico fellow – Whitby, I think his name is – came up to me just as I was coming to bed; he asked me if I would go up with him and have a look at the old boy.'

He paused awkwardly, and Abbershaw suddenly realized that it was a question of professional etiquette that was embarrassing him.

'I thought they'd be bound to have got you up there already,' the boy continued, 'so I chased up after the fellow and found the Colonel stretched out on the bed, face covered up and all that. Gideon was there too, and as soon as I got up in the room I grasped what it was they wanted me for. Mine was to be the signature on the cremation certificate.'

'Cremation? They're in a bit of a hurry, aren't they?'

Prenderby nodded.

'That's what I thought, but Gideon explained that the old boy's last words were a wish that he should be cremated and the party should continue, so they didn't want to keep the body in the house a moment longer than was absolutely necessary.'

'Wanted the party to go on?' repeated Abbershaw stupidly. 'Absurd!'

The young doctor leant forward. 'That's not all by any means,' he said. 'When I found what they wanted, naturally I pointed out that you were the senior man and should be first approached. That seemed to annoy them both. Old Whitby, who was very nervous, I thought, got very up-stage and talked a lot of rot about "*Practising* MDs", but it was the foreigner who got me into the really unpleasant hole. He pointed out, in that disgustingly sticky voice he has, that I was a guest in the house and could hardly refuse such a simple request. It was all damn cheek, and very awkward, but eventually I decided to rely on your decency to back me up and so . . .' He paused.

'Did you sign?' Abbershaw said quickly.

Prenderby shook his head. 'No,' he said with determination, adding explanatorily: 'They wouldn't let me look at the body.'

'What?' Abbershaw was startled. Everything was tending in the same direction. The situation was by no means a pleasant one.

'You refused?' he said.

'Rather.' Prenderby was inclined to be angry. 'Whitby talked a lot of the usual bilge – trotted out all the good old phrases. By the time he'd finished, the poor old bird on the bed must have been dead about a year and a half according to him. But he kept himself between me and the bed, and when I went to pull the sheet down, Gideon got in my way deliberately. Whitby seemed to take it as a personal insult that I should think even an ordinary examination necessary. And then I'm afraid I lost my temper and walked out.'

He paused, and looked at the older man awkwardly. 'You see,' he said, with a sudden burst of confidence, 'I've never signed a cremation certificate in my life, and I didn't feel like starting on an obviously fishy case. I only took my finals a few months ago, you know.'

'Oh, quite right, quite right.' Abbershaw spoke with conviction. 'I wonder what they're doing?'

Prenderby grinned.

'You'll probably find out,' he said dryly. 'They'll come to you now. They thought I should be easier to manage, but having failed – and since they're in such a hurry – I should think you were for it. It occurred to me to nip down and warn you.'

'Good of you. Thanks very much.' Abbershaw spoke genuinely. 'It's a most extraordinary business. Did it look like heart failure?'

Prenderby shrugged his shoulders.

'My dear fellow, I don't know,' he said. 'I didn't even see the face. If it was heart failure why shouldn't I examine him? It's more than fishy, you know, Abbershaw. Do you think we ought to do anything?'

'No. That is, not at the moment.' George Abbershaw's round and chubby face had suddenly taken on an expression which immediately altered its entire character. His mouth was firm and decided, and there was confidence in his eyes. In an instant he had become the man of authority, eminently capable of dealing with any situation that might arise.

'Look here,' he said, 'if you've just left them they'll be round for me any moment. You'd better get out now, so that they don't find us together. You see,' he went on quickly, 'we don't want a row here, with women about and that sort of thing; besides, we couldn't do anything if they turned savage. As soon as I get to town I can trot along and see old Deadwood at the Yard and get everything looked into without much fuss. That is, of course, once I've satisfied myself that there is something tangible to go upon. So if they press me for that signature I think I shall give it 'em. You see, I can arrange an inquiry afterwards if it seems necessary. It's hardly likely they'll get the body cremated before we can get on to 'em. I shall go up to town first thing in the morning.'

'That's the stuff,' said Prenderby with enthusiasm. 'If you don't mind, I'll drop down on you afterwards to hear how things have progressed. Hullo!'

He paused, listening. 'There's someone coming down the passage now,' he said. 'Look here, if it's all the same to you I'll continue the melodrama and get into that press.'

He slipped into the big wardrobe at the far end of the room and closed the carved door behind him just as the footsteps paused in the passage outside and someone knocked.

On opening the door, Abbershaw found, as he had expected, Dr Whitby on the threshold. The man was in a pitiable state of nerves. His thin grey hair was damp and limp upon his forehead, and his hands twitched visibly.

'Dr Abbershaw,' he began, 'I am sorry to trouble you so late at night, but I wonder if you would do something for us.'

'My dear sir, of course.' Abbershaw radiated good humour, and the other man warmed immediately.

'I think you know,' he said, 'I am Colonel Coombe's private physician. He has been an invalid for some years, as I dare say you are aware. In point of fact, a most unfortunate thing has happened, which although we have known for some time that it must come soon, is none the less a great shock. Colonel Coombe's seizure this evening has proved fatal.'

Abbershaw's expression was a masterpiece: his eyebrows rose, his mouth opened.

'Dear, dear! How very distressing!' he said with that touch of pomposity which makes a young man look more foolish than anything else. '*Very* distressing,' he repeated, as if another thought had suddenly struck him. 'It'll break up the party, of course.'

Dr Whitby hesitated. 'Well,' he said, 'we had hoped not.'

'Not break up the party?' exclaimed Abbershaw, looking so profoundly shocked that the other hastened to explain.

'The deceased was a most eccentric man,' he murmured confidentially. 'His last words were a most urgently expressed desire for the party to continue.'

'A little trying for all concerned,' Abbershaw commented stiffly.

'Just so,' said his visitor. 'That is really why I came to you. It has always been the Colonel's wish that he should be cremated immediately after his decease, and, as a matter of fact, all preparations have been made for some time. There is just the formality of the certificate, and I wonder if I might bother you for the necessary signature.'

He hesitated doubtfully, and shot a glance at the little red-haired man in the dressing-gown. But Abbershaw was ready for him.

'My dear sir, anything I can do, of course. Let's go up there now, shall we?'

All traces of nervousness had vanished from Whitby's face, and a sigh of relief escaped his lips as he escorted the obliging Dr Abbershaw down the long, creaking corridor to the Colonel's room.

It was a vast old-fashioned apartment, high-ceilinged, and not too well lit. Panelled on one side, it was hung on the other with heavy curtains, ancient and dusty. Not at all the sort of room that appealed to Abbershaw as a bed-chamber for an invalid.

A huge four-poster bed took up all the farther end of the place, and upon it lay something very still and stiff, covered by a sheet. On a small table near the wide fire-place were pen and ink and a cremation certificate form; standing near it was Jesse Gideon, one beautiful hand shining like ivory upon the polished wood.

Abbershaw had made up his mind that the only way to establish or confute his suspicions was to act quickly, and assuming a brisk and officious manner he strode across the room rubbing his hands.

'Heart failure?' he said, in a tone that was on the verge of being cheerful. 'A little unwonted excitement, perhaps – a slightly heavier meal – anything might do it. Most distressing – most distressing. Visitors in the house too.'

He was striding up and down as he spoke, at every turn edging a little nearer the bed.

'Now let me see,' he said suddenly. 'Just as a matter of form, of course . . .' On the last word, moving with incredible swiftness, he reached the bedside and flicked the sheet from the dead man's face.

The effect was instantaneous. Whitby caught his arm and dragged him back from the bed, and from the shadows a figure that Abbershaw had not noticed before came out silently. The next moment he recognized Dawlish, the man who looked like Beethoven. His face was still expressionless, but there was no mistaking the menace in his attitude as he came forward, and the young scientist realized with a little thrill of excitement that the veneer was off and that he was up against an antagonistic force.

The moment passed, however, and in the next instant he had the situation in hand again, with added advantage of knowing exactly where he stood. He turned a mildly apologetic face to Whitby.

'Just as a matter of form,' he repeated. 'I like to make a point of seeing the body. Some of us are a little too lax, I feel, in a matter like this. After all, cremation is cremation. I'm not one of those men who insist on a thorough examination, but I just like to make sure that a corpse is a corpse, don't you know.'

He laughed as he spoke, and stood with his hands in his pockets, looking down at the face of the man on the bed. The momentary tension in the room died down. The heavy-faced Dawlish returned to his corner, Gideon became suave again, and the doctor stood by Abbershaw a little less apprehensively.

'Death actually took place up here, I suppose?' Abbershaw remarked conversationally, and shot a quick sidelong glance at Whitby. The man was ready for it, however.

'Yes, just after we carried him in.'

'I see.' Abbershaw glanced round the room. 'You brought him up in his chair, I suppose? How wonderfully convenient those things are.' He paused as if lost in thought, and Dawlish muttered impatiently.

Gideon interposed hastily.

'It is getting late,' he said in his unnaturally gentle voice. 'We must not keep Dr Abbershaw –'

'Er – no, of course not,' said Whitby, starting nervously.

Abbershaw took the hint.

'It is late. I bid you good night, gentlemen,' he murmured, and moved towards the door.

Gideon slipped in front of it, pen in hand. He was suave as ever, and smiling, but the little round eyes beneath the enormous shaggy brows were bright and dangerous.

Abbershaw realized then that he was not going to be allowed to refuse to sign the certificate. The three men in the room were determined. Any objections he might raise would be confuted by force if need be. It was virtually a signature under compulsion.

He took the pen with a little impatient click of the tongue.

'How absurd of me, I had forgotten,' he said, laughing as though to cover his oversight. 'Now, let me look, where is it? Oh, I see – just here – you have attended to all these particulars, of course, Dr Whitby.'

'Yes, yes. They're all in order.'

No one but the self-occupied type of fool that Abbershaw was pretending to be could possibly have failed to notice the man's wretched state of nervous tension. He was quivering and his voice was entirely out of control. Abbershaw wrote his signature with a flourish, and returned the pen. There was a distinct sigh of relief in the room as he moved towards the door.

On the threshold he turned and looked back.

'Poor young Petrie knows all about this, I suppose?' he inquired. 'I trust he's not very cut up? Poor lad.'

'Mr Petrie has been informed, of course,' Dr Whitby said stiffly. 'He felt the shock – naturally – but like the rest of us I fancy he must have expected it for some time. He was only a relative by his aunt's marriage, you know, and that took place after the war, I believe.'

'Still,' said Abbershaw, with a return of his old fussiness of manner, 'very shocking and very distressing – very distressing. Good night, gentlemen.'

On the last words he went out and closed the door of the great sombre room behind him. Once in the corridor, his expression changed. The fussy, pompous personality that he had assumed dropped from him like a cloak, and he became at once alert and purposeful. There were many things that puzzled him, but of one thing he was perfectly certain. Colonel Gordon Coombe had not died of heart disease.

Chapter 5
The Mask

Abbershaw made his way quietly down the corridor to Wyatt's room. The young man had taken him into it himself earlier in the day, and he found it without difficulty.

There was no light in the crack of the door, and he hesitated for a moment before he knocked, as if undecided whether he would disturb its occupant or not, but at length he raised his hand and tapped on the door.

There was no reply, and after waiting a few minutes he knocked again. Still no one answered him, and obeying a sudden impulse, he lifted the latch and went in.

He was in a long, narrow room with a tall window in the wall immediately facing him, giving out on to a balcony. The place was in darkness save for the faint light of a newly risen moon, which streamed in through the window.

He saw Wyatt at once. He was in his dressing-gown, standing in the window, his arms outstretched, his hands resting on either side of the frame.

Abbershaw spoke to him, and for a moment he did not move. Then he turned sharply, and for an instant the moonlight fell upon his face and the long slender lines of his sensitive hands. Then he turned round completely and came towards his friend.

But Abbershaw's mood had changed: he was no longer so determined. He seemed to have changed his mind.

'I've just heard,' he said, with real sympathy in his tone. 'I'm awfully sorry. It was a bit of a shock, coming now, I suppose? Anything I can do, of course . . .'

Wyatt shook his head.

'Thanks,' he said, 'but the old boy's doctor had been expecting it for years. I believe all the necessary arrangements have been made for some time. It may knock the life out of the party pretty thoroughly, though, I'm afraid.'

'My dear man.' Abbershaw spoke hastily. 'We'll all sheer off first thing tomorrow morning, of course. Most people have got cars.'

'Oh, don't do that.' Wyatt spoke with sudden insistence. 'I understand my uncle was very anxious that the party should go on,' he said. 'Really, you'd be doing me a great service if you'd stay on till Monday and persuade the others to do the same. After all, it isn't even as if it was his house. It's mine, you know. It passed to me on Aunt's death, but my uncle, her husband, was anxious to go on living here, so I rented it to him. I wish you'd stay. He would have liked it, and there's no point in my staying down here alone. He was no blood relative of mine, and he had no kin as far as I know.' He paused, and added, as Abbershaw still looked dubious, 'The funeral and cremation will take place in London. Gideon has arranged about that; he was his lawyer, you know, and a very close friend. Stay if you can, won't you? Good night. Thanks for coming down.'

Abbershaw went slowly back to his room, a slightly puzzled expression in his eyes. He had meant to tell Wyatt his discoveries, and even now he did not know quite why he had not done so. Instinct told him to be cautious. He felt convinced that there were more secrets in Black Dudley that night than the old house had ever known. Secrets that would be dangerous if they were too suddenly brought to light.

He found Prenderby sitting up for him, the ash-tray at his side filled with cigarette-stubs.

'So you've turned up at last,' he said peevishly. 'I wondered if they'd done a sensational disappearing act with you. This house is such a ghostly old show I've been positively sweltering with terror up here. Anything transpired?'

Abbershaw sat down by the fire before he spoke.

'I signed the certificate,' he said at last. 'I was practically forced into it. They had the whole troupe there, old Uncle Tom Beethoven and all.'

Prenderby leant forward, his pale face becoming suddenly keen again.

'They are up to something, aren't they?' he said.

'Oh, undoubtedly.' Abbershaw spoke with authority. 'I saw the corpse's face. There was no heart trouble there. He was murdered – stuck in the back, I should say.' He paused, and hesitated as if debating something in his mind.

Prenderby looked at him curiously. 'Of course, I guessed as much,' he said, 'but what's the other discovery? What's on your mind?'

Abbershaw looked up at him, and his round grey-blue eyes met the boy's for an instant.

'A darned queer thing, Prenderby,' he said. 'I don't understand it at all. There's more mystery here than you'd think. When I twitched back the sheet and looked at the dead man's face it was darkish in that four-poster, but there was light enough for me to see one thing. Extreme loss of blood had flattened the flesh down over his bones till he looked dead – very dead – and that plate he wore over the top of his face had slipped out of place and I saw something most extraordinary.'

Prenderby raised his eyes inquiringly. 'Very foul?' he said.

'Not at all. That was the amazing part of it.'

Abbershaw leaned forward in his chair and his eyes were very grave and hard. 'Prenderby, that man had no need to wear that plate. His face was as whole as yours or mine!'

'Good God!' The boy sat up, the truth slowly dawning on him. 'Then it was simply –'

Abbershaw nodded.

'A mask,' he said.

Chapter 6

Mr Campion Brings the House Down

Abbershaw sat up for some time, smoking, after Prenderby left him, and when at last he got into bed he did not sleep at once, but lay staring up into the darkness of the beamed ceiling – thinking.

He had just fallen into a doze in which the events of the evening formed themselves into a fantastic nightmare, when a terrific thud above his head and a shower of plaster upon his face brought him hurriedly to his senses.

He sat up in bed, every nerve alert and tingling, waiting for the next development.

It came almost immediately.

From the floor directly above his head came a series of extraordinary sounds. It seemed as if heavy pieces of furniture were being hurled about by some infuriated giant, and between the crashes Abbershaw fancied he could discern the steady murmur of someone cursing in a deep, unending stream.

After a second or so of this he decided that it was time to get up and investigate, and slipping on his dressing-gown he dashed out into the corridor, where the grey light of morning was just beginning to pierce the gloom.

Here the noise above was even more distinct. A tremendous upheaval seemed to be in progress.

Not only Abbershaw had been awakened by it; the whole house appeared to be stirring. He ran up the staircase in the direction from which the noise was coming to discover that an old-time architect had not built another room above the one in which he slept but a wide gallery from which a second staircase descended. Here he was confronted by an extraordinary scene.

The man-servant he had noticed so particularly on the evening before was grappling with someone who was putting up a very stout resistance. The man was attacking his opponent with an amazing ferocity. Furniture was hurled in all directions, and as Abbershaw came up he caught a stream of oaths from the infuriated footman.

His first thought was that a burglar had been surprised red-handed, but as the two passed under a window in their violent passage round the place, the straggling light fell upon the face of the second combatant and Abbershaw started with surprise, for in that moment he had caught a glimpse of the vacant and peculiarly inoffensive features of Mr Albert Campion.

By this time there were many steps on the stairs, and the next moment half the house-party came crowding round behind Abbershaw; Chris Kennedy in a resplendent dressing-gown was well to the fore.

'Hullo! A scrap?' he said, with something very near satisfaction in his voice, and threw himself upon the two without further preliminaries.

As the confusion increased with this new development Abbershaw darted forward and, stooping suddenly, picked up something off the floor by the head of the second staircase. It was very swiftly done, and no one noticed the incident.

Chris Kennedy's weight and enthusiasm brought the fight to an abrupt finish.

Mr Campion picked himself up from the corner where he had been last hurled. He was half strangled, but still laughing idiotically. Meanwhile, Chris Kennedy inspected the butler, whose stream of rhetoric had become much louder but less coherent.

'The fellow's roaring tight,' he announced, upon closer inspection. 'Absolutely fighting-canned, but it's wearing off a bit now.'

He pushed the man away from him contemptuously, and the erstwhile warrior reeled against the stair-head and staggered off down out of sight.

'What's happened? What's the trouble?' Wyatt Petrie came hurrying up the passage, his voice anxious and slightly annoyed.

Everybody looked at Mr Campion. He was leaning up against the balustrade, his fair hair hanging over his eyes, and for the first time it dawned upon Abbershaw that he was fully dressed, and not, as might have been expected, in the dinner-jacket he had worn on the previous evening.

His explanation was characteristic.

'Most extraordinary,' he said, in his slightly high-pitched voice. 'The fellow set on me. Picked me up and started doing exercises with me as if I were a dumb-bell. I thought it was one of you fellows joking at first, but when he began to jump on me it percolated through that

I was being massacred. Butchered to make a butler's beano, in fact.'

He paused and smiled fatuously.

'I began to hit back then,' he continued. 'The bird was tight, of course, but I'm glad you fellows turned up. I didn't like the idea of him chipping bits off the ancestral home with me.'

'My dear fellow, I'm frightfully sorry this has happened. The man shall be discharged tomorrow. I'll see to it.' Wyatt spoke with real concern, but Abbershaw was not nearly so easily satisfied.

'Where did he get at you?' he said, suddenly stepping forward. 'Where were you?'

Mr Campion met the question with charming ingenuousness.

'Just coming out of my room – that's the door, over there,' he said. 'I opened it and walked out into a war.'

He was buttoning up his waistcoat, which had been ripped open in the fight, as he spoke.

Abbershaw glanced at the grandfather clock at the head of the staircase. It showed the hour at eight minutes past four. Mr Campion followed the direction of his eyes.

'Yes,' he said foolishly, 'I – I always get up early.'

'Amazingly early,' said Abbershaw pointedly.

'I was, this morning,' agreed Mr Campion cheerfully, adding by way of explanation, 'I'm one of those birds who can never sleep in a strange bed. And then, you know, I'm so afraid of ghosts. I didn't see any, of course,' he went on hastily, 'but I said to myself as I got into bed last night, "Albert, this place smells of ghosts," and somehow I couldn't get that idea out of my head all night. So as soon as it began to get light I thought a walk was indicated, so I got up, dressed, and sallied forth into the fray.' He paused and yawned thoughtfully. 'I do believe I shall go back to bed now,' he remarked as they all stared at him. 'I don't feel much like my walk now. In fact, I don't feel much like anything. Bung-ho, everybody, Uncle Albert is now closing down until nine-thirty, when the breakfast programme will begin, I hope.' On the last word he waved his hand to them and disappeared into his own room, shutting the door firmly behind him.

As Abbershaw turned to go back to his bedroom he became aware of a slender figure in a dressing-gown at his side. It was Meggie. Seized by a sudden impulse, he spoke to her softly.

'Who brought Campion down?'

She looked at him in surprise.

'Why, Anne,' she said. 'I told you. They arrived together about the same time that I did. Why the interest? Anything I can do?'

Abbershaw hesitated.

'Well, yes,' he said at last. 'She's a friend of yours, isn't she?'

Meggie nodded.

'Rather; I've known her for years.'

'Good,' said Abbershaw. 'Look here, could you get her to come down into the garden? Meet me down there in half an hour in that shrubbery we found last night? There's one or two things I want to ask her. Can you manage that for me?'

'Of course.' She looked up at him and smiled; then she added, 'Anything happened?'

Abbershaw looked at her, and noticed for the first time that there was a faintly scared expression in her narrow brown eyes, and a sudden desire to comfort her assailed him. Had he been a little less precise, a little less timid in these matters, he would probably have kissed her. As it was, he contented himself by patting her hand rather foolishly and murmuring, 'Nothing to get excited about,' in a way which neither convinced her nor satisfied himself.

'In half an hour,' she murmured and disappeared like a fragile ghost down the corridor.

Chapter 7

Five o'clock in the Morning

George Abbershaw stood in front of the fire-place in his bedroom and looked down into the fast-greying embers amongst which some red sparks still glowed, and hesitated irresolutely. In ten minutes he was to meet Meggie and Anne Edgeware in the garden. He had until then to make up his mind.

He was not a man to do anything impulsively, and the problem which faced him now was an unusual one.

On the mantelpiece near his head lay a small leather wallet, the silk lining of which had been ripped open and something removed, leaving the whole limp and empty. Abbershaw looked down on a sheaf of paper which he held in one hand, and tapped it thoughtfully with the other.

If only, he reflected, he knew exactly what he was doing. The thought occurred to him, in parenthesis, that here arose the old vexed question as to whether it was permissible to destroy a work of art on any pretext whatsoever.

For five minutes he deliberated, and then, having made up his mind, he knelt down before the dying fire and fanned the embers into a flame, and after coolly preparing a small bonfire in the grate stood back to watch it burn.

The destruction of the leather case was a problem which presented more difficulties. For a moment or two he was at a loss, but then taking it up he considered it carefully.

It was of a usual pattern, a strip of red leather folded over at either end to form two inner pockets. He took out his own case and compared the two. His own was new; an aunt had sent it to him for his birthday, and in an excess of kindliness had caused a small gold monogram stud to be made for it, a circular fretted affair which fastened through the leather with a small clip. This stud Abbershaw removed, and, gouging a hole in the red wallet, effected an exchange.

A liberal splodging with ink from his fountain pen completed the disguise, and, satisfied that no one at a first or second glance would recognize it, he ripped out the rest of the lining, trimmed the edges with a pair of nail scissors, and calmly transferred his papers, with the exception of a letter or two, to it, and tucked it in his pocket. His own wallet he put carefully into the inner pocket of his dinner-jacket, hanging up in the wardrobe.

Then, content with his arrangements, he went softly down the wide staircase and let himself out into the garden.

Meggie was waiting for him. He caught a glimpse of her red-gold hair against the dark green of the shrubbery. She was dressed in green, and despite his preoccupation with the affairs on hand, he noticed how very much it suited her.

'Anne is just coming,' she said, 'I expect her any moment. I hope it's something important you want to ask her. I don't think she'll relish getting up just to see the sun rise.'

Abbershaw looked dubious.

'I'm afraid that didn't occur to me,' he said. 'It is important, as it happens, although it may not sound so.'

The girl moved a step closer to him.

'I told *you*,' she said, looking up into his face. 'Tell me. What are the developments?'

'I don't know,' he said, '. . . yet. There's only one thing I can tell you, and that will be common property by breakfast-time. Colonel Coombe is dead.'

The girl caught her breath sharply, and looked at him with fear in her brown eyes.

'You don't mean he was . . . ?' She broke off, not using the word.

Abbershaw looked at her steadily.

'Dr Whitby has pronounced it heart failure,' he said. The girl's eyes widened, and her expression became puzzled.

'Then – then the dagger –?' she began.

'Ssh!' Abbershaw raised his hand warningly, for in the house a door had creaked, and now Anne Edgeware, a heavily embroidered Chinese dressing-gown over her frivolous pyjamas, crossed the grass towards them.

'Here I am,' she said. 'I had to come like this. You don't mind, do you? I really couldn't bring myself to put on my clothes at the hour I usually take them off. What's all the fun about?'

Abbershaw coughed: this kind of girl invariably embarrassed him.

'It's awfully good of you to come down like this,' he said awkward-ly. 'And I'm afraid what I am going to say will sound both absurd and impertinent, but if you would just take it as a personal favour to me I would be eternally grateful.' He hesitated nervously, and then hurried on again. 'I'm afraid I can't offer you any explanation at the moment, but if you would just answer one or two questions and then forget I ever asked them, you would be rendering me a great service.'

The girl laughed.

'How thrilling!' she said. 'It sounds just like a play! I've got just the right costume too, haven't I? I feel I shall break out into song at any moment. What is it?'

Abbershaw was still ill at ease, and he spoke with unwonted timidity.

'That's very good of you. As a matter of fact I wanted to ask you about Mr Campion. I understood that he's a friend of yours. Excuse me, but have you known him long?'

'Albert Campion?' said Anne blankly. 'Oh, he's not a friend of mine at all. I just gave him a lift down here in "Fido" – that's my car.'

Abbershaw looked puzzled.

'I'm sorry. I don't quite understand,' he said. 'Did you meet him at the station?'

'Oh no.' The girl was amused. 'I brought him all the way down. You see,' she went on cheerfully, 'I met him the night before we came down at the "Goat on the Roof" – that's the new night-club in Jermyn Street, you know. I was with a party, and he sort of drifted into it. One of the lads knew him, I think. We were all talking, and quite suddenly it turned out that he was coming down here this week-end. He was fearfully upset, he said: he'd just run his bus into a lorry or something equally solid, so he couldn't come down in it. So I offered him a lift – naturally.'

'Oh, er – naturally,' said Abbershaw, who appeared to be still a little bewildered. 'Wyatt invited him, of course.'

The girl in pyjamas looked at him, and a puzzled expression appeared on her doll-like face.

'Oh no,' she said. 'I don't think so – in fact I'm sure he didn't, because I introduced them myself. Not properly, you know,' she went on airily. 'I just said, "Hullo, Wyatt, this thing is Albert Campion," and "Albert, this is the man of the house," but I could swear they didn't know each other. I think he's one of the Colonel's pals – how is the poor old boy, by the way?'

Neither Abbershaw nor Meggie spoke, but remained looking dubiously ahead of them, and Anne shivered.

'Here, I'm getting cold,' she said. 'Is that all you wanted to know? Because if it is, I'll get in, if you don't mind. Sunrises and dabbling in the dew aren't in my repertoire.'

She laughed as she spoke, and Abbershaw thanked her. 'Not a word, mind,' he said hastily.

'Not a hint,' she promised lightly, and went fluttering off across the lawn, the Chinese robe huddled about her.

As soon as she was out of earshot Meggie caught Abbershaw's arm.

'George,' she said, 'the Colonel didn't invite Albert Campion here.'

He turned to her sharply.

'How do you know?' he demanded.

The girl spoke dryly.

'Because,' she said, 'the Colonel himself pointed Campion out to me and asked who he was. Why, George,' she went on suddenly, as the idea occurred to her, *'nobody* asked him – he hasn't any business here at all!'

Abbershaw nodded.

'That's just exactly what had occurred to me,' he said, and relapsed into silence.

They walked slowly back to the house together, Meggie quiet and perturbed, her brown eyes narrowed and thoughtful; Abbershaw walking with his hands clasped behind his back, his head bowed.

He had had, he supposed, as much association with crime and criminals as any man of his age, but never, in any of his previous experiences of crime mysteries, had he been placed in a position which required of him both initiative and action. On other occasions an incident had been repeated to him and he had explained it, a problem had been put before him and he had solved it. Now, for the first time in his life he had to pick out his own questions and answer them himself. Every instinct in him told him to do something, but what exactly he ought to do he did not know.

They had almost reached the heavy iron-studded door which led into the hall, when a smothered exclamation from the girl made him stop suddenly and look up. The next instant he had stepped back into the shadow of some overgrown laurels by the house and drawn the girl back after him.

Out of the garage, silent as a cloud of smoke, had come the incredible old car which Abbershaw had noticed on the previous evening.

The man-servant who had created the scene with Mr Campion not an hour before was at the wheel, and Abbershaw noticed that for a man who had been murderously drunk so recently he was remarkably fresh and efficient.

The car drew up outside the main door of the mansion not ten paces from where they stood, hidden by the greenery. The man got out and opened the door of the car. For some minutes nothing happened, then Gideon appeared followed by Dawlish and Doctor Whitby, bearing between them a heavy burden.

They were all fully dressed, and appeared to be in a great hurry. So engrossed were they that not one of them so much as glanced in the direction of the laurel clump which hid the two onlookers. Whitby got into the back of the car and drew the blinds carefully over the windows, then Dawlish and Gideon lifted the long heavy bundle in after him and closed the door upon it.

The great car slid away down the drive, and the two men stepped back noiselessly into the house and disappeared.

The whole incident had taken perhaps three minutes, and it had been accomplished with perfect silence and precision.

Meggie looked up at Abbershaw fearfully.

'What was that?' she said.

The violence of his reply surprised her.

'Damn them!' he said explosively. 'The only piece of real evidence there was against them. That was the body of Colonel Coombe.'

Chapter 8

Open Warfare

Breakfast that morning showed every promise of being a gloomy and uncomfortable meal.

Wyatt had discreetly announced his uncle's death, and the news had circulated amongst the guests with inevitable speed.

The general opinion was that a tactful farewell and a speedy departure was the obvious procedure of the day. The story of the old man's last wish had not tended greatly to alter anyone's decision, as it was clear that no party was likely to be a success, or even bearable in such circumstances. The wishes of the dead seemed more kindly in intention than in fact.

Wyatt seemed very crestfallen, and a great deal of sympathy was felt for him; events could not well have turned out more unfortunately for him. He sat at the end of the table, a little paler than usual, but otherwise the same graceful, courteous scholar as ever. He wore the coloured tie of one of the more obscure Oxford clubs, and had not attempted to show any outward signs of mourning.

Albert Campion, looking none the worse for his nocturnal adventure, sat next to Anne Edgeware. They were talking quietly together, and from the sullen look upon Chris Kennedy's handsome face it was evident to anybody who cared to see that the irrepressible young lady was indulging in the harmless feminine sport of encouraging one admirer in order to infuriate and thereby gain the interest of another more valued suitor – even though the occasion was so inauspicious. Mr Campion was amazingly suited to his present role, and in low tones they planned their journey back to town together. Coming departures were indeed a subject for the general conversation of the rather dispirited assembly in the big sunlit hall.

Michael Prenderby was late for breakfast, and he came in, a trifle flushed and hurried, and took his place at the table between little Jeanne Dacre, his fiancée, and Martin Watt, the black-haired beaky youngster whom Meggie had described as 'Just a stray young man'. He was, in point of fact, a chartered accountant in his father's office, a pleasing youth with more brains than energy.

Neither Gideon nor Dawlish had appeared, nor had places been set for them, but the moment that Prenderby sat down and the number of the guests was completed, the door opened and the two men who most interested Abbershaw in the house that day walked into the room.

Dawlish came first, and in the sunlight his face appeared more unprepossessing than it had seemed on the evening before. For the first time it became apparent what an enormous man he was.

He was fat to the point of grossness, but tall with it, and powerfully built. The shock of long grey hair, brushed straight back from the forehead, hung almost to his shoulders, and the eyes, which seemed to be the only live thing in his face, were bright now and peculiarly arresting.

Gideon, who came in behind him, looked small and insignificant by comparison. He was languid and sinuous as before, and he glanced over the group of young people round the table with a thoughtful, mildly appraising eye, as if he were estimating their combined weight – or strength.

Wyatt looked up as they came in and bade them a polite 'Good morning'. To everyone's surprise they ignored him.

Dawlish moved ponderously to the top of the table, where he stood looking round at the astonished faces, with no expression on his own.

'Let there be silence,' he said.

The words were so utterly unexpected and out of keeping with the situation that it is probable that a certain amount of amusement would have greeted them had not the tone in his deep Teutonic voice been singularly menacing.

As it was, the silence was complete, and the German went on, his expression still unchanged so that it seemed that his voice came to them through a mask.

'Something has been lost,' he said, dividing the words up as he uttered them and giving equal emphasis to each. 'It must be returned to me. There is no need to explain what it is. Whoever has stolen it will know of what I speak.'

At this colossal piece of impudence a sensation ran round the table, and Wyatt sprang to his feet. He was livid with anger, but he kept his voice under perfect control, and the polished intensity of his icy tone contrasted sharply with the other's heavy rudeness.

'Mr Dawlish,' he said, 'I think your anxiety to recover your property has upset your sense of proportion. Perhaps you are aware that you are a guest in a house that is mine, and that the people that you have just insulted are my guests also. If you will come to me after breakfast – before you go – I will do all I can to institute a proper search for the thing you have mislaid.'

The German did not move. He stood at the head of the table and stared unblinkingly at the man before him.

'Until it is returned to me nobody leaves this house,' he said, the same solid force behind his tone. Wyatt's snub he did not appear to have heard. A faint wave of colour passed over the young man's pale face, and he turned to the others, who were staring from one to the other in frank astonishment.

'I must apologize,' he said. 'I ask you to forgive this extraordinary display. My uncle's death appears to have turned this unfortunate man's brain.'

Dawlish turned.

'That young man,' he said. 'Let him sit down and be quiet.'

Gideon smiled at Wyatt, and the look on his grey decadent face was an insult in itself.

'My dear Mr Petrie,' he said, and his peculiarly oily voice was suave and ingratiating, 'I don't think you quite realize the position you are in, you and your friends. Consider: this house is two miles from the public road. There is no telephone. We have two women servants and six men and a gate-keeper. All of these people are in Mr Dawlish's employ. Your cars have been drained of petrol. I am afraid you are entirely helpless.' He paused, and allowed his glance to take in the amazed expressions round the table.

'It would be better,' he continued, 'to listen rationally, for I must warn you, my friend Mr Dawlish is not a man who is accustomed to any opposition to his wishes.'

Wyatt remained on his feet; his face had grown slowly paler, and he was now rigid with barely controlled fury.

'Gentlemen, this farce has gone on long enough,' he said, in a voice which quivered in spite of himself. 'If you will please go away we will get on with our breakfast.'

'Sit down!'

The words were uttered in a sudden titanic bellow, though but for the obvious fact that Gideon was incapable of producing so much noise there was nothing upon Benjamin Dawlish's face to betray that it was he who had shouted.

Wyatt started; the limit of his patience had come. He opened his mouth to speak, to assert his authority. Then, quite suddenly, he dropped back into his chair, his eyes dilating with as much surprise as fear. He was looking into the black barrel of a revolver.

The German stood stolidly, absolutely immobile, the dangerous little weapon levelled in one ponderous hand. 'Here,' he said in his unwieldy English, 'there is one who has what I seek. To him I speak. When he returns to me what he has taken you shall all go free. Until then no one leaves this house – no one at all.'

In the silence which followed this extraordinary announcement Jesse Gideon moved forward.

'If Mr Dawlish were to receive his property immediately it would save us all a great deal of inconvenience,' he murmured.

For several seconds there was no movement in the room, and the singing of the birds in the greenery outside the windows became suddenly very noticeable.

Then Albert Campion coughed discreetly and handed something wrapped up in his table napkin to the girl who sat next to him.

She passed it to her neighbour, and in utter stillness it went the whole length of the table until Gideon pounced on it avidly and set it before the German on the table. With a grunt of satisfaction the big man thrust the revolver into his coat pocket and threw aside the white napery. Then an exclamation of anger escaped him, and he drew back so that Mr Campion's offering lay exposed.

It was a breakfast egg, the very one, in fact, which the fatuous young man had been on the verge of broaching when the extraordinary interruptions had occurred.

The effect was instantaneous; the reaction from the silent tension of a moment before complete.

The entire table shook with laughter.

The German stood stiffly as before. There was still no expression of any sort upon his face, and his little eyes became dull and lifeless.

Gideon, on the other hand, betrayed his anger vividly. His eyes were narrowed with fury and his long thin lips were drawn back over his teeth like an angry dog's. Gradually the laughter subsided. Benjamin Dawlish's personality was one that could not be ignored for long. When at last there was perfect silence in the room he put his hand in his pocket and drew out his revolver again.

'You laugh,' he said heavily. 'I do not laugh. And she, the little one,' he tossed the gun in his hand with incredible delicacy for one who looked so clumsy, '*she does not laugh either*.'

The last words were uttered with such amazing ferocity that his hearers started involuntarily, and for an instant there appeared upon the heavy face, which hitherto had seemed immovable, an expression of such animalic violence that not one at that table looked him in the eyes.

A moment later his features had relapsed into their usual stolidity, and followed by Jesse Gideon he walked slowly from the room.

As the door closed behind them, the silence became painful, and at last a fitful, uneasy conversation broke out.

'What an unpleasant old bird!' said Prenderby, looking at Abbershaw. He spoke lightly, but there was a worried expression in his eyes; one hand rested over his fiancée's, who sat very pale by his side apparently on the verge of tears. Even Anne Edgeware's magnificent sang-froid seemed a little shaken, and Meggie, although the least alarmed of the three girls, looked very white.

Wyatt was still angry. He gave up trying to apologize for the incident, however, and joined with the others in discussing it.

'He's loony, of course,' said Martin Watt lazily. 'Campion got his goat beautifully, I thought.'

'Still, even if he is potty, if what he says is true, things are going to be pretty sportive,' remarked Chris Kennedy cheerfully. 'I fear I may be called upon to bash his head in.'

Abbershaw rose to his feet.

'I don't know what you think, Wyatt,' he said, 'but it occurs to me that it might be an idea if we all went into the other room and talked this thing over. The servants won't disturb us there. I don't think there's any real danger,' he went on reassuringly, 'but perhaps we ought to find out if what Gideon says about the cars is true.'

Chris Kennedy got up eagerly.

'I'll toddle down and discover, shall I?' he said. 'Really – I should like to,' he added, as Wyatt regarded him doubtfully, and he went off whistling.

The party adjourned to the next room as Abbershaw had suggested. They still talked lightly, but there was a distinctly constrained atmosphere amongst them. Jeanne was frankly scared, Anne Edgeware out of her depth, and the rest apprehensive.

Abbershaw was the last to step into the enormous hall that was now a blaze of sunlight. It poured in through long diamond-paned windows, glinted on the polished floor, and shone softly on Tudor rose and linenfold. But it was not these which caught his eye and made him start back with a half-concealed exclamation.

Over the far fire-place, set in the circle of lanceheads, its clear blade dazzling in the sun and gleaming as brightly as if it had never left its plaque, sinister and beautiful, was the Black Dudley Dagger.

Chapter 9

Chris Kennedy Scores a Try Only

As soon as Abbershaw had recovered from his first surprise, he turned to Meggie. She was standing just beside him, the others having split up into little groups talking quietly together. 'Did you come in here this morning,' he said, 'after we came in from the garden?'

She nodded, and he saw that she was trembling slightly. 'Yes,' she whispered, 'and – and *it* was here then, hanging just where it is now. I – I couldn't help coming in to see. Someone must have put it back – in the night.'

Her voice died away in a sob on the last word, and he laid a hand on her arm.

'Scared?' he said.

She met his eyes bravely.

'I'm glad you're here too,' she said simply.

A wave of pleasure swept over Abbershaw, and he coloured, but he did not speak. The gravity of the situation was by no means lost to him. He was the eldest of the party, and, moreover, he knew more about the events of the last twelve hours than probably anyone else in the room.

Something told him to keep quiet about his discoveries, however; he realized that they were up against dangerous men. Mr Benjamin Dawlish, as he styled himself, was no ordinary individual, and, at the moment, he was angry.

The main idea now was to get away at all costs; Abbershaw was sure of it.

He had not dreamed that the late Colonel's extraordinary friends would dare to take this extreme course, but since they had done so, he was not fool enough to think that they would risk the possibility of being overpowered; their forces must be very strong.

Once out of the house he himself could get an immediate inquiry instituted by the highest authorities. If the police could be informed without their captors' knowledge, so much the better, but the principal problem was escape, and that, in the present circumstances, did not appear to be any too simple.

There was, of course, one way of obtaining freedom; he felt the battered red wallet in his pocket now, but he was loth to take that path, for it meant the escape of what he felt certain was a leader of one of the most skilful criminal organizations in the world. So far he had been working in the dark, and if he gave in now, that darkness would never be lightened. It would mean complete surrender. The mystery would remain a mystery.

He glanced down at Meggie.

'We'll lick 'em yet,' he said.

She laughed at him.

'Or die in the attempt.'

Abbershaw appeared vastly relieved.

'That's how I feel,' he said.

It was at this moment that Mr Campion made the entire party one group again by a single fatuous remark.

'Of course,' he said affably, 'I suppose nobody has pinched anything.'

'I've got two bits of soap in my room,' murmured Prenderby, 'but I shouldn't think that's what the old bird's after by the look of him. And look here, Wyatt,' he added suddenly, 'there's something damned queer about something else! I suppose you know –'

Abbershaw interposed hastily.

'The whole thing is a bit queer, Michael,' he said, fixing the boy with his eyes. Prenderby took the hint, and was silent, but Wyatt turned to him.

'I'm beyond apologizing,' he said. 'The whole business is quite out of my experience. My uncle asked me to bring a party down for this week-end. He had often done so before. I have met Gideon here before, but never exchanged more than half a dozen words with him. As for that Hun, Dawlish, he's a complete stranger.'

Prenderby, to whom the words had sounded like a reproach, coloured, and what might have been an uncomfortable pause was covered by the sudden return of Chris Kennedy. He was in high good humour. His handsome young face was flushed with excitement, and the others could not banish the suspicion that he was enjoying the situation thoroughly.

'They *have*, the blighters!' he said, bursting into the group. 'Not a drain of juice in any of the buses. Otherwise they're all right, though.

"Exhibit A" has vanished, by the way – crumbled into dust, I should think – but apart from that they're all there.'

'Meet anyone?' said Martin.

'Not a soul,' said Kennedy cheerfully, 'and little Christopher Robin has an idea. If I asked you for a drink, Petrie, would you give me ginger-beer?' There was an air of suppressed jubilation in his tone as he spoke.

'My dear fellow . . .' Wyatt started forward. 'I think you'll find all you want here,' he said, and led the way to a cupboard set in the panelling of the fire-place. Kennedy stuck his head in it, and came out flushed and triumphant. 'Two Scotch and a "Three Star" Brandy,' he said, tucking the bottles under his arm. 'It's blasphemy, but there's no other way. Get to the window, chicks, and Uncle Christopher will now produce the rabbit.'

'What are you going to do with that stuff?' said Watt, who was not an admirer of the athletic type. 'Fill yourself up with it and run amok?'

Kennedy grinned at him over his shoulder; he was already half out of the room.

'No fear!' he said, pausing with his hand on the door-handle. 'But the Salmson is. Watch the garage. Keep your eyes upon the perform-ance, ladies and gentlemen. This trick cannot be repeated.'

The somewhat bewildered little group regarded him doubtfully.

'I'm afraid I don't follow you even now,' said Martin, still coldly. 'I'm probably infernally thick, but I don't get your drift.'

Michael Prenderby suddenly lifted his head.

'Good Lord!' he said. 'I do believe you might do it. What a stunt!'

'That's what I thought,' said Kennedy.

He went out, and they heard him racing down the corridor.

Abbershaw turned to Michael.

'What's the idea?' he said.

Prenderby grinned.

'He's going to use the booze as juice,' he said. 'Rather an idea, don't you think? A car like that ought to run on pure spirit, I suppose. Let's watch him.'

He led the way to the windows and the others followed him. By craning their necks they could just see the doors of the barn, both of which stood open.

For some minutes nothing happened, and Martin Watt was just beginning to assure himself that his first impression of Kennedy's ideas in general was going to be justified when a terrific back-fire sounded from the garage.

'Good heavens!' said Abbershaw. 'He's going to do it.'

Someone began to laugh.

'What a pack of fools they'll look,' said Prenderby.

Another small explosion sounded from the garage, and the next moment the little car appeared in a cloud of blue smoke, with Mr Kennedy at the wheel. It was moving slowly but triumphantly, and emitting a stream of back-fires like a machine-gun.

'Isn't he marvellous?'

Anne Edgeware clasped her hands as she spoke, and even Martin Watt admitted grudgingly that 'the lad had initiative'. Kennedy waved to them, and they saw his face flushed and excited as a child's. As he changed gear the car jerked forward and set off down the drive at an uneven but ever-increasing pace.

'That'll show 'em,' said Prenderby with a chuckle.

'They haven't even tried to stop him,' said little Jeanne Dacre.

At that moment Mr Kennedy changed into top gear with a roar, and immediately there was a sharp report, followed by a second, which seemed to come from a window above their heads. Instantly, even as they watched it, the Salmson swerved violently, skidded drunkenly across the drive and turned over, pitching its occupant out upon the grass beside the path.

'Good God!'

Michael Prenderby's voice was hoarse in the silence.

Martin Watt spoke quickly.

'Dawlish's gun. They've got him. The Hun was in earnest. Come on, you fellows.'

He thrust open the window and leapt out upon the lawn, the men following him.

Chris Kennedy was already picking himself up when they reached him. He was very white, and his left hand grasped his other wrist, from which the blood was streaming.

'They got my near-side front wheel and my driving arm,' he gasped, as they came up. 'There's a bloke somewhere about who can shoot like hell.'

He swayed a little on the last word, and smiled valiantly. 'Do you mind if we get in?' he murmured. 'This thing is turning me sick.'

They got him back to the house and into the room where they had all been standing. As they crossed the lawn, Abbershaw, glancing up at the second-floor windows, fancied he saw a heavy expressionless face peering out at them from behind the dark curtains.

The rescue party was considerably subdued. They were beginning to believe in the sincerity of Mr Benjamin Dawlish's remarks.

Kennedy collapsed into a chair, and, after saving him from the tender ministrations of Anne Edgeware, Abbershaw was just about to set out in search of warm water and a dress shirt to tear up as a bandage, when there was a discreet tap on the door and a man-servant entered bearing a complete surgical outfit together with antiseptic bandages and hot water.

'With Mr Gideon's compliments,' he said gravely, and went out.

Kennedy smiled weakly.

'Curse their dirty politeness,' he said, and bowed his head over his injured wrist.

Abbershaw removed his coat and went over to the tray which the man had brought.

'Hullo!' he said. 'There's a note. Read it, Wyatt, will you, while I get on with this. These are Whitby's things, I suppose. It almost looks as if he was expecting trouble.'

Wyatt took the slip of paper off the tray and read the message aloud in his clear even voice.

'*We are not joking. No one leaves this house until we have what we want.*'

'There's no signature,' he added, and handed the note to Prenderby, who looked at it curiously.

'Looks as if they *have* lost something,' he said. 'What the devil is it? We can't help 'em much till we know what it is.'

No one spoke for a moment.

'Yes, that's true,' said Martin Watt at last, 'and the only thing we know about it is that it isn't an egg.'

There was a faint titter of laughter at this, but it soon died down; the party was beginning to realize the seriousness of their position.

'It must be something pretty fishy, anyway,' said Chris Kennedy, still white with the pain of his wound which Abbershaw was now bandaging. 'Else why don't they describe it so that we can all have a hunt round? Look here, let's go to them and tell them that we don't know what their infernal property is. They can search us if they like, and when they find we haven't got it they can let us go, and by God, when they do I'll raise hell!'

'It is precisely for that reason that I'm not inclined to endorse that suggestion, Kennedy,' said Abbershaw without looking up from the bandage he was winding. 'Our friends upstairs are very determined, and they're not likely to risk a possible visit from the police before they have got what they want and have had reasonable time to make a good getaway.'

Martin Watt raised his hand.

'One moment,' he said, 'let us do a spot of neat detective work. What the German gentleman with no manners has lost must be very small. "And why, my dear Sherlock?" you ask. Because, my little Watsons, when our obliging young comrade, Campion, offered them an egg wrapped up in a table napkin they thought they'd holed in one. It isn't the Black Dudley diamonds, I suppose, Petrie?'

'There aren't any,' said Wyatt shortly. 'Damn it all!' he burst out with a sudden violence. 'I never felt so helpless in my life.'

'If only we had a few guns,' mourned Chris Kennedy, whose wound even had not slaked his thirst for a scrap. 'Then we might make an attempt to rush 'em. But unarmed against birds who shoot like that we shouldn't have an earthly.'

'It's not such a bad thing for you that we're not armed, my lad,' said Abbershaw, straightening his shoulders and stepping back from the table. 'You don't want too much excitement with an arm like that. You've lost enough blood already. If I were you, I'd try and get a spot of sleep. What's your opinion, Prenderby?'

'Oh, sleep, by all means,' said Michael, grinning, 'if he can get it, which doesn't seem likely.'

They were all standing round the patient on the hearth-rug, with their backs to the fire-place, and for the moment Kennedy was the centre of interest.

Hardly were the words out of Prenderby's mouth when they were suddenly and startlingly confirmed by an hysterical scream from Anne Edgeware.

'He's gone!' she said wildly, as they turned to her. Her dark eyes were dilated with fear, and every trace of her usual sophisticated and slightly blasé manner had disappeared.

'He was standing here – just beside me. He spoke to me a second ago. He couldn't have got past me to the door – I was directly in his way. He's just vanished. Oh, God – I'm going potty! I think – I . . .' She screamed again.

'My dear girl!'

Abbershaw moved to her side. 'What's the matter? Who's vanished?'

The girl looked at him in stupid amazement. 'He went from my side just as if he had disappeared into the air,' she repeated. 'I was just talking to him – I turned away to look at Chris for a moment – I heard a sort of thud, and when I turned round he'd gone.'

She began to cry noisily.

'Yes, but who? Who?' said Wyatt impatiently. 'Who has vanished?'

Anne peered at him through her tears.

'Why, *Albert!*' she said, and burst into louder sobbing. 'Albert Campion. They've got him because he made fun of them!'

Chapter 10

The Impetuous Mr Abbershaw

A hasty search revealed the fact that Mr Campion had indeed disappeared, and the discovery, coupled with Chris Kennedy's experience of the morning, reduced the entire company to an unpleasant state of nerves. The terrified Anne Edgeware and the wounded rugby blue comforted each other in a corner by the fire. Prenderby's little fiancée clung to his hand as a frightened child might have done. The others talked volubly, but every minute the general gloom deepened.

In the midst of this the lunch gong in the outer hall sounded, as if nothing untoward had happened. For some moments nobody moved. Then Wyatt got up. 'Well, anyway,' he said, 'they seem to intend to feed us – let's go in, shall we?'

They followed him dubiously into the other room, where a cold luncheon had been prepared at the long table. Two men-servants waited on them, silent and surly, and the meal was a quiet one. No one felt in the mood for trivialities, and Mr Campion was not there to provide his usual harmless entertainment.

There was a certain amount of apprehension, also, lest Mr Dawlish might reappear and the experience of breakfast be repeated. Everyone felt a little relieved, therefore, when the meal ended without a visitation. The explanation of this apparent neglect came ten minutes or so later, when Martin Watt, who had gone up to his room to replenish his cigarette-case, came dashing into the hall where they were all sitting, the lazy expression for once startled out of his grey eyes.

'I say,' he said, 'the blighters have searched my room! Had a real old beano up there by the look of it. Clothes all over the place – half the floor boards up. I should say the Hun has done it himself – it looks as if an elephant had run amok there. If I were you people I'd trot up to your rooms and see if they've done the thing thoroughly.'

This announcement brought everybody to their feet. Wyatt, who still considered himself the host of the party, fumed impotently. Chris

Kennedy swore lurid deeds of revenge under his breath, and Prenderby and Abbershaw exchanged glances. Abbershaw smiled grimly. 'I think perhaps we had better take Watt's suggestion,' he said, and led the way out of the hall.

Once in his room he found that their fears had been justified. His belongings had been ransacked, his meticulously arranged suitcase lying open on its side, and his clothes strewn in all directions. The door of the big oak press with the carved front, which was built into the wall and took up all one end of the room, stood open, its contents all over the floor.

A wave of uncontrollable anger passed over him, and with that peculiarly precise tidiness which was one of his most marked characteristics he began methodically to put the room straight again.

Prisoners they might be, shots could be fired, and people could disappear apparently into thin air, none of these could shake him, but the sight of his belongings jumbled into this appalling confusion all but unnerved him completely.

He packed up everything he possessed very neatly, and stowed it in the press, then, slamming the heavy oaken door, he turned the key in the lock, and thrust it into his pocket.

It was at this precise moment that an extraordinary mental revolution took place in Abbershaw.

It happened as he put the cupboard key in his pocket; during the actual movement he suddenly saw himself from the outside. He was naturally a man of thought, not of action, and now for the first time in his life he was thrust into a position where quick decisions and impulsive actions were forced from him. So far, he realized suddenly, he had always been a little late in grasping the significance of each situation as it had arisen. This discovery horrified him, and in that moment of enlightenment Dr George Abbershaw, the sober, deliberate man of science, stepped into the background, and George Abbershaw the impulsive, energetic enthusiast came forward to meet the case.

He did not lose his head, however. He realized that at the present juncture infinite caution was vital. The next move must come from Dawlish. Until that came they must wait patiently, ready to grasp at the first chance of freedom. The present state of siege was only tenable for a very short time. For a week-end Black Dudley might be safe from visitors, tradespeople, and the like, but after Monday inquiries must inevitably be made. Dawlish would have to act soon.

There was the affair of Albert Campion. Wyatt had been peculiarly silent about him, and Abbershaw did not know what to make of it at all. His impulse was to get the idiot back into their own circle at all costs, but there was no telling if he had been removed or if he had vanished of his own free will. No one knew anything about him.

Abbershaw went slowly out of the room and down the corridor to the staircase, and was just about to descend when he heard the unmistakable sound of a woman crying.

He paused to listen, and discovered that the noise came from behind a door on his left.

He hesitated.

Half an hour before, a fear of being intrusive would have prevented him from doing anything, but a very considerable change had taken place in him in that time, and he listened again.

The sound continued.

The thought dawned upon him that it was Meggie; he fancied that this was her room, and the idea of her alone and in distress banished his last vestige of timidity and caution. He knocked at the door.

Her voice answered him.

'It's George,' he said, almost defiantly. 'Anything the matter?'

She was some seconds opening the door, and when at last she came he saw that although she had hastily powdered her face the tear-stains were still visible upon it.

For one moment Abbershaw felt that he was going to have a relapse into his old staid self, but he overcame it and there was an expression of fiery determination in his chubby round face which astonished the girl so much that her surprise showed in her eyes. Abbershaw recognized it, and it annoyed him.

In a flash he saw himself as she must have seen him all along, a round, a self-important little man, old for his years, inclined to be pompous, perhaps – terrible thought – even fussy. A horrible sense of humiliation swept over him and at the same time a growing desire to teach her she was wrong, to show her that she had been mistaken, to prove to her that he was a man to be reckoned with, a personality, a man of action, vigorous, resourceful, a he-man, a . . . !

He drew a deep breath.

'I can't have you crying like this,' he said, and picked her up and kissed her.

Meggie could not have responded more gracefully. Whether it was relief, shock, or simply the last blow to her tortured nerves, he never knew, but she collapsed into his arms; at first he almost thought she had fainted.

He led her firmly down the long corridor to the wide window-seat at the far end. It was recessed, and hung with heavy curtains. He sat down and drew her beside him, her head on his shoulder.

'Now,' he said, still bristling with his newly discovered confidence, 'you're going to escape from here tomorrow certainly, if not tonight, and you're going to marry me because I love you! I love you! I love you!'

He paused breathlessly and waited, his heart thumping against his side like a schoolboy's.

Her face was hidden from him and she did not speak. For a moment the awful thought occurred to him that she might be angry with him, or even – laughing.

'You – er – you will marry me?' he said, a momentary anxiety creeping into his tone. 'I'm sorry if I startled you,' he went on, with a faint return of his old primness. 'I didn't mean to, but I – I'm an impetuous sort of fellow.'

Meggie stirred at his side, and as she lifted her face to him he saw that she was flushed with laughter, but there was more than mere amusement in her brown eyes. She put her arm round his neck and drew his head down.

'George, you're adorable,' she said. 'I love you ridiculously, my dear.'

A slow, warm glow spread all over Abbershaw. His heart lolloped in his side, and his eyes danced.

He kissed her again. She lay against his breast very quiet, very happy, but still a little scared.

He felt like a giant refreshed – after all, he reflected, his first essay in his new role had been an unparalleled success.

Chapter 11

One Explanation

That evening, after tea had been served in ominous silence by the same two men-servants who had waited at lunch, Michael Prenderby crossed the room and spoke confidentially to Abbershaw.

'I say,' he said awkwardly, 'poor old Jeanne has got the wind up pretty badly. Do you think we've got an earthly chance of making a bolt for it?' He paused, and then went on again quickly, 'Can't we hatch out a scheme of some sort? Between you and me, I'm feeling a bit desperate.'

Abbershaw frowned.

'We can't do much at the moment, I'm afraid,' he said slowly; but added, as the boy's expression grew more and more perturbed, 'Look here, come up and smoke a cigarette with me in my room and we'll talk it over.'

'I'd like to.' Prenderby spoke eagerly, and the two men slipped away from the others and went quietly up to Abbershaw's room.

As far as they could ascertain, Dawlish and the others had their headquarters in the vast old apartment which had been Colonel Coombe's bedroom and the rooms immediately above and below it, into which there seemed no entrance from any part of the house that they knew.

Even Wyatt could not help them with the geography of Black Dudley. The old house had been first monastery, then farmstead, and finally a dwelling-house, and in each period different alterations had been made.

Besides, before the second marriage of his aunt, the enormous old place had been shut up, and it was not until shortly before her death that Wyatt first stayed at the place. Since then his visits had been infrequent and never of a long enough duration to allow him to become familiar with the numberless rooms, galleries, passages, and staircases of which the place was composed.

Prenderby was getting nerves, his fiancée's terror was telling on him, and, of course, he knew considerably more of the ugly facts of the situation than any one of the party save Abbershaw himself.

'The whole thing seemed almost a joke this morning,' he said petulantly. 'That old Hun might have been a music-hall turn then, but I don't mind confessing that I've got the wind up now. Hang it all,' he went on bitterly, 'we're as far away from civilization here as we should be if this was the seventeenth century. The modern "Majesty of the Law" and all that has made us so certain of our own safety that when a trap like this springs we're fairly caught. Damn it, Abbershaw, brute force is the only real power, anyway.'

'Perhaps,' said Abbershaw guardedly, 'but it's early yet. Some opportunity is bound to crop up within the next twelve hours. I think we shall see our two troublesome friends in gaol before we're finished.'

Prenderby glanced at him sharply.

'You're very optimistic, aren't you?' he said. 'You talk as if something distinctly promising had happened. Has it?'

George Abbershaw coughed.

'In a way, yes,' he said, and was silent. Now, he felt, was not the moment to announce his engagement to Meggie.

They had reached the door of the bedroom by this time, and further inquiries on Prenderby's part were cut short by a sudden and arresting phenomenon.

From inside the room came a series of extraordinary sounds – long, high-pitched murmurs, intermingled with howls and curses, and accompanied now and then by a sound of scuffling.

'My God!' said Prenderby. 'What in the name of good fortune is that?'

Abbershaw did not answer him.

Clearly the move which he had been expecting had been made.

With all his new temerity he seized the door-latch and was about to fling it up, when Prenderby caught his arm.

'Go carefully! Go carefully!' he said, with a touch of indignation in his voice. 'You don't want to shove your head in it, whatever it is. They're armed, remember.'

The other nodded, and raising the latch very cautiously he thrust the door gently open.

Prenderby followed him; both men were alert and tingling with expectation.

The noise continued; it was louder than before, and sounded peculiarly unearthly in that ghostly house.

Abbershaw was the first to peer round the door and look in.

'Good Lord!' he said at last, glancing back over his shoulder at Prenderby, 'there's not a soul here.'

The two men burst into the room, and the noise, although muffled, became louder still.

'I say!' said Prenderby, suddenly startled out of his annoyance, 'it's in *there*!'

Abbershaw followed the direction of his hand and gasped.

The extraordinary sounds were indubitably proceeding from the great oak press at the far end of the room – the wardrobe which he had locked himself not two hours before and the key of which was still heavy in his pocket. He turned to Michael.

'Shut the door,' he said. 'Lock it, and take the key.' Then he advanced towards the cupboard.

Michael Prenderby stood with his back against the door of the room, waiting.

Very gingerly Abbershaw fitted the huge iron key into the cupboard, turned over the lock, and wrenched the door open, starting back instantly.

The noise stopped abruptly.

There was a smothered exclamation from Prenderby and both men stood back in utter amazement.

There, seated upon a heavy oaken shelf in a square cavity just large enough to contain him, his hair over his eyes, his clothes dishevelled, his inane face barely recognizable, was Mr Albert Campion.

For several seconds he did not move, but sat blinking at them through the lank strands of yellow hair over his eyes. Then it was that Abbershaw's memory revived.

In a flash it came to him where he had seen that vacuous, inoffensive face before, and a slow expression of wonderment came into his eyes.

He did not speak, however, for at that moment Campion stirred, and climbed stiffly out into the room.

'No deception, ladies and gentlemen,' he said, with a wan attempt at his own facetiousness. 'All my own work.'

'How the devil did you get in there?' The words were Prenderby's; he had come forward, his eyes fixed upon the forlorn figure in child-like astonishment.

'Oh – influence, mostly,' said Campion, and dropped into a chair. But it was evident that a great deal of his spirit had left him.

Obviously he had been badly handled, there were crimson marks round his wrists, and his shirt showed ragged beneath his jacket.

Prenderby opened his mouth to speak again, but a sign from Abbershaw silenced him.

'Dawlish got you, of course?' he said, with an unwonted touch of severity in his tone.

Mr Campion nodded.

'Did they search you?' Abbershaw persisted.

'Search me?' said he. A faintly weary expression came into the pale eyes behind the large spectacles. 'My dear sir, they almost had my skin off in their investigations. That Hun talks like comic opera but behaves like the Lord High Executioner. He nearly killed me.' He took his coat off as he spoke, and showed them a shirt cut to ribbons and stained with blood from great weals across his back.

'Good God!' said Abbershaw. 'Thrashed!' Instantly his magisterial manner vanished and he became the professional man with a case to attend to.

'Michael,' he said, 'there's a white shirt amongst my things in that cupboard, and water and boracic on the wash-stand. What happened?' he continued briefly, as Prenderby hurried to make all preparations for dressing the man's injuries.

Mr Campion stirred painfully.

'As far as I can remember,' he said weakly, 'about four hundred years ago I was standing by the fire-place talking to Anne What's-her-name, when suddenly the panel I was leaning against gave way, and the next moment I was in the dark with a lump of sacking in my mouth.' He paused. 'That was the beginning,' he said. 'Then I was hauled up before old Boanerges and he put me through it pretty thoroughly; I couldn't convince him that I hadn't got his packet of love-letters or whatever it is that he's making such a stink about. A more thorough old bird in the questioning line I never met.'

'So I should think,' murmured Prenderby, who had now got Campion's shirt off and was examining his back.

'When they convinced themselves that I was as innocent as a new-born babe,' continued the casualty, some of his old cheerfulness returning, 'they gave up jumping on me and put me into a box-room and locked the door.' He sighed. 'I sleuthed round for a bit,' he went on, while they listened to him eagerly. 'The window was about two thousand feet from the ground with a lot of natty ironwork on it – and finally, looking round for a spot soft enough for me to lie down without yowling, I perceived an ancient chest, under the other cardboard whatnots and fancy basketwork about the place, and I opened it.' He paused, and drank the tooth-glass of water which Prenderby handed to him.

'I thought some grandmotherly garment might be there,' he continued. 'Something I could make a bed of. All I found, however, was something that I took to be a portion of an ancient bicycle – most unsuitable for my purpose. I was so peeved that I jumped on it with malicious intent, and immediately the whole show gave way and I made a neat but effective exit through the floor. When I got the old brain working again, I discovered that I was standing on the top of a flight of steps, my head still half out of the chest. The machinery was the ancients' idea of a blind, I suppose. So I shut the lid of the trunk behind me, and lighting a match toddled down the steps.'

He stopped again. The two men were listening to him intently.

'I don't see how you got into the cupboard, all the same,' said Prenderby.

'Nor do I, frankly,' said Mr Campion. 'The steps stopped after a bit and I was in a sort of tunnel – a ratty kind of place; the little animals put the wind up me a bit – but eventually I crawled along and came up against a door which opened inwards, got it open, and sneaked out into your cupboard. That didn't help me much,' he added dryly. 'I didn't know where I was, so I just sat there reciting "The Mistletoe Bough" to myself, and confessing my past life – such sport!' He grinned at them and stopped. 'That's all,' he said.

Abbershaw, who had been watching him steadily as he talked, came slowly down the room and stood before him.

'I'm sorry you had such a bad time,' he said, and added very clearly and distinctly, 'but there's really no need to keep up this bright conversation, *Mr Mornington Dodd.*'

For some seconds Mr Campion's pale eyes regarded Abbershaw blankly. Then he started almost imperceptibly, and a slow smile spread over his face.

'So you've spotted me,' he said, and, to Abbershaw's utter amazement, chuckled inanely. 'But,' went on Mr Campion cheerfully, 'I assure you you're wrong about my magnetic personality being a disguise. There is *absolutely no fraud*. I'm like this – always like this – my best friends could tell you.'

This announcement took the wind out of Abbershaw's sails; he had certainly not expected it.

Mr Campion's personality was a difficult one to take seriously; it was not easy, for instance, to decide when he was lying and when he was not. Abbershaw had reckoned upon his thrust going home, and although it had obviously done so he did not seem to have gained any advantage by it.

Prenderby, however, was entirely in the dark, and now he broke in upon the conversation with curiosity.

'Here, I say, I don't get this,' he said. 'Who and what is Mr Mornington Dodd?'

Abbershaw threw out his hand, indicating Mr Albert Campion.

'That gentleman,' he said, 'is Mornington Dodd.'

Albert Campion smiled modestly. In spite of his obvious pain he was still lively.

'In a way yes, and in a way no,' he said, fixing his eyes on Abbershaw. 'Mornington Dodd is one of my names. I have also been called the "Honourable Tootles Ash", which I thought was rather neat when it occurred to me. Then there was a girl who used to call me "Cuddles" and a man at the Guards Club called me something quite different –'

'Campion, this is not a joke.' Abbershaw spoke sternly. 'However many and varied your aliases have been, now isn't the time to boast of them. We are up against something pretty serious now.'

'My dear man, don't I know it?' said Mr Campion peevishly, indicating the state of his shoulders. 'Even better than you do, I should think,' he said dryly.

'Now look here,' said Abbershaw, whose animosity could not but be mollified by this extraordinary naïveté, 'you know something about this business, Campion – that is your name, I suppose?'

'Well – er – no,' said the irrepressible young man. 'But,' he added, dropping his voice a tone, 'my own is rather aristocratic, and I never use it in business. Campion will do quite well.'

Abbershaw smiled in spite of himself.

'Very well, then, Mr Campion,' he said, 'as I remarked before, you know something about this business, and you're going to tell us here and now. But my dear lad, consider,' he went on as the other hesitated, 'we're all in the same boat. You, I presume, are as anxious to get away as anyone. And whereas I am intensely interested in bringing Dawlish and his confederates to justice, there is no other delinquency that I am concerned with. I am not a policeman.'

Mr Campion beamed. 'Is that so?' he inquired.

'Certainly it is,' said Abbershaw. 'I am a consultant only as far as the Yard is concerned.'

Mr Campion looked vastly relieved.

'That's rather cheered me up,' he said. 'I liked you. When I saw you pottering with your car I thought, "There's a little joss who might be quite good fun if he once got off the lead", and when you mentioned Scotland Yard just now all that good impression just faded away.'

He paused, and Abbershaw cut in quickly.

'This doesn't get us very far,' he said quietly, 'does it? You know the explanation of this extraordinary outrage. Let's have it.'

Mr Campion regarded him frankly.

'You may not believe me,' he said, 'but I don't know quite what they're driving at even now. But there's something pretty serious afoot, I can tell you that.'

It was obvious that he was telling the truth, but Abbershaw was not satisfied.

'Well, anyway, you know one thing,' he said. 'Why are you here? You just admitted yourself it was on business.'

'Oh, it was,' agreed Campion, 'most decidedly. But not my business. Let me explain.'

'I wish to God you would,' said Prenderby, who was utterly out of his depth.

'Well then, chicks, Uncle Albert speaking.' Campion leant forward, his expression more serious than his words. 'Perhaps I ought to give you some little idea of my profession. I live, like all intelligent people, by my wits, and although I have often done things that mother wouldn't like, I have remembered her parting words and have never been vulgar. To cut it short, in fact, I do almost anything within reason – for a reasonable sum, but nothing sordid or vulgar – quite definitely nothing vulgar.'

He glanced at Abbershaw, who nodded, and then went on.

'In this particular case,' he said, 'I was approached in London last week by a man who offered me a very decent sum to get myself included as unobtrusively as possible into the house-party this week-end and then to seize the first opportunity I could get of speaking to my host, the Colonel, alone. I was to make sure that we were alone. Then I was to go up to him, murmur a password in his ear, and receive from him a package which I was to bring to London immediately – unopened. I was warned, of course,' he continued, looking up at Abbershaw. 'They told me I was up against men who would have no compunction in killing me to prevent me getting away with the package, but I had no idea who the birds were going to be or I shouldn't have come for any money. In fact when I saw them at dinner on the first night I nearly cut the whole job right out and bunked back to town.'

'Why? Who are they?' said Abbershaw.

Mr Campion looked surprised.

'Good Lord, don't you know?' he demanded. 'And little George a Scotland Yard expert, too. Jesse Gideon calls himself a solicitor. As a matter of fact he's rather a clever fence. And the Hun is no one else but Eberhard von Faber himself.'

Prenderby still looked blank, but Abbershaw started.

'The "*Trois Pays*" man?' he said quickly.

'And "*Der Schwarzbund*". And "The Chicago Junker", and now our own little "0072" at the Yard,' said Mr Campion, and there was no facetiousness in his tone.

'This means nothing to me,' said Prenderby.

Mr Campion opened his mouth to speak, but Abbershaw was before him.

'It means, Michael,' he said, with an inflection in his voice which betrayed the gravity in which he viewed the situation, 'that this man controls organized gangs of crooks all over Europe and America, and he has the reputation of being utterly ruthless and diabolically clever. It means we are up against the most dangerous and notorious criminal of modern times.'

Chapter 12

'Furthermore . . .' said Mr Campion

After the little silence that followed Abbershaw's announcement, Prenderby spoke.

'What's in this mysterious package they've lost?' he said.

Abbershaw looked at Mr Campion inquiringly.

'Perhaps you could tell us that,' he said pointedly.

Albert Campion's vacuous face became even more blank than usual.

'I don't know much about it,' he said. 'My client didn't go into all that, naturally. But I can tell you this much, it's something sewn in the lining of a red leather wallet. It felt to me like paper – might have been a couple of fivers, of course – but I shouldn't think so.'

'How do you know?' said Prenderby quietly.

Mr Campion turned to him cheerfully.

'Oh, I collected the doings all right,' he said, 'and I should have got away with them if little George here hadn't been a car fiend.'

Abbershaw frowned.

'I think you'd better explain,' he said.

'Explain?' said Mr Campion. 'My dear chicks, there was nothing in it. As soon as I saw old Uncle Ben and his friends at the table my idea was to get the package and then beat it, manners or no manners, so when the story of the Ritual came up I thought "and very nice too" and suggested the game. Then while all you people were playing "Bats in the Belfry" with the ancestral skewer, I toddled over to the old boy, whispered "Inky-Pinky" in his ear, got the wallet, and made a beeline for the garage.'

He paused and sighed.

'It was all very exhilarating,' he went on easily. 'My only trouble was that I was afraid that the wretched game would come to an end before I got away. With great presence of mind, therefore, I locked the door leading to the servants' quarters so that any serenade on the dinner gong would not bring out the torchlight procession immediately. Then I toddled off down the passage, out of the side door, across the garden, and arrived all girlish with triumph at the garage and walked slap-bang into our Georgie looking like an illustration out of *How to Drive in Three Parts, Send No Money*.'

He stopped and eyed Abbershaw thoughtfully.

'I got the mental machinery to function with a great effort,' he continued, 'and when I had it ticking over nicely I said to myself, "Shall I tonk this little cove on the cranium, and stuff him under the seat? Or shall I leap past him, seize the car, and go home in it?" And neither stunt seemed really promising. If I bunked, I reasoned, George would rouse the house or chase me in one of the other cars. I couldn't afford to risk either just then. The only other expedient therefore was to tonk him, and the more I looked at him the less I liked the notion. Georgie is a sturdy little fellow, a pugnacious little cove, who might quite easily turn out to be a fly-weight champ, somewhere or other. If I was licked I was absolutely sunk, and even if I won we were bound to make a hell of a noise and I was most anxious not to have any attention focused on me while I had that pocket-book.'

'So you came back to the house with me meaning to slip out later?' said Abbershaw.

'George has made the bell ring – three more shots or a packet of Gold Flake,' said Mr Campion facetiously. 'Of course I did; and I should have got away. All would have been as merry as a wedding bell, in fact,' he went on more sadly, 'if that Anne woman had not decided that I was just the sort of harmless mutt to arouse jealousy safely with Mr Kennedy without giving trouble myself. I couldn't escape her – she clung. So I had to wait until I thought everyone would be asleep, and then, just as I was sneaking out of my room, that precious mock butler of theirs came for me with a gun. I knocked it out of his hand, and then he started to jump on me. They must have rumbled by that time that the old boy had got rid of the packet, and were on the look-out for anyone trying a moonlight flit.'

He paused, a faintly puzzled expression passed over his face. 'I could have sworn he got the packet,' he said; 'anyway, in the fight I lost it. And that's the one thing that's really worrying me at the moment – what has happened to that wallet? For if the man who calls himself Dawlish doesn't get what he wants, I think we are all of us for a pretty parroty time.'

He stopped and looked at Abbershaw steadily.

'It doesn't seem to be of any negotiable value,' he said, 'and as far as I can see, the only people who are interested in it are my client and

Dawlish, but I can tell you one thing. It does interest them very much, and to get hold of it I don't believe they'd stick at anything.'

'But what was it?' persisted Prenderby, who was more puzzled than ever by these explanations.

Campion shook his head.

'I don't know,' he said, 'unless it was the Chart of the Buried Treasure, don't you know.'

Abbershaw got up from his chair and paced slowly up and down the room.

'There's only one weak spot in your story, Campion,' he said suddenly. 'It sounds like Gospel apart from that. But there is one thing I don't understand. It's this: Why didn't you have a revolver on you when you came out into the garage?'

'Answered in one,' said Mr Campion. 'Because I hadn't one: I never carry guns.'

'Do you mean to say that you set out on an infernally dangerous game like this without one?' Abbershaw's voice was incredulous.

Mr Campion became momentarily grave.

'It's a fact,' he said simply. 'I'm afraid of them. Horrible things – guns. Always feel they might go off in a fit of temper and I should be left with the body. And no bag to put it in either. Then poor little Albert would be in the soup.' He shuddered slightly.

'Let's talk about something else,' he said. 'I can keep up my pecker in the face of anything else but a corpse.'

Prenderby and Abbershaw exchanged glances, and Abbershaw turned to where the young man with the tow-coloured hair and the unintelligent smile sat beaming at them through his glasses.

'Campion,' he said, 'you know, of course, that Colonel Coombe died last night? Do you know how he died?'

Mr Campion looked surprised.

'Heart, wasn't it?' he said. 'I thought the old bird had been scratching round the grave for the last year or so.'

Abbershaw's expression did not change.

'Oh,' he said, 'if that is all you know it may surprise you to hear that he was murdered – while the Dagger Ritual was going on.'

'Murdered!'

Every trace of frivolity had vanished from Albert Campion's face. There was no mistaking the fact that the news had appalled him, and he looked at Abbershaw with undisguised horror in his pale eyes.

'Murdered?' he repeated. 'How do you know?'

'I saw him,' said Abbershaw simply. 'They wanted a signature on the cremation certificate, and got me in for it. They wouldn't let me examine the body, but I saw the face and neck and I also saw his invalid chair.' His eyes were fixed on Campion the whole time he was speaking. 'Then there was the dagger itself,' he said. 'There was blood on the dagger, and blood on the cushions of the chair, but even if I had not known of these, the body, though I saw so little of it, would have convinced me that he had been murdered. As perhaps you know,' he went on, 'it is my job to explain how men die, and as soon as I saw that dead grey face with the depleted veins I knew that he had died of some wound. Something that would bleed very freely. I should say it was a stab in the back, myself.'

The change in Mr Campion was extraordinary; he pulled himself together with an effort.

'This is horrible,' he said. 'I suppose they got him when they discovered that he had parted with the package. Pretty quick work,' he added thoughtfully. 'I wonder how they rumbled him so soon.'

There was silence for a moment or two after he had spoken, then Prenderby looked up.

'The store they set by that package must be enormous, on the face of it,' he said. 'Clearly they'll do anything for it. I wonder what their next move will be?'

'He's searched our rooms,' said Abbershaw, 'and I believe he intended to lock us in the dining-room and search us immediately after, but his experiences in the bedrooms taught him the utter impossibility of ever making a thorough search of a house like this. It couldn't be done in the time he had at his disposal. I think he realizes that his only chance of getting hold of what he wants is to terrorize us until someone hands it over.'

'Then I hope to goodness whoever has got it gets the wind up soon,' said Prenderby.

Campion nodded and sat down gingerly on the edge of the bed. 'I expect he'll have you people up one at a time and bully the truth out of you until he gets what he wants,' he said.

'For a great crook he hasn't proved very methodical, so far,' said Abbershaw. 'He might have known from the first that there'd be no point in churning everybody's clothes up.'

Albert Campion leaned forward. 'You know, you fellows don't understand this bright specimen of German culture,' he said, with more gravity than was usual in his falsetto voice. 'He's not used to little details of this sort. He's the laddie at the top – the big fellow. He just chooses his men carefully and then says, "You do this", and they do it. He doesn't go chasing round the country opening safes or pinching motor-cars. I don't believe he even plans the *coups* himself. He just buys criminal brains, supplies the finance, and takes the profits. That's why I can't understand him being here. There must have been something pretty big afoot, or he'd have had a minion in for it. Gosh! I wish I was well out of it.'

Abbershaw and Prenderby echoed his wish devoutly in their hearts, and Prenderby was the first to speak.

'I wonder whom he'll start on first,' he said thoughtfully.

Campion's pale eyes flickered.

'I fancy I could tell you that,' he said. 'You see, when they couldn't get anything out of me, except banalities, they decided that I was about the fool I looked, and just before a couple of thugs, armed to the teeth, bundled me off to the box-room, I heard a certain amount of what they said. Jesse Gideon had apparently gone carefully over the crowd, and prepared a dossier about each one of us. I came first on the list of people about which nothing was known, and the next was a girl. She wasn't a friend of Petrie's apparently, and the enemy couldn't place her at all.'

'Who – who was that?'

Abbershaw was staring at the speaker, his eyes grown suddenly hard. A terrible apprehension had sent the colour to his face. Campion glanced at him curiously.

'That red-haired girl who met us in the passage when we came back from the garage. What's her name – Oliphant, isn't it? Meggie Oliphant. She's the next to be for it, I believe.'

Chapter 13
Abbershaw Sees Red

'My God, Abbershaw, he was right! They've got her!'

Ten minutes after Mr Campion had first suggested that Meggie might be the next victim, Prenderby ran into Abbershaw in the corridor outside the girl's room. 'I've been all over the house,' he said. 'The girls say that she went up to her room an hour ago to lie down. Now there's not a sign of her about.'

Abbershaw did not speak.

In the last few minutes his face had lost much of its cherubic calm. An entirely new emotion had taken possession of him. He was wildly, unimaginably angry.

Never, in all his life before, had he experienced anything that could compare with it, and even as Prenderby watched him he saw the last traces of the cautious methodical expert vanish and the new, impulsive, pugnacious fighter come into being.

'Michael,' he said suddenly, 'keep an eye on Campion. His story may be absolutely true – it sounds like it – but we can't afford to risk anything. Keep him up in my room so that he can hide in the passage if need be. You'll have to smuggle food up to him somehow. Cheer the others up if you can.' Prenderby looked at him anxiously.

'What are you going to do?' he said.

Abbershaw set his teeth.

'I'm going to see them,' he said. 'There's been enough of this mucking about. There is going to be some sort of understanding, anyway. Damn it all! They've got my girl!' Turning on his heel he strode off down the passage.

A green-baize door cut off that portion of the house where Dawlish had established his headquarters. He passed through it without any interruption, and reached the door of the room that had once been Colonel Coombe's bedchamber.

He tapped on it loudly, and it was opened immediately by a man he had never seen before, a heavy bull of a fellow whom he guessed to be one of the servants.

'What do you want?' he demanded suspiciously.

'Mr Dawlish,' said Abbershaw, and attempted to push past him.

A single blow, violent as a mule kick, sent him flying back against the opposite wall of the corridor, and the giant glowered at him.

'Nobody comes in 'ere,' he said. 'Mr Dawlish isn't seeing anybody for another hour at least,' he added with a laugh that sent Abbershaw cold as he grasped its inference.

'Look here,' he said, 'this is very important. I must get in to Mr Dawlish. Does this interest you?'

He drew a notecase from his pocket as he spoke. The man advanced towards him and stood glaring down at him, his heavy red face darker than ever with anger.

Suddenly his hand shot out and Abbershaw's throat was encased in a band of steel.

'You just 'aven't realized, you and your lot downstairs, what you're playing about wiv,' he said. 'This 'ere isn't no Sunday School hunt-the-thimble-set-out. There's nine of us, we're armed, and *he* isn't jokin'.' The hand round Abbershaw's throat tightened as the thug thrust his face close against his victim's.

''E ain't ordered about by nobody. Makes 'is own laws, 'e does. *As* you'll soon find out. At the moment 'e's busy – talking to a lady. And when 'e's done wiv 'er I'll take your message in to 'im and not before. Now get out – if I 'aven't killed yer.'

On the last words he flung the half-strangled Abbershaw away from him as if he had been a terrier, and, re-entering the room, slammed the door behind him, shooting home the bolts.

Abbershaw scrambled to his feet, flung himself against the door, beating it with his hands, in a paroxysm of fury.

At last he paused in despair: the heavy oak would have withstood a battering ram. He stood back, helpless and half-maddened with apprehension for Meggie's safety.

Then from somewhere far away he fancied he heard a muffled cry.

The effect upon him was instantaneous. His impotent fury vanished and he became once more cold and reasoning. His one chance of saving her was to get round the other way: to break in upon Dawlish's inquisition from an unguarded point, and, once there, declare all he knew about the red wallet and the fate of its contents, regardless of the revenge the German would inevitably take.

Campion had been imprisoned conceivably somewhere near the room where Dawlish had dealt with him. It was just possible, therefore, that the passage through the cupboard would lead him to Meggie.

He turned quickly: there was no time to be lost; even now Dawlish might be trying some of the same methods of urging a confession as he had employed upon Campion earlier in the day. The thought sickened him and he dashed down the passage into his own room.

Brushing the astonished Campion aside, he threw open the cupboard door and pressed against the back of the shelf steadily.

It gave before his weight and swung open, revealing a dark cavity behind.

He took out his pocket torch and flashed it in front of him. The passage was wood-lined and very dusty. Doubtless it had not been used for years before Campion stumbled upon it by chance that afternoon.

It was narrow also, admitting only just enough space for a man to pass along it, crawling on his hands and knees. But Abbershaw set off down it eagerly.

The air was almost unbearably musty, and there was a scuttling of rats in front of him as he crawled on, shining the torch ahead of him as he went. At length he reached the steps of which Campion had spoken. They were steep and solid, leading straight up into the darkness which had opened above his head.

He mounted them cautiously, and a moment later found himself cut off by an apparently solid floor over him.

A closer examination, however, showed a catch, which, upon being released, allowed the trap to drop slowly open, so that he had to retreat some steps in order to avoid its catching him.

The machinery which Campion had referred to as a 'piece of old bicycle' was in fact an ancient iron device, worked with a pedal, for opening the trap. As soon as he had lifted this hatch, Abbershaw hauled himself into the open space above it which he knew must be the chest itself. The lid was down, and he waited for some moments, breathless, listening. He could hear nothing, however, save the scuffling of the rats behind him, and at length, very cautiously, he put his hands above his head, pressed the lid up an inch or two, and peered out.

No one appeared to be about, and he climbed silently out of the box. He was in a longish vaulted room, one of the relics of the days when Black Dudley had been a monastery. Its stone walls were unpanelled, and a small window high up was closely barred. It was, as Campion had said, used as a box-room, and filled with lumber of every description.

Abbershaw looked round eagerly for a door, and saw it built almost next door to the fire-place in the wall opposite him.

It was small, iron, hinged, and very heavy.

He tried it cautiously, and found to his relief that it was unlocked. So Campion's escape had been discovered, he reflected, and went warily. He let himself out cautiously; he had no desire to be apprehended before he reached Dawlish himself.

The door opened out on to a small stone landing in which were two similar doors. A steep spiral staircase descended almost at his feet.

He listened attentively, but there was no sound, and he decided that Dawlish's inquisition could not be taking place on that floor. He turned down the steps, therefore, treading softly and hugging the wall. Once round the first bend, he heard a sound which made him stiffen and catch his breath – the muffled murmur of voices somewhere quite close. He went on eagerly, his ears strained to catch the first recognizable word.

The stairs ended abruptly in a small oak door to the right of which a narrow passage led off into the darkness.

Through the door he could hear clearly Dawlish's deep German voice raised menacingly.

Abbershaw took a deep breath, and pressing up the latch, carefully pushed the door open. It swung silently on well-greased hinges, and he passed through it expecting to find himself in the Colonel's bedroom.

To his surprise he came out into what appeared to be a large cupboard. The air in it was insufferably hot, and it dawned upon him that he was in one of those hiding-places that are so often to be found in the sides of ancient fireplaces. Doubtless it was just such another cache that had swallowed up Campion when he disappeared off the hearthrug in the hall. Perhaps the mysterious passage behind him led directly down to that great sombre room.

From where he stood, every sound in the room without was distinctly audible.

Dawlish's voice, bellowing with anger, sounded suddenly quite near to where he stood.

'Speak!' it said. 'What do you know? All of it – all of it. Keep nothing back.' And then, explosively, as if he had turned back to someone else in the room – 'Stop her crying – make her speak.'

There was a soft, short, unmistakable sound, and Meggie screamed. A blinding flash of red passed before Abbershaw's eyes, and he hurled himself against the wooden panel nearest him. It gave way before him, and he shot out into the midst of Dawlish's inquiry like a hand grenade.

Chapter 14
Abbershaw Gets His Interview

When Abbershaw picked himself up he discovered that he was not in Colonel Coombe's bedroom as he had supposed, but in a smaller and more luxurious apartment presumably leading off it.

It was lined with books, and had been used apparently as a study or library.

At a heavy oak table-desk set across one end sat Dawlish, his face mask-like as ever, and his ponderous hands resting among the papers in front of him.

Before him stood Jesse Gideon, looking down at Meggie, who sat on a chair; a man Abbershaw had never seen before leaning over her.

She had been crying, but in spite of her evident terror there was a vestige of spirit in her narrow brown eyes, and she held herself superbly.

Abbershaw's somewhat precipitate entrance startled everybody, and he was on his feet again before Dawlish spoke.

The German's dull, expressionless eyes rested on his face.

'You,' he said, in his peculiarly stilted English. 'How foolish you are. Since you have come out of your turn you may stay. Sit down.'

As the young man stared at him he repeated the last words violently, but without any movement or gesture.

The man was almost unbelievably immobile.

Abbershaw remained where he was.

His anger was slowly getting the better of him, and he stood there stiffly, his flaming red hair on end and his round face white and set.

'I insist that you listen to me,' he said. 'This terrorizing of women has got to stop. What are you gaining by it, anyway? Have you learnt anything of value to you from this girl?' His voice rose contemptuously. 'Of course you haven't. You're making fools of yourselves.'

The German looked at him steadily, unblinkingly, not a muscle of his face moved.

'Gideon,' he said, 'tell me, who is this foolish red-headed young man who so loves to hear his own voice?'

Gideon glided forward obsequiously and stood beside the desk, his grey face and glittering eyes hideous beneath his white hair. He used his hands as he talked, emphasizing his words with graceful fluttering gestures.

'His name is George Abbershaw,' he said. 'He is a doctor of medicine, a pathologist, an expert upon external wounds and abrasions with especial regard to their causes. In this capacity he has been often consulted by Scotland Yard. As a university friend of Wyatt Petrie's, there is no reason to suppose that he came here with any ulterior motive.'

The German continued to regard Abbershaw steadily.

'He is not a detective, *ja*?'

'No.' Gideon spoke emphatically. 'That is obvious. English detectives are a race apart. They are evident at the first glance. No one who knew anything about the English Police Force could possibly suspect Dr Abbershaw of holding any rank in it.'

The German grunted.

'So,' he said, and returned to Abbershaw, 'you are just an ordinary headstrong young man who, like the others downstairs, is under the impression that this affair is a melodrama which has been especially devised in order that they may have the opportunity of posing heroically before the young ladies of your party. This is an old house, suitable for such gaming, but I, one of the chief actors in your theatre, I am not playing.'

He paused, and Abbershaw was conscious of a faint change in his face, although he did not appear to have moved a muscle.

'What does it matter to me,' he continued, 'if you hide yourselves in priestholes or spring upon me out of cupboards? Climb from one room to another, my friend, make yourself dusty in disused passages, attempt to run your motor-cars upon alcohol: it does me no harm. My only interest is in a package I have lost – a thing that can be of no use to anyone but myself and possibly one other man in the world. It is because I believe that there is in this house someone who is in the employ of that other man that I am keeping you all here until I recover my property.'

The dull, rasping voice stopped for a moment, and Abbershaw was about to speak when Dawlish again silenced him.

'To recover that property,' he repeated, 'at *whatever cost*. I am not playing a game. I am not jumping out of cupboards in an attempt to be heroic. I am not pretending. I think the boy who attempted to drive off in his motor-car and the madman who escaped from the room upstairs where I had locked him understood me. The girl here, too, should begin to understand by now. And the rest of you shall be convinced even as they have been.'

Abbershaw's anger had by no means died down under this harangue, and when he spoke his voice was frigid and very formal.

'If you carry out those threats, Herr Eberhard von Faber,' he said, 'you will be wasting your time.'

Gideon started violently at the name, but the German did not appear even to have heard.

'I had your packet,' Abbershaw continued bitingly.

They were listening intently, and he fancied he discerned a change in Dawlish's dull eyes.

'And in the morning before you had the audacity to place us under this restraint I destroyed it in the grate in my bedroom.' He paused, breathless; the truth was out now, they could do what they liked with him.

The German's reply came, very cold and as contemptuous as his own.

'In the present situation you cannot expect to be believed,' he said. 'Do not they tell me after every crime in which great public interest is taken at least four or five imbeciles approach the police, confessing to it? Forgive me if I say that you remind me of one of those imbeciles, Dr Abbershaw.'

He laughed on the last word, and the effect of the deep-throated chuckle emerging from that still expressionless face was curiously inhuman.

Abbershaw thrust his hand into his pocket and drew out the red wallet. To his astonishment neither Dawlish nor his two subordinates betrayed any sign of recognition, and with a feeling approaching dismay he realized that this was not what they had visualized as the container of the thing they sought. He opened it, drew out his own papers, and laid the case upon the desk in front of the German.

'The papers you were looking for were sewn inside the lining of this wallet,' he said. 'I ripped them out and destroyed them.'

There was silence for a moment after he had spoken, and Gideon leant forward and picked up the case in his pale, exquisitely tapering fingers.

'It is too small,' he pronounced at last, turning to the German.

Dawlish spoke without taking his eyes off Abbershaw. It was impossible to tell what he was thinking.

'If you are not lying, young man with red hair,' he said, 'will you explain to me why you saw fit to destroy the papers that were concealed in that pocket-case? Did you read them?'

'They were in code,' said Abbershaw sullenly.

Gideon shot a swift glance at him under his bushy eyebrows, and then turned to Dawlish.

'Code?' he said. Still the German did not look at him, but remained staring at Abbershaw unblinkingly.

'There may have been a code message in the wallet,' he said, 'and you may have destroyed it. But I do not think it is likely that it had anything to do with my business down here; unless . . .'

For the first time during that conversation he turned to Gideon. 'Coombe,' he said, and there was sullen ferocity in his tone, 'he may have succeeded at last.'

Gideon started.

'Double-crossed?' he said, and his voice died away in a question.

'We don't know.'

The German spoke fiercely. 'I have no faith in this young fool's story – he's only concerned with the girl. Is Whitby back yet?'

'No,' said Gideon. 'We can't expect him yet.'

'So.' Dawlish nodded. 'We must keep them till he comes. He may be able to recognize this case. Whose initials are these?'

'Mine,' said Abbershaw. 'You'll find that they are clipped on at the back. I put them on myself.'

Gideon smiled.

'A very singular thing to do, Dr Abbershaw,' he said. 'And may I ask where you got this wallet?'

Abbershaw hesitated. For the moment he was in a quandary. If he told the truth he could hardly help incriminating Campion, and in view of that young man's present condition it was inhuman to betray him.

'I found it,' he said at last, realizing at once how lame the explanation must sound. Gideon shrugged his shoulders. 'This man is wasting our time,' he said. 'No, it is Petrie you should examine, as I have told you all along. He's just the type *they* would choose. What shall we do with these two?'

'Put them in the other room – not the one the young lunatic got out of,' said Dawlish. 'You came through the passage from the fire-place in the hall, I suppose,' he added, turning heavily to Abbershaw, who nodded. 'We must wait for Whitby to see this case,' he continued, 'then we will consider what is to be done.'

The stranger who had been standing at Meggie's side laid a hand on her shoulder.

'Come,' he said, jerking her to her feet.

Abbershaw turned on him furiously, only to find a revolver pressed against his ribs. They were heading towards the staircase behind the fire-place by which he had come, but when they reached the threshold Dawlish spoke again.

'Dr Abbershaw,' he said, 'come here.'

Unwillingly, the young man turned and stood before the desk, looking down at the florid Teutonic face with the dull corpse-like eyes.

'So you are an expert often referred to by Scotland Yard.'

The German spoke with curious deliberation.

'I have heard of you. Your name has been mentioned in several cases which have interested me deeply. You gave evidence in the Waterside-Birbeck murder, didn't you?'

Abbershaw nodded.

'And in the Sturges affair?'

'Yes.'

'Had it not been for you, Newman would never have been hanged?'

'Very probably not.'

A slightly deeper colour seemed to flood the expressionless face.

'Three of my best men,' he said. 'I am very glad to have met you, Dr Abbershaw. Put them in the small room, Wendon, and lock the door very carefully. When I have a little more time to speak I have promised myself another interview with you, Dr Abbershaw.'

Chapter 15

Doctor Abbershaw's Deductions

The room into which Meggie and Abbershaw were thrust so uncere-
moniously in the middle of the night was one of the three which
opened out on to the small winding staircase leading down to Colonel
Coombe's study.

It was comparatively empty, containing only a pile of disused
tapestries and old curtains, two or three travelling trunks and a chair.

Here, as in the other room, the window was high up in the wall and
iron-barred. There was a second door in the room but it appeared to
be heavily bolted on the other side. Abbershaw made a thorough
investigation of the room with his torch, and then decided that escape
was impossible, and they sat down on the tapestry in silence.

Until now they had not spoken very much, save for a brief account
from Abbershaw of his interview with Campion and his journey
through the passage from his cupboard. Meggie's story was simpler.
She had been seized on her way up to her room and dragged off
through the green-baize door to be questioned.

Neither felt that much was to be gained from talking. The German
had convinced them of the seriousness of their position, and Abbershaw was overcome with self-reproach for what he could only feel was
his own fault. Meggie was terrified but much too plucky to show it.

As the utter silence of the darkness descended upon them, however,
the girl laid her hand on Abbershaw's arm. 'We'll be all right,' she
murmured. 'It was wonderful of you to come and get me out like that.'

Abbershaw laughed bitterly. 'I didn't get you very far,' he said.

The girl peered at him through the shadow.

'Oh, I don't know,' she said. 'It's better up here than it was down
there.'

Abbershaw took her hand and spoke with unusual violence. 'My
God, they didn't hurt you?' he said.

'Oh no, nothing much.'

It was evident from her voice that she was trying to make light of a
terrible experience. 'I was frightened more than hurt,' she said, 'but it

was good to see you. Who are they, George? What are they doing here? What's it all about?'

Abbershaw covered his face with his hands and groaned in the darkness.

'I could kick myself,' he said. 'It's all my fault. I did an absurd, a foolhardy, lunatic thing when I destroyed those papers. I didn't realize whom we were up against.'

The girl caught her breath.

'Then what you said was true?' she said. 'You did destroy what they are looking for?'

'Yes.' Abbershaw spoke savagely. 'I've behaved like an idiot all the way through,' he said. 'I've been too clever by half, and now I've got you, of all people – the person I'd rather die for than see any harm come to – into this appalling situation. I hit on the truth,' he went on, 'but only half of it, and like a fool I acted upon my belief without being sure. Oh, my God, what a fool I've been!'

The girl stirred beside him and laid her head on his shoulders, her weight resting in the hollow of his arm. 'Tell me,' she said.

Abbershaw was only too glad to straighten out his own thoughts in speech, and he began softly, keeping his voice down lest there should be listeners on the landing behind the bolted door.

'It was Colonel Coombe's murder that woke me up,' he said. 'And then, when I saw the body and realized that the plate across his face was unneeded and served as a disguise, I realized then that it was crooks we had to deal with, and casting about in my mind I arrived at something – not quite the truth – but very near it.'

He paused and drew the girl closer to him.

'It occurred to me that Dawlish and Gideon might very well be part of the famous Simister gang – the notorious bank thieves of the States. The descriptions of two of the leaders seemed to tally very well, and like a fool I jumped to the conclusion that they were the Simister gangsters. So that when the documents came into my hands I guessed what they were.'

The girl looked at him.

'What were they?' she said.

Abbershaw hesitated.

'I don't want to lay down the law this time,' he said, 'but I don't see how I can be wrong. In these big gangs of crooks the science of thieving has been brought to such perfection that their internal management resembles a gigantic business concern more than anything else. Modern criminal gangs are not composed of amateurs – each man has his own particular type of work at which he is an expert. That is why the police experience such difficulty in bringing to justice the man actually responsible for a crime, and not merely capturing the comparatively innocent catspaw who performs the actual thieving.'

He paused, and the girl nodded in the darkness. 'I see,' she said.

Abbershaw went on, his voice sunk to a whisper.

'Very big gangs, like Simister's, carry this cooperative spirit to an extreme,' he continued, 'and in more cases than one a really big robbery is planned and worked out to the last detail by a man who may be hundreds of miles away from the scene of the crime when it is committed. A man with an ingenious criminal brain, therefore, can always sell his wares without being involved in any danger whatsoever. The thing I found was, I feel perfectly sure, a complete crime, worked out to the last detail by the hand of a master. It may have been a bank robbery, but of that I'm not sure. It was written in code, of course, and it was only from the few plans included in the mass of written matter – and my suspicions – that I got a hint of what it was.'

Meggie lifted her head.

'But would they write it down?' she said. 'Would they risk that?'

Abbershaw hesitated.

'I admit that worried me at first,' he said, 'but consider the circumstances. Here is an organization, enormous in its resources, but every movement of which is bound to be carried out in absolute secrecy. A lot of people sneer at the efficiency of Scotland Yard, but not those who have ever had cause to come up against it. Imagine an organization like this, captained by a mind simple, forceful, and eminently sensible. A mind that only grasps one thing at a time, but which deals with that one thing down to the last detail, with the thoroughness of a Hun.'

'Dawlish?' said Meggie.

Abbershaw nodded in the darkness.

'Yes,' he said. 'Mr Benjamin Dawlish is one of his names.' He paused, and then went on again with new enthusiasm, 'Then imagine the brains of his gang,' he continued, 'the man with the mind of a genius plus just that one crooked kink which makes him a criminal instead of a diplomat. It is most important that this one man of all others shall evade the police.'

Meggie nestled closer to him.

'Go on,' she said.

Abbershaw continued, his voice hardly raised above a whisper, but intense and vehement in the quietness.

'He must be kept away from the gang then, at all costs,' he said. 'So why not let him live at some out-of-the-way spot in the guise of an innocent old gentleman, an invalid, going out for long drives in his ramshackle old car for his health's sake; but in reality changing his personality on the road and becoming for a few hours an entirely different person? Not always the same man, you understand,' he explained, 'but adopting whatever guise seemed most suitable for the actual detail in hand. A respectable suburban householder eager to open a small account when it was necessary to inspect a certain bank manager's office; an insurance man when a watchman was to be interviewed; a jovial, open-handed man-about-town when clerks were to be pumped. And all these different personalities vanishing into thin air as soon as their work was done, each one of them merging into the quiet inoffensive old invalid driving about in his joke of a car.'

His voice died away in the darkness, and Meggie stiffened.

'The Colonel,' she whispered.

'Yes,' murmured Abbershaw. 'I'm sure of it. He was the designer of the crimes. Dawlish organized them, and a carefully trained gang carried them out. The arrangements had to be written out,' he went on, 'because otherwise it would entail the Colonel spending some considerable time with the gang explaining his schemes, whereas it was much better that they should not know him, or he them. You see,' he went on suddenly, 'that's what Dawlish had to guard against – double-crossing. Old Coombe's plans had a definite market value. They were worth money to any criminal gang who could get hold of them, and, as I have said, to minimize any danger of this, Coombe was kept here, practically as a prisoner, by Dawlish. I dare say the only time he saw any member of the gang was when Gideon and some other member as witness came down here to collect the finished scheme for one robbery, or to discuss the next. On such occasions it was Coombe's practice to invite Wyatt to bring down a house-party as a blind to distract attention from any of his other visitors, who may in some cases have been characters "known to the police".' He stopped and sighed. 'So far,' he said, 'I was practically right, but I had made one tremendous error.'

'And that?' The girl's voice quivered with excitement.

'That,' said Abbershaw gravely, 'was the fatal one of taking Dawlish for Simister. Simister is a rogue about whom there are as many pleasant stories as unpleasant ones, but about Eberhard von Faber no one ever laughs. He is, without exception, the most notorious, unsavoury villain this era has produced. And I have pitched us all – you too – into his hands.'

The girl repressed a shudder, but she clung to Abbershaw confidently.

'But why,' she said suddenly, 'why didn't they succeed? Why didn't the Colonel give Dawlish the papers and the whole thing work out according to plan?'

Abbershaw stirred.

'It would have done,' he said, 'but there *was* double-crossing going on. The Colonel, in spite of his body-guard – Whitby and the butler – must have got into communication with Simister's gang and made some arrangement with them. I'm only guessing here, of course, but I should say that the Colonel's plans were never allowed outside the house and that his attitude towards Simister must have been, "I will sell them if you can get them without implicating me". So Simister employed our friend, Mr Campion, to smuggle himself into Wyatt's party without being recognized by Dawlish.'

Meggie sat up. 'I see,' she said, 'but then, George, who murdered the Colonel?'

'Oh, one of the gang, of course – evidently. When they discovered that he had double-crossed them.'

The girl was silent for a moment, then:

'They were very quick,' she said thoughtfully.

Abbershaw jerked his chin up. This was a point which it had never occurred to him to question.

'What do you mean?' he demanded.

Meggie repeated her former observation.

'They were very quick,' she said. 'If the Colonel didn't have a heart attack he was murdered when we were playing with the dagger. Before I had the thing in my hand, in fact. Did they see the old man part with the papers? And if so, why did they kill him and not Albert Campion?'

Abbershaw was silent. This point of view had not occurred to him. As far as he knew, apart from the single affair on the landing, they had not spotted Albert Campion at all.

'Besides,' said Meggie, 'if you remember, Dawlish seemed to be surprised when something you said suggested that Coombe had double-crossed them.'

Abbershaw nodded: the incident returned to his mind. Meggie went on speaking, her voice very low.

'So Albert Campion was the murderer,' she said.

Abbershaw started.

'Oh, no,' he said. 'I don't think that for a moment. In fact I'm sure of it,' he went on, as he remembered the scene – it seemed incredible that it was only that afternoon – when Mr Campion had heard of the Colonel's murder.

'I'm sure of it,' he repeated, 'and besides,' he added, as the extenuating circumstances occurred to him, 'why should von Faber have taken all those precautions to conceal someone else's crime?'

Meggie was silent at this, and Abbershaw continued. 'There's no doubt that the Colonel intended to cheat the gang,' he said. 'The documents were exquisite pieces of work, written on the finest paper in a hand so small that it would have taken a reading glass to follow the words. It was in code – not one I know, either – and it was only the tiny plans that gave the clue to what it was. All sewn into the lining of a pocket-book which Dawlish didn't recognize when I showed it to him. Oh, what a fool I was to destroy it!'

The regret in his tone was very poignant, and for some seconds the girl did not speak. Then she moved a little nearer to him as if to compensate him for any embarrassment her question might cause him.

'Why did you?' she said at last.

Abbershaw was silent for some time before he spoke. Then he sighed deeply.

'I was a crazy, interfering, well-meaning fool,' he said, 'and there's no more dangerous creature on the face of the earth. I acted partly on impulse and partly because it really seemed to me to be the best thing to do at the moment. I had no idea whom we were up against. In the first place I knew that if I destroyed it I should probably be preventing a crime at least; you see, I had no means, and no time, to decipher it and thereby obtain enough information to warn Scotland Yard. I didn't even know where the bank to be robbed was situated, or if indeed it was a bank. I knew we were up against pretty stiff customers, for one man had already been murdered, presumably on account of the papers, but I had no idea that they would dream of attempting anything so wholesale as this.'

He paused and shook his head.

'I didn't realize then,' he continued, 'that there had been any double-crossing going on, and I took it for granted that the pocket-book would be recognized instantly. Situated as we were then, too, it was reasonable to suppose that I could not hold out against the whole gang, and it was ten chances to one that they would succeed in getting back their plans and the scheme would go forward with me powerless to do anything. Acting entirely upon the impulse of the moment, therefore, I stuffed the plans into the grate and set fire to them. That was just before I went down to speak to you in the garden. Now, of course, Dawlish won't believe me, and if he did, I'm inclined to believe he would take his revenge upon all of us. In fact, we're in a very nasty mess. If we get out of here we can't get out of the house, and that Hun is capable of anything. Oh, my dear, I wish you weren't here.'

The last words broke from him in an agony of self-reproach. Meggie nestled closer to his shoulder.

'I'm very glad I am,' she said. 'If we're in for trouble let's go through it together. Look, we've been talking for hours – the dawn's breaking. Something may turn up today. Don't these people ever have postmen or milkmen or telegram-boys or anything?'

Abbershaw nodded.

'I've thought of that,' he said, 'but I think everyone like that is stopped at the lodge, and anyhow today's Sunday. Of course,' he added brightly, 'in a couple of days there'll be inquiries after some of us, but it's what von Faber may do before then that's worrying me.'

Meggie sighed.

'I don't want to think,' she said. 'Oh, George,' she added pitifully, 'I'm so terribly tired.'

On the last word her head lolled heavily against his breast, and he realized with sudden surprise that she was still a child who could sleep in spite of the horror of the situation. He sat there with his back against the wall supporting her in his arms, staring out across the fast-brightening room, his eyes fixed and full of apprehension.

Gradually the room grew lighter and lighter, and the sun, pale at first, and then brilliant, poured in through the high window with that warm serenity that is somehow peculiar to a Sunday morning. Outside he heard the faraway lowing of the cattle and the lively bickering of the birds.

He must have dozed a little in spite of his disturbing thoughts, for he suddenly came to himself with a start and sat up listening intently, his ears strained, and an expression of utter bewilderment on his face.

From somewhere close at hand, apparently in the room with the bolted door, there proceeded a curious collection of sounds. It was a hymn, sung with a malicious intensity, unequalled by anything Abbershaw had ever heard in his life before. The voice was a feminine one, high and shrill; it sounded like some avenging fury. He could make out the words, uttered with a species of ferocious glee underlying the religious fervour.

> 'Oh vain all outward sign of grief,
>   And vain the form of prayer,
> Unless the heart implore relief
>   And Penitence be there.'

And then with still greater emphasis:

> 'We smite the breast, we weep in vain,
>   In vain in ashes mourn,
> Unless with penitential pain –'

The quavering crescendo reached a pinnacle of self-righteous satisfaction that can never be known to more forgiving spirits.

> 'Unless with penitential pain
>   The smitten soul be torn.'

The last note died away into silence, and a long drawn-out 'Ah-ha-Ha-men' followed it.

Then all was still.

Chapter 16
The Militant Mrs Meade

'Good heavens, what was that?'

It was Meggie who spoke. The noise had awakened her and she sat up, her hair a little wilder than usual and her eyes wide with astonishment.

Abbershaw started to his feet.

'We'll darned soon find out,' he said, and went over to the second door and knocked upon it softly.

'Who's there?' he whispered.

'The wicked shall perish,' said a loud, shrill, feminine voice, in which the broad Suffolk accent was very apparent. 'The earth shall open and they shall be swallowed up. And you won't come into this room,' it continued brightly. 'No, not if you spend a hundred years a-tapping. And why won't you come in? 'Cause I've bolted the door.'

There was demoniacal satisfaction in the last words, and Abbershaw and Meggie exchanged glances.

'It's a lunatic,' whispered Abbershaw.

Meggie shuddered.

'What a horrible house this is,' she said. 'But talk to her, George. She may know how to get us out.'

'Her chief concern seems to be not to let us in,' said Abbershaw, but he returned to the door and spoke again.

'Who's there?' he said, and waited, hardly hoping for an answer, but the voice replied with unexpected directness:

'That's a thing I won't hide from anybody,' it said vigorously. 'Daisy May Meade's my name. A married woman and respectable. A church-going woman too, and there's some that's going to suffer for what's been going on in this house. Both here, *and* in the next world. The pit shall open and swallow them up. Fire and brimstone shall be their portion. The Lord shall smite them.'

'Very likely,' said Abbershaw dryly. 'But who are you? How did you get here? Is it possible for you to get us out?'

Apparently his calm, matter-of-fact voice had a soothing effect upon the vengeful lady in the next room, for there was silence for some moments, followed by an inquisitive murmur in a less oracular tone.

'What be you doing of?'

'We're prisoners,' said Abbershaw feelingly. 'We've been shut up here by Mr Dawlish, and are most anxious to get out. Can you help us?'

Again there was silence for some moments after he had spoken, then the voice said considerately, 'I've a good mind to have the door open and have a look at ye.'

'Good heavens!' said Abbershaw, startled out of his calm. 'Do you mean to say that you can open this door?'

'That I can,' said the voice complacently. 'Didn't I bolt it myself? I'm not having a lot of foreigners running round me. I told the German gentleman so. Oh, they shall be punished. "To the devil you'll go," I told them. "Fire and brimstone and hot irons," I said.'

'Yes, I know,' said Abbershaw soothingly, 'but have you any idea how we can get out?'

A grunt of consideration was clearly audible through the door. 'I will have a look at ye,' said the voice with sudden decision, and thereupon there began a fearsome noise of chains, bolts, and the scraping of heavy furniture, which suggested that Mrs Meade had barricaded herself in with a vengeance. Soon after there was a creaking and the door swung open an inch or two, a bright black eye appearing in the crack. After a moment or so, apparently satisfied, Mrs Meade pushed the door open wide and stood upon the threshold looking in on them.

She was a striking old woman, tall and incredibly gaunt, with a great bony frame on which her clothes hung skimpily. She had a brown puckered face in which her small eyes, black and quick as a bird's, glowed out at the world with a religious satisfaction at the coming punishment of the wicked. She was clothed in a black dress, green with age, and a stiff white apron starched like a board, which gave her a rotundity of appearance wholly false. She stood there for some seconds, her bright eyes taking in every nook and corner of the room. Apparently satisfied, she came forward.

'That'll be your sister, I suppose,' she said, indicating Meggie with a bony hand, 'seeing you've both red hair.'

Neither of the two answered, and taking their silence for assent, she went on.

'You're visitors, I suppose?' she demanded. 'It's my belief the devil's own work is going on in this house. Haven't I seen it with me own eyes? Wasn't I permitted – praise be the Lord! – to witness some of it? It's four shall swing from the gallows, their lives in the paper, before there's an end of this business.'

The satisfaction in her voice was apparent, and she beamed upon them, the maliciousness in her old face truly terrible to see. She was evidently bursting with her story, and they found it was not difficult to get her to talk.

'Who are you?' demanded Abbershaw. 'I know your name, of course, but that doesn't make me much wiser. Where do you live?'

'Down in the village, three mile away,' said the redoubtable Mrs Meade, beaming at him. 'I'm not a regular servant here, and I wouldn't be, for I've no need, but when they has company up here I sometimes come in for the week to help. My time's up next Wednesday, and when I don't come home my son'll come down for me. That's the time I'm waiting for. Then there'll be trouble!'

There was grim pleasure in her tone, and she wagged her head solemnly.

'He'll have someone to reckon with then, the German gentleman will. My son don't hold with foreigners nohow. What with this on top of it, and him being a murderer too, there'll be a fight, I can tell you. My son's a rare fighter.'

'I shouldn't think the Hun would be bad at a scrap,' murmured Abbershaw, but at the same time he marvelled at the complacency of the old woman who could time her rescue for four days ahead and settle down peacefully to wait for it.

There was one phrase, however, that stuck in his mind.

'Murderer?' he said.

The old woman eyed him suspiciously and came farther into the room.

'What do you know about it?' she demanded.

'We've told you who we are,' said Meggie, suddenly sitting up, her clever pale face flushing a little and her narrow eyes fixed upon her face.

'We're visitors. And we've been shut up here by Mr Dawlish, who seems to have taken over charge of the house ever since Colonel Coombe had his seizure.'

The old woman pricked up her ears.

'Seizure?' she said. 'That's what they said it was, did they? The fiery furnace is made ready for them, and they shall be consumed utterly. I know it wasn't no seizure. That was murder, that was. A life for a life, and an eye for an eye, a tooth for a tooth, that's the law, *and* they shall come to it.'

'Murder? How do you know it was murder?' said Abbershaw hastily. The fanatical forebodings were getting on his nerves.

Once again the crafty look came into the little black eyes and she considered him dubiously, but she was much too eager to tell her story to be dissuaded by any suspicions.

'It was on the Friday night,' she said, dropping her voice to a confidential monotone. 'After dinner had been brought out, Mrs Browning, that's the housekeeper, sent me upstairs to see to the fires. I hadn't been up there more than ten minutes when I came over faint.' She paused and eyed the two defiantly.

'I never touch liquor,' she said, and hesitated again. Abbershaw was completely in the dark, but Meggie had a flash of intuition, born of long experience of Mrs Meade's prototypes.

'But as you weren't well you looked about for something to revive you?' she said. 'Of course. Why not?'

Mrs Meade's dubious expression faded.

'Of course,' she said. 'What else was I to do?'

'What else indeed?' said Meggie encouragingly.

'What did I do?' said the old woman, lapsing once more into the rhetorical form she favoured. 'I remembered that in the Colonel's study – that's through his bedroom, you know – there was a little cupboard behind the screen by the window, where he kept a drop of Scotch whisky. That's soothing and settling to the stomach as much as anything is. So, coming over faint, and being in the Colonel's bedroom, I went into the study, and had just poured myself out a little drop when I heard voices, and the German gentleman with his friend Mr Gideon and Dr Whitby come in.' She stopped again and looked at Meggie.

'I didn't holler out,' she said, 'because it would have looked so bad – me being there in the dark.'

Meggie nodded understandingly, and Mrs Meade continued.

'So I just stayed where I was behind the screen,' she said. 'Mr Gideon was carrying a lamp and he set it down on the desk. They was all very excited, and as soon as Dr Whitby spoke I knew something was up. "What an opportunity," he said, "while they're playing around with that dagger he'll just sit where he is. We're safe for fifteen minutes at least." Then the German gentleman spoke. Very brusque he is. "Get on with it," says he. "Where does he keep the stuff?"'

Mrs Meade paused, and her little black eyes were eloquent. 'Imagine the state I was in, me standing there with the bottle in me 'and,' she said. 'But the next moment Dr Whitby set me at peace again. "In the secret drawer at the back of the desk," he said. I peeked round the edge of the screen and saw 'im fiddling about with the master's desk.' She fixed Meggie with a bright black eye. 'I *was* upset,' she said. 'If it hadn't been for the whisky and the way it would have looked I'd 'ave gone out, but as it was I couldn't very well, and so I stayed where I was, but I listened. For I said to myself, "The humblest of us are sometimes the ministers of the Lord," and I realized someone would have to be brought to justice.'

Her self-righteousness was so sublime that it all but carried her hearers away with it, and she went on, whilst they listened to her, fascinated.

'I saw them open the drawer and then there was such a swearing set-out that I was ashamed. "It's gone," said Mr Gideon, and Dr Whitby he started moaning like an idiot. "He always kept them here," he kept saying over and over again. Then the German, him that's for Hell Fire as sure as I'll be with the Lambs, he got very angry. "You've played the fool enough," he said, in such a loud voice that I nearly cried out and gave myself away. "Go and fetch him," he said. "Bring him up here. I've had enough of this playing."'

Mrs Meade paused for breath.

'Dr Whitby's rather a sullen gentleman,' she continued, 'but he went off like a child. I stood there, my knees knocking together, wishing me breathing wasn't so heavy, and praying to the Lord to smite them for their wickedness, while the German gentleman and Mr Gideon were talking together in a foreign language. I couldn't understand it, of course,' she added regretfully, 'but I'm not an old fool, like you might imagine. Though I'm sixty-two I'm pretty spry, and I could tell by the way they was waving their hands about and the look on their faces and the sound of their voices that the German gentleman was angry about something or other, and that Mr Gideon was trying to soothe 'im. "Wait," he said at last, in a Christian tongue, "he'll have it on him, I tell you." Well! . . .' She paused and looked from one to the other of her listeners, her voice becoming more dramatic and her little black eyes sparkling. Clearly she was coming to the cream of her narrative.

'Well,' she repeated, when she was satisfied that they were both properly on edge, 'at that moment the door was flung open and Dr Whitby came back, white as a sheet, and trembling. "Chief! Gideon!" he said. "He's been murdered! Stabbed in the back!"'

Mrs Meade stopped to enjoy the full effect of her announcement.

'Were they surprised?'

Abbershaw spoke involuntarily.

'You be quiet and I'll tell 'ee,' said Mrs Meade, with sudden sternness. 'They was struck silly, I can tell you. The German gentleman was the first to come to his senses. "Who?" he said. Mr Gideon turned on him then. "Simisters?" he says, as if asking a question.'

Meggie and Abbershaw exchanged significant glances, while Mrs Meade hurried on with her narrative, speaking with great gusto, acting the parts of the different speakers, and investing the whole gruesome story with an air of self-righteous satisfaction that made it even more terrible.

'The German gentleman wasn't pleased at that,' she continued, 'but it was he who kept his head, as they say. "And the papers," said he. "Were they on him?" "No," says the doctor. "Then," said the German gentleman, "get him upstairs. No one must leave the house till we get back the papers." "Don't let anyone know he's dead, then," said Mr Gideon. "Say it's heart attack – anything you like." "There's blood about," said Dr Whitby – "bound to be." "Then clear it up," says Mr Gideon. "I'll help you. We must hurry before the lights go up."'

On the last word her voice sank to a whisper, but the stagey horror with which she was trying to invest the story did not detract from the real gruesomeness of the tale. Rather it added to it, making the scene down in the lamplit panelled room seem suddenly clear and very near to them.

Meggie shuddered and her voice was subdued and oddly breathless when she spoke.

'What happened then?'

Mrs Meade drew herself up, and her little black eyes burned with the fire of righteousness.

'Then I could hold my tongue no longer,' she said, 'and I spoke out. "Whoso killeth any person, the murderer shall be put to death by the mouth of witnesses," I said, and stepped out from behind the screen.'

Abbershaw's eyes widened as the scene rose up in his mind – the fanatical old woman, her harsh voice breaking in upon the three crooks in that first moment of their bewilderment.

'They were terrified, I suppose,' he said.

Mrs Meade nodded, and an expression of grim satisfaction spread over her wrinkled old face.

'They *was*,' she said. 'Mr Gideon went pale as a sheet, and shrank away from me like an actor on the stage – Dr Whitby stood there stupid like, his eyes gone all fishy and his mouth hanging open . . .' She shook her head. 'You could see there was guilt there,' she said, 'if not in deed, in the *heart* – the German gentleman was the only one to stay his natural colour.'

'And then?' Meggie hardly recognized her own voice, so toneless was it.

'Then he come up to me,' the old woman continued, with a return of indignation in her voice. 'Slowly he come and put his great heavy face close to mine. "You be off," said I, but that didn't stop him. "How much have you heard?" said he. "All of it," says I, "and what's more I'm going to bear witness."'

Mrs Meade took a deep breath.

'That did it,' she said. 'He put his hand over my mouth and the next moment Dr Whitby had jumped forward and opened the cupboard by the fire-place. "Put her in here," said he; "we can see to her after we've got *him* upstairs."'

'You struggled, of course,' said Abbershaw. 'It's extraordinary someone in the house didn't hear you.'

Mrs Meade regarded him with concentrated scorn.

'Me struggle, young man?' she said. 'Not me. If there's going to be any scrabbling about, I said to myself, better leave it to my son who knows something about fighting, so as soon as I knew where I was I hurried up the stairs and shut myself in here. "You can do what you like," I said to the German gentleman through the door, "but I'm staying here until Wednesday if needs be, when my son'll come for me – then there'll be summat to pay, I can tell you!"'

She paused, her pale cheeks flushing with the fire of battle, as she remembered the incident. 'He soon went away after that,' she went on, wagging her head. 'He turned the key on me, but that didn't worry me – I had the bolts on my side.'

'But you couldn't get out?' interrupted Meggie, whose brain failed before this somewhat peculiar reasoning.

'O' course I couldn't get out,' said Mrs Meade vigorously. 'No more'n could he come in. As long as my tongue's in my head someone'll swing for murder, and I'm quite willing to wait for my son on Wednesday. They won't get in to me to kill me, I reckon,' she continued, with a flicker of pleasure in her eyes, 'and so when my son comes along there'll be someone to help cast out the wicked. I ain't a-holding my tongue, not for nobody.'

'And that's all you know, then?' said Meggie.

'All?' Mrs Meade's tone was eloquent. 'Some people'll find it's quite enough. Those three didn't actually do the murder, but there's someone in the house who did, and –' She broke off sharply and glanced from one to the other. 'Why're you two lookin' at one 'nother so?' she demanded.

But she got no reply to her question. Meggie and Abbershaw were regarding each other fixedly, the same phrase in the old woman's remark had struck both of them, and to each it bore the same terrible significance. 'Those three didn't actually do the murder, but there's someone in the house who did.' Dawlish, Gideon, Whitby were cleared of the actual crime in one word; the servants were all confined in their own quarters – Albert Campion insisted that he locked the door upon them. Who then could be responsible? Albert Campion himself – or one of their own party? Neither spoke – the question was too terrifying to put into words.

Chapter 17

In the Evening

The disturbing discovery which Meggie and Abbershaw had made in Mrs Meade's story silenced them for some time. Until the old woman's extraordinary announcement ten minutes before, the division between the sheep and the goats had been very sharply defined. But now the horrible charge of murder was brought into their own camp. On the face of it, either Albert Campion or one of the young people in the house-party must be the guilty person.

Of course there was always the saving hope that in his haste Campion had locked one of the servants out instead of confining them all to their quarters as he had intended. But even so, neither Abbershaw nor the girl could blind themselves to the fact that in the light of present circumstances the odds were against the murderer lying in that quarter.

The entire staff of the house was employed by von Faber or his agents, that is to say that they were actually of the gang themselves. Coombe was an asset to them – it was not in their interests to kill him.

And yet, on the other hand, if the gang had not committed the murder they certainly covered up all traces of it. Mrs Meade's story had deepened the mystery instead of destroying it.

Meggie looked at Abbershaw.

'If we could only get out,' she murmured. Abbershaw nodded briskly. Conjectures and theories could wait until afterwards; the main business in hand at the moment was escape, if not out of the house at least back to the others.

He turned to the old woman.

'I don't suppose there's any chance of getting out through there?' he suggested, indicating the inner room in the doorway of which she still stood.

She shook her head.

'There's nobbut a fire-place and a door,' she said, 'and you'll not get through the door because I've bolted it and he's locked it. You can have a look at the fire-place if you like, but the chimney'll only land you up on the roof even if you could get up it; best wait till Wednesday till my son comes.'

Abbershaw was inclined to enlighten her on the chances her son was likely to have against the armed Herr von Faber, but he desisted, and contented himself by shaking his head. Meggie, ever practical, came forward with a new question.

'But do you eat? Have you been starved all this time?' she said.

Mrs Meade looked properly aggrieved.

'Oh, they bring me my victuals,' she said; 'naturally.'

Apparently the event of her being starved out of her stronghold had not occurred to her. 'Lizzie Tiddy brings me up a tray night and morning.'

'Lizzie Tiddy?' Abbershaw looked up inquiringly. 'Who's that?'

A smile, derisive and unpleasant, spread over the wrinkled face. 'She's a natural,' she said, and laughed.

'A natural?'

'She's not right in her head. All them Tiddys are a bit crazed. Lizzie is the wust.'

'Does she work here?' Meggie's face expressed her disapproval.

Mrs Meade's smile broadened into a grin, and her quick eyes rested on the girl.

'That's right. No one else wouldn't ha' had her. She helps Mrs Browning, the housekeeper, washes up and such-like.'

'And brings up the food?' There was an eagerness in Abbershaw's tone. An idiot country girl was not likely to offer much resistance if they made an attempt to escape as soon as she opened the door.

Mrs Meade nodded.

'Ah, Lizzie brings up the tray,' she said. 'She sets it on the floor while she unlocks my door, then I pull the bolts back and open it ever such a little, and then I pull the tray in.'

It was such a simple procedure that Abbershaw's spirits rose.

'When does this happen?' he said. 'What time of day?'

'Half after eight in the morning and half after eight at night.'

He glanced at his watch.

'She's due now, then, practically?'

Mrs Meade glanced up at the window. 'Shouldn't be at all surprised,' she agreed. 'Light looks about right. I'll go back to my own room, then, if you don't mind. Best not to let anybody know that I've been havin' any truck wi' you.'

On the last word she turned her back on him, and after closing the door, connecting the two rooms, silently, they heard her softly pressing the bolts home.

'What an extraordinary old woman,' whispered Meggie. 'Is she mad, do you think?'

Abbershaw shook his head.

'No,' he said. 'I almost wish she were. But she's certainly not crazy, and I believe every word of her story is absolutely true. My dear girl, consider – she certainly hasn't the imagination to invent it.'

The girl nodded slowly.

'That's true,' she said, and added suddenly, 'but, George, you don't really believe that those dreadful men didn't kill Colonel Coombe?'

Abbershaw looked at her seriously.

'I don't see why they should, do you?' he asked. 'Think of it in the light of what we know.'

'Then that means that either Albert Campion or – oh, George, it's horrible!'

Abbershaw's face grew even more serious.

'I know,' he said, and was silent for a minute or so. 'But that is not what is worrying me at the moment,' he went on suddenly, as though banishing the thought from his mind. 'I've got you into this appalling mess, and I've got to get you out of it – and that, unless I'm mistaken, is Lizzie Tiddy coming up the stairs now.'

The girl held her breath, and for a moment or two they stood silent, listening. There was certainly the sound of footsteps on the stone landing outside, and the uneasy rattle of crockery on an unsteady tray. Abbershaw's hand closed round the girl's arm.

'Now,' he whispered, 'keep behind me, and at your first opportunity nip out of here into the room immediately on your left and go straight for the chest I told you of. You can't miss it. It's in the corner and enormous. I'll follow you.'

The girl nodded, and at the same moment the key turned in the lock, and whatever hopes Abbershaw had entertained vanished immediately. The door opened some two inches, and there appeared in the aperture the muzzle of a revolver.

Abbershaw groaned. He might have known, he told himself bitterly, that their captors were not absolute fools. The girl clung to him and he could feel her heart beating against his arm. Gradually the door opened wider, and a face appeared above the gun. It was the stranger whom Dawlish had addressed as Wendon on the day before. He stood grinning in at them, the gun levelled directly at Meggie.

'Any monkey-tricks and the girl goes first,' he said. 'It's the Guvnor's orders. He's reserving you, mate, for 'is own personal attention. That's one of the reasons why he's feeding you. Now then, my girl, push the tray under and hurry about it.'

The last remark was addressed to someone behind him, although he never for a moment took his eyes off Abbershaw and the girl. There was a scuffling in the passage outside, and then a narrow tray appeared upon the floor. It came sliding towards them through the crack in the door, and Abbershaw was suddenly conscious of a pair of idiot eyes, set in a pale, vacant face, watching him from behind it.

His impulse was to leap forward and risk the revolver, but the man had him helpless since it was Meggie whom he covered. Slowly the door closed, and on the moment that the gun disappeared Abbershaw sprang forward fiercely, but it was a forlorn hope. The heavy door slammed to, and they heard the lock shoot home.

There was food on the tray: a pile of sandwiches, and a jug of water. Meggie stood listening for a moment, then she whispered sharply:

'George, they don't take the same precautions with her. Perhaps if we got in there we could get past them.'

Abbershaw darted across the room to the other door, then his face changed.

'She's bolted us out, of course,' he said, 'and besides, we're too late now. We must wait till they come this evening. Oh, my dear, I'm so sorry I got you into all this.'

The girl smiled at him, but she did not reply, and presently, since in spite of their precarious position they were very hungry, they sat down and began to eat.

And then the long weary day dragged on. Mrs Meade did not seem to be inclined for further conversation, and they knew that sooner or later Dr Whitby and the man who had driven him must return, and the red-leather wallet be identified. What would happen then they could only conjecture, but since Dawlish was already prejudiced against Abbershaw he was not likely to be unmoved when he discovered the story of the burning of the papers to be true.

But it was Meggie's position that chiefly disturbed Abbershaw. Whatever they did to him, they were not likely to let her return to civilization knowing what she did about them. The others, after all, so far as Dawlish knew, realized little or nothing of the true position. Campion had succeeded in convincing them that he was no more than the fool he looked, and they knew nothing of his disclosures to Abbershaw and Prenderby.

The chances, therefore, were against them releasing the girl, and Abbershaw's brain sickened at the thought of her possible fate. Escape was impossible, however, and there was nothing in the room that could in any way be manufactured into a weapon. The window, even had it been large enough to permit a man's climbing through it, looked out on to a sheer drop of seventy feet on to the flags below.

There seemed nothing for it but to settle down and wait for Dawlish to make the next move.

As the morning passed and then afternoon without any change, save for a few martial and prophetic hymns from Mrs Meade, their spirits sank deeper than ever; and it grew dark.

Clearly Whitby had not yet returned, and Abbershaw reflected that he might quite possibly have experienced some trouble with the cremation authorities, in which case there were distinct chances of the police coming to their rescue. He wondered, if that occasion should arise, what Dawlish would do – if he would remove Meggie and himself, or simply make a dash for it with his own gang, risking detection afterwards.

On the face of it, he reflected, as he considered what he knew of the man, both from what he had heard and his own experience, the chances were against Meggie and himself being left to tell their story. The prospects looked very black.

And then, quite suddenly, something happened that set his heart beating wildly with new hope, and made him spring to his feet with Meggie at his side, their eyes fixed upon the door, their ears strained to catch every sound.

From inside the room where Mrs Meade had fortified herself, there came an extraordinary sound.

A gentle scraping followed by a burst of shrill indignation from the old woman herself, and the next moment, clear and distinct, a slightly nervous falsetto voice said briskly, 'It's all right, my dear madam, I'm not from the assurance company.'

Meggie grasped Abbershaw's arm.

'Albert Campion!' she said.

Abbershaw nodded: the voice was unmistakable, and he moved over to the inner door and tapped upon it gently.

'Campion,' he called softly, 'we're in here.'

'That's all right, old bird, I'm coming. You couldn't call the old lady off, could you?'

Campion's voice sounded a little strained.

'She seems to think I'm not the sort of person you ought to know. Can't you tell her that many a true heart beats beneath a ready-made suit?'

'Mrs Meade.'

Abbershaw raised his voice a little.

'Mr Campion is a friend of ours. Could you let him in to us?'

'You keep strange company,' came the woman's strident voice from the other side of the door. 'A man that creeps down a chimney upon a body isn't one that I'd put up with.'

Abbershaw and Meggie exchanged glances. Apparently Mr Campion had descended from the skies.

Then the absurd voice came out to them again, raised a little in indignation.

'But even if your son is coming, my dear old bird,' he was saying, 'there's really no reason why my friends and I should not meet before that happy moment. After all, I too have a mother.' The exact significance of his last remark was not apparent, but it seemed to work like a charm upon the old woman, and with a few mumbled words she opened the door, and Albert Campion stood upon the threshold, beaming at them.

'I don't think I'll come in,' he said cheerfully. 'This lady seems crazy for me to meet her son and I'm afraid that she may compel me to do so by locking me in with you if I get far enough out of the room for her to shut this door. And as the laddie is not expected to call till Wednesday, I don't want him to get his diploma from me in person. I think if you're both ready, we'll all go back the way I came.'

'Down the chimney?' said Meggie, in some trepidation.

'Through the chimney,' corrected Campion, with pride. 'I've been fooling about all day trying to find the "money-back" handle – and now I've got the two coppers,' he added brightly, grinning at the two red-headed young people before him. 'You can't possibly dislike puns more than I do,' he went on hastily. 'Let's get back, shall we? This is an unhealthy spot.'

They followed him into the old woman's room. She stood glaring at them suspiciously with her little bright eyes.

'Where are you going?' she demanded. 'I don't know as 'ow I ought to let ye go.'

'Aren't you coming with us?' said Meggie quickly. 'Surely you want to get away from those dreadful men at once? You'll be much safer with us.'

'What? And miss seeing my son beat 'em up?' said Mrs Meade contemptuously. 'Not me, miss. Besides,' she added sharply, 'I don't know as I'm not safer with the German gentleman than I am with a natural.' She pointed to Campion suggestively. 'Lizzie Tiddy's not the only half-wit in this house. Chimney-climbing –!' Her remark reminded them, as they turned to where an old stone fire-place, wide and primitive, stood on one side of the small room. It seemed at first utterly impracticable as a means of exit, but Campion led them over to it with a certain pride.

'Look,' he said. 'It's so simple when you think of it. The same chimney serves for both this room and the room behind it, which is no other, ladies and gentlemen, than the one which Mr Campion performed his now famous disappearing trick in. Admission four-pence. Roll up in your hundreds. In fact,' he went on more seriously, 'virtually speaking, both rooms have the same fire-place separated only by this little wall arrangement – quite low, you see – to divide the two grates, and topped by a thin sheet of iron to separate the flames.'

He paused, and surveyed them owlishly through his horn-rimmed spectacles. 'I discovered, all by myself and with no grown-up aid, that this natty device was removable. I lifted it out, and stepped deftly into the presence of this lady on my right, whose opening remark rather cooled my ardour.'

'I said "The wicked shall be cast into hell",' put in Mrs Meade, 'and so they shall. Into a burning fiery furnace, same as if that grate there was piled up with logs and you a-top of them.'

This remark was addressed to Abbershaw, but she turned with tremendous agility upon Campion. '*And* the fools,' she said, 'the Lord 'isself couldn't abide fools.'

Campion looked a little hurt.

'Something tells, me,' he said in a slightly aggrieved tone, 'that I am not, as it were, a popular hero. Perhaps it might be as well if we went. You'll bolt your door again, won't you?' he added, turning to the old woman.

'You may lay I will,' said she meaningly.

'Are you sure you won't come with us?'

It was Meggie who spoke, and the old woman eyed her less fiercely than she had done the others.

'Thank you, I'll bide where I am,' she said. 'I know what I'm up to, which is more than you do, I reckon, trapezing round with a pair of gorbies.'

Campion touched the girl's arm.

'Come,' he said softly. 'I thought I heard someone. I'll go first, then you follow me.'

He stepped up on the stone hob as he spoke, and then swung his leg over the brick back of the grate which they now saw was little over three feet high, and disappeared out of sight. Meggie followed him, and Abbershaw sprang after her. Within three minutes they had emerged into the boxroom and Campion raised the lid of the chest in the far corner.

Meggie suffered herself to be led down the dusty passage, Campion in front of her, and Abbershaw behind.

As they went, they heard the cracked voice of Mrs Meade chanting vigorously to herself:

> 'While the wicked are confounded
> Doomed to flames of woe unbounded,
> Call me with Thy saints surrounded.
> Ah-ha-Ha-ha-men.'

Chapter 18

Mr Kennedy's Council

When Albert Campion and his two refugees crawled out at the far end of the passage, they found the cupboard door open and the entire crowd assembled in the bedroom without, waiting for them. Anne Edgeware threw herself across the room towards Meggie with a little squeaky cry that was part sympathy, part relief. Prenderby's little Jeanne had not been a reassuring companion.

The strain of the last twenty-four hours had told upon them all. The atmosphere in the wide, old-fashioned room was electric, and Campion's somewhat foolish voice and fatuous expression struck an incongruous note.

'Goods as per instructions,' he said brightly, as he scrambled out of the cupboard. 'Sign along the dotted line please.'

As soon as they were all in the room, however, he shut the cupboard door carefully, betraying that he was especially anxious that no sound should percolate through into the little boxroom they had just left.

Chris Kennedy was the first to speak. He was a little flushed, and there was an air of suppressed excitement about him that showed that his wounded arm no longer damped his spirits.

'Now we're all here,' he said, 'we can get right down to this thing and work out a scheme to get us out of here and those customers what they deserve. I'm for a fight.'

'Here, I say, hold on a minute, my son,' drawled Martin Watt, 'let's all start fair. What have you two lost souls been up to, first of all?' he went on, turning to Meggie and Abbershaw. 'How did our little Albert get hold of you? No bickering, I hope?'

'No, all done by kindness,' said Mr Campion cheerfully; 'there was only one dragon in my path, a female of the species, and full of good words. Most of them new to me,' he added thoughtfully. The portion of Abbershaw's story which the little doctor felt inclined to tell did not take very long. The others also had had their adventures; Martin Watt seemed to have instituted himself spokesman, and as soon as the other had finished he began.

'We've had sport, too, in our own way. Old Dachshund Dawlish has had us up one at a time, you know, heard our catechism and our family history, searched our pockets and let us go again. He has also locked us all up in the central big hall and had another go at our rooms. Old Prenderby tried to square a servant and got the business end of a gun in his tummy by way of retort. The girls have been overhauled by a ghastly old housekeeper woman and a loony maid. And last but not least, we had a confidential lecture from Gideon, who gave us the jolliest little character-sketch of his pal that one can imagine.'

He paused, and a faint smile at the recollection passed over his indolent face.

'According to him, the old boy is a cross between Mr Hyde, Gilles de Rais, and Napoleon, but without the finesse of any of the three. On the whole I'm inclined to agree with him,' he continued, 'but a fat lot of good it's doing him or us, for that matter, because he can't find his package and we can't get home to our mommas. I told him that, but he didn't seem to see the argument. I'm afraid he's rather a stupid man.'

Abbershaw nodded.

'Perhaps he is,' he said, 'but at the same time he's a very dangerous one. I may as well tell you fellows,' he went on, with sudden determination in his grey eyes, 'there's something that's on my conscience. I had those papers – they were papers, as a matter of fact – the first morning we were down here, and I burnt them. I told him what I'd done when I went in to see him yesterday, but he wouldn't believe me.'

He paused and looked round him. Campion's pale eyes were goggling behind his enormous spectacles, and Wyatt met Abbershaw's appealing glance sympathetically. The rest were more surprised than anything else, and, on the whole, approving.

Campion voiced the general thought.

'Do you know what they were – the papers, I mean?' he said, and there was something very like wonderment in his tone. Abbershaw nodded.

'They were all written in code, but I had a pretty shrewd idea,' he said, and he explained to them the outline of his ideas on the subject.

Campion listened to him in silence, and when he had finished glanced across and spoke softly.

'You burnt them?' he said dreamily, and then remarked, as if he had switched on to an entirely new subject, 'I wonder if the smoke from five hundred thousand pounds in notes looks any different from any other sort of firing.'

Abbershaw glanced at him sharply.

'Five hundred thousand pounds?' he said.

'Why not?' said Campion lightly. 'Half a crown here, half a crown there, you know. It soon tells up.'

The others turned to him, attributing the remark to his usual fatuity, but Abbershaw met the pale eyes behind the big spectacles steadily and his apprehension increased. It was not likely that Mr Campion would be far out in his estimation since he knew so much about the affair.

Five hundred thousand pounds. The colossal sum brought home to him the extent of the German's loss, and he understood the crook's grim determination to recover the lost plans. He had not thought that the men were playing for such great stakes. In a flash he saw the situation as it really was, and his next words were sharp and imperative.

'It's more important than I can say that we should get out of here,' he said. 'In fact we've *got* to get out of here at once. Of course I know it's been the idea all along, but now it's imperative. At any moment now Whitby may return, and Dawlish will be convinced that I told him the truth yesterday. And then heaven only knows what he will do. Our one hope is to get out before Whitby comes back.'

'There's only one way, I've been saying it all along.' It was Chris Kennedy who spoke. He was seated on the end of the bed, his knees crossed, and his young face alert and eager. 'We shall have to make a straight fight for it,' he said. 'It's our only hope. No one trying to sneak out on his own to inform the local Bobby would have an earthly. I've thought of that. They'd spot us and we know they don't mind shooting.'

'There's a suit of armour in the hall,' suggested Campion suddenly. 'I'll put it on and toddle forth into the night, if you like. They could pot at me as much as they pleased. How about that?'

Abbershaw glanced at him sharply, but there was no trace of a sneer on the pleasant vacuous face, and he looked abashed when Kennedy spoke a little brutally.

'Sorry,' he said, without looking round, 'we haven't got time for that sort of stuff now. We're in a devilish unpleasant situation and we've got to get the girls and ourselves out of it. I tell you, a straight fight is the only thing for it. Look here, I've got it all taped. We've got our first chance coming in a moment. We've had dinner every night so far, so I expect we can reasonably suppose that we'll get it again tonight. Two fellows wait on us then. They're both armed, we know, and judging from the way they treated Michael they know how to use their guns all right.'

'Why, they're not very tricky, are they?' said Mr Campion, a faint expression of surprise appearing in his face. 'I understood you just pressed the trigger and – pop! – off it went.'

Chris Kennedy granted him one withering look and went on with his scheme.

'There's only one way to handle these customers, therefore,' he said. 'The first thing is to overpower those two and get their guns. Six of us ought to be able to do that. Then the two best shots had better take those revolvers and scout round for the others. The important thing is, of course, that the first bit of work is done in absolute silence. I believe that once we get those two guns we can lay 'em all by the heels. We shall be prepared, we shall be organized – they won't. What do you say?'

There was a moment or two of silence. Martin Watt was the first to speak.

'Well, I'm for it,' he said.

'So am I,' said Wyatt quietly.

Abbershaw hesitated, and Prenderby too was silent, whilst Albert Campion remained mild and foolish-looking as if he were looking in on the scene from outside.

Abbershaw was thinking of Meggie. Prenderby too had his fiancée clinging to his arm. Mr Campion appeared to be thinking of nothing at all.

'After all, it does seem to be our only chance.'

It was Prenderby who spoke, and the words stirred Abbershaw. What the boy said was perfectly true. He turned to Kennedy.

'All right,' he said, 'I'm with you.'

Kennedy looked pointedly at Albert.

'And you?' he said.

Albert shook his head. 'Oh, I'm not standing out,' he said. 'I don't like these rough games, but I don't shirk them when they're thrust on me. What do we all do?'

Mr Kennedy appeared to have the whole plan clear in his mind.

'It's quite simple,' he said, leaning his chin in his unwounded hand and bending forward, an intent expression in his eyes.

'Let *me* shape your career for you!' quoted Mr Campion brightly. Kennedy reddened angrily and dropped the pose, but he went on doggedly.

'My idea,' he said, 'is that three go down to dinner with the girls. I'm afraid they'll have to come or the men will smell a rat. They start food, and the other three fellows wait outside the door until one of their laddies is at work on the side table and the other serving the dishes at the big table. At that moment someone knocks a glass on to the flags. That's the signal. Then the blokes outside the door charge in and seize the carver. One of 'em gets his arm. Another stuffs a hanky in his mouth, and the third stands by to slog him over the head if necessary. Hang it, we can't go wrong like that. The only thing is they mustn't suspect us. We've got to take them by surprise. It's the simplest thing going as long as we don't make a row.'

'Yes,' said Mr Campion, standing up with sudden solemnity. 'A very clever idea, but what we have to ask ourselves is: Is it quite fair? Three men on to one. Come, come, we must remember that we are British, and all that. Perhaps we could each tie a hand behind our backs – or shall I offer them single combat instead?'

Chris Kennedy rose to his feet, and walking across to Mr Campion spoke quietly but vigorously.

Mr Campion blushed.

'I didn't think you'd take it like that. You will have it your own way, of course. I shan't say anything.'

'You'd better not,' said Kennedy, and walked back to his seat. 'Abbershaw, you, Michael, and Mr Campion had better go down with the girls, and Wyatt, Martin, and I will wait for the signal of the broken glass. Who's going to do that? It had better be a girl. Miss Oliphant, will you do it?'

Meggie nodded.

'As soon as one man is at the carving-table and the other serving us,' she said.

Kennedy smiled at her. 'That's it,' he said. 'Now is that clear?' he went on, glancing around him, his eyes dancing with excitement. 'Abbershaw, you get the bloke's arms, Prenderby, you're responsible for gagging the sportsman! –'

'Yes?' said Campion, who was apparently gibbering with excitement. 'And what can I do?'

'You stand by,' said Kennedy, with something suspiciously like a sneer on his handsome young face.

'Oh, very well,' said Mr Campion, looking considerably disappointed. 'I'll stand ready to dot the fellow with a bottle if necessary.'

'That's the idea,' agreed Chris Kennedy somewhat grudgingly, and returned to the others. 'Of course,' he said, 'it'll be a bit of a shock for the two lackey-thugs to see you all turning up bright and happy after your adventures; still, I think the idea is to walk in as if nothing had ever happened. You can indulge in a certain amount of bright conversation if you like, to put them off the scent. That's where you'll come in useful,' he added, turning to Campion. 'Talk as much as you like. That's the time to be funny.'

'Righto,' said Mr Campion, brightening visibly. 'I'll show them my two-headed penny. I'll be awfully witty. "They laughed when I sat down at the piano, but when I began to play they knew at once that I had taken Kennedy's Patent Course. How they cheered me on –"'

'Oh, shut up,' said Martin Watt, grinning good-naturedly. 'The fun starts at dinner, then. Oh, and by the way, when we've pinched these fellows' guns, what do we do with the laddies? Leave them lying about?'

'I've thought of that,' said the indefatigable Kennedy; 'we tie 'em up. I've been collecting portmanteau straps. That'll do it, you'll find. We'll lash 'em both into chairs and leave 'em there.'

'Yes,' said Martin, 'and next? When we've fixed up all that, what happens next?'

'Then somebody takes charge of the girls,' said Kennedy. 'They lock themselves in some safe room – Miss Oliphant's bedroom just at the head of the stairs, for instance. Then the rest of us form into two parties with a revolver each and storm the servants' quarters, where, with a certain amount of luck, we shall get another gun or two. Then we can let out at some of these lads who amble round keeping an eye on us after dinner. We'll tie 'em up and raid old Dawlish's quarters.'

He paused and looked round him, smiling.

'As soon as we've got everyone accounted for, we get the girls and sheer out of the house in a body. How's that?'

'Sounds lovely,' said Mr Campion, adding after a pause, 'so simple. It'll be rather awkward if someone makes a noise, though, won't it? I mean you might have the entire gang down on you at the one-gun-per-three-men stage.'

Kennedy snapped at him. He was thoroughly tired of Mr Campion's helpful suggestions.

'There just hasn't got to be any noise,' he said, 'that's the point. And by the way, I think you're the man to stay with the girls.'

There was no mistaking his inference, but to Abbershaw's surprise Mr Campion seemed to jump at the idea.

'Righto,' he said, 'I shall be delighted.'

Chris Kennedy's answering remark was cut short, rather fortunately, Abbershaw felt, by a single and, in the circumstances, highly dramatic sound – the deep booming of the dinner gong.

Chapter 19

Mr Campion's Conjuring Trick

The six young people went down to the big dining-hall with a certain amount of trepidation. Jeanne clung to Prenderby, the other two girls stuck together, and Abbershaw was able to have a word or two with Mr Campion.

'You don't like the idea?' he murmured.

The other shrugged his shoulders.

'It's the risk, my old bird,' he said softly. 'Our pugilistic friend doesn't realize that we're not up against a gang of racecourse thugs. I tried to point it out to him but I'm afraid he just thought I was trying to be funny. People without humour always have curious ideas on that subject. However, it may come off. It'll be the last thing he'll expect us to do, anyway, and if you really have burnt that paper it's the best thing we could do.'

'I suppose you think I'm a fool,' said Abbershaw, a little defiantly. Campion grinned.

'On the contrary, young sir, I think you're a humorist. A trifle unconscious, perhaps, but none the worse for that.'

Their conversation ended abruptly, for they had reached the foot of the staircase and were approaching the dining-room.

The door stood open, and they went in to find the table set for all nine of them, and the two men who had acted as footmen during the week-end awaiting their coming. They sat down at the table. 'The others won't be a moment, but we'll start, please,' said Campion, and the meal began.

For some minutes it seemed as if the funereal atmosphere which surrounded the whole house was going to damp any attempt at bright conversation that anyone might feel disposed to make, but Mr Campion sailed nobly into the breach.

Abbershaw was inclined to wonder at him until he realized with a little shock that considering the man's profession the art of talking rubbish in any circumstances might be one of his chief stock-in-trades.

At the moment he was speaking of food. His high voice worked up to a pitch of enthusiasm, and his pale eyes widened behind his horn-rimmed spectacles.

'It all depends what you mean by eating,' he was saying. 'I don't believe in stuffing myself, you know, but I'm not one of those people who are against food altogether. I knew a woman once who didn't believe in food – thought it was bad for the figure – so she gave it up altogether. Horrible results, of course; she got so thin that no one noticed her around – husband got used to being alone – estrangement, divorce – oh, I believe in food. I say, have you seen my new trick with a napkin and a salt-cellar – rather natty, don't you think?'

He covered a salt-cellar with his napkin as he spoke, made several passes over it, a solemn expression on his face, and then, whisking the napery away, disclosed nothing but shining oak beneath.

His mind still on Mr Campion's profession, Abbershaw was conscious of a certain feeling of apprehension. The salt-cellar was antique, probably worth a considerable sum.

Mr Campion's trick was not yet over, however. A few more passes and the salt-cellar was discovered issuing from the waistcoat of the man-servant who happened to be attending to him at the time.

'There!' he said. 'A pretty little piece of work, isn't it? All done by astrology. For my next I shall require two assistants, any live fish, four aspidistras, and one small packet of Gold Flake.' As he uttered the last words he turned sharply to beam around the table, and his elbow caught Meggie's glass and sent it crashing to the floor.

A little breathless silence would have followed the smash had not he bounded up from his chair immediately and bent down ostensibly to gather up the fragments, jabbering the whole time. 'What an idiot! What an idiot! Have I splashed your dress, Miss Oliphant? All over the floor! What a mess, what a mess! Come here, my man, here: bring a dust-pan and broom with you.' He was making such a fuss and such a noise that no one had noticed the door open, and the somewhat self-conscious entry of Chris Kennedy's little band. No one, that is, save Campion, who from his place of vantage half-way under the table had an excellent view of the feet.

At the moment when Martin Watt leapt forward at the man by the carving table, Campion threw his arms round the other man-servant's legs just below the knees, and jerked him back on to the flags with an almost professional neatness. Within two seconds he was seated astride the man's chest, his knees driven into the fleshy part of his arms, whilst he stuffed a handkerchief into his mouth. Abbershaw and Prenderby hurried to his assistance and between them they strapped the man into a chair, where he sat glaring at them, speechless and impotent.

Kennedy's party, though less neat, had been quite as successful, and Chris himself, flushed with excitement, now stood with his man's loaded revolver in his hand.

'Have you got his gun?' he said, in a voice which sounded hoarse even to himself, as he indicated Campion's captive.

'No,' said Abbershaw, and began his search. Two minutes later he looked up, disappointed.

'He hasn't one,' he said at last, and even the man himself seemed surprised.

Kennedy swore softly and handed the gun which he held to Martin.

'You'd better have it,' he said. 'I'm hopeless with my right arm gone. Now, then, Campion, will you go upstairs with the girls? Abbershaw, you'd better go with them. As soon as you've seen them safely locked in the room, come back to us. We're making for the servants' quarters.'

They obeyed in silence, and Abbershaw led Campion and the three girls quietly out of the room, across the hall, and up the wide staircase. On the first landing they paused abruptly. Two figures were looming towards them through the dimness ahead. It was Jesse Gideon and the heavy, red-faced man whom Abbershaw had encountered outside Dawlish's door in his search for Meggie. They would have passed in silence had not Gideon spoken suspiciously in his smooth silken voice.

'Dinner is over early?' he said, fixing his narrow glittering eyes on Meggie.

She replied coldly that it was, and made as if to pass on up the stairs, but Gideon evidently intended to prolong the conversation, for he glided in front of her so that he and the surly ruffian beside him barred her progress up the stairs from the step above the one on which she was standing.

'You are all so eager,' Gideon continued softly, 'that it almost looks like an expedition to me. Or perhaps it is one of your charming games of hide-and-seek which you play so adroitly,' he added, and the sneer on his unpleasant face was very obvious. 'You will forgive me saying so I am sure,' he went on, still in the same soothing obsequious voice, 'but don't you think you are trying Mr Dawlish's patience a little too much by being so foolish in your escapades? If you are wise you will take my advice and keep very quiet until it pleases him to release you.'

He spoke banteringly, but there was no mistaking the warning behind his words, and it was with some eagerness that Abbershaw took Meggie's arm and piloted her between the two men. His one aim at the moment was to get the girl safely to her room.

'We understand you perfectly, Mr Gideon,' he murmured. Gideon's sneer deepened into a contemptuous smile and he moved aside a little to let them pass. Abbershaw deliberately ignored his attitude. He wanted no arguments till the girls were safe. They were passing silently, therefore, when suddenly from somewhere beneath them there sounded, ugly and unmistakable, a revolver shot.

Instantly Gideon's smiling contempt turned to a snarl of anger as all his suspicions returned – verified.

'So it is an expedition, is it?' he said softly. 'A little explanation, if you please.'

Abbershaw realized that once again they were caught, and a feeling of utter dejection passed over him.

Suddenly from the darkness behind him a high, rather foolish voice that yet had a certain quality of sternness in it said quickly, 'Don't talk so much. Put 'em up!'

While Abbershaw stood looking at them, Gideon and his burly companion, with mingled expressions of rage and amazement on their faces, raised their hands slowly above their heads.

'Quick, man, get their guns!'

The words were uttered in Abbershaw's ear by a voice that was still vaguely foolish. He obeyed it instantly, removing a small, wicked little weapon from Gideon's hip pocket and a heavy service revolver from the thug's.

'Now then, turn round. Quick march. Keep 'em right up. I'm a dangerous man and I shoot like hell.'

Abbershaw glanced round involuntarily, and saw what Gideon and his companion must have done some minutes before – Albert Campion's pleasant, vacuous face, pale and curiously in earnest in the faint light, as he peered at them from behind the gleaming barrel of a heavy Webley.

'Shove the girls in their room. Give Miss Oliphant the little pistol, and then come with me,' he murmured to Abbershaw, as the strange procession set off up the stairs.

'Steady,' he went on in a louder voice to the two men in front of him. 'No fancy work. Any noise either of you makes will be voluntary suicide for the good of the cause. It'll mean one man less to tie up, anyway. I'm taking them up to my room,' he murmured to Abbershaw. 'Follow me there. They're slippery beggars and two guns are better than one.'

Abbershaw handed Gideon's little revolver to Meggie, which she took eagerly.

'We'll be all right,' she whispered. 'Go on after him. They're terrible people.'

'For God's sake wait here till we come, then,' he whispered back. She nodded, and for a moment her steady brown eyes met his.

'We will, old dear. Don't worry about us. We're all right.'

She disappeared into the room with Jeanne and Anne Edgeware, and Abbershaw hurried after Campion considerably reassured. Meggie was a wonderful girl.

He reached Campion just in time to get the bedroom door open and to assist him to get the two into the room. 'Now,' said Campion, 'it's getting infernally dark, so we'll have to work fast. Abbershaw, will you keep watch over these two gentlemen. I'm afraid you may have to fire at the one on the right, he's swearing so horribly – while I attend to Mr Gideon's immediate needs. That worthy enthusiast, Chris Kennedy, has pinched all my straps, and though I hate to behave as no guest should, I'm afraid there's no help for it. The Black Dudley linen will have to go.'

As he spoke he stripped the clothes from the great four-poster bed, and began to tear the heavy linen sheets into wide strips. 'If you could persuade Mr Gideon to stand with his back against the post of this bed,' he remarked at length, 'I think something might be done for him. Hands still up, please.'

Ten minutes later, a silent mummy-like figure, stretched against the bedpost, arms bandaged to the wood high above his head, an improvised gag in his mouth, was all that remained of the cynical little foreigner.

Mr Campion seemed to have a touch of the professional in all he did. He stood back to survey his handiwork with some pride, then he glanced at their other captive.

'Heavy, unpleasant-looking bird,' he remarked. 'I'm afraid he's too heavy for the bed. Isn't there something we can shove him into?'

He glanced round the room as he spoke, and their captive fancied that Abbershaw's eyes followed his, for he suddenly lunged forward and caught the doctor, who was unused to such situations, round the ankles, sending him sprawling. The heavy gun was thrown out of Abbershaw's hand and the thug reached out a great hairy fist for it.

He was quick, but Campion was before him. With a sudden cat-like movement he snatched up the weapon, and as the other came for him, lunging forward, all his ponderous weight behind his fist, Campion stepped back lightly and then, raising his arm above his head, brought down the butt of the pistol with all his strength upon the close-shaven skull.

The man went down like a log as Abbershaw scrambled to his feet, breathless and apologetic.

'My dear old bird, don't lose your Organizing Power, Directive Ability, Self-Confidence, Driving Force, Salesmanship, and Business Acumen,' chattered Mr Campion cheerfully. 'In other words, look on the bright side of things. This fruity affair down here, for instance, has solved his own problem. All we have to do now is to stuff him in a cupboard and lock the door. He won't wake up for a bit yet.'

Abbershaw, still apologetic, assisted him to lift the heavy figure into a hanging cupboard, where they deposited him, shutting the door and turning the key.

'Well, now I suppose we'd better lend a hand with the devilry downstairs,' said Mr Campion, stretching himself. 'I haven't heard any more shots, have you?'

'I don't know,' said Abbershaw. 'I fancied I heard something while you were dealing with – er – that last customer. And I say, Campion, I haven't liked to ask you before now, but where the devil did you get that gun from?'

Mr Campion grinned from behind his enormous spectacles. 'Oh, that,' he said, 'that was rather fortunate as it happened. I had a notion things might be awkward, so I was naturally anxious that the guns, or at least one of them, should fall into the hands of someone who knew something about bluff at any rate.'

'Where did you get it from?' demanded Abbershaw. 'I thought only one of those men in the dining-room had a gun?'

'Nor had they when we tackled 'em,' agreed Mr Campion. 'I relieved our laddie of this one earlier on in the meal, while I was performing my incredible act with the salt-cellar, in fact. It was the first opportunity I'd had, and I couldn't resist it.'

Abbershaw stared at him.

'By Jove,' he said, with some admiration, 'while you were doing your conjuring trick you picked his pocket.'

Mr Campion hesitated, and Abbershaw had the uncomfortable impression that he reddened slightly.

'Well,' he said at last, 'in a way, yes, but if you don't mind – let's call it *léger de main*, shall we?'

Chapter 20

The Round-Up

As Abbershaw and Campion made their way slowly down the staircase to the first floor, the house seemed to be unnaturally silent. The candles in the iron sconces had not been lighted, and the corridors were quite dark save for a faint greyness here and there when the open doors of a room permitted the faint light of the stars to penetrate into the gloom.

Abbershaw touched his companion's arm.

'How about going through the cupboard passage to the boxroom and then down the staircase into Dawlish's room through the fireplace door?' he whispered. 'We might take him by surprise.' Mr Campion appeared to hesitate. Then his voice, high and foolish as ever, came softly through the thick darkness.

'Not a bad notion, doctor,' he said, 'but we're too late for that, I'm afraid. Hang it all, our friends' target practice downstairs must have given the old boy a hint that something was up. It's only natural. I think we'd better toddle downstairs to see how the little ones progress. Walk softly, keep your gun ready, and for heaven's sake don't shoot unless it's a case of life or sleep perfect sleep.'

On the last word he moved forward so that he was a pace or two ahead of Abbershaw, and they set off down the long corridor in single file.

They reached the head of the staircase without hindrance and paused for a moment to listen.

All beneath them was silent, the husky, creaky quiet of an old house at night, and Abbershaw was conscious of an uneasy sensation in the soles of his feet and a tightening of his collar band.

After what seemed an interminable time Campion moved on again, hugging the extra shadow of the wall, and treading so softly that the ancient wood did not creak beneath him. Abbershaw followed him carefully, the gun clenched in his hand. This sort of thing was manifestly not in his line, but he was determined to see it through as creditably as he was able. He might lack experience, but not courage.

A sudden stifled exclamation from Mr Campion a pace or so ahead of him made him start violently, however; he had not realized how much the experience of the past forty-eight hours had told on his nerves.

'Look out!' Campion's voice was barely audible. 'Here's a casualty.'

He dropped silently as he spoke, and the next moment a little pin-prick of light from a minute electric torch fell upon the upturned face of the body upon the stairs.

Abbershaw felt the blood rise and surge in his ears as he looked down and recognized Chris Kennedy, very pale from a gash over his right temple.

'Dotted over the beam with the familiar blunt instrument,' murmured Campion sadly. 'He was so impetuous. Boys will be boys, of course, but – well, well, well.'

'Is he dead?' Abbershaw could not see the extent of the damage, and he hardly recognized his own voice, it was so strained and horror-stricken.

'Dead?' Mr Campion seemed to be surprised. 'Oh, dear me, no – he's only out of action for a bit. Our friends here are artists in this sort of thing, and I rather fancy that so far Daddy Dawlish has decided against killing off his chicks. Of course,' he went on softly, 'what his attitude will be now that we've taken up the offensive deliberately I don't like to suggest. On the whole I think our present policy of complete caution is to be maintained. Hop over this – he's as safe here as anywhere – and come on.'

Abbershaw stepped carefully over the recumbent figure, and advanced softly after the indefatigable Mr Campion.

They had hardly reached the foot of the staircase, and Abbershaw was speculating upon Campion's plan of campaign, when their direction was suddenly decided for them. From the vicinity of the servants' quarters far below them on their left there came a sudden crash which echoed dully over the entire house, followed by a volley of shots and a hoarse scream as of a man in pain or terror.

Albert Campion paused abruptly.

'That's done it!' he said. 'Now we've *got* to lick 'em! Come on, Doc.' On the last word he darted forward, Abbershaw at his heels. The door in the recess under the stairs was shut but unlocked, and on opening it they found themselves in a narrow stone corridor with a second door at the far end.

The noise was increasing; it sounded to Abbershaw as if a pitched battle were taking place somewhere near at hand.

The second door disclosed a great stone kitchen lit by two swinging oil lamps. At first Abbershaw thought it was deserted, but a smothered sound from the far end of the room arrested him, and he turned to see a heavy, dark-eyed woman and an hysterical weak-faced girl gagged and bound to wooden kitchen chairs in the darkest corner of the room.

These must be Mrs Browning and Lizzie Tiddy; the thought flitted through his mind and was forgotten, for Mr Campion was already at the second door, a heavy iron-studded structure behind which pandemonium seemed to have broken loose.

Mr Campion lifted the iron latch, and then sprang aside as the door shot open to meet him, precipitating the man who had been cowering against it headlong into the room. It was Wendon, the man who had visited Meggie and Abbershaw in their prison room early that morning.

He struggled to his feet and sprang at the first person he caught sight of, which unfortunately for him was Campion himself. His object was a gun, but Mr Campion, who seemed to have a peculiar aversion to putting a revolver to its right use, extricated himself from the man's hold with an agility and strength altogether surprising in one of such a languid appearance, and, to use his own words, 'dotted the fellow'.

It was a scientific tap, well placed and of just adequate force; Wendon's eyes rolled up, he swayed forward and crashed. Abbershaw and Campion darted over him into the doorway.

The scene that confronted them was an extraordinary one.

They were on the threshold of a great vaulted scullery or brew-house, in which the only light came from a single wall lamp and a blazing fire in the sunken hearth. What furniture there had been in the room, a rickety table and some benches, was smashed to firewood, and lay in splinters all over the stone floor.

There were seven men in the room. Abbershaw recognized the two he had last seen bound and gagged in the dining-hall, two others were strangers to him, and the remaining three were of his own party.

Even in the first moment of amazement he wondered what had happened to their guns.

The two prisoners of the dining-room had been relieved of theirs, he knew, but then Martin Watt should be armed. Wendon, too, had had a revolver that morning, and the other two, quick-footed Cockneys with narrow suspicious eyes, should both have had weapons, surely.

Besides, there were the shots he had just heard. There was evidence of gunfire also. Michael Prenderby lay doubled up on a long, flat stone sink which ran the whole length of the place some three feet from the floor. Martin Watt, every trace of his former languidness vanished, was fighting like a maniac with one of the erstwhile prisoners in the shadow at the extreme end of the room; but it was Wyatt who was the central figure in the drama.

He stood balanced on the edge of the sink in front of Michael. The flickering firelight played on the lines of his lank figure, making him seem unnaturally tall. His longish hair was shaken back from his forehead, and his clothes were blood-stained and wildly dishevelled; but it was his face that most commanded attention. The intellectual, clever, and slightly cynical scholar had vanished utterly, and in its place there had appeared a warrior of the Middle Ages, a man who had thrown his whole soul into a fight with fanatical fury.

In his two hands he wielded a wooden pole tipped at the end with a heavy iron scoop, such as are still used in many places to draw water up out of wells. It was clearly the first thing that had come to his hand, but in his present mood it made him the most formidable of weapons. He was lashing out with it with an extraordinary fury, keeping the three men at bay as if they had been yelping dogs, and as an extra flicker from the fire lit up his face afresh it seemed to Abbershaw that it was transformed; he looked more like the Avenging Angel than a scholar with a well scoop.

Campion whipped out his gun, and his quiet high voice sounded clearly through the noise.

'Now then, now then! Put 'em up!' he said distinctly. 'There's been enough fun here for this evening. Put 'em up! I'm firing,' he added quietly, and at the same moment a bullet flashed past the head of the man nearest Wyatt and struck the stone wall behind him. The effect was instantaneous. The noise ceased, and slowly the four members of Dawlish's gang raised their hands above their heads.

Gradually Wyatt's uplifted weapon sank to the ground and he dropped down off the sink and collapsed, his head between his knees, his arms hanging limply by his sides.

Martin Watt came reeling into the circle of light by the fire, somewhat battered and dishevelled but otherwise unhurt.

'Thank God you've come,' he said breathlessly, and grinned. 'I thought our number was up.'

Mr Campion herded his captives into a straight line along one wall.

'Now if you fellows will hold them up,' he said pleasantly, 'I will repeat my celebrated rope trick. For this performance I shall employ nothing less than actual rope, which I see, is all ready waiting for me.'

As he spoke he was unfastening the hank of clothes line which hung ready for use near the fire. He handed Martin his gun, while Abbershaw, more alert this time, held up their captives. As he corded up the four, Martin Watt, still breathless, recounted briefly the events which had led up to the scene they had just witnessed.

'We got into the kitchen first,' he said. 'There didn't seem to be a soul about except the women. They started to scream the place down though, so we tied 'em up. It wasn't till we'd done that that we realized that Chris wasn't with us. We guessed he'd met trouble, so we started to go back. We hadn't got half-way across the room, though, before the door burst open and a man came in.'

He paused and took a deep breath.

'I told him to put up his hands or I'd fire at him,' he went on jerkily, 'but he didn't. He just came for me, so I did fire. I didn't hit him, of course – I didn't mean to – but the noise seemed to start things up generally. There seemed to be footsteps all round us. We didn't know where to shove the cove. The door into here seemed handy and we'd just got him inside when these four charged in on us from the kitchen passage. Michael had got the first fellow's gun by that time. He lost his head a bit, I guess, and blazed at them – shooting wildly over their heads most of the time. Then one of the fellows got him and he curled up on the sink over there with his gun underneath him. By this time, however, I'd got 'em fairly well under control, God knows how.'

The boy spoke modestly, but there were indications of 'how' upon the faces of their captives.

'I got them to stick up their hands,' he continued, 'and then I yelled to Wyatt to get their guns.'

He paused, and glanced at the silent figure hunched up on the flags.

'Poor old chap,' he said. 'I think he went barmy – almost ran amok. He got the guns all right – there were only two of them – and before I could stop him or yell at him even, he had chucked them into that bricked-in place over there. See what it is? A darn great well – I heard them splash ages after they went in. I bawled at him, but he yelled out what sounded like "Sweet Seventeen" or something equally potty, grabbed that scoop, and began to lay about with it like a loony.' He shook his head and paused for breath. 'Then a foul thing happened,' he went on suddenly. 'One of them came for me – and I warned him I'd shoot, and finally I tried to, but the thing only clicked in my hand. The shot I had already fired must have been the last. Then we closed. When you came in the other three were trying to get at Prenderby for his gun – he was knocked out, you know – and old Wyatt was lashing round like the flail of the Lord. Then, of course, you just finished things off for us.'

'A very pretty tale of love and war,' murmured Mr Campion, some of his old inanity returning. ' "Featuring Our Boys. Positively for One Night Only." I've finished with the lads now, Doc. – you might have a look at the casualties.'

Abbershaw lowered his revolver, and approached Prenderby with some trepidation. The boy lay on the stone sink dangerously doubled up, his face hidden. A hasty examination, however, disclosed only a long superficial scalp wound. Abbershaw heaved a sigh of relief.

'He's stunned,' he said briefly. 'The bullet grazed along his temple and put him out. We ought to get him upstairs, though, I think.'

'Well, I don't see why we shouldn't,' said Martin cheerfully. 'Hang it, our way is fairly clear now. Gideon and a thug are upstairs, you say, safely out of the way; we have four sportsmen here and one outside; that's seven altogether. Then the doctor lad and his shover are still away presumably, so there's only old Dawlish himself left. The house is ours.'

'Not so eager, not so eager!' Albert Campion strolled over to them as he spoke. 'Old Daddy Dawlish is an energetic bit of work, believe me. Besides, he has only to get going with his Boy Scout's ever-ready, self-expanding, patent pocket-knife and the fun will begin all over again. No, I think that the doc. had better stay here with his gun, his patient and the prisoners, while you come along with me. I'll take Prenderby's gun.'

'Righto,' said Martin. 'What's the idea, a tour of the works?'

'More or less,' Campion conceded. 'I want you to do a spot of ambulance work. The White Hope of our side is draped tastefully along the front stairs. While you're gathering up the wreckage I'll toddle round to find Poppa von Faber, and on my way back after the argument I'll call in for the girls, and we'll all make our final exit *en masse.* Dignity, Gentlemen, and British Boyhood's Well-known Bravery, Coolness, and Distinction are the passwords of the hour.'

Martin looked at him wonderingly. 'Do you always talk bilge?' he said.

'No,' said Mr Campion lightly, 'but I learnt the language reading advertisements. Come on.'

He led the way out of the brewhouse into the kitchen, Martin following. On the threshold he paused suddenly, and an exclamation escaped him.

'What's happened?' Abbershaw darted after them, and the next moment he, too, caught his breath.

Wendon, the man Campion had laid out not ten minutes before, and left lying an inert mass on the fibre matting, had vanished utterly. Campion spoke softly, and his voice was unusually grave.

'He didn't walk out of here on his own,' he said. 'There's not a skull on earth that would withstand that tap I gave him. No, my sons, he was fetched.' And while they looked at him he grinned.

'To be continued – evidently,' he said, and added lightly, 'Coming, Martin?'

Abbershaw returned to his post in the brewhouse, and, after doing all he could for the still unconscious Prenderby, settled down to await further developments.

He had given up reflecting upon the strangeness of the circumstances which had brought him, a sober, respectable London man, into such an extraordinary position, and now sat staring ahead, his eyes fixed on the grey stone wall in front of him.

Wyatt remained where he had collapsed; the others had not addressed him, realizing in some vague subconscious way that he would rather that they left him alone.

Abbershaw had forgotten him entirely, so that when he raised himself suddenly and staggered to his feet the little red-haired doctor was considerably startled. Wyatt's face was unnaturally pale, and his dark eyes had become lack-lustre and without expression.

'I'm sorry,' he said quietly. 'I had a brain storm, I think – I must get old Harcourt Gieves to overhaul me if we ever get back to London again.'

'If we ever get back?' The words started out of Abbershaw's mouth. 'My dear fellow, don't be absurd! We're bound to get back some time or other.' He heard his own voice speaking testily in the silence of the room, and then with a species of forced cheerfulness foreign to him.

'But now I think we shall be out of the house in an hour or so, and I shall be delighted to inform the county police of this amazing outrage.'

Even while he spoke he wondered at himself. The words and the voice were those of a small man speaking of a small thing – he was up against something much bigger than that.

Further conversation was cut short by the arrival of Martin with the now conscious but still dazed Kennedy. The four prisoners remained quiet, and after the first jerky word of greeting and explanation there was no sound in the brewhouse, save the crackling of the fire in the great hearth.

It was Abbershaw himself who first broke the silence. It seemed that they had waited an age, and there was still no audible movement in the house above them.

'I hope he's all right,' he said nervily.

Martin Watt looked up.

'An extraordinary chap,' he said slowly. 'What is he?'

Abbershaw hesitated. The more he thought about Mr Albert Campion's profession the more confused in mind he became. It was not easy to reconcile what he knew of the man with his ideas on con-men and that type of shady character in general. There was even a possibility, of course, that Campion was a murderer, but the farther away his interview with Mrs Meade became, the more ridiculous and absurd that supposition seemed. He did not answer Martin's question, and the boy went on lazily, almost as if he were speaking to himself.

'The fellow strikes one as a congenital idiot,' he said. 'Even now I'm not sure that he's not one; yet if it hadn't been for him we'd all be in a nasty mess at the present moment. It isn't that he suddenly stops fooling and becomes serious, though,' he went on, 'he's fooling the whole time all right – he *is* a fool, in fact.'

'He's an amazing man,' said Abbershaw, adding as though in duty bound, 'and a good fellow.' But he would not commit himself further, and the silence began again.

Yet no one heard the kitchen door open, or noticed any approach, until a shadow fell over the bright doorway, and Mr Campion, inoffensive and slightly absurd as ever, appeared on the threshold.

'I've scoured the house,' he murmured, 'not a soul about. Old Daddy Hun and his pal are not the birds I took them for. They appear to have vamoosed – I fancy I heard a car. Ready?'

'Did you get the women?' It was Abbershaw who spoke. Campion nodded. 'They're here behind me, game as hell. Bring Prenderby over your shoulder, Watt. We'll all hang together, women in the centre, and the guns on the outside; I don't think there's anyone around, but we may as well be careful. Now for the wide open spaces!'

Martin hoisted the unconscious boy over his shoulder and Abbershaw and Wyatt supported Kennedy, who was now rapidly coming to himself, between them. The girls were waiting for them in the kitchen. Jeanne was crying quietly on Meggie's shoulder, and there was no trace of colour in Anne Edgeware's round cheeks, but they showed no signs of panic. Campion marshalled the little force into advancing order, placing himself at the head, Meggie and Jeanne behind him, with Abbershaw on one side and Martin and Anne on the other, while Wyatt and Kennedy were behind.

'The side door,' said Campion. 'It takes us nearest the garage – there may be some juice about now. If not, we must toddle of course. The tour will now proceed, visiting the Albert Memorial, Ciro's, and the Royal Ophthalmic Hospital . . .'

As he spoke he led them down the stone passage-way, out of the door under the stairs, and down the corridor to the side door, through which Abbershaw had gone to visit the garage on the fateful night of the Dagger Ritual.

'Now,' he said, as with extraordinarily silent fingers he manoeuvred the ponderous bars and locks on the great door, 'this is where the orchestra begins to play soft music and the circle shuffles for its hats as we fall into one another's arms – that's done it!'

On the last word the hinges creaked faintly as the heavy door swung inwards. The night was pitch dark but warm and pleasant, and they went out eagerly on the gravel, each conscious of an unspeakable relief as the realization of freedom came to them.

'My God!' The words were uttered in a sob as Campion started forward.

At the same moment the others caught a shadowy glimpse of the radiator of a great car not two yards ahead of them. Then they were enveloped in the glare of enormous headlights, which completely blinded them.

They stood dazed and helpless for an instant, caught mercilessly and held by the glare.

A quiet German voice spoke out of the brightness, cold, and inexplicably horrible in its tonelessness.

'I have covered the girl with red hair with my revolver; my assistant has the woman on the left as his aim. If there is any movement from anybody other than those I shall command, we shall both fire. Put your hands over your heads. Everybody! . . . So.'

Chapter 21

The Point of View of Benjamin Dawlish

It was all over very quickly.

There was no way of telling if the cold merciless voice behind the blinding lights was speaking truth or no, but in the circumstances it was impossible not to regard it.

The little party stood there, hands raised above their heads; then hurrying footsteps echoed down the stone corridor behind them and their erstwhile prisoners surrounded them.

The German had lied when he spoke of his assistant, then. The man must have slipped into the house by the other door and released the men in the brewhouse.

'You will now go up to a room on the top floor to which my men will lead you. Anyone who makes the least attempt to escape will be shot instantly. By "shot" I mean shot dead.'

The voice of Benjamin Dawlish came clearly to them from behind the wall of light. The icy tonelessness which had made the voice so terrible on the first hearing was still there and Abbershaw had a vision of the expressionless face behind it, heavy and without life, like a mask.

The spirit of the little group was momentarily broken. They had made their attempt and failed in the very moment when their success seemed assured.

Again unarmed, they were forced back into the house and placed in a room on the top floor at the far end of the long gallery where Albert Campion had had his fight with the butler. It was a long narrow room, oak-panelled, but without a fire-place, and lighted only from a single narrow iron-barred window.

Even as Abbershaw entered it, a feeling of misgiving overcame him. Other rooms had possibilities of escape; this held none.

It was completely empty, and the door was of treble oak, iron-studded. It had doubtless been used at one time as a private chapel, possibly in those times when it was wisest to hold certain religious ceremonies behind barred doors.

The only light came from a hurricane lantern which one of the men had brought up with him. He set it on the floor now so that the room was striped with grotesque shadows. The prisoners were herded down to the end of the room, two men keeping them covered the whole time.

Martin Watt set Prenderby down in a corner, and Jeanne, still crying quietly, squatted down beside him and took his head in her lap. Abbershaw darted forward towards their captors.

'This is absurd,' he said bitterly. 'Either let us interview Mr Dawlish downstairs or let him come up to us. It's most important that we should come to a proper understanding at last.'

One of the men laughed.

'I'm afraid you don't know what you're talking about,' he said in a curiously cultured voice. 'As a matter of fact I believe Mr Dawlish is coming up to talk to you in a moment or so. But I'm afraid you've got a rather absurd view of the situation altogether. You don't seem to realize the peculiar powers of our chief.'

Wyatt leaned against the oak panelling, his arms folded and his chin upon his breast. Ever since the incident in the brewhouse he had been peculiarly morose and silent. Mr Campion also was unusually quiet, and there was an expression on his face that betrayed his anxiety. Meggie and Anne stood together. They were obviously very frightened, but they did not speak or move. Chris Kennedy fumed with impotent rage, and Martin Watt was inclined to be argumentative.

'I don't know what the damn silly game is,' he said, 'but whatever it is it's time we stopped playing. Your confounded "Chief" may be the great Pooh-Bah himself for all I care, but if he thinks he can imprison nine respectable citizens for an indefinite period on the coast of Suffolk without getting himself into serious trouble he's barmy, that's all there is to it. What's going to happen when inquiries start being made?'

The man who had spoken before did not answer, but he smiled, and there was something very unpleasant and terrifying about that smile.

Further remarks from Martin were cut short by steps in the corridor outside and the sudden appearance of Mr Benjamin Dawlish himself, followed by Gideon, pale and stiff from his adventure, but smiling sardonically, his round eyes veiled, and his wicked mouth drawn all over to one side in the 'O' which so irritated Abbershaw.

'Now look here, sir.' It was Martin Watt who spoke. 'It's time you had a straight talk with us. You may be a criminal, but you're behaving like a lunatic, and –'

'Stop that, young man.'

Dawlish's deep unemotional voice sounded heavily in the big room, and instantly the boy found that he had the muzzle of a revolver pressed against his ribs.

'Shut up,' a voice murmured in his ear, 'or you'll be plugged as sure as hell.'

Martin relapsed into helpless silence, and the German continued. He was still unblinking and expressionless, his heavy red face deeply shadowed in the fantastic light. He looked at them steadily from one to the other as if he had been considering them individually, but there was no indication from his face or his manner to betray anything of his conclusions.

'So,' he said, 'when I look at you I see how young you all are, and it does not surprise me any longer that you should be so foolish. You are ignorant, that is why you are so absurd.'

'If you've come here to be funny –' Martin burst out, but the gun against his ribs silenced him, and the German went on speaking in his inflexible voice as if there had been no interruption.

'Before I explain to you what exactly I have ordained shall happen,' he said, 'I have decided to make everything quite clear to you. I do this because it is my fancy that none of you should consider I have behaved in any way unreasonably. I shall begin at the beginning. On Friday night Colonel Coombe was murdered in this house while you were playing in the dark with that ancient dagger which hangs in the hall. It was with that dagger that he was killed.'

This announcement was news to some of his hearers, and his quick eyes took in the expressions of the little group before him. 'I concealed that murder,' he continued deliberately, 'because at that time there were several very excellent reasons why I should do so. It would have been of very great inconvenience to me if there had been an inquest upon Coombe, as he was in my employ, and I do not tolerate any interference, private or official, in my affairs. Apart from that, however, the affair had very little interest for me, but I should like to make it clear now that although I do not know his identity, the person who killed Gordon Coombe is in this room facing me. I say this advisedly because I know that no one entered the house from outside that night, nor has any stranger left it since, and even had they not perfect alibis there is no reason why I should credit it to one of my own people.'

His inference was clear, and there was a moment of resentment among the young people, although no one spoke. The German went on with inexorable calm.

'But as I have said,' he repeated, in his awkward pedantic English, 'that does not interest me. What is more important to me is this. Either the murderer stole a packet of papers off the body of his victim, or else Colonel Coombe handed them at some time or other in that evening to one of you. Those papers are mine. I think I estimate their value to me at something over half one million pounds. There is one other man in the world to whom they would be worth something approaching the same value. I assume that one of you here is a servant of that man.'

Again he paused, and again his small round eyes scrutinized the faces before him. Then, apparently satisfied, he continued. 'You will admit that I have done everything in my power to obtain possession of these papers without harming anyone. From the first you have behaved abominably. May I suggest that you have played hide-and-seek about the house like school-children? And at last you have annoyed me. There are also one or two among you' – he glanced at Abbershaw – 'with whom I have old scores to settle. You have been searched, and you have been watched, yet no trace of my property has come to light. Therefore I give you one last chance. At eleven o'clock tomorrow morning I leave this house with my staff. We shall take the side roads that will lead us on to the main Yarmouth motor way without passing through any villages. If I have my property in my possession when I go, I will see that you can contrive your release for yourselves. If not –'

He paused, and they realized the terrible thing that was coming a full second before the quiet words left his lips.

'I shall first set fire to the house. To shoot you direct would be dangerous – even charred skeletons may show traces of bullet fractures. No, I am afraid I must just leave you to the fire.'

In the breathless silence that followed this announcement Jeanne's sobs became suddenly very audible, and Abbershaw, his face pale and horror-stricken, leapt forward.

'But I told you,' he said passionately. 'I told you. I burnt those papers. I described them to you. I burnt them – the ashes are probably in my bedroom grate now.'

A sound that was half a snarl, half a cry, broke from the German, and for the second time they saw the granite composure of his face broken, and had a vision of the livid malevolence behind the mask.

'If I could believe, Dr Abbershaw,' he said, 'that you could ever be so foolish – so incredibly foolish – as to destroy a packet of papers, a portion of whose value must have been evident to you, then I could believe also that you could deserve no better fate than the singularly unpleasant death which most certainly awaits you and your friends unless I am in possession of my property by eleven o'clock tomorrow morning. Good night, ladies and gentlemen. I leave you to think it over.'

He passed out of the room on the last words, the smirking Gideon on his heels. His men backed out after him, their guns levelled. Abbershaw dashed after them just as the great door swung to. He beat upon it savagely with his clenched fists, but the oak was like a rock.

'Burn?' Martin's voice broke the silence, and it was almost wondering. 'But the place is stone – it can't burn.'

Wyatt raised his eyes slowly.

'The outer walls are stone,' he said, and there was a curious note in his voice which sent a thrill of horror through everyone who heard it. 'The outer walls are stone, but the rest of it is oak, old, well-seasoned oak. It will burn like kindling wood in a grate.'

Chapter 22

The Darkest Hour

'The time,' said Mr Campion, 'is nine o'clock.'

Chris Kennedy stretched himself wearily.

'Six hours since that swine left us,' he said. 'Do you think we've got an earthly?'

There was a stir in the room after he had spoken, and almost everybody looked at the pale-haired bespectacled young man who sat squatting on his haunches in a corner. Jeanne and Prenderby were alone unconscious of what was going on. The little girl still supported the boy's head in her lap, with her timid little figure crouched over him, her face hidden.

Albert Campion shook his head.

'I don't know,' he said, but there was no hopefulness in his tone, and once again the little group relapsed into the silence that had settled over them after the first outburst which had followed von Faber's departure.

Whatever their attitude had been before, they were all now very much alive to the real peril of their position.

Von Faber had not been wasting his time when he had spoken to them, and they had each been struck by the stark callousness which had been visible in him throughout the entire interview.

At last Campion rose to his feet and came across to where Meggie and Abbershaw were seated. Gravely he offered Abbershaw his cigarette-case in which there was a single cigarette neatly cut into two pieces.

'I did it with a razor blade,' he said. 'Rather neat, don't you think?'

Abbershaw took the half gratefully and they shared a match.

'I suppose,' said Campion suddenly, speaking in a quiet and confidential tone, 'I suppose you did really burn that junk, Doc.'

Abbershaw glanced at him sharply.

'I did,' he said. 'God forgive me. When I think what I'm responsible for I feel I shall go mad.'

Mr Campion shrugged his shoulders.

'My dear old bird,' he said, 'I shouldn't put too much stress on what our friend von Faber says. He doesn't seem to me to be a person to be relied upon.'

'Why? Do you think he's just trying to frighten us?'

Abbershaw spoke eagerly, and the other shook his head.

'I'm afraid not, in the sense you mean,' he said. 'I think he's set his heart on this little conflagration scene. The man is a criminal loony, of course. No, I only meant that probably, had someone handed over his million-dollar book of the words, the Guy Fawkes celebrations would have gone forward all the same. I'm afraid he's just a nasty vindictive person.'

Meggie shuddered, but her voice was quite firm.

'Do you mean to say that you really think he'll burn the house down with us up here?' she said.

Campion looked up at her, and then at Abbershaw.

'Not a nice type, is he?' he murmured. 'I'm afraid we're for it, unless by a miracle the villagers see the bonfire before we're part of it, or the son of our friend in the attic calls earlier than was expected.'

Meggie stiffened.

'Mrs Meade,' she said. 'I'd forgotten all about her. What will Mr Dawlish do about her, do you suppose?'

Mr Campion spoke grimly.

'I could guess,' he said, and there was silence for a while after that.

'But how terrible!' Meggie burst out suddenly. 'I didn't believe that people like this were allowed to exist. I thought we were civilized. I thought this sort of thing couldn't happen.'

Mr Campion sighed.

'A lot of people believe things like that,' he said. 'They imagine the world is a well-ordered nursery with Scotland Yard and the British Army standing by to whack anybody who quarrels or uses a naughty word. I thought that at one time, I suppose everybody does, but it's not like that really, you know. Look at me, for example – who would dream of the cunning criminal brain that lurks beneath my inoffensive exterior?'

The other two regarded him curiously. In any other circumstances they would have been embarrassed. Abbershaw was the first to speak.

'I say,' he said, 'if you don't mind my asking such a thing, what on earth made you take up your – er – present profession?'

Mr Campion regarded him owlishly through his enormous spectacles.

'Profession?' he said indignantly. 'It's my vocation. It seemed to me that I had no talent for anything else, but in this line I can eke out the family pittance with tolerable comfort. Of course,' he went on suddenly, as he caught sight of Meggie's face, 'I don't exactly "crim", you know, as I told the doc. here. My taste is impeccable. Most of my commissions are more secret than shady. I occasionally do a spot of work for the Government, though, of course, that isn't as lucrative as honest crime. This little affair, of course, was perfectly simple. I had only to join this house-party, take a packet of letters from the old gentleman, toddle back to the Savoy, and my client would be waiting for me. A hundred guineas, and all clean fun – no brain-work required.' He beamed at them. 'Of course I knew what I was in for,' he went on. 'I knew that more or less as soon as I got down here. I didn't expect anything quite like this, though, I admit. I'm afraid the Gay Career and all that is in the soup.'

He spoke lightly, but there was no callousness in his face, and it suddenly occurred to Abbershaw that he was doing his best to cheer them up, for after a moment or two of silence he remarked suddenly:

'After all, I don't see why the place should burn as he says it will, and I know people do escape from burning houses because I've seen it on the pictures.'

His remarks were cut short by a thundering blow upon the door, and in the complete silence that followed, a voice spoke slowly and distinctly so that it was audible throughout the entire room.

'You have another hour,' it said, 'in which to restore Mr Dawlish's property. If it is not forthcoming by that time there will be another of these old country-mansion fires which have been so frequent of late. It is not insured and so it is not likely that anyone will inquire into the cause too closely.'

Martin Watt threw himself against the door with all his strength, and there was a soft amused laugh from outside.

'We heard your attempts to batter down the door last night,' said the voice, 'and Mr Dawlish would like you to know that although he has perfect faith in it holding, he has taken the precaution to reinforce it considerably on this side. As you have probably found out, the walls, too, are not negotiable and the window won't afford you much satisfaction.'

'You dirty swine!' shouted Chris Kennedy weakly from his corner, and Martin Watt turned slowly upon his heel and came back into the centre of the room, an expression of utter hopelessness on his face.

'I'm afraid we're sunk,' he said slowly and quietly and moved over towards the window, where he stood peering out between the bars.

Wyatt sat propped up against the wall, his chin supported in his hands, and his eyes fixed steadily upon the floor in front of him. For some time he had neither moved nor spoken. As Abbershaw glanced at him he could not help being reminded once again of the family portraits in the big dining-hall, and he seemed somehow part and parcel of the old house, sitting there morosely waiting for the end.

Meggie suddenly lifted her head.

'How extraordinary,' she said softly, 'to think that everything is going on just the same only a mile or two away. I heard a dog barking somewhere. It's incredible that this fearful thing should be happening to us and no one near enough to get us out. Think of it,' she went on quietly. 'A man murdered and taken away casually as if it were a light thing, and then a criminal lunatic' – she paused and her brown eyes narrowed – 'I hope he's a lunatic – calmly proposes to massacre us all. It's unthinkable.'

There was silence for a moment after she had spoken, and then Campion looked at Abbershaw.

'That yarn about Coombe,' he said quietly. 'I can't get over it. Are you sure he was murdered?'

Abbershaw glanced at him shrewdly. It seemed unbelievable that this pleasant, inoffensive-looking young man could be a murderer attempting to cast off any suspicion against himself, and yet, on the face of Mrs Meade's story, the evidence looked very black against him.

As he did not reply, Campion went on.

'I don't understand it at all,' he said. 'The man was so valuable to them . . . he must have been.'

Abbershaw hesitated, and then he said quietly:

'Are you sure he was – I mean do you *know* he was?'

Campion's pale eyes opened to their fullest extent behind his enormous glasses.

'I know he was to be paid a fabulous sum by Simister for his services,' he said, 'and I know that on a certain day next month there was to be a man waiting at a big London hotel to meet him. That man is the greatest genius at disguise in Europe, and his instructions were to give the old boy a face-lift and one or two other natty gadgets and hand him a ticket for the first transatlantic liner, complete with passport, family history, and pretty niece. Von Faber didn't know that, of course, but even if he did I don't see why he should stick the old gentleman in the gizzard, do you? The whole thing beats me. Besides, why does he want to saddle us with the nasty piece of work? It's the sort of thing he'd never convince us about. I don't see it myself. It can't be some bright notion of easing his own conscience.'

Abbershaw remained silent. He could not forget the old woman's strangely convincing story, the likelihood of which was borne out by Campion's own argument, but the more he thought about the man at his side, the more absurd did an explanation in that direction seem.

A smothered cry of horror from Martin at the window brought them all to their feet.

'The swine,' he said bitterly, turning to them, his face pale and his eyes glittering. 'Look. I saw Dawlish coming out of the garage towards the house. He was carrying petrol cans. He intends to have a good bonfire.'

'Good God!' said Chris Kennedy, who had taken his place at the window. 'Here comes a lad with a faggot. Oh, why can't I get at 'em!'

'They're going to burn us!'

For the first time the true significance of the situation seemed to dawn upon little Jeanne, and she burst into loud hysterical sobbing which was peculiarly unnerving in the tense atmosphere. Meggie crossed over to her and attempted to soothe her, but her self-control had gone completely and she continued to cry violently.

Anne Edgeware, too, was crying, but less noisily, and the tension became intolerable.

Abbershaw felt for his watch, and was about to draw it out when Albert Campion laid a hand over his warningly. As he did so his coat sleeve slipped up and Abbershaw saw the dial of the other's wristwatch. It was five minutes to eleven.

At the same moment, however, there were footsteps outside the door again, and this time the voice of Jesse Gideon spoke from without.

'It is your last chance,' he said. 'In three minutes we leave the house. You know the rest. What shall I say to Mr Dawlish?'

'Tell him to burn and to be damned to him!' shouted Martin.

'Very appropriate!' murmured Mr Campion, but his voice had lost its gaiety, and the hysterical sobs of the girl drowned the words.

And then, quite suddenly, from somewhere far across the fields there came a sound which everybody in the room recognized. A sound which brought them to their feet, the blood returning to their cheeks, and sent them crowding to the window, a new hope in their eyes.

It was the thin far-off call of a hunting horn.

Martin, his head jammed between the bars of the narrow window, let out a whoop of joy.

'The Hunt, by God!' he said. 'Yes – Lord! There's the pack not a quarter of a mile away! Glory be to God, was that a splodge of red behind that hedge? It was! Here he comes!'

His voice was resonant with excitement, and he struggled violently as if he would force himself through the iron bars.

'There he is,' he said again; 'and yes, look at him – look at him! Half the county behind him! They're in the park now. Gosh! They're coming right for us. Quick! Yell to 'em! God! They mustn't go past! How can we attract them! Yell at 'em! Shout something! They'll be on us in a minute.'

'I think,' murmured a quiet, rather foolish voice that yet had a note of tension in its tone, 'that in circumstances like this a "view-halloo" would be permissible. Quickly! Now, are you ready, my children? Let her go!'

There was utter silence after the shout died away upon the wind, and then Campion's voice behind them murmured again:

'Once more. Put your backs into it.'

The cry rang out wildly, agonizingly, a shout for help, and then again there was stillness.

Martin suddenly caught his breath.

'They've heard,' he said in a voice strangled with excitement. 'A chap is coming over here now.'

Chapter 23

An Error in Taste

'What shall I shout to him?' said Martin nervously, as the solitary horseman came cantering across the turf towards the house. 'I can't blab out the whole story.'

'Yell, "We're prisoners,"' suggested Kennedy, 'and, "Get us out for the love of Mike."'

'It's a young chap,' murmured Martin. 'Sits his horse well. Must be a decent cove. Here goes.'

He thrust his head as far out of the window as the bars would permit, and his clear young voice echoed out across the grass.

'Hello! Hello! Hell-o! Up here – top window! Up here! I say, we're prisoners. A loony in charge is going to burn the house down. For God's sake give the alarm and get us out.'

There was a period of silence, and then Martin spoke over his shoulder to the others:

'He can't hear. He's coming closer. He seems to be a bit of an ass.'

'For heaven's sake get him to understand,' said Wyatt. 'Everything depends on him.'

Martin nodded, and strained out of the window again.

'We're locked in here. Prisoners, I tell you. We –' he broke off suddenly and they heard him catch his breath.

'Dawlish!' he said. 'The brute's down there talking to him quietly as if nothing were up.'

'We're imprisoned up here, I tell you,' he shouted again. 'That man is a lunatic – a criminal. For heaven's sake don't take any notice of him.'

He paused breathless, and they heard the heavy German voice raised a little as though with suppressed anger.

'I tell you I am a doctor. These unfortunate people are under my care. They are poor imbeciles. You are exciting them. You will oblige me by going away immediately. I cannot have you over my grounds.'

And then a young voice with an almost unbelievable county accent spoke stiffly:

'I am sorry. I will go away immediately, of course. I had no idea you – er – kept lunatics. But they gave the "view-halloo" and naturally I thought they'd seen.'

Martin groaned.

'The rest of the field's coming up. The pack will be past in a moment.'

Mr Campion's slightly falsetto voice interrupted him. He was very excited. '*I* know that voice,' he said wildly. 'That's old "Guffy" Randall. Half a moment.'

On the last word he leapt up behind Martin and thrust his head in through the bars above the boy's.

'Guffy!' he shouted. 'Guffy Randall! Your own little Bertie is behind these prison bars in desperate need of succour. The old gentleman on your right is a fly bird – look out for him.'

'That's done it!'

Martin's voice was triumphant.

'He's looking up. He's recognized you, Campion. Great Scott! The Hun is getting out his gun.'

At the same moment the German's voice, bellowing now in his fury, rose up to them.

'Go away. You are trespassing. I am an angry man, sir. You are more than unwise to remain here.'

And then the other voice, well bred and protesting.

'My dear sir, you have a friend of mine apparently imprisoned in your house. I must have an explanation.'

'Good old Guff –' began Mr Campion, but the words died on his lips as the German's voice again sounded from the turf beneath them.

'You fool! Can none of you see when I am in earnest? Will that teach you?'

A pistol shot followed the last word, and Martin gasped.

'Good God! He hasn't shot him?' The words broke from Abbershaw in horror.

Martin remained silent, and then a whisper of horror escaped the flippant Mr Campion.

'Shot him?' he said. 'No. The unmitigated arch-idiot has shot one of the hounds. Just caught the tail end of the pack. Hullo! Here comes the huntsman with the field bouncing up behind him like Queen Victoria rampant. Now he's for it.'

The noise below grew to a babel, and Albert Campion turned a pink, excited face towards the anxious group behind him.

'How like the damn fool Guffy,' he said. 'So upset about the hound he's forgotten me.'

He returned to his look-out, and the next moment his voice resounded cheerfully over the tumult.

'I think they're going to lynch Poppa von Faber. I say, I'm enjoying this.'

Now that the danger was less imminent, the spirits of the whole party were reviving rapidly.

There was an excited guffaw from Martin.

'Campion,' he said, 'look at this.'

'Coo!' said Mr Campion idiotically, and was silent.

'The most militant old dear I've ever seen in all my life,' murmured Martin aloud. 'Probably a Lady Di-something-or-other. Fourteen stone if she weighs an ounce, and a face like her own mount. God, she's angry. Hullo! She's dismounting.'

'She's coming for him,' yelped Mr Campion. 'Oh, Inky-Pinky! God's in His Heaven, all's right with the world. She's caught him across the face with her crop. Guffy!' The last word was bellowed at the top of his voice, and the note of appeal in it penetrated through the uproar.

'Get us out! And take care for yourselves. They're armed and desperate.'

'With you, my son.'

The cheering voice from outside thrilled them more than anything had done in their lives before, and Martin dropped back from the window, breathless and flushed.

'What a miracle,' he said. 'What a heaven-sent glorious miracle. Looks as if our Guardian Angel had a sense of humour.'

'Yes, but will they be able to get to us?' Meggie spoke nervously. 'After all, they are armed, and –'

'My dear girl, you haven't seen!' Martin turned upon her. 'He can't murder half the county. There's a crowd outside the house that makes the place look like the local horse show. Daddy Dawlish's stunt for putting the fear of God into Campion's little friend has brought the entire Hunt down upon him thirsting for his blood. Looks as if they'll get it now, too. Hullo! Here they come.'

His last words were occasioned by the sound of footsteps outside, and then a horrified voice said clearly:

'Good heavens! What's the smell of kerosene?'

Several heavy blows outside followed. Then there was the grating of bolts and the heavy door swung open.

On the threshold stood Guffy Randall, a pleasant, horsy young man with a broken nose and an engaging smile. He was backed by half a dozen or so eager and bewildered horsemen.

'I say, Bertie,' he said, without further introduction, 'what's up? The passage out here is soaked with paraffin, and there's a small mountain of faggots on the stairs.'

Martin Watt grasped his arm.

'All explanations later, my son,' he said. 'The one thing we've got to do now is to prevent Uncle Boche from getting away. He's got a gang of about ten, too, but they're not so important. He's the lad we want, and a little sheeny pal of his.'

'Righto. We're with you. Of course the man's clean off the bean. Did you see that hound?'

'Yes,' said Martin soothingly. 'But it's the chappie we want now. He'll make for his car.'

'He won't get to it yet awhile,' said the new-comer grimly. 'He's surrounded by a tight hedge composed of the oldest members, and they're all seeing red – but still, we'll go down.'

Campion turned to Abbershaw.

'I think the girls had better come out,' he said. 'We don't want any mistakes at this juncture. Poor old Prenderby too, if we can bring him. The place is as inflammable as gun-cotton. I'll give you a hand with him.'

They carried the boy downstairs between them.

As Randall had said, the corridors smelt of paraffin and there were enormous faggots of dry kindling wood in advantageous positions all the way down to the hall. Clearly Herr von Faber had intended to leave nothing to chance.

'What a swine!' muttered Abbershaw. 'The man must be crazy, of course.'

Albert Campion caught his eye.

'I don't think so, my son,' he said. 'In fact I shouldn't be at all surprised if at this very moment our friend Boche wasn't proving his sanity pretty conclusively . . . Did it occur to you that his gang of boy friends have been a little conspicuous by their absence this morning?'

Abbershaw halted suddenly and looked at him.

'What are you driving at?' he demanded.

Mr Campion's pale eyes were lazy behind his big spectacles.

'I thought I heard a couple of cars sneaking off in the night,' he said. 'We don't know if old Whitby and his Dowager Daimler have returned – see what I mean?'

'Are you suggesting Dawlish is here *alone?*' said Abbershaw.

'Not exactly alone,' conceded Campion. 'We know Gideon is still about, and that county bird with the face like a thug also, but I don't expect the others are around. Consider it! Dawlish has us just where he wants us. He decides to make one last search for his precious package, which by now he realizes is pretty hopelessly gone. Then he means to make the place ready for his firework display, set light to it and bunk for home and mother; naturally he doesn't want all his pals standing by. It's not a pretty bit of work even for those lads. Besides, even if they do use the side roads, he doesn't want three cars dashing from the scene at the same time, does he?'

Abbershaw nodded.

'I see,' he said slowly. 'And so, now –'

The rest of his sentence was cut short by the sound of a shot from the turf outside, followed by a woman's scream that had more indignation than fear in it. Abbershaw and Campion set down their burden in the shadow of the porch and left him to the tender ministrations of Jeanne while they dashed out into the open.

The scene was an extraordinary one.

Spread out in front of the gloomy, forbidding old house was all the colour and pageantry of the Monewdon Hunt. Until a moment or two before, the greater part of the field had kept back, leaving the actual interviewing of the offender to the Master and several of the older members, but now the scene was one of utter confusion.

Apparently Herr von Faber had terminated what had proved to be a lengthy and heated argument with a revolver shot which, whether by accident or by design, had pinked a hole through the Master's sleeve, and sent half the horses in the field rearing and plunging; and then, under cover of the excitement, had fled for the garage, his ponderous form and long grey hair making him a strange, grotesque figure in the cold morning sun.

When Abbershaw and Campion burst upon the scene the first moment of stupefied horror was barely over.

Martin Watt's voice rang out clearly above the growing murmur of anger.

'The garage . . . quickly!' he shouted, and almost before the last word had left his lips there was the sound of an engine 'revving' violently. Then the great doors were shattered open, and the big Lanchester dived out like a torpedo. There were three men in it, the driver, Dawlish, and Gideon. Guffy Randall sprang into his saddle, and, followed by five or six of the younger spirits, set off at a gallop across the turf. Their intention was obvious. With reasonable luck they could expect to cut off the car at a point some way up the drive.

Campion shouted to them warningly, but his voice was lost in the wind of their speed, and he turned to Abbershaw, his face pale and twisted with horror.

'They don't realize!' he said, and the doctor was struck with the depth of feeling in his tone. 'Von Faber won't stop for anything – those horses! God! Look at them now!'

Guffy Randall and his band had drawn their horses up across the road in the way of the oncoming car.

Campion shouted to them wildly, but they did not seem to hear. Every eye in the field was upon them as the great grey car shot on, seeming to gather speed at every second.

Campion stood rigidly, his arm raised above his head.

'He'll charge 'em,' he murmured, and suddenly ducked as though unable to look any longer. Abbershaw, too, in that moment when it seemed inevitable that men and horseflesh must be reduced to one horrible bloody mêlée, blinked involuntarily. They had reckoned without horsemanship, however; just when it seemed that no escape were possible the horses reared and scattered, but as the car swept between them Guffy's lean young form shot down and his crop caught the driver full across the face.

The car leapt forward, swerved over the narrow turf border into a small draining ditch, and, with a horrible sickening grind of smashing machinery, overturned.

Chapter 24

The Last of Black Dudley

'I'm sorry to 'ave 'ad to trouble you, sir.'

Detective-Inspector Pillow, of the County Police, flapped back a closely written page of his notebook and resettled himself on the wooden chair which seemed so small for him as he spoke. Abbershaw, who was bending over the bed in which Prenderby lay, now conscious and able to take an interest in the proceedings, did not speak.

The three of them were alone in one of the first-floor rooms of Black Dudley, and the Inspector was coming to the end of his inquiry.

He was a sturdy, red-faced man with close-cropped yellow hair, and a slow-smiling blue eye. At the moment he was slightly embarrassed, but he went on with his duty doggedly.

'We're getting everybody's statements – in their own words,' he said, adding importantly and with one eye on Abbershaw, 'The Chief is not at all sure that Scotland Yard won't be interested in this affair. 'E is going to acquaint them with the facts right away, I believe . . . I know there's no harm in me telling *you* that, sir.'

He paused, and cast a wary glance at the little red-haired doctor.

'Oh, quite,' said Abbershaw hastily, adding immediately: 'Have you got everything you want now? I don't want my patient here disturbed more than I can help, you understand, Inspector.'

'Oh, certainly not, sir – certainly not. I quite understand.'

The Inspector spoke vehemently, but he still fingered his notebook doubtfully.

'There's just one point more, sir, I'd like to go into with you, if you don't mind,' he said at last. 'Just a little discrepancy 'ere. Naturally we want to get everything co'erent if we can, you understand. This is just as a matter of form, of course. Only you see I've got to hand my report in and –'

'That's all right, Inspector. What is it?' said Abbershaw encouragingly.

The Inspector removed his pencil from behind his ear and, after biting the end of it reflectively for a moment, said briskly: 'Well, it's about this 'ere tale of a murder, sir. Some of the accounts 'ave it that the accused, Benjamin Dawlish, believed to be an alias, made some rather startling accusations of murder when you was all locked up together on the evening of the 27th, that is, yesterday.'

He paused and looked at Abbershaw questioningly. The doctor hesitated.

There were certain details of the affair which he had decided to reserve for higher authorities since he did not want to risk the delay which a full exposure now would inevitably cause.

Whitby and the driver of the disguised Rolls had not returned. Doubtless they had been warned in time.

Meanwhile the Inspector was still waiting.

'As I take it, sir,' he said at length, 'the story was a bit of "colour", as you might say, put in by the accused to scare the ladies. Perhaps you 'ad some sort of the same idea?'

'Something very much like that,' agreed Abbershaw, glad to have evaded the awkward question so easily. 'I signed the cremation certificate for Colonel Coombe's body, you know.'

'Oh, you did, did you, sir. Well, that clears that up.'

Inspector Pillow seemed relieved. Clearly he regarded Abbershaw as something of an oracle since he was so closely associated with Scotland Yard, and incidentally he appeared to consider that the affair was tangled enough already without the introduction of further complications.

'By the way,' said Abbershaw suddenly, as the thought occurred to him, 'there's an old woman from the village in one of the attics, Inspector. Has she been rescued yet?'

A steely look came into the Inspector's kindly blue eyes.

'Mrs Meade?' he said heavily. 'Yes. The party 'as been attended to. The local constable 'as 'er in charge at the moment.' He sniffed. '*And* 'e's got 'is 'ands full,' he added feelingly. 'She seems to be a well-known character round 'ere. A regular tartar,' he went on more confidentially. 'Between you and me, sir' – he tapped his forehead significantly – 'she seems to be a case for the County Asylum. It took three men half an hour to get 'er out of the 'ouse. Kept raving about 'ell-fire and 'er son comin' of a Wednesday or something, I dunno. 'Owever, Police-Officer Maydew 'as 'er in 'and. Seems 'e understands 'er more or less. 'Er daughter does 'is washing, and it's well known the old lady's a bit queer. We come across strange things in our work, sir, don't we?'

Abbershaw was properly flattered by this assumption of colleagueship.

'So you expect Scotland Yard in on this, Inspector?' he said.

The policeman wagged his head seriously.

'I shouldn't be at all surprised, sir,' he said. 'Although,' he added, a trifle regretfully, 'if they don't hurry up I shouldn't wonder if there wasn't much for them to do except to attend the inquest. Our Dr Rawlins thinks 'e may pull 'em round, but 'e can't say yet for certain.'

Abbershaw nodded.

'It was Dawlish himself who got the worst of it, wasn't it?' he said.

'That is so,' agreed the Inspector. 'The driver, curiously enough, seemed to get off very lightly, I thought. Deep cut across his face, but otherwise nothing much wrong with 'im. The Chief's been interviewing 'im all the morning. Jesse Gideon, the second prisoner, is still unconscious. 'E 'as several nasty fractures, I understand, but Dawlish got all one side of the car on top of 'im and the doctor seems to think that if he keeps 'im alive 'is brain may go. There's not much sense in that, I told 'im. Simply giving everybody trouble, I said. Still, we 'ave to be 'umane, you know. How about Mr Prenderby, sir? Shall I take 'is statement later?'

Prenderby spoke weakly from the bed.

'I should like to corroborate all Dr Abbershaw has told you,' he said. 'Do you think you could make that do, Inspector?'

'It's not strictly in accordance with the regulations,' murmured Pillow, 'but I think under the circumstances we might stretch a point. I'll 'ave your name and address and I won't bother you two gentlemen no more.'

After Prenderby's name, age, address, and telephone number had been duly noted down in the Inspector's notebook, Abbershaw spoke.

'I suppose we may set off for Town when we like, then?' he said.

'Just whenever you like, sir.'

The Inspector shut his notebook with a click, and picking up his hat from beneath his chair, moved to the door.

'I'll wish you good day, then, gentlemen,' he said, and stalked out.

Prenderby looked at Abbershaw.

'You didn't tell him about Coombe?' he said.

Abbershaw shook his head.

'No,' he said.

'But surely, if we're going to make the charge we ought to do it at once? You're not going to let the old bird get away with it, are you?'

Abbershaw looked at him curiously.

'I've been a damned fool all the way through,' he said, 'but now I'm on ground I understand, and I'm not going to live up to my record. You didn't hear what Dawlish said to us last night, but if you had, and if you had heard that old woman's story, I think you'd see what I'm thinking. He didn't murder Coombe.'

Prenderby looked at him blankly.

'My head may be still batty,' he said, 'but I'm hanged if I get you. If the Hun or his staff aren't responsible, who is?'

Abbershaw looked at him fixedly, and Prenderby was moved to sarcasm.

'Anne Edgeware, or your priceless barmy crook who showed up so well when things got tight, I suppose,' he suggested.

Abbershaw continued to stare at him, and something in his voice when he spoke startled the boy by its gravity.

'I don't know, Michael,' he said. 'That's the devil of it, I don't know.'

Prenderby opened his mouth to speak, but he was cut short by a tap on the door. It was Jeanne and Meggie.

'This will have to wait, old boy,' he murmured as they came in. 'I'll come round and have a talk with you if I may, when we get back.'

'May Michael be moved?' It was Meggie who spoke. 'I'm driving Jeanne up to Town,' she explained, 'and we wondered if we might take Michael too.'

Prenderby grinned to Abbershaw.

'As one physician to another,' he said, 'perhaps not. But speaking as man to man, I don't think the atmosphere of this house is good for my aura. I think with proper feminine care and light conversation only, the journey might be effected without much danger, don't you?'

Abbershaw laughed.

'I believe in the feminine care,' he said. 'I'd like to come with you, but I've got the old AC in the garage, so I must reconcile myself to a lonely trip.'

'Not at all,' said Meggie. 'You're taking Mr Campion. Anne and Chris are going up with Martin. Chris's car is hopeless, and Anne says she'll never drive again until her nerves have recovered. The garage man is taking her car into Ipswich, and sending it up from there.'

'Where's Wyatt?' said Prenderby.

'Oh, he's staying down here – till the evening, at any rate.' It was Jeanne who spoke. 'It's his house, you see, and naturally there are several arrangements to make. I told him I thought it was very terrible of us to go off, but he said he'd rather we didn't stay. You see, the place is quite empty – there's not a servant anywhere – and naturally it's a bit awkward for him. You'd better talk to him, Dr Abbershaw.'

Abbershaw nodded.

'I will,' he said. 'He ought to get away from here pretty soon, or he'll be pestered to death by journalists.'

Meggie slipped her arm through his.

'Go and find him then, dear, will you?' she said. 'It must be terrible for him. I'll look after these two. Come and see me when you get back.'

Abbershaw glanced across the room, but Jeanne and Michael were too engrossed in each other to be paying any attention to anything else, so he bent forward impetuously and kissed her, and she clung to him for a moment.

'You bet I will,' he said, and as he went out of the room he felt himself, in spite of his problems, the happiest man alive.

He found Wyatt alone in the great hall. He was standing with his back to the fire-place, in which the cold embers of yesterday's fire still lay.

'No, thanks awfully, old boy,' he said, in response to Abbershaw's suggestion. 'I'd rather stay on on my own if you don't mind. There's only the miserable business of caretakers and locking up to be seen to. There are my uncle's private papers to be gone through, too, though Dawlish seems to have destroyed a lot of them. I'd rather be alone. You understand, don't you?'

'Why, of course, my dear fellow . . .' Abbershaw spoke hastily. 'I'll see you in Town no doubt when you get back.'

'Why, yes, I hope so. You do see how it is, don't you? I must go through the old boy's personalia.'

Abbershaw looked at him curiously.

'Wyatt,' he said suddenly, 'do you know much about your uncle?'

The other glanced at him sharply.

'How do you mean?' he demanded.

The little doctor's courage seemed suddenly to fail him.

'Oh, nothing,' he said, and added, somewhat idiotically, he felt, 'I only wondered.'

Wyatt let the feeble explanation suffice, and presently Abbershaw, realizing that he wished to be alone, made his adieux and went off to find Campion and to prepare for the oncoming journey. His round cherubic face was graver than its wont, however, and there was a distinctly puzzled expression in his grey eyes.

It was not until he and Campion were entering the outskirts of London late that evening that he again discussed the subject which perplexed him chiefly.

Mr Campion had chatted in his own particular fashion all the way up, but now he turned to Abbershaw with something more serious in his face.

'I say,' he said, 'what *did* happen about old Daddy Coombe? No one raised any row, I see. What's the idea? Dawlish said he was murdered; you said he was murdered; Prenderby said he was murdered. Was he?'

His expression was curious but certainly not fearful, Abbershaw was certain.

'I didn't say anything, of course, to the old Inspector person,' Campion went on, 'because I didn't know anything, but I thought you fellows would have got busy. Why the reticence? *You* didn't do it by any chance, did you?'

'No,' said Abbershaw shortly, some of his old pompousness returning at the suggestion of such a likelihood.

'No offence meant,' said Mr Campion, dropping into the vernacular of the neighbourhood through which they were passing. 'Nor none taken, I hope. No, what I was suggesting, my dear old bird, was this: Are you sleuthing a bit in your own inimitable way? Is the old cerebral machine ticking over? Who and what and why and wherefore, so to speak?'

'I don't know, Campion,' said Abbershaw slowly. 'I don't know any more than you do who did it. But Colonel Coombe was murdered. Of that I'm perfectly certain, and – I don't think Dawlish or his gang had anything to do with it.'

'My dear Holmes,' said Mr Campion, 'you've got me all of a flutter. You're not serious, are you?'

'Perfectly,' said Abbershaw. 'After all, who might not have done it, with an opportunity like that, if they wanted to? Hang it all, how do I know that you didn't do it?'

Mr Campion hesitated, and then shrugged his shoulders.

'I'm afraid you've got a very wrong idea of me,' he said. 'When I told you that I never did anything in bad taste, I meant it. Sticking an old boy in the middle of a house-party parlour-game occurs to me to be the height of bad form. Besides, consider, I was only getting a hundred guineas. Had my taste been execrable I wouldn't have risked putting my neck in a noose for a hundred guineas, would I?'

Abbershaw was silent. The other had voiced the argument that had occurred to himself, but it left the mystery no clearer than before.

Campion smiled.

'Put me down as near Piccadilly as you can, old man, will you?' he said.

Abbershaw nodded, and they drove on in silence.

At last, after some considerable time, he drew up against the kerb on the corner of Berkeley Street. 'Will this do you?' he said.

'Splendidly. Thanks awfully, old bird. I shall run into you some time, I hope.'

Campion held out his hand as he spoke, and Abbershaw, overcome by an impulse, shook it warmly, and the question that had been on his lips all the drive suddenly escaped him.

'I say, Campion,' he said, 'who the hell are you?'

Mr Campion paused on the running-board and there was a faintly puckish expression behind his enormous glasses.

'Ah,' he said. 'Shall I tell you? Listen – do you know who my mother is?'

'No,' said Abbershaw, with great curiosity.

Mr Campion leaned over the side of the car until his mouth was an inch or two from the other man's ear, and murmured a name, a name so illustrious that Abbershaw started back and stared at him in astonishment.

'Good God!' he said. 'You don't mean that?'

'No,' said Mr Campion cheerfully, and went off striding jauntily down the street until, to Abbershaw's amazement, he disappeared through the portals of one of the most famous and exclusive clubs in the world.

Chapter 25

Mr Watt Explains

After dinner one evening in the following week, Abbershaw held a private consultation on the affair in his rooms in the Adelphi.

He had not put the case before his friend, Inspector Deadwood, for a reason which he dared not think out, yet his conscience forbade him to ignore the mystery surrounding the death of Colonel Coombe altogether.

Since von Faber and his confederates were wanted men, the County Police had handed over their prisoners to Scotland Yard; and in the light of preliminary legal proceedings, sufficient evidence had been forthcoming to render the affair at Black Dudley merely the culminating point in a long series of charges. Every day it became increasingly clear that they would not be heard of again for some time.

Von Faber was still suffering from concussion, and there seemed every likelihood of his remaining under medical supervision for the term of his imprisonment at least.

Whitby and his companion had not been traced, and no one, save himself, so far as Abbershaw could tell, was likely to raise any inquiries about Colonel Coombe.

All the same, although he had several excellent reasons for wishing the whole question to remain in oblivion, Abbershaw had forced himself to institute at least a private inquiry into the mystery.

He and Meggie had dined together when Martin Watt was admitted.

The girl sat in one of the high-backed Stuart chairs by the fire, her brocade-shod feet crossed, and her hands folded quietly in her lap.

Glancing at her, Abbershaw could not help reflecting that their forthcoming marriage was more interesting to him than any criminal hunt in the world.

Martin was more enthusiastic on the subject of the murder. He came in excited, all trace of indolence had vanished from his face, and he looked about him with some surprise.

'No one else here?' he said. 'I thought we were going to have a pukka consultation with all the crowd present – decorations, banners, and salute of guns!'

Abbershaw shook his head.

'Sorry! I'm afraid there's only Prenderby to come,' he said. 'Campion has disappeared, Anne Edgeware is in the South of France recuperating, Jeanne doesn't want to hear or think anything about Black Dudley ever again, so Michael tells me, and I didn't think we'd mention the thing to Wyatt, until it's a certainty at any rate. He's had his share of unpleasantness already. So you see there are only the four of us to talk it over. Have a drink?'

'Thanks.' Martin took up the glass and sipped it meditatively. It was evident from his manner that he was bubbling with suppressed excitement. 'I say,' he said suddenly, unable to control his eagerness any longer, 'have you folk twigged the murderer?'

Abbershaw glanced at him sharply.

'No,' he said hesitatingly. 'Why, have you?'

Martin nodded.

'Fancy so,' he said, and there was a distinctly satisfied expression in his grey eyes. 'It seems pretty obvious to me, why –'

'Hold hard, Martin.'

Abbershaw was surprised at the apprehension in his own voice, and he reddened slightly as the other two stared at him.

Martin frowned.

'I don't get you,' he said at last. 'There's no special reason against suspecting Whitby, is there?'

'Whitby?'

Abbershaw's astonishment was obvious, and Meggie looked at him curiously, but Martin was too interested in his theory to raise any question.

'Why, yes,' he said. 'Whitby. Why not? Think of it in cold blood, who was the first man to find Colonel Coombe dead? Who had a better motive for murdering him than anyone else? It seems quite obvious to me.' He paused, and as neither of them spoke went on again, raising his voice a little in his enthusiasm.

'My dear people, just think of it,' he insisted. 'It struck me as soon as it occurred to me that it was so obvious that I've been wondering ever since why we didn't hit on it at once. We should have done, of course, if we hadn't all been having fun in our quiet way. Look here, this is exactly how it happened.'

He perched himself on an armchair and regarded them seriously.

'Our little friend Albert is the first person to be considered. There is absolutely no reason to doubt that fellow's word, his yarn sounds true. He showed up jolly well when we were in a tight place. I think we'll take him as cleared. His story is true, then. That is to say, during Act One of the drama when we were all playing "touch" with the haunted dagger, little Albert stepped smartly up, murmured "Abracadabra" in the old man's ear and collected the doings, leaving the Colonel hale and hearty. What happened next?' He paused and glanced at them eagerly. 'See what I'm driving at? No? Well, see column two – "The Remarkable Story of the Aged and Batty Housemaid!" Now have you got it?'

Meggie started to her feet, her eyes brightening.

'George,' she said, 'I do believe he's got it. Don't you see, Mrs Meade told us that she had actually seen Whitby come in with the news that the Colonel was stabbed in the back. Why – why it's quite clear –'

'Not so fast, not so fast, young lady, *if* you please. Let the clever detective tell his story in his own words.'

Martin leant forward as he spoke and beamed at them triumphantly.

'I've worked it all out,' he said, 'and, putting my becoming modesty aside, I will now detail to you the facts which my superlative deductions have brought to light and which only require the paltry matter of proof to make them as clear as glass to the meanest intelligence. Get the scene into your mind. Whitby, a poor pawn in his chief's hands, a man whose liberty, perhaps his very life, hangs upon the word of his superior, von Faber; this man leads his chief to the Colonel's desk to find that precious income-tax form or whatever it was they were all so keen about, and when he gets there the cupboard is bare, as the classics have it.' Martin, who had been gradually working himself up, now broke into a snatch of imaginary dialogue:

'"It must be on Coombe himself," growls the Hun,' he began.

'"Of course," agrees the pawn, adding mentally: "Heaven pray it may be so," or words to that effect. "Go and see, *you*!" venoms the Hun, and off goes Whitby, fear padding at his heels.'

He paused for breath and regarded them soberly.

'Seriously, though,' he continued with sudden gravity. 'The chap must have had a nasty ten minutes. He knew that if anything had gone wrong and old Coombe had somehow managed to double-cross the gang, as guardian he was for it with von Faber at his nastiest. Look now,' he went on cheerfully, 'this is where the deduction comes in; as I work it out, as soon as Whitby entered the darkened part of the house, someone put the dagger in his hand and then, I should say, the whole idea occurred to him. He went up to old Coombe in the dark, asked him for the papers; Coombe replied that he hadn't got them. Then Whitby, maddened with the thought of the yarn he was bound to take back to von Faber, struck the old boy in the back and, after making a rapid search, took the dagger, joined in the game for thirty seconds, maybe – just enough time to hand the thing on to somebody – and then dashed back to Faber and Gideon, with his news. How about that?'

He smiled at them with deep satisfaction – he had no doubts himself.

For some minutes his audience were silent. This solution was certainly very plausible. At last Abbershaw raised his head. The expression on his face was almost hopeful.

'It's not a bad idea, Martin,' he said thoughtfully. 'In fact, the more I think about it the more likely it seems to become.'

Martin pressed his argument home eagerly.

'I feel like that too,' he said. 'You see, it explains so many things. First of all, it gives a good reason why von Faber thought that one of our crowd had done it. Then it also makes it clear why Whitby never turned up again. And then it has another advantage – it provides a motive. No one else had any *reason* for killing the old boy. As far as I can see he seems to have been very useful to his own gang and no harm to anybody else. Candidly now, don't you think I'm obviously right?'

He looked from one to the other of them questioningly.

Meggie was frowning.

'There is just one thing you haven't explained, Martin,' she said slowly. 'What happened to the dagger? When it was in my hand it had blood on it. Someone snatched it from me before I could scream, and it wasn't seen again until the next morning, when it was all bright and clean again and back in its place in the trophy.'

Martin looked a little crestfallen.

'That had occurred to me,' he admitted. 'But I decided that in the excitement of the alarm whoever had it chucked it down where it was found next morning by one of the servants and put back.'

Meggie looked at him and smiled.

'Martin,' she said, 'your mother has the most marvellous butler in the world. Plantagenet, I do believe, would pick up a blood-stained dagger in the early morning, have it cleaned, and hang it up on its proper nail, and then consider it beneath his dignity to mention so trifling a matter during the police inquiries afterwards. But believe me, that man is unique. Besides, the only servants there were members of the gang. Had they found it we should probably have heard about it. Anyway, they wouldn't have cleaned it and hung it up again.'

Martin nodded dubiously, and the momentary gleam of hope disappeared from Abbershaw's face.

'Of course,' said Martin. 'Whitby may have put it back himself. Gone nosing around during the night, you know, and found it, and thinking, "Well, we can't have this about," put it back in its proper place and said no more about it.' He brightened visibly. 'Come to think of it, it's very likely. That makes my theory all the stronger, what?'

The others were not so easily convinced.

'He might,' said Meggie, 'but there's not much reason why he should go nosing about at night, as you say. And even so it doesn't explain who took it out of my hand, does it?'

Martin was shaken but by no means overwhelmed.

'Oh, well,' he said airily, 'all that point is a bit immaterial, don't you think? After all, it's the main motive and opportunity and questions that are important. Anyone might have snatched the dagger from you. It is one of those damn fool gallant gestures that old Chris Kennedy might have perpetrated. It might have been anyone playing in the game. However, in the main, I think we've spotted our man. Don't you, Abbershaw?'

'I hope so.'

The fervency of the little doctor's reply surprised them.

Martin was gratified.

'I *know* I'm right,' he said. 'Now all we've got to do is to prove it.'

Abbershaw agreed.

'That's so,' he said. 'But I don't think that will be so easy, Martin. You see, we've got to find the chap first, and without police aid that's going to be a well-nigh impossible job. We can't bring the Yard into it until we've got past theories.'

'No, of course not,' said Martin. 'But I say,' he added, as a new thought occurred to him, 'there is one thing, though. Whitby was the cove who had the wind-up, wasn't he? No one else turned a hair, and if there was a guilty conscience amongst the gang, surely it was his?'

This suggestion impressed his listeners more than any of his other arguments. Abbershaw looked up excitedly.

'I do believe you're right,' he said. 'What do you think, Meggie?'

The girl hesitated. As she recollected Mrs Meade's story of the discovery of the murder, Martin's theory became rapidly more and more plausible.

'Yes,' she said again. 'I believe he's hit it.'

Martin grinned delightedly.

'That's fine,' he said. 'Now all we've got to do is to find the chap and get the truth out of him. This is going to be great. Now what's the best way to get on to the trail of those two johnnies? Toddle round to all the crematoriums in the country and make inquiries?'

The others were silent. Here was a problem which, without the assistance of Scotland Yard, they were almost powerless to tackle.

They were still discussing it when, fifteen minutes later, Michael Prenderby walked in. His pale face was flushed as if from violent exertion and he began to talk eagerly as soon as he got into the room.

'Sorry I'm late,' he said; 'but I've had an adventure. Walked right into it in the Lea Bridge Road. I stopped to have a plug put in and there it was staring at me. I stared at it – I thought I was seeing things at first – until the garage man got quite embarrassed.'

Martin Watt regarded the new-comer coldly.

'Look here, Michael,' he said with reproach. 'We're here to discuss a murder, you know.'

'Well?' Prenderby looked pained and surprised. 'Aren't I helping you? Isn't this a most helpful point?'

Abbershaw glanced at him sharply.

'What are you talking about?' he said.

Prenderby stared at him.

'Why, the car, of course,' he said. 'What else could it be? The car,' he went on, as they regarded him uncomprehendingly for a moment or so. '*The* car. The incredible museum specimen in which that precious medico carted off the poor old bird's body. There it was, sitting up looking at me like a dowager-duchess.'

Chapter 26

'Cherchez la Femme'

'If you'd only keep quiet,' said Michael Prenderby, edging a chair between himself and the vigorous Martin who was loudly demanding particulars, 'I'll tell you all about it. The garage is half-way down the Lea Bridge Road, on the left-hand side not far past the river or canal or whatever it is. It's called "The Ritz" – er – because there's a coffee-stall incorporated with it. It's not a very big place. The usual type – a big white-washed shed with a tin roof – no tiles or anything. While the chap was fixing the plug the doors were open, so I looked in, and there, sitting in a corner, a bit like "Dora" and a bit like a duchess, but unmistakably herself, was Colonel Coombe's original mechanical brougham.'

'But are you sure?'

Martin was dancing with excitement.

'Absolutely positive.' Prenderby was emphatic. 'I went and had a look at the thing. The laddie in the garage was enjoying the joke as much as anyone. He hadn't had time to examine it, he said, but he'd never set eyes on anything like it in his life. I didn't know what to do. I didn't think I'd wait and see the fellows without telling you because I didn't know what schemes you were hatching, so I told the garage man that I'd like to buy the bus as a museum piece. He told me that the people who brought it in were coming back for it some time tonight and he'd tell them. I thought we'd get down there first and be waiting for them as they came in. Of course the old car may have changed hands, but even so –'

'Rather!' Martin was enthusiastic. 'We'll go down there right away, shall we? All of us?'

'Not Meggie,' said Abbershaw quickly. 'No,' he added with determination, as she turned to him appealingly. 'You had your share of von Faber's gang at Black Dudley, and I'm not going to risk anything like that again.'

Meggie looked at him, a faintly amused expression playing round the corners of her mouth, but she did not attempt to argue with him: George was to be master in his own home, she had decided.

The three men set off in Prenderby's small Riley, Abbershaw tucked uncomfortably between the other two.

Martin Watt grinned.

'I've got a gun this time,' he said. 'Our quiet country week-end taught me that much.'

Abbershaw was silent. He, too, had invested in an automatic, since his return to London. But he was not proud of the fact, since he secretly considered that its purchase had been a definite sign of weakness.

They wormed their way through the traffic, which was mercifully thin at that time of night, although progress was by no means easy. A clock in Shoreditch struck eleven as they went through the borough, and Martin spoke fervently.

'Good lord, I hope we don't miss them,' he said, and added with a chuckle, 'I bet old Kennedy would give his ears to be on this trip. How far down is the place, Prenderby?'

'Not far now,' said Michael, as he swung into the unprepossessing tram-lined thoroughfare which leads to the 'Bakers' Arms' and Wanstead.

'And you say the garage man was friendly?' said Abbershaw.

'Oh, perfectly,' said Prenderby, with conviction. 'I think we can count on him. What exactly is our plan of campaign?'

Martin spoke airily.

'We just settle down and wait for the fellows, and when they come we get hold of them and make them talk.'

Abbershaw looked dubious. Now that he was back in the civilization of London he was inclined to feel that the lawless methods of Black Dudley were no longer permissible, no matter what circumstances should arise. Martin had more of the adventurous spirit left in him, however. It was evident that he had made up his mind about their plan of campaign.

'The only thing these fellows understand is force,' he said vigorously. 'We're going to talk to 'em in their mother tongue.'

Abbershaw would have demurred, but at this moment all conversation was suspended by their sudden arrival at the garage. They found 'The Ritz' still open, though business even at the coffee-stall was noticeably slack.

As soon as the car came to a standstill, a loose-limbed, raw-boned gentleman in overalls and a trilby hat came out to meet them.

He regarded them with a cold suspicion in his eyes which even Prenderby's friendly grin did not thaw.

'I've come back to see about the old car I wanted to buy –' Prenderby began, with his most engaging grin.

'You did, did you?' The words were delivered with a burst of Homeric geniality that would have deceived nobody. 'But, it's not for sale, see! You'd better back your car out, there's no room to turn here.'

Prenderby was frankly puzzled; clearly this was the last reception he had expected.

'He's been told to hold his tongue,' whispered Martin, and then, turning to the garage man, he smiled disarmingly. 'You've no idea what a disappointment this is to me,' he said. 'I collect relics of this sort and by my friend's description the specimen you have here seems to be very nearly perfect. Let me have a look at it at any rate.'

He slipped hastily out of the car as he spoke and made a move in the direction of the darkened garage door.

'Oh no, you don't!' The words were attended by the suspicious and unfriendly gentleman in the overalls and at the same moment Martin found himself confronted with the whole six-foot-three of indignant aggressiveness, while the voice, dropping a few tones, continued softly, 'There's a lot of people round here what are friends of mine. Very particular friends. I'd 'op it if I was you.'

Martin stared at him with apparent bewilderment.

'My dear man, what's the matter?' he said. 'Surely you're not the type of fellow to be unreasonable when someone asks you to show him a car. There's no reason why I should be wasting your time even.'

He chinked some money in his pocket suggestively. The face beneath the trilby remained cold and unfriendly.

'Now look 'ere,' he said, thrusting his hands into his trousers pockets through the slits in his overalls, 'I'm telling you, and you can take it from me or not as you please. But if you do take it, and I 'ope for your sake you do, you'll go right away from this place. I've got my reasons for telling you – see?'

Martin still seemed bewildered.

'But this is extraordinary,' he said, and added as if the thought had suddenly occurred to him, 'I suppose this doesn't interest you?'

A crackle of notes sounded as he spoke and then his quiet lazy voice continued. '*So* attractive I always think. That view of the Houses of Parliament on the back is rather sweet – or perhaps you like this one better – or this? I've got two here printed in green as well. What do you say?'

For a moment the man did not answer, but it was evident that some of his pugnacity had abated.

'A fiver!' he said, and went on more reasonably after a considerable pause. 'Look here, what *is* this game you're up to? What's your business is your business and I'm not interfering, but this I 'ope and arsk. I don't want any fooling around my garage. I've got 'undreds of pounds' worth of cars in 'ere and I've got my reputation to think of. So no setting fire to anything or calling of the police – see? If I let you in 'ere to 'ave a look at that car that's got to be understood.'

'Why, of course not. Let us have a look at the car at any rate,' said Martin, handing him the notes.

The man was still doubtful, but the money had a warming and soothing effect upon his temper.

'Are you all coming in?' he said at last. 'Because if so you'd better hurry up. The owners may be back any time now.'

This was a step forward at any rate. Abbershaw and Prenderby climbed out of the Riley and followed Martin with the visibly softening proprietor into the garage.

The man switched on the light and the three surveyed the miscellaneous collection of cars with interest.

'There she is,' said Prenderby, his voice betraying his excitement. 'Over in that corner there. Now, I ask you, could you miss her anywhere?'

The others followed the direction of his eyes and an exclamation broke from Martin.

'She certainly has IT,' he said. 'Once seen never forgotten.' He turned to the garage proprietor. 'Have you looked at her, Mr – er – er –?' he hesitated, at a loss for the name.

''Aywhistle,' said the man stolidly, 'and I ain't. I don't know anything about 'er nor don't want to. Now, 'ave you seen enough to keep you 'appy?'

Martin looked at him curiously.

'Look here, Captain,' he said. 'You come over here. I want to show you something if you haven't seen it already.'

He moved over to the old car as he spoke, Mr Haywhistle following him unwillingly. Martin pulled up the bonnet and pointed to the engine.

'Ever seen anything like that before?' he said.

Mr Haywhistle looked at the machinery casually and without interest at first. But gradually his expression changed and he dropped upon his knees and peered underneath the car to get a glimpse of the chassis. A moment or two later he lifted a red face towards them which wore an expression almost comic in its surprise.

'Gawd lumme!' he said. 'A bloomin' Rolls.'

Martin nodded and an explanation of these 'Young Nobs' interest in the affair presented itself to the garage owner:

'Pinched it, did he?' he said. 'Oh! I see now. But I pray and arsk you, sir, don't 'ave any rowin' in 'ere. I've 'ad a bit of trouble that way already – see?' He looked at them appealingly.

Martin turned to the others.

'I don't think we need do anything in here, do you?' he said. 'If Mr Haywhistle will let us wait in his yard at the side, with the gates open, as soon as Whitby comes out we can follow him. How's that?'

'That suits me fine,' said Mr Haywhistle, looking at them anxiously. 'Now I'll tell you what,' he went on, clearly eager to do all that he could to assist them now that he was not so sure of himself. 'This is wot 'e says to me. Early this morning, about eight o'clock, 'e comes in 'ere with the car. My boy put 'er in for 'im, so I didn't 'ear the engine running. I came in just as 'e was leaving instructions. As far as I could gather he intended to meet a friend 'ere late tonight and they was going off together in the car as soon as this friend turned up. Well, about eight o'clock tonight, this gentleman 'ere,' – he indicated Prenderby – ''e calls in and spots the car and mentioned buying it. Of course I see where 'is artfulness comes in now,' he added, beaming at them affably. ''Owever, I didn't notice anything fishy at the time so when the owner of the car comes in about 'alf an hour ago I tells him that there was a gentleman interested in the old bus. Whereupon 'e went in the air – a fair treat. "Tell me," says 'e, "was 'e anything like this?" Thereupon 'e gives a description of a little red-'eaded cove, which I see now is this gentleman 'ere.'

He nodded at Abbershaw. 'Perhaps it's your car, sir?' he suggested.

Abbershaw smiled non-committally, and Mr Haywhistle went on.

'Well, what eventually transpired,' he said ponderously, 'was this. I was not to show 'is property to anybody, and a very nasty way 'e said it too. 'E said 'e was coming back this side of twelve and if 'is friend turned up before him I was to ask 'im to wait.'

Abbershaw looked at his watch.

'We'd better get into the yard straight away,' he said.

Mr Haywhistle glanced up at a big clock on the bare whitewashed wall.

'Lumme, yes,' he said. '''Alf a minute, I'll come and 'elp you.'

With his assistance they backed the Riley into the dark yard by the side of 'The Ritz' and put out their lights.

'You get into 'er and sit waiting. Then as soon as they come out on the road you can nip after them – see?' he said.

Since there was nothing better to do they took his advice and the three sat silent in the car, waiting.

Martin was grinning to himself. The promise of adventure had chased the lazy expression out of his eyes and he appeared alert and interested. Prenderby leant on the steering wheel, his thin pale face utterly expressionless.

Abbershaw alone looked a little perturbed. He had some doubts as to the Riley's capabilities as far as chasing the disguised Rolls were concerned. He was also a little afraid of Martin's gun. He realized that they were on a lawless errand since they were acting entirely without proof, and any casualties that might occur would be difficult to explain afterwards even to so obliging a person as Inspector Deadwood.

He was disturbed in his reflections by Martin's elbow gently prodded into his ribs. He looked up to see a tall burly figure, in a light overcoat and a cap pulled down well on his head, standing in the wedge of light cast through the open doorway of the garage.

'"The butler",' whispered Prenderby excitedly.

Abbershaw nodded; he too had recognized the man.

Mr Haywhistle's manner was perfect.

''Ere you are, sir,' they heard him say cheerfully. 'Your friend won't be long. Said 'e'd be round just before twelve. I shouldn't stand out there,' he went on tactfully, as the man showed a disposition to look about him. 'I'm always 'aving cars swing in 'ere without looking where they're going. I can't stop 'em. It's dangerous you know. That's right. Come inside.'

As the two figures disappeared, a third, moving rapidly with quick, nervous steps, hurried in out of the darkness.

The three men in the car caught a glimpse of him as he passed into the garage. It was Whitby himself.

'Shall I start the engine?' murmured Prenderby.

Martin put a warning hand on his.

'Wait till they start theirs,' he said. 'Now.'

Michael trod softly on the starter and the Riley began to purr.

'Keep back, see which way they turn, and then after them,' Martin whispered sharply. 'Hullo! Here they come!'

Even as he spoke there was the soft rustle of wheels on the concrete and then the curious top-heavy old car glided softly and gently into the road, taking the direction of Wanstead, away from the city.

Prenderby dropped in the clutch and the Riley slipped out of its hiding-place and darted out in pursuit, a graceful silver fish amid the traffic.

Chapter 27
A Journey by Night

For the first few miles, while they were still in the traffic, Prenderby contented himself with keeping the disguised Rolls in sight. It would be absurd, he realized, to overtake them while still in London, since they were acting in an unofficial capacity and he was particularly anxious not to arouse the suspicions of the occupants of the car in front of them.

He went warily, therefore, contriving always to keep a fair amount of traffic between them.

Martin was exultant. He was convinced by his own theory, and was certain that the last act of the Black Dudley mystery was about to take place.

Prenderby was too much absorbed by the details of the chase to give any adequate thought to the ultimate result.

Abbershaw alone was dubious. This, like everything else connected with the whole extraordinary business, appalled him by its amazing informality. He could not rid his mind of the thought that it was all terribly illegal – and besides that, at the back of his mind, there was always that other question, that problem which had caused him so many sleepless nights since his return to London. He hoped Martin was right in his theory, but he was sufficiently alarmed by his own secret thought to wish not to put Martin's idea to the test. He wanted to think Martin was right, to find out nothing that would make him look elsewhere for the murderer.

As they escaped from the tramway lines and came out into that waste of little new houses which separates the city from the fields, they and the grotesque old car in front were practically alone on the wide ill-lighted roads.

It was growing cold and there was a suggestion of a ground mist so that the car in front looked like a dim ghost returned from the early days of motoring.

As the last of the houses vanished and they settled down into that long straight strip of road through the forest, Prenderby spoke:

'How about now?' he said. 'Shall I open out?'

Martin glanced at Abbershaw.

'What do you think?' he said.

Abbershaw hesitated.

'I don't quite see what you intend to do,' he said. 'Suppose you succeed in stopping them, what are you going to say? We have no proof against the man and no authority to do anything if we had.'

'But we're going to get proof,' said Martin cheerfully. 'That's the big idea. First we stop them, then we sit on their heads while they talk.'

Abbershaw shook his head.

'I don't think we'd get much out of them that way,' he said. 'And if we did it wouldn't be evidence. No, if you take my advice you'll run them to earth. Then perhaps we'll find something, although really, my dear Martin, I can't help feeling –'

'Let's kick him out, Prenderby,' said Martin, 'He's trying to spoil the party.'

Abbershaw grinned.

'I think we're doing all we can do,' he said. 'After all it's no good letting them out of our sight.'

Prenderby sighed.

'I wish you'd decided to overtake,' he said. 'This is a marvellous road. It wouldn't hurt us to be a bit nearer, anyway, would it?'

Martin nudged him gently.

'If you want to try your speed, my lad,' he said, 'here's your opportunity. The old lady has started to move.'

The other two glanced ahead sharply. The Rolls had suddenly begun to move at something far beyond her previous respectable rate. The red tail-light was already disappearing into the distance.

Prenderby's share in the conversation came to an abrupt end. The Riley began to purr happily and they shot forward at an ever-increasing pace until the speedometer showed sixty.

'Steady!' said Martin. 'Don't pass them in your excitement. We don't want them to spot us either.'

'What makes you so sure that they haven't done so already?' said Abbershaw shrewdly, and added as they glanced at him inquiringly, 'I couldn't help thinking as we came along that they were going very leisurely, taking their time, when there was plenty of other traffic on the road. As soon as we were alone together they began to move. I believe they've spotted us.'

Prenderby spoke without looking round.

'He's right,' he said. 'Either that or they're suddenly in the deuce of a hurry. I'm afraid they're suspicious of us. They can't possibly know who we are with lights like these.'

'Then I say,' cut in Martin excitedly, 'they'll try to dodge us. I'd get as near as you can and then sit on their tail if I were you.'

Abbershaw said nothing and the Riley slowly crept up on the other car until she was directly in her head-lights. The Rolls swayed to the side to enable them to pass, but Prenderby did not avail himself of the invitation. Eventually the big car slackened speed but still Prenderby did not attempt to pass.

The next overture from the Rolls was as startling as it was abrupt. The little rear window opened suddenly and a bullet hit the road directly in front of them.

Prenderby swerved and brought the Riley almost to a full stop.

'A pot-shot at our front tyre,' he said. 'If he'd got us we'd have turned over. Martin, I believe you're on the right tack. The cove is desperate.'

'Of course I'm right,' said Martin excitedly. 'But don't let them get away, man, they'll be out of sight in a minute.'

'Sorry,' said Prenderby obstinately, 'I'm keeping my distance. You don't seem to realize the result of a tyre-burst at that pace.'

'Oh, he won't do it again,' said Martin cheerfully. 'Besides, he's a rotten shot anyway.'

Prenderby said no more, but he was careful to keep at a respectable distance from the Rolls.

'They'll start moving now,' said Martin. 'We shall have our work cut out if we're going to be in at the death. Look out for the side turnings. Do you know this road at all?'

'Pretty well,' said Prenderby. 'He's heading for Chelmsford, I should say, or somewhere round there. I think he'll have some difficulty in shaking us off.'

The big car ahead was now speeding away from them rapidly and Prenderby had his hands full to keep them anywhere in sight. In Chelmsford they lost sight of it altogether and were forced to inquire of a policeman in the deserted High Street.

The placid country bobby took the opportunity of inspecting their licence and then conceded the information that a 'vehicle of a type now obsolete, and bearing powerful lamps' had passed through the town, taking the Springfield road for Kelvedon and Colchester some three minutes before their own arrival.

The Riley sped on down the winding road through the town, Martin cursing vigorously.

'Now we're sunk,' he said. 'Missed them sure as Pancake-tide. They've only got to nip into a side road and shut off their lamps and we're done. In fact,' he went on disconsolately, 'I don't know if there's any point in going on at all now.'

'There's only one point,' cut in Abbershaw quietly. 'If by chance they are going somewhere definite – I mean if they want to get to a certain spot in set time – they'll probably go straight on and trust to luck that they've shaken us off.'

'That's right,' said Martin. 'Let's go on full tilt to Colchester and ask there. No one could miss a bus like that. It looks as if it ought not to be about alone. Full steam ahead, Michael.'

'Ay, ay, sir,' said Prenderby cheerfully and trod on the accelerator.

They went through Witham at a speed that would have infuriated the local authorities, but still the road was ghostly and deserted. At length, just outside Kelvedon, far away in the distance there appeared the faint haze of giant head-lights against the trees.

Martin whooped.

'A sail, a sail, captain,' he said. 'It must be her. Put some speed into it, Michael.'

'All right. If we seize up or leave the road, on your head be it,' said Prenderby, through his teeth. 'She's all out now.'

The hedges on either side of them became blurred and indistinct. Finally, in the long straight strip between Marks Tey and Lexden, they slowly crept up behind the big car again.

'That's her all right,' said Martin; 'she's crawling, isn't she? Comparatively, I mean. I believe Abbershaw's hit it. She's keeping an appointment. Look here, let's drop down and shut off our head-lights – the sides will carry us.'

'Hullo! Where's he off to now?'

It was Michael who spoke. The car ahead had taken a sudden turn to the right, forsaking the main road.

'After her,' said Martin, with suppressed excitement. 'Now we're coming to it, I do believe. Any idea where that leads to?'

'No,' said Michael. 'I haven't the least. There's only a lane there if I remember. Probably the drive of a house.'

'All the better.' Martin was enthusiastic. 'That means we have located them anyway.'

'Wait a bit,' said Michael, as, dimming his lights, he swung round after the other car. 'It's not a drive. I remember it now. There's a signpost over there somewere which says, "To Birch", wherever "Birch" may be. Gosh! No speeding on this road, my children,' he added suddenly, as he steered the Riley round a concealed right-angle bend in the road.

The head-lights of the car they were following were still just visible several turns ahead. For the next few miles the journey developed into a nightmare. The turns were innumerable.

'God knows how we're going to get back,' grumbled Michael. 'I don't know which I prefer; your friend with the gun or an attempt to find our way back through these roads before morning.'

'Cheer up,' said Martin consolingly. 'You may get both. Any idea where we are? Was that a church we passed just now?'

'I thought I heard a cow,' suggested Abbershaw helpfully.

'Let's catch 'em up,' said Martin. 'It's time something definite happened.'

Abbershaw shook his head.

'That's no good, my dear fellow,' he said. 'Don't you see our position? We can't stop a man in the middle of the night and accuse him of murder without more proof or more authority. We must find out where he is and that's all.'

Martin was silent. He had no intention of allowing the adventure to end so tamely. They struggled on without speaking.

At length, after what had seemed to be an interminable drive, through narrow miry lanes with surfaces like ploughed fields, through forgotten villages, past ghostly churches dimly outlined against the sky, guided only by the glare ahead, the darkness began to grey and in the uncertain light of the dawn they found themselves on a track of short springy grass amid the most desolate surroundings any one of them had ever seen.

On all sides spread vast stretches of salting covered with clumps of rough, coarse grass with here and there a ragged river or a dyke-head.

Far ahead of them the old black car lumbered on.

Martin sniffed.

'The sea,' he said. 'I wonder if that old miracle ahead swims? A bus like that might do anything. That would just about sink us if we went to follow them.'

'Just about,' said Michael dryly. 'What do we do now?'

'I suppose we go on to the bitter end,' said Martin. 'They may have a family house-boat out there. Hullo! Look at them now.'

The Rolls had at last come to a full stop, although the head-lights were still streaming out over the turf.

Michael brought the Riley up sharply.

'What now?' he said.

'Now the fun begins,' said Martin. 'Get out your gun, Abbershaw.'

Hardly had he spoken when an exclamation came down the morning to them, followed immediately by a revolver shot which again fell short of them.

Without hesitation Martin fired back. The snap of his automatic was instantly followed by a much larger explosion.

'That's their back tyre,' he said. 'Let's get behind the car and play soldiers. They're sure to retaliate. This is going to be fun.'

But in this he was mistaken. Neither Whitby nor his companion seemed inclined for further shooting. The two figures were plainly discernible through the fast-lightening gloom, Whitby in a long dust coat and a soft hat, and the other man taller and thinner, his cap still well down over his face.

And then, while they were still looking at him, Whitby thrust his hand into his coat pocket and pulled out a large white handkerchief which he shook at them solemnly, waving it up and down. Its significance was unmistakable.

Abbershaw began to laugh. Even Martin grinned.

'That's matey, anyway,' he said. 'What happens next?'

Chapter 28
Should a Doctor Tell?

Still holding the handkerchief well in front of him, Whitby came a pace or two nearer, and presently his weak, half-apologetic voice came to them down the wind.

'Since we've both got guns, perhaps we'd better talk,' he shouted thinly. 'What do you want?'

Martin glanced at Abbershaw.

'Keep him covered,' he murmured. 'Prenderby, old boy, you'd better walk behind us. We don't know what their little game is yet.'

They advanced slowly – absurdly, Abbershaw could not help thinking – on that vast open salting, miles from anywhere.

Whitby was still the harassed, scared-looking little man who had come to ask Abbershaw for his assistance on that fateful night at Black Dudley. He was, if anything, a little more composed now than then, and he greeted them affably.

'Well, here we are, aren't we?' he said, and paused. 'What do you want?'

Martin Watt opened his mouth to speak; he had a very clear notion of what he wanted and was anxious to explain it.

Abbershaw cut him short, however.

'A word or two of conversation, Doctor,' he said.

The little man blinked at him dubiously.

'Why, yes, of course,' he said, 'of course. I should hate to disappoint you. You've come a long way for it, haven't you?'

He was so patently nervous that in spite of themselves they could not get away from the thought that they were very unfairly matched.

'Where shall we talk?' continued the little doctor, still timidly. 'I suppose there must be quite a lot of things you want to ask me?'

Martin pocketed his gun.

'Look here, Whitby,' he said, 'that is the point – there are lots of things. That's why we've come. If you're sensible you'll give us straight answers. You know what happened at Black Dudley after you left, of course?'

'I – I read in the papers,' faltered the little figure in front of them. 'Most regrettable. Who would have thought that such a clever, intelligent man would turn out to be such a dreadful criminal?'

Martin shook his head.

'That's no good, Doc.,' he said. 'You see, not everything came out in the papers.'

Whitby sighed. 'I see,' he said. 'Perhaps if you told me exactly how much you know I should see precisely what to tell you.'

Martin grinned at this somewhat ambiguous remark.

'Suppose we don't make things quite so simple as that,' he said. 'Suppose we both put our cards on the table – all of them.'

He had moved a step nearer as he spoke and the little doctor put up his hand warningly.

'Forgive me, Mr Watt,' he said. 'But my friend behind me is very clever with his pistol, as you may have noticed, and we're right in his range now, aren't we? If I were you I really think I'd take my gun out again.'

Martin stared at him and slowly drew his weapon out of his pocket.

'That's right,' said Whitby. 'Now we'll go a little farther away from him, shall we? You were saying –?'

Martin was bewildered. This was the last attitude he had expected a fugitive to take up in the middle of a saltmarsh at four o'clock in the morning.

Abbershaw spoke quietly behind him.

'It's Colonel Coombe's death we are interested in, Doctor,' he said. 'Your position at Black Dudley has been explained to us.'

He watched the man narrowly as he spoke but there was no trace of surprise or fear on the little man's face.

He seemed relieved.

'Oh! I see,' he said. 'You, Doctor Abbershaw, would naturally be interested in the fate of my patient's body. As a matter of fact, he was cremated at Eastchester, thirty-six hours after I left Black Dudley. But, of course,' he went on cheerfully, 'you will want to know the entire history. After we left the house we went straight over to the registrar's. He was very sympathetic. Like everybody else in the vicinity he knew of the Colonel's weak health and was not surprised at my news. In fact, he was most obliging. Your signature and mine were quite enough for him. He signed immediately and we continued our journey. I was on my way back to the house when I received – by the merest chance – the news of the unfortunate incidents which had taken place in my absence. And so,' he added with charming frankness, 'we altered our number plates and changed our destination. Are you satisfied?'

'Not quite,' said Martin grimly.

The nervous little doctor hurried on before they could stop him.

'Why, of course,' he said, 'I was forgetting. There must be a great many things that still confuse you. The exact import of the papers that you, Doctor Abbershaw, were so foolhardy as to destroy? Never revealed, was it?'

'We know it was the detailed plan of a big robbery,' said Abbershaw stiffly.

'Indeed it was,' said Whitby warmly. 'Quite the largest thing our people had ever thought of undertaking. Have you – er – any idea what place it was? Everything was all taped out so that nothing remained to chance, no detail left unconsidered. It was a complete plan of campaign ready to be put into immediate action. The work of a master, I assure you. Do you know the place?'

He saw by their faces that they were ignorant, and a satisfied smile spread over the little man's face.

'It wasn't my secret,' he said. 'But naturally I couldn't help hearing a thing or two. As far as I could gather von Faber's objective was the Repository of the Bullion for the Repayment of the American Debt.'

The three were silent, the stupendousness of the scheme suddenly brought home to them.

'Then,' continued Whitby rapidly, 'there was Colonel Coombe's own part in von Faber's affairs. Perhaps you don't know that for the greater part of his life Colonel Coombe had been under von Faber's influence to an enormous extent, in fact I think I might almost say that he was dominated absolutely by von –'

'It's not Colonel Coombe's life, Doctor Whitby, which interests us so particularly,' cut in Martin suddenly. 'It's his death. You know as well as we do that he was murdered.'

For an instant the nervous garrulousness of the little doctor vanished and he stared at them blankly.

'There are a lot of people interested in that point,' he said at last. 'I am myself, for one.'

'So we gathered,' murmured Martin, under his breath, while Abbershaw spoke hastily.

'Doctor Whitby,' he said, 'you and I committed a very grave offence by signing those certificates.'

'Yes,' said Whitby, and paused for a moment or so, after which he brightened up visibly and hurried on. 'But really, my dear sir, in the circumstances I don't see that we could have done anything else, do you? We were the victims of a stronger force.'

Abbershaw disregarded the other's smile and spoke steadily.

'Doctor Whitby,' he said, 'do you know who murdered Colonel Coombe?'

The little doctor's benign expression did not alter.

'Why, of course,' he said. 'I should have thought that, at least, was obvious to everybody – everybody who knew anything at all about the case, that is.'

Abbershaw shook his head.

'I'm afraid we must plead either great stupidity or peculiarly untrusting dispositions,' he said. 'That is the point on which we are not at all satisfied.'

'But my dear young people –' for the first time during that interview the little man showed signs of impatience. 'That is most obvious. Amongst your party – let us say, Mr Petrie's party, as opposed to von Faber's – there was a member of the famous Simister gang of America. Perhaps you have heard of it, Doctor Abbershaw. Colonel Coombe had been attempting to establish relations with them for some time. In fact, that was the reason why I and my pugnacious friend behind us were placed at Black Dudley – to keep an eye upon him. During the progress of the Dagger Ritual, Simister's man eluded our vigilance and chose that moment not only to get hold of the papers, but also to murder the unfortunate Colonel. That, by the way, was only a title he adopted, you know.'

The three younger men remained unimpressed.

Martin shook his head.

'Not a bad story, but it won't wash,' he said. 'If one of our party stabbed the old boy, why do you all go to such lengths to keep it so quiet for us?'

'Because, my boy,' said Whitby testily, 'we didn't want a fuss. In fact, the police on the scene was the last thing we desired. Besides, you seem to forget the extraordinary importance of the papers.'

Again Martin shook his head.

'We've heard all this before,' he said; 'and it didn't sound any better then. To be perfectly frank, we are convinced that one of your people was responsible. We want to know who, and we want to know why.'

The little doctor's face grew slowly crimson, but it was the flush of a man annoyed rather than a guilty person accused of his crime.

'You tire me with your stupidity,' he said suddenly. 'Good God, sir, consider it. Have you any idea how valuable the man was to us? Do you know what he was paid for his services? Twenty thousand pounds for this coup alone. Simister would probably have offered him more. You don't hear about these things. Government losses rarely get into the papers – certainly not with figures attached. Not the smallest member of our organization stood to gain anything at all by his death. I confess I was surprised at Simister's man, unless he was double-crossing his own people.'

For a moment even Martin's faith in his own theory was shaken.

'In that case,' said Abbershaw unexpectedly, 'it will doubtless surprise you to learn that the man employed by Simister to obtain the package had a complete alibi. In fact, it was impossible for him ever to have laid hands upon the dagger.'

'Impossible?' The word broke from Whitby's lips like a cry, but although they were listening to him critically, to not one of them did it sound like a cry of fear. He stared at them, amazement in his eyes.

'Have you proof of that?' he said at last.

'Complete proof,' said Abbershaw quietly. 'I think you must reconsider your theory, Doctor Whitby. Consider how you yourself stand, in the light of what I have just said.'

An expression of mild astonishment spread over the insignificant little face. Then, to everybody's surprise, he laughed.

'Amateur detectives?' he said. 'I'm afraid you've had a long ride for nothing, gentlemen. I confess that my position as accessory after the fact is a dangerous one, but then, so is Doctor Abbershaw's. Consider the likelihood of your suggestion. Have you provided me with a motive?'

'I suggest,' said Martin calmly, 'that your position when von Faber discovered that your prisoner had "eluded your vigilance", as you call it, would not have been too good.'

Whitby paused thoughtfully.

'Not bad,' he said. 'Not bad at all. Very pretty. But' – he shook his head – 'unfortunately not true. My position with Coombe dead was "not good" as you call it. But had Coombe been alive he would have had to face the music, wouldn't he? It was von Faber's own fault that I ever left his side at all.'

This was certainly a point which they had not considered. It silenced them for a moment, and in the lull a sound which had been gradually forcing itself upon their attention for the last few moments became suddenly very apparent – the steady droning of an aeroplane engine.

Whitby looked up, mild interest on his face.

It was now quite light, and the others, following his gaze, saw a huge Fokker monoplane flying low against the grey sky.

'He's out early,' remarked Prenderby.

'Yes,' said Whitby. 'There's an aerodrome a couple of miles across here, you know. Quite near my house, in fact.'

Martin pricked up his ears.

'Your house?' he echoed.

The little doctor nodded.

'Yes. I have a small place down here by the sea. Very lonely, you know, but I thought it suited my purpose very well just now. Frankly, I didn't like the idea of your following me and it made my friend quite angry.'

'Hullo! He's in difficulties or something.'

It was Prenderby who spoke. He had been watching the aeroplane, which was now almost directly above their heads. His excited cry made them all look up again, to see the great plane circling into the wind.

There was now no drone of the engine but they could hear the sough of the air through the wires, and for a moment it seemed as if it were dropping directly on top of them. The next instant it passed so near that they almost felt its draught upon their faces. Then it taxied along the ground, coming to a halt in the glow of the still burning head-lights of the big car.

Instinctively, they hurried towards it, and until they were within twenty yards they did not realize that Whitby's confederate had got there first and was talking excitedly to the pilot.

'Good God!' said Martin suddenly stopping dead in his tracks. The same thought struck the others at precisely the same instant.

Through the waves of mingled anger and amazement which overwhelmed them, Whitby's precise little voice came clearly.

'I observe that he carries a machine-gun,' he remarked. 'That's what I like about these Germans – so efficient. In view of what my excitable colleague has probably said to the pilot, I really don't think I should come any nearer. Perhaps you would turn off our head-lights when you go back, they have served their purpose. Take the car too if you like.'

He paused and beamed on them.

'Good-bye,' he said. 'I suppose it would annoy you if I thanked you for coming to see me off? Don't do that,' he added sharply, as Martin's hand shot to his side pocket. 'Please don't do that,' he repeated more earnestly. 'For my friends would most certainly kill you without the least compunction, and I don't want that. Believe me, my dear young people, whatever your theories may be, I am no murderer. I am leaving the country in this melodramatic fashion because it obviates the inconveniences which might arise if I showed my passport here just at present. Don't come any nearer. Good-bye, gentlemen.'

As they watched him go, Martin's hand again stole to his pocket.

Abbershaw touched his arm.

'Don't be a fool, old man,' he said. 'If he's done one murder, don't encourage him to do another, and if he hasn't, why help him to?'

Martin nodded and made a remark which did nobody any credit.

They stood there watching the machine with the gun trained upon them from its cockpit until it began to move again; then they turned back towards the Riley.

'Right up the garden,' said Martin bitterly. 'Fooled, done brown, put it how you like. There goes Coombe's murderer and here are we poor mutts who listened trustingly while he told us fair stories to pass the time away until his pals turned up for him. I wish we'd risked that machine-gun.'

Prenderby nodded gloomily.

'I feel sick,' he said. 'We spotted him and then he got away with it.'

Abbershaw shook his head.

'He got away certainly,' he said. 'But I don't think we've got much cause to regret it.'

'What do you mean? Think he didn't kill him?'

They looked at him incredulously.

Abbershaw nodded.

'I know he didn't kill him,' he said quietly.

Martin grunted.

'I'm afraid I can't agree with you there,' he said. 'Gosh! I'll never forgive myself for being such a fool!'

Prenderby was inclined to agree with him, but Abbershaw stuck to his own opinion, and the expression on his face as they drove silently back to Town was very serious and, somehow, afraid.

Chapter 29

The Last Chapter

In the six weeks which followed the unsatisfactory trip to the Essex Marshes, Abbershaw and Meggie were fully occupied preparing for their wedding, which they had decided should take place as soon as was possible.

Prenderby seemed inclined to forget the Black Dudley affair altogether: his own marriage to Jeanne was not far distant and provided him with a more interesting topic of thought and conversation, and Martin Wyatt had gone back to his old haunts in the City and the West End.

Wyatt was in his flat overlooking St James's, apparently immersed as ever in the obscurities of his reading.

But Abbershaw had not forgotten Colonel Coombe.

He had not put the whole matter before his friend, Inspector Deadwood of Scotland Yard, for a reason which he was unable to express in definite words, even to himself.

An idea was forming in his mind – an idea which he shrank from and yet could not wholly escape.

In vain he argued with himself that his thought was preposterous and absurd; as the days went on and the whole affair sank more and more into its true perspective, the more the insidious theory grew upon him and began to haunt his nights as well as his days.

At last, very unwillingly, he gave way to his suspicions and set out to test his theory.

His procedure was somewhat erratic. He spent the best part of a week in the reading-room of the British Museum; this was followed by a period of seclusion in his own library, with occasional descents upon the bookshops of Charing Cross Road, and then, as though his capacity for the tedium of a subject in which he was not naturally interested was not satiated, he spent an entire week-end in the Kensington house of his uncle, Sir Dorrington Wynne, one-time Professor of Archaeology in the University of Oxford, a man whose conversation never left the subject of his researches.

Another day or so at the British Museum completed Abbershaw's investigations, and one evening found him driving down Whitehall in the direction of the Abbey, his face paler than usual, and his eyes troubled.

He went slowly, as if loth to reach his destination, and when a little later he pulled up outside a block of flats, he remained for some time at the wheel, staring moodily before him. Every moment the task he had set himself became more and more nauseous.

Eventually, he left the car, and mounting the carpeted stairs of the old Queen Anne house walked slowly up to the first floor.

A man-servant admitted him, and within three minutes he was seated before a spacious fire-place in Wyatt Petrie's library.

The room expressed its owner's personality. Its taste was perfect but a little academic, a little strict. It was an ascetic room. The walls were pale-coloured and hung sparsely with etchings and engravings – a Goya, two or three moderns, and a tiny Rembrandt. There were books everywhere, but tidily, neatly kept, and a single hanging in one corner, a dully burning splash of old Venetian embroidery.

Wyatt seemed quietly pleased to see him. He sat down on the other side of the hearth and produced cigars and Benedictine.

Abbershaw refused both. He was clearly ill at ease, and he sat silent for some moments after the first words of greeting, staring moodily into the fire.

'Wyatt,' he said suddenly, 'I've known you for a good many years. Believe me, I've not forgotten that when I ask you this question.'

Wyatt leaned back in his chair and closed his eyes, his liqueur glass lightly held in his long, graceful fingers. Abbershaw turned in his chair until he faced the silent figure.

'Wyatt,' he said slowly and evenly, 'why did you stab your uncle?'

No expression appeared upon the still pale face of the man to whom he had spoken. For some moments he did not appear to have heard.

At last he sighed and, leaning forward, set his glass down upon the little book-table by his side.

'I'll show you,' he said.

Abbershaw took a deep breath. He had not been prepared for this; almost anything would have been easier to bear.

Meanwhile Wyatt crossed over to a small writing-desk let into a wall of bookshelves and, unlocking it with a key which he took from his pocket, produced something from a drawer; carrying it back to the fire-place, he handed it to his visitor.

Abbershaw took it and looked at it with some astonishment.

It was a photograph of a girl.

The face was round and childlike, and was possessed of that peculiar innocent sweetness which seems to belong only to a particular type of blonde whose beauty almost invariably hardens in maturity.

At the time of the portrait, Abbershaw judged, the girl must have been about seventeen – possibly less. Undeniably lovely, but in the golden-haired unsophisticated fashion of the medieval angel.

The last face in the world that he would have suspected Wyatt of noticing.

He turned the thing over in his hand. It was one of those cheap, glossy reproductions which circulate by the thousand in the theatrical profession.

He sat looking at it helplessly; uncomprehending, and very much at sea.

Wyatt came to the rescue.

'Her stage name was "Joy Love",' he said slowly, and there was silence again.

Abbershaw was still utterly perplexed, and opened his mouth to ask the obvious question, but the other man interrupted him, and the depth and bitterness of his tone surprised the doctor.

'Her real name was Dolly Lord,' he said. 'She was seventeen in that photograph, and I loved her – I do still love her – most truly and most deeply.' He added simply, 'I have never loved any other woman.'

He was silent, and Abbershaw, who felt himself drifting further and further out of his depth at every moment, looked at him blankly. There was no question that the man was sincere. The tone in his voice, every line of his face and body proclaimed his intensity.

'I don't understand,' said Abbershaw.

Wyatt laughed softly and began to speak quickly, earnestly, and all in one key.

'She was appearing in the crowd scene in *The Faith of St Hubert*, that beautiful little semi-sacred opera that they did at the Victor Gordon Arts Theatre in Knightsbridge,' he said. 'That's where I first saw her. She looked superb in a snood and wimple. I fell in love with her. I found out who she was after considerable trouble. I was crazy about her by that time.'

He paused and looked at Abbershaw with his narrow dark eyes in which there now shone a rebellious, almost fanatical light.

'You can call it absurd with your modern platonic-suitability complexes,' he said, 'but I fell in love with a woman as nine-tenths of the men have done since the race began and will continue to do until all resemblance of the original animal is civilized out of us and the race ends – with her face, and with her carriage, and with her body. She seemed to me to fulfil all my ideals of womankind. She became my sole object. I wanted her, I wanted to marry her.'

He hesitated for a moment and looked at Abbershaw defiantly, but as the other did not speak he went on again. 'I found out that in the ordinary way she was what they call a "dancing instructress" in one of the night-clubs at the back of Shaftesbury Avenue. I went there to find her. From the manager in charge I discovered that for half a crown a dance and anything else I might choose to pay I might talk as long as I liked with her.'

Again he hesitated, and Abbershaw was able to see in his face something of what the disillusionment had meant to him.

'As you know,' Wyatt continued, 'I know very little of women. As a rule they don't interest me at all. I think that is why Joy interested me so much. I want you to understand,' he burst out suddenly with something akin to savagery in his tone, 'that the fact that she was not of my world, that her accent was horrible, and her finger-nails hideously over-manicured would not have made the slightest difference. I was in love with her: I wanted to marry her. The fact that she was stupid did not greatly deter me either. She was incredibly stupid – the awful stupidity of crass ignorance and innocence. Yes,' he went on bitterly as he caught Abbershaw's involuntary expression, 'innocence. I think it was that that broke me up. The girl was innocent with the innocence of a savage. She knew nothing. The elementary civilized code of right and wrong was an abstruse doctrine to her. She was horrible.' He shuddered, and Abbershaw fancied that he began to understand. An incident that would have been ordinary enough to a boy in his teens had proved too much for a studious recluse of twenty-seven. It had unhinged his mind.

Wyatt's next remark therefore surprised him.

'She interested me,' he said. 'I wanted to study her. I thought her extraordinary mental state was due to chance at first – some unfortunate accident of birth and upbringing – but I found I was wrong. That was the thing that turned me into a particularly militant type of social reformer. Do you understand what I mean, Abbershaw?'

He leant forward as he spoke, his eyes fixed on the other man's face.

'Do you understand what I'm saying? The state of that girl's mentality was not due to chance – it was *deliberate*.'

Abbershaw started.

'Impossible,' he said involuntarily, and Wyatt seized upon the word.

'Impossible?' he echoed passionately. 'That's what everybody would say, I suppose, but I tell you you're wrong. I went right into it. I found out. That girl had been trained from a child. She was a perfect product of a diabolical scheme, and she wasn't the only victim. It was a society, Abbershaw, a highly organized criminal concern. This girl, my girl, and several others of her kind, were little wheels in the machinery. They were the catspaws – specially prepared implements with which to attract certain men or acquire certain information. The thing is horrible when the girl is cognizant of what she is doing – when the choice is her own – but think of it, trained from childhood, minds deliberately warped, deliberately developed along certain lines. It's driven me insane, Abbershaw.'

He was silent for a moment or so, his head in his hands. Abbershaw rose to his feet, but the other turned to him eagerly.

'Don't go,' he said. 'You must hear it all.'

The little red-haired doctor sat down immediately.

'I found it all out,' Wyatt repeated. 'I shook out the whole terrible story and discovered that the brains of this organization were bought, like everything else. That is to say, they had a special brain to plan the crime that other men would commit. That appalled me. There's something revolting about mass-production anyway, but when applied to crime it's ghastly. I felt I'd wasted my life fooling around with books and theories, while all around me, on my very doorstep, these appalling things were happening. I worked it all out up here. It seemed to me that the thing to be done was to get at those brains – to destroy them. Lodging information with the police wouldn't be enough. What's the good of sending brains like that to prison for a year or two when at the end of the time they can come back and start afresh? It took me a year to trace those brains and I found them in my own family, though not, thank God, in my own kin . . . my aunt's husband, Gordon Coombe. I saw that there was no point in simply going down there and blowing his brains out. *He* was only the beginning. There were others, men who could organize the thing, men who could conceive such an abominable idea as the one which turned Dolly Lord into Joy Love, a creature not quite human, not quite animal – a machine, in fact. So I had to go warily. My uncle was in the habit of asking me to take house-parties down to Black Dudley, as you probably know, to cover his interviews with his confederates. I planned what I thought was a perfect killing, and the next time I was asked I chose my house-party carefully and went down there with every intention of putting my scheme into action.'

'You *chose* your house-party?'

Abbershaw looked at him curiously as he spoke.

'Certainly,' said Wyatt calmly. 'I chose each one of you deliberately. You were all people of blameless reputation. There was not one of you who could not clear himself with perfect certainty. The suspicion would therefore necessarily fall on one of my uncle's own guests, each of whom had done, if not murder, something more than as bad. I thought Campion was of their party until we were all prisoners. Until Prenderby told me, I thought Anne Edgeware had brought him, even then.'

'You ran an extraordinary risk,' said Abbershaw.

Wyatt shook his head.

'Why?' he said. 'I was my uncle's benefactor, not he mine. I had nothing to gain by his death, and I should have been as free from suspicion as any of you. Of course,' he went on, 'I had no idea that things would turn out as they did. No one could have been more surprised than I when they concealed the murder in that extraordinary way. When I realized that they had lost something I understood, and I was desperately anxious that they should not recover what I took to be my uncle's notes for the gang's next coup. That is why I asked you to stay.'

'Of course,' said Abbershaw slowly, 'you were wrong.'

'In not pitching on von Faber as my first victim?' said Wyatt.

Abbershaw shook his head.

'No,' he said. 'In setting out to fight a social evil single-handed. That is always a mad thing to do.'

Wyatt raised his eyes to meet the other's.

'I know,' he said simply. 'I think I am a little mad. It seemed to me so wicked. I loved her.'

There was silence after he had spoken, and the two men sat for some time, Abbershaw staring into the fire, Wyatt leaning back, his eyes half-closed. The thought that possessed Abbershaw's mind was the pity of it – such a good brain, such a valuable idealistic soul. And it struck him in a sudden impersonal way that it was odd that evil should beget evil. It was as if it went on spreading in ever-widening circles, like ripples round the first splash of a stone thrown into a pond.

Wyatt recalled him from his reverie.

'It was a perfect murder,' he said, almost wonderingly. 'How did you find me out?'

Abbershaw hesitated. Then he sighed. 'I couldn't help it,' he said. 'It was too perfect. It left nothing to chance. Do you know where I have spent the last week or so? In the British Museum.'

He looked at the other steadily.

'I now know more about your family history than, I should think, any other man alive. That Ritual story would have been wonderful for your purpose, Wyatt, if it just hadn't been for one thing. It was not true.'

Wyatt rose from his chair abruptly, and walked up and down the room. This flaw in his scheme seemed to upset him more than anything else had done.

'But it might have been true,' he argued. 'Who could prove it? A family legend.'

'But it wasn't true,' Abbershaw persisted. 'It wasn't true because from the year 1100 until the year 1603 – long past the latest date to which such a story as yours could have been feasible, Black Dudley was a monastery and not in the possession of your family at all. Your family estate was higher up the coast, in Norfolk, and I shouldn't think the dagger came into your possession until 1650 at least, when an ancestor of yours is referred to as having returned from the Papal States laden with merchandise.'

Wyatt continued to pace up and down the room.

'I see,' he said. 'I see. But otherwise it was a perfect murder. Think of it – Heaven knows how many fingerprints on the dagger handle, no one with any motive – no one who might not have committed the crime, and by the same reasoning no one who might. It had its moments of horror too, though,' he said, pausing suddenly. 'The moment when I came upon Miss Oliphant in the dark – I had to follow the dagger round, you see, to be in at the first alarm. I saw her pause under the window and stare at the blade, and I don't think it was until then that I realized that there was blood on it. So I took it from her. It was an impulsive, idiotic thing to do, and when the alarm did come the thing was in my own hand. I didn't see what they were getting at at first, and I was afraid I hadn't quite killed him, although

I'd worked out the blow with a medical chart before I went down there. I took the dagger up to my own room. You nearly found me with it, by the way.'

Abbershaw nodded.

'I know,' he said. 'I think it was instinct, but as you came in from the balcony I caught a glimpse of something in your hand, and although I didn't see what it was, I couldn't get the idea of the dagger out of my mind.'

'Two flaws,' said Wyatt, and was silent.

The atmosphere in the pleasant room had become curiously cold, and Abbershaw shivered. The sordid glossy photograph lay upon the floor, and the pretty childish face with the expression of innocence which had now become so sinister smiled up at him from the carpet.

'Well, what are you going to do?'

It was Wyatt who spoke, pausing abruptly in his feverish stride.

Abbershaw did not look at him.

'What are *you* going to do?' he murmured.

Wyatt hesitated.

'There is a Dominican Foundation in the rocky valley of El Puerto in the north of Spain,' he said. 'I have been in correspondence with them for some time. I have been disposing of all my books this week. I realized when von Faber passed into the hands of the police that my campaign was ended, but –'

He stopped and looked at Abbershaw; then he shrugged his shoulders.

'What now?' he said.

Abbershaw rose to his feet and held out his hand.

'I don't suppose I shall see you again before you go,' he said. 'Good-bye.'

Wyatt shook the outstretched hand, but after the first flicker of interest which the last words had occasioned his expression had become preoccupied. He crossed the room and picked up the photograph, and the last glimpse Abbershaw had of him was as he sat in the deep armchair, crouching over it, his eyes fixed on the sweet, foolish little face.

As the little doctor walked slowly down the staircase to the street his mind was in confusion. He was conscious of a strong feeling of relief, even although his worst fears had been realized. At the back of his head, the old problem of Law and Order as opposed to Right and Wrong worried itself into the inextricable tangle which knows no unravelling. Wyatt was both a murderer and a martyr. There was no one who could decide between the two, in his opinion.

And in his thoughts, too, were his own affairs: Meggie, and his love for her, and their marriage.

As he stepped out into the street, a round moon face, red and hot with righteous indignation, loomed down upon him out of the darkness.

'Come at last, 'ave yer?' inquired a thick sarcastic voice. 'Your name and address, *if* you please.'

Gradually it dawned upon the still meditative doctor that he was confronted by an excessively large and unfriendly London bobby.

'This is your car, I suppose?' the questioner continued more mildly, as he observed Abbershaw's blank expression, but upon receiving the assurance that it was, all his indignation returned.

'This car's been left 'ere over an hour to my certain personal knowledge,' he bellowed. 'Unattended and drawn out a foot from the kerb, which aggravates the offence. This'll mean a summons, you know' – he flourished his notebook. 'Name and address.'

Abbershaw having furnished him with this information, he replaced the pencil in its sheath and, clicking the book's elastic band smartly, continued his homily. He was clearly very much aggrieved.

'It's people like you,' he explained, as Abbershaw climbed into the driving seat, 'wot gives us officers all our work. But we're not goin' to have these offences, I can tell you. We're making a clean sweep. Persons offending against the Law are not going to be tolerated.'

He paused suspiciously. The slightly dazed expression upon the face of the little red-haired man in the car had suddenly given place to a smile.

'Splendid!' he said, and there was unmistakable enthusiasm in his tone. 'Really, really splendid, Officer! You don't know how comforting that sounds. My fervent wishes for your success.' And he drove off, leaving the policeman looking after him, wondering a little wistfully if the charge in his notebook should not perhaps have read, 'Drunk in charge of a car'.

Mystery Mile

To P. Y. C. and A. J. G.
Partners in Crime

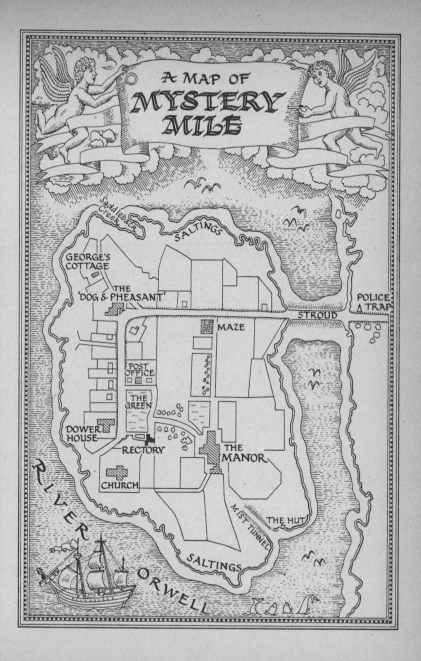

Chapter 1

Among Those Present

'I'll bet you fifty dollars, even money,' said the American who was sitting nearest the door in the opulent lounge of the homeward-bound *Elephantine*, 'that that man over there is murdered within a fortnight.'

The Englishman at his side glanced across the sea of chairs at the handsome old man they had been watching. 'Ten pounds,' he said. 'All right, I'll take you. You've no idea what a safe little place England is.'

A slow smile spread over the American's face. 'You've got no idea what a dangerous old fellow Crowdy Lobbett is,' he said. 'If your police are going to look after him they'll have to keep him in a steel bandbox, and I don't envy them that job. It's almost a pity to take your money, though I'm giving you better odds than any Insurance Corporation in the States would offer.'

'The whole thing sounds fantastic to me,' said the Englishman. 'But I'll meet you at Verrey's a fortnight today and we'll make a night of it. That suit you?'

'The twenty-second,' said the American, making a note of it in his book. 'Seems kind of heathen celebrating over the old man's corpse. He's a great old boy.'

'Drinking his health, you mean,' said the Englishman confidently. 'Scotland Yard is very spry these days. That reminds me,' he added cheerfully, 'I must take you to one of our night clubs.'

On the other side of the ship's lounge the loquacious Turk who had made himself such a nuisance to his fellow passengers since they put out from New York was chattering to his latest victim.

'Very courageous of him to come down for the concert,' he was saying. 'He's a marked man, you know. I don't think there's any doubt about that. Four murders in his household within the past month and each time his escape was a miracle.'

His victim, a pale young man who seemed to be trying to hide behind his enormous spectacles, woke out of the reverie into which he had fallen ever since the talkative Oriental had first tackled him and surveyed his persecutor owlishly. 'Not that nice old gentleman over there?' he said. 'The one with the white hair? Four murders in his house within a month? That ought to be stopped. He's been told about it, I suppose?'

Since this was the first remark with which the young man had favoured him, the bore jumped to the conclusion that he had inadvertently stumbled on a mental case. It was inconceivable to him that anyone should not have heard of the now famous Misfire Murders, as the Press had starred them, which had filled the New York papers for the past four weeks. The young man spoke.

'Who is the stormy old petrel?' he said.

His companion looked at him with some of the delight which a born gossip always feels upon finding an uninformed listener. His heavy red face became animated and he cocked his curious pear-shaped head, which alone betrayed his nationality, alertly on one side.

'That fine old man, typical of the best type of hard-bitten New Englander,' he began in a rhetorical whisper, 'is none other than Judge Crowdy Lobbett. He has been the intended victim of an extraordinary series of crimes. I can't understand how you've missed reading about it all.'

'Oh, I've been away in Nebraska for my health,' said the young man. 'He-man stuff, you know,' he added in his slightly falsetto voice.

He spoke with the utmost gravity, and the old man nodded unsuspectingly and continued.

'First his secretary, seated in his master's chair, was shot,' he said slowly. 'Then his butler, who was apparently after his master's Scotch, got poisoned. Then his chauffeur met with a very mysterious accident, and finally a man walking with him down the street got a coping stone on his head.' He sat back and regarded his companion almost triumphantly. 'What do you say to that?' he demanded.

'Shocking,' said the young man. 'Very bad taste on someone's part. Rotten marksmanship, too,' he added, after some consideration. 'I suppose he's travelling for health now, like me?'

The Turk bent nearer and assumed a more confidential tone.

'They say,' he mumbled, in an unsuccessful attempt to keep his voice down, 'that it was all young Marlowe Lobbett could do to get his father to come to Europe at all. I admire a man like that, a man who's not afraid of what's coming to him.'

'Oh, quite!' said the young man mildly. 'The neat piece of modern youthing with the old gentleman is the son you spoke of, I suppose?'

The Turk nodded.

'That's right, and the girl sitting on his other side is his daughter. That very black hair gives them a sort of distinction. Funny that the boy should be so big and the girl so small. She takes after her mother, one of the Edwardeses of Tennessee, you know.'

'When's the concert going to begin?'

The Turk smiled. He felt he had consummated the acquaintanceship at last.

'My name is Barber,' he said. 'Ali Fergusson Barber – a rather stupid joke of my parents, I have always thought.'

He looked inquiringly at his companion, hoping for a similar exchange of confidence, but he was unrewarded. The young man appeared to have forgotten all about him, and presently to the Oriental's complete disgust, he drew a small white mouse from the pocket of his jacket and began to fondle it in his hands. Finally he held it out for Mr Barber's inspection.

'Rather pretty, don't you think?' he said. 'One of the cabin boys lent it to me. He keeps it to remind him of his brother, Haig. He calls it Haig, after him.'

Mr Barber looked down his immense nose at the little creature, and edged away from it.

The young man said no more, for already a very golden-haired lady with pince-nez was playing the Sixth Hungarian Rhapsody with a certain amount of acid gusto.

Her performance was greeted with only mild enthusiasm, and the Turk overcame his repugnance to the noise sufficiently to lean over and inform the young man that there were several stage stars travelling and no doubt the programme would improve as it went on. For some time, however, his optimism was unrewarded.

At length the fussy, sandy-haired young man who was superintending the performance came forward with the announcement that Satsuma, the world-famous Japanese conjurer, was to perform some of his most celebrated illusions, and the audience's patience was craved while the stage was made ready for him.

For the first time Mr Barber's companion seemed to take an intelligent interest in the proceedings and he joined enthusiastically in the applause.

'I'm potty about conjurers,' he remarked affably. 'Haig will like it too, I fancy. I'm most interested to see the effect upon him.'

Mr Barber smiled indulgently.

'You are making jokes,' he said naïvely.

The young man shot him a quick glance from behind his spectacles. 'I do a little conjuring myself,' he went on confidentially. 'And I once knew a man who could always produce a few potatoes out of the old topper, or a half bottle of Bass. He once got in some champagne that way, but it wasn't much of a brand. Hullo! what's going on up there?'

He peered at the platform with childlike interest.

Several enthusiastic amateurs, aided by an electrician, were engaged in setting up the magician's apparatus on the small stage. The piano had to be moved to make way for the great 'disappearing' cabinet, and the audience watched curiously while the cables were connected and the various gaily-coloured cupboards and boxes were set in position.

The magician himself was directing operations from behind a screen, and at length, when the last scene-shifter had departed, he came forward and bowed ceremoniously.

He was tall for a Japanese, and dark-skinned, with a clever face much too small for him.

Mr Barber nudged the young man at his side.

'Old Lobbett doesn't let his troubles damp his interest, does he?' he rumbled, as he glanced across the room to where the man who had been the subject of so much speculation sat forward in his chair. His keenness and excitement were almost childlike, and after a moment or two, dissatisfied with his view of the stage, he left his seat and walked up to the front row, where he stood watching. Mr Barber's companion made no comment. He appeared to be engrossed in his small pet mouse, which he held up, apparently with the idea of allowing the little animal to watch the performance.

The magician began with one or two sleight-of-hand tricks, presenting each illusion with a topical patter.

'Very clever. Very clever,' murmured Mr Barber in his stentorian undertone. 'They say those tricks are handed down from generation to generation. I think it's all done with mirrors myself.'

His acquaintance did not reply. He was sitting bolt upright, staring at the stage through his heavy glasses.

Satsuma produced ducks, goldfish, pigeons, and even a couple of Japanese ladies, with amazing dexterity, and the distressing Mr Barber beat his fat hands together delightedly, while far across the room old Lobbett also was clearly enchanted.

Eventually the magician came forward to the front of the tiny stage and made the announcement which always preceded his most famous trick.

'Ladies and gentlemen,' he began, 'it has only been by the kind co-operation of the electrical staff on board that I am now able to show you this most remarkable trick – the greatest I have ever performed.'

He stepped back a pace or two and tapped the huge disappearing cabinet which had taken up the greater part of the stage during his entire act. He touched a button hidden in the moulding, and immediately the cabinet was illuminated until it glowed all over in a series of diagonal designs of light.

The Japanese beamed upon his audience.

'By the aid of this cabinet,' he said, 'I will make to disappear not just one of my assistants, but any one of you who will come up and help me.' He paused to let his full meaning sink in upon his audience. 'I will make them to disappear and to reappear,' he went on. 'And if, after the experience, any one of them can explain how the miracle was performed, then' – with a great gesture of solemnity – 'I throw myself into the sea.'

He waited until the polite laughter had subsided, and then went on briskly.

'Who will come first? You, sir, you?' he added, pointing out Mr Barber, who was by far the most conspicuous person before him.

The Turk shook his head and laughed.

'Ah! no, my boy. No. I am too old for these adventures.'

The Japanese smiled and passed on. The pale young man in the spectacles jumped up, however.

'I'll disappear,' he said, in his somewhat foolish voice. 'I think Haig would like to,' he murmured to the Oriental by way of explanation.

He went forward eagerly, but paused, as there was some commotion across the room. Judge Lobbett, in spite of his son's obvious disapproval, was already halfway up the steps to the stage. He also paused as the young man appeared, and the two men stood irresolute until the magician, coming forward, beckoned them both on to the stage.

'One after the other,' he said easily. 'The first to come, the first to be served.'

He helped the judge up as he spoke, and the pale young man leaped up beside them.

'I say,' he said nervously, 'would you mind if my pet went first?'

He held up the white mouse as he spoke, while the audience,

thinking it was some intentional comic relief, tittered complacently.

Satsuma smiled also, but his English was not equal to the situation, and, ignoring the young man, he led Judge Lobbett over to the cabinet.

'Haig,' announced the foolish-looking young man in a loud voice, 'will be more than disappointed if he's not allowed to go first. This is his birthday and he's been promised the best and the first of everything. Surely, sir,' he went on, turning to the old man, 'you wouldn't deprive my young friend of his birthday thrill?'

Judge Lobbett contented himself by regarding the young man with a slow cold smile for some seconds, but the other appeared not in the least abashed.

Meanwhile, with a flourish from the orchestra, Satsuma touched the cabinet with his wand and the doors swung open, disclosing a safe-like metal-lined compartment whose grilled sides shone in the brilliant light.

'Now, ladies and gentlemen,' said the magician, turning to his audience, 'I shall invite this gentleman' – he indicated the older man – 'to step in here. Then I shall close these doors. When I open them again he will be gone. You shall search the whole ship, ladies and gentlemen, the stage, under the stage – you shall not find him. Then I will shut the doors once more. Once more they will fly open, and this gentleman shall be back again as you see him now. Moreover, he will not be able to tell you where he has been hiding. Now, sir, if you please.'

'What?' said the irrepressible young man, darting forward, consternation in his pale eyes. 'Can't Haig go first? Are you going to disappoint him after all?'

The audience was becoming restive, and Lobbett turned upon the importunate one, mildly annoyed.

'I don't know who you are, sir,' he said, in a low tone, 'but you're making a darn nuisance of yourself. I'm genuinely interested in this experiment, and I think everyone else is. Go and play with your mouse on deck, sir.'

On the last word he turned and stepped towards the cabinet, the doors of which stood open to receive him. The man who, by this time, was regarded by everyone in the room as a source of embarrassment, seemed suddenly to lose all sense of decorum.

With an angry exclamation he elbowed the unsuspecting old man out of the way, and before the magician could stop him deliberately dropped the small white mouse upon the glittering floor of the cabinet.

Then he stepped back sharply.

There was a tiny hiss, only just loud enough to be heard among the audience: a sickening, terrifying sound.

For a moment everyone in the lounge held his breath. With a convulsive movement the mouse crumpled up on the polished steel grille, where it slowly blackened and shrivelled before their eyes.

There was an instant of complete stupefaction.

The significance of this extraordinary incident dawned slowly. The men upon the platform to whom the thing had been so near stiffened with horror as the explanation occurred to them.

Marlowe Lobbett was the first to move. He sprang on to the platform by his father's side and stood with him looking down at the charred spot on the cabinet floor.

It was at this moment that the pale young man with the spectacles, apparently grasping the situation for the first time, let out a howl of mingled grief and astonishment.

'Oh! my poor Haig! What has happened to him? What has happened to him?' He bent forward to peer down into the cabinet.

'Look out, you fool!' Judge Lobbett's voice was unrecognizable as he caught the incautious young man by his collar amd jerked him backwards. 'Can't you see!' His voice rose high and uncontrolled. 'That cabinet is live! Your pet has been electrocuted!'

The words startled everyone.

An excited murmur followed a momentary silence. Then a woman screamed.

Concert officials and ship's officers hurried on to the platform. The noise became greater, and a startled, bewildered crowd swept up to the platform end of the room.

Judge Lobbett and his tall son were surrounded by an excited group of officials.

Satsuma chattered wildly in his own tongue.

The pale young man with the spectacles appeared to be on the verge of fainting with horror. Even the complacent Mr Barber was shaken out of his habitual affability. His heavy jaws sagged, his greasy eyes grew blank with astonishment.

All the time the cabinet remained glowing with a now evil radiance, bizarre and horrible, a toy that had become a thing of terror.

The arrival of the chief engineer roused the general stupor. He was a lank Belfast Irishman, yellow-haired, lantern-jawed, and deaf as a post. He gave his orders in the hollow bellow of a deaf man and soon reduced the affair to almost a commonplace.

'McPherson, just clear the lounge, will you? I don't want anyone to remain but those intimately concerned. There's been a small accident here in the temporary fittings,' he explained soothingly to the bewildered crowd which was being gently but firmly persuaded out of the lounge by an energetic young Scotsman and his assistants.

'There's something very wrong with the insulation of your cupboard,' he went on, addressing the Japanese severely. 'It's evidently a very dangerous thing. Have you not had trouble with it before?'

Satsuma protested violently, but his birdlike twittering English would have been unintelligible to the engineer even had he been able to hear it.

Meanwhile a small army of mechanics was at work. The chief entered into an incomprehensible technical discussion with them, and their growing astonishment and consternation told more plainly than anything else could have done the terrible tragedy that had only just been averted by the timely sacrifice of the unfortunate Haig.

It was impossible not to be sorry for the Japanese. There could be no doubt of the sincerity of his wretchedness. He hovered round the electricians, half terrified of the consequences of what had happened and half fearful for the safety of his precious apparatus.

Marlowe Lobbett, whose patience had been slowly ebbing, stepped up to the chief and shouted in his ear.

'I don't know if you've heard,' he began, 'but back in New York there have been several unsuccessful attempts upon my father's life. This affair looks very like another. I should be very glad if you could make certain where the responsibility lies.'

The chief turned upon him.

'My dear sir,' he said, 'there's no question of responsibility. The whole thing's an extraordinary coincidence. You see that cable on the floor there?' He pointed to the exposed part of a cable resting upon the parquet floor of the platform. 'If, in shifting the piano, the cabinet hadn't been moved a little so that the one place where the insulation had worn off the cabinet made a connection with it, the affair could never have happened. At the same time, if it hadn't been for the second purely accidental short, the other contact could not have been made.' He indicated a dark stain on the polished grille of the cabinet. 'But,' he went on, fixing the young American with a vivid blue eye, 'you're not suggesting that someone fixed the whole thing up on the very slender chance of getting your father in there, are you?' The chief was considerably more puzzled than he dared to admit. But since no harm had been done he was not anxious to go into the matter too thoroughly for the ship's sake.

Old Judge Lobbett laid his hand on his son's arm.

'This isn't quite the time to discuss this, my boy,' he said. 'Someone knew I couldn't resist a conjuror. But I don't think we'll discuss it here.'

He glanced round as he spoke, and the chief, following the direction of his eyes, suddenly caught sight of the pale young man with the horn-rimmed spectacles who was still standing foolishly by the dismantled cabinet. The officer frowned.

'I thought I gave orders for the lounge to be cleared,' he said. 'May I ask, sir, what you've got to do with this affair?'

The young man started and coloured uncomfortably.

'Well, it was my mouse,' he said.

It was some time before the chief could be made to understand what he was saying, but when at last he did he was hardly sympathetic.

'All the same, I think we can manage without you,' he said bluntly.

The dismissal was unmistakable, and the pale young man smiled nervously and apologized with a certain amount of confusion. Then he crept off the platform like his own mouse, and had almost reached the door before young Marlowe Lobbett overtook him.

The young American had left his father and sister on the platform and came up eagerly. His dark-skinned face and piercing eyes gave him almost a fierce expression, and the pale young man in the spectacles had an impression of someone abounding in energy that was not solely physical.

'I'd like to thank you,' he said, holding out his hand. 'And,' he added bluntly, 'I'd like to talk to you. I'm greatly indebted to you, but I don't see quite where you come in on this. What's your game? Who are you?'

The pale young man looked, if possible, even more foolish than before.

'My game?' he said. 'I don't quite know what you mean. I toss a few cabers, and tiddle a wink occasionally, and I'm a very fair hand at shove-halfpenny.'

He paused.

Marlowe Lobbett was looking at him steadily.

'This is more serious for me than it is for you,' he said slowly.

The pale young man grew suddenly very red and uncomfortable.

'I've got a card here somewhere.' He took a handful of miscellaneous odds and ends out of his coat pocket, and selecting a visiting card handed it gravely to Marlowe.

'My trade card,' he said, 'if there's anything I can do for you, ring me up. I don't suppose we shall meet again on board. We bus conductors feel dreadfully out of place here.'

Then, grinning fatuously, he bowed and disappeared through the doorway out of sight, leaving the other staring after him.

The whole conversation had taken less than ten seconds.

Undecided whether the stranger was genuine or not, young Lobbett glanced at the card in his hand. It was immaculate and beautifully engraved:

MR ALBERT CAMPION
Coups neatly executed
Nothing sordid, vulgar or plebeian
Deserving cases preferred
Police no object

PUFFINS CLUB
THE JUNIOR GREYS

On the back a phone number had been scribbled:

Regent 01300.

Chapter 2

The Simister Legend

After half an hour's experience of the vagaries of the London telephone service Marlowe Lobbett could hear the telephone bell ringing
in some far-off room in the great city which seemed to be huddling
round his hotel as if it were trying to squeeze the life out of it.

At last he heard the welcome click at the far end of the wire and a
thick and totally unexpected voice said huskily, 'Aphrodite Glue
Works speaking.'

Marlowe Lobbett sighed. 'I want Regent 01300,' he said.

'That's right,' said the voice. ''Oo do you want?'

The young man glanced at the card in front of him, and a wave of
disappointment overwhelmed him. He had cherished the idea that he
could rely upon the man who had come to his father's rescue so
successfully on board the *Elephantine*.

'No, it's all right,' he said. 'I only wanted to speak to a Mr Albert
Campion.'

'Oh?' The voice became confidential immediately. 'Could I have
yer name, please, sir?'

Very puzzled, Marlowe Lobbett gave his name. The voice became
more deferential than before. 'Listen carefully, sir,' it said in a
rumbling whisper. 'You want Bottle Street Police Station. You know
where that is, don't you? – off Piccadilly. It's the side door on the left.
Right up the stairs. You'll see the name up when you come to it. No.
No connection with the police station – just a flat on top. Pleased to see
you right away. Goo'-bye, sir.'

There was a second click and he was cut off.

The girl seated on the edge of the table by the instrument looked at
her brother eagerly. She was dark, but whereas he was tall and heavily
built, with the shoulders of a prize-fighter, she was petite, finely and
slenderly fashioned.

'Did you get him?' she asked anxiously. 'I'm scared, Marlowe.
More scared than I was at home.'

The boy put his arm round her. 'It's going to be all right, kid,' he said. 'The old man's obstinacy doesn't make it any easier for us to look after him. I was rather hopeful about this Campion fellow, but now I don't know what to think. I'll see if I can find him, anyhow.'

The girl clung to him. 'Be careful. You don't know anyone here. It might be a trap to get you.'

The boy shook his head. 'I fancy not,' he said.

She was still not reassured. 'I'll come with you.'

Marlowe shook his head. 'I wouldn't,' he said. 'It may be a wild-goose chase. Stay here and look after Father. Don't let him go out till I come back.'

Isopel Lobbett nodded. 'All right,' she said. 'But hurry.'

The taxi route from the Strand to Piccadilly is not a long one, and Marlowe found himself outside the police station in the narrow cul-de-sac sooner than he had anticipated. The 'door on the left', he decided, must be the yellow portal which stood open showing a flight of wooden stairs, scrubbed white, leading up into darkness. After the first flight of steps he came upon a carpet, at the third there were pictures on the wall, and he began to have the uncomfortable impression that he had stumbled into some private house, when he suddenly came to a stop before an attractively carved oak door upon which there was a small brass plate, neatly engraved with the simple lettering:

MR ALBERT CAMPION, MERCHANT
GOODS DEPT

When he saw it he realized with a shock how forlorn he had expected his errand to be. He tapped upon the door with more vigour than he had intended.

It was opened immediately by the young man in the horn-rimmed spectacles himself. He was attired in what appeared to be a bathrobe, a stupendous affair of multi-coloured Turkish towelling.

'Hallo!' he said. 'Seeing London? I come next in importance after the Tower, I always think. Come in.' He dragged his visitor into a room across the tiny passage and thrust him into a deep comfortable armchair by the fire. As he mixed him a drink he rambled on inconsequentially without allowing the other to get a word in.

'I have to live over a police station because of my friends. It's a great protection against my more doubtful acquaintances.'

In spite of his agitation and the importance of his errand, Marlowe could not help noticing the extraordinary character of the room in which he sat. It was tastefully, even luxuriously, furnished. There were one or two delightful old pieces, a Rembrandt etching over the bureau, a Steinlen cat, a couple of original cartoons, and a lovely little Girtin.

But amongst these were scattered a most remarkable collection of trophies. One little group over the mantelpiece comprised two jemmies, crossed, surmounted by a pair of handcuffs, with a convict's cap over the top. Lying upon a side table, apparently used as a paper knife, was a beautiful Italian dagger, the blade of which was of a curious greenish-blue shade, and the hilt encrusted with old and uncut gems.

Campion picked it up. 'That's the Black Dudley dagger,' he said. 'An old boy I met was stuck in the back with that, and everyone thought I'd done the sticking. Not such fun. I suppose you've seen most of the sights of London by now,' he went on. 'There's my Great-aunt Emily. I've often thought of running a good cheap char-à-bancs tour round her.'

Marlowe Lobbett did not smile. 'You'll forgive me,' he said, 'but can't we drop this fooling? I've come to you as a last chance, Mr Campion.'

The boy's gravity was sobering, but his irrepressible host, after a momentary expression of contrition had passed over his face, began once more. 'Rather – anything I can do for you,' he said affably. 'I undertake almost anything these days. But nothing sordid. I will not sell that tinted photograph of myself as Lord Fauntleroy. No. Not all your gold shall tempt me. I am leaving that to the Nation. Patriotism, and all that sort of rot,' he chattered on, proffering a particularly dangerous-looking cocktail. 'All my own work. It contains almost everything except tea. Now, young sir, what can I do for you?'

Marlowe accepted the drink. 'I say,' he said, 'do you always talk like this?'

Mr Campion looked abashed. 'Almost always,' he said. 'People get used to it in time. I can't help it, it's a sort of affliction, like stammering or a hammer toe. My friends pretend they don't notice it. What did the police say to you this morning?'

The last question was put so abruptly that Marlowe Lobbett had not time to conceal his surprise. 'What do you know about it?' he demanded. 'How do you know that I visited your police headquarters this morning?'

Mr Campion advanced with great solemnity and gingerly removed a tiny piece of fluff from his visitor's overcoat with his thumb and forefinger. 'A police hair, my dear Watson,' he said. 'I noticed it as soon as you came in. Since then my brain has been working. I suppose they funked it?' he went on with sudden directness.

Marlowe glanced up. 'They wouldn't guarantee his safety,' he said.

Mr Campion shook his head. 'I don't altogether blame them,' he said soberly. 'Your own police in New York weren't handing out any insurance certificates, were they?'

'No,' said Marlowe. 'That is the main reason why I got the old boy over here. Our Big Noise over there told me that in his opinion they were playing cat-and-mouse with father and that they'd get him just whenever they pleased. You see,' he burst out impatiently, 'it's mostly the old boy's fault. He won't stand for any reasonable restraint. He won't let the police look after him in their way. You see, he's never been afraid of –' He hesitated, and added the word 'them' with a peculiar intonation. 'And he's not going to begin now. He's not crazy. He just feels that way about it. You see what I'm up against.'

'Not quite,' said Mr Campion thoughtfully. 'How come, boy? How come?'

Marlowe stared at him in astonishment. 'Do you mean to say you don't *know*?' he said. 'I don't understand you at all, Mr Campion. When you saved my father on the *Elephantine* surely you had some idea of what was up?'

'Well, naturally,' said the owner of the flat airily, 'but not very much. I met an old burgling friend of mine on board and he pointed out a fellow graduate of his, as it were, who had suddenly got very pally with old Hanky Panky the Magician. Like all professional men, we took an intelligent interest in the fellow's technique, and, well, I just borrowed friend Haig in case of emergencies. Do you know,' he rattled on, 'I believe that mouse was fond of me? I am glad it was a sudden death. By the way,' he continued, 'may I ask, was it because of my stupendous platform appearance that you came to me today?'

Marlowe Lobbett hesitated. 'Not altogether,' he admitted. 'In fact, when I was talking to Chief Inspector Deadwood at Scotland Yard this morning and I found that they couldn't promise to protect the old boy without a regular police guard, which father would never stand, I appealed to him as a man to tell me of someone to whom I could go.'

Mr Campion chuckled. 'Good for him,' he said. 'Behold Albert Campion, CID – i.e. Cell in Dartmoor,' he explained regretfully. 'But it hasn't come to that yet. You know of course who "they" are?' he said suddenly.

Marlowe Lobbett was becoming used to these lightning changes of mood. He nodded, his shrewd dark eyes fixed upon the spectacles which hid Mr Campion's seriousness from him. 'Simister.' He spoke the word so softly that it sounded like a whisper. Mr Campion was silent for some moments, and Marlowe Lobbett suddenly leaned forward in his chair.

'Mr Campion,' he said, 'can you tell me about this man Simister? What is he? A gangster? A master crook? Is he a single personality at all? In New York they say his records go back for over a hundred years, and that no such person exists. According to them a powerful gang is using the word as a sort of trade name. Tell me,' he went on. 'Does he exist?'

A laugh escaped Mr Campion. 'My dear man,' he said, 'somewhere on this earth there is a man called Simister. He may be a devil – a bogle – anything you like, but he's as real a power of evil as dope is. I'm not saying this to chill your youthful ardour,' he went on, 'but it's most dangerous to underrate an enemy. This is all I know about him. I've talked to crooks and I've talked to policemen – I've even talked to members of his own gang – but I've never met anyone yet who has set eyes on him. Apparently he's a voice on the telephone, a shadow on the road, the gloved hand that turns out the light in the crook play; but with one big difference – he's never caught. There are thousands of amazing yarns told about him, and in not one of them does a hint of his face ever appear. They say no one ever escapes him.'

Marlowe moved uneasily in his chair. 'I've heard that,' he said, 'and that's why I've come to you – as a last chance, if you'll forgive me saying so. Can you do anything for me?'

Mr Campion eyed him owlishly, but he did not give a direct reply. 'There's one thing I don't get,' he said. 'Why your father?'

Marlowe Lobbett rose to his feet and walked up and down the room. 'That's what gets me,' he said. 'It's nothing I can help. It's nothing money can undo. It's a sort of revenge.'

Campion nodded. 'I see,' he said gravely. 'Anything else?'

'I'm not sure,' Marlowe spoke helplessly. 'You see,' he went on with sudden confidence, 'I've found all this out with difficulty. It goes back a long time. When I was a kid of course I hadn't much idea of what father was up to. I've only recently dug out the truth from him, and he won't admit much, even to me. Apparently the old boy has been fighting the Simister Gang all his life. He was the only weapon the police really had. When they got a gangster dad gave it to him hot. He wasn't unjust, you understand, he was just hard where they were concerned. But he couldn't make any real impression on them. Quite suddenly – it was after the Steinway trial (he wasn't trying that, you know, he was just advising; that was after he had retired) – they went for him. We've lived in terror for him for over six months,' he finished quietly.

'Not a Mothers' Union Outing,' said Mr Campion appreciatively, and added more gravely, 'Is that all?'

Marlowe Lobbett hesitated. 'Well, the rest is only conjecture,' he said.

'Let's have it,' said Mr Campion.

Marlowe sat down again and lit a cigarette, which he did not smoke.

'Well, you must understand,' he began hesitatingly, 'my father has said nothing to me to give me this idea. I don't know anything for certain but from several things that have happened lately I believe that he's got something pretty definite on the Simister Gang. You see,' he went on abruptly, ' "advisory work" is such a vague term. I can't help feeling that it may mean that he's been devoting himself to investigations about these Simister people. He probably wouldn't admit it for fear of scaring us. I believe the old boy tumbled on something. I've been trying to figure out what it could be, and it's occurred to me that he might have stumbled on some clue as to the actual identity of this Simister fellow himself.'

Mr Campion took off his spectacles and his pale eyes regarded his visitor in frank astonishment. 'I hope for your sake that what you think is not true. If, as you said at first, the Simister Gang is after your father out of sheer temper, i.e. revenge, that's one thing. There's a chance for him. But if, as you suggest now, he's got a line on them, then I'm afraid that the fabulous sums spent in hiring Mr Campion's assistance would be a mere waste of money. Consider,' he went on – 'what can you expect me to do? I tell you quite candidly, your only chance is to get the old boy into Brixton Jail, and that wouldn't be fun for him.'

Marlowe Lobbett rose to his feet. 'I see,' he said. 'I told you you were my last hope.'

Mr Campion hesitated. 'I'd like to have a whack at Simister,' he said.

The young American turned to him quickly. 'Well, here's your chance,' he said. 'It may be a forlorn chance, but after all, the mischief isn't done yet.'

'My dear young optimist,' said Mr Campion admonishingly, 'in effect you're saying, "Here's a nice war; come and sit in it".'

He was interrupted from further comment by a tap at the outer door.

'The one-thirty,' said Mr Campion. 'Excuse me.'

He went out of the room and returned immediately with a racing edition of the *Evening Standard* in his hand. He was smiling. 'Now I can dress,' he explained cheerfully. 'I had my shirt on the Archdeacon!'

His eye travelled down the stop-press column. Suddenly his expression changed and he handed the paper to his visitor.

'Well-known American's Narrow Escape', it ran:

Judge Crowdy Lobbett, the well-known American visitor, narrowly missed a serious accident when a taxicab mounted the pavement outside his hotel in the Strand and crashed into a shop window this morning at twelve o'clock. No one was injured.

'My God!' Marlowe Lobbett started for the door. 'They don't know where I am – I didn't leave your address. Isopel will be terrified. I must get along to them at once.'

Mr Campion had disappeared into his bedroom, which led off the room where they had been talking.

'Wait for me,' he shouted. 'I shan't be a second.'

Marlowe Lobbett appeared in the doorway. 'I don't quite get you.'

'I'm in this,' said Mr Campion.

Chapter 3

Mystery Mile

On the grey marshy coast of Suffolk, fifteen miles from a railway station, and joined to the mainland by the Stroud only, a narrow road of hard land, the village of Mystery Mile lay surrounded by impassable mud flats and grey-white saltings.

The name was derived from the belt of ground mist which summer and winter hung in the little valleys round the small hill on which the village stood. Like many Suffolk hamlets, the place was more of an estate than a village. The half-dozen cottages, the post office, and the Rectory were very much outbuildings of the Manor House, the dwelling of the owner of the Mile.

In olden times, when the land had been more profitable, the squire had had no difficulty in supporting his large family of retainers, and, apart from the witch burnings in James I's reign, when well-nigh a third of the population had suffered execution for practices more peculiar than necromantic, the little place had a long history of peaceful if gradually decaying times.

The families had intermarried, and they were now almost as much one kin as the Pagets themselves.

The death of the present squire's father, Giles Paget, had left his young son and daughter the house and worthless lands, with little or no money to keep them up, and some twenty or thirty villagers who looked to them as their natural means of support.

The Manor, hidden in the thick belt of elms which surrounded it, had but one lamp shining from the big casement windows. It was a long, low, many-gabled building, probably built round 1500 and kept in good repair ever since. The overhung front sheltered rose trees under its eaves, and the lintels of the windows were low and black, enhancing the beauty of the moulded plaster surrounding them.

In the library, round the fireplace with the deep-set chimney seat, the squire and his sister were entertaining the rector.

The squire was twenty-three. Giles Paget and his sister Biddy were twins. As they sat together they looked startlingly modern against the dark oak-furnished room which had not been materially altered for centuries.

Giles was a heavily built, fair youngster whose sturdiness suggested a much larger man. He had a square-cut face, not particularly handsome, but he had a charming smile.

Biddy was possessed of an animation unusual in a country girl. Tall as her brother, with a figure like a boy's, she had a more practical outlook on life than had been born into the Paget family for centuries.

Their visitor, the Reverend Swithin Cush, rector of Mystery Mile, sat and beamed at them. He was a lank old man, with a hooked nose and deep-set twinkling black eyes surrounded by a thousand wrinkles. His long silky white hair was cut by Biddy herself when it got past his collar, and his costume consisted of a venerable suit of plus-fours, darned at knees and elbows with a variety of wools, and a shining dog collar, the one concession he made to 'the cloth'. His only vanity was a huge signet ring, a bloodstone, which shone dully on his gnarled first finger. For nearly fifty years he had baptized, wedded, and buried the people of the isthmus. The village was conservative, not to say medieval in its religious opinions, and the old chained Bible in the little late-Norman church was the only book of the law they considered at all.

The subject of discussion round the fire in the library was the paper Giles Paget held in his hand.

'St Swithin can now see the telegram,' said Biddy; 'the first Mystery Mile has seen since Giles won the half-mile. I don't know how Albert's going to get here, Giles; the Ipswich taxies don't like the Stroud at night.'

The rector took the telegram and read it aloud, holding the paper down to the fire to catch the light from the flames.

LISTEN KIDDIES UNCLE HAS LET HOUSE STOP RING OUT WILD BELLS STOP SEND NO FLOWERS STOP ARRIVING NINE THIRTY STOP SHALL EXPECT FOOD AND RARE VINTAGES STOP OBEDIENTLY YOURS EVA BOOTH.

'If I know anything about Albert,' said the rector, 'he'll arrive on a broomstick.'

Biddy sighed. 'Think he has let the house?' she said. 'I never dreamed he would take us seriously. I do hope we get something for it. Cuddy's third daughter's having another baby in September. That's another for the bounty. These ancient customs are a bit hard on the budget.'

' "The Lord will provide," ' said the rector regretfully, 'is a tag which is not found in the Vulgate. But I have great faith in Albert.'

Biddy chuckled. 'St Swithin,' she said. 'Albert is a fishy character and no fit associate for a dignitary of the Church.'

The old man smiled at her, and his small black eyes twinkled and danced in the firelight.

'My daughter,' he said, 'out of evil cometh good. There is no reason why we should not sit in the shadow of the Bay Tree while it flourishes. Although,' he went on seriously, 'our very good friend Albert is a true son of the Church. In the time of Richelieu he would no doubt have become a cardinal. His associates are not solely criminals. Look at us, for instance.'

Giles broke in. 'Oh no,' he said, 'he's not a crook. Not exactly, I mean,' he added as an afterthought.

'He's not a detective either,' said Biddy. 'As a matter of fact, he's really a sort of Universal Aunt, isn't he? "Your adventures undertaken for a small fee." Oh, I like Albert.'

Giles grinned.

'I know you do,' he said. 'She's prepared a school treat for him in the next room, St Swithin. One of these days she'll put us in a home and go off with him.'

Biddy laughed and regarded them shrewdly out of the corners of her brown eyes.

'I might,' she said, 'but he's comic about women.' She sighed.

'He's a comic chap altogether,' said Giles. 'Did I tell you, St Swithin, the last time I saw him we walked down Regent Street together, and from the corner of Conduit Street to the Circus we met five people he knew, including a viscountess and two bishops? Each one of them stopped and greeted him as an old pal. And every single one of them called him by a different name. Heaven knows how he does it.'

'Addlepate will be glad to see him,' said Biddy, patting the head of a sleek chestnut-brown dog who had just thrust his head into her lap. The dog looked self-conscious at hearing his name, and wagged his stump of tail with feverish enthusiasm.

Giles turned to the rector. 'Albert said he tried to train Addlepate for crime before he gave it up as a bad job and brought him down to us. He said the flesh was willing but the mind was weak. I shall never forget,' he went on, pulling at his pipe, 'when we were up at Cambridge, hearing Albert explain to the porter after midnight that he was a werewolf out on his nightly prowl who had unexpectedly returned to his own shape before he had time to bound over the railings. He kept old . . .'

The sound of a motor horn among the elms outside interrupted him. Biddy sprang to her feet. 'There he is,' she said, and ran out to open the door to him herself. The other two followed her.

Through the rustling darkness they could just make out the outlines of a small two-seater, out of which there rose to greet them the thin figure they expected. He stood up in the car and posed before them, one hand upraised.

'Came Dawn,' he said, and the next moment was on the steps beside them. 'Well, well, my little ones, how you have grown! It seems only yesterday, St Swithin, that you were babbling your infant prayers at my knee.'

They took him into the house, and as he sat eating in the low-ceilinged dining-room they crowded round him like children. Addlepate, grasping for the first time who it was, had a mild fit of canine hysterics by himself in the hall before he joined the others.

By common consent they left the question of the letting of the house until Mr Campion should mention it, and as he did not bring up the subject, but chattered on inconsequentially about everything else under the sun, there was no talk of it until they were once more seated round the library fire.

Mr Campion sat between Giles and Biddy. The firelight shone upon his spectacles, hiding his eyes. Giles leaned back in his chair, puffing contentedly at his pipe. The girl sat close to their new guest, Addlepate in her lap, and the old rector was back in his corner. Sitting there, the firelight making a fine tracery of his face, he looked like a Rembrandt etching.

'Well, about this Estate Agency business,' said Mr Campion, 'I've got something to put up to you kids.' His tone was unusually serious.

'I know what you're thinking,' he said. 'You're wondering where the slow music comes in. It's like this. It so happened that I wanted a country house in a remote spot for a particularly peppy job I've got on hand at the moment. Your announcement that you'd have to let the ancestral home occurred to me, and I thought the two stunts worked in together very well. Giles, old boy, I shall want you to help me. Biddy, could you clear out, my dear, and go and stay with an aunt or something? For a fortnight or so, I mean – until I know how the land lies?'

The girl looked at him with mild surprise in her brown eyes. 'Seriously?' she said.

He nodded. 'More serious than anything in the world.'

Biddy leaned back in her chair. 'You'll have to explain,' she said. 'I don't want to miss anything.'

Mr Campion took Biddy's hand with awful solemnity. 'Woman,' he said, 'this is *men's* work. You'll keep your little turned-up neb out of it. Quite definitely and seriously,' he went on, 'this is not your sort of show, old dear.'

'Suppose you don't blether so much,' said Giles; 'let's have the facts. You're so infernally earnest that you're beginning to be interesting for once.'

Mr Campion got up and wandered up and down the room, his steps sounding sharply on the polished oak floor.

'Now I'm down here,' he said suddenly, 'and I see you dear old birds all tucked up in the ancestral nest, I've got an attack of conscience. I ought not to have done this, but since I have I'd better make a clean breast of it.'

The others turned and stared at him, surprised by this unusual outburst.

'Look here,' he went on, planting himself back in his chair, 'I'll tell you. You read the newspapers, don't you? Good! Well, have you heard of Judge Lobbett?'

'The old boy they're trying to kill?' said Giles. 'Yes. You know I showed it to you this morning, St Swithin. Are you in that, Albert?'

Mr Campion nodded gravely. 'Up to the neck,' he said, adding hastily, 'on the right side, of course. You know the rough outline of the business, don't you? Old Lobbett's stirred up a hornet's nest for himself in America and it's pretty obvious they've followed him here.' He shot a glance at Giles. 'They're not out to kill him, you know – not yet. They're trying to put the fear of God into him and they've picked an infernally tough nut. In fact,' he went on regretfully, 'if he wasn't such a tough nut we wouldn't have such a job. I'm acting for the son, Marlowe Lobbett – a very decent cove; you'll like him, Giles.' He paused and looked round at them. 'Have you got all that?'

They nodded, and he continued: 'The old boy won't stand any serious police protection. He himself is our chief difficulty. At first I thought he was going to sink us, but quite by chance I stumbled on a most useful sidelight in his character. The old boy has got a bee in his bonnet about folk-lore – ancient English customs – all that sort of thing. Marlowe introduced me to him as a sort of guide to rural England. Said he'd met me on the boat coming over, as of course he had. Anyway, I've let him the house. There's a title of Lord of the Manor that goes with it, isn't there?'

Giles glanced up. 'There is something like that, isn't there, St Swithin?'

The old man nodded and smiled. 'There's a document in the church to that effect,' he said. 'I don't know what good it is to anybody nowadays, though.'

'Old Judge Lobbett liked it, anyway,' said Mr Campion. 'It gives the place a sort of medieval flavour. But I'll come to that later. All that matters now is that the old bird has taken the place off your hands at fourteen quid a week. And if he knew as much as I do he'd realize he got it cheap.'

Giles sat up. 'You expect trouble?' he said.

Mr Campion nodded. 'I don't see how we can escape it,' he said. 'You see,' he went on hastily, 'I had to get the old boy out of the city and down here, because in a place like this if there're any strangers knocking about we know at once. Look here, Giles, I shall need you to help me.'

Giles grinned. 'I'm with you,' he said. 'It's time something happened down here.'

'And I'm in it too,' said Biddy, that expression of determination which the others knew so well appearing at the corners of her mouth.

Mr Campion shook his head. 'Sorry, Biddy,' he said, 'I couldn't have that. You don't know what you'd be letting yourself in for. It was only in a fit of exuberance that I went into it myself.'

Biddy sniffed. 'I'm staying,' she said. 'Judge Lobbett has a daughter, hasn't he? If she's going to be in it, so am I. Besides, what would you three poor fish do without me? We'll move over to the Dower House.'

Mr Campion turned to the rector. 'Bring your influence to bear, St Swithin. Tell her that this is stern stuff – no place for the tender sex.'

The old man shook his head. 'In the words of the poet, "I do remain as neuter",' he said. 'Personally, I always obey her.'

Mr Campion looked abashed. 'You're making it very awkward for me,' he said. 'I'd never have done it if I'd dreamed that I was bringing you into it, Biddy.'

The girl laid her hand upon his knee. 'Don't be a fool,' she said. 'You silly old dear, I'm with you to the death. You know that.'

Mr Campion almost blushed, and was silent for an appreciable space of time. The rector brought him back to the subject on hand. 'Let us be specific,' he said. 'No doubt you have your own dark secrets, Albert, but what are we expected to do?'

Mr Campion plunged into the details of his scheme. 'First of all,' he said, 'we've got to keep the old boy here. And that means we've got to keep him interested. St Swithin, I rely on you for the archaeology and whatnots. Show him the village trophies. Get out the relics of the witch burnings and polish up the stocks. Make it all bright and homely for him. Then there's the doubtful Romney in the drawing room. Get his opinion on that. He's a delightful old cove, but obstinate as sin.'

He hesitated. 'What he's really interested in,' he went on after a pause, 'is actual folk-lore and superstition. Haven't you any prize yokels who know a few ancient wisecracks? – old songs and that sort of thing?'

Giles glanced up. 'Plenty of those,' he said. 'Did I tell you, Biddy, I set George to cut down that dead thorn at the end of the home paddock this morning? When I passed by at lunchtime he grinned at me, as pleased as Punch – he'd been all the morning at it. "How are you going, George?" said I. "Foine, Master Giles," he said, "I can cut that down quicker than that took to grow." When I said, "So I should hope," he seemed quite offended. We might pass him off as the original Old Saw himself.'

'That's the sort of thing,' Campion agreed. 'But I warn you to go carefully. The old boy's no fool. This sort of thing's his hobby. You'd be surprised how much more the average American knows about England than we do.'

The Reverend Swithin Cush coughed dryly. 'There is enough here to interest a genuine antiquary for some time,' he said. 'How long do you expect him to stay? Is the length of his visit indefinite?'

Mr Campion became suddenly vague. 'I don't know,' he said. 'I've cracked up the place a lot, but he may give us one swift look and go home, and then *bang* goes little Albert's fourpence an hour and old Lobbett's sweet young life, most likely. Oh, I forgot. He'll be here the day after tomorrow. Can you be ready in time, Biddy?'

The girl sighed. 'Just,' she said. 'It'll be a bit of a camp at the Dower House.'

They sat discussing their plans until after midnight, when the old rector rose stiffly out of his chair.

'Biddy, I'll have my hurricane,' he said. 'You ought all to be in bed now if you're going to move tomorrow.'

The girl fetched the storm lantern, and they watched him disappearing into the darkness – a gaunt, lonely figure, his white hair uncovered, the lantern bobbing at his side like a will-o'-the-wisp.

As they came back into the shadowy hall, Mr Campion grinned. 'Dear old St Swithin,' he said. 'You've known him since you were muling and puking in Cuddy's arms, haven't you?'

Biddy answered him. 'Yes,' she said. 'He's getting old, though. Alice – that's his housekeeper, you know – says he's gone all Russian lately. "Like a broody hen," she said.'

'He must be hundreds of years old,' said Albert. 'There's an idea in that. We might pass him off as the original St Swithin himself. Dropped in out of the rain, as it were.'

'Go to bed,' said Biddy. 'The machinery wants a rest.'

Up in the chintz-hung bedroom the oak floor was sloping and the cool air was fragrant with lavender, toilet soap, and beeswax. Mr Campion did not get into the four-poster immediately, but stood for some time peering out into the darkness.

At last he drew a small, much-battered notebook from an inside pocket and scribbled 'St S'. For some time he stood looking at it soberly, and then deliberately added a question mark.

Chapter 4

The Lord of the Manor

'Although you're a foreigner, which can't be helped, and therefore it ain't loikely that you'll be used to our ways, all the same we welcome you. We do 'ope you'll live up to the old ways and do all you can for us.'

The speaker paused and wiped round the inside of his Newgate fringe with a coloured handkerchief. 'Now let's sing a 'ymn,' he added as an afterthought.

He was standing by himself at the bottom of his cottage garden, his face turned towards the meadows which sloped down sleekly to the grey saltings. After a while he repeated his former announcement word for word, finishing with an unexpected 'Morning, sir,' as a thin, pale-faced young man with horn-rimmed spectacles appeared upon the other side of the hedge.

'Morning, George,' said Mr Campion.

George Willsmore surveyed the newcomer thoughtfully. He was a gnarled old man, brown and nobbled as a pollarded willow, with great creases bitten into his face, which was surrounded by a thick hearthbrush of a beard. As the oldest able member of the family of which the village was mainly composed, he considered himself a sort of mayor, and his rural dignity was enhanced by a curious sententiousness of utterance.

'You come upon me unawares,' he said. 'I was sayin' over a few words I be goin' to speak this afternoon.'

'Really?' Mr Campion appeared to be interested. 'You're thinking of making a speech of welcome, George?'

'Summat like that,' conceded the old man graciously. 'Me and the rector was 'avin a talk. 'E was for singin'. And me bein' churchwarden, seems only right, seems, I should do the greetin'. Him bein' a foreigner, 'e mightn't understand the others.'

'There's something in that, of course,' said Mr Campion, who had followed the old man's reasoning with difficulty.

George continued.

'I put on some new clo'es. Seems like 'tis a good idea to look smart. I be a wunnerful smart old man, don't you think?'

He turned himself about for Mr Campion's inspection. He was dressed in a pair of tight corduroy trousers which had once been brown, but were now washed to creamy whiteness, a bright blue collarless gingham shirt, and one of his late master's white waistcoats which hung loosely round his spare stomach. His straw hat, built on the Panama principle, had a black ribbon round it and a bunch of jay's feathers tucked into the bow.

'How's that?' he demanded with badly concealed pride.

'Very fine,' agreed the young man. 'All the same, I wouldn't make your speech if I were you, George. I was coming down to have a talk with you about this business. Aren't there some customs, maypolings and whatnot, suitable for this afternoon?'

The old man pushed back his straw hat, revealing an unexpectedly bald head, the crown of which he rubbed meditatively with the edge of his hat.

'Not give the speech?' he said with disappointment. 'Oh well, sir, I reckon you know best. But I'd 'ave done it right well, that I would. I do be a powerful talkative old man. But the time for maypolin's past,' he went on, 'and Pharisees' Day, that ain't come yet.'

The young man sighed. 'None of these – er – feasts are movable?' he suggested hopefully.

George shook his head. 'No, you can't alter they days. Not for nobody,' he added with decision.

Mr Campion regarded the old man with great solemnity. 'George,' he said, 'take my advice and make an effort. It wouldn't be a bad idea if you could think of some sort of turnip-blessing ceremony. You're a smart man, George.'

'Aye,' said the old man with alacrity, and remained in deep thought for some time. 'No, there be nothin',' he said at last. 'Nothin' but maybe the Seven Whistlers.'

'Seven Whistlers?' said Mr Campion with interest. 'What's that? Who are they?'

The old man studied his hat intently for some time before replying. 'Seven Whistlers, sir,' he said at last. 'No one knows if they be ghosts or Pharisees – that be fairies, if you take me. You 'ear 'em passin' overhead about this time of year. Whistlin'. Least, you only 'ears six on 'em. The seventh's got a kind o' whoop in it, trailin' away like a barn owl, terrible to 'ear, and when you 'ears that, that's the end of the world. Only no one's ever 'eard it yet.'

'That sounds all right,' said Mr Campion. 'But it doesn't get us more forrarder, does it, George?'

An unexpectedly crafty expression appeared upon the old man's venerable face. 'Toime was,' he said, 'when the old squoire used to give a barrel o' beer for they Seven Whistlers. Just about round this time of the year it was, now I come to think on it.' He paused and looked at Mr Campion hopefully.

'For the Seven Whistlers?' said the young man dubiously.

The old man broke into hasty explanations.

''Twas so, only they Seven Whistlers they never came to drink it, so it had to be drinked up by the poor, for fear of that goin' sour.'

'I see,' said Mr Campion, who had begun to comprehend. 'The poor, I suppose, were the villagers?'

'Aye.' George paused, and remarked after some consideration, 'Master Giles and Miss Biddy most likely wouldn't know anything about it if you asked 'em. Doubt not they 'eard o' the Seven Whistlers, but not of the beer. You understand, sir?'

'Perfectly,' said Mr Campion. 'It occurs to me, George, that you and I might get on very well together. You have the flair, if I may say so. You've got a brother, haven't you?'

'Oh 'Anry?' said Mr Willsmore with contempt. 'I'm the clever one. 'Anry is not. I'm the man for you, sir.'

Mr Campion regarded him gravely. 'I believe you are,' he said.

They remained deep in conversation together for some time.

When the young man walked back over the rough grass he was considerably easier in his mind than before. As he approached the house he was surprised to see a long black Daimler outside the oak door. He hurried forward. Biddy met him in the hall.

'Albert, he's a dear,' she said. 'They're in the library with Giles now. I've been looking for you everywhere. They've been here nearly an hour. We've shown them all over the house and they're just charming about it. The boy's awfully handsome, don't you think?'

'Nonsense!' said Mr Campion. 'You should see me in my new moustache. Quite the latest thing, my dear. Only ten-three. Illusion guaranteed. I'm being ringed for it. Mother need never know.'

'Jealous!' said Biddy. 'Come and see them.'

He followed her down the stone-paved corridor to where the library door stood ajar.

Judge Lobbett stood looking out across the lawn. The sun glinted on his face, on the pictures let into the panelling, and on the sherry glasses on the table.

'It's a lovely place,' he said, turning as Albert and Biddy came in. 'Good morning, Mr Campion. I congratulate you on your choice on our behalf.' He turned to the young people. Biddy had crossed over to her brother and they stood together with their backs to the fireplace, looking wonderfully alike.

'Seems I'm turning you out of your homestead,' he said bluntly. 'Are you sure you want to let?'

Biddy smiled at him, her brown eyes meeting his gratefully.

'It's awfully nice of you to say that,' she said, 'but we've got to let. Did Albert warn you, you'll be taking over half our responsibilities as far as the village is concerned? We just couldn't do it as Dad did before the war. The money won't go so far. Being squire at Mystery Mile is rather like being papa to the village.'

The old man smiled at her. 'I'll like it,' he said.

Biddy sighed. 'You don't know what a relief it is to know that someone's got the house who really likes it.'

Judge Lobbett turned to his daughter, a slim little figure wrapped in furs. 'If you don't think you'll find it too quiet –'

Isopel glanced at him, and a faint scared smile passed over her face. 'Not too quiet?' she said meaningly, and a sigh escaped her.

Meanwhile Marlowe Lobbett had crossed over to Mr Campion and the two young men stood talking together.

'You weren't followed?' Mr Campion spoke softly.

Marlowe shook his head. 'I think they were waiting for us,' he said. 'Your policemen held up a car directly behind us. The chauffeur you found us is a genius. We got out of the city in no time. Anyone following us would have had an almighty job.'

Biddy's voice broke in upon their conversation. 'We'll leave the place to you now. You'll find Mrs Whybrow's prepared everything for you. She's a wonderful housekeeper. You've all promised to come to dinner with us this evening, haven't you?' she went on, turning to Isopel. 'The Dower House is only just across the park. Old Mr Cush, the rector, will be there. In his Sunday clothes, I hope. You ought to meet him.'

Isopel clung to her hand as they said good-bye. After the terrible experiences of the last few months this pleasant sleepy old house with its young untroubled owners was very comforting. 'I'm so glad you're

here,' she said impulsively. The other girl shot her a swift comprehending glance.

'Don't worry,' she murmured. 'You don't know Albert.'

Mr Campion and the Pagets walked down the gravelled drive and
passed over the village green where the pump stood to the Dower
House. A high yew hedge hid it from the green, and all the main
windows faced the other side of the house, looking over an old walled
garden.

Mr Campion looked greatly relieved. 'Thank goodness the old bird
fell for the house!' he said. 'Naturally I couldn't get him to agree to
take the place for any length of time before he'd seen it, but we
couldn't have him running up and down to town setting our homicid-
al pal on his track immediately. What do you think of them, Giles?'

'Nice old boy,' said Giles. 'Not unlike the Governor, only American. Same direct way of looking at you and saying exactly what
comes into his head. I didn't have much talk with young Lobbett, but
he seemed all right. But oh boy! what a girl!'

Biddy and Mr Campion exchanged glances. 'Yuth! Yuth!' said she.
'I like her. She must have been having a nerve-racking time.'

Giles nodded. 'I was thinking that,' he said. 'Time there was
someone to look after her.'

'That's the spirit,' said Mr Campion, adding with sudden gravity,
'Biddy, I wish you'd clear out. Old Cuddy has lived at the Dower
House so long she'll be able to look after us without any trouble.'

Biddy shook her head. 'You still expecting excitement?'

Mr Campion nodded. 'We can't escape it,' he said. 'Won't you go
and leave us to it, old dear?'

Biddy was determined. 'Find something else to be inane about,' she
said. 'As I said before, I'm with you to the death.'

Mr Campion did not smile. 'I wish you wouldn't say that,' he said.
'It puts the wind up me – all this harping on mortality. Whenever I see
a white flower nowadays I think, "Albert, that might be for you".'

'Would you say her eyes were blue or brown or a sort of a heather
mixture?' said Giles.

Chapter 5

The Seven Whistlers

The drawing-room at the Dower House, small, cosy, and lined with white panelling, was lit that evening with candles only, and their flickering light was kind to the faded rose tapestry and the India carpet which had once been the pride of a great-great-grandmother of Biddy's. There was a fire in the old-fashioned grate, and the whole room looked particularly inviting when they came in from dinner.

Swithin Cush and Judge Lobbett were talking enthusiastically as they followed the young people. They had delighted each other with a mutual display of archaeological fireworks all through dinner and were still engrossed in their subject.

The rector had appeared in his Sunday clothes in response to an urgent message from Biddy, and his venerable green-black clerical coat of ancient cut enhanced his patriarchal air.

They had been discussing the Royal Letter which entitled the incumbent of the Mansion to be styled Lord of the Manor. Old Lobbett was deeply interested, and the two elder men bent over the faded parchment, sharing their enthusiasm for the relic.

Biddy and Isopel sat side by side on the high-backed settee while the three younger men talked together on the far side of the fireplace.

'By the way,' said Marlowe, 'we had a visit from a deputation this afternoon. Two old fellows came up to see us, apparently representing the villagers, with an extraordinary yarn about free beer that was apparently doled out at this time of the year. It was something about "Owl Friday", as far as we could gather.'

Biddy and Giles exchanged glances. 'I bet that's George,' said Giles. 'Disgusting old cadger!'

'That's right,' said Marlowe. 'George and a man apparently called "'Anry". But George was the head man.'

Biddy began to apologize. 'They're dreadful,' she said helplessly. 'They're inveterate beggars. I hope you sent them away.'

Marlowe shook his head. 'The old boy rather liked them,' he said. 'It showed they were friendly, anyway. They were talking about old customs practically all the afternoon. At least, George was. 'Anry's comments were unintelligible.'

'Henry's a bokel,' said Biddy. 'That was father's word. It means half a barmy, half a yokel.'

After a while the conversation died down and the little party sat in that pleasant silence which is induced by warmth and well-being. And then, from far away over the marshes came a sound, almost lost and diffused in the air – a soft, long-drawn-out whistle.

No one appeared to hear it, but Mr Campion's pale eyes flickered behind his spectacles, and he shifted slightly in his chair, his ear turned to the window.

Within ten seconds the sound came again, a little nearer, more distinguishable. Still no one spoke in the warm peaceful room, but the atmosphere of security had vanished for one of the party at least. Again the whistle sounded, still far away, but appreciably nearer.

Suddenly Isopel looked up. 'An owl,' she said. 'Did you hear it?'

Giles listened. 'Yes, there it is again,' he said. 'It's flying this way,' he added, as the sound was repeated, this time no farther away than the park.

Mr Campion rose and walked over to the window, and it did not escape Biddy that he stood at the side of the sash, so that he could not be seen easily from without. For the sixth time the unearthly sound was repeated.

And then, while they were all listening, a curious sense of apprehension stealing over every one of them, a sudden blood-curdling wail was uttered somewhere within the garden, long-drawn-out like the others, but with a definite quaver in the middle.

'God bless my soul!' said Swithin Cush, sitting up suddenly. 'What was that?'

Mr Campion turned from the window. 'That, if I am not very much mistaken,' said he, 'is a visitor.'

Hardly had the words passed from his lips than a loose wire creaked uneasily somewhere over their heads and the next moment a bell pealed hollowly, echoing noisily over the house.

No one moved or spoke. In the hall outside they heard the sound of feet and the click of the lock as someone opened the door. Then there was a murmur of voices, a soft insidious tone mingled with the strident Suffolk accent. Then the door of the room in which they sat opened and old Cuddy, flustered and excited, appeared on the threshold.

She was a spare, scrupulously tidy old lady, with a round red face and a lot of combs in her scant hair. She wore a black apron over a particularly vivid magenta woollen frock.

She came in, and striding across the room handed Biddy a card on a small brass platter. The girl took it in astonishment, Mr Campion coming up behind her.

She read it aloud:

'MR ANTHONY DATCHETT, PALMIST'.

Chapter 6

The Man in Dress Clothes

'Anthony Datchett?' said Mr Campion, reading over Biddy's shoulder. 'Not a gate-crasher, I hope. I personally superintended all the invitations. He can't come palming at this time of night.'

Giles looked relieved. 'Oh, that's *the* palmist?' he said. 'He must be rather a character. I met Guffy Randall at the Dog Trials last week; he was telling me about him then.'

'A fortune teller?' said Judge Lobbett, joining in. 'That's interesting. A gipsy?'

'Oh no, sir!' Old Cuddy was startled out of her silence. 'He's a gentleman, with a car as big as yours, sir.'

'Yes, that's right,' said Giles. 'He's an extraordinary chap. Apparently he turns up after dinner at country houses and shells out the past and present for five bob a time. Anyway, that sort of thing. Rather funny: he told Guffy Randall that a beautiful creature was going to throw him over and he was going to be pretty seriously hurt by it. Guffy was quite rattled. He didn't ride to hounds for a fortnight, and it wasn't until Rosemary Waterhouse broke off their engagement that he realized what the chap meant. He was awfully relieved.'

Marlowe Lobbett laughed. 'Let's have him in,' he said, and glanced at Campion questioningly.

The young man in horn-rimmed spectacles was lounging against the back of the settee where the two girls were sitting.

'Since Owl Friday falls on a Wednesday this year,' he said, 'and that, I understand, means trouble anyhow, we may as well see him and hear the worst.'

Cuddy bustled off. Then the door with its faded tapestry portière swept open, making a quiet rustling sound. Everyone sat forward instinctively, and a sudden cold draught from the open hall door passed through the room.

On the threshold a man stood smiling at them. As they looked at him the vague feeling of apprehension which had descended upon them when they heard the warning cry over the marshes now grew into a reality, and yet there was nothing in the stranger's appearance that was obviously alarming.

Small, slight, immaculately dressed in well-cut tails, he might have been any age. His face was covered with a reddish-brown curling beard; sparse and silky, it formed two small goat curls at the point of his chin, and above it his lips appeared, narrow and shapely, disclosing even teeth.

The face would have been attractive had it not been for the eyes. They were small, slightly oblique, and of a pale indeterminate colour with extremely small pupils.

The stranger came forward. 'I am so glad that you decided to see me,' he said, and for the first time they heard clearly the voice that had been a murmur outside. It was low and soft, peculiarly insinuating, and yet not altogether unpleasing.

Mr Campion regarded him speculatively.

'Perhaps I had better introduce myself more fully,' the stranger went on. 'My name is Anthony Datchett. I am an itinerant palmist. It is my custom to tell fortunes for a small fee –' He paused and glanced round the room, his curious eyes resting at last upon Giles. 'I should be delighted if one or two of you would consent to let me give a reading. If I do, I can promise you one thing. The truth.'

He was still looking at Giles as he finished speaking, and the others were surprised to see the boy get up immediately and cross over to him. He was not mesmerized; there was no suggestion of any trance or coma, yet he seemed completely subjected to the stranger.

Giles held out his hands. 'Tell me,' he said.

The stranger glanced towards the deep window-seat at the far end of the room. 'Certainly,' he said. 'Shall we go over there? I don't like an audience for my readings,' he explained, smiling at the others. 'It prevents one from being frank, I feel.'

'The only man who ever told my fortune,' said Mr Campion, 'was an income-tax collector.'

The stranger turned. 'Did he tell you about the Seven Whistlers?' he said.

No flicker of surprise appeared upon Mr Campion's rather foolish face, and the stranger glanced round swiftly, but nowhere had the thrust gone home. He walked over to the window-seat with Giles beside him, and was presently engrossed in the boy's hand.

Mr Campion perched himself beside Biddy on the arm of the settee in a direct line between the fortune teller and Judge Lobbett.

'The time has come,' he began, the fatuous expression returning to his face, 'when I think our distinguished visitors ought to hear my prize collection of old saws, rustic wisecracks, and gleanings from the soil. After years of research I am able to lay before you, ladies and gentlemen, one or two little gems. Firstly:

> When owd Parson wears two coats
> It be a powerful year for oats.

Consider the simplicity of that!' he continued with complete seriousness. 'The little moral neatly put, the rustic spirit of prophecy epitomized in a single phrase. And then of course:

> Owl hoots once up in the rafter,
> 'Nother hoot be comin' after.

That needs no comment from me.'

They laughed, eager to escape the tension of the last few minutes. At the far end of the room the murmur of the fortune teller went on steadily.

Mr Campion continued. He chattered without effort, apparently completely lost to the rest of the world.

'I knew a man once,' he said, 'who managed by stealth to attend a Weevil Sabbath at Mould. He went prepared to witness fearful rites, but when he got there he found it wasn't the genuine thing at all, but the yearly outing of the Latter Day Nebuchadnezzars, the famous grass-eating society. He didn't see a single weevil.'

He would have gone on had not Giles suddenly returned to the group. His expression was one of incredulous amazement.

'This is astounding,' he said. 'The chap seems to know all about me – things I hadn't told to anybody. Biddy, you must get him to tell your fortune.'

Some of the uneasiness the occupants of the room had felt at the arrival of their strange visitor began to disappear, but all the same there was no great eagerness on anyone's part to hurry over to the strange slight figure in the window-seat whose eyes seemed to be gazing at them all impartially.

It was at this moment that the attention of the party focused upon the rector. He had not moved nor spoken, but a change had taken place in his appearance. Biddy, glancing at him casually, was appalled by a look of great age which she had never noticed before. His jaw seemed to have sunk, his eyelids became grey and webby.

To their surprise he rose to his feet and walked a little unsteadily across the room to the fortune teller, who appeared to be waiting for him.

As the soft murmur began again Giles began to talk enthusiastically about his experience. 'He's an amazing chap,' he said quietly.

'What did he tell you?' said Campion.

'Well.' Giles was childlike in his mystification. 'What really got me was when he said I was thinking of entering a horse for the Monewdon Show next month. I know, of course, that's fairly obvious. But he told me I wouldn't send my favourite mare as I'd intended, but I'd send a hunter. That's really most extraordinary, because I went down to look at Lilac Lady just before dinner and I made up my mind that I couldn't get her into really decent condition in the time. I was wondering if I wouldn't enter St Chris, or let it go this year. I hadn't mentioned that to a soul.' He laughed. 'It's crazy, isn't it? He also told me the usual bunk – to beware of wagging tongues, and so on. He hinted at some sort of scandal, I thought. I didn't quite get it. I wonder what he's telling old St Swithin.'

He glanced over his shoulder to where the fortune teller sat upright in the window-seat, the candlelight making fantastic shadows on his unusual face. He was speaking in the same subdued monotone, which they could hear quite plainly without being able to distinguish the words.

They could not see the rector's face. He was bending forward, his hands cupped before the stranger.

'He seems interested all right,' said Marlowe.

Biddy laughed. 'Doesn't he?' she said. 'I do hope he's promising him plenty of adventures. He has led such a good quiet life.'

'I doubt if he'd like it,' said Giles. 'Tranquillity has always been St Swithin's note.'

'That seems to be the note of the whole place,' said Judge Lobbett, and sighed.

'Hullo, they've finished,' Marlowe said, as the rector and the stranger came down the room together. The fortune teller was smiling, suave and completely at ease. Swithin Cush looked thoughtful.

Biddy turned to him smiling. 'What sort of luck did you have, St Swithin?' she said.

The old man put a hand on her shoulder. 'My dear, I'm too old to have any fortune at all,' he said. He pulled out his old turnip watch. 'I must go to bed,' he remarked. 'I know you won't mind.' He turned to Judge Lobbett. 'We keep early hours in the country.'

He spoke the words absently as if he did not expect any reply, and while the others gathered round the fortune teller he returned once more to the girl. 'Good night, my dear,' he said. 'Give my love to Giles.'

She looked up at him without surprise. He often said unexpected things; but as she did so she caught his eyes before he had time to lower them, and for an instant she was afraid.

The old man departed, taking his storm lantern from Cuddy in the hall, although the night was fine and moonlit.

The fortune teller still dominated the room, and the old man's going made very little impression. The stranger's quiet, even voice was raised a little in surprise.

'I did not realize that it was so late,' he said. 'It was a longer drive here than I expected. I can tell only one more fortune. I will read the hand aloud so that you can all hear. Let it be someone to whom I can promise nothing but happiness.' He turned to Isopel. 'Will you permit me to tell yours?'

The girl looked at him dubiously, but with Giles at her side and Marlowe and Mr Campion leaning over the settee behind her, it seemed ridiculous to be afraid.

The stranger took her hand in his own, and when he turned his palm uppermost they saw with a little surprise that the natural fold of his hand made no permanent crease. The skin was smooth and unlined.

'I was right,' he said, holding the girl's small hand out for inspection. 'You have had troubles; they will end, though not perhaps as you expect. You will love, you will be loved. I see you in strange company at least twice in your life. The thing you remember most clearly,' he went on with sudden intensity, 'is lying on a bed of thick fur with the head of an animal looking down at you. Isn't that so?'

Judge Lobbett and his daughter exchanged astonished glances, and a smothered exclamation escaped Marlowe. Giles and Biddy glanced at their visitor inquiringly, and after some hesitation Isopel explained. 'When I was a child,' she said, 'we were on holiday in the Rockies. I got lost. A trapper found me and I stayed in his cabin for a few hours until father found me. The trapper told me to lie down, and I rested on a heap of skins by the fire. There was a bear skin on the wall with a roughly stuffed head. I couldn't take my eyes off it. It was terrible, grotesque, and out of shape. It's one of my most usual nightmares. I don't know how you knew,' she finished, staring at the fortune teller, her dark eyes widening as she realized the wonder.

The stranger smiled and went on. His voice revealed a soothing quality.

'You will have your dark hour,' he said, 'but it will pass. There is serenity for you. Beware of strangers, although you will not marry one of your own people. Your domains will be wide, and you will know the peace which is the lowing of kine over small meadows. That is your fortune. It is a pity that I cannot promise as much to you all.'

He spoke the last words softly, and although his tone was unchanged, the soothing effect of Isopel's reading was completely spoiled, and an unpleasant flavour remained.

He made his adieux immediately afterwards, and Giles and Marlowe settled with him, paying the trifling sum he demanded with some surprise.

The car disappeared down the narrow road. As it passed, the whistle that had heralded its approach sounded once more from the garden. The seven cries were repeated one after the other, each fainter and farther off than the one before. Mr Campion and Giles were standing with Marlowe.

'Seven,' said Giles. 'The Seven Whistlers. That means the end of the world, so they say.'

'That means he's gone,' said Mr Campion with relief. 'My respected friends George and 'Anry, with their five sons, have performed their spot of policing with great success. No one comes over the Stroud at night in future without our knowing on the moment. These blessed lads are posted every five hundred yards along the road. The moment a stranger passes any one of them – well, it's Owl Friday. Trespassers will be persecuted, you see.'

They went back towards the door laughing. Biddy met them on the threshold. Judge Lobbett and his daughter were behind her, and a stout perplexed old woman who had evidently entered by the back way hovered at her side.

Biddy was pale and her brown eyes spoke unnamed terrors. There was something in her hand which she held out to her brother.

'Giles,' she said, 'look at this. Alice has just brought it over.'

The boy took the crumpled piece of paper and the big old-fashioned ring she gave him. It lay gleaming in his hand.

'"Giles and Albert come over alone,"' he read slowly.

A look of horror suddenly dawned in his face.

'St Swithin!' he said breathlessly. 'His ring! He would never part with that unless —'

The words were silenced by a sound which reached them clearly through the open window, sharp and unmistakable. A gunshot on the night air.

Chapter 7

By the Light of the Hurricane

The old woman screamed, a shrill stifled sound in her throat. They caught a fleeting impression of her face, still and horrified, as if carved out of red sandstone, her small black eyes dilated. She suddenly started for the door.

Mr Campion laid a hand upon her arm. He was unnaturally quiet in his movements, his face expressionless.

'Wait, Alice,' he said. 'Giles and I will go first.'

'Leave I go,' said the old woman, wrenching her arm away. 'Leave I go, I tell 'ee.'

Biddy came forward. 'Stay here, Alice,' she said gently. 'Stay here. He said they were to go alone.'

Alice suffered herself to be led back into the room. Judge Lobbett stood between his two children, an inscrutable expression on his face. Isopel clung to him. Marlowe looked on gravely, ready to help when the occasion should arise.

Mr Campion touched Giles upon the shoulder. 'Come along,' he said. They hurried out of the house together.

The Rectory lay across the green, standing back from the road down a long ill-kept gravelled drive lined with heavy shrubberies and tall trees. The house appeared to be in darkness as they approached, but the front door stood open under the ivy-covered porch.

Mr Campion turned to Giles. 'Let me go first,' he said softly. 'You never know.'

Giles hung back unwillingly, but he did not attempt to remonstrate. Campion went on into the dark house alone.

In front of him a door stood open through which the room beyond was faintly visible.

He went in.

A moment or so later he reappeared on the porch. Giles caught a glimpse of his face in the moonlight.

'Come in, will you, old boy?' he said quietly, and Giles knew that the question which had been on his lips had been answered.

The two men went quietly into the house. The old rector's study was the only room with any light in it, and that was given only by the hurricane lantern which he had brought from the Dower House such a short while ago. It stood upon the heavy writing table shedding a diffused light over parts of the sombre place. It was a big rectangular room with a fireplace at one end and a bay window at the other and bookshelves ranged all along the intervening walls.

The desk was set parallel to the fireplace, and the rector's old chair with its dilapidated leather seat was pushed back from it as if he had just risen. The fire glowed dully in the grate.

Giles looked round anxiously.

'Where?' he began, and Campion pointed silently to a door corresponding to the one through which they had entered, on the other side of the fireplace. Giles recognized it as leading to the tiny robing-room which a thoughtful ancestor of his own had built off the study. The door was closed, and from under it there issued a thin dark trickle of blood on the worn brown linoleum.

Giles walked over and opened the door. He struck a match and held it high. The flickering light filled the tiny apartment for an instant and died out. His hand fell to his side. Then he shut the door unsteadily and turned to Campion. His face was very pale, and he moistened his lips with his tongue nervously.

'His old shotgun,' he said.

Campion nodded.

'In his mouth – tied a string to the trigger. It's the usual way.' The boy sank down in the chair. 'Suicide?' he said. 'My God – old St Swithin!'

Campion stood staring at the closed door. 'Why?' he said. 'In the name of all that's extraordinary, *why*?'

A step in the hall startled them both. Alice Broom, the housekeeper, appeared on the threshold. Her black eyes fixed them questioningly.

'He shot hisself?' she burst out. 'I saw the old gun was gone, but I never thought. Oh, dear Lord, have mercy on his soul!' She flopped down on her knees where she was and covered her face with her hands.

The sight of her helplessness brought Giles to himself. He and Campion lifted her up, and together they led her to the chair by the desk. She started away from it like a frightened sheep.

'Not in his chair. I'll not sit in his chair,' she said hysterically. 'The chair of the dead!'

The unexpectedness of her superstition breaking through her grief startled them oddly. They sat her down in the armchair by the fireplace, where she sat sobbing quietly into her cupped hands.

Campion took command of the situation.

'Look here, Giles,' he said, 'we shall want a doctor and the police. You haven't either in the village, have you?'

Giles shook his head. 'No. We shall have to get old Wheeler over from Heronhoe. The nearest bobby's there, too. Campion, this is ghastly. Why did he do it? Why did he do it?'

The other pointed to a letter propped up against the inkstand on the desk, next to the lantern. It was addressed in Swithin Cush's spidery old-fashioned writing:

HENRY TOPLISS, ESQ.

'Who's that? The coroner?' he demanded. Giles nodded, and again the incredulous expression passed over his face.

'He must have done it quite deliberately,' he said. 'I can't understand it. You don't think that fortune teller —'

Campion put his hand up warningly. There was the sound of feet in the hall.

Biddy came first, the others behind her. Her face was white and twisted with anxiety. She glanced round the room and her eye fell upon the closed door almost immediately. With a little cry she advanced towards it. Campion darted forward and drew her back.

'No, old dear, don't go in,' he said softly. 'You can't do anything.' The hand he held grew cold and the slender fingers bit into his flesh.

Campion put his arm round her until Isopel Lobbett came up, and, slipping her hand through Biddy's, led her to a chair by the fire.

Judge Lobbett and Marlowe came forward and Giles explained the situation to them as well as he could.

The old man was horrified.

'This is terrible,' he said. 'Terrible! I —' Words seemed to fail him, and he stood silent for a moment, rendered completely helpless by the shock. Gradually his old practical self reasserted itself. 'Isopel,' he said gently, 'take Miss Paget back to the Dower House and stay there with her, my dear, while we see what's to be done here.'

Campion joined the two younger men. 'Giles,' he said, 'if you and Marlowe would take a car and go in to Heronhoe and bring back a doctor and the police, that's as much as we can do. I'll get Alice up to her room. And then, if you don't mind, sir,' he added, turning to old Lobbett, 'we'll wait for them here.'

The two younger men jumped at the chance of doing something, and hurried off.

Isopel and Biddy went back to the Dower House. Biddy did not cry, but her face had not lost the strained twisted look which had been noticeable when she first came into the Rectory.

Campion watched her out of the doorway and then turned his attention to Alice. The problem of her disposal would have presented untold difficulties had it not been suddenly solved by the unexpected appearance of George. The old man had heard the shot while watching in the Dower garden and had followed Judge Lobbett over.

Hat in hand, his eyes goggling, he listened to the curt explanation Campion gave him.

'Rector dead,' he said, and repeated the words over and over again to himself, the horror and shock which he felt slowly becoming visible on his face.

'I'll take Al-us along,' he said at last. 'She's my sister. My wife'll take care o' she. She's looked after he so long this'll come like a shock to her, like.'

He helped the old woman to her feet and guided her with awkward elaborateness out of the room.

'Good night. Good night,' he said.

Campion hurried after him. 'George,' he said, 'don't rouse the village, will you?'

The old man turned on him.

'No, sir. 'Tis best in time like this to keep the mouth shut till after police be gone.'

With which unexpected remark he clumped off. Campion went back to the study and Judge Lobbett.

The old man stood by the fireplace, one hand upon the heavy oak mantel. Campion lit the candles in the iron sticks on the shelf, and then sat down quietly on the other side of the fireplace and took out a cigarette.

'This is a bad business,' said the old man suddenly; 'a terrible bad business. Death seems to follow me as gulls follow a ship.'

Campion said nothing. He had thrown a log of wood upon the fire and the gentle crackling as the bark caught was the only sound of the big dimly-lit room. On the brown oilcloth behind him the thin stream of blood congealed slowly.

Judge Lobbett cleared his throat.

'Of course, you know,' he began, 'I'm not a fool. I know Marlowe's got you to bring me down here. I didn't say anything because I like this sort of life. But if I'd dreamed that I should bring a tragedy like this into the lives of such kindly homely folk, nothing would have induced me to come here. I feel it can't be a coincidence,' he added abruptly, 'and yet there seems no doubt that it was suicide.'

Campion spoke quietly.

'It was suicide. No doubt at all, I think. He left a letter to the coroner.'

'Is that so?' The old man looked up sharply. 'It was premeditated, then. Have you any idea why he did it?'

'None at all.' Campion spoke gravely. 'This is the most astounding thing I've ever experienced. If I hadn't seen that letter I should have said it was a brainstorm.'

Crowdy Lobbett sat down in the chair opposite the younger man and rested his elbows on his knees, his big hands locked tightly together.

'I reckon you and I ought to understand one another before we go any farther,' he said. 'Of course I remember you on board ship. That was a very smart piece of work of yours, and I'm more than grateful. But I feel I've been following your instructions without knowing where I'm going long enough. I meant to have a talk with you this evening anyhow, even if this terrible thing hadn't made it imperative. Marlowe engaged you to look after me. I'll say I know that much. You're not a policeman, are you?'

'Hardly,' said Mr Campion. 'I believe I was recommended to your son by Scotland Yard, though,' he added with a faint smile. 'I'm not quite a private detective, you know. I suggested that you come here because I believe that you'll be safer here than anywhere, and that your family will run less risk.'

Judge Lobbett looked at him sharply.

'You can't understand me letting Isopel into it, can you?' he said. 'Where else would she be safer than where I can watch over her myself?'

Mr Campion offered no opinion.

'Just how much do you know?' said Judge Lobbett.

The young man looked more thoughtful. 'I know enough to realize that it's not revenge pure and simple that they're after you for,' he said at last. 'That's patent from common or garden Holmic deduction. In

New York they were trying to frighten you. That points to the fact that you had a line on them.' He paused and eyed the other man questioningly. Lobbett signed to him to go on and he continued: 'Then I think they must have decided that, had you a definite line, you'd have used it before,' he said. 'They decided to kill you. You escaped. One of the first things you did when you got to London was to consult MacNab, the cipher expert. That put the wind up them again. They want to know what you hold first, then they want your blood. I should say myself,' he added, 'that you've got a clue from one of Simister's gang which you can't decipher yourself as yet. Isn't that so?'

Lobbett stared back at him in astonishment.

'I don't mind telling you,' he said, 'that when I first saw you, Mr Campion, I thought you were the biggest goddam fool ever made; but I'm now beginning to wonder if you're not some sort of telepathy expert.' He leaned forward. 'I'll say you're right, and I may as well tell you MacNab didn't help me any, but he was the first man I felt I could trust to see what I had. I've got one end of the string, you see, but if any of that crowd should get wind of what it is they'd cut it higher up and then the one chance I've got of stopping this thing at the head would be lost for ever. As it is, the thing's no more use to me than so much junk. And I daren't and won't confide in any of you youngsters.'

The determined expression on the judge's face and the obstinate lines about his mouth made the younger decide in an instant that, upon this point at any rate, he would be as stubborn as a mule.

'You intend, I suppose,' he said, 'to stay here until you've found the solution to your crossword?'

Judge Lobbett nodded. 'I certainly had that idea,' he said. 'But after the terrible affair this evening I don't know what to say.' He glanced at Campion. 'Look here,' he said. 'In your opinion what sort of chance have I got of getting my man if I stay here?'

The younger man rose to his feet. 'One,' he said, an unusually convincing tone in his voice. 'You're in England, and I don't think it would be any too easy for our friend Simister to do anything on a very big scale. He couldn't get half his best people out of your country, for instance, so there's just one chance in a hundred that he'll do the job himself. The mountain may come to Mahomet for once; and in that case I doubt whether anyone is in any real danger except yourself.'

Judge Lobbett nodded to the closed door behind the younger man. 'Maybe so,' he said, 'but what about that?'

Campion remained silent for some moments, his hands thrust deep in his pockets.

'I fancy,' he said at last, hesitating as if he were weighing every word, 'that there's something more than ordinarily mysterious about that. Poor old boy!'

Chapter 8

The Envelope

The change in the drawing-room in the Dower House was extraordinary. The cosiness, the peace had vanished. The fire had burned down to a few red and grey coals, the candles had shrunk in their sticks, and the room was cold and desolate.

The two girls sat huddled together in the window-seat. Biddy was not crying; she sat up stiffly, her back against the folded wooden shutter. Her face was very pale, and the same twisted, suffering expression was still engraved upon it.

The other girl sat close to her, her small hand resting upon her knee.

'I can't tell you how unbelievable it is,' Biddy burst out suddenly, keeping her voice down instinctively as if she feared to be overheard. 'It's so unlike him. I didn't think he had a care in the world, and no greater worry than the attendance at the Sunday school. Why should he have done this horrible, horrible thing?'

Isopel could not answer her.

'To think of it! He must have known when he said good night to me. He must have gone over there deliberately, written the letter to Mr Topliss, sent Alice over here with that note, and then gone into that little cupboard all by himself and – oh –'

She leaned back against the shutter and closed her eyes.

Isopel nodded. 'I know,' she said. The lashes drooped over her dark eyes and a sombre expression passed over her young face. 'For the last six weeks I've lived in an atmosphere like this. I'm growing callous, I think. At first, Schuyler, father's secretary. I'd known him since I was a kid. They found him in dad's chair, shot through the head.' She shuddered. 'They must have shot him through the window from a block opposite. Ever since then it's been one after the other. Wills – the butler; then our new chauffeur, and then Doc Wetherby, who was walking down the street with father. I was scared then. But afterwards, on board ship and at our hotel in London, I was so frightened I thought I should go out of my mind. And then when we came down here it seemed like an escape.' She sighed. 'That house of yours across the park, and this one – they were so quiet, undisturbed for centuries, it seemed that nothing terrible could happen in them. But now we've brought you this horror. Sometimes I feel' – her voice sank to a whisper – 'that we've roused the devil. There's some ghastly evil power dogging us, something from which we can't escape.'

She spoke quite seriously, and the gravity of her voice, coupled with the tragedy which had overwhelmed her, infected the other girl with some of her terror.

'But,' said Biddy, struggling to regain her common sense, 'St Swithin killed himself. There's no doubt of that, they say. If it were a murder it wouldn't be so horrible. Oh,' she said irrelevantly, 'I wish Giles would come back.'

A gentle tap on the door startled them both. Old Cuddy appeared with a tray. The old woman's hands trembled. She had been told of the tragedy and had reacted to it in her own practical way.

'I've brought you both a cup of cocoa, Miss Biddy,' she said.

She set the tray down beside them and without further words began to make the fire and refill the emptying candlesticks. They drank the cocoa gratefully. The heavy stimulant soothed their nerves and they sat quiet until far away over the silhouetted hedge tops they saw the faint glow of headlights against the sky. The light came nearer until they heard the car whisper past the house. Then all was black again.

'Who will they have got? The doctor and the sheriff?' said Isopel nervously.

Biddy shook her head. 'It'll be Dr Wheeler and Peck, the Heronhoe policeman, I suppose,' she said; and quite suddenly she turned her face towards the shutter and wept.

In the study across the green Dr Wheeler, a short, thick-set, oldish man with a natural air of importance, set his bag down upon the desk and took off his coat.

Peck, the Heronhoe police-constable, red-faced and perspiring with unaccustomed responsibility, clutched his notebook unhappily.

Giles and Marlowe had followed them into the room and now stood gravely in the doorway. Giles introduced Judge Lobbett and Albert Campion.

The doctor nodded to them curtly.

'This is bad,' he said. 'Terrible. Not like the old man. I saw him only the other day. He seemed quite cheerful. Where's the body, please?' He spoke briskly.

Giles indicated the door of the robing-room. 'We've left him just as he fell, sir. There was nothing to be done. He – he's practically blown his head off.'

The little doctor nodded. 'Yes, quite,' he said, taking the affair completely into his capable hands. 'We shall need some light, I suppose. Peck, bring the lantern, will you?'

His deference to their susceptibilities was not lost upon the others, and they were grateful.

The closet door swung open and the doctor, stepping carefully to avoid the stream of blood, went in, the constable walking behind him, the lantern held high.

Some of the horror that they saw was communicated to the four who now stood upon the hearthrug waiting. Dr Wheeler reappeared within a few minutes, Peck following him, stolid and unmoved.

The doctor shook his head. 'Very nasty,' he said quietly. 'Death must have been absolutely instantaneous, though. We must get him out of there. We'll need a shed door, and if you could get a sheet, Giles – How's Biddy?' he broke off. 'Is she all right? Over at the Dower House? I'll go in and see her before I go.'

Giles explained that Isopel was with her, and the old man, who had known the brother and sister since they were children, seemed considerably relieved. Campion and Marlowe went through the dark stone kitchens of the Rectory. They let themselves into the brick yard, and lifting a toolshed door off its hinges brought it carefully into the house. Giles was upstairs in search of a sheet: they could hear him stumbling about on the uneven floors.

With the constable holding the light, they assisted the doctor to lift the gruesome sightless thing on to the improvised stretcher. The doctor had thrown a surplice that had been hanging on the wall over all that remained of the old man before Giles returned with the sheet.

They laid the stretcher on a hastily arranged trestle of chairs at the far end of the room. Campion swung the great shutters across the windows, and then without speaking they trooped off to the scullery to wash.

Peck was particularly anxious to avoid troubling the Pagets and their friends any more than was absolutely necessary, and when he once more produced his notebook it was with an air of apology.

'There's just one or two things I'll have to make a note of,' he began, clearing his throat nervously. 'You'd say the gun was fired by the deceased 'imself?'

'Oh, yes, no doubt about that.' The doctor was struggling into the coat Giles held for him. 'You'll go to Mr Topliss, Peck? Tell him I'll 'phone him in the morning.'

'Mr Cush left a letter for Mr Topliss,' said Campion, pointing to the big yellow envelope on the desk. The policeman moved forward clumsily to take it, and the doctor sighed with relief.

'I expect that'll make it all very simple,' he said. 'I was afraid from the look of things there might be a lot of tedious questioning for you all. This'll probably mean only a formal inquest.'

The constable slipped the letter into his pocket. 'I'll ride out to Mr Topliss first thing,' he said. 'There's just one thing, 'owever, if you don't mind. Where was you all when the shot was fired?'

'All together,' said Giles, 'in the drawing-room at the Dower House just across the green there.'

'I see,' said Peck, writing laboriously. 'And the housekeeper, Mrs Broom, where was she?'

'She was with us,' said Giles. 'She brought a message from St Swithin – I mean Mr Cush.'

'Oh?' said the constable with interest. 'What was that?'

Giles handed him the slip of paper and the countryman held it to the light. '"Giles and Albert come over alone,"' he read. 'Albert – that'll be you, sir?' he said, turning to Campion.

'Yes,' the young man nodded. 'As soon as we got the message we heard the shot.'

'I see. And that was when you was over at the Dower House? That makes it seem very deliberate, don't it, sir?' said Peck, turning to the doctor.

'There's no doubt that it was deliberate.' The medical man spoke emphatically.

'And you two gentlemen found the body, I suppose?' said Peck, coming to the end of his entries with relief. 'No idea of cause or reason, sir, I suppose?' he added, turning to Giles.

'None at all,' said Giles.

'Mr Topliss's letter will explain all that, be sure,' said Dr Wheeler, pulling on his gloves with an air of finality. 'I'll go over to your sister now, Giles.'

At this juncture the question of who was to remain with the body of the old rector became a pressing one. Giles and Campion sat down, one on either side of the fireplace, and prepared for the vigil, and would have stayed there alone in spite of Marlowe's generous offer to remain with them, had not Alice, the old housekeeper, appeared in the doorway.

She had got over her first outburst of grief, and the stolid stoicism of the countrywoman who accepts birth and death, spring and winter in the same spirit had come to her rescue. Her red face was set and unmoved.

'You go to your bed, Master Giles,' she said. 'I'm staying.' She waved aside his protestations. 'I looked arter him in loife. I'll look arter him in death,' she said. 'He's old,' she explained quaintly. 'He wouldn't loike nobody but me. Good night to you.'

They accepted their dismissal.

Campion was the last to leave, and some thought of the old woman alone with the horror passing through his mind, he turned to her and whispered a few words of warning.

She looked at him, faint surprise showing in her small eyes. 'I shan't be afeard o'him,' she said. 'What if there's blood? 'Tis his, ain't it? I looked arter him since I were a young woman, but no doubt you meant well. Good night.'

He followed the others out into the drive. They walked in silence over to the Dower House, where the doctor was soothing the two girls in his brisk professional manner.

Old Lobbett moved quietly over to Campion. 'I'll take my girl up to the Manor,' he said. 'I guess we won't intrude on you people any longer. Get Miss Paget to go to bed. There's nothing like sleep. Time for talking in the morning.'

With the departure of the Lobbetts the affair assumed a more intimate aspect. Giles sat with his arm round Biddy. Campion stood on the hearthrug, one elbow on the mantelpiece.

The doctor and Peck departed with the reassurance that all needful arrangements would be made.

'Now,' said Giles explosively, 'what in the name of creation does it all mean?'

Biddy turned to Campion appealingly. 'What does it all mean, Albert? How did it happen? You knew him almost as well as we did. Why did he do it?'

Campion thrust his hand into his coat pocket and produced a bulky yellow envelope and handed it to them.

It was addressed, 'For Giles, Biddy, and Albert Campion', and was marked in the corner 'Confidential'.

'This was lying on the desk beside the note for the coroner,' he said.

'I thought it best to keep it till we were alone. You open it, Giles.'

The boy tore open the flap with unsteady fingers and drew out the contents. There was a second envelope marked 'Giles', a folded paper for Biddy, and something hard wrapped in a piece of notepaper for Campion. Giles handed them out gravely.

Biddy glanced at her message. There were only two lines. The old man's writing was shaky and almost illegible.

Tell Albert about our longest walk [it ran]. God bless you, my dear.

She handed the slip of paper to Campion, an expression of utter bewilderment on her face. 'He must have suddenly gone mad,' she said. 'How horrible – over there in the dark.'

Campion took the message from her and stared at it. Then he shook his head.

'He wasn't mad, Biddy. He was trying to tell us something, something that he didn't want anyone but us to know. Perhaps this will help us.' He began to unwrap the little package which bore his name. He drew off the paper and a murmur of surprise escaped him. He held out the little object in the palm of his hand.

It was a single ivory chessman, the red knight.

Chapter 9
'In Event of Trouble . . .'

'What does it mean?' Biddy sat back in her chair, her eyes fixed upon the little ivory figure in Campion's hand.

Giles was startled also. 'I recognize it, of course,' he said. 'It's one of his best set – the ones we seldom played with. What do you think, Albert?'

Campion dropped the chessman into his coat pocket. 'Suppose you read your letter?' he suggested.

Giles ripped open the thick envelope he held in his hand. 'Of course,' he said.

To everyone's surprise he drew out two sheets of closely written paper upon which the ink was dried and black. The letter had evidently been written some time before. Giles read it aloud, his young voice husky in the chill room.

'MY DEAR BOY:

'If ever you read this letter it will be because I shall have committed a crime the magnitude of which I realize fully. If, however, it does come to this, I ask you to believe that it was because I preferred to go to my death with my health and sanity than to weary out a tortured existence in which I should be a burden to you all, and a wretchedness to myself.

'I have known for a long time that I was a victim of a malignant and incurable disease, and my increasing fear has been that it would enfeeble not only my body but my mind. I ask you and Biddy to forgive me. I shall leave a note for the coroner which should relieve you from any ordeal in the court. However . . .

'This is underlined,' said Giles.

'. . . *in the event of any serious trouble* arising directly after my death, send Albert Campion to my old friend Alaric Watts, the Vicar of Kepesake in Suffolk, who will know the correct procedure in this situation.

'Something is crossed out here,' said Giles, holding the paper up to the light. 'The "this" has been put in afterwards. As far as I can see it looks as if he had first written "in so terrible a situation". Then it goes on, getting very wobbly towards the end.

'In any case I do most particularly ask your forgiveness and your prayers. My temptation was great. I succumbed to it. All my love to you, my children.
                                                                ST SWITHIN.

P.S. – My will, bequeathing my few belongings, is in my desk.'

'That's all,' said Giles.

Biddy broke the silence. There were tears in her eyes, but she spoke firmly. 'Albert, the whole thing's a mistake; it's not true.'

Campion looked at her thoughtfully. 'How do you mean?' he said.

'I mean' – Biddy's voice rose a little – 'St Swithin was no more ill than you or I. He's hiding something, or shielding someone, or –' Her voice died away into silence.

Campion took the letter from Giles and spread it out on the table in front of him. 'It's been written a long time,' he said, 'before we'd heard of the Lobbetts. Not long after your father died, I should say.'

Biddy was sitting bolt upright, her eyes shining. 'That doesn't alter it,' she said. 'St Swithin's never been ill in his life. I've never heard him complain even of a headache. He's been moody lately, a little strange, but not ill. Besides, why did he choose such a curious time to kill himself? Just after that – that man was here.'

The brother and sister looked at Campion. He sat regarding them, his pale eyes grave behind his spectacles.

'My dear old birds,' he said, 'I don't know him. You say you've heard of him, Giles?'

The boy nodded. 'Yes. From all over the county. I told you about Guffy, and a man who had a place round by Hadleigh spoke of him. He's been going for several years, I believe, off and on. He turned up at Maplestone Hall on Christmas Day and was a great success. That's when Guffy saw him.'

'Maplestone Hall?' said Campion, looking up. 'Wasn't there a bit of a row there a month or so ago? I thought I read something about it.'

Giles nodded. 'A libel case or something,' he said. 'Something fishy, anyway. Guffy had some rambling yarn about it.'

Biddy leaned across the table and put her hand on Campion's arm. 'Albert,' she said, 'that man killed St Swithin.'

'But my dear old girl,' he protested gently. 'We had watchers all along the road and the seven whistles came quite clearly. Besides, it was obviously a suicide. There's no getting away from it.'

'Oh, I *know*.' Biddy spoke impatiently. 'I know. I'm not saying that poor old St Swithin didn't shoot himself over there in the dark, but it was the man who really did it. That terrible man with the little red beard. He told him something. While we were all sitting here laughing round the fire, he said something that made St Swithin go right out and kill himself. I know it, I'm sure of it.'

Campion hesitated. 'It's too far-fetched,' he said.

'Do you think he was just an ordinary fortune teller?' Biddy's tone implied her opinion of the theory.

Campion shook his head. 'Oh no, I don't believe that for a moment. That bird, whoever he was, was up to some most fishy stunt. Oh no,' he went on thoughtfully, 'he was no ordinary gipsy's warning. That neat little exercise in telepathy was a stout piece of work. A chap like that could earn a fortune. And yet, what did he get at Maplestone Hall last Christmas? Certainly not fifty quid. And what did he get tonight? Oh no, he was up to some really nasty nap and double. I can't help feeling that he came to spy out the nakedness of the land.' His hand closed over Biddy's and he smiled at her wryly from behind his spectacles. 'Dear old St Swithin was too small game for him, I think, Biddy.'

'Then do you believe this?' Biddy tapped the letter lying on the table.

For some time Campion was silent. 'Not altogether,' he said at last. 'Where is Kepesake, Giles?'

'About twenty miles across country. It's not far from Bury. It's a tiny little village on the Larksley Estate. The story goes that an ancient Larksley, setting off to some war or other, left it to his mistress as a keepsake. I remember old Watts. He used to come over here and preach sometimes. He's an authority on Church history, I believe. Quite a nice old boy.'

'I think,' said Campion, 'that a visit is indicated. "In the event of any serious trouble" sounds ominous, without leading us anywhere.'

'And the red chessman?' said Giles.

Albert Campion drew the ivory knight out of his pocket and set it on the table before them. It was small, beautifully carved, and of a slightly unusual pattern, the horse's head being much more realistic than in most pieces. It was stained a bright scarlet and stood vivid and beautiful upon the polished walnut table. Giles picked it up and turned it over and then weighed it in his hand.

'It's too light to contain anything,' he said. 'Besides, that's such a fantastic idea. I'm afraid he was quite right, Biddy. The old boy had some disease that was affecting his mind and suddenly it sent him clean crazy.'

'That won't wash.' Biddy spoke vehemently. 'If St Swithin had actually thought he was ill he would have gone straight to Dr Wheeler. He believed in doctors. When he got that lump on his foot that he thought might be gout he was off to Heronhoe within the hour. The Shrine of Aesculapius he used to call it, you know.'

'How do you know he hasn't been to Wheeler?' Giles objected.

Biddy shot a withering glance at him. 'How could he, without us knowing? I should have had to drive him if he'd gone, and if Wheeler had come within a mile of the Rectory the village would have been full of it. That man – that man with the horrible red beard – I'm sure he is the real explanation. That chessman means something. The very fact that he sent it to Albert proves something.'

Giles looked at Campion. 'You think that fortune teller chap came here because of Judge Lobbett?' he asked.

Campion nodded. 'It doesn't seem unlikely.'

'And yet,' Giles persisted, 'you said yourself that he was a brilliant man. Could he be an ordinary spy? I never heard that Guffy Randall's fortune teller had a red beard. Straight, Campion, is there a chance that he could be Simister himself?'

Campion raised his head and his pale eyes did not waver.

'Well, there's always a chance, isn't there?' he said.

He got up and walked over to the fireplace and kicked a smouldering log in the grate. 'That's all there is to it for tonight,' he said. 'There's nothing else to be done as far as I can see. Unless –' he swung round, a frown upon his face – 'I'd forgotten. Of course. Perhaps the most important thing of all. Your message, Biddy. What did it mean?'

For an instant she looked at him blankly, she had forgotten the last of the three curious bequests. She took up the slip of paper from her lap, where it had been lying.

'Tell Albert about our longest walk. God bless you, my dear.'

'Your longest walk? Where was it? Where did you go?'

Campion spoke eagerly, coming across the room to her and looking down into her face.

The girl strove to compose her mind. 'We've gone for so many walks,' she began desperately. 'We've walked all over the place together. We got lost on the saltings one night. Alice came out to meet us with a hurricane. That must have been the time,' she went on suddenly. 'We reckoned we'd done fifteen miles.'

Campion shook his head. 'That doesn't tell us much. What else happened? Where did you go?'

The girl struggled to remember. 'We crossed the Stroud and went off on the farther saltings,' she said slowly. 'We went on for miles until we came to a belt of quick mud. Then we turned back. I remember it now. The sky grey and the water the same colour, the drab mud with the saltings brown beside it and the dykes cut out in red. Then there was the great pool of "soft". That was all.'

Campion was looking at her intently. 'Think, Biddy,' he said. 'Think, my sweet. Was that all? How did you know when you came to the quick mud, for instance?'

'Oh, there was a board up, you know. There always is.' She spoke carelessly, but then an expression of horror spread over her face. 'Oh, I see now,' she said breathlessly. 'The board said "Danger", Albert.'

Chapter 10
The Insanity of Swithin Cush

Giles and Judge Lobbett walked one on either side of Dr Wheeler out of the long room at the thatched 'Dog and Pheasant', and down the flint road towards the green and the Dower House.

It was still early. The inquest had taken scarcely half an hour and the village was still discussing the affair in the tap-room.

The morning was very sunny, although it was cold for late May and the last of the May-blossom trembled in a chill wind.

Dr Wheeler talked volubly. He found Judge Lobbett the best of audiences. The American had the great gift of being interested in everything with which he came into contact, and the doctor was only too anxious to give his opinions.

'A significant case,' he was saying. 'I don't like parsons as a rule. Too narrow. But Swithin Cush was an entirely different proposition, don't you know. I've known him ever since I came to this part of the country thirty years ago. I attended him once only that I remember. A strained tendon in his foot. A more healthy, hearty-living old man I never saw. And yet he gets an idea into his mind, imagines all sorts of things, and then goes and blows his head off.'

Judge Lobbett shot a bright sidelong glance at him.

'Then there was absolutely no trace of any disease?'

'Not at all, sir.' The doctor spoke emphatically. 'Just as I told Topliss in the court there. There was no reason why he shouldn't have gone on living perfectly healthily for another twenty years. And yet it's one of the most common forms of delusion,' he went on. 'I always put it down myself to the fact that the emotion of fear acts more noticeably on the digestive organs than on any other. Once a man is afraid that he has a malignant growth, he'll have plenty of physical corroboration to convince him. A pity! He had only to come to me, and I could have reassured him. Poor Biddy!' he went on. 'She won't take this easily, I'm afraid. They were great friends, she and the old man. He did his best to take your father's place, Giles.'

Giles did not reply, and Lobbett nodded.

'My girl's with her over at the Dower House,' he said. 'They get on very well together, those two.' He stooped and threw a stone for Addlepate, who had waited in the bar for Giles during the inquest and now gambolled foolishly in the dust.

'Remarkable what a durned fool that dog is,' he observed, as the mongrel darted off in pursuit, changed his mind, and returned to walk sedately behind them, his nose very close to the road. The doctor looked back at him.

'The silly part about that is,' he said, 'that I don't believe he can smell a thing.'

Lobbett laughed. 'He's Campion's dog, isn't he?' he said.

The doctor nodded. 'They say like dog, like master,' he observed dryly.

As they reached the Dower House they saw Mr Campion's little car standing outside the gate. The young man himself was bending over the open bonnet, flushed and heated. Marlowe and Biddy stood with Isopel in the porch watching him.

'Hullo, he's back!' said Giles, hurrying forward to where Addlepate was already prostrated before the car, all four legs waving in the air.

As the two older men advanced more slowly towards the group a figure emerged from the thatched post office and village shop and hurried towards them. He was a large white-looking man with fair hair so closely cropped that he appeared almost bald.

This was Mr Kettle, the village 'foreigner': that is to say, he was not a Suffolk man, but had been born, so it was believed, as far away as Yarmouth, a good forty miles off. His excessive politeness and his superiority made him the most unpopular man in the village community. He lived with his daughter, a sour-faced young woman, white and flabby as himself, and between them they managed not only the post office but the only shop for six miles.

He came through the long grass of the green at a dignified amble and bounded on to the road two or three paces ahead of the judge and the doctor.

'Letter, sir,' he said breathlessly, disclosing a Norfolk accent, over which a certain veneer of 'refeenment' had been spread. 'The second post 'as just come. And popping my 'ead out of the door, sir, I said to my daughter, I said, "there's the new squire".' He laid an unpleasant unction on the last word, and his attempt to curry favour was sickeningly transparent. He gasped again for breath, and hurried on.

'And my daughter, sir, she said, "Take it over to him, dad". And so I did.'

He handed the square white envelope to the judge as he finished speaking and stood squelching his white hands together, a ridiculous smirk on his face.

'We 'ave a very nice little shop 'ere, sir, and any time you're wanting anything up at the Manor 'all, sir, we shall only be too 'appy to send it up.'

The judge, who had listened in some bewilderment to this oration, his ears unaccustomed to the two distinct accents, the one affected and the other natural, felt in his pocket, having come to the conclusion, in common with so many other visitors to Europe, that the safe rule is, 'When in doubt, tip'.

Mr Kettle, who had determined to be obliging at all costs, refused the coin magnificently. 'Oh no, sir,' he said. 'Only too 'appy to do anything for you. Any time of the night or day, sir.' And turning, he ran off through the long grass, flapping his hands against his sides as he ran.

The doctor went to join the others. They were gathered round Giles.

'Yes, "Suicide during temporary insanity",' he was saying as the doctor came up. 'Topliss was very decent, I thought. It didn't take very long. Alice was there, very cut up. George's wife took her home. I've brought the doc. in to lunch, Biddy. How long has Albert been back?'

'Only about ten minutes.' It was Campion himself who spoke. 'The bit of sardine tin that keeps my carburettor from leaking into the mag. has slipped its bootlace. I shall be a minute or so. Some of the rigging has come adrift.'

Giles went over to him, and together they bent over the miscellaneous collection of hairpins and string that seemed to make Campion's car go.

'Well?' he murmured. 'Did you see him – Alaric Watts, I mean?'

'Yes,' said Campion, producing a small fountain of petrol from the carburettor, 'but there's no lift in the fog in his direction. He was very grieved at his old pal's death, but that's about all. He knows no more than we do.'

'That means, then,' said Giles, 'that St Swithin was really insane when he wrote us.'

'Yes,' said Campion thoughtfully, 'either that or else –' He glanced at his friend over the top of his spectacles. 'Or else the "serious trouble" has not yet arisen.'

Giles did not reply. Campion straightened his back and stood looking after the others, who, at Biddy's invitation, were disappearing into the house.

'Giles,' he said suddenly, 'do you like that American chap?'

'Marlowe? One of the best. I like him immensely. Biddy and I were talking about him this morning. She admires that type, you know.'

'That's what I mean,' said Campion. 'Now if I were to grow a beard,' he went on with apparent seriousness, 'what colour would you suggest? Something with lure, to cover all this up?' He indicated his face with a gesture. 'Let's go in, shall we? I hate to be out of anything.'

They reached the morning-room, where they were all gathered, drinking sherry as an aperitif. Judge Lobbett was speaking as they entered.

'I'm real sorry about this. I forgot every word about my letter to this firm. The picture got me interested, and as Miss Biddy had suggested it I wrote to them asking for the expert to be sent, directly before we all came over here that night. The things that happened after that put it right out of my mind.' He put a typewritten letter down upon the table. 'This note says their expert will arrive here by car tomorrow afternoon. I can easily put him off. I should feel it kind of ungracious to have him around at a time like this.'

'Is that about the pseudo-Romney?' Biddy came forward. 'Because if so, please don't let this – this terrible thing make any difference. St Swithin never disobliged anyone in his life and I know he'd hate to do it now.'

She spoke quietly, but with such conviction that it made it impossible for the old man to refuse her.

Giles nodded. 'That's true,' he said. 'Biddy's right about St Swithin. How I feel about it is: we can't do anything. Let's get away from the horror of it if we can.'

Marlowe picked up the letter. 'It says here, "The famous international expert, Mr A. Fergusson Barber"!'

'Eh?' said Mr Campion.

Biddy turned to him with interest. 'Do you know him?'

Mr Campion sighed. 'I've met him,' he said. 'He was on the *Elephantine*. As far as pictures are concerned he may be the Big Bezezuz himself, but as a guide, philosopher, and friend he's a menace.'

Marlowe grinned. 'He's a bore?'

'A bore?' said Mr Campion. 'He's worse than a movie star's confessions.'

Chapter 11
The Maze

They were having tea on the lawn at the Manor the following day. Judge Lobbett had insisted that his 'landlords', as he called them, should be present when the art expert arrived. The old man was anxious to do all he could to dispel the gloom which had settled over the Dower House, and since Giles himself had expressed the desire to carry on as usual, he was all the more eager to help.

Mr Campion had accompanied the twins as a matter of course, and Addlepate escorted them.

They had sat long over their tea and it was almost six o'clock when they arose. The sun was dropping behind the house, the last blaze of yellow light shone over the garden, gilding the green leaves and warming the pale browns of the tree stems. Some of the peace and contentment of the evening settled upon them.

'Isn't it lovely?' Isopel spoke enthusiastically.

Campion followed her gaze round the wide shrub-encircled lawn, through the high trees to the parkland beyond.

'Charming,' he said. 'I knew a man once, though, who said the country wasn't the country without paper bags. He was a millionaire at the time, having made all his money in the jellied-eel business. The only country he knew was Burnham Beeches and Epping on a bank holiday. When he had made his fortune and bought a big estate in Surrey he wasn't at all satisfied with it. The staff was in an awful stew until one of the secretaries imported half a ton of orange skins, a few peanut shells, and a gross or so of paper bags. That transformed the place, and the old boy's lived there very happily ever since. It's all a question of ideals, you know.'

Judge Lobbett rose from his deck chair. 'How about a walk round the estate?' he said. 'George tells me there's a maze over on the east side of the park.'

'So there is,' said Giles. 'Though I'm afraid it's not in very good condition. It hasn't been clipped for the last year or so.'

'It's still there, though,' said Biddy. 'Shall we go and have a look at it?'

They trooped off over the lawn to the narrow paved walk which, enclosed by low hedges, led through the parkland to a second and larger orchard and kitchen garden on the east side. At the far end of a wide strip of grass in which fruit trees stood they saw the maze before they reached it – a great square of yew, the dense bushes, which had once been trimmed as square as a marble block, now overgrown and uneven.

'It's quite big,' said Biddy. 'It stretches down the rest of the field on one side, and there's the road at the end. We used to play here a lot when we were children.'

She turned to find herself speaking only to Mr Campion. Judge Lobbett had gone on a little way in front. Giles and Isopel lagged behind. Marlowe had not come with them.

When she saw him her expression changed. She linked her arm through his. 'You haven't found out anything – about St Swithin, or the red chessman?'

Campion's arm gripped hers. 'Biddy,' he said softly, 'promise me. Never, never, never say anything about the red chessman to anyone. Never. Promise me.'

She looked at him sharply, a suggestion of fear in her eyes. He smiled at her reassuringly. 'Don't worry, old dear. Nothing to get the wind up about. But you must give me that promise.'

He did not attempt to disguise the seriousness of his tone.

'I promise,' she said, 'and Giles –?'

'That's all right,' said Campion; 'he's wise. He won't even mention it amongst ourselves.'

Mr Campion allowed his vacuous expression to fade for an instant. 'I say, Biddy, can you ever forgive me for getting you into this?'

She shot him one of her sharp inquiring glances. 'Then you think St Swithin had something to do with this – this other affair?'

Mr Campion did not look at her. 'How could he?' he said. But he spoke dully and without conviction.

'Is this the entrance?' Judge Lobbett's shout made them both look up. The old man was standing against the yew hedge, his light flannel suit outlining him sharply against the sombre background.

'That's right,' Biddy shouted back. 'I'm afraid you'll have to push your way through, here and there. Do you want to know the key?'

'No, I'll find my way myself.' He disappeared into the green walls on the last word. 'It's going to be easy,' he called, his voice only slightly muffled by the hedges.

'My own tour,' said Mr Campion, 'which our impetuous friend has missed, will be personally conducted by the greatest living authority on Barratry, Trigonometry, and the Kibbo Kift. I shall charge a small fee –'

Giles coming up with Isopel shouted, 'Found the centre, Mr Lobbett?'

'I'm just on it.' The reply came back from the middle of the dense square of yew. 'It's not very overgrown. There ought to be a lot of birds' nests here.'

'They're not fond of yew,' Biddy remarked.

'I don't believe it's got a middle,' came the judge's voice. 'Are you coming?'

'Righto.' It was Giles who called back. 'But the key is, turn to the left whenever possible.'

Mr Campion looked at him coldly. 'Cheating,' he said. 'Don't forget the old college, Brother. What would the boys of St Agatha's say? Remember our proud school motto, *"Floreat Fauna"*, which being translated means, of course, "Grow, you little beasts".'

Giles was about to retort when Biddy, who had been looking in the direction from which they had come, interrupted him.

'Oh, look,' she said. 'He's arrived.'

They looked round to see Marlowe coming down the path towards them, and beside him, smiling, self-important, and talking volubly, was Mr Fergusson Barber.

An expression of dismay appeared on Isopel's face. 'Oh, I remember him now,' she said. 'He was the bore at our table on the *Elephantine*. Look at Marlowe.'

The others smiled. The young American's disgust was evident. His keen dark face wore a dubious look, and he made no attempt to interrupt Mr Barber's flow. The expert carried a large flat picture case under his arm, but it did not hamper the freedom of his gesticulations.

'Hullo!' Campion murmured to Giles. 'He's brought some pictures to sell. I bet he says they're Cotmans. Whenever I see a leather case like that I say, "Hullo. The Great Defunct has been at it again."'

By this time Marlowe and the expert were upon them. Mr Barber bowed gravely to the ladies, and recognizing Campion, greeted him as a brother.

'We meet again, my friend,' he rumbled. 'You think I don't remember you,' he continued in the same gusty bellow, 'but I never forget a name or a face. Nothing ever escapes me. No, no, don't remind me. You told me your name just as you were leaving, I remember. Ah, yes, I have it. Mr Memorial – Albert Memorial.'

Everyone looked at Campion accusingly. That gentleman seemed not in the least abashed.

'How absurd of me,' he said. 'I gave you my address by mistake. My name is Campion. Albert Campion. You see how the error occurred.'

Although his gravity was perfect the others were not as successful, and the Oriental glanced at them suspiciously. Biddy reddened, and kicked Mr Campion gently to relieve her feelings.

'You want to see Judge Lobbett, don't you?' she said, turning to Mr Barber. 'He's exploring the maze. I'll call him.'

Mr Barber appeared interested. 'In the maze?' he said. 'Ah, yes, I see now. He is in the bush, as the Australians say.'

'Well, we're all a little up the garden this afternoon,' said Mr Campion.

Marlowe introduced the others hastily, and Giles inquired politely if the visitor had had a good run down.

'Magnificent!' Mr Barber threw out a fat hand. 'I did not realize it was so far. That is why I am a little late. Then I was held up by a police trap just on the far side of the road that joins this place to the mainland. I saw no sense in it. I told the policeman so. On a main road, yes, but at the beginning of a tiny village which leads nowhere, there is no point in it. Unless, why, of course' – his face broadened into a grin – 'I understand. They are there to protect Judge Lobbett.'

As soon as he had spoken he realized the bad taste of his remark. He opened his mouth and was about to make bad worse by apologizing when the situation was saved by Mr Campion.

'Had you got your licence?' he said. 'It means rather a lot to us,' he went on with embarrassing earnestness. 'Police funds are rather low, and we need a good fine or two to set us on our feet again. Even a five-bob touch would help,' he added wistfully.

Mr Barber laughed uproariously. 'What a joke, what a joke!' he said. 'I was all right. I could not be touched, in either sense of the word. I too make jokes,' he added, a little proudly.

'Well, where is Dad?' said Marlowe. 'He must have had enough of the maze by now. Hullo, Dad! Half a minute!'

His voice sounded clearly over the still sunlit garden. There was an echo at the point where he stood, and his own words came back mockingly across the fields. There was no reply.

'He's foxing,' said Isopel. 'He's got lost.'

'Let's go in and get him out,' said Biddy. 'I bet he hasn't found the centre.'

'But he must have done,' said Giles. 'I shouted the key to him. Call again, Marlowe.'

'Here, Dad! seriously' – Marlowe's voice rose. 'Here's a visitor to see you. You must come out.'

Once again the echo was his only reply.

A faintly scared expression flickered into Isopel's eyes. 'I suppose he's all right?' she said.

Her alarm passed from one to the other of them. The smile left Campion's face, and he hurried forward to the opening in the yew hedge.

'Mr Lobbett,' he shouted, 'answer us, please. You're scaring us.'

They listened with more anxiety now, a growing presentiment of danger becoming more and more firmly fixed in their minds.

'He does not answer,' said Mr Barber idiotically.

Biddy hurried forward. 'Come on, Giles,' she said. 'We can find our way through the place. I'll go straight to the centre, you go down the blind alleys.' She disappeared into the green fastness, Giles at her heels. The others congregated at the mouth of the maze, listening breathlessly. Isopel called suddenly, her voice shrill and appealing.

'Daddy! Daddy! Answer me.'

Marlowe's face grew very pale, and he put his arm around the girl.

'This is crazy,' he said. 'He must be there. There's no other way out, is there?'

'I don't think so.' Campion spoke with unaccustomed seriousness. 'A maze never has a second door.'

Biddy's voice silenced him. 'I'm here at the centre,' she said. 'There's no sign of him, Giles.'

'Half a moment,' the boy's voice answered her. 'No luck yet. Try that false exit from the centre.'

The search went on in feverish silence. Mr Campion, who had hitherto been standing rather foolishly before the entrance to the maze, now turned to Marlowe and Isopel. 'You go round to that side,' he said, 'and I'll cut round this. He may have found some opening.'

'What shall I do?' said Mr Barber.

'You stay here and give us a call if you see anyone come out,' said Campion, and started off round the east side of the maze. He climbed the hedge with some difficulty and scrambled along the ditch by the field. The minutes passed quickly. Campion met Marlowe in the road which skirted the fourth side of the yew puzzle. Their expressions betrayed their lack of success.

'It's absurd,' Marlowe said, as if in answer to some unspoken question. 'We're getting the wind up about nothing, of course. The whole darned place is as sound as an icebox. There isn't any way out except the one he went in by. He must be in there. He's playing the fool with us. I guess he doesn't't realize how jumpy we are.' The words were belied by his tone.

Mr Campion seemed stupefied.

'We'll get round to the others,' he said. 'He'll probably be with them.'

A light step on the road behind them made them swing round expectantly. It was Biddy. Her face was pale, her brown eyes dark and startled.

'Albert,' she said breathlessly, 'he's gone. We've combed the maze, Giles and I, and there's not a trace of him. It's as if he'd disappeared into the earth.'

Chapter 12

The Dead End

'It's no good hanging about the maze any longer.' Biddy spoke helplessly. 'He can't be here.'

She and Isopel were standing in the entrance to the yew puzzle. Mr Campion had dashed down to interview the police trap on the far side of the Stroud. Giles was still searching every corner of the maze with dogged obstinacy, and Marlowe was scouring the grounds. Mr Barber, a stolid expression of surprise upon his face, was seated bolt upright in a deck chair upon the lawn, his leather case upon his knee, considerably bewildered by the whole affair. Addlepate, as upon all other occasions when he might conceivably have been useful, had entirely disappeared.

Isopel had grown very pale. She looked more like her brother than ever. Her features seemed to have become sharper and her eyes larger in the last ten minutes.

Biddy was frankly flustered.

'But it's impossible,' she said, her voice rising a little on the final word. 'He *can't* have gone. It's like magic.'

Isopel shook her head and her lips moved silently. She seemed to be struggling for words.

'They've followed us – here. I knew we couldn't get away from them. I knew – I –'

She put out her hand as if to save herself, and Biddy, catching a glimpse of her face, moved forward just in time to catch her before she collapsed.

Faced with a problem with which she could deal, Biddy's practical nature reasserted itself. She let the other girl down gently into a sitting position and thrust her head between her knees. A shout to Giles brought him stumbling out of the maze.

He let out a short nervous exclamation when he saw the girl on the grass, and came running towards them. He looked at Biddy with eyes full of horror.

'Good heavens, she's not dead, is she?' he said.

'Of course not, you fool,' said Biddy, whose nervousness had turned into irritation. 'Pick her up and carry her into the house. She's only fainted. Poor kid, she's frightened out of her life. And so am I, Giles. Where on earth is he?'

Giles did not appear to be listening to her. He was looking down at the white-faced girl whose head lolled so heavily against his shoulder, and whatever he was thinking, he did not confide it to Biddy. He carried Isopel into the house and set her down on her bed, where he left her to his sister's ministrations, then went back stolidly to the maze, which his own faith in cold reason would not allow him to leave.

He stepped into the dark bushes and found his way along the narrow paths, going over and over ground that he had already searched. At length, pausing in a cul-de-sac on the west side, he remained for some time regarding the hedge before him speculatively. One of the yew trees was dead and there was a decided hole near the ground, leading into the ditch that skirted the hay field which flanked the garden. He scrambled through it himself: it was a comparatively simple matter. The discovery relieved him to a certain extent; it eliminated that element which Biddy had called 'magic' and which had been so abhorrent to his prosaic mind.

The ditch in which he found himself was dry and had recently been cleared. He could see up and down it unimpeded, on his left as far as the road and on his right to the end of the field, some two hundred yards distant. The hay was ready for cutting, and as he stood in the ditch it waved above him higher than his head. It would be perfectly possible for a small army to have hidden in the wide dry ditch without being seen from the road, but there was no evidence of a struggle of any sort.

Unsatisfied, Giles returned to the maze the way he had come. He searched the cul-de-sac carefully.

While he was standing there undecided he heard Campion's voice shouting from the roadway, 'Hullo! Anyone in there?'

He called back eagerly, 'Any luck?'

'Not a trace. It's the durndest mad thing I ever struck.' It was Marlowe who answered. 'And you?'

'I don't know,' said Giles. 'Come down the ditch at the side of the hay field and I'll show you.' He turned, squatting down in the opening by the dead yew. Presently they came along, stumbling through the ditch, Campion in particular slipping about considerably on the uneven ground.

'See this?' said Giles. 'This is the only way anybody could get in or out, bar the entrance, as far as I can see, and I've gone through the place with a comb. The question is, how did anyone get him out without his making the least sound or putting up any struggle? There's no sign of a row here, you see, and we didn't hear a whisper.'

'And we haven't told you the most extraordinary thing of all yet,' said Marlowe. 'There were two old cops there and they swear that not a vehicle or pedestrian has left Mystery Mile since four o'clock this afternoon. And that's not all. I've been up to George's brother, 'Anry, who's been sitting outside the inn at the corner of the road there, and he swears that he hasn't seen a soul except Mr Barber, who stopped to ask him the way and seems to have impressed him considerably.'

Giles stared at him. 'Then he must be on the estate,' he said, and the thought seemed to relieve him. 'He couldn't have lost his memory or something, could he? Has he ever gone off like this before?'

This attempt to attribute the affair to a natural cause was a new idea. Marlowe seized it hopefully. 'No,' he said, 'he hasn't. Suppose he had a brainstorm? The things he's been through lately would be enough to bring it on. He might easily have gone wandering off on his own. Couldn't we turn out the village and have a hunt for him? I can't believe that he could stray lost for long in a little place like this.'

'Of course,' said Giles slowly, 'there's the estuary, you know. Could they have got him off in a boat?'

'That won't be difficult to trace,' said Campion. 'Two or three men with a prisoner would be noticed in a place like this. When was high tide, Giles?'

'That's what I was thinking,' the boy replied. 'It was high tide about five. It must have been still well up at the time he disappeared. We'll get the village out, anyway. They're certain to know if there have been any strangers around. There are only about six rowboats in the place, now I come to think of it. It's such a long way to the water across the saltings. I say,' he went on abruptly, 'don't you think we'd better tell all this to Isopel? About the idea of a brainstorm, I mean. She came over faint out here about twenty minutes ago, and I carried her in. She's with Biddy now, but I feel that if we could reassure her, even a little bit, we ought to.'

They were filing out of the maze as he spoke, and they turned towards the house.

'Of course,' said Marlowe, 'the staff's hunting round the place now. We may hear something any minute.'

It was only then that the others realized the strain under which he was labouring. 'Something's bound to turn up,' said Mr Campion reassuringly. But his pale face was expressionless and there was a trace of alarm in his eyes.

They found the house in considerable commotion. Biddy came running out to meet them. After they had reported their discoveries to her, and she had satisfied herself that no more could be done at the moment, she turned to them.

'I've shoved some cold food on the table. You'd better eat it. I'm trying to make Isopel eat, too. Perhaps if you all sit down you'll be able to think of something. Nothing's even logical at present.'

As they went into the dining-room they were startled to see the smiling Mr Barber rise out of the window-seat.

'Oh!' said Biddy, surprised into frankness. 'I'd forgotten all about you. I'm so sorry.'

'Not at all.' Mr Barber spoke complacently. 'I will wait until Mr Lobbett can see me. You see,' he went on confidentially, 'I have here something that I think will interest him.' He tapped the leather case significantly. 'The works of Cotman are only now beginning to be fully appreciated. But since their worth has become known the samples of this genius have naturally become rare. I think I may say that the discovery of a hitherto unknown painting of his Greta period is an event, the importance of which can hardly be overestimated. Now' – with a magnificent gesture he proceeded to unlock the silver catches – 'you shall judge for yourselves.'

The expressions of bewilderment which had appeared upon the faces of his audience gave place to those of incredulity as they realized that his mind was on some picture or other that he had come down with the intention of selling.

Marlowe stepped up to him. 'You'll forgive us,' he said. 'I thought you understood. My father has mysteriously –' He jibbed at the word 'disappeared'. 'I mean we can't find him.'

Mr Barber smiled and spread out his hands. 'It does not matter,' he said. 'I will wait.'

Marlowe lost his patience. 'Don't you understand?' he said. 'We don't know where he is.'

Mr Barber's reproachful smile did not vanish. 'I have come down to value the other picture,' he said. 'There will be no compulsion to buy my Cotman. I think I will wait, having come so far.'

His cheerful non-acceptance of the facts was too much for them.

Giles repressed a violent desire to shout at him. Marlowe turned away helplessly. 'Oh, wait then,' he said, and quite obviously dismissed the man from his mind.

Mr Barber bowed and sat down again, nursing his precious case.

Addlepate's single sharp imperative bark, demanding entrance, startled them all. 'Curse him!' said Giles, getting up out of force of habit to open the door. No one looked at the little dog as he came padding in. They were eating mechanically, almost in silence, waiting for the coherent frame of mind which Biddy had foretold.

'Oh, down, darling, down!' Biddy spoke irritably as the only creature in the room faintly interested in food pawed her arm.

'Ah,' said Mr Barber conversationally. 'The dog. The animal sacred to the English.'

No one took any notice of the opening, but Giles glanced moodily at the little mongrel, vaguely seeking inspiration there.

His reward was sudden and startling. Folded through the ring of the dog's collar, and indubitably placed there by human hand, was a small twist of paper.

Before he could speak, Campion had seen it also. He called the dog over to him. They watched him fascinated as he unwound the strip of paper and spread it out upon the tablecloth.

They left their seats and crowded round him, leaning over his shoulder. It was a page torn from a notebook, and the few words were scrawled as if the sender had written under great difficulty. Marlowe read out the message in a shaking voice:

'Am safe if blue suitcase is not lost.'

'I don't quite get this last bit,' said Marlowe. 'The paper's got crumpled. Oh, wait a bit – yes, I see it now.'

'Keep the police out of this. Safer without.'

They exchanged frightened glances.

'Is it your father's writing?' It was Giles who spoke.

'Yes, that's his hand all right. The leaf's torn from his notebook, too, I think.' Marlowe raised his eyes and looked round at them, bewilderment and incredulity mingling on his face. 'Not a sign of anyone on the roads, not a trace of a stranger in the place, and then out of the air – this,' he said huskily. 'What do you make of it? I feel I've gone mad.'

Chapter 13

The Blue Suitcase

It was very nearly dawn before the last of the yellowing hurricane lanterns which had been bobbing over the saltings and in every nook and cranny of Mystery Mile took the path across the park and came to a stop outside the big kitchen door at the back of the hall. There were ten of them, carried by the entire male population of the village, with the exception of two old men who were bedridden and a few small boys.

They were an untidy red-faced crowd, considerably wearied by their night of search, but intensely interested in the proceedings.

The distinction between the two main families, the Willsmores and the Brooms, was sharply defined: the Willsmores, lank dark people with quick beady eyes and a knowing expression; the Brooms, sturdier, more stolid, with large red bovine faces, and every variety of fair hair from red to yellow.

Cuddy, who had come over from the Dower House to help Mrs Whybrow, the Manor housekeeper, bustled about preparing tea or mulled beer for each newcomer.

The outer kitchen where they were assembling was one of those great stone outbuildings without which no East Anglian house is complete. It was tacked on to the rest of the Manor and was stone-floored with a great brick fireplace whose chimney was built out into the room. The trestle tables had been pushed back against the whitewashed walls, and forms and settles dragged round the roaring fire.

Mrs Whybrow was a housewife of the old school, and black hams of her own curing hung from the centre beam, high above their heads. The beer barrel was in the room, and the great kettles of boiling water steamed on the wide hearthstone.

The housekeeper and Cuddy were sisters; both old women had entered the service of the Paget family when they were girls, and they considered themselves quite as much a part of it as any of the household. As they hurried round now, doling out the great white mugs of beer and hunks of home-made bread and yellow cheese, they looked marvellously alike with their greying hair and their stiff aprons crackling as they moved.

George and 'Anry were well to the fore, as became George's dignity. They sat side by side. 'Anry was the younger by a year or so. He was considerably less proud of himself than his brother, and was afflicted with a certain moroseness which, coupled with his natural inarticulate tongue, made him something of a man of mystery in the village. He was a simple old fellow with a goatee instead of a fringe, which he eschewed out of deference to George, mild brown eyes, and, when he permitted it, a slow and rather foolish smile.

Mr Kettle, the postmaster, who had come in after the others with a great show of exhaustion, sat some little distance away from the crowd. He drank his beer from a glass, a circumstance which seemed to make the beverage more genteel to his way of thinking. He also wore a bowler hat, and had wrapped himself up in an immense grey-and-white striped scarf.

''E looks like an owd badger,' remarked George in an undertone to 'Anry. The observation was quite loud enough to reach Mr Kettle, but he remained magnificently aloof and offered no retaliation.

One of the Broom boys, a great sandy-haired lout with the beginnings of a beard scattered over his chin like golden dust, repeated the jest, and the party tittered hysterically while George preened himself. Wit, he considered, was one of his strongest points.

'If yow'd a' found summat o' the foreigner instead o' 'tending yow was barmy, you'd ha' summat more to tell Mr Giles when he come in,' said Cuddy sharply, forsaking her company accent for her native sing-song. 'I heard him and Mr Marlowe comin' in a minute ago.'

A gloom fell over the party as they recollected the matter on hand.

'I had I owd dog on ut,' remarked one of the Brooms, a great hulking cross-eyed fellow with a red moustache. ''E didn't find nobbut. 'E kept leadin' I back to I own house.'

'Owd dog go by smell,' said George contemptuously, and once again there was laughter.

Cuddy banged a china mug down upon the table, her kindly old face paling with anger. 'I'm ashamed o' the whole lot on yow,' she said, her voice rising. 'Don't none of yow realize that the foreign gentleman's lost? An' yow set here guzzling and laughing yow'sel's sillier'n yow was before.'

''E ain't a foreigner,' said George. ''E talks same as I do.'

'Anyone as don't be born 'ere is a foreigner, ain't they?' said the man with the red moustache, squinting viciously at Mr Kettle.

'T'other gentleman wot come s'afternoon was a proper foreigner,' said 'Anry, speaking entirely without the aid of George. ''E couldn't 'ardly understand what I said to un. 'E got riled with I. I couldn't 'elp laughin'.'

'Yow'll 'elp ut this minute,' said Cuddy quickly. 'Here come the house folk.' Her sharp ears had caught the sound of Giles's voice in the passage, and the talk died down immediately, so that there was perfect silence in the kitchen when the wooden latch clicked, and Giles, followed by Marlowe, came into the room.

They too had been out on the saltings all night. The two young men looked pale and worried as they pushed their way into the group.

'Anything to report?' Giles's voice slipped down a tone or two and there was the suspicion of a country accent in some of the words he used. 'Now,' he went on, 'anyone who's seen anything unusual about the place, speak up right away. Let's hear about it.'

There was silence in the room. The group shifted uneasily and glanced uneasily at one another.

'Us ain't seen nothin',' said George. 'It do be a wonder.' He spoke with a certain amount of satisfaction. Giles was nettled.

'It's no wonder you couldn't find him, George,' he said. 'He can't have disappeared into thin air, though. There must be some trace of him about the place.'

'I could find 'im if annybody could,' said George. 'I be a wunnerful smart old man. But neither me nor 'Anry, we didn't see nothin'.'

'I'm afraid the man's right, sir.' Mr Kettle's unpleasant voice was raised from his corner. 'I myself 'ave been over all the principal means of exit from the estate and there is no trace as far as I can see. As you know, sir, we are practically an island, only more cut off, if I may say so, on account of the mud at low tide. You can depend upon it that we have done our best. Ever since I left my little shop, sir, at eight o'clock, I have walked —'

'Yes, yes, I know. That was very good of you,' said Giles brusquely. He disliked Mr Kettle quite as much as any of the village. 'But the question I'm trying to get at is, have there been any strangers seen on the estate since yesterday morning?'

There was silence again in the big kitchen, and then 'Anry suddenly became violently agitated. He grew very red, and struggled for his words.

'Master Giles – I seen un. In a car wi' great red wheels. 'E stopped I and 'e said to I, "Where's the big 'ouse?" and I said to 'e, suspicious-like, "What do yow want ut for?" and – and –'

'Oh, you're talking about Mr Barber,' said Giles. 'We know about him, 'Anry. He's in the next room now.'

George nudged his brother self-righteously. 'You be a fool, 'Anry,' he said, wagging his head complacently. 'Anry cast his eyes down and looked supremely uncomfortable.

'How about boats?' said Giles. 'Did anybody see a row-boat or any other kind round here between six and seven yesterday evening?'

'No, sir.' It was George who spoke, and the others agreed with him. 'We was nearly all on us t'home, you see, sir,' explained one of the Willsmores. 'We was gettin' our tea 'bout that time.'

'You was out, George,' said 'Anry.

George nodded. 'I were. I were down by owd mist tunnel, Master Giles, right lookin' on the water, as you might say. And I didn't see nothin', like I would 'a' done 'ad there been a boat there. Come to think,' he went on reflectively, 'I come right round from t'lower meadows, so if there'd been a boat a-pullin' away from the shore I couldn't 'elp but see ut. No, sir,' he finished, 'I doubt there wasn't no boat left 'ere last night.'

'Half a minute,' said Marlowe. 'What's the mist tunnel?'

George answered. 'That be a pocket, as you might say, sir. A bit of a dip, like, in the salting. The mist do lie there. Summer and winter, 'tis always the same. It be a wunnerful place for snares. It used to be, I mean,' he corrected himself as he caught Giles's eye upon him.

'And you were down there, you say?' said Marlowe, 'and you didn't see a soul?'

'Nothin',' said George. 'Nothin' anywheres.'

He passed his mug to Cuddy without a word. She took it from him and set it in the big stone sink which ran all along one side of the room.

The old man left his seat and walked gingerly over the stones towards her. 'That warn't for washin',' he said. 'I've been tellin' of Master Giles, and tellin' of makes I thirsty.'

Marlowe turned to Giles. 'It's no good,' he said. 'They don't know anything. We'd better get back to the others. Those girls ought to get some sleep if possible.'

They left the crowded kitchen and went back into the library, where Biddy lay dozing in a chair. She started up when they came in. 'Any luck?' she said eagerly.

Their faces told her their news.

'Where are the others?' Giles glanced round the room.

'In the garden. As soon as it got light Isopel wanted to go out searching again. Albert wouldn't let her go alone. Mr Barber went to bed. I put him in the honeysuckle room. Isopel and I thought it was the best thing to do.'

Giles crossed over to the window and looked out: it was just light. There was still a greyness over everything, and the air was fresh and sweet. He caught sight of Isopel and Campion coming up through the trees towards the house. Campion was bending forward, looking at the girl, and Giles fancied he heard her laugh. There was nothing unusual in it; most people laughed with or at Mr Campion, and yet he felt surprised, almost resentful. The situation had no funny side that he could see.

They came in two or three minutes later. Isopel was grave as before, but Giles's resentment against Campion grew. He had certainly succeeded in reassuring her where he himself had failed.

'See here,' said Marlowe, 'this thing's getting more and more peculiar every way you look at it. I must admit our crowd of sleuths aren't over-gifted, but it is their own back gardens they've been searching, isn't it? There's no boat been seen about, and none of those belonging to Mystery Mile are missing. Nor were any of them out yesterday.'

'You know,' said Biddy, suddenly sitting up, 'what we're all doing is to ignore that note Addlepate brought in. There're three suppositions: either Mr Lobbett has really been kidnapped and managed to scribble a few lines to warn us, or else he went quite mad and wrote it because he imagined the whole thing, or else someone else wrote it to put us off.'

'She's right, you know,' said Marlowe. 'We've been jibbing at that note. But dad wrote it, sure enough. And on a page of his own notebook, too. I'd like to believe,' he went on slowly, 'that dad had written that sanely, even though it meant that he had fallen into their hands. But I can't believe it, because there's no sign of them. You don't tell me a stranger wouldn't be noticed in a place like this. A cartload of men strong enough to get dad away would be the most conspicuous thing in the scenery for miles. He must have crawled out of that maze alone, fixed the note on the dog's collar – heaven knows when – and then disappeared as if he'd dropped into a quicksand.'

As he spoke the others started, and Mr Campion and the twins exchanged glances. The explanation which had occurred to all of them at some time during the search had not been mentioned by any of them. As in many other places on the east coast, there were several spots of 'soft' in the black mud which lay round Mystery Mile, and in these quick patches it was quite possible for a man to be sucked under and completely buried within a few minutes.

No one cared to suggest this possibility. Marlowe drew the sheet of paper from his pocket. ' "The blue suitcase," ' he said – 'that's quite safe, isn't it, Isopel?'

The girl nodded. 'Yes. Biddy and I brought it down here. We thought it would be safer.' She smiled wryly. 'I don't envy anyone trying to steal it. It weighs about a hundredweight. It's over in that corner.' She pointed to the far end of the room, where the heavy leather suitcase with a blue canvas cover stood beside a bookcase.

'That's it,' said Marlowe. 'That's the one he was so anxious about all through the voyage. I think we'd better open it.'

Isopel looked dubious. 'I don't think he'd like it, Marlowe.'

'I just can't help that.' The boy spoke emphatically. 'I've got to find out what this whole thing is about.'

He strode across the room and took the case by the handle. The weight of it surprised him, and instead of lifting it he dragged it into the centre of the room. The others watched him, fascinated, as he dragged off the blue canvas cover and disclosed a leather-bound steel case with a lock that ran all one side of the box.

The boy looked at it doubtfully. 'Now we're sunk,' he said. 'There's no key, of course. Father had that with him.'

Giles and Biddy glanced at Mr Campion, who was standing modestly in the background.

'It'll take a locksmith to do this,' said Marlowe, 'or a crook,' he said bitterly.

Once again the brother and sister looked at their friend inquiringly. He came forward, looking slightly uncomfortable.

'This sort of thing looks awfully bad,' he said. 'I never show off in the ordinary way.'

'Do you mean you can do it?' Isopel's look of wide-eyed astonishment brought a faint colour to Mr Campion's cheek.

'Perhaps if you would all turn your backs –' he murmured, taking out a small piece of wire and what appeared to be a penknife from his pocket.

'You're not going to do it with that? It's only got two blades,' said

Biddy, staring at the knife, her curiosity overcoming her anxiety.

'Inaccurate,' said Mr Campion. 'Two blades *and* a thing for taking nails out of horses' hooves. Whenever I see a horse hoof I take out this natty little instrument and –' As he was talking he was bending over the delicate lock, his thin fingers working with unbelievable rapidity. 'I prod,' he went on, 'and prod – and – *hup!* – out she comes! *Voilà!*'

A sharp click accompanied the last word as the spring lock shot back. Marlowe slipped down upon his knees before the case to raise the lid.

As he lifted the heavy steel covering he disclosed a layer of newspaper. The others pressed round eagerly, hoping for at least some glimmer in the mystery which surrounded them.

Marlowe drew off the paper carefully. Filling the entire case, and neatly stacked in half-dozens, were some forty or fifty, gaudily bound children's books. It looked like the supply for an infants' school-prize day.

Marlowe stretched out his hand and drew out a book gingerly as if he suspected it to contain some hidden explosive. He turned the leaves over: it was entitled *Robinson Crusoe Told to the Children*, and appeared to be perfectly genuine. They took out one book after another, turning over the pages of each. They were all in the same binding, some new, some patently second-hand, and appeared to be the complete output of a library called 'The Kiddies' Own'.

They were little green books profusely decorated with designs in gold, and pasted on the front of each was a coloured illustration of the story within. They consisted mostly of famous tales, simplified and bowdlerized for young people's consumption.

Campion and the others turned each copy over, hunting vainly for any mark in the margin or message scribbled on the flyleaves.

They hardly spoke, but went on steadily scouring every volume, until they sat back and looked at each other in bewilderment. The most exhaustive and methodical search had revealed only that no copy differed to any great extent from its fellows.

Marlowe looked at Campion helplessly. 'What do you make of it?' he said.

Mr Campion glanced round at all of them. They were looking at him appealingly, asking for an explanation. He threw out his hands. 'My dear old birds,' he said, 'I think I'm losing my speed. This finds you where it leaves me at present – high and dry. It all looks like good clean reading to me.'

Chapter 14
Campion to Move

Mr Campion was hidden in the high-backed Queen Anne chair in the faded drawing-room at the Dower House, and Biddy did not notice him at first when she came bustling in.

It was not until she caught sight of his long thin legs sprawled out across the hearthrug that she realized that he was there. She pounced on him immediately.

'Albert, if you don't get rid of Mr Barber for the Lobbetts this day I shall have a nervous breakdown. I can't bear it.'

He sat back in his chair and grinned at her.

'You won't,' he said. 'You've got more real nervous stamina than all the rest of us put together.'

Biddy did not smile. She remained staring down at him, a peculiar intensity in her eyes.

'You're a beast, Albert,' she said. 'I used to be awfully fond of you. I'd never seen you at work before. Now I think you're callous and – oh, and horrible!'

She was speaking hurriedly, her voice very near tears.

'There's Isopel and Marlowe nearly ill with grief and anxiety about their father for the last two days,' she hurried on, 'and all you do is to organize silly little searches over the island and advise them not to call the police. You're making so little fuss about it that that idiot Barber doesn't even believe that Mr Lobbett has disappeared.'

Mr Campion did not speak. He sat huddled in the corner of his chair, blinking at her behind his spectacles.

'Well, what are you going to do?' Biddy looked down at him angrily.

He rose to his feet, and walking up to her suddenly put his arm around her neck and kissed her vigorously. She gasped at him, astonishment predominating over every other emotion.

'What – what are you doing?' she expostulated, breaking away from him.

'Rough stuff,' said Mr Campion, and walked out of the room with unusual dignity. In the doorway he paused and looked back at her. 'You'll be sorry when you see me in my magenta beard,' he said.

Still puzzled, flustered and annoyed, she watched him from the porch as he crossed the green and entered the park gates. Mr Campion swaggered consciously until he was well out of sight of the Dower House, when his shoulders drooped; he walked more slowly, and he allowed himself a profoundly mournful expression, which persisted until he reached the Manor.

Marlowe was waiting for him.

'I've got it all set, as we said last night,' he said. 'There's one snag in it, however. Mr Barber wants to come up with us. He's taken some photographs of the Romney and he wants to get a second opinion on them. He insists on driving us up. What shall we do?'

Mr Campion seemed not in the least put out. 'That's a good idea,' he said. 'Perhaps we can lose him in Town. I don't know about Isopel, but Biddy seems to have taken a dislike to him.'

'Isopel's shown signs of strain, too,' said Marlowe. 'They've had to listen to him more than we have. Do you feel confident of this trip to the city?'

'It all depends on what you mean by "confident",' said Mr Campion. 'I certainly feel that we shall have more chance of finding out where we are, through a few well-placed inquiries in Town, than we shall if we sit here and wait for something else to happen. If we leave Giles in charge he'll look after the girls quite as well as ever we could. He's hot dogs on the England, Home, and Beauty Act. I think if we get rid of Mr Barber for them that'll be about the best thing we can do.'

'Giles knows all about it then?' said Marlowe.

Mr Campion nodded. 'I put a bit of sugar on his nose and said "Trust", and away I came.'

Marlowe grinned. 'They're charming folks,' he said. 'I've got the greatest admiration for Biddy.'

He paused abruptly, but Mr Campion made no comment.

He did not appear to have heard, and the conversation did not continue, for at that moment Mr Barber appeared, bustling out of the doorway to the waiting car. He was smiling and self-engrossed as ever, and the leather case was still under his arm.

'My friends, I have kept you waiting.' He apologized profusely. 'I hope you have persuaded Mr Campion to be of our party, Mr

Lobbett. I am a chauffeur *par excellence*, I assure you. I drive, as you say, as well as the devil. I shall run you to London, take you where you will, and at six or seven o'clock I shall be ready to drive you back again.'

Marlowe's jaw dropped. 'But I thought, Mr Barber,' he said, 'that you had seen all you wanted to of the Romney?'

Mr Barber's bushy eyebrows rose. 'But no,' he said, 'I am just begun. Besides, you must remember, I am acting for your father. Until I see him I shall not consider that I have carried out my commission. You see' – he tapped his leather case mysteriously – 'I have something here that I know will interest him.'

Marlowe glanced at Mr Campion, who sighed but offered no comment, and the three climbed into the car. Biddy saw them flash past the Dower House, and her resentment against Mr Campion grew as her curiosity was piqued.

Mr Barber lived up to his word. His driving was really remarkable. They reached London before lunch in spite of their late start, and Mr Barber, who had his own ideas of what was the most important place in the city, drew up with a flourish outside Simpson's.

Lunch with Mr Barber proved to be a greater ordeal than a journey in his company. Freed from the restraint of being a guest, his behaviour became skittish. He playfully threw a piece of bread at a man several tables away whom he fancied he recognized, and was childishly amused when he discovered his mistake. He also pocketed a fork as a souvenir, an incident that horrified Mr Campion, at whom the Oriental winked delightedly. He continued in this sportive fashion throughout the meal, and as they came out into the Strand disclosed to the bewildered Marlowe that the loose pockets of his ulster contained at least four crescent rolls which he had secreted.

'Not a bad bag,' remarked Mr Campion appraisingly. 'How's the time going, by the way?'

The Oriental put his hand into his waistcoat pocket and felt for the immense gold watch he usually carried. The change in his expression was ludicrous. His heavy jaw fell open, his eyes goggled.

'My watch – my watch – it's gone,' he said. 'I must have dropped it in there.' He turned and hurried back into the restaurant with extraordinary agility for so cumbersome a man.

Mr Campion watched him disappear, then he turned to Marlowe with a sigh of relief. 'He'll be no end of a time looking for it,' he said. 'I put it under the tablecloth. Come on.' And before the other had realized what had happened he had piloted him out into the roadway and hailed a taxi.

'I'm afraid you got rather a curious impression of my place last time you came,' said Mr Campion, as they climbed the stairs.

'Do you just walk out of this place and shut the door?' said Marlowe with interest. 'I didn't see a janitor here.'

'Oh, you didn't meet the family,' said Mr Campion. 'I forgot. They'll both be in.' He threw open the oak door as he spoke, and Marlowe followed him into the room in which they had first discussed the whole thing. There was no sign of a human being.

However, the young American became aware that someone was watching him with intense interest. He felt the scrutiny of a quizzical and speculative eye. He spun round nervily to find himself confronted by a venerable and wicked-looking jackdaw, who balanced himself sedately on the high back of a chair and regarded the visitor, his head cocked on one side.

'That's Autolycus,' said Mr Campion. 'My chaplain. A brilliant chap, but, like our friend Barber, a kleptomaniac. I don't know where my major domo is.'

He went out to the doorway and called, 'Lugg!'

There was a heavy step in the passage, and the next moment the largest and most lugubrious individual Marlowe had ever seen appeared on the threshold. He was a hillock of a man, with a big pallid face which reminded one irresistibly of a bull terrier. He was practically bald, but by far the most outstanding thing about him was the all-pervading impression of melancholy which he conveyed. He was somewhat unconventionally clothed in what looked remarkably like a convict's tunic, apparently worn as a house-coat over an ordinary suit.

Campion grinned at him. 'Still in your blazer?' he said pleasantly.

The man did not smile.

'I thought you was alone, sir,' he said, revealing a sepulchral voice. 'I put it on, sir, when attending to the bird's cage,' he remarked to Marlowe. 'It may interest you to know, sir,' he added, once more addressing his master, 'that during yer absence 'e's laid an egg.'

'No?' said Mr Campion. 'Don't you believe it, Lugg. He pinched it from a pigeon to deceive you. He's pulling your leg. I've known Autolycus for years. He's not that kind of a bird.' He turned to Marlowe. 'Autolycus and I are always trying to cheer Lugg up,' he said. 'We prepare little surprises like this for him. Now, Lugg, suppose you mix us a drink and tell us the news. By the way, Marlowe, you've met Uncle Beastly before. He told you he was the Aphrodite Glue Works once, but that was only his fun. Lugg,' he went on, his manner changing, 'I want some information about one or two people. There's a fortune-teller chap who works country houses, who has awakened my interest. But most particularly I want an authority on the American side. Who do you suggest, Lugg?'

'Well, in my opinion, sir, though you won't take it, I'm sure' – the tone was once more aggrieved – 'if I was you, I'd apply to Thos Knapp. It's wonderful wot 'e picks up, one way and another.'

Mr Campion's pale face flushed. 'I'll be hanged if I do,' he said with unusual heat. 'There are some people at whom even I draw the line. As I've told you before, Lugg, we do not associate with Mr Knapp.'

'Wot did I tell you?' said Mr Lugg, unexpectedly turning to Marlowe. ''E won't be guided by me. Keeps me as a pet about the 'ouse, 'e does.'

'I know,' said Mr Campion suddenly. 'Our old friend Stanislaus. Get me on to the Yard.'

'Imperialism,' muttered Mr Lugg bitterly. But he took up the telephone and gave the magic number. His voice assumed a husky, confidential tone.

'Mr Ash – Mr Tootles Ash to speak to Detective-Inspector Stanislaus Oates, *if* you please. 'Ullo, sir, yes, sir, it's me, sir. Very nicely, sir, thank you. Very nicely, sir, too. Laid an egg, sir. Oh *no*, sir. Mr Tootles is 'ere, sir.'

Mr Campion took the receiver.

'Hullo, Stanislaus,' he said cheerfully. 'How's the son and heir? Another tooth? Wonderful! I say, Stanislaus, do you know anything about a chap called Datchett?' His face became animated as he listened. 'That's him! – a chap with a curling red beard . . . Blackmail? Why don't you get him? Oh, I see . . . What had he got on Mrs Cary at Maplestone Hall? Eh? Yes, of course he was in it, you ought to know that . . . Yes, well, go all out for him, and when you get him, bring up the subject of the Reverend Swithin Cush . . . I don't know; that's what I want to find out. All the best. Oh – they say "Delila's" a good thing for tomorrow. So long.'

He rang off. 'Well, that's something,' he said. 'I think a concise history of our friend old Baa Baa Blacksheep might be a good idea. And the man who can probably tell us more about him than anyone is the best old Sherlock of them all – old W. T.'

Within a few minutes he was chatting affably. 'Hullo, is that you, W. T.? Hewes speaking. Sorry to disturb your millennium, but in your adventurous youth did you ever come across a man called Fergusson Barber? I should say he's an Armenian or a Turk of some sort. He might be a dealer . . . Oh, was he? Even as a young man? You remember him well? Kleptomaniac? I rather gathered that myself.'

The old detective's voice sounded so clearly over the wire that some of the words reached Marlowe.

'Will steal anything of small value,' he said. 'Seems to have a passion for bread . . .'

Campion took up the conversation, and for some time the listener could not follow the talk. When at last he rang off, Campion sighed. 'Barber seems a funny old cuss,' he said. 'It seems that W. T. met him over an affair at the Lord Mayor's banquet. If you pinch the cutlery at a restaurant it doesn't matter much, but start taking home souvenirs from the Mansion House and no one is amused. Apparently the old chap has establishments all over the place. Dabbles in every sort of dealing and collecting. W. T. says he has a harem, but spreads it about over the earth. But now,' he went on, the old anxious look returning to his eyes, 'to the one really fundamental and serious matter in hand – your father. Lugg, who can tell us anything about the Simister crowd?'

Mr Lugg raised his eyes in pious horror. 'Now I warn yer,' he said, his voice becoming plaintive, 'I warn yer. You're ignorant compared with me. You don't know. They're a nasty lot, leave 'em alone. Yer own mother couldn't give yer better advice.'

'My hat, I wouldn't like to hear her advice on this question,' said Mr Campion scandalized. 'Come on, pull yourself together. What can we do?'

'I shall wear a black band round me 'at for yer,' said Mr Lugg. 'The funeral cards'll cost a bit, 'avin' all your different names on 'em.'

'Mon, you're makin' a fearrful exhibition o' yersel,' said Mr Campion. 'I think perhaps we will have a chat with Mr van Houston.'

'Very good, sir. 'E calls 'imself "'Omer, the society photographer", now.' Lugg took out a dilapidated notebook and looked out the number.

Mr Campion took the instrument, and a long and animated conversation ensued in what was apparently a French argot.

He finished, and hanging up the receiver, returned to Marlowe. 'That sounds most promising,' he said, 'but it's hardly cheerful.

Apparently there's great activity in certain quarters. I think we're on the right tack. Lugg, has anyone of the fraternity been away recently, except for the usual reasons?'

Mr Lugg considered. 'Now you come to mention it, sir,' he said, 'I was talkin' about that down at the club only last night. There's been a notable absence among the really nasty customers lately. Ikey Todd an' is lot. Very significant, I thought it.'

'Very,' said Mr Campion. 'Did you hear any other funny stories at this club of yours?'

'Well, since you're being nosey, as you might say,' said Mr Lugg affably, 'I did 'ear that Ropey is back in the country.'

'Ropey?' said Mr Campion questioningly. Then a slow expression of disgust passed over his face. 'Not the man who –'

Lugg nodded. 'That's 'im. "'Tis an infamy that such a bloke as you should live," said the Beak. You know 'im.'

'Yes, I do,' said Campion, ignoring Lugg's effort at local colour.

Marlowe looked at him dubiously. 'I haven't got much of all this. What does it all amount to?'

Mr Campion considered. 'We've got daylight on one or two interesting points,' he said. 'In the first place, we know who Mr Datchett is. He's a blackmailer, though what he had on poor old Swithin Cush is more than I can possibly imagine. I think he must have been a spy in his spare time. Then we've placed Mr Barber, but that doesn't help us any. And last, and most important, we've discovered that there is a move on amongst those gentlemen who can be hired for any really unpleasant job. So Simister isn't working altogether with his own men. He must be doing this as a kind of side line to protect himself. The attacking army isn't a very bright lot. I don't know about the brains behind it. On the whole the prospect looks brighter than I expected to find it.'

There was a tap at the outside door, and Lugg went to open it.

'Say I've gone to Birmingham for my health,' said Mr Campion.

Lugg returned in an instant, an orange envelope in his hand. He handed it to Campion, who tore open the flap and glanced at the contents. As he read, a sharp exclamation escaped him and he became paler than before. He passed the telegram silently to Marlowe. It ran:

COME AT ONCE STOP BODY FOUND STOP BIDDY.

Chapter 15

The Exuberance of Mr Kettle

Biddy met them at Ipswich Station in Judge Lobbett's big Daimler.

'I knew you wouldn't mind my bringing this,' she said somewhat unexpectedly to Marlowe as they came across the station yard.

'My dear girl –' Marlowe looked at her in amazement. 'I want to know all about it. Where did they find him?'

Biddy stared at him. 'I don't understand,' she said.

'We're talking about the body,' said Campion. 'You wired us.'

The girl's bewilderment increased. 'I wired you we'd found a clue,' she said. 'There's no trace of Mr Lobbett himself.'

Marlowe drew the telegram from his pocket and handed it to her. She read it through and turned to them, her cheeks reddening.

'Oh, my dear, how you must have been tortured all the way down,' she said impetuously. 'This is Kettle. His daughter found the clothes, and he's so excited about it he's gone nearly insane. I think my wire to you ran more or less like this: "Come at once. Important clue. Meet you four-thirty train." I wondered why you wired me.'

Marlowe wiped the perspiration off his forehead.

'Now about this discovery,' said Mr Campion. 'Just what is it? What did Kettle's daughter find?'

'She found Mr Lobbett's clothes,' said Biddy; 'the suit he disappeared in, I mean. They were soaked with sea water and torn, and I'm afraid there's blood on them, Marlowe. But that doesn't mean he's dead, does it?' she went on eagerly, and Campion, glancing down, saw that she had laid her hand upon Marlowe's arm.

'Not necessarily, of course.'

Campion's voice was slightly irritated. 'Where did Miss Kettle make this interesting discovery?'

'Up the Saddleback Creek. I wired you at once. As a matter of fact, we were frightened, Isopel and I. She's all right now. Giles is with her. I never dreamed Kettle would send a crazy wire like that one.'

Marlowe looked bewildered. 'I thought,' he said, 'that a postmaster could get into serious trouble for a thing like that.'

'So he can,' said Campion grimly. 'Something tells me that he's going to get it. Didn't you fill in a form, Biddy?'

'No, I took it in to him on a piece of paper. I expect my scribble was partly to blame. You know how I write when I'm excited.' She smiled wryly at Campion. 'You've no idea how dithery he is. He's only a silly old man, Albert.'

Mr Campion did not reply, but his expression was dubious.

They got into the car and went back to the house.

Campion followed Marlowe into the white-panelled room, where on the round table stood a large tin tray, on which was a suit of clothes still wet with sea water. Marlowe glanced at Campion, a sharp quick look, full of apprehension.

'It's his suit, sure enough,' he said.

Campion nodded. A gloomy expression had come into his eyes. He thrust his hands deep into his pockets and stared darkly at the tray with its contents.

'Nothing in the pockets, I suppose?' he said.

'No, nothing at all,' said Isopel. 'The clothes must have been rifled before they were discovered. All the pockets were pulled inside out.'

Marlowe was still turning over the muddy flannel. 'Hullo!' he said, and held up the waistcoat, in which there was a jagged little hole surrounded by dark ominous stains. Mr Campion came over to the table and bent over the garment. He made no comment, and Biddy nudged him.

'Don't torture them,' she whispered. 'What does it all mean?'

His reply was silenced by a commotion in the hall outside.

'My good woman' – Mr Kettle's voice reached them, raised in protest. 'My good woman, show me in immediately. I am needed in there, and I 'ave every reason to suppose that my presence is awaited eagerly.'

'I ain't showin' anyone in without Master Giles's word. You ought to be 'shamed o' yowself, Kettle, forcin' your way in 'pon a bereaved family. They don't want to see you now.' Cuddy's voice, shrill and contemptuous, answered him.

'Shall I go and send him away?' said Biddy.

Campion glanced at Marlowe. 'If you don't mind,' he began, 'I think it would be an idea if we interviewed old Cleversides ourselves.'

Marlowe nodded. 'Certainly, if you think there's anything to be gained by it,' he said, and opened the door. 'Come in, Mr Kettle, will you?'

The unprepossessing postmaster shot one delighted glance at the angry Cuddy and stalked into the room with the air of a conqueror. He was clutching his bowler hat, and was still in his overcoat which he had put on to hide his apron.

''Ere I am, sir,' he said to Marlowe. There was a faint tinge of colour in his flaccid face. 'I saw the car turn into the drive and I put on me 'at and run after you, sir. I knew you'd be wantin' the truth. My daughter, sir, she found the remains, as you might say.' His eyes were watering and his lips twitching with excitement.

'Is your daughter here?' said Campion with unusual peremptoriness.

'No, sir.' Mr Kettle assumed an air of parental indignation. 'Wot?' he said, with great dignity. 'Think, sir. 'Ow could I subject the poor girl to look on once again that 'orror that 'as turned 'er from a 'ealthy woman, sir, to a mere wreck of 'er former self?'

In spite of the anxiety of the situation there was something extremely laughable in Mr Kettle's rhetorical outburst.

He lent an air of theatricality to a scene that would otherwise have been too terrible.

'No, sir, she is not 'ere,' he continued. 'And I may add, sir,' he went on with gathering righteousness, 'that she was in such an 'elpless state, sir, such a nasty 'opeless condition, sir, that I left 'er to mind the post office and come myself. I would like to mention also, sir,' he added, fixing a malignant eye upon Giles, 'that although I 'ave offered myself to be the messenger, no one 'as, as yet, sent for the police. It will look very suspicious, sir, when they do come. Although you are the son of the dead man, sir' – he swung round upon Marlowe on the words – 'it'll look nasty.'

'What dead man?' said Mr Campion, coming forward. He had developed a magisterial air that contrasted very oddly with his appearance. 'Have you got the body?'

'Me, sir? Oh no, sir.' Mr Kettle was not in the least abashed. 'When we find that I dare say we'll know who killed 'im.'

'Oh yes?' said Mr Campion with interest. 'How was he killed?'

'With a dagger, sir.' Mr Kettle made the startling announcement in a breathless whisper.

'How do you know?' said Mr Campion.

Mr Kettle rested one hand upon the table and assumed the attitude of a lecturer. 'I 'ave the detective mind, sir,' he said. 'I form my theories and they work out in accordance.'

'That's rather nice,' said Mr Campion. 'I must do that.'

Mr Kettle ignored him. 'To begin with, let us start with the discovery of this clue.' He waved his hand towards the table. 'My daughter, sir, an innocent girl, unsuspecting, goes for a walk, sir. This is the seaside, she thinks; why shouldn't she walk there?'

'No reason at all,' said Mr Campion. He was standing with one hand on Marlowe's shoulder, and the American's keen, clever face wore an expression of enlightenment.

'Well, she went along the beach – that is, on the edge of the saltings – on the sea wall, in fact. Imagine 'er for yourselves, careless, free –'

'Oh, cut the cackle,' said Giles. 'Tell us what happened.'

'I'm speakin' of my daughter, sir,' said Mr Kettle with dignity.

'You're also speaking of this lady's father,' said Giles. 'You'll say what you know, and then clear out.'

A particularly nasty expression came into Mr Kettle's white face.

'You're the wise one, sir,' he said. 'I shall be a witness at the inquest, don't forget. It's going to be very significant, I may say.'

'I'm sure it is,' said Mr Campion soothingly. 'Suppose you tell us about those deductions of yours.'

The postmaster was mollified. 'My knowledge is based on these instructive facts, sir,' he said. 'Look at this jagged hole, right over the region of the heart. Was that made by a knife, or was it not? It was, sir. See those stains all round? If you don't know what that is, I can tell you. It's blood – 'eart's blood, sir.'

Once more Giles was about to break out angrily, but this time it was Isopel who restrained him.

'What does that show, sir? The victim was stabbed to death with a knife. Then again, these clothes are soppin' wet with sea water. What does that show?'

'That they've been in the sea,' suggested Mr Campion.

'Exactly, sir, you've 'it it in one. Mr Lobbett was taken out in a boat, stabbed through the heart, and thrown into the water.'

'Where he undressed,' said Mr Campion, 'being careful to remove his braces. So far I think that's perfectly clear. However, there are several other little matters that'll have to be explained before we call in Scotland Yard. In the first place, there's this knife thrust. Rather a curious incision, don't you think? A little hole nicked with a pair of scissors and then made larger with a table knife. And then these bloodstains. The poor man seems to have bled from outside his clothes. The inside, you see, is pretty clean. But the gore on the outside is sensational. I wonder who's been killing chickens lately?'

Mr Kettle sat down on the edge of a chair, his face immovable. Mr Campion continued.

'There is something fishy about this – a whole kettle of fishiness, I might say. Someone's been playing the fool with you. I should go back to the post office.'

Mr Kettle got up, picked up his bowler hat, and walked quietly out of the room.

Campion turned to Isopel and Marlowe and spoke with genuine contrition. 'Will you forgive me for making you listen to all that?' he said. 'But I had to do it to find out how much the local Sherlock knew.'

'Then what do you make of these?' Marlowe indicated the soaking garments.

'An extraordinary bad fake on somebody's part,' said Mr Campion. 'I never saw such amateur work. This isn't your New York friends: it looks more like home product to me. I suppose you haven't been offering a reward by any chance?'

'No,' said Marlowe. 'But you can't get away from it, Campion,' he broke out. 'That's the suit he was wearing.'

'I know,' said Mr Campion. 'That's the only thing that makes it interesting. I think if you'll excuse me I'll go down to the village and make a few investigations.'

'Are you going to interview Kettle again?' Biddy spoke curiously.

'I hardly think so,' said Mr Campion. He smiled at her. 'He's not the only interesting character in the place.'

Chapter 16
The Wheels Go Round

Giles and Isopel were sitting in the window-seat in the morning-room, holding hands.

The sunlight poured in upon them, and the village of Mystery Mile was as peaceful as if nothing untoward had ever happened upon the whole island. They were alone. Biddy was at the Dower House, and Mr Campion off once more upon his investigations in the village.

The rustle of car wheels outside on the drive startled the two, and Isopel, who caught a fleeting glance of a putty-coloured body and crimson wings, turned to Giles looking utterly dismayed.

'Oh, my dear,' she said. 'He's come back!'

'Who? Your father?' Giles was ever more physically than mentally alert.

'No. That was Mr Barber.'

The young squire bounced to his feet.

'Good Lord!' he said. 'What cheek that chap has! I'll kick him out.'

He advanced towards the door, but it was opened before he reached it. Mr Barber, complete with satchel and the most important smile imaginable, appeared upon the threshold.

'Mr Paget,' he said, holding out his hand. 'Let me be the first to congratulate you.'

Giles, taken completely off his guard, reddened and glanced sheepishly at Isopel.

'I don't know how you knew –' he began. But Mr Barber was still talking. 'My boy, I have the proof – the proof positive. The thing's genuine. I should like to arrange for the sale with you.'

It was only at this moment that Giles realized that he had been mistaken and that Mr Barber was not talking about the all-important subject of which his own mind was full.

Isopel slipped her arm through his. 'It's the picture, dear,' she whispered.

'Of course I'm talking about the picture,' said Mr Barber testily.

'Come and see it for yourselves.' He bustled out of the room as he spoke, leading them into the cool drawing-room on the other side of the house.

The portrait hung over the mantelpiece: a long-dead Mistress Paget, who smiled at them with foolish sweetness from out of her monstrous gold frame. She wore a diaphanous scarf over her golden hair, and one slender hand caressed a little white dog who nestled in the folds of her oyster-coloured gown.

Mr Barber was visibly excited. 'As soon as I saw it,' he said, his eyes watering profusely, 'I said to myself, "This is the moment of my career. Here is an undiscovered Romney, one of the finest I have ever seen." I must see Judge Lobbett immediately and make my report. I'm afraid my little Cotmans sink into obscurity beside this master.'

'Look here,' said Giles, managing to get a word in when Mr Barber paused to breathe, 'this is all very fine but you don't seem to understand. We can't be bothered with little things like this just now. You don't appear to have grasped the fact that Mr Lobbett has disappeared. Naturally we can't consider doing anything till he's found.'

'Disappeared?' said Mr Barber, the fact apparently dawning on him for the first time.

'Yes,' said Giles irritably. 'And his blood-stained clothes were found in a pool yesterday.'

The effect upon Mr Barber was extraordinary. His mouth fell open, his eyes bulged, and he sat down suddenly upon the edge of a chair as if his feet would not support him.

'I didn't believe you,' he said blankly. 'I thought you were all joking with me. So many people are afraid of anyone who might want to sell them a picture. I thought Mr Lobbett was away on some visit. When Mr Campion and young Lobbett gave me the slip in London they were joking. Campion jokes so often. This is terrible – terrible! Where are the police?'

Giles hesitated, and then spoke stiffly. 'We decided that there was no need for them at present.'

Mr Barber raised his eyebrows. 'Oh, then, I see you know where he is?' he said. 'You thought it would be best for him to disappear for a little while?'

'Certainly not,' said Giles. 'But we've the finest – er – private detective in the world investigating for us.'

Mr Barber appeared to be quite as much bewildered as before. 'Oh,

I see,' he said. 'But in these circumstances, for whom am I acting? I mean,' he added a little helplessly, 'what is my position here?'

The easy-going good-tempered Giles relented. 'Oh, that'll be all right,' he said cheerfully. 'Suppose you go back to town tomorrow and send me in a list of your expenses?'

'But the Romney?' said Mr Barber, his voice rising to a squeak.

A hint of the long line of independent landowners behind him was apparent in Giles just then, as he stood squarely under the picture, his brows contracted. 'It's hung there for the last hundred years, and it can stay there a year or so longer if necessary,' he said. 'I've told you, sir, that I can't be bothered about it now.'

'But it's worth a fortune,' objected Mr Barber.

'I don't care what it's worth,' said Giles stubbornly. 'I shall have to wait until all this is settled before I think about anything else. I'll write you then. Will that do?'

It was evident that Mr Barber felt that he was dealing with a lunatic. 'You must forgive my insistence,' he said with dignity, 'but the commission. If you would allow me to take the picture –'

'No, I'm hanged if I will,' said Giles, his irritation returning.

'Then let me take more photographs. There are so many people who will be interested.' The expert's tone was supplicating. 'I can prepare the market. Surely, surely you will not forbid me to do that?'

'Oh, do what you like,' said Giles, 'only don't move the picture.'

He put his arm through Isopel's and was leading her out of the room when they met Marlowe in the doorway.

His dark handsome face was more than usually serious.

'Seen Biddy?' he asked.

'She's down at the Dower House,' said Giles. 'Anything I can do?'

'No. That's all right.' Marlowe did not stop, but hurried on his way, leaving the young man engrossed in Isopel and Mr Barber standing before the Romney, his pudgy feet well apart, his hands clasped behind his back, and upon his face an expression of rapt, almost idolatrous, admiration.

Fifteen minutes later found Marlowe striding across the park, where he encountered Mr Campion. The pale foolish-looking young man came along thoughtfully, whistling plaintively to himself.

'Hullo,' he said cheerfully. 'I've just thought of something. Listen –

> As Sir Barnaby Rowbotham died,
> He turned and he said to his maid,

The Albert Memurrial
Is the place for my burrial,
The first on the left, just inside.

There's uplift for you. It's the message that counts.'

Marlowe did not appear to have heard. 'I say,' he said, 'have you seen Biddy?'

Mr Campion looked hurt. 'No soul for Higher Things,' he murmured. 'No, I've been sleuthing about the village, and I believe that I have lighted upon something.' He paused. 'You're not listening to me,' he said regretfully.

'No,' said Marlowe. 'I'm sorry, Campion, and I don't want to make a fuss, but I can't find Biddy anywhere. She's gone.'

'Gone?'

Marlowe glanced up to find Campion staring at him. His vacuous face was transformed by an expression of puzzled consternation and incredulity.

'Absurd,' he said at last. 'How long have you been looking for her?'

'All the morning,' said Marlowe. 'The fact is,' he went on, the words blurring a little in his embarrassment, 'she'd promised to meet me. We were going down to the Saddleback Creek. But this isn't – ordinary caprice. She's not that sort of kid.'

Mr Campion shot him a swift glance.

'No,' he said quietly, and was silent.

'But she's gone. I tell you I've been everywhere. I've asked everybody. She hasn't been seen all the morning. Cuddy says that she last saw her after breakfast when she went into the drawing-room to write letters.'

'Letters?' Campion spun round on the word. Behind his spectacles his pale eyes had become narrow and hard. 'Are you sure?' he said, and his voice was more serious than Marlowe had ever heard it.

'Why, yes,' he went on. 'Cuddy says that she went straight in to her desk first thing after breakfast. Why –'

'Come on,' said Mr Campion. He was already heading for the village at a brisk trot.

'Ought to be shot!' he said breathlessly to Marlowe as they raced over the slippery turf together. 'Never dreamed they'd act so soon. Was coming back to hold a committee meeting. Taking my time over it.'

When they reached the park gates he came to a halt.

'I think, just to make sure that we're not making fools of ourselves, we'll drop into the Dower House,' he said. 'Cuddy may have made a mistake. This looks very nasty, Marlowe.'

They hurried across the green and into the Dower House where Cuddy met them in the hall. The old woman was red-faced and annoyed.

'Have you seen Miss Biddy, sir?' she said, fixing on Campion. 'She was coming into the kitchen to give me a hand with the huffikins at twelve o'clock,' she said, 'and here have I been waiting with my oven hot and the dough spoiling for the last three-quarters of an hour. I suppose I'd better get on with them alone.'

The apprehension in Mr Campion's pale eyes deepened.

'I was looking for Biddy myself, Cuddy,' he said. 'When did you see her last?' Marlowe had gone on into the drawing-room, and the old woman glanced after him.

'I told Mr Lobbett,' she said: 'not since just after breakfast.' Her quick eyes took in Campion's expression, and she came a little closer to him. 'Looks like you ain't goin' to have no chance,' she said, dropping her voice confidentially. 'Be more serious-like. You can't tell what's goin' to please a girl.'

Campion did not smile. 'May the best man win, you know, Cuddy,' he said with apparent gravity.

'Yes, and I'm afraid he will,' said she. 'When you see Miss Biddy tell her I couldn't wait no longer.'

She bustled off, and Campion hurried after Marlowe.

'She must have been writing here,' he said. 'Look.' He pointed to the open inkstand, the sheets of notepaper carelessly strewn about, and the empty stamp book lying on the polished wood. 'There you are,' he said. 'Campion, if anything happens to that girl, I'll commit murder.'

'That,' said Mr Campion, 'is the spirit. Come on.'

Chapter 17

'Gent on a Bike'

The interior of Mr Kettle's shop, which was also the post office of Mystery Mile, provided one of those scenes of mingled profusion and constriction which can be equalled only by any other English village general shop. The whole place was hardly more than ten feet square, a little low room into which customers stepped down some inches from the garden path.

The wide counter divided the room in half, and over it, from floor to ceiling, the entire stock of bacon, hardware, boiled sweets, flypapers, bread, and groceries were displayed without any attempt at order.

The post office consisted of a wired-off enclosure at one end of the counter, the iron rail of which was decorated with licensing notices and pension forms.

An open doorway at the back of the shop revealed a glimpse of a small neat room decorated with a particularly unlovely grey-and-green wallpaper, a pair of aspidistras, and a model of a white horse given away with a whisky advertisement.

It was through this doorway that Mr Kettle advanced upon Campion and Marlowe as they stepped down into the shop.

A change in him was apparent immediately.

His pallor was even more striking than before, and there was a slightly shifty, troubled look in his pale eyes.

'What can I do for you, gentlemen?' he said, the nervousness in his voice unmistakable. Marlowe leaned across the counter, when a touch on his arm restrained him.

'Miss Paget left her purse in here, she thinks, Mr Kettle,' said Campion pleasantly. 'We shall have to have all this cleared away, you know' – he waved his hand at the miscellaneous collection round him, and rambled on foolishly. 'Where's the exit in case of fire? Most dangerous, all this litter about the place. Now where's that purse?'

'She didn't leave anything 'ere, sir.' Mr Kettle's voice was emphatic.

'Fine!' said Campion with sudden enthusiasm. 'Now we know where we are. Is she still in the house?'

Mr Kettle did not look at him, and Marlowe suddenly noticed that he was squinting horribly. He was standing perfectly still, his great flabby hands spread out upon the counter. Campion bent a little nearer and repeated his question softly.

'Is she still in the house?'

A thin stream of saliva trickled out of the corner of Mr Kettle's mouth, and Marlowe, who until now had been utterly bewildered, realized with a shock that the man was paralyzed with terror. The sight nauseated him, but Campion was less impressed.

'Don't be a fool, Kettle,' he said sharply. 'We've only got to turn you over to the police. Better save a lot of bother and take us to her at once.'

The effect of this threat upon the man was as startling as his terror had been. He started back from them with an angry sound that was midway between a snarl and a hiccough. His fear had turned to a peculiarly vindictive type of satisfaction.

'That's right! Bring in the police!' he said with unexpected violence. 'Search the 'ouse! Turn me 'ole shop upside down. Stick your noses into every 'ole and corner of the place. And when you've finished that *I* shall 'ave something to say to the police. Where's Mr Lobbett, eh? 'Oo 'ushed up the parson's suicide? Why didn't you show them clothes to the police? You daren't bring the police 'ere! You . . . !'

The outburst came to an end at last, and a transformed Mr Kettle stood glaring at them across the two feet of worn counter. Gone and forgotten was his servility.

Mr Campion seemed entirely unmoved. He stood, his hands in his pockets, looking if anything a little more strikingly inane than usual. 'It wouldn't be the Heronhoe police,' he said. 'I think the county people would be interested.'

Mr Kettle remained unimpressed. 'No police will worry me,' he said. 'I've got nothing 'ere to 'ide.'

'Good!' said Campion. 'Now we understand one another better than ever.' His next remark seemed entirely casual. 'You sell biscuits, I see, Mr Kettle?'

Marlowe glanced at his friend questioningly, only to find that he was regarding the postmaster fixedly. The young American was not prepared for the third change in Mr Kettle: his terror returned, and he looked at the pale young man before him in blank astonishment.

'There, there,' said Mr Campion soothingly. 'Here's a nice old lady coming down the path, Kettle. Pull yourself together. She'll want to be served. No self-respecting woman will buy a stamp off you if you squint like that.'

He had hardly finished speaking when Alice Broom came rustling into the shop. She nodded to the young men.

'Soda, please, Mr Kettle,' she said. 'Nice after the rain, isn't it? How's your pore feet today?' She was evidently in a talkative mood, and Campion seemed disposed to pander to it.

'I've been telling Mr Kettle he doesn't look any too bobbish,' he said. 'What do you think, Alice? Excitement isn't healthy, is it?'

'I don't know what excitement he'll be gettin' down 'ere,' she said. 'I've got a bone to pick with un, too,' she added, the thought suddenly occurring to her. 'I sent round last night askin' for a box to keep my rarebits in. 'E wouldn't let I have un, an' I seed he this mornin' packin' off crate after crate into that biscut van.'

Campion turned to Marlowe. 'Another Old English custom for you,' he said. 'We have our biscuits here by the crate.'

Alice shook her head at him. ''E's makin' game on you, sir,' she said. 'Biscuts come in tins. Yes, biscuts come in tins.'

She repeated the phrase with a certain amount of satisfaction, and waddled out of the shop with a cheerful 'Goodday, sirs.'

Campion beamed at Mr Kettle. 'Biscuits come in tins,' he said. 'And Mr Kettle returns the empty crates. That's very interesting. I shouldn't be surprised if they didn't send a special van from London for them, eh?'

Mr Kettle moistened his lips. 'I don't know what you've been 'earing –' he began desperately.

Campion grinned. 'Our Albert hasn't been hearing anything – he's been seeing,' he said. 'Suppose we go into that artistic little room through there, and go into the whole question peacefully and without fear of interruption?'

Mr Kettle did not move, nor did he make any protest when Marlowe lifted the counter flap and the two young men walked into the inner room.

'Come in,' said Campion pleasantly, holding the door open for him.

The postmaster followed them silently. Campion shut the door behind him and set a chair. 'I don't suppose the windows will open,' he observed. 'What a pity, Kettle! You'd have got the smell of chloroform out by this time. As it is, I should think it would linger for days.'

Kettle did not speak, and a change came over Campion's face.

He leaned forward.

'If she's been hurt, Kettle, I'll break my rule and kill you! Now then, animal, tell us all about it.'

Mr Kettle sat on the edge of his chair, his large hands spread out on the table, and looked neither to right nor to left.

'Come on,' said Campion. 'We know practically everything. Out with it.'

Still Mr Kettle remained silent, his mouth twitching. Marlowe took a step forward. 'You'll tell us here and now,' he said, 'or I'll smash you to pulp.'

'No need,' said Campion. 'What is he now? I see I may as well repeat the procedure to you, Kettle. We'll start at the beginning. A suit of clothes came into your hands, and you thought you'd be clever with them. You were – my hat you were. So thunderingly clever that you set not only us but your own dirty employers buzzing round your head. I gave you credit for so much stupidity, but what I didn't believe was that you'd be fool enough to tell your own people about it yourself.' He turned to Marlowe. 'That's where I miscalculated the time. Now,' he went on, returning to his victim, 'you got orders to kidnap the first one of us that came into the shop, you and your precious daughter were to chloroform him, and I suppose the rest of the business was perfectly simple.'

It was evident from the look of wonderment on the postmaster's face that so far Campion had been very near the truth.

'Having captured Biddy,' continued Mr Campion, 'no doubt you telephoned some apparently innocent message to Heronhoe, or wherever the van was waiting, and along came the one vehicle that wouldn't be questioned by the police on the Stroud – a reputable-looking trade van. You loaded your crates into it, one of which contained the poor kid. Now then, where did they take her to?'

He had taken off his spectacles, and as he leaned across the table to the shivering man his pale eyes were bright and hard.

Mr Kettle made an inarticulate sound; his mouth sagged open.

'If they find out you know all this they'll kill me,' he slobbered at last. 'Oh, Mr Campion, sir' – he grovelled across the table, his hands plucking at the cloth – 'don't let them ever know – don't let them ever know!'

'Where have they taken her?' repeated Campion.

'I don't know.' Mr Kettle was on the verge of tears: there was no doubting his sincerity. 'I never seen either of 'em before. I get my orders by phone, in code. I wouldn't 'a' done it if I could 'a' 'elped it – reelly I wouldn't. I couldn't 'elp it – I 'ad to obey 'em.'

Mr Campion rose from the table where he had been seated.

'I believe him,' he said gloomily. 'I think perhaps the nastiest thing we can do is to leave him to his unspeakable pals.'

'I'd tell you,' wailed Mr Kettle. 'I'd tell you anything if only I knew it.'

'I believe you would,' said Campion contemptuously. 'I'm afraid there's no doubt they've kept you in the dark all right. They're not such fools that they don't know the type they've got working for them. Come on, Marlowe. He'll keep his mouth shut for his own sake.'

Marlowe, as they strode across the green, looked at his companion curiously. 'How much of this yarn of Kettle's did you know when you went into the store?' he said.

Campion frowned. 'Not as much as I ought to have done,' he said bitterly. 'And there's still a link I don't get. I told you, it was misjudging Kettle's abysmal idiocy that put me out. I knew they couldn't have got going on the job so soon after the discovery of the clothes unless they had heard about it at the same time we did; and that was only possible if our friend Kettle told them himself. As he'd made such a hash of it, I didn't dream he would. But he did, and I should think from the look of him that they had come down hot and strong.'

'Then it was Kettle who doctored those clothes?'

'Not a doubt of it. Though heaven only knows how he got hold of them. The only thing that matters at the moment is Biddy,' he went on suddenly, lifting up his head. 'Get her back and then we can start.'

'I'm with you there,' said Marlowe with conviction. 'What are you going to do?'

Campion shrugged his shoulders impatiently. 'God only knows,' he said. 'The old mental machinery seems to have conked out altogether.'

They walked on in silence. As they came into the house through the conservatory door which stood open they heard Mrs Whybrow's voice raised, high and suspicious. She was talking to someone in the inner hall.

'Mr Campion? I don't know if 'e's in, but I'll take your name if you'll give it me. Who shall I say 'as called?'

A bright unpleasant voice answered her, indescribable in its cockney self-assurance.

'Don't say any name. Just go up to 'im, put yer 'ead close to 'is ear, and say, soft-like, "Gent on a bike".'

Chapter 18

The Unspeakable Thos

Mr Campion, standing in the outer hall, remained for a moment perfectly silent, listening.

'Who is it?'

Mr Campion took off his spectacles and wiped them with a tasteful line in silk handkerchiefs. 'That, my unfortunate friend,' he said gloomily, 'is the unspeakable Thos. Thos T. Knapp. T. stands for "tick".'

'Why, if it ain't my old sport Bertie!' said the voice, appreciably nearer. 'I 'eard your pipe from out 'ere, my lovely.'

Simultaneously with this last announcement, Mr Thos Knapp himself appeared in the doorway, where he stood looking in on them with bright, sharp, sparrow-like eyes. He was an undersized young man with a broken snub nose and an air of undefatigable jauntiness. His clothes must have been the pride of the Whitechapel Road: fantastically cut garments, they comprised a suit of a delicate shade of purple, together with a fancy tie designed in shot silk by a man with a warped imagination, and the ensemble neatly finished off by bright yellow shoes of incredible length and narrowness.

Mr Campion surveyed him against the venerable dark oak panelling. 'Quite the little knut, isn't he?' he said pleasantly.

Mr Knapp removed a large, flat, buff superstructure and smiled at Marlowe, revealing an astonishing assortment of teeth.

''E's a spark, ain't 'e?' he said, jerking his head towards Campion affably. 'Pleased to meet you, I'm sure. Well, Bertie, I've come down for a bit of private conversation with you. Nice little place you've got 'ere. I didn't 'alf 'ave a time findin' it on my bike. I left it outside. By the way, I suppose it'll be safe? I 'ad to pinch the bike in Ipswich or I shouldn't 'ave got 'ere at all. Wonderful quiet place. I didn't even 'ave to paint it. I often feel you and me could do something in these parts, Bertie.'

'How did you know I was here?' said Campion.

'Ah!' Mr Knapp put his head upon one side and spoke with

exaggerated caution. 'You may know, Bertie, that from time to time I come across bits of information.' He glanced at Marlowe questioningly.

Campion nodded. 'That's all right,' he said. 'One of us.'

'Is that so?' Mr Knapp shook hands with Marlowe once more.

'On the American side,' Campion explained easily. 'But what I want to know is how you found me here.'

'Now then, now then, not so eager,' said Mr Knapp playfully. 'As a matter o' fac', Magersfontein Lugg put me on to you. And a very good job 'e did, too. I've got something that will interest you, Bertie.'

Campion shook his head. 'I'm sorry, Knappy,' he said, 'but nothing that isn't directly connected with the job I'm on at the moment ever interests me.'

'Well!' said Mr Knapp indignantly. 'Well! Bit free, aren't yer? Bit free? Wot d'yer think I come down 'ere for? Fifteen miles on a ruddy bicycle. Are you teetotal in this 'ouse?'

Marlowe grinned. 'Bring him into the study,' he said. 'I'll get some beer.' He went off, and Mr Knapp looked after him appreciatively.

'A nice chap to work with, I should think,' he said. 'You're always lucky, you are, Bertie. Lovely place, nice people, food and drink *ad lib*. It isn't as though you was smart or anything. It's luck, that's what it is.'

'Now look here,' said Campion. 'Out with it. What's the information? Remember, if it's any more of your filthy Rubinstein tricks I'll chuck you out as I told you I would. I'm not interested, see?'

'All right,' said Mr Knapp, 'I only 'appened to 'ear something directly connected with you and this 'ere Lobbett business, so I come all the way to see yer.'

Mr Campion's interest was now thoroughly aroused. 'Hold on a moment,' he said. 'This sounds more like it.'

'Wot did I tell yer?' said Mr Knapp. 'You an' me 'ave worked in the past, Bertie. We're after the same style, we are. We understand one another.'

Mr Campion made no comment, and at this moment Marlowe's voice from the other end of the corridor so distracted Mr Knapp that he was completely uncommunicative until he found himself seated at the heavy oak table in the library, a glass at his side.

'That's right,' he said, wiping his mouth. 'When I die, don't forget, Bertie – wreath of 'ops. Now, I dessay I'm 'olding you up. You know my terms, old sport.'

He nodded to Campion, who signed to him to continue.

'Well, then, we won't go into my methods before strangers' – he winked at Campion – 'but yesterday afternoon I 'appened to over'ear a very curious conversation.'

'On the telephone?' said Campion.

'Natcherally. Private line wot I was interested in. Never got much off it before – only recently been installed. But wot I 'eard was this – roughly, you understand.'

He paused, and produced a small shabby notebook. 'I cops in 'arfway through, you get me, so I didn't 'ear the beginning. There was two voices, one soft and smooth as you like, and the other sounded like it was disguised. Assumed foreign accent, I reckoned. This last one seemed to be the boss. "Wot?" 'e was sayin', "that man's a fool – get rid of 'im. Who sent the clothes?" Then the other chap says, "There was no message, only the 'andwritin' on the label". Then the boss says, "Well, that's the man you want, isn't it?"'

Mr Knapp looked up. 'This didn't seem no use to me,' he continued. 'And then, quite sudden, the boss says, "'Oo's this Albert Campion?" and the other chap says, "I'll find out about 'im". Then of course I was interested, but they didn't say much more after that. All I 'eard was the boss say, "If it was the girl's writin' get 'er up an' put 'er through it. You can arrange that. She must know somethink. As soon as you 'ear anythink, communicate with me in the usual way," says the voice. Then 'e rings off.'

Marlowe looked at Campion, but his eyes were hidden behind his glasses and his face was expressionless. 'Look here, Thos,' he said, 'where did you hear all this?'

Mr Knapp shook his head and appealed to Marlowe. 'Artful, ain't 'e?' he said. 'Before we go any further I want to know just 'ow interested you are in this. 'Ow do we stand?'

Campion sighed. 'Thos, you make me writhe,' he said. 'How much do you want?'

Mr Knapp rose to his feet. 'I'll tell you wot,' he said, 'I'll be a gent too. I'll come in with you. I can be a good sport when I like. I've often wanted to work with you again, Bertie,' he went on, somewhat lugubriously. 'Do you remember –?'

Mr Campion coughed. 'We won't go into that now,' he said. 'Let me point something out to you. Unless you know where these people were speaking from this information is no more than we know already.'

'Wait a minute,' said Mr Knapp. '*Wait* for it. That is just exactly wot I do know. And I'm makin' you a gentlemanly offer – wot I wouldn't if I didn't know you. I'll come in with you. When we're successful you coughs up and you coughs up 'andsome. 'Ow's that?'

'Fine,' said Mr Campion. 'But what do you imagine we're up to?'

Mr Knapp hesitated. 'Seems I'm doin' all the talkin',' he said. 'But since I know you, Bertie, I'll say that one of yer little party 'ere is about to be took off to 'ave a particularly nasty time. Is there a young woman down 'ere?'

Marlowe spoke before Campion could stop him. 'As a matter of fact,' he said, 'Miss Paget has already disappeared.'

'Ho?' said Mr Knapp, his eyes flickering. 'So you wasn't comin' across, Bertie? Well, I'll treat you fair, if you don't me. Fifty quid for that address, and another fifty when we get the girl back. Then I'll 'elp you, for the sake of old times. Saved me ruddy life, 'e did once,' he added conversationally to Marlowe. 'Stuffed me down a drain and kept me there till danger was past. I've never forgot that. Now what do you say to that, Bert?'

'Since we're all on the make,' said Campion slowly, 'I'll give you a piece of information for your first fifty and the second fifty down when we get the girl.'

'Wot information?' said Mr Knapp cautiously.

'A little matter of "snide",' said Campion lightly. 'I think you ought to know about it.'

All the bounce left Mr Knapp. 'I'm on,' he said softly. 'Come across. That's my old man, you know. Break 'is 'eart if anythink 'appened to that business.'

'That's right,' said Campion affably. 'You're the heir, aren't you?'

'Come across,' said Mr Knapp doggedly.

'They're watching the building. I'd get your grandfather to move if I were you. Etching presses are very suspicious.'

''Ow do I know you're not kiddin'?'

'Well you can always stay and find out,' said Campion carelessly. 'But there's a new flower-seller at the end of the street, and an invalid man spends most of his time in a wheel chair on the balcony of the house opposite.'

'I see,' said Mr Knapp thoughtfully. 'I see. Gawd! 'Ood a' thought of that after all these years!' He seemed lost in contemplation. Campion brought him back to earth.

'Suppose you give us the address.'

'Thirty-two Beverley Gardens, Kensington, W8.' He spoke without hesitation. 'It's a nice little 'ouse. Swell part. I 'ad a look at it as I come past. Three floors an' a basement. Steps up to front door. Easiest entrance by the roof. I got it all taped for you. I was workin' it all out as I come down, just in case.'

He unfolded a grubby sheet of paper from his notebook. The other two bent over it.

'Now this 'ere,' he said, tapping a series of hieroglyphics with a distressing forefinger, 'this gives you the 'ole plan of the roofs. This 'ouse is where I 'ang out. It backs almost directly on to Beverley Gardens. If we made my place the 'eadquarters – I'm on the top floor – we could nip across them roofs as easy as kiss yer 'and. They won't think of keepin' an eye on the roof, but I see a couple o' heavy blokes watchin' the place as I come past and I dessay there's 'arf a dozen others inside. Money no object, it looked to me. I know the plan o' the house, too,' he went on, 'because all that row is built on the same idea and the last one's empty. I gave it the once-over in case there was any decent fittings left behind. Now just 'ere there's a skylight which looks like wot we want. That gives into a sort of boxroom – the smallest of two attics. Outside that door there's the stairs that goes down on to the first landing. After that –'

He was interrupted by Giles, who thrust his head round the door. 'I suppose you know lunch has been waiting for half an hour?' he said. 'Where's Biddy? I thought she was with you, Marlowe.'

He stopped short at the sight of Mr Knapp. Campion beckoned him into the room and closed the door behind him. 'Look here, old boy,' he said, 'we've got to get up to London as quick as we can. Don't get the wind up, but they've got Biddy.'

It was some moments before Giles comprehended. Campion explained all they knew of her disappearance, and gradually the slow anger kindled in the boy's eyes.

'My God, someone'll pay for this,' he said. 'I'll thrash that little whelp Kettle within an inch of his life.'

Campion frowned. 'My dear old bird,' he said, 'we shall need all the spitefulness you can muster this evening. Get her back first. Our friend here seems to have been doing a spot of borough surveying on our behalf. By the way' – he turned to Knapp – 'I suppose you've got all the necessary penknives and whatnots?'

Mr Knapp's expression was eloquent. 'Wot d'you take me for?' he said. 'I got all my uncle's stuff after 'e was pinched. Wot we want' – he ticked the items off on his fingers – 'is a couple o' jemmies, a small 'ook ladder, and 'arf a dozen life preservers, assorted sizes. A good old-fashioned outfit. Wot surprises me, you know, Bert,' he went on, suddenly changing his tone, 'is that these people should kidnap anyone. It ain't their line by a long chalk.'

Campion swung round on him. 'Who do you think they are?'

''Oo do I *know* they are,' said the visitor. 'A new lot – blackmail, I shouldn't wonder. The chap tells fortunes – a bloke with a red beard.'

'Anthony Datchett?'

'Is that wot 'e calls 'imself?' Mr Knapp was unimpressed. 'The only thing I thought was funny was 'im goin' in for this sort of thing at all. Seems to me 'e's doin' a job for someone, same as I'm doin' a job for you.'

'Answered in one,' said Campion. 'As far as intelligence is concerned you're coming on, Thos.'

'That's right, flatter me,' said Mr Knapp, without enthusiasm.

'What I can't understand,' broke in Giles explosively, 'is why they took Biddy. There were all the rest of us about – why pitch on her?'

'That's easy,' said Knapp. 'I told these chaps that at the beginning. She sent a parcel of clothes by post, wot was mucked about with. Which is, I take it, wot they want to know about.'

The three others exchanged glances.

'Clothes?' said Giles. 'He must mean Judge Lobbett's clothes – the suit Kettle said he'd found. Biddy sent them away by post?' He sat down heavily in a chair and looked at them blankly.

'I deliberately refuse to consider that question,' said Marlowe. 'Find her first.'

Chapter 19
The Tradesmen's Entrance

Mr Campion's council of war was made unexpectedly stormy by Giles. Until now he had borne the nightmare experiences of the past few days with comparative equanimity, but the latest development was too much for him: it seemed to have aroused every spark of obstinacy in his nature.

'Look here,' he said. 'I'm sorry to be uncivil, but it does strike me as being very fishy that the moment my sister disappears up comes Mr Knapp with the details for rescuing her all worked out pat. How do you know that he's not in with these people?'

'Now, calm yerself, calm yerself,' said the accused one soothingly. 'An' don't interrupt me, Bertie,' he added, waving a hand to silence Campion. 'This gent's asked me a straight question; 'e's entitled to a straight answer. Fishy it may look, but it ain't really. And why? I'll tell you.' He came over to the young man and caught him by the lapel with a slightly greasy thumb and forefinger. 'Magersfontein Lugg an' me 'as been pals for some years. Union of bonds, as you might say.' He winked at Campion knowingly. 'Last week 'e come to me an' 'e said "Our friend Bertie"– 'e works for Bertie: cleans the 'ouse up an' gives the place a tone – "Our friend Bertie," 'e says, "is off on some very nasty business. 'E 'asn't told me nothing, but you, bein' a knowin' one, might keep yer eyes open." So I 'ave.'

He stood back from Giles and grinned as though he felt he had completely allayed any doubts in the young man's mind. Giles, however, was unimpressed.

'That's all very well,' he said, 'but what could you do?'

'Oh, I see!' Mr Knapp's tone was more intimate than ever. 'P'r'aps I'd better introduce myself. I used to work for the Government on the telephone repairs. Then me an' the Postmaster-General, we 'ad a bit of a tiff an' I retired from public life an' service for a spell. When I come out I thought I'd make use of my electrical knowledge, an' I've worked up a very tidy little connection. You may not know it, but all over London there's 'undreds of private wires, some of 'em straight, some fishy.' He paused. 'Now do you get me?'

'No,' said Giles.

Mr Knapp grinned at Marlowe and tapped his forehead significantly. 'That's where'e wants it,' he remarked pleasantly. 'Well, I'll tell you. It's the easiest thing to listen on to a wire, if you knows the way. You'd be surprised at the stuff I pick up. Filthy goin's-on in 'igh life wot you wouldn't believe.'

Without speaking, Giles looked at Campion, who smiled in spite of himself at his friend's expression.

'Well,' continued Mr Knapp, 'me bein' on the lookout, it ain't really surprisin' that I 'appened to 'ear something of interest. I come down as quick as I could, 'opin' to be a prevention rather than a cure. But since things 'ave 'appened as they 'ave 'appened we're doin' what we can to make the best of it. Take my tip, old son, and leave the arrangements to Bertie – 'e's got the kind of mind for a do of this sort. I remember once –'

Mr Campion interrupted him hastily. 'Keep your jokes for your profession,' he said. 'Now look here. The proceeding is, I take it, something like this –'

'If you know the address of the house, why not call the police in?' said Giles.

'Because, oh heart – and head – of oak,' said Campion gently, 'we don't know if Biddy's there, in the first place, and in the second, they're bound to have some perfectly good get-away. The only thing to do to prevent the poor kid from being longer in their hands than we can help is to get her out ourselves if she's there, and if she isn't, to scout about till we do find her. We're evidently on their track.'

Giles folded his arms and stared gloomily before him.

'All right, get on with it,' he said. 'What do you suggest?'

Mr Campion perched himself on the table, where he sat with his knees drawn up a little, peering round at them through his spectacles.

'We shall have to go carefully,' he said. 'You see, according to Knapp, ever since yesterday afternoon Mr Datchett and his chorus boys have been making investigations concerning our Albert. If they discover some of his pet names they will be on the watch for us pretty closely. They may even have someone watching us here. I don't think Kettle will be much good to them any more, but there's bound to be someone else on the road just over the Stroud. Therefore we must not parade ourselves. The simplest thing, I fancy, is for us to appeal to old Baa Baa Blacksheep, who I see is still with us. They'd never suspect him, so if we could get him to take you all the way to Knapp's we'd be fairly safe.' He laughed. 'Isopel will have to come with us. We daren't leave her here. I think the best place for her is my flat; it's over a police station, you know. I'll drive her there myself in my own bus, so that anyone on the look-out for us will only know that Isopel and I have gone off and Mr Barber has returned to London. That's straight enough.'

'Then they'll think that all the rest of us are down here?' said Giles.

Campion beamed at him. 'That's the idea. Of course they may not be watching, but it's as well to take the precaution,' he said. 'Now, that's all set, then, if you people agree to it.'

Marlowe nodded. 'I'm with you,' he said. 'Isopel and I have put ourselves completely in your hands all along and I believe you'll pull us through.'

Campion grinned. 'For these kind words, many thanks,' he said. 'There's only one snag in it,' he went on, 'and that is our little picture-postcard expert.'

'I think I can manage him' – Marlowe spoke confidently. 'I'll go and talk to him. I'd like to see Isopel too.'

He went out of the room, leaving the others still conferring.

'I see the idea, Bertie.' Mr Knapp pushed the beer away from him regretfully. 'You take this other girl to safety an' pick up the one or two things you'll need at your place, an' I'll manage this bunch. I'll 'ave 'em all primed up. I don't like workin' with amateurs, but there's nothin' like beef in a rough 'ouse. My old ma'll be up there, you know. She'll give us a 'and with the get-away if necessary. There's not much she don't know.'

Mr Campion looked sceptical, but he did not speak, and presently Marlowe came into the room with Mr Barber.

'Certainly,' he said, 'I will give anybody a lift to London.'

'So I should 'ope,' muttered Mr Knapp. 'Now I reckon the earlier we start the better. So pull yer socks up, mates.'

Mrs Whybrow received careful instructions from Giles. She was not to go into the village, no one was to know that they were not all still in the house. She was a sensible woman and took her instructions placidly.

Campion packed the three men, Giles and Marlowe with Mr Knapp, into the back of Mr Barber's car.

'The police won't stop an out-going car on the Stroud. Mr Barber, we shall be eternally grateful to you.'

The old man bent towards him and spoke in a confidential rumble.

'My dear sir,' he said, 'if you could persuade Mr Paget to consent to allow me to handle the sale of his picture, the gratitude would be entirely mine.'

He drove off, and Campion turned to Isopel. She was standing waiting for him, wrapped up in a fur coat, although it was summer. She looked very small and terrified standing there, her white face peering out from the dark fur of her high collar.

He smiled at her. 'Scared?' he said.

'No.' She shook her head. 'Not any more. That part of me has gone numb.'

He frowned. 'That's bad. Do you think you could do something for me? I want you to drive this car from here over the Stroud. I shall do a neat impersonation of a parcel at your feet. There's no danger. I just don't want anyone in the village to know that I've left the house.'

She nodded. 'Why, surely.'

Mr Campion doubled himself up at the bottom of the car. 'She's the easiest thing in the world to drive,' he murmured. 'There's one gear that I know of. Any other handle you pull you get your money back.'

The journey from Mystery Mile to the Ipswich road passed without excitement, and Mr Campion emerged from his hiding-place. 'Now I'll take her,' he said. 'You've managed her marvellously. I've never known her to move for a woman before. It's a sort of jealousy, I think.'

Isopel did not appear to be listening to him.

'Mr Campion,' she said, 'you're not talking about this – this terrible thing that has happened to Biddy because you're afraid of frightening me. But don't think about that, please. I want to do all I can to help. Marlowe is in love with her, you know. I think they fell for each other when they first met.'

The car was racing along the main Woodbridge-Ipswich road, and the young man did not take his eyes off the giddy stretch before them.

'You mean they'd probably want to marry?' he said.

'Oh yes, I think so. Isn't it funny that he and she should feel like that when I and –'

She paused abruptly, and Mr Campion did not press her to continue. She sat back in the car, a thoughtful look in her dark eyes. Suddenly she turned again.

'I suppose,' she said jerkily, 'that no one knows about – about the red knight, do they?'

'Don't forget your promise.' The words were spoken lightly

enough, but there was no mistaking the sincerity beneath them. 'No one, in the world, must know anything about that.'

She caught her breath. 'I'm sorry,' she said, 'but sometimes I feel so terribly afraid.'

'Don't worry. I'll get her back if it's the last thing I do.' The vigorous determination in his voice surprised her, and she turned to him, but Mr Campion's face was as pleasantly vacuous and inane as it had ever been.

He made for a garage on the east side of Regent Street.

'I hope you won't mind,' he said, beaming down at her as they emerged into Piccadilly Circus, 'but I'm afraid I shall have to take you into my place by the tradesmen's entrance. You never know at a time like this who may be watching the front door. This is another dark secret, by the way. I think I'll have to insist that you stay at my flat,' he went on. 'It's the one really safe place in London for you. There's a police station downstairs. I'm only taking you in the back way so that no one will see me. I don't want any ovation from the populace.'

He pointed her across the road and down one of the small turnings on the opposite side, and paused at last before what looked to Isopel like a small but expensive restaurant. They went in, and, passing through a line of tables, entered a smaller room leading off the main hall where favoured patrons were served. The place was deserted, and Mr Campion approached the service door and held it open for her.

'I must show you my little kitchenette,' he said. 'It's too *bijou* for anything.'

Isopel looked round her. On her right was an open doorway disclosing a vast kitchen beyond, on her left a narrow passage leading apparently to the manager's office. Campion walked in.

A grey-haired foreigner rose to meet him. It was evident that he recognized the young man, but to the girl's surprise he did not speak to him. He led them silently into an inner room and threw open a cupboard doorway.

'I'll go first.' Campion spoke softly. With a great show of secrecy the foreigner nodded, and, standing back, disclosed what appeared to be a very ordinary service lift which was apparently used principally for food. One of the shelves had been removed, and Mr Campion climbed into the opening with as much dignity as he could muster.

'See Britain first,' he said oracularly, and pressed the button so that, as if the words had been a command, he shot up suddenly out of sight.

Isopel opened her mouth to speak, but the foreigner placed a finger on his lips and looked about him with such an expression of apprehension that she was silenced immediately. Within a minute the lift reappeared, a big blue cushion in the bottom of it. A voice floated down the shaft. 'My second name is Raleigh. *Houp*, Elizabeth!'

The mysterious foreigner helped the girl into the lift as if he feared that at any moment they might be attacked. The journey was not so uncomfortable as it looked, and as she felt herself being drawn up into the darkness, Isopel's sense of the ridiculous was touched and she began to laugh.

'That's fine,' said Campion, helping her out into the dining-room of his flat. 'Was old Rodriguez too much for your gravity? He's a wonderful chap. He owns that restaurant, and makes a damn good thing out of it – the old robber! The only way I get him to let me use the lift as an entrance is by pretending it's a case of life or death. He has a secret thirst for adventure, and my little goings and comings by the back door give him no end of a thrill. As a matter of fact, a previous tenant here had the lift put in to have his food sent up. Rodriguez is a nice chap, but he will act his part, which becomes a little trying at times. Now look here,' he went on, conducting her into the other room. 'You'll be quite all right here. Lugg, I fancy, is already at the scene of operations, but you'll have Autolycus to keep you company. You'll have to watch your jewellery, that's all. It's living with Lugg that does it.'

He was bustling about the room as he spoke, selecting various odds and ends from a Sheraton bureau at the far end of the room and a deep cupboard by the fireplace.

'If you get hungry, just shout down the lift. If you get scared, just shout out of the window. If anyone should call, don't open the door. Especially not to an old gentleman with an aerial to his top hat and natty black gaiters. That's my wicked uncle. You can see everyone who comes in the mirror on the inside of the door. It works on the periscope principle. All done with a few common chalks.'

Isopel watched him as he pottered about the room. For some moments the girl seemed on the verge of speaking. At last she found her courage.

'Mr Campion,' she said, 'don't let Giles do anything silly – or Marlowe either, of course,' she added hastily. 'You'll look after them?'

'As if they were my own sons, madam,' said Campion, beaming at her. 'Both young gentlemen will be under the direct care of the Matron.'

She laughed, but her eyes were still anxious. 'You see,' she burst out suddenly, the colour suffusing her face, 'you don't know how dreadfully worrying it is to be in love.'

Mr Campion crossed over to the lift. She could see him through the open doorway from where she sat. He climbed in with great dignity, and sat there, looking ineffably comic, his knees drawn up to his chin, as he regarded her owlishly from behind his spectacles.

'That's all you know, young woman,' he said solemnly, and shut the hatch.

Chapter 20

The Profession

The glories of Pedigree Mews had departed for ever. There were not even children playing in the uneven brick sink which formed the street, and the whole place had a furtive and surly aspect.

It lay at right angles to the blind alley which was Beverley Mews on the one side, and Wishart Street, which wriggled down into Church Street, Kensington, on the other. A dangerous and depressing spot.

Mr Campion glanced up and down the row. There was not a soul in sight. Number Twelve A was a dilapidated doorway in the corner between the two mews.

He pushed open the door, and entered into a passage smelling horribly of damp and cats. In front of him was a square patch of light revealing the tiny yard of the house, probably even more execrable than the passage itself. Just before the yard entrance he stumbled upon a dirty flight of stairs which wound a narrow way up into the building. Here the odours became more intense and were mingled with others even less attractive. Mr Campion ascended gingerly, keeping clear of the walls. As he reached the top floor, which consisted of two rooms, the doors of which formed two sides of a tiny square landing, he heard the unmistakable voice of Thos T. Knapp himself, clearly intent on being hospitable.

'Mother, make room on the bed for Mr Barber. 'E don't look 'appy in the corner there.'

Campion paused and whistled softly. The door was opened immediately, and Mr Lugg came edging his way out. He was even more gloomy than before, and he regarded Mr Campion appraisingly.

'Think you're clever, don't you?' he remarked in a throaty rumble. 'When you're goin' into a really nasty business, 'oo do you get round you? Two ruddy amateurs and somethin' out of a carpet shop. Gawd, you should see wot's goin' on in there.' He clicked his tongue against his teeth contemptuously. '*Don't* lean against that wall,' he added hastily. 'It's *me* wot looks after yer clothes, don't forget.'

'Look here,' said Campion mildly, 'this nursemaid impersonation of yours is getting on my nerves. Why did you get Knapp into this when I told you not to?'

'It was done afore you spoke.' Lugg was not in the least abashed. 'The day you gets plugged is the day I lose my job. I'm lookin' after you, see? I believe you've beat me this time, though,' he added lugubriously. 'S'pose I bring Thos out and we 'ave a talk in the other room? There's an atmosphere of 'appy-go-lucky in there wot neely makes me sick.'

Without waiting for a reply, he put his head round the door and made an inarticulate sound. Mr Knapp appeared at once.

''Ullo, Bertie,' he said pleasantly. 'We ain't 'arf got a little party in 'ere. My old ma says she feels she's got all 'er sons round 'er again.'

Mr Lugg raised his hand. 'Pleasantries is over,' he said. 'Take 'im into the other room, Thos, and we'll 'ave a talk.'

'Righto.' Mr Knapp threw open the door of the second room. 'Plenty of time – 'opeless to try anythin' in this light. This 'ere is wot I call my workshop. Nice little place, ain't it?'

The room into which he conducted them was about ten feet square, low-ceilinged and as dirty as the approach had suggested. There were two long trestle tables which practically filled it, and upon these were odd pairs of earphones, vast quantities of wire, electric plugs, a home-made switchboard, and any amount of other odds and ends, all more or less in direct connection with Mr Knapp's unpleasant hobby.

'There you are,' he said, throwing out a hand. 'All give me by the Government in unconscious recognition of my services. There's one of the old Bell telephones over there – come from Clerkenwell – interestin' relic.'

'Stop yer reminiscences,' said Mr Lugg. ''Oo do you think you are? A retired admiral? This 'ere's business. I expect trouble, I don't mind tellin' you. I see yer 'ouse is Twelve A. Thirteen that ought to be by rights.'

'Shut up,' said Mr Knapp with unexpected bad temper. 'There's a thirteen 'igher up the street. Bloke's in quod.'

'I hear you've got Mr Barber in the next room,' said Campion. 'What's the idea? Have you any objects of virtue up here, Thos?'

'I 'ate jokes about sex,' said Mr Knapp sententiously. 'No, I brought 'im up 'ere because I thought 'is car might be 'andy if we 'ad to 'urry off. I couldn't very well keep it and not 'im. When dealin' with gents you 'ave to be a gent, so I says, "Come up an' see mother". 'E's not 'appy in there, but mother'll keep 'im quiet. She's as good as a bull pup.'

'Cut the guff,' said Mr Lugg. ''Oo the 'ell cares, anyway?'

Mr Knapp pulled himself together. ''Eave yerself over this 'ere bench an' take a look out o' the window. D'you see where we are? No? Well, that's the end 'ouse of Beverley Gardens, that is. Now run yer eye along.' He was holding Campion firmly by the shoulder as he spoke. 'Stand well back so as no one don't see you from the window. Now that 'ouse with the blue curtain to the top window – see it? – that's the 'ouse we want. It's not much of a climb,' he went on. 'This 'ere ledge outside 'ere goes straight along till we get to the flat roof of the shop. Mother can do it easy, so you ought to.'

'Then there's a spot of mountaineering,' said Campion.

'That's right,' said Mr Knapp. 'That'll be easy enough. I got me ladder 'ere. There's plenty o' rubber shoes about, too.'

'I brought mine with me,' said Mr Lugg, taking a pair of mysteriously constructed rubber clogs from a brown-paper parcel which he carried.

Mr Knapp looked at him with undisguised amusement. 'Gawd! You don't use them old things, do you? I ain't seen those since I was a nipper. Wotcher, Spring'eel Jack!'

'Think yer clever, don't you?' said Mr Lugg. 'These are an heirloom, that's wot these are.'

Campion turned away from the window. 'When do we start?' he said. 'As soon as it gets dark? Round about half-past ten?'

'That's about it,' said Mr Knapp. 'Nearly everyone's out o' doors or at any rate downstairs about that time.'

'I think we'd better join the lady,' said Campion. 'And I tell you, Knapp, you'd better keep your exuberance down a bit. Those two kids in the next room are both deeply interested in the girl, so don't let them do anything silly if you can prevent it.'

'Am I likely to?' said Mr Knapp with contempt. 'I'm in, too, ain't I? I've showed 'em the plan o' the works an' they seemed quite intelligent to me. Oh, well, it won't be the first time you an' me's been in a rough 'ouse, Bertie, will it? Do you remember, Lugg, you an' me in that 'ouse in Chiswick? Old girl three flights up kept 'anging over the banister screamin' like a train. "Rapine!" she shouts. A great big cop was sittin' on my chest, but I couldn't 'elp laughin'.'

Mr Lugg snorted contemptuously, and Campion pushed his way into the other room.

At first sight the happy-go-luckiness to which Mr Lugg had alluded was painfully apparent. This room, only a foot or so larger than the one they had just left, served the Knapp family as a complete domicile. In spite of the heat of the day, the window was tightly closed, and a saucepan boiled upon the gas stove. It was impossible to see clearly across the room for tobacco smoke and certain bedraggled pieces of laundry were suspended from an impromptu clothes-line. A large iron bedstead blocked one corner of the room, a smaller one prevented the door from opening properly on the other side, and the mother's and son's complete wardrobes were hung up along the farther wall.

In the midst of this discomfort Mrs Knapp presided affably over a worn and impatient gathering. She was a vast florid person clad in an assortment of garments, each one of which attempted to do only half the duty for which it had originally been intended. Her face was chiefly remarkable for some three or four attempts at a beard which grew out of large brown moles scattered over her many chins.

She was seated upon the larger bed, and beside her, dignified but uncomfortable, was the unfortunate Mr Barber.

Giles and Marlowe greeted Campion with relief.

'Thank heaven you've come!' said the American. 'Isn't it time we started?'

'My dear old bird, I'm palpitating for the fray,' said Campion emphatically. 'But it's absolutely no use starting in the daylight because we shouldn't get there. We shall have to wait for some considerable time longer.'

'This is damnable,' said Marlowe. 'Poor kid, you don't know what they may be doing to her. It makes me mad.' He ground his heel savagely into the floor.

'You sit down, matey, an 'ave a friendly game o' cards.' Mr Knapp was doing his best to be reassuring. 'I'd go an' 'ave a mike round for you, but it's too light as yet. We can't do anythin'.'

'Suicide to go out now,' added Mr Lugg sepulchrally. 'We professionals, we know.'

Giles was sitting on a piece of newspaper carefully spread over the boards, his knees drawn up to his chin and an utterly dejected expression on his face. 'Gosh, I shall be glad when we can start,' he said feelingly.

'You won't, once the time comes,' said Mr Lugg with disquieting solemnity. 'We're goin' to be for it tonight. I've got that feelin'.'

Mrs Knapp turned upon him and emitted such a stream of blasphemies that everyone except her son was startled.

'Mother's superstitious,' said Knapp. 'She don't like premonitions.'

The lady, having recovered her serenity, smiled at them toothily. It was at this moment that Mr Barber staggered to his feet.

'I do not wish to appear unsporting,' he said, 'but really I think I had better go. I feel that I shall not be of any further service to you.'

The Knapps turned upon him as one person.

'You stay where you are. If you go now you'll give the 'ole show away,' said Thos. 'Mother, pass the gentleman yer bottle.'

Mr Barber was forced back. He sat looking round in helpless misery. Mrs Knapp took no notice of her son's last remark, much to the Oriental's relief, and a sticky pack of cards was produced.

'Nothink like poker,' said Mr Knapp. 'An' remember, gentlemen, this is a friendly game.'

'It seems almost a waste of time,' said Mr Lugg, drawing up a broken-backed chair.

Marlowe moved over to Campion. 'You're sure this is the best thing?' he murmured. 'I feel ready to burst.'

Campion bent towards him, and for a moment he saw the seriousness in the pale eyes behind the big spectacles. 'It's our only chance, old bird,' he said. 'We're going the moment we've the least hope.'

Marlowe glanced at him sharply. 'You expect serious trouble?'

'I expect a small war,' said Campion frankly.

Chapter 21

Mr Campion's Nerve

'Argue as much as you like, mother,' said Mr Knapp. 'Five queens is five queens. If these gentlemen will accept the fact that some o' the old pack 'ave got mixed in we'll say no more about it. Personally, I think the time's gettin' on.'

'That's right,' said Mr Lugg. 'I'll be gettin' me boots off.'

The atmosphere of the small room, which had been steadily thickening for the past two hours, was now positively sulphurous. Mr Barber, after several unsuccessful attempts to make a graceful departure, had resigned himself to his unwholesome fate. Mrs Knapp was keeping her eye on him.

Marlowe and Giles, who were profoundly relieved at the idea of doing something, at last rose to their feet, whilst the lady of the party gathered up her winnings unashamedly.

Now that the moment of action was approaching, Messrs Lugg and Knapp took charge of the proceedings with the air of specialists. Knapp produced a couple of life preservers and gave Marlowe and Giles a few well-thought-out words of instruction.

'Just a gentle tap, reelly,' he said – '*be'ind* the ear – or over it – or above it – administered firmly and with precision.'

They removed their coats at Mr Knapp's suggestion. The seriousness of the affair began to assume its proper proportion.

Campion removed his glasses.

'I see so much better without them,' he explained, and set about changing his shoes.

Mother Knapp began to move about with feline quietness, producing rubber-soled shoes and small tots of rum and water.

'Now, look 'ere,' said her son, when they had all assembled in the back room. 'We goes carefully *an'* quietly, takin' our time, an' no mistakes. Keep off the skyline as much as possible, 'eads low, as a rule. Once there, I nips in first, bein' fairly light an' 'avin' a knowledge of the 'ouse. Then I comes out an' tells you 'ow the land lies, an' 'an's over my command to Bertie, as you might say.'

'And I?' said Mr Barber from the doorway. 'Really I –'

Mrs Knapp appeared behind him. 'You stay with me, dearie,' she said. 'Till they come back.' All five of Mrs Knapp's teeth appeared in a devastating smile. 'You'll stay with me, won't you, lovey?' she said, and gently drew the unfortunate Oriental into the other room.

Mr Knapp continued. 'Now then, me first, Bertie second. Then you two lads, then Lugg. Don't forget, soft on the slates an' quiet on the tiles. If you 'ear me whistle, stop dead, an' lie as flat as you can. Now, are you ready?'

'Any more for the "Skylark"?' murmured Mr Campion. 'Lovely drying day.'

Mr Knapp raised the window gently and crawled out on to the ledge. After a moment of suspense they heard his whisper: 'All clear. Come on.'

'Railin's with spikes on under 'ere, shouldn't be surprised,' said Mr Lugg huskily from the background. 'Gently does it.'

The night was clear but moonless. There were people in the farther streets, and a rumble of traffic came to them. Nearly all the windows that lay beneath their path were dark, as Mr Knapp had predicted.

Ahead of them to the east the lights of London made a glow in the sky. The air was warm, and the scents of the great city – fruit, face powder, petrol fumes, and dust – were not too unpleasantly mixed together.

The going was not so much perilous as awkward, after the first giddy twenty feet or so of parapet. Mr Knapp unfolded a collapsible ladder which he was apparently used to carrying, since he managed its conveyance with extraordinary skill. On it they climbed up from the lower roofs of the shops to the flat lead-covered tops of the houses in Beverley Gardens. Mr Lugg, bringing up the rear, left it in position for the return.

The trip was not without its thrills. As Mr Knapp dropped lightly on to the roof of the second house in the row, a woman's voice, old and querulous, shouted at him through an open window:

'Who's there?'

'London Telephone Service, ma'am. Breakdown gang. Tracing a wire.' Mr Knapp's cheerful tone would have satisfied the most timid.

There was a satisfied grunt from the darkness, and they pushed on again. The sweat was pouring off Giles's face. Both he and Marlowe were law-abiding souls, and were it not for the all-important motive which now impelled them, neither of them would have dreamed of assisting in such an enterprise.

'It's the next 'ouse after this,' murmured Mr Knapp, and paused abruptly, nudging Campion. 'Absolutely askin' for it – this lot,' he said, indicating the skylight of the roof on which they now stood. It was wide open. He bent over it and idly ran his torch round the dark room. It appeared to be a studio. The little circle of light rested upon a side table, where, beside a telephone, stood a decanter and a siphon.

'Wot a spot o' luck if we wasn't busy,' he remarked casually. 'Afraid we shan't be so 'appy next door.'

One by one they clambered over the narrow stone coping which separated the two roofs.

'Gently does it – gently,' Mr Knapp whispered as the two amateurs climbed somewhat nervily over it. 'Keep yer 'eads down. 'Ere we are, then,' he went on to Campion. 'I ain't actually been 'ere afore, you understand, but I got a nice pair o' binoculars at my place – a present from my old colonel. I've always felt 'e meant to give 'em to me. Now, a jemmy or a diamond, d'you think?'

'Diamond,' said Mr Lugg. 'Less noisy. There's no one underneath. Sure this is the 'ouse?'

'Shut up, 'Appy,' said Mr Knapp. Now that the procedure had been decided upon he set to work with a silent and a practised hand.

The tension among the onlookers became strained, as he drew out a piece of glass on a rubber sucker, slipped in his hand, and raising the catch gently laid the window back upon the leads. All was dark and silent inside the house.

'Not a bit o' light showin' anywhere,' said Mr Lugg, who had investigated both sides of the building from the roof. 'Now then, Thos, in with you. I'll see you buried decent.'

Mr Knapp made a careful survey of the interior of the room below, which appeared empty, and then, gripping the lintel firmly in both hands, swung gently into the air and dropped noiselessly into the room.

'Lie flat,' commanded Lugg. 'You don't know nothing, none of you. Be ready to nip off like 'ell if there's a row.'

There was a soft click from the room below them, and the tiny circle of Mr Knapp's torch was seen no more. They waited listening, every nerve strained, anxious to catch the least sound from the silent house below them. The minutes passed with agonizing slowness. Still Mr Knapp did not return.

At last even Lugg began to show signs of uneasiness.

'Thos ain't the chap to stay in a nasty spot fer fun,' he muttered nervously. Marlowe edged nearer, Giles behind him.

'Can't we go in?' he said. 'After him?'

'You'll stay where you are,' growled Mr Lugg.

Campion, who was bending over the dark square of the open skylight, suddenly dodged back. *'Cave,'* he whispered.

An unnatural stillness fell over the whole party. No one breathed. At last a welcome whisper sounded out of the darkness.

'Give us a hand, matey.'

Lugg and Campion thrust down an arm each, and the next moment Mr Knapp, nimble and monkey-like in the darkness, scrambled softly out on the leads beside them. His rapid breathing was the first thing they noticed.

'Keep low,' said Mr Lugg. 'Keep low.'

They were lying flat upon the roof, and Giles, whose face came suddenly very close to Knapp's, saw that he was considerably shaken.

'She's in there all right.' His squeaky cockney voice was ominously subdued. It rekindled the apprehension in the minds of all his hearers.

Marlowe moved forward involuntarily, and Campion himself stiffened where he lay close to the skylight.

'They've got 'er on the next floor down,' said Mr Knapp. 'I didn't find 'em at first. The bloke with the red beard is all alone in a sort of drawin'-room they've got lower down. I come back, an' as I reached the second floor I 'eard a sort o' guggly noise, an' I found there was a long room that runs the 'ole width o' the 'ouse, along the front. It 'ad a kind of 'arf glass over the door, a curtain coverin' it. That's 'ow I missed it goin' down. I nipped up on a chair an' 'ad a look.'

He paused, and his voice when he continued was pitched a tone or so lower.

'There was six or seven o' 'em,' he said, 'all nasty-lookin' coves. Ikey Todd 'isself an' two or three of 'is pals. There's a long table down the middle o' the room. The girl's sittin' at one end of it, tied into a chair. They're all askin' 'er questions, one after the other – old-fashioned police methods. An' sittin' on the other end o' the table was that dirty little Ropey. 'E's got a fishin' rod in 'is 'and. I couldn't quite see wot 'e'd got on the end of it – looked like a needle or something. 'E was wavin' it about in front of 'er eyes, looked like 'e'd scratched 'er face with it once or twice already. Made me sick to look at it.'

After the first chill of horror which his story produced upon his hearers, each reacted to it after his own way. Lugg and Campion knew as well as Mr Knapp the sort of men with which they had to deal.

Giles and Marlowe, on the other hand, merely realized that the girl who was extraordinarily dear to them both was being subjected to a particularly ghastly torture in a room beneath their feet.

Before any of the other three had time to prevent them, they hurled themselves one after the other down into the attic and charged into the house like a couple of bulls.

Lugg and Knapp clutched at each other.

'Shall we nip off?' said Knapp nervously. 'They've done it now.'

Even the redoubtable Lugg hesitated. As a man of experience he knew what the mêlée below stairs was likely to resemble.

'Wot's that?' Knapp, already nervy, almost screamed. The two men, swinging round, were just in time to see a slight figure drop silently over the coping on to the next roof.

'It's Bertie,' said Mr Knapp, ' 'ooking it.'

The faithful Lugg was shaken to the core. Then, as the noise below suddenly broke into an uproar, he caught his friend by the collar and thrust him into the attic.

'Come on,' he said. 'Lost 'is nerve for a spell. See it 'appen in the war. We've got to take blasted good care we don't lose ours. Now then, pile up them boxes for a bloke leavin' in an 'urry. I told you wot'd come of bringin' amateurs. Last man up locks this 'ere door.'

As he spoke he was moving about with incredible swiftness, dragging the odd lumber in the room to under the open skylight, to facilitate an exit.

Somewhere beneath them Biddy screamed. The sound touched the last spot of chivalry in Mr Lugg's unsentimental heart.

'Come on, Thos,' he said. ' 'It anythink you see, and 'it like 'ell – s'long as it ain't me.'

Chapter 22

The Rough-house

Messrs Lugg and Knapp descended the narrow stairs to the second floor with considerably more caution than their immediate predecessors had shown, although this care was now slightly ridiculous, since the noise proceeding from the room below contradicted any idea that the occupants were listening for a further attack.

As they reached the landing they saw their objective immediately. The room was brilliantly lit, and crowded with people. They crept along the passage, keeping out of the shaft of light from the doorway. As they approached, a man staggered out and collapsed over the banisters, and the noise within the room increased in fury. Somewhere in the throng a voice was swearing continuously in a high-pitched stream, the monotonous tone sounding clearly above the deeper voices and the crashes of overturning furniture.

''Ere goes,' whispered Mr Lugg, hitching his trousers and grasping his life preserver. 'I ain't 'eard any shootin' yet.'

'They daren't risk it 'ere,' muttered Knapp, sliding along the wall behind the larger man to the doorpost, round which he peered.

Giles and Marlowe had evidently charged straight through the surprised gangsters and made for Biddy. At the moment when Lugg and Knapp arrived, the girl was still bound to her chair, and the two young men, although remaining beside her, were not making any further progress towards getting her out. They were both badly cut about. Giles's cheek was laid open to the bone, and Marlowe was laying about him with his left hand, his right arm hanging limply at his side.

Clearly they had only managed to get into the room by the suddenness of their attack. The angry gangsters had only just collected themselves.

An immense Jew standing with his back to the doorway suddenly raised his voice above the din. 'Put 'em up quick, both of you. Sit on 'em, boys.'

He stepped back a pace, his gun levelled, and Mr Lugg, seizing the opportunity, darted into the room and caught him a vicious blow just above the ear. He grunted like a pig and sprawled forward.

Knapp made a dive for the gun, but a heavy boot descended on his wrist and the revolver was snatched out of his grasp. The next instant the butt descended vigorously on the back of his head, and he went down without a sound.

The prompt dispatch of his partner stirred Mr Lugg to fury. Flinging out his left hand, he brought down a heavy picture frame over the sprawling figures, which, while it did no appreciable good to the cause, added most successfully to the confusion.

'The Guv'nor'll be up in a minute,' shouted a voice. ''Old 'em till then! 'E'll deal with 'em. 'Tain't the police.'

'The police'll be here any minute, you blighters!' yelled Giles. He was growing visibly fainter every second from loss of blood, but he was still game and struck about him savagely. Even as he spoke a man closed with him and they rolled on to the floor together.

The position of the rescue party seemed hopeless. There were still two gangsters without immediate adversaries, one of whom had a gun, and Biddy remained fastened in her chair. Marlowe was fighting like a maniac in spite of his injured arm. The sweat was trickling into his eyes, and his black hair hung over his face in damp strands.

It was at the precise moment when Ropey was kneeling upon Lugg's outstretched arms and was slowly but surely forcing his neck back, and strangulation seemed certain, that without sound or warning all light in the place disappeared.

'Switch don't work,' said a voice out of the darkness, 'Look out! There's somethin' comin' up the stairs.'

Lugg finding himself under the chair in which the girl sat, set to work to unfasten the bonds, his fingers moving deftly in the darkness.

Fighting ceased momentarily, and there was a general movement towards the door. There seemed to be the sound of many feet coming up the stairs.

'Is that you, Guv'nor?' A strangled voice from the room spoke eagerly.

'In here, officer, in here.' The voice was unrecognizable, and at the same moment a torch shone into the room.

'The police!' shouted someone, and there was a stampede to the doorway. The first man out sprawled and went down like a log.

''Ere,' said another voice, 'there's only one of 'em. Out 'im!'

The last words were drowned by a small explosion – not very loud, but curiously ominous in sound. The torch went out, and almost immediately everyone in the room became aware of something insidious in the atmosphere which choked and suffocated them.

Someone attempted to light a match, and a startled exclamation broke from him. 'Smoke!' he shouted. 'Fire!'

'Pull yourselves together,' shouted a second voice. 'Someone's foolin' us. It's the Guv'nor.'

The fumes became more and more intense. Giles, staggering to his feet, heard a whisper that put new life in him:

'Return tickets ready, please. Get the girl out, you fool.'

The voice was unmistakably Campion's, and at the same time a flying chair crashed against the curtained window. A tinkle of glass sounded in the street below.

Giles felt someone brush past him. He stretched out his hand and touched a silk sleeve. He seized it with an exclamation.

Lugg's voice growled at him softly under the tumult.

'You come on quick. I've got 'er.'

The overpowering smoke had now suffused the landing and the floors above and below. The natural instinct of the gangsters was to get downstairs, as the quickest means of access to the street. The raiding party, on the other hand, made for the roof. Under the cover of the confusion escape was comparatively easy.

In the boxroom Giles and Lugg found Mr Knapp as they came struggling up with Biddy.

'I was waitin' for you,' he said, with an attempt at his old cheerfulness. 'I ain't 'arf 'ad a sock on the 'ead. That was Bertie down there, Lugg.'

'Shut up, and get the girl out on the roof.' Mr Lugg was in no mood for conversation. His face was glistening with sweat, and his eyes were shifty with apprehension.

Giles looked round him dizzily. 'Where's Marlowe?' he said weakly. 'We must get him out. I'll go down again.' He turned to the door unsteadily, but on the last word his voice trailed off and he sank down on the boards.

'Now there's two of 'em.' Mr Lugg's tone had returned to normal. 'First of all, lock this 'ere door. The others must look after theirselves. We'll clear this lot away. Stop 'im bleedin', if you can. We don't want a trail be'ind us.'

Knapp sniffed. 'Gawd! wot a picnic,' he commented. 'Come on, then – up we go.'

Meanwhile, downstairs chaos continued. The smoke had made the first room uninhabitable, and the darkness which persisted all over the house was made thicker and more impenetrable by the fumes.

Terrified men had broken windows and burst open doors in the hope of diffusing the suffocating clouds. No one understood in the least what had happened.

Marlowe, staggering along the upper landing, cannoned into a man who was standing by the open window. He started back.

'Wait for the wagon,' said a voice softly out of the darkness. 'Wait for the wagon and we'll all take a ride.'

'Campion!' Before the word was out of his mouth a hand was placed over his lips. All around them in the smoke there were scufflings and any amount of profanity. Retreat was impossible. The whole house seemed to be in a turmoil. Added to the seven men who had been in the long room there were now reinforcements from below, coughing and shouting in the choking vapour.

'Don't let 'em get away!' The shout was from downstairs.

'We're cut off,' whispered Marlowe. 'We shall suffocate.'

Campion kicked him softly, and at the same moment at the far end of the street below a fire bell's hysterical clangour echoed noisily.

'Fire!' The cry seemed to rise up from all parts of the dignified street. Campion and Marlowe, gasping for air at the open window, saw the engines pull up, the brass helmets moving with magnificent swiftness.

'Fire!' The cry was spreading to the house.

Campion touched Marlowe on the shoulder. 'Emergency Exit,' he murmured, and swung lightly out on to the sill. Marlowe followed him more slowly. This new development was entirely unexpected.

Their appearance on the window-ledge caused a sensation among the crowd gathering in the street below. From outside, the fire appeared to be a very serious one. Great billows of smoke poured out of every window and ventilation grille. Mr Campion looked down at the yellow clouds with a certain pride. 'Not bad for an amateur show,' he said. 'I've often speculated on the chances of crossing the smoke bomb with the common stink variety. What an offspring! But I forget,' he went on with sudden seriousness. 'Register "Fireman, save my child"; this is too much like "The Boy stood on the Burning Deck". Put some pep into it. Quiver a bit; go quaggly about the knees but for the love of Mike don't fall!'

He began to wave frantically, and the crowd below made reassuring signs. Just as the ladders were shifted into position there was a movement behind them. Campion swung round and caught the face that loomed out of the mists towards them with his rubber truncheon. The face did not reappear.

'Look out,' said Marlowe, and leaned back as the top of a crimson ladder hovered in mid-air and came down within a foot of them.

'Tell them the end is not yet,' said Campion. 'Off we go.'

As they descended, the sound of crashing glass and woodwork floated up to them from below. The door and windows of the lower floors were apparently securely bolted, and the firemen were breaking in.

So great was the excitement at this incident that their arrival on the ground floor did not do much to increase it.

All the same, a small portion of the crowd pressed about them, and the fireman who collected them at the foot of the ladder inquired anxiously if there were others inside.

Mr Campion's reply set the hopes of a spectacle-loving public ablaze.

'House crammed full,' he said seriously. 'More smoke than fire, I imagine. It's a man's club, you know – a lot of retired military men – all sticking to their posts.'

'You wasn't one of the brave ones,' said a miserable-looking little man in the crowd. 'I don't blame you neither. Fool'ardy, I call it.'

Campion glanced back at the house. The hoses were pouring water into the darkened building, and firemen were already entering.

'Hullo!' he shouted suddenly. 'What's that they've got there? A corpse?'

Marlowe turned to look with the rest of the crowd which surged forward, but he felt himself firmly grasped by the upper arm and forced forward through the oncoming mass. The arrival of a couple of policemen pressing back the tide finally covered their escape.

As he reached the open street Campion's voice sounded in his ear.

'Now, since we've rung the bell pretty effectively, old bird,' he murmured, 'this, I think, is where we run away.'

Chapter 23

And How!

The scene in Mr Knapp's back room was not unlike a dressing station when Marlowe and Campion arrived.

Giles, still very white and shaky, was receiving experienced first aid at the capable hands of Mr Lugg, while Mr Knapp was examining a lump upon his head in an oak-framed mirror, whose usefulness was considerably lessened by the fact that the words 'Bass's Bottled Ales' were printed across it in large letters.

Mrs Knapp was bending over Biddy, administering small quantities of rum in an egg-cup. Mr Barber alone remained where they had left him. The expression upon his face was inscrutable. He had evidently resigned himself to a situation which was completely beyond his comprehension.

Campion was frankly relieved to see them back. His entry was hilarious, and they all turned towards him with an eagerness which told of the anxiety they had felt at his prolonged absence.

Biddy rose to her feet and came towards them. 'Oh, I'm so glad,' she said breathlessly. She took Campion's hand, but her real interest was plainly centred in Marlowe.

'You're hurt!' she said, all her anxiety returning. He grimaced at her and smiled. 'It looks worse than it is,' he said lightly.

With her help he wriggled out of his coat and displayed a nasty wound in the forearm. The others gathered round him.

'I'll see to that,' said Lugg. 'An' you lie down, miss. You don't look any too good. Now then, Pretty,' he went on, turning to Mr Knapp, 'leave off titivating an' give us a 'and.'

'Lay off,' said his friend bitterly. 'I've got a lump 'ere as big as a 'en's egg. Still,' he continued, brightening, 'it was worth it. Not 'arf a bad show, it wasn't, Ma. You ought to 'ave been there.'

'Blow me if I know wot 'appened,' said Mr Lugg conversationally as he applied a great swab to Marlowe's arm. 'I nipped straight off with the girl as the Guv'nor told me.' He turned to Campion. 'I wasn't 'arf glad to 'ear you when you come up. What 'appened to you an' this young spark 'ere?'

'I'm afraid it was my fault,' said Marlowe. 'I went back to scrag that damned man. I suppose you came after me, Campion?'

'Not exactly,' said that young man modestly. 'I couldn't help staying to see the fire engines. You've no idea what a torchlight tattoo there was after you other people left. Marlowe and I were received like royalty.'

'Fire?' said Mr Knapp, looking up. 'There wasn't no real fire, was there?'

'Wasn't there, by heck?' said Giles. 'I thought we were going to be suffocated.'

Marlowe grinned. 'That was him,' he said, pointing at Campion.

'I did it with my little smoke bomb,' said Campion proudly. 'This room, begging your pardon, Knapp, was nothing to it.'

'Wot beats me,' said Mr Knapp, ignoring the last remark, 'is 'ow the bloomin' engines got there so quick.'

'That,' said Campion again, 'was me too. As soon as these young hopefuls got up their Charge of the Light Brigade, what did little Albert do? He nipped off.'

'I know,' said Mr Knapp. 'I seen you.'

'Quite,' said Campion, putting on his spectacles once more and surveying the little man through them coldly. 'And with your sordid mind, Thos, you doubtless conceived the idea that I had quitted. But no, you wronged me, Jasper Strange. I dropped through that open skylight in the next house which you found for me, and I picked up the telephone and I said, "I'm so sorry to trrrouble you, but I'm afraid there's a fire at Number Thirty-two. The building is well ablaze. Could you send someone round to see to it?" The people at the other end seemed quite impressed and I came back. I dropped in just in time to see the two old contemptibles go into action. It occurred to me that there was too much light about the place, so I toddled downstairs to see about it. On the way I met old Gingerbeard. After a few short words of greeting I showed him my trick with the truncheon. He fell for it, and I went to do my electrical work. Then I ambled back doing my celebrated imitation of the British Police Force. The rest was quite simple,' he added, beaming upon them fatuously. 'I dropped my little Kloos bomb. Up went the fire balloon. You showed the lady out, and Marlowe and I stayed for the washing up. Any questions?'

'Albert, you're wonderful!', Biddy, standing with her arm tucked into Marlowe's, spoke admiringly. 'You all are. If you knew how terrified I was – I –'

Campion placed a finger on his lips and glanced at the Knapps. Biddy comprehended, and turned the phrase off.

'I was glad to see you,' she said. 'I don't know yet where we are or how we got here.'

'Seems to me,' said Mr Lugg, inspecting Giles, 'that I shall 'ave to take this youngster off to old Doc Redfern. A spot o' stitchin' is wot 'e wants.'

Giles and Biddy exchanged glances, and Campion, guessing the question in their minds, spoke reassuringly. 'The best man you could have,' he said. 'He makes a specialty of this sort of thing.'

'A good man? 'E's a bloomin' marvel,' said Mr Lugg pugnaciously. 'If it 'adn't been for Doc Redfern, I'd be walkin' about in four separate bits. I'll take 'im right off now. See you round at the flat. You come along, mate. 'E's a beauty specialist, that's wot 'e is.'

'Perhaps,' said Mr Barber, rising at the first opportunity, 'I had better give the rest of you a lift to Mr Campion's flat.'

He spoke so hopefully that Marlowe grinned. No one had taken much notice of him since their return, and it was almost with surprise that Campion turned to him.

'That's a fine idea,' he said. 'I'm afraid we've given you an awful lot of trouble, Mr Barber, but you see, we've had a bit of trouble ourselves.'

The Oriental looked at him as if he thought he were an idiot, but he moved towards the door, and the others followed him.

Campion stayed behind to talk to Knapp. When he came downstairs at last, the others were already packed into the car. Giles and Lugg caught a taxi in Church Street.

'Good night, all,' shouted Mr Knapp from the window.

As Mr Barber's car passed the top of Beverley Gardens the engines were still drawn up outside Number Thirty-two.

'Still playing Snakes and Ladders, I see,' said Campion cheerfully. 'I wonder what explanation they'll give the authorities. That ought to trouble Mr Datchett, I fancy.'

'Datchett?' said Biddy quickly. 'The fortune teller? Is that who it was?'

'Mr Datchett it was,' said Campion grimly. 'About the worst type imaginable – a blackmailer.'

'Of course, our friend Thos is –' began Marlowe softly.

Mr Campion grimaced at him. 'What do you want to bring that up for?' he said, and they drove on in silence.

By tacit consent no word was spoken of Biddy's adventure. Campion seemed to wish to keep the matter as much to themselves as possible.

It was about one o'clock when they reached the dark entrance beside the police station.

'Thank you, no.' There was a note of complete finality in Mr Barber's reply when they asked him to come in. 'You will forgive me, but I feel I should like a Turkish bath.' He hesitated, and looked at Biddy. 'I had hoped to obtain your brother's consent to my handling the sale of his picture,' he said wistfully.

Biddy stared at him. Had she not been so exhausted she would have laughed. This sudden explanation of his presence in the midst of such an extraordinary adventure touched her sense of the absurd.

'I think I can promise you that will be all right,' she said. 'Thank you so much for all you've done for us.'

Mr Barber beamed. 'I shall hold you to that promise,' he said. 'You have no idea of the value, the exquisite state of preservation, the –'

Campion touched his arm. 'Not now, old boy,' he said wearily. 'Go to bye-byes. Nice long day tomorrow.'

Marlowe and Biddy were already climbing the stairs. Campion turned into the doorway and walked slowly after the others. He climbed leisurely, his face was lined and sweat-marked: the ordeal of the last few hours had left its mark.

When he arrived, Isopel, white and tired from her long vigil, had already got the door open.

'You've done it!' she said hysterically. 'Oh, Biddy, thank God they've got you back! Where's Giles?' she added nervously as Campion closed the door behind him.

'He's all right,' said Marlowe reassuringly. 'Lugg will bring him round in a moment.'

'Bring him round?' Her eyes widened. 'He's hurt?'

'Not badly.' It was Biddy who spoke. 'His cheek's cut. Oh, Isopel, they were marvellous.' She threw herself down into an armchair and covered her face with her hands. 'Now it's all over,' she said, 'I do believe I'm going to cry.'

Marlowe perched himself on the arm of her chair and put a hand on her shoulder soothingly.

'Food,' said Mr Campion. 'When depressed, eat. Full story of the crime in the later editions. Isopel, have you had any food?'

The girl shook her head. 'I – I wasn't hungry.'

'That makes it more difficult. Rodriguez has gone home to roost long ago. We must see what Lugg eats.' He disappeared into the back of the flat. All this time he had studiously avoided Biddy, and it suddenly dawned upon Isopel what he had meant when he made his slightly comic exit down the lift shaft.

'What a gastronomic failure the British Burglar is,' he remarked, reappearing. 'A tin of herrings, half a Dutch cheese, some patent bread for reducing the figure, and several bottles of stout. Still, better than nothing. There's some Benedictine in that cupboard by you, Marlowe. The whisky's there, too, and there's a box of biscuits somewhere. Night scene in Mayfair flat – four herring addicts, addicting. Of course, a wash isn't a bad idea,' he went on, looking down at himself. 'Isopel, look after Biddy in my room, and we'll see what we can get off on the towels in the bathroom, Marlowe. Our hostess was doubtless a good mother, but as a housewife she was a menace.'

'I'll say you're right,' said Marlowe. 'With all due deference, I guess I'll have to burn these clothes.'

'It was a bit like that,' Campion agreed. 'I've got a spot of gent's natty suiting in the next room if you'd care for it.'

Giles and Lugg returned about an hour later, when they had washed and fed. The boy was bandaged pretty thoroughly, and Isopel fluttered about him in a manner which he found most gratifying.

Mr Lugg looked round the flat in disgust. 'You 'ave bin 'avin' a picnic, ain't you?' he remarked. 'Washin' for one thing, and eatin' my best bit o' cheese for another. A cheese like that lasts me thirty days without the op. Good job me an' the young un 'ad a bit at a coffee stall, otherwise cheese rind an' 'erring juice'd be our portion, as the Scriptures 'ave it.'

'The time has come,' said Campion, ignoring him, 'when we gather round Biddy and hear the worst. Look here, old dear,' he went on, looking at the girl, 'I don't want you to talk now if it's going to knock you up any more. We're as safe here as anywhere for the time being.'

The girl looked at him gratefully. 'I'm all right,' she said. 'I've been telling Isopel in the next room, and I must get it off my chest to you all, or I shall think that I went mad and imagined the whole thing.'

'Stupendous,' said Campion. 'Imagine we're a Sunday paper. Spare us nothing. Not a single gruesome detail.'

They had drawn round the girl, who was lying propped up on the Chesterfield. Marlow sat on the back of the couch, Isopel on the floor beside her, Campion straddling a chair before her, and Giles and Lugg on either side of him.

Biddy looked at them helplessly. 'The awful part of it is,' she said, 'I can remember so little. I'll tell you all I can. I went into the post office at home.'

'That was this morning,' said Giles. 'Or rather, yesterday morning, now, I suppose.'

She looked at him blankly. 'It must be longer ago than that,' she said. 'Why, I –'

'Never mind,' said Marlowe gently. 'I guess we know what happened at Kettle's.'

'That's more than I do,' said Biddy. 'It seems so long ago. I remember he told me he had something to show me if I would come into the inner room for a moment. I went in, of course – naturally. Then I think someone must have jumped upon me from behind, and I can't remember anything else at all until I woke up feeling most dreadfully sick in a sort of box. I thought I was in a coffin. I was terrified. It was like all the bad dreams I'd ever had. I kicked and screamed, and they let me out. I was in a room – it must have been in that house you came to. I was feeling horribly sick, and I had a filthy taste in my mouth. I was still doped a bit, I suppose.'

Marlowe made an inarticulate sound, and she smiled up at him faintly.

'I'm better now,' she said. 'And, oh, I'll tell you something, Albert,' she went on hurriedly, 'they weren't the right people. I mean, they weren't the people who got Mr Lobbett. They were a different lot. They thought I knew where he was. That's what they kept questioning me about. They wouldn't believe that I didn't know anything.'

'Hold on a moment,' said Giles. 'There's something here that's got to be cleared up, Biddy. What made them think that you knew?'

There was an unconscious movement among the group round the girl on the couch. This question, which had been forgotten in the excitement of the past few hours, now returned to their minds with redoubled importance. Looking at Biddy it seemed impossible to connect her with any duplicity.

She frowned at them. 'I couldn't quite make that out,' she said. 'It was something about my handwriting.'

'See here,' said Marlowe, 'it's up to us to explain to Biddy all that we know. Remember, we've only got Knapp's word for it, but he says he overheard a phone message which said that you had posted a parcel containing the suit dad was wearing when he disappeared. That's roughly why you were kidnapped.'

Biddy shook her head. 'I'm none the wiser,' she said. 'I sent no parcel. And yet Kettle could hardly mistake my handwriting – he's seen it so often.'

'Well, did you write anything?' said Giles. 'Who have you written to lately?'

Biddy remained thoughtful. 'No one,' she said at last. 'I paid a few bills. Unless – oh, Giles – it couldn't be George? He couldn't –'

Campion became interested immediately. 'George couldn't what?' he said.

'George couldn't write,' said Biddy. 'Amongst other things. But, Albert, he couldn't be mixed up in this. That's fantastic.'

'Couldn't write?' said Marlowe. 'That's fantastic, if you like.'

'But I did write something for George,' said Biddy. 'You see, poor old St Swithin used to write all his letters for him – make up his bills and everything. He came to me with a sticky label. I remember when it was – it was the morning after Mr Lobbett disappeared. I remember that because I was so tired. It seemed to me absurd that anyone could be thinking of ordinary things, like sending off a parcel.'

'That's fine,' said Campion. 'Do you remember the address?'

'Yes,' said Biddy. 'It was sent to Mrs Pattern. That's his daughter, the one who married the garage man and went to Canvey Island. I send her things sometimes. He told me he was sending her some roots.'

'A funny time of year to send roots,' said Giles.

Biddy nodded. 'It is,' she confessed. 'But of course I didn't notice it at the time. The whole thing seems crazy even now. He can't know anything about it, Giles – we've known him all our lives.'

'The old devil probably found the clothes and sent them off without saying anything. That's about it,' said Giles. 'All the same, he'll have to explain himself pretty thoroughly.'

'Even so,' said Marlowe, 'wouldn't this chap Kettle know who sent the parcel? George must have posted it himself.'

'That doesn't follow,' said Giles. 'He used to take all the letters from the Manor, and the Dower House, too, for that matter. He called for them when he passed. He's done it for years. It's one of his jobs.'

'That's about the explanation,' said Campion. 'Carry on, old dear. How long were they cross-questioning you?'

The fear returned to the girl's eyes. 'It seemed days,' she said. 'I can't tell you how long it was really. It was that awful little man who frightened me most.'

An expression of satisfaction appeared in Marlowe's face. 'He'll never do it again,' he said. 'I don't understand, Biddy. Were they at you the whole time?'

'Yes. I was tied up when they took me out of the box. I felt most desperately ill. I think I fainted.'

'What did you tell them?' said Campion.

'What could I tell them? They wanted to know where Mr Lobbett was. I didn't know. I told him we thought he had been kidnapped, and they laughed at me. They made all sorts of threats and promises. Oh, it – it was horrible.'

For a moment she seemed about to break down, but controlled herself. 'I never understood before,' she burst out suddenly, 'how real it all is. St Swithin's death left me numbed and stupid, I think. When Mr Lobbett disappeared and that absurd message arrived, and then the clothes turned up, my mind didn't seem to register it all. But then, when they were questioning me, I suddenly grasped how desperately serious they were. Do you realize, all of you, that either their leader, whom I didn't see, or Mr Lobbett, is bound to die? It's a death game.'

Although this thought had come to them all at different times, Biddy's point-blank acknowledgement of it startled them considerably.

Campion got up. 'That's what I've known all along,' he said in a tone utterly unlike his usual flippancy.

'They didn't get anything out of me,' said Biddy, 'because I didn't know anything. But if I had' – she looked round at them, her brown eyes wide and honest – 'I would have told. I was just scared stiff. I was frightened they were going to kill me or put my eyes out. You do understand me, don't you?'

'Perfectly,' said Marlowe. 'And you're quite right, too. Campion, we can't bring Biddy and Giles into it any longer. We –'

Giles interrupted him. 'We're staying. I'm speaking for Biddy, I know, but I think we understand one another.'

'We're staying,' repeated the girl. 'I insisted on being in it. I feel quite brave, now you've rescued me,' she added, laughing nervously.

Mr Lugg, who had absented himself during the latter part of the conversation, now returned. 'I got a mornin' paper,' he said. 'It's just past three. "Mystery Fire at Kensington" is our little do. Listen to this:

'The Kensington Fire Brigades were called out last night to a mysterious outbreak which occurred at 32 Beverley Gardens, W8. Two interesting features are reported. The dense clouds of smoke which were thought to be caused by fire were produced by chemical means. The second mysterious feature is that several men were removed from the house in an unconscious condition not altogether caused by the fumes. The police are investigating the incident.

'Couple o' inches, that's all we get,' said Mr Lugg. 'A lovely show like that – a couple o' inches. Wait until the *News o' the World* publish my life. "*I was drove to it,*" says famous crook.'

He threw the paper down contemptuously. Marlowe picked it up and was turning to the stop press when a picture on the back page attracted his attention. He studied it intently.

'Good Lord!' he said suddenly. 'I thought that was dad.'

Campion bounded to his feet and was beside him in an instant.

'Where?' he said, snatching the paper with altogether uncalled-for excitement.

'Here,' said Marlowe, pointing over his shoulder at the photograph of a man evidently caught unexpectedly, glancing back as if at some sudden sound. The caption was not particularly enlightening:

Giant Diplodocus in Suffolk – Our special photographer, with long-distance camera, manages to catch a glimpse of archaeologists at work. Great secrecy is still being maintained by the Hon. Elwin Cluer over the remarkable discovery in his grounds at Redding Knights, near Debenham, Suffolk.

'It's infernally like him,' said Giles, joining the other two.

'Like him,' said Mr Campion, stammering. 'Don't you see, my babes in the wood, the ultimately improbable and ghastly has occurred on this blessed night of all nights?'

'It's damnably like him,' said Marlowe.

'Of course it is.' Mr Campion was shouting in his consternation. 'It *is* him. I put him there.'

Chapter 24

'Once More Into the Breach, Dear Friends'

For some moments after Mr Campion's startling announcement no one spoke.

'You'd better explain, Albert,' said Isopel at last.

'I suppose I had,' Campion agreed. 'We shall have to get a move on pretty quickly, too. We shan't be the only people to spot this disgusting example of newspaper nosery. This rag has a couple of million circulation. I'm desperately sorry, all of you,' he went on hurriedly, as they sat staring at him. 'I've added to the anxiety of the past day or two, but it couldn't be helped. It wasn't that I didn't trust you, but I wanted you all to live up to your parts. I didn't know what steps they'd take to get information from us, and I wanted to be quite sure that you were all genuinely in the dark.'

'But he disappeared in front of us,' said Biddy. 'I was with you. You were talking to me.'

'He helped,' admitted Campion. 'He and George really did the thing between them. A good old-fashioned put-up job, in fact. You see,' he went on, turning to Marlowe, 'things were getting too hot.'

'They pinked us the first evening you got down – Datchett turned up. I didn't recognize him, and for the moment he put the wind up me. I thought he might be the Big Bezezus himself. Then poor old St Swithin shot himself. I was in the dark over that – I am still, up to a point. It's quite obvious now that this chap and his pals are being employed by Simister, and for a very good reason. This chap had just the outfit that the Big Noise needed. He seems to have a collection of informers all over the country – gossips, small agents, and the like. Kettle was one of them. That sort of reptile provided him with his best clients. They collected the evidence; Datchett collected the blackmail. Not a certificate "U" production.'

'I don't quite get this,' said Marlowe. 'Did that fortune teller try to force the old minister to double-cross us?'

'That's about it,' said Campion. 'He probably realized that Kettle would be precious little help to him, apart from spotting us in the first place, and he wanted St Swithin to give him the goods from inside.'

'And St Swithin shot himself rather than do it?' said Giles.

Campion hesitated. 'I'm afraid,' he said at last, 'that it was a pretty substantial threat which Datchett held over him. I fancy the old boy must have been sucked dry long before this. It was obviously some sort of exposure that he feared and he had no means to buy himself off any longer.'

'But what could he have feared?' said Biddy. 'It's absurd.'

'We can't tell what it was, old dear' – Campion spoke gently – 'but what I do know is that his last thought was to help us, and he did it in a most effective and practical manner. He sent us sound advice which arrived in the rather melodramatic fashion that it did only because he was so desperately anxious that only the person who was directly concerned should understand it.'

'That was you,' said Giles.

Campion nodded.

'I wasn't any too quick on the up-take,' he said. 'The messages didn't come in their right order. Yours, Biddy, "Danger", should have come first. That was to break any illusions we may have had about Datchett as a fortune teller. Then there was Alaric Watts – one of the most interesting old men I've met for a long time. When in doubt, I fancy, St Swithin appealed to Alaric Watts, though he never took his principal trouble to him. And then, of course, there was the red knight. I didn't get that until I went over to see Watts. It appears that he has a great pal next door who is an old fossil monger. In his somewhat hefty back garden the early Britons built a church, bits of which he ferrets up from time to time. While they were on one of these pot-hunting expeditions they dogged up a toenail as big as a dining table, which cheered things up all round. The press got wind of it, and old Cluer – that's the man I've been talking about – barricaded himself in and made a kind of fortress. No one was allowed in or out without their GFS badge.

'St Swithin, God bless him, knew all this, and it had probably occurred to him before that it was just the place for anyone who wanted to avoid publicity for a bit. He dared not see us again, for fear of losing his nerve. That's why he wrote.'

'But why did he send a chessman?' said Marlowe.

'If you'll look at the paper over there,' said Campion, 'you'll see. The name of the estate next door to Alaric Watts is Redding Knights. There's a stream there where the old tin-hats used to have a wash and brush-up, I understand. That was St Swithin's only way of telling us without writing the name, which might conceivably have been seen by anybody. That explains why I wanted you all to be as secret as an oyster about it.'

'Good Lord, you knew the whole time!' said Marlowe.

Giles looked at Isopel. The girl coloured faintly and met his glance.

'I knew too,' she said. 'Albert told me the next morning.'

'Toujours le Polytechnic,' said Mr Campion hurriedly.

'How on earth did you manage it?' said Biddy.

'It was the little grey books that did it,' said Campion. 'After half an hour's reading my head swelled up. Within two hours I had qualified as a motor salesman, whereas before I used to sell pups. After three days –'

'Chuck it!' said Giles. 'How did you do it?'

'The ordinary Bokel Mind,' began Mr Campion oracularly. 'Deep, mysterious, and replete with low cunning though it is, is nothing compared to the stupendous mental machines owned by those two losses to the criminal world, George Willsmore, and 'Anry, his brother – who pips him easily in the matter of duplicity, by the way. In all my wide experience I have never come across two such Napoleons of deceit. They staged and arranged the whole affair, whilst I looked on and admired. Such technique!

'I persuaded your father,' he went on. 'I pointed out that if I had a clear field and him out of danger, there was just a chance that our friends might be persuaded to show their hands. They have, up to a point, but not far enough. The old boy was very sporting, and, as I said, George and 'Anry did the rest. The remarkable disappearing act was nothing like as difficult as it looked, thank heaven! You must remember, both time and place were prearranged. 'Anry discovered the dead yew, and devised the whole scheme. George was waiting for your father inside the maze. Mr Lobbett's tour was personally conducted by him. They toddled down that ditch which you discovered so inopportunely, Giles, only instead of going on to the road they ambled along the side of the hay field. The grass, being pretty high then, together with the depth of the dyke, hid them completely. From that they got quite easily into the mist tunnel without being observed. There's a hut down there, isn't there, Giles? Well, he changed there, since yokel garbage was absolutely necessary. 'Anry's wife's brother from Heronhoe was waiting in a rowboat just where the mist tunnel runs into the creek. It was high tide, you remember. He paddled your father down the river to a strip of coast where our good friend Alaric Watts was waiting for him in a car. There you are – quite easily done. 'Anry fixed the note on Addlepate's collar. That was your father's idea. I confess that, knowing the animal, I was dubious about that part of the scheme, but it worked all right.'

Giles was looking at him in undisguised horror.

'George and 'Anry got Mr Lobbett into a boat where the mist tunnel runs into the creek?' he said. 'I didn't know anyone would dare it.'

Campion eyed him curiously.

'I don't get you.'

Giles shrugged his shoulders.

'It's the most dangerous bit of "soft" on the coast,' he said. 'The sea's encroaching every day, so it's impossible to mark it. I'm always expecting that old hut to disappear.'

'I didn't know that,' said Campion quietly. 'I've underestimated those two. They're Machiavellis. Anyhow, they got him away safely, all right. George's one lapse occurred in that matter of the suit. He had orders to destroy it, but having a son-in-law who is a Brummel of Canvey Island, his frugal mind suggested that the clothes might come in useful for him. That's how the rather serious misunderstanding which led to Biddy's abduction occurred.'

'Kettle simply untied the parcel, then?' said Marlowe.

Campion nodded. 'I imagine he was going through all our correspondence at the time. I chatted to George on the subject. He swore to me that he'd buried the clothes in the mud. Kettle, he insisted, must have dug them up again. That story didn't wash, but it put me straight on to Kettle's track; however, like an ass, I wasn't fast enough.'

'Sounds like a bit o' the Decameron to me,' said Mr Lugg unexpectedly. 'Without the fun, as you might say.'

'It is a bit of a mouthful,' said Giles, 'coming on top of everything else. What's the next move? We're all pretty well dead-beat, and I state here and now that the girls are out of it for the future.'

'Quite right,' said Campion. '"Over my dead body," as Lugg would say.'

'I'm all for that,' said Marlowe.

The two girls were too tired to protest. Biddy was already more than half asleep.

'I suggest,' said Mr Campion, 'that I go down to Redding Knights straight away. I think we've got about four hours' start. That's why I haven't been hurrying. Oh, they're sure to get wind of that photograph,' he went on, answering Giles's unspoken question. 'That's one of those certain things. Half the crooks in London probably know there's a reward in a certain quarter for information about the judge. I'll set off right away, then.'

'I'll bring a couple o' pennies down for yer eyes,' said Mr Lugg, 'and I'll see you laid out proper.'

'You'll stay where you are,' said Campion. 'You're going to be a ladies' maid for a day or two. A mixture of ladies' maid and bulldog.' He turned to the girls. 'You couldn't be safer in Wormwood Scrubs.'

'That's right,' said Mr Lugg. 'I'll get my 'armonium out to-morrer. Give 'em a spot of music to cheer 'em up.'

'Must you all go?' Biddy looked at Campion imploringly.

Giles interrupted his reply. 'Marlowe and I are going with Campion,' he said stubbornly.

'That's so.' The young American nodded. He went over to Biddy, and for a moment they spoke together.

'I say, there's one thing,' said Giles suddenly, looking up. 'Are you going to do all your rescue work in your giddy two-seater?'

'Don't insult her,' said Mr Campion. 'I've had her since she was a tricycle. Still, I hardly think she's fit for Flying Squad work. You will now shut your eyes, and Uncle Albert will do one of his pret-ty con-jur-ing tricks, kid-dies. Lugg, I think this is just about the time to catch Brother Herbert, don't you?'

Mr Lugg became supercilious immediately. 'Very likely,' he said, adding gratuitously: 'Sittin' up 'arf the night, excep' on business, is my idea of a vice.' He went to the telephone. After listening for some moments his expression changed to one of bitterest contempt, and he held the receiver some distance from his ear. 'Mr Rudolph would like to speak to 'is brother,' he said. There was an indistinct reply, and Mr Lugg's scowl darkened and his little eyes glittered with sudden anger. 'Yus, and look nippy about it, my young gent's gent,' he said bitterly; then, turning to Campion, he mimicked a voice of horrible refinement: ''is Lordship is 'avin' 'is 'air curled and may be some moments comin' to the phone.'

'Hair curled?' said Campion.

'I dunno. Cleanin' is teeth or somethink silly. 'Ere 'e is, sir.'

Campion took the phone.

'Hullo, Sonny Boy,' he said, grinning into the instrument. 'Did she accept you? It'll cost you seven and sixpence. Better buy a dog. Yes, boy, I said *dog*. I say, where's the Bentley? Could you send her round? No, Wootton can leave her here. Oh, and by the way, Ivanhoe, now you're sober you might point out to the family that you can only disinherit an offspring once. One offspring – one disinheritance. Make that quite clear. Yes, I know it's four o'clock in the morning. You'll send the bus at once, won't you? Yes, the business is looking up. I'm going to buy some braces with your crest on if the present boom continues. Cheerio, old son. I shall expect the car in five minutes. Good-bye.'

He rang off. 'Once more into the breach, dear friends,' he said, smiling at them. 'We'll take some brandy in a flask, Lugg. Look after the ladies. Don't let them out. We won't be more than a couple of days at the most.'

'Two young females in this 'ere flat,' said Lugg. 'Well!'

'Shocking!' agreed Campion. 'I don't know what my wife would say.'

Marlowe stared at him. 'Good Lord, you haven't a wife, have you?' he said.

'No,' said Mr Campion. 'That's why I don't know what she'd say. Get your coats on, my little Rotarians.'

Chapter 25

The Bait

They drove all through the dawn: out of the city into Essex, and from Essex into Suffolk.

Marlowe and Giles dozed in the back of the Bentley. Campion sat at the wheel, his natural expression of vacant fatuity still upon his face.

But throughout that long drive, in spite of his weariness, his mind was working with unusual clarity, and by the time they turned into the drive he had come to an important decision.

They stumbled out of the car, sleepy and dishevelled, to find themselves outside an old house, ivy-covered and half hidden by towering cedars. There was an air of darkness and shadow in the big garden, of privacy undisturbed for centuries.

An old man admitted them to the house, accepting Campion's explanation with quiet deference.

'Mr O'Rell is having breakfast with the vicar, sir,' he said. 'Will you come this way?'

'That's your father's *nom de guerre*,' murmured Campion to Marlowe. 'I wanted to call him Semple MacPherson, but he wouldn't stand for it.'

They followed the man into a room which ran all along one side of the house. The outside wall had been taken down to allow space for a long creeper-covered conservatory, and it was here, sitting at the top of the stone steps leading down to a sloping lawn, that they found Judge Lobbett and his host at breakfast.

Old Crowdy Lobbett sprang up at the sight of them. His delight at seeing his son again was evident, but on seeing Giles's bandaged face he turned to Campion with considerable anxiety.

'Isopel and Miss Paget – are they all right?'

Marlowe answered him. 'Quite safe now, dad. But Biddy had a terrible experience. Things have moved some.'

The old man was eager for explanations, but Alaric Watts came forward and he paused to introduce him.

Marlowe, once he realized that it was safe to speak before the vicar, sketched a rough outline of the affair in Kensington.

Crowdy Lobbett listened to him with growing excitement. At the end he rose to his feet and strode restlessly down the room.

'This is terrible!' he said. 'Terrible! Always others. I seem to escape myself, but wherever I go, whoever comes in contact with me seems to suffer. I spread this danger like a plague.'

'Oh, well, we're all right for the present,' said Giles, with an attempt at cheerfulness. 'Marlowe and I aren't really hurt, and Biddy and Isopel are perfectly safe for the time being. It's what's going to happen next that's worrying us.'

Old Lobbett turned inquiringly to Campion, who had been unusually silent ever since their arrival. The young man smiled at him.

'We've been spilling so many beans for your sake that we've forgotten the pork,' he said. 'It's the morning papers that have brought us down here.' He produced the back page of the famous daily from his pocket and handed it to the judge.

An exclamation escaped the old man as he saw the photograph Campion indicated, and he handed it to the vicar.

'Disgusting!' said Alaric with sudden heat. 'Disgusting! It's an ichthyosaurus, not a diplodocus. They'll be calling it an iguanodon next. Cluer will be furious about this.'

'Anyhow, it's a darn good portrait,' said Mr Campion. 'That's the real trouble.'

The seriousness of this new development was by no means lost upon Crowdy Lobbett. He had been lulled into a false security by the peace of Kepesake and by the absorbing interest of his new friends. His very blue eyes had grown darker, and the lines were deepening upon his still handsome face.

'It's no good,' he said. 'This can't go on any longer. I made up my mind that if this last scheme of yours failed, Campion, or if the danger threatened any of you youngsters, I should face this thing alone and take what's coming to me. It's the only way to buy immunity for those about me.'

Campion let the other two finish their outbursts against this suggestion without making any contribution towards it. At length his silence became noticeable, and they turned to him. Giles was angry.

'Good Lord, Campion, you're not saying that you agree with this ghastly idea?' he said. 'We wouldn't stand it for a minute, sir,' he went on, turning to the judge. 'We're in it now. We'll see it through to the end. You're with us in that, aren't you, Campion?'

Campion shook his head slowly, and was about to speak, when the vicar interrupted him.

'No doubt you would prefer to discuss your affairs without me,' he said softly. 'I shall be in my study when you want me.' He went quietly out of the room; as the door closed behind him Giles and the father and son turned towards Mr Campion once more.

The effects of the night's work had told upon him physically. There were dark shadows in his pale face, and behind the heavy glasses his eyes were inexpressibly weary. But his spirit was as effervescent as ever, and his voice, when he spoke, had lost none of its light-heartedness.

'This rather ticklish question,' he began, 'has been dragged up before I meant it to be. Natheless, as they say in the writs, since the matter has now come to a head, let's dot it. I think, if you don't mind, sir,' he went on, glancing at the judge, 'a review of our transactions to date is clearly indicated. There're one or two facts that are important and must be properly filed for reference.'

Judge Lobbett, who had now become accustomed to the young man's somewhat misleading business manner, signalled to him to go on.

'First of all,' said Campion, 'Old Airy-fairy Simister, who, as we all know, is anxious to remain a kind of Machiavellian Mrs Harris, has a theory that you have a line on his birth certificate. So you have, but since it's written in Esperanto, or something, you can't read it. He doesn't know what you've got hold of, and realizes that he wouldn't recognize it if he saw it.' He paused and glanced round at them. 'Any boy who does not follow that, please put up his hand. All got there? Good! I'll carry on. He realized it was impossible to kidnap you in New York without running undue risk, so he hit on the ingenious little plan of scaring you out of action. That proving unsatisfactory, he invented a sensational killing on board ship. The untimely end of my poor Haig finished that idea for him. Now we come to Mystery Mile.' He talked on hurriedly, peering at them anxiously through his heavy spectacles.

'There, as we know, we were spotted straight away, and poor old St Swithin got it in the neck, more by luck than judgement on Simister's part, I fancy. There's a mystery there we haven't fathomed yet, by the way.'

He paused for breath.

Judge Lobbett was bending forward intently. Campion continued:

'To return to little Albert,' he said. 'How did the famous sleuth go to work? First of all he gained the confidence of our client here. How did he do this? He detailed to Mr Lobbett senior the facts appertaining to the putting-away of Joe Gregory, a gentleman who crossed upon the same boat unspotted by anyone except his own dirty soul and myself.'

The judge turned to Marlowe. 'That was so,' he said. 'Until Campion convinced me of that I thought he was some young adventurer who had got hold of you. I don't suppose you remember hearing about Gregory. I sent him down for a long term some years ago. He was one of Simister's men. When I found that out it impressed me very considerably.'

'Thousands of these splendid testimonials at our head office,' murmured Campion, and continued: 'It was through this, then, that Our Hero and the Guv'nor got down to business on the disappearing act. Mr Lobbett agreed with me that our best chance was to make them show their hand a bit. This was done by our sensational vanishing performance at the maze. So far so good. The clever detective's splendid ruse worked sensationally, apart from one or two nasty bloomers which resulted in Biddy's adventure.

'Then, as the movies have it, "Chance with her Fateful Finger, Like a Cheap Loud Speaker, Bellowed our Little Secret to the Waiting World", and now you and little Albert are in the *bouillabaisse*.'

'You really expect them any minute, I suppose?' said Marlowe.

'Hardly,' said Mr Campion judicially. 'We learned a good deal *via* Knapp and Biddy. In the first place, we discovered that Old Holy Smoke, the Voice in the Dark, was using our friend Datchett and his neat little organization, plus a pretty selection of thugs. That is to say that we know exactly who our enemies are with the single exception of our little Sim himself, who, by the way, is probably some well-known and respected person, like the Premier, or Mr Home, of the Home and Colonial.'

'You don't think he's got any of his own men over here?' It was Judge Lobbett who spoke.

'It all depends on what you mean,' said Campion. 'I'm not sure whether Mr Datchett isn't one of his own men. Certainly, he is second in command at the moment. And that is where we come to our second slight advantage. If ever anyone had his headquarters and staff mucked up completely, the man is Datchett. He himself is probably not yet convalescent. That gives us time, anyway. It also gives us the blessed possibility that the Big Bezezus himself will turn up to make a personal affair of it. It's well on the cards, I think.'

'Still I don't get your idea,' said Marlowe, cutting in. 'What's your plan of campaign?'

Campion hesitated and looked at the judge. 'I want you to come back to Mystery Mile with me. I choose Mystery Mile because it's our own ground, so to speak. They'd attack *us*. We shouldn't be endangering anyone else, for I'm certain Simister's not the man to go yokel baiting. Either we get them or they get us. Any development will be pretty speedy, certainly sensational, and probably final. What do you say?'

A gleam had appeared in the old man's eyes. This was the sort of proposition that appealed to his forthright personality.

'I'm on,' he said.

'So am I,' said Marlowe.

'You can count on me,' chimed in Giles.

Campion shook his head. 'Sorry,' he said to Marlowe, 'but your father and I go alone or not at all. That's the final scheme.'

'Yes, that's final,' said old Lobbett. 'See here, Marlowe, I'm in this because I can't and won't help it. Someone's got to look after Isopel. It's not only because you're my son and a man likes to feel that there's someone carrying on if anything happens to him, but you've got work to do. You've got Isopel and all my affairs to look after.'

The boy looked at him helplessly.

'But I can't let you and Campion go alone into this, dad. Why Campion?'

'Oh, orders taken for this sort of thing daily,' said the irrepressible young man airily. 'You seem to forget my professional status.'

'That's so,' said the judge. 'You and Paget, Marlowe, are out of it.'

'Rot!' said Giles. 'I'm coming, even if I only go back to live in the Dower House as I've a perfect right to. None of you knows your way about Mystery Mile as I do. I'm the man you want. I've two arms still useful, which is more than Marlowe has. My head never was much good, anyway.'

Mr Campion looked thoughtful. 'There's something in that,' he said.

'What about your sister?' said old Lobbett.

Giles hesitated and glanced at Marlowe. 'I think she'll be all right,' he said.

Lobbett looked sharply at his son. 'Is that so?' he said. 'Then you cut back to the city as soon as you've had a rest. What do you say about young Paget, Campion?'

'I don't see that we can prevent him coming,' Campion said slowly. 'It's a far, far better thing, and all that, you know, Giles.'

'I don't like it,' said Marlowe.

'"Efficiency" is my watchword,' said Mr Campion. 'Who arrested Jack Sheppard? Who convicted Charlie Peace? Who trailed Palmer the Poisoner? Who brought Jack the Ripper triumphantly to Justice? Who stopped mixed ping-pong in the Polytechnic? Don't heckle me, I only ask you. Who? For the next thrilling instalments see *Polly's Paper*, twopence every Tuesday.'

'That settles it,' said Lobbett. 'Now, Campion, what's the next move?'

'Sleep, Nature's sweet restorer,' said the young man quite seriously. 'The learned cleric must be prevailed upon to put us up today. We'd better arrive at Mystery Mile at night. I think we're safe here until then. Marlowe, you'd better rest, too. We'll put you out at the nearest railway station on our way.'

'Hell to you!' said Marlowe. 'I don't think I shall ever sleep again.'

'Amateur,' said Mr Campion happily. 'I shall slumber like a babe.'

There was no difficulty about accommodation in the old Vicarage. Within half an hour the adventurers were established in a bedroom whose stripped beams and plaster walls were cool and silent.

When the three awoke they found that a repast had been prepared for them which would not have dissatisfied a small medieval army going into battle.

It was nearly nine o'clock when they finished their meal. There were no reports of any strangers in the village, and Campion became thoughtful.

'They must have watched the flat,' he said. 'I thought there was a man there. Quite likely they had a bit of a hangover from last night. We may not see a sign for a day or two.'

'I wish I was in this,' said Marlowe for the hundredth time. 'My arm isn't nearly as stiff as I thought it would be.'

His father turned upon him. 'We settled that this morning, son,' he said. 'You pack right back to the city and take this letter with you to Isopel.'

'You're out of it,' said Giles. 'I feel primed up to hit something. God help Kettle if nothing more serious arrives.'

'There's a train for you, Marlowe,' said Campion, 'at Woodbridge at half-past ten. We shall get back to Mystery Mile about an hour later. Are you all ready?'

They nodded. The realization of the seriousness of the expedition returned to their minds, and although Campion remained as flippant as ever, the others were quiet.

Alaric Watts unbarred his gate and let the great Bentley creep noiselessly out.

They stopped only a minute to put Marlowe down at Woodbridge. Marlowe and his father, who had been sitting in the back of the car in close conversation, merely shook hands.

Giles bent towards the younger man. 'Look after the kid,' he said, and added awkwardly, 'All my love to Isopel if anything happens.'

Marlowe nodded. 'I envy you, old boy,' he said sincerely. 'Any message, Campion?'

'Tell Biddy, "Smiling, the boy fell dead",' said Mr Campion. 'Should I do so, of course. Tell her she can have Autolycus,' he added more seriously. 'Lugg, too, if she likes. The woman could hardly hope to forget me if she had those two about the house.'

On the last word he swung the car round out of the tiny station yard towards Mystery Mile.

It was at that precise moment that back in the Vicarage at Kepesake the Reverend Alaric Watts pored over an ultra-late telegram which the postmaster had only just brought over himself, 'to oblige'.

It was addressed to Campion, Redding Knights. It had been delivered at the Hall, and Cluer had sent the postmaster over to the Vicarage.

The old vicar had hesitated before he read it, but as the postmaster volunteered the information that it was urgent, he finally slit open the flimsy envelope.

RETURNING MYSTERY MILE STOP [IT RAN]. COME TO US AT ONCE STOP. URGENT. BIDDY. YSOBEL.

Alaric Watts turned to the postmaster. 'The post office makes funny mistakes,' he said testily. 'The lady spells her name I-S-O-P-E-L.'

'That's 'ow it come, that's 'ow it was sent.' The man spoke stolidly. 'If there's a mistake, it was made by the sender.'

Although he did not know it, the postmaster of Kepesake and Redding Knights was amazingly justified in this observation.

Chapter 26

One End of the String

The Bentley crept slowly towards Mystery Mile. As they drew nearer, the faint cold smell of the sea reached them. The night had become extraordinarily dark, but it was close and thundery, and the sense of oppression which hung over them all was intensified by the heavy atmosphere.

Crowdy Lobbett bent forward and touched Campion on the shoulder. 'Now that Marlowe is right out of it,' he said, 'I shall be prepared to tell you everything I know. You understand that?'

Campion promptly pulled the car into the side and stopped. He turned round in his seat and faced the older man.

'You've no notion what a good idea that is,' he said. 'If you don't mind, I think here is the time to let us have it.' He switched off the headlights and composed himself to listen.

The judge nodded in the darkness. 'That's how I see it,' he said. 'Now I'll tell you, and you'll see just how awkwardly I've been placed. I don't know if Marlowe told you that all through my career as a judge in the States I've had a reputation for my handling of these Simister gangsters. We could never find out who this alleged Simister is.'

He paused. 'That was the thing that we were always trying to find out about them – the identity of this mysterious leader. One day I got hold of something which looked like a clue. It was after I had retired. The police had what you would call over here, I suppose, a standing committee, especially appointed to investigate this lot. As an authority on these people, I was invited to join it. We had special facilities for the questioning of prisoners.

'There was a man in the state jail named Coulson. He was doing a term for implication in a very nasty case of dope smuggling in which several policemen had been shot. He was a Simister man.

'While in prison Coulson developed internal trouble which turned out to be cancer. He was dying in the penitentiary infirmary when I was approached by the committee to visit him, which I did. He was particularly anxious to die in his own home, wanted to spend his last days with his wife. I went into the matter and found that he was too far gone to do any more harm, so I obtained the necessary release and struck a bargain with him.'

He peered through the darkness at them. They were listening intently.

'He swore to me that he had something which he believed was a clue to the identity of Simister himself.'

'At last, after a lot of trouble and persuasion, I got hold of it. As soon as I saw it I thought he'd been making a fool of me. But he was so earnest that I was gradually forced to believe that the ridiculous thing in my hands was in some sort of way a line on our little problem.'

'Fine!' said Mr Campion. 'But what does your little *billet doux* consist of?'

The judge moved in his seat. 'A kid's fairy-story book,' he said.

Giles stirred.

'In the blue suitcase?' he said.

'Marlowe told me he opened it,' said the old man. 'Yes, that's so. I bought the whole series – there was a list of them in the back of the first book. I've read every word of those books, hunted for every kind of cipher, and neither I nor your great expert, MacNab, could make anything of it.'

Campion stared at him through the darkness. 'Good Lord, was it one of those we saw?' he said. 'We'll push back at once. I'd no idea you'd left your clue at Mystery Mile.'

'It was the safest thing to do,' the old man pointed out. 'While it remained there among the other books it was impossible for anyone to tell which was the key copy unless one knew. If I'd been caught with that one book the inference would have been pretty obvious. That's why I used to carry it like that with all the others. It was the safest way I could think of.'

'All the same, I think we'll get on,' said Campion. 'A bedtime story with a point. I must have a go at it. I got seven-and-six for an acrostic once.'

He started the engine and they drove off with more speed than before. The night had now reached a pitch of darkness unusual in the summer months. The sky was thick with clouds and the air was sultry in spite of the cool tang of the sea which reached them every now and again.

This, combined with their sense of approaching danger, made the drive a thrilling and unnerving experience. The whole countryside seemed to be stirring. Birds and animals slept uneasily in the heat and there were rustlings and little squeals from the roadside as they passed, and strange cries from the woods as the night birds prepared for the storm.

They reached the Stroud unchallenged. Campion glanced at Giles beside him. 'No police on the road. What's this – economy? or has someone been busy? I wish my Seven Whistlers were still operating. I think we'd better push on.'

Giles breathed heavily through his nose.

'Nothing else for it, now,' he said. 'If this storm doesn't break pretty soon I shall explode. It may hang like this all night. They do down here sometimes. It always makes me feel like murdering someone.'

'That's the idea,' said Campion cheerfully. 'I fancy you're going to get your chance.' He swung the car round the bend and they mounted the long low hill to the village.

The village was in darkness as they passed. The park, with great trees towering over the narrow drive, seemed unfamiliar, ominous, and uneasy.

'Lights,' said Giles suddenly. 'Lights in the drawing-room, I think. What are they up to?'

Campion shut off his engine, and the car rolled on a few yards and stopped. He jumped out on to the grass and spoke softly.

'I think we'd better approach with caution,' he said. 'I'll go and reconnoitre outside that window. It may be nothing, of course.'

He spoke lightly enough, but it was plain that he was by no means satisfied that all was well.

For a few moments he was lost in the darkness, and there was no shadow across the shaft of light from the drawing-room window, which gilded the green boles of the elms. At length they heard his voice again quite close to them, whispering in a tone unusually agitated.

'We're for it,' he murmured. 'We've gone and put our little necks into it like bunnies in a snare. Look here.'

They followed him across the lawn, treading softly on the springy turf. The silence in the house was terrible, though the lights still glared out unwinkingly. They crept up to the drawing-room window and peered in.

The sight within was an extraordinary one.

The room was brightly lighted. From where they stood they could just see the Romney. The beautiful girl with her sweet, stupid smile simpered in her frame, and before the picture, sprawled out in a little Louis XVI armchair, was Mr Barber. His great head was thrown back, disclosing the thick bull throat beneath his beard.

'Who the heck is that, anyway?' murmured the judge. Campion explained.

'Is he dead?' Giles heard his own voice break as he whispered.

'I think not,' said Campion. 'He's breathing pretty heavily. He looks as if he'd been drugged.'

Judge Lobbett craned forward a little too far, and his shadow fell across the stream of light. Campion jerked him back.

'Come round here,' he whispered. He led them round the back of the house to the kitchen windows. There, too, the lights were burning. Once again they peered in.

Mrs Whybrow sat at the kitchen table, her head resting on the boards, her arms hanging limply at her sides.

'Good God, they've got her too!' Giles ejaculated.

'Comfort me with chloroform,' said Campion cryptically. 'Wait a minute, and I'll go and play peep-bo round the house. I'm afraid we've come and settled in the very middle of it. Look here, Giles, I'm going to bring out that blue suitcase if I can lift it. Meanwhile, should I not return said Our Hero, you, Giles, will not obey your natural ass instincts and attempt to clear off in the Bentley, but you will use the only other exit which is not known to everybody, and that is *via* the mist tunnel. George and 'Anry have had orders to have a boat there ever since the search for Mr Lobbett was abandoned. I never knew when we'd need it. In the words of the immortal Knapp, "Good night, all".'

The judge caught his sleeve. 'The book you want is called *Sinbad the Sailor and Other Stories*,' he said.

The fatuousness of the title at such a moment was not lost on Mr Campion. 'That sounds like me,' he said. 'In view of the scene in the drawing-room it really ought to have been *The Sleeping Beauty*.'

He disappeared noiselessly round the side of the house. Giles and old Lobbett flattened themselves against the wall and waited. The boy was breathing like a horse, and his heart was thumping so loudly that he felt he must shake the foundations of the house.

Lobbett was calmer, but he was by no means impervious to the excitement of the moment. He drew a gun out of his hip pocket and waited.

Still there was no sound from the house. The minutes went by. Giles was quivering with impatience, and the wound in his cheek had begun to throb.

All sense of time left them. It seemed hours since Campion had disappeared. At last a board creaked in the house and Giles started violently. Next moment someone dropped lightly on the ground at their feet.

The judge whipped up his revolver, but it was Campion's whisper which greeted him out of the darkness.

'The Sleeping Beauty good and proper inside, the Babes in the Wood outside,' he murmured. 'Rummiest job I've ever seen. It serves old Barber right for overzealous attention to business. He seems to have put up a bit of a struggle. There's a chair or so overturned. I don't understand it. There's not a soul moving in the house.' He lowered his voice still further. 'I've got the book. Now, then, it's your one chance. Down the mist tunnel.'

Giles did not move. 'It's suicide in the dark like this,' he said. 'You don't know that "soft", Campion.'

'I've got a storm lantern I pinched out of the kitchen. We'll light it when we get down there,' said Campion. 'It's hopeless to go back by the car. That's their bright idea, I fancy.'

Judge Lobbett nodded towards the window. 'What about those people in there?'

'I know,' admitted Campion. 'All the same I don't think they're in any real danger. Our friends are evidently not going to hurt them or they'd have done it before now. We're in a trap and we must get out of it as best we can. It's not safe even to try to get back to the village.'

All round them the dark garden was whispering. They had no idea where the enemy might be hidden. They could hardly hope that their coming had not been eagerly awaited. No one could have missed seeing their headlights as they came across the Stroud. Perhaps even now they were being observed, perhaps at any moment the attack would come.

Neither Giles nor Judge Lobbett had doubted for an instant the wisdom of Campion's remark when he had pointed out that the enemy were probably guarding the way back. Mr Datchett and his followers were clearly not the only subordinates their mysterious enemy possessed.

They obeyed Campion without question.

'Carry on, Sergeant,' said Giles. 'I don't like the navigation scheme, but we'll have a shot at it.'

'Hang on to Uncle Albert, then,' said Campion. 'This isn't going to be a pleasant country walk. The snake-in-the-grass stuff is on our programme.'

They set off, Campion leading. Their progress was slow and nerve-racking. Every sound startled them. Every moment they expected something to leap at them out of the darkness.

Campion paused constantly to listen, but the house behind them was as silent as ever.

When they entered the maze he produced a torch and Giles took the lead. They found the gap and struggled out into the dry ditch on the farther side. The heat and breathlessness of the air had become intolerable. It felt as if a great hot compress had been placed over the little isthmus.

Giles was bathed in sweat, and even old Lobbett breathed uneasily.

Campion alone showed no outward sign of excitement. He padded along stealthily, keeping up a fair pace.

The hay was still standing, and they turned down into the deep channel of which Mr Lobbett had made use before. The ditch was quite dry and their passage was easy.

They dropped out at last into the mist tunnel.

This wide dip in the saltings, which had been at one time an old river bed, was now quite dry and covered with short wiry grass, very slippery to the feet. Now, as ever, it was half filled with a fine white ground mist, only discernible in the darkness by its dank, marshy taste and smell.

'This place is pretty ghastly in the daytime,' muttered the judge. 'It's like the Valley of the Shadow of Death at night.'

'Keep it pleasant, Guv'nor, keep it pleasant,' quavered Mr Campion, unexpectedly shrill.

'Look out.' Giles's voice was quiet. 'We're getting near now. Keep close in.'

All around them the saltmarsh sucked and chattered horribly, and still farther ahead the disturbed sea birds wailed disconcertingly at uneven intervals.

Presently Giles stopped. 'It's not safe any farther without the lantern,' he said. 'Your little torch isn't strong enough. I tell you, Campion, this is quick mud we're coming to. You can sink up to your waist, up to your neck, or out of sight altogether, and nothing but a couple of horses and a cart-rope can save you.'

They paused and lit the lantern.

'Now,' said Campion, as he replaced the glass in its wire shield and the lantern gave out its uncertain yellow light through the fine mist, 'speed, my old sea dogs. All aboard for Paris, Dijon, Lyons, Macon, Victoria, Clapham Junction, Marseilles, and the Gates of Gold. *En voitures.*'

The flippancy sounded bizarre, almost terrifying in the fetid, breathless atmosphere.

'We're in luck,' said Giles. 'The tide's more than three-quarters' way up. Keep well in, keep well in.'

They were standing nearly opposite the little hut where so few days before old Lobbett had changed his clothes before joining George in the rowboat. The grass had come to an end, and all around them was the mud, squelching and gurgling as the sea came nearer and nearer.

'Up to here you're safe.' Giles spoke emphatically. 'From now on, for God's sake look out. This is the hard side. All round the hut on the sea side the "soft" begins. It stretches across here unevenly. It shifts, you know, but I'm afraid we've got to risk that.'

Campion was peering forward into the circle of light thrown by the lantern. There was a thin white line on the mud a few feet ahead showing dimly through the mist. It was the oncoming tide.

'How high does this come?' said Campion, indicating it.

'Up to where the grass stops,' said Giles. 'It stops just short of the hut, except in September in the neap tides. Can you see the boat?'

'There it is,' said the judge, preparing to step forward.

Giles jerked him back. 'You've got to feel it step by step now,' he said. 'Hold the lantern high, Campion.'

The boat was rocking gently, just clear of the bottom, only a few yards out.

Giles ripped off his shoes and stockings. 'I'll have more chance if I find the "soft",' he explained. Then he stepped forward gingerly, trying each step with the utmost caution.

Campion glanced back over his shoulder. Far back among the trees he fancied he saw moving lights.

'Hurry,' he whispered softly, 'hurry.'

Giles went on steadily. Once he started back, plunged, and righted himself. He reached the boat and clambered in.

'It's all right if you walk straight at me,' he said. 'Come on. I daren't bring her in nearer or she'll ground.'

Campion gripped the older man's arm. 'Off you go,' he said. 'Just set your mind on the boat and get there. Tell Giles to make for Heron

Beach, or if he can't in this light to get out into the stream and stay there.'

It was not until the judge had completed his unsteady journey to the bobbing rowboat that he realized that Campion was still standing on the bank, lantern in hand.

'Come on,' said Giles, raising his voice.

'Shut up, you fool! Row out or I'll plug you – with my water pistol.' Campion's whisper had a peculiarly carrying quality, although he was so far away they heard him perfectly.

'Rot!' Giles proceeded to draw in.

'For the love of Mike, get on! No heroics.' Campion's voice was imploring. 'You haven't a minute to spare and everything depends on it. You'll spoil everything. Trust your Uncle Albert.'

'Boy, you can't do this.' Crowdy Lobbett's tone was dangerously obstinate.

'Giles,' commanded Campion, 'pull straight if you don't want us all murdered, and stay out, whatever you hear. If that dear old stowaway of yours makes any noise, for the love you bear his daughter, dot him on the head with an oar.'

Giles had known Campion for many years. So far he had never disobeyed him. This, he realized, was quite obviously the last moment at which to waver. He made up his mind.

' Dipping the oars softly into the water, he pulled out to the centre of the estuary.

Campion waved the lantern to him enthusiastically. Giles's last glimpse of him was of a lank wild figure standing upon the bank, the hurricane held above his head in a ridiculous gesture.

'I loved Ophelia!' he bellowed with great dramatic effect. 'It's the tobacco that counts!'

With which cryptic utterance he walked quietly back along the edge of the bank, dropped into the mist tunnel, and advanced towards the hut. He climbed the wooden steps and hung the hurricane carefully upon the corner of the door so that the light could be clearly seen for some distance. Then, taking his torch out of his pocket, he stepped in.

The hut, which was built up on piles some four feet high, contained a rough flat table, supported by one leg and a couple of hinges in the wall. On one side was a shelf set low enough to form a seat.

The young man looked round him carefully. Apart from a certain amount of odd boat tackle and an empty wooden box, the place was quite empty. The only other thing of interest was the fact that the floor boards at the back of the hut, directly under the form, had been removed, doubtless to prevent the sea from carrying it away at phenomenally high tides.

Campion sat down on the form, and placing his lighted torch beside him on the table, took out the child's book that he had brought from the house.

Sinbad the Sailor and Other Stories. He turned over the pages one by one, past Frontispiece, Dedication, Preface, and Editor's Note. The list of contents caught his eye – children's stories that he had known all his life. Anything more fatuous at a time like this it was impossible to imagine.

His eye wandered down the list. 'Sinbad the Sailor', 'Aladdin and His Wonderful Lamp'. Suddenly his glance became fixed.

A title leaped up at him from the page. He put his hand over it and stared out into the darkness. His face was blank, his eyes dull behind his spectacles.

'I've gone mad,' he said aloud, his voice strangely subdued. 'It's happened at last. I'm insane. "Ali Fergusson Baba and the Forty Thieves".'

Chapter 27
Late Night Finale

Campion, alone in the hut on the marshes, listened to the dying ring of his own voice, and then taking off his spectacles he wiped his face with a huge pocket handkerchief, and stared into the little haze of light which the hurricane made outside the narrow door.

Minutes passed, and he remained there looking blankly ahead of him: the silence was unbearable. Then very softly out in the darkness beyond the screen of light something moved. Instantly he sat up stiffly, listening, his head thrust forward.

At first he fancied that he had heard no more than the movement of some wild thing on the saltings, or the ominous clucking of the mud, but the sound came again, nearer this time and more distinct – footsteps on the short wiry grass.

Campion thrust the book he held into his jacket pocket. His torch followed it. He sat silent, waiting.

Someone trod softly on the wooden steps leading up to the hut; he could hear the creak of the ancient wood as it trembled under a heavy weight.

The next instant the lantern was snatched from its mooring, and a shape, ponderous and elephantine, stood in the doorway.

Mr Barber was barely recognizable. The genial, rather stupid old gentleman had vanished, and in his place there looked out at the young man at the table something mocking and incredibly evil hiding within this monument of flesh.

'You are alone?' he said inquiringly. 'You are very clever, my friend.'

Campion grinned at him; his expression was if possible even more fatuous than usual.

'Spoken like a true gent,' he said. 'If you would sign that for me it might do me a lot of good.'

The man who called himself Ali Fergusson Barber moved over to the table, where he set down the lamp and stood towering above the pale young man, who appeared dwarfed and negligible beside him.

'Perhaps it is as well,' he said. 'I fancy it is time that you and I had a little discussion together, Mr Rudolph K—.' He mentioned a name which so startled the young man before him that he betrayed himself with an exclamation.

The older man smiled faintly. 'I have here, my young friend,' he said, drawing a paper out of his pocket, 'a most interesting dossier. I assure you it contains some very remarkable reading. You and I have both made the same mistake. We underestimated each other, Mr —.'

'Shall we say Campion?' said the young man, his vacant smile returning. 'Now perhaps, since we're getting so matey, we'll go into another matter. Who the hell are you?'

The other man laughed, and just for a moment there was a trace of the old art expert in his face. The next moment it had vanished again, and he was once more this new and vivid personality.

'I am a man of integrity,' he said. 'I have never made the mistake of using an alias. It would be silly of me to try and disguise myself, and also very tiring. I live my own life.'

Campion shrugged his shoulders. 'You know your own limitations better than I do,' he said. 'Still, I could have suggested another name for you. Sit down and make youself comfortable. There's a soap box over there.'

Mr Barber accepted the seat. 'I suppose you've got Lobbett away by sea, as you did before,' he said easily. 'That was very clever of you, Mr Campion. We shall have no difficulty in dealing with that old gentleman, I fancy. But my chief interest at the moment is in you.'

The change in the man was extraordinary. It occurred to Campion that no disguise he might have adopted could have concealed him half as effectively as this remarkable new personality, which he seemed to drop and adopt at will.

'As you have no doubt guessed,' he went on, 'I am a representative of one of the cleverest organizations in the world. In fact, I believe that you were once commissioned by us on a rather delicate mission in an affair at a house called Black Dudley. On that occasion you failed. What was the cause I do not know, but perhaps that explains why we took your entrance into this particular business as so negligible a matter. It may interest you to know that I and my superiors have now considered it worth while to offer you a position in our organization.'

'Sign along the dotted line,' said Mr Campion. 'Please tear carefully. Nothing genuine without this signature.'

The face before him was expressionless. Mr Barber's altered voice went on. 'That rather irritating humour of yours – I suppose that's involuntary.'

'That's a remark that might have been better put,' said the young man.

'I suppose that it is an asset,' the other man remarked judicially. 'But a distressing price to have to pay for business efficiency.'

'In replying to yours of the fifth ult,' said Campion, 'I take it that you are making me an offer?'

His visitor nodded. 'Exactly,' he said. 'This man Lobbett is making himself a nuisance to our organization. We believe that he has, or thinks he has, a key to a secret so important that it is impossible for me to discuss it with you. I don't need to tell a man of your intelligence any more. A settlement of this affair would be the best introduction you could have, and I can assure you personally that you will never regret it.'

'I suppose I should live in?' remarked Campion thoughtfully. 'All found, washing done by the firm, and perhaps a Circassian or two thrown in when times were good?'

The older man folded his hands. 'I appreciate your humour,' he said seriously. 'Your remuneration would be in no sense inadequate. I should like to point out that your alternative is complete exposure. What do you say?'

'Cheek,' said Mr Campion. 'Now I'm going to talk. First of all, how did it happen that you were waiting for us with your neat little put-up job? And why? Bit of a bow at a venture, wasn't it?'

'Not at all. I knew my telegram would bring you. Women are a great handicap in affairs of this sort, Mr Campion.'

'Oh yes, of course.' The young man spoke hastily, an inkling of what had happened occurring to him.

'I admit you were too quick for me,' the other continued. 'Foolishly I imagined that you would search the house for the young women and then appeal to me. I should have been easy to revive. We had received the information that the document which old Lobbett set such store upon was a bulky affair. I argued therefore that he would have left it at the house, carefully hidden. Since it was useless for me to search for something I should not recognize, I waited for Mr Lobbett himself to show it to me.'

Although the conversation had been comparatively amicable, the atmosphere in the little hut had grown steadily more electric. Outside the breathlessness which comes before a storm had become stifling. A flash of sheet lightning lit up the marshes.

'Not bad,' said Campion suddenly. 'But not good either. The situation is becoming clear to me. I am to appear in the gossip columns or do your dirty work for you. I suppose you've been to Pinkertons about me?'

Suddenly he began to laugh. 'All the same,' he said, 'even if I do appear in the What Shall We Do With Our Boys? section, I'm not sure that it won't have been worth it. You were with us all through our spot of fun last night. I shall see you to my dying day sitting next to Mrs Knapp. I wouldn't have missed it for anything.'

A slow flush passed over the Oriental's face: the first sign of anger he had betrayed. 'I considered it best to let you carry out your rather childish little rescue,' he said. 'I thought it valuable to be in your confidence. I, too, consider it was worth it.'

Campion leaned back a little. 'On the whole I suppose you're pretty pleased with yourself?' he said. 'But you're not going to get Our Little Albert on the staff. Now consider your own position for a bit. Here you are, chucking your weight about in the middle of a marsh, far away from home and mother. Suppose I bang you on the head and go home and say no more about it?'

Mr Barber smiled faintly. 'I don't think you'll do that,' he said. 'You must remember I've studied your record pretty closely. I think that a body would be very difficult for a man in your position to explain. Your friends at Scotland Yard would hardly outweigh the record of your curious profession. On the other hand, I am a man of unblemished character, and everyone knows who I am.'

'Except Our Albert,' said Campion, with a lightning change of tone.

Something in his manner silenced the man opposite him, and the little hut was suddenly uncannily still.

'Do you remember a man called Coulson?' Campion was speaking softly. 'The only man to whom you ever half betrayed yourself? My second name is Morgiana, Mr Ali Baba.'

No muscle of the Oriental's heavy face moved. 'I do not understand you,' he said. 'You are still making jokes.'

'That's where you're wrong, my captive Helen.' Campion still spoke lightly, but every second now was tingling with suppressed excitement. At any moment the storm might break.

'You admitted that you didn't know what sort of key the estimable

Judge Lobbett had,' Campion continued. 'I can clear things up for you a bit. His precious clue is perfectly *bona fide*. It's clear enough to anybody who knows you. In fact, your name is the hidden word in the acrostic. Now, I think, in view of everything, we're properly introduced. How now, brown cow?'

That the man was shaken there could be no doubt. After the first shock he pulled himself together with amazing control.

'You are what they call over here "too clever by half", young man,' he said heavily. 'It says in my dossier that it is one of your peculiarities that you never carry a gun. I think you are wise, with such a varied record as yours. It would be interesting to learn if it is true.'

'Talking of confidences,' said Mr Campion airily, 'since I see that one of us is going to cop in for it shortly, there are several things I'd like to know. For instance, I would like to know – as a last favour – how have you managed to keep so quiet about yourself all this time? Accounts of you go back, they say, for the past hundred years. You're pushing along, but you haven't come all that way, surely?'

Mr Barber seemed to become positively affable. Outside great drops of rain had begun to fall. The lightning was becoming more frequent.

'I am in no hurry,' he said. 'Perhaps I will tell you. I must remain here till after this storm, at any rate. But I am afraid I must withdraw my offer.'

'Spoken, I take it, as a sort of funeral oration?' said Mr Campion. 'Let's have something from the heart.'

Mr Barber sighed. 'You are either a very brave man,' he said, 'or you are even more foolish than you pretend to be.'

'Pure courage,' said Mr Campion modestly. 'I wasn't going to point it out, but since you brought it up –'

Mr Barber silenced him with a gesture.

'I am glad that this opportunity has occurred,' he said slowly. 'The desire to confide is very strong in a man of my temperament, Mr Campion. I have never before found myself in a situation in which it was safe for me to indulge this particular desire.'

Campion nodded gravely. The Oriental was fast becoming more and more expansive. He seemed to have grown into a larger, more sophisticated personality than ever before. Now at last it did not seem absurd to connect him with the mysterious figure whose name had been a byword in police circles for so many years.

'I am the only man,' he said, looking at Campion, a slight hint of pride in his eyes, 'who ever turned my particular business into something as pleasurable as any other more legitimate concern. That is to say,' he went on with surprising contentment, 'I am as safe, as well respected, and as undisturbed as any other man of my wealth. I go where I like, live as I choose. I have a villa with a hanging garden on the Bosphorus, the most delightful of Queen Anne houses in Chelsea. My apartment in New York is one of the loveliest in that most expensive of cities. I have a positive palace in California, and my château behind Juan-les-Pins is famous throughout France. I am an authority on pictures, and I have the finest collection of Reynoldses in the world. My amusements are many. I am a respected citizen in every district where I have a house. I have many friends. And yet' – he shrugged his shoulders – 'there is no one in whom I dare confide absolutely. But that is my only disadvantage. For the rest, if I made my money out of oil, motor cars, what difference would it make?'

Campion appeared impressed. 'Your business is done entirely through agents, I suppose?' he said. 'I can understand carrying it on, but I don't see how you started it. You are the financier of the show? You buy the brains on one side and the executive power on the other?'

'That is so.' Mr Barber nodded. 'It is a great pity, my friend,' he remarked, 'that I should have to kill you. I find you quite intelligent. The question you raise is a simple one. My father was the original Simister.'

Campion stared at him, and for a moment he seemed about to laugh.

'Good Lord!' he said, 'you inherited it?'

'Why not?' The Oriental spread out his hands. 'There seems to me to be nothing ridiculous in the idea that a man should leave his son a business of this kind any more than any other concern. I never take part in any of my – shall we say? – business transactions, save at the very beginning. My father preserved my anonymity most carefully. When he died I carried on. I do not think that anybody realized that a change had taken place. You see, the organization must necessarily be very scattered and secret. That is how I have preserved my identity.'

'Wonderful!' said Campion, whose eyes were dancing. 'Forgive me, Mr Barber, but have you any family?'

The old man hesitated. 'No, there is no one to follow me.'

'Hard lines,' said Campion sympathetically.

Mr Barber shrugged his shoulders. 'I am very much of an individualist, and' – he laughed confidently – 'I shall live to be very old.'

Campion leaned across the table.

'Forgive my asking,' he said. 'But what's to prevent my killing you, as soon as we stop being matey? I mean, when you dot me one, why shouldn't I dot you one back? Suppose I risk being found with the body? I'm younger than you are, and probably more gifted at horseplay.'

'I do not think you are so well armed.' There was something terrifying in the calm satisfaction of the tone in which the words were uttered. Mr Barber's large face was mild and affable.

'Let me explain. In the first place, Mr Campion, I have heard that it was your custom to carry a child's water pistol manufactured to look like a genuine service revolver. I confess I was amused when I heard this. So amused that I also had my little joke. I too possess a water pistol, Mr Campion. It is at this moment trained directly upon your face. I would like to mention in passing that I am considered a remarkable shot. I did not wish to copy you exactly, however, and my pistol maintains a particularly corrosive fluid. It is not humanly possible to stand up against such a fire, and in your confusion an ordinary bullet will finish you easily.'

Campion had not stirred, but a muscle at the hinge of his jaw twitched violently.

'I didn't realize that you'd planned this *conversazione*,' he said at last.

The man opposite him fancied that his tone had lost some of its buoyancy.

'Nor had I,' he said easily. 'I had hoped that it would not be necessary.'

Campion breathed more heavily.

It was not long after midnight, he guessed. Mystery Mile would not be stirring for another five hours at least. Giles, he felt sure, would obey instructions. The remote chance of anyone's noticing the lighted hut in the rainstorm was negligible. For once in Mr Campion's eventful life he was almost subdued.

'Don't be afraid of boring me,' he said, with a vigorous attempt at his old flippancy. 'I love these peeps behind the scenes. Oh, by the way, there is no use wasting your time unduly in bothering the old gentleman, in whose employ I am. The clue he had to your identity was a copy of a child's book – absolutely harmless in itself – and unintelligible to anybody who didn't already suspect you. He thought there was a code message hidden in it, and still thinks so. The book is in my pocket now.'

The Oriental's eyes regarded him narrowly. 'Do not have any illusions about my little toy, my friend,' he said. 'Stand up. Put your hands above your head.'

Campion obeyed him. Mr Barber stood up also and from under the edge of the table, where his hand had levelled it, there appeared what was, in the circumstances, the most dangerous-looking weapon Campion had ever seen. It was a small glass syringe. Any doubts he might have had as to the truth of the other man's threat were instantly dispelled.

'In your left pocket, I see.' The voice was smooth and almost caressing. With his left hand he removed the book deftly.

'Sit down,' he went on. 'Now that we understand one another perfectly our conversation will be so much more pleasant.'

'What little gents we both are,' said Mr Campion. 'Tell me, do you do all your murders like this?'

Mr Barber moved his left hand deprecatingly. 'I work from my desk as a rule. I know everything: I am behind every *coup* of any consequence. It was only because Mr Lobbett very foolishly wrote for an art expert that, on receiving that information, I decided to take part personally. I am enjoying the experience immensely.'

Campion did not reply. Mr Barber continued.

'I was also not very satisfied with my agent, Datchett. I have neglected that little branch of my organization. A man brilliant in his own line, but not a good servant. I ought to have known all about you long ago.'

The first hint of a smile appeared on Mr Campion's face. 'Stupendous!' he murmured. 'A sort of departmental store. "Don't Miss Our Bumper Blackmail Basement. Wholesale Murder, First Floor. Kidnapping and Hosiery on Your left."'

Mr Barber was not listening to him. His left hand still rested upon the little green-and-gold-bound children's book. He tapped it gently with a heavy forefinger.

'It recalls an incident which I had forgotten – an accident of twenty years ago. Coulson was the only man with whom I ever had direct personal dealings. I was comparatively young, and this desire to confide was very strong in me. One day he asked me if I knew the identity of Simister himself – if I had ever seen him. Foolishly, I confessed that I had. Ever afterwards he bothered me for the truth.

Frankly, I was amused by it, and one day I pointed to this book which lay upon the counter of a second-hand bookshop which was his headquarters. I fancy he thought I had brought the book with me. "There is your clue," said I. I never saw him again. The incident had slipped my memory completely, which shows one, my friend Campion,' he added with sudden sententiousness, 'that a foolish act is much more dangerous than an evil one.'

Campion nodded.

'There's one more thing I'd like to know,' he said. 'What had your friend Datchett got against old Swithin Cush?'

Mr Barber shrugged his shoulders.

'How should I know?' he said. 'A lot of Datchett's business shocked me. It was so small. That Kettle – he should never have been entrusted with anything. I was ashamed that he should be even remotely in my service.'

'That's the spirit,' said Campion. 'I was interested in Swithin Cush, it seemed to me impossible that such a man should have a secret.'

Mr Barber shook his head. 'A secret is never impossible,' he observed. 'Look at me, for instance.'

'If it's not being nosey,' the young man remarked slowly, 'I should be very interested to know how you intend to get away with your reputation all pure and virgie and our Albert's poor little mucked-up corp. lying about? I may be crude, but the question of the body has always worried me.'

'That will not be difficult.' The Oriental spoke confidently. 'After I had sent the telegram which I knew would bring you here, my agents came down here, waited until the village had retired – and then set upon the servants and drugged them as you found them. They had orders to do that and then remove themselves. I arrived upon the scene immediately afterwards. To them, as to everyone else, I am Fergusson Barber, the art expert. I waited for you, as you found me. What more simple, then? I shall go back, change my boots, which will be necessary after this rain. I shall even drug myself.'

'Don't forget the footmarks,' said Mr Campion. 'They're very hot on them over here.'

Mr Barber nodded. 'I had thought of that,' he agreed. 'But you ought to know that to follow footmarks on a saltmarsh is an impossibility. My alibi will be perfect – especially since both Judge Lobbett and young Paget saw me at the same time you did.'

The Turk spoke quite seriously. 'I shall have a beautiful Romney as a memento of my visit. It is quite genuine, by the way – one of the loveliest specimens I have ever seen. I shall have it put up for sale, discredited by good authorities – it may be necessary to substitute a copy for that – and sold quite cheaply to one of my agents.

'But the time moves on, my friend. It sounds as if the storm were clearing. Such a delightful conversation – it is a pity that it should ever have to close.'

'Something occurs to me,' said Campion, looking up. 'I have just composed my epitaph, you might see if you could get it put over my grave. No vulgar antique lettering either; good Roman Caps. Now listen carefully, because I should hate you to get it wrong.'

He was speaking with intense seriousness, and the Turk was amused. His veering eyes watched the young man tolerantly, but always he held the deadly syringe ready for the first sign of violence.

'No text,' said Campion. 'Just this, neatly and sincerely inscribed:

Here lie I, poor Albert Campion,

don't forget to get the scansion right.'

He recited the rhyme earnestly, his long thin hand beating out the rhyme on the rough table:

'Death was bad, but Life – *was champion!*'

On the last word his voice rose to a note of triumph, and with a gesture of amazing swiftness he swept the lamp from the table, dropping his head sharply as he did so.

Instantly something soft and horrible splattered over his shoulder, and the acid burning through his clothes ate deep into the flesh beneath, an almost paralyzing agony. The lantern crashed on the floor and, the draught catching it, went out, leaving the hut in complete darkness.

Campion wriggled towards the gap in the floor boards. It was his one hope. The pain in his shoulder was crippling him. He was terrified lest his senses should give way before it and he should faint.

In the darkness the man who a moment before had been chatting affably to him hovered, ready to kill.

Campion found the gap with his foot. Savagely he jerked himself towards it, and at the instant Barber fired. The gun had a silencer on it, but a flash of flame cut through the darkness. The place was too small for there to be a chance for the younger man to escape. The bullet entered his body.

The Oriental heard the stifled grunt of his victim as he slid helplessly through the opening on the marsh beneath.

Unaware of this second exit, he fired again, bullet after bullet.

The silencer was most effective. He had no cause to fear an alarm and he was determined to dispatch his man.

When at last he paused there was an ominous silence in the hut.

'Clever, my friend, clever to the end!' He spoke softly, but there was a peculiarly horrible satisfaction in his tone.

Still holding the gun cautiously, he drew a match-box from his pocket, his spent torch being useless. The tiny spurt of flame flickered for an instant, and went out in the draught. He moved to the edge of the gap under the bench and once more struck a match. This time the flame lasted longer.

Campion lay upon his back on the fast-reddening grass. His spectacles had fallen off and his eyes were closed, his face livid in the momentary light. Just for an instant the Turk hesitated. He had fired five times. There was one shot left in his gun. He debated if he should use it. There was no way of making sure if the man were dead unless he went out to him.

As he knelt looking down, the little green-and-gold book which he had snatched up in his first rush from the table slipped from his pocket where he had hurriedly thrust it and fell out on to the figure below.

That decided him. He clambered carefully to his feet and crossed the hut.

In the doorway he paused, feeling for the steps. He descended carefully.

Once on the grass he attempted to strike another light, but the rain which was still falling lightly rendered it impossible. He stepped out blindly to the left, unconsciously taking the shorter way round the hut. He took a step forward, then another, the short thick grass still beneath his feet.

As he took the third step a sudden sense of impending danger seized him, and he tried vainly to swing his weight back. A moment before he might have succeeded, but the turf beneath his feet was slippery.

He staggered and plunged forward over the three-foot drop of ragged earth into the stretch of slimy mud which lay beneath – that very stretch, paler and smoother-looking than the rest, which Giles had been so fearful of finding not an hour before. Unconscious of the imminent danger, he struggled to right himself, his only fear being that his alibi would be more difficult to establish now that his clothes were soaked with sea water and slime.

All round him the mud sucked and chattered to itself in its quiet guttural tongue. The rain continued to fall. He was alone between clay and sky.

He fought fiendishly to escape, realizing suddenly that the slime was past his waist. He beat out wildly with his arms and touched nothing but the foetid stuff. It reached his shoulders, and oblivious of any other danger he screamed aloud, calling upon Campion, straining his lungs until he felt that the village must hear.

The mud gurgled and spat. Little rivulets of water burst up through it. He slipped deeper; in a moment it must reach his chin. He forced his arms down, an instinct telling him that he might so gain a moment's respite. The stuff was closing about him, sucking him gently, firmly, and with horrible slowness into its slimy breast. He dared not scream now, lest the very movement should drag him under.

It was at that second that, far below, his foot touched the hard. He stiffened all over, a new hope returning. The difficulty of breathing was intense; as if it felt itself cheated, the mud pressed him, flattened him with its enormous weight.

Still, hope was returning, a wild, reckless desire for life, whatever it might bring with it.

The rain stopped.

Cramps were racking him, but he dared not relax the muscles that alone held him above the morass.

Far over his head the clouds parted. The tail end of the storm which had passed over them had dispersed itself. It became a little lighter.

He stared ahead of him. His eyes strained out of their sockets. His face was distorted, his mouth gaping, the veins standing out in great ridges under his pallid skin.

Not a foot away from him was a thick white line, irregular, more terrible, more relentless than the mud itself, the tide.

He watched it. Every spark of life that was left in him concentrated against this last and most dreadful foe. It retreated a little way, only to rush forward again within an inch of his face, splashing him with brine.

He forced up every fighting nerve that was in him. His frenzied scream startled the wild birds, and echoed, a cry of death, into the silent rooms of the Manor itself, acres distant across the saltings, and died away hollowly in the stillness of the early morning.

The waves retreated once more, and this time returned frothing, laughing, smothering over his mouth.

Chapter 28

Moral

'Two teeth?' said the man from Scotland Yard with contempt. 'He's got seven. Three at the bottom, four at the top. Mary and I are crazy about him. You'll have to come round and see him as soon as you can get out again.'

He was sitting forward in the big chair, before one of the first of autumn's fires, in the flat at Bottle Street.

'I'll come down next week. I'm all right now.' The slightly high-pitched voice was more hollow than it had been, but it had not lost that suggestion of exuberance which had always been its characteristic. Campion was almost completely hidden in the depths of his high-backed Toby chair. Only now and again when the firelight flickered did the other man get a glimpse of his face. It was still desperately haggard from his long illness. Ali Barber's bullet had pierced his lung and the mending had been slow. But his old sparkle had returned and his eyes behind his horn-rimmed spectacles were once more amused and very much alive.

His companion smiled at him. 'You were damned lucky to come out of that as well as you did,' he said. 'You were always lucky.'

'I'm very grateful to the boys for getting me out of it so quietly,' murmured Campion with genuine gratitude. He sighed. 'I was afraid I was going to get a medal.'

'More kicks than ha'pence in our job,' said the other. 'It's something to lay to your credit, though. There wasn't a doubt that it was the right man. We've been tracing the sources of his income among other things. Marvellous!' he remarked dreamily, leaning forward and knocking the ashes of his pipe out on the hearth.

Campion chuckled. 'You ought to start a copybook, Stanis,' he said. 'But I really thought I was for it that time when I fell through the floor. I recited God Save the King, sang the old school song, muttered the family motto – "No Rubbish to be Shot Here" – and passed out. Any further developments in the Datchett case?'

'Lugg told me I wasn't to talk shop.'

The man from Scotland Yard looked round him nervously. Lugg, in his new rôle as hospital attendant, was a truly terrifying personage. As he was nowhere in sight the man continued softly.

'I wanted to tell you about that,' he said. 'He went to pieces at his trial – I don't suppose you've seen the papers. He got the limit. I don't think there'll be any appeal either. We got all the witnesses we wanted from the Maplestone Hall affair. There was no need to go into that other business.'

Campion glanced up sharply. 'Swithin Cush?'

The other man nodded.

'That was interesting if you like,' he said. 'In the house at Kensington there were masses of stuff dealing with all sorts of things. Wherever possible we bunged the papers back to the right owners and said no more about it. We're not out to stir up scandals. We got our man where we wanted him, and that was right enough. But the old man had his secret all right. The last thing you'd guess in a thousand years. He wasn't a parson.'

Campion stared at him.

'He wasn't a parson?' he repeated blankly. 'They've pulled your leg again, Stanis.'

'No. It's quite true.' The other man shook his head. 'An impersonation story fifty years old. There were two brothers – Swithin Cush just ordained, Welwyn Cush, too poor to take the 'varsity course. Swithin died, apparently quite suddenly, from heart trouble. The two brothers were living alone together in rooms in Kensington. The dead man had just been appointed to his first curacy in a Norfolk village. The younger man had a great friend in the daughter of the house, and it was she, I fancy, who put the idea up to him. He allowed the dead man to be buried in his name, and took his job. There was only a year between the brothers, and they seem to have resembled each other very closely. No one appears to have doubted Welwyn for a moment and the years slipped by as they do in the country. The life was congenial to him, the vicar liked him, and he was a great favourite with the parishioners. Five or six years later he was appointed to Mystery Mile, and his history there I suppose you know much better than I do. The older he got the safer he was. The only person who knew his secret was the woman in Kensington. She died only about a year or so ago. Her name was Aggie Saunders, and very much the class of person you'd imagine.' He glanced at Campion, who was sitting forward in his chair, his eyes goggling. He continued.

'She could not resist reminding him from time to time of the power she held over him by deliberately referring to the secret in long rambling letters to him. He replied to these imploring her not to write anything so incriminating.

'I fancy that she found that a letter on this subject invariably brought a reply from him, and therefore harped upon it shamelessly. When she felt that her time was drawing to an end she packed up all these letters of his and sent them to him, choosing, by extraordinary bad luck, the first week of Kettle's appointment as postmaster.

'Kettle simply pinched the letters and packed them off to Datchett. From which time the poor old boy you knew as Swithin Cush couldn't have had a moment's peace. How's that?'

Campion was silent for a moment, lost in amazement. 'Good Lord!' he said at last, and repeated softly, 'Good Lord!'

'Blackmail is the filthiest of all crimes,' said the man from Scotland Yard. 'I'm glad Datchett got what was coming to him.'

Campion regarded his visitor awkwardly.

'This raises a rather delicate question re Births, Marriages, and Deaths in Mystery Mile, doesn't it?' he said. 'What are your people doing with the letters?'

Detective Inspector Stanislaus Oates shrugged his shoulders. He seemed almost official in his vagueness. 'Whatever criticism anybody ever makes about Scotland Yard,' he said, 'they can't call us mischief makers. We protect the peace: that's our job. I don't fancy we shall go into it any further. It would make a lot of unpleasantness all round, and a scandal in the Church, which is always to be avoided. I'm not an authority on ecclesiastical law – I suppose it would be a case for the archbishop if it ever came out.'

At the words 'ecclesiastical law' Campion pricked up his ears. For the first time he realized the meaning of the mysterious phrase in Swithin Cush's letter to Giles: *'In the event of any serious trouble . . . send to Alaric Watts . . . who will know the correct proceeding.'* This was the serious trouble of which the old man had been afraid.

'Of course,' the inspector went on, 'the authorities may decide to take the matter to the Church. I think it would only mean some sort of minor bill being passed. It's not an important thing now, but it was serious enough for him.'

Campion did not speak. He realized more than anyone how serious it had been for the old man, so beloved by his bigoted congregation.

'I suppose you're very satisfied?' The detective inspector dismissed the subject airily. 'Apart from your wound and the old rector's death you're not sorry it happened. If you hadn't got old Lobbett and his kids down to Mystery Mile a lot of things would never have happened.'

'There's something in that,' said Campion, so thoughtfully that the other man glanced at him shrewdly.

'What's worrying you?' he said.

'I had such a nice death scene,' said Mr Campion unexpectedly. 'I feel that the curtain's gone up and exposed me crawling off. No more fun until the next performance, Stanis, and I'm not sure I wouldn't rather be in the stalls for that.'

'A spot of brandy'll put you right – that's nerves,' said the other cheerfully, but he had made a mistake in his diagnosis.

They chatted for some time longer, and eventually the Scotland Yard man took his leave. Campion lay back in his chair and reflected upon the tragic story of Swithin Cush.

'As perfect a parson as ever lived,' he reflected. 'And a damned old fraud at the same time, God bless him!'

After some time he took an envelope from his dressing-gown pocket and reopened it. Biddy's handwriting was not of the best. It might have been a schoolgirl's letter. He re-read it slowly:

Home.
Sunday.

MY DEAR ALBERT:

Lugg tells me you're allowed out, in a really marvellous epistle which begins 'Dear Madham' and ends 'Well duckie, I must close now'. We're coming up to see you again on Friday. Mystery Mile looks marvellous now, all the leaves turning and apples waiting to be picked. The D'arcy Spice that St Swithin planted in the courtyard is bearing this year. They'll be just eatable when you come down, though why you ever wanted to convalesce in London I don't know.

The new rector is a dear. Four kids, and an exceptional wife (for a parson). He's going to officiate on *the great occasion*. Only a month now. Isopel's going to have a short frock and I'm going to have a long one. A real country do, with a party for the village and George and 'Anry as sidesmen.

Giles is going to get an awful lot for the Romney, it seems. It's impossible to believe that that ghastly man could have been right about anything, but I'm not going to write about him or anything connected with that dreadful time, although of course if it hadn't happened I shouldn't have found Marlowe.

I'm bursting with happiness now, but I wish you were down here with us. Giles says that we shall have to watch you or you'll come in a Boy Scout uniform to the wedding, but you won't will you? He says you turned up as a Salvation Army General when Bunny Wright married Lady Rachel. You won't do anything silly this time, promise, because I mean – oh, well, please don't, anyway.

Cuddy's daughter had her baby, quite a beauty. Mr Lobbett (I'm beginning to call him 'Poppa', which seems to be American for 'Daddy', 'Daddy' meaning something else) gave it the Bounty. *And* (this will please you) she wanted to call the poor little beast 'Nuptial' because of our weddings, but we persuaded her not to, so it's going to be called 'Bridget Isopel' instead.

Addlepate has got a new collar because he got the old one off and ate it, or tried to, anyhow he did it in.

There doesn't seem to be anything more to say, although such heaps of glorious things are happening. I miss old St Swithin dreadfully. He would have enjoyed this. Alice is looking after the new people at the Rectory. And do you know I do believe Cuddy is having an affair with the new postmaster who came when Kettle went. He isn't married, or at least not now. He has two children that Cuddy is always washing for him.

And you did all this, you wonderful old thing. Marlowe and I thank you from the bottom of our hearts and so do the others. We'll never forget it. All the best.

Lots of love, old dear,
BIDDY

There was a postscript on her letter, written in Marlowe's precise, educated hand:

Coming to town with this abandoned woman, Friday. Everything OK. The dad wants to know where he can buy some more port like that '98 stuff in the cellar. The doc says it will give him gout. He says 'What's gout?'

Yrs ever,
M. K. L.

The other two had signed the letter. It was a family epistle. From time immemorial Biddy's letters had been like that – frank, unconscious affairs which anyone might read.

Campion thrust the wad of notepaper back into his pocket, and glanced up to find Mr Lugg looking down at him with lugubrious interest.

'That's a warnin',' he said. 'There's a moral in that, there is. Find the Lady is a Mug's game, that's wot this 'as shown you, and don't you forget it neither.'

Campion ignored him.

'Two wedding presents,' he remarked. 'I shall have to send you out on to the tiles again, Lugg.'

'I wish you would,' said that worthy with unexpected vigour. 'Buy, buy, buy – it gives me the 'ump. That letter's from that girl you was rather sweet on, ain't it? You know, wot you want, if you must 'ave a woman about the place, is a nice sensible 'omely 'ospital nurse. Someone who'll do the washin' up for us.'

'Shut up, Lugg,' said Campion. 'What about those wedding presents? Silver, I suppose.'

Lugg was dubious.

'Don't 'ave it inscribed, whatever you do,' he remarked feelingly. 'Can't pop it, can't sell it, no one even wants to pinch it. It does silver right in, inscribin' does. There's a sight too much of it these days. I'll think of something.'

Campion remained silent for some time. 'Lugg,' he said at last, 'suppose I retired? This profession of mine puts people off.'

Mr Lugg's expression silenced him. The old lag was staring at him, his eyes bulging, his jaw dropped.

'You've 'ad a relapse. I'll mix you something.'

'Stop!' Campion put up his hand. 'Don't be a fool, Lugg. I'm serious.'

'That's un'ealthy in itself,' said Lugg, and trotted out of the room.

Campion sat down again. He took the letter from his pocket and threw it into the fire. Folding his hands on his knees, he watched it burn. Then he moved restlessly in his chair. Von Faber in Broadmoor, Simister dead – for the moment he felt like Alexander, sighing for new worlds to conquer.

At this instant Lugg returned. He appeared considerably subdued, and a little troubled. In his hand he held a card.

'Not 'arf a funny bloke outside,' he said in a hoarse whisper. 'A foreigner. Shall I chuck a brick at 'im?'

'I don't know,' said Campion. 'Let's have a look at that.'

Lugg parted with the slip of pasteboard unwillingly. A glance at it brought a sparkle in Mr Campion's eyes, and a flush of pleasure appeared in his cheeks. He swept past Lugg and threw open the door.

In a moment he reappeared with a man about his own age, dark and distinguished-looking, with a somewhat military carriage.

They were talking together with great animation in a tongue which Mr Lugg afterwards described as 'monkey talk'. It was evident that they had known each other for some time.

After the first moment or so the stranger produced a letter, a massive grey-white envelope, sealed and bound with crimson tape.

He bowed and withdrew a pace or two as the Englishman cut it carefully open. The single sheet of paper within was crested with the arms of a famous European royal house, but the few lines were scribbled in English:

Salutations. My dear fellow, I am in despair. State Trip to Indo-China indicated. Fed to the teeth. Could you impersonate me, as before?

Yours ever, R.

PS – Trouble expected, if that appeals to you. For the love of Ike (I think you call him) come and help me.

Mr Campion folded the missive carefully, and dropped it into the fire after Biddy's. He was obviously elated. He turned to his visitor and beamed. Crossing to his desk, he wrote a few words on a sheet of notepaper and slipped it into an envelope, which he sealed carefully. Then he exchanged a few more civilities with his visitor, and the stranger departed.

As the door closed behind him Campion turned to his inquisitive aide.

'Lugg,' he said joyously, 'you may kiss our hand.'

Look to the Lady

To Orlando

Look to the Lady

To Orlando

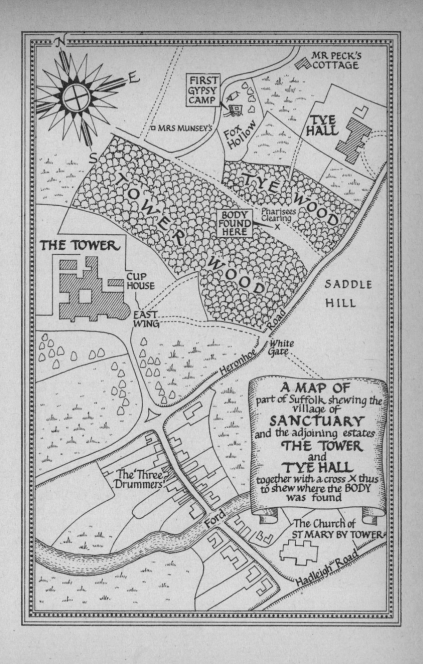

Chapter 1

'Reward for Finder?'

'If you'll accept this, sir,' said the policeman, pressing a shilling into the down-and-out's hand, 'you'll have visible means of support and I shan't have to take you along. But,' he added with a delightful hint of embarrassment, 'I'll have to ask you to move on; the Inspector is due round any minute.'

Percival St John Wykes Gyrth, only son of Colonel Sir Percival Christian St John Gyrth, Bt, of the Tower, Sanctuary, Suffolk, reddened painfully, thrust the coin into his trouser pocket, and smiled at his benefactor.

'Thank you, Baker,' he said. 'This is extraordinarily kind of you. I shan't forget it.'

'That's all right, sir.' The man's embarrassment increased. 'You gave me five pounds the night you was married.' He opened his mouth as though to continue, but thought the better of it, and the young man's next remark indicated clearly that he was in no mood for reminiscences.

'I say, where the devil can I sit where I shan't be moved on?'

The policeman glanced nervously up South Molton Street, whence even now the dapper form of the Inspector was slowly approaching.

'Ebury Square – just off Southampton Row,' he murmured hastily. 'You'll be as safe as houses there. Good night, sir.'

The final words were a dismissal; the Inspector was almost upon them. Val Gyrth pulled his battered hat over his eyes, and hunching his shoulders, shuffled off towards Oxford Street. His 'visible means of support' flopped solitarily in the one safe pocket of his suit, a suit which had once come reverently from the hands of the tailor whose shop he was passing. He crossed into Oxford Street and turned up towards the Circus.

It was a little after midnight and the wide road was almost deserted. There were a few returning revellers, a sprinkling of taxicabs, and an occasional late bus.

Val Gyrth chose the inside of the pavement, keeping as much in the shadow as possible. The summer smell of the city, warm and slightly scented like a chemist's shop, came familiarly to his nostrils and in spite of his weariness there was an impatience in his step. He was bitterly angry with himself. The situation was impossible, quixotic and ridiculous. Old Baker had given him a shilling to save him from arrest as a vagrant on his own doorstep. It was unthinkable.

He had not eaten since the night before, but he passed the coffee-stall outside the French hat shop in the Circus without a thought. He had ceased to feel hungry at about four o'clock that afternoon and had been surprised and thankful at the respite. The swimming sensation which had taken the place of it seemed eminently preferable.

The pavement was hot to that part of his foot which touched it through the hole in an expensive shoe, and he was beginning to limp when he turned down by Mudie's old building and found himself after another five minutes' plodding in a dishevelled little square whose paved centre was intersected by two rows of dirty plane trees, beneath which, amid the litter of a summer's day, were several dilapidated wooden benches. There were one or two unsavoury-looking bundles dotted here and there, but there were two seats unoccupied. Val Gyrth chose the one under a street lamp and most aloof from its fellows; he sank down, realizing for the first time the full sum of his weariness.

A shiver ran through the dusty leaves above his head, and as he glanced about him he became obsessed with a curious feeling of apprehension which could not be explained by the sudden chill of the night. A car passed through the square, and from far off beyond the Strand came the mournful bellow of a tug on the river. None of the bundles huddled on the other seats stirred, but it seemed to the boy, one of the least imaginative of an unimaginative race, that something enormous and of great importance was about to happen, or was, indeed, in the very act of happening all round him; a sensation perhaps explainable by partial starvation and a potential thunder-storm.

He took off his hat and passed his fingers through his very fair hair, the increasing length of which was a continual source of annoyance to him. He was a thick-set, powerful youngster in his early twenties, with a heavy but by no means unhandsome face and an habitual expression of dogged obstinacy; a pure Anglo-Saxon type, chiefly remarkable at the moment for a certain unnatural gauntness which accentuated the thickness of his bones.

He sighed, turned up his coat collar, and was about to lift his feet out of the miscellaneous collection of paper bags, orange skins and cigarette cartons on to the bench, when he paused and sat up stiffly, staring down at the ground in front of him. He was conscious of a sudden wave of heat passing over him, of an odd shock that made his heart jump unpleasantly.

He was looking at his own name, written on a battered envelope lying face upwards among the other litter.

He picked it up and was astonished to see that his hand was shaking. The name was unmistakable. 'P. St J. W. Gyrth, Esq.' written clearly in a hand he did not know.

He turned the envelope over. It was an expensive one, and empty, having been torn open across the top apparently by an impatient hand. He sat staring at it for some moments, and a feeling of unreality took possession of him. The address, 'Kemp's, 32a Wembley Road, Clerkenwell, E C I', was completely unfamiliar.

He stared at it as though he expected the words to change before his eyes, but they remained clear and unmistakable: 'P. St J. W. Gyrth, Esq.'

At first it did not occur to him to doubt that the name was his own, or that the envelope had been originally intended for him. Gyrth is an unusual name, and the odd collection of initials combined with it made it impossible for him to think that in this case it could belong to anyone else.

He studied the handwriting thoughtfully, trying to place it. His mind had accepted the astounding coincidence which had brought him to this particular seat in this particular square and led him to pick up the one envelope which bore his name. He hunted among the rubbish at his feet in a futile attempt to find the contents of the envelope, but an exhaustive search convinced him that the paper in his hand was all that was of interest to him there.

The hand puzzled him. It was distinctive, square, with heavy downstrokes and sharp Greek E's; individual handwriting, not easily to be forgotten. He turned his attention to the postmark, and the bewildered expression upon his young face became one of blank astonishment. It was dated the fifteenth of June. Today was the nineteenth. The letter was therefore only four days old.

It was over a week since he had possessed any address. Yet he was convinced, and the fact was somehow slightly uncanny and unnerving, that someone had written to him, and someone else had received the letter, the envelope of which had been thrown away to be found by himself.

Not the least remarkable thing about a coincidence is that once it has happened, one names it, accepts it, and leaves it at that.

Gyrth sat on the dusty seat beneath the street lamp and looked at the envelope. The rustling in the leaves above his head had grown fiercer, and an uncertain wind ricocheted down the square; in a few minutes it would rain.

Once again he was conscious of that strange sensation of being just on the outside of some drama enacted quite near to him. He had felt it before tonight. Several times in the past few days this same uneasy feeling had swept over him in the most crowded streets at the height of noon, or at night in the dark alleyways of the city where he had tried to sleep. Experienced criminals recognize this sensation as the instinctive knowledge that one is being 'tailed', but young Gyrth was no criminal, nor was he particularly experienced in anything save the more unfortunate aspects of matrimony.

He looked again at the address on the tantalizing envelope: '32a Wembley Rd, Clerkenwell.' This was not far from where he now sat, he reflected, and the impulse to go there to find out for himself if he were not the only P. St J. W. Gyrth in the world, or, if he was, to discover who was impersonating him, was very strong.

His was a conservative nature, however, and perhaps if the experience had happened to him in ordinary circumstances he would have shrugged his shoulders and taken no further active interest in the matter. But at the moment he was down-and-out. A man who is literally destitute is like a straw in the wind; any tiny current is sufficient to set him drifting in a new direction. His time and energies are of no value to him; anything is worth while. Impelled by curiosity, therefore, he set off across the square, the storm blowing up behind him.

He did not know what he expected to find, but the envelope fascinated him. He gave up conjecturing and hurried.

Clerkenwell in the early hours of the morning is one of the most unsavoury neighbourhoods in the whole of East Central London, which is saying a great deal, and the young man's ragged and dishevelled appearance was probably the only one which would not have attracted the attention of those few inhabitants who were still abroad.

At length he discovered a pair of policemen, of whom he inquired the way, gripping their colleague's shilling defiantly as he did so. They directed him with the unhurried omniscience of their kind, and he eventually found himself crossing a dirty ill-lit thoroughfare intersected with tramlines and flanked by the lowest of all lodging-houses, and shabby dusty little shops where everything seemed to be second-hand.

Number 32a turned out to be one of the few establishments still open.

It was an eating-house, unsavoury even for the neighbourhood, and one stepped down off the pavement a good eighteen inches to reach the level of the ground floor. Even Val Gyrth, now the least cautious of men, hesitated before entering.

The half-glass door of the shop was pasted over with cheap advertisements for boot polish and a brand of caramel, and the light from within struggled uncertainly through the dirty oiled paper.

Gyrth glanced at the envelope once more and decided that there was no doubt at all that this was his destination. The number, 32a, was printed on a white enamelled plaque above the door, and the name 'Kemp's' was written across the shop front in foot-high letters.

Once again the full sense of the absurdity of his quest came over him, and he hesitated, but again he reflected that he had nothing to lose and his curiosity to appease. He turned the door-handle and stepped down into the room.

The fetid atmosphere within was so full of steam that for a moment he could not see at all where he was. He stood still for some seconds trying to penetrate the haze, and at last made out a long dingy room flanked with high, greasy pew seats, which appeared to be empty.

At the far end of the aisle between the tables there was a counter and a cooking-stove from which the atmosphere obtained most of its quality. Towards this gastronomic altar the young man advanced, the envelope clutched tightly in his coat pocket.

There was no one in sight, so he tapped the counter irresolutely. Almost immediately a door to the right of the stove was jerked open and there appeared a mountain of a man with the largest and most lugubrious face he had ever seen. A small tablecloth had been tied across the newcomer's stomach by way of an apron, and his great muscular arms were bare to the elbow. For the rest, his head was bald, and the bone of his nose had sustained an irreparable injury.

He regarded the young man with mournful eyes.

'This is a nice time to think about getting a bit of food,' he observed more in sorrow than in anger, thereby revealing a sepulchral voice. 'Everything's off but sausage and mash. I'm 'aving the last bit o' stoo meself.'

Gyrth was comforted by his melancholy affability. It was some time since an eating-house keeper had treated him with even ordinary humanity. He took the envelope out of his pocket and spread it out on the counter before the man.

'Look here,' he said. 'Do you know anything about this?'

Not a muscle of the lugubrious face stirred. The mountainous stranger eyed the envelope for some time as if he had never seen such a thing before and was not certain if it were worth consideration. Then, turning suddenly, he looked the boy straight in the eyes and made what was in the circumstances a most extraordinary observation.

'I see,' he said clearly, and with a slightly unnecessary deliberation, '*you take the long road.*'

Gyrth stared at him. He felt that some reply was expected, that the words had some significance which was lost upon him. He laughed awkwardly.

'I don't quite follow you,' he said. 'I suppose I am tramping, if that's what you mean? But I came to inquire about this envelope. Have you seen it before?'

The big man ventured as near a smile as Gyrth felt his features would permit.

'Suppose I 'ave?' he said cautiously. 'Wot then?'

'Only that it happens to be addressed to me, and I'm anxious to know who opened it,' said Gyrth shortly. 'Can you tell me who collected it?'

'Is that your name?' The big man placed a heavy forefinger upon the inscription. 'I suppose you couldn't prove it, could yer?'

Gyrth grew red and uncomfortable. 'I can't get anyone to identify me, if that's what you mean, and I haven't got a visiting-card. But,' he added, 'if you care to take my tailor's word for it there's the tab inside my coat here.'

He unbuttoned the threadbare garment and turned down the edge of the inside breast pocket, displaying a tailor's label with his name and the date written in ink across it. In his eagerness he did not realize the incongruity of the situation.

The sad man read the label and then surveyed his visitor critically.

'I suppose it *was* made for yer?' he said.

Gyrth buttoned up his coat. 'I've got thinner,' he said shortly.

'Awright. No offence,' said the other. 'I believe yer – some wouldn't. Name o' Lugg meself. Pleased to meet yer, I'm sure. I got another letter for you, by the way.'

He turned round ponderously, and after searching among the cups and plates upon the dresser behind him, he returned bearing a similar envelope to the one which Gyrth had put down upon the counter. It was unopened.

The young man took it with a sense of complete bewilderment. He was about to tear the seal when the gentleman who had just introduced himself with such light-hearted friendliness tapped him on the shoulder.

'Suppose you go and sit down,' he observed. 'I'll bring yer a spot o' coffee and a couple o' Zepps in a smoke screen. I always get peckish about this time o' night meself.'

'I've only got a shilling –' Gyrth began awkwardly.

Mr Lugg raised his eyebrows.

'A bob?' he said. 'Where d'you think you're dining? The Cheshire Cheese? You sit down, my lad. I'll do you proud for a tanner. Then you'll 'ave yer "visible means" and tuppence to spare for emergencies.'

Gyrth did as he was told. He edged on to one of the greasy benches and sat down before a table neatly covered with a clean newspaper bill. He tore at the thick envelope with clumsy fingers. The smell of the place had reawakened his hunger, and his head was aching violently.

Three objects fell out upon the table; two pound notes and an engraved correspondence card. He stared at the card in stupefaction:

> Mr Albert Campion
> At Home

– and underneath, in the now familiar square handwriting:

> Any evening after twelve.
> Improving Conversation.
> Beer, Light Wines, and Little Pink Cakes.
> Do come.

The address was engraved:

> 17, Bottle Street, w 1
> (Entrance on left by Police Station).

Scribbled on the back were the words: 'Please forgive crude temporary loan. Come along as soon as you can. It's urgent. Take care. A. C.'

Val Gyrth turned the card over and over.

The whole episode was becoming fantastic. There was a faintly nonsensical, Alice-through-the-Looking-Glass air about it all, and it did just cross his mind that he might have been involved in a street accident and the adventure be the result of a merciful anaesthetic.

He was still examining the extraordinary message when the gloomy but also slightly fantastic Mr Lugg appeared with what was evidently his personal idea of a banquet. Gyrth ate what was set before him with a growing sense of gratitude and reality. When he had finished he looked up at the man who was still standing beside him.

'I say,' he said, 'have you ever heard of a Mr Albert Campion?'

The man's small eyes regarded him solemnly. 'Sounds familiar,' he said. 'I can't say as I place 'im, though.' There was a stubborn blankness in his face which told the boy that further questioning would be useless. Once again Gyrth took up the card and the two bank-notes.

'How do you know,' he said suddenly, 'that I am the man to receive this letter?'

Mr Lugg looked over his shoulder at the second envelope. 'That's yer name, ain't it?' he said. 'It's the name inside yer suit, any'ow. You showed me.'

'Yes, I know,' said Val patiently. 'But how do you know that I am the Percival St John Wykes Gyrth –?'

'Gawd! It don't stand for all that, do it?' said Mr Lugg, impressed. 'That answers yer own question, my lad. There ain't two mothers 'oo'd saddle a brat with that lot. That's your invitation ticket all right. Don't you worry. I should 'op it – it's gettin' late.'

Gyrth considered the card again. It was mad, of course. And yet he had come so far that it seemed illogical not to go on. As though to clinch the matter with himself he paid for his food out of his new-found wealth, and after tipping his host prodigally he bade the man good night and walked out of the deserted eating-house.

It was not until he was outside the door and standing on the pavement that the problem of transportation occurred to him. It was a good three miles across the city to Piccadilly, and although his hunger was sated he was still excessively tired. To make the situation more uncomfortable it was very late and the rain had come in a sullen downpour.

While he stood hesitating, the sound of wheels came softly behind him.

'Taxi, sir?'

Gyrth turned thankfully, gave the man the address on the card, and climbed into the warm leather depths of the cab.

As he sank back among the cushions the old feeling of well-being stole over him. The cab was speeding over the glistening roads along which he had trudged so wearily less than an hour before. For some minutes he reflected upon the extraordinary invitation he had accepted so unquestioningly. The ridiculous card read like a hoax, of course, but two pounds are not a joke to a starving man, and since he had nothing to lose he saw no reason why he should not investigate it. Besides, he was curious.

He took the card out of his pocket and bent forward to read it by the light from the meter lamp. He could just make out the scribbled message: 'Come along as soon as you can. It's urgent. Take care.'

The last two words puzzled him. In the circumstances they seemed so ridiculous that he almost laughed.

It was at that precise moment that the cab turned to the right in Gray's Inn Road and he caught a glimpse of a quiet tree-lined Bloomsbury square. Then, and not until then, did it dawn upon him with a sudden throb and quickening of his pulse that the chance of picking up a taxi accidentally at three o'clock in the morning in Wembley Road, Clerkenwell was one in a million, and secondly, that the likelihood of an ordinary cabman mistaking him in his present costume for a potential fare was nothing short of an absurdity. He bent forward and ran his hand along the doors. There were no handles. The windows too appeared to be locked.

Considerably startled, but almost ashamed of himself for suspecting a danger for which he was hardly eligible, he rapped vigorously on the window behind the driver.

Even as Gyrth watched him, the man bent over his wheel and trod heavily on the accelerator.

Chapter 2

Little Pink Cakes

Val sat forward in the half-darkness and peered out. The old cab was, he guessed, travelling all out at about thirty-five miles an hour. The streets were rain-swept and deserted and he recognized that he was being carried directly out of his way.

On the face of it he was being kidnapped, but this idea was so ridiculous in his present condition that he was loth to accept it. Deciding that the driver must be drunk or deaf, he thundered again on the glass and tried shouting down the speaking tube.

'I want Bottle Street – off Piccadilly.'

This time he had no doubt that his driver heard him, for the man jerked his head in a negative fashion and the cab rocked and swayed dangerously. Val Gyrth had to accept the situation, absurd though it might be. He was a prisoner being borne precipitately to an unknown destination.

During the past eighteen months he had discovered himself in many unpleasant predicaments, but never one that called for such immediate action. At any other time he might have hesitated until it was too late, but tonight the cumulative effects of starvation and weariness had produced in him a dull recklessness, and the mood which had permitted him to follow such a fantastic will-o'-the-wisp as his name on a discarded envelope, and later to accept the hardly conventional invitation of the mysterious Mr Campion, was still upon him. Moreover, the kindly ministrations of Mr Lugg had revived his strength and with it his temper.

At that moment, hunched up inside the cab, he was a dangerous person. His hands were knotted together, and the muscles of his jaw contracted.

The moment the idea came into his head he put it into execution.

He bent down and removed the heavy shoe with the thin sole, from which the lace had long since disappeared. With this formidable weapon tightly gripped in his hand, he crouched in the body of the cab, holding himself steady by the flower bracket above the spare seats. He was still prodigiously strong, and put all he knew into the blow. His arm crashed down like a machine hammer, smashing through the plate glass and down on to the driver's skull.

Instantly Gyrth dropped on to the mat, curling himself up, his arms covering his head. The driver's thick cap had protected him considerably, but the attack was so sudden that he lost control of his wheel. The cab skidded violently across the greasy road, mounted the pavement and smashed sickeningly into a stone balustrade.

The impact was terrific: the car bounded off the stone-work, swayed for an instant and finally crashed over on to its side.

Gyrth was hurled into the worn hood of the cab, which tore beneath his weight. He was conscious of warm blood trickling down his face from a cut across his forehead, and one of his shoulders was wrenched, but he had been prepared for the trouble and was not seriously injured. He was still angry, still savage. He fought his way out through the torn fabric on to the pavement, and turned for an instant to survey the scene.

His captor lay hidden beneath the mass of wreckage and made no sound. But the street was no longer deserted. Windows were opening and from both ends of the road came the sound of voices and hurrying footsteps.

Gyrth was in no mood to stop to answer questions. He wiped the blood from his face with his coat-sleeve and was relieved to find that the damage was less messy than he had feared. He slipped on the shoe, which he still gripped, and vanished like a shadow up a side street.

He finished the rest of his journey on foot.

He went to the address in Bottle Street largely out of curiosity, but principally, perhaps, because he had nowhere else to go. He chose the narrow dark ways, cutting through the older part of Holborn and the redolent alleys of Soho.

Now, for the first time for days, he realized that he was free from that curious feeling of oppression which had vaguely puzzled him. There was no one in the street behind him as he turned from dark corner to lighted thoroughfare and came at last to the cul-de-sac off Piccadilly which is Bottle Street.

The single blue lamp of the Police Station was hardly inviting, but the door of Number Seventeen, immediately upon the left, stood ajar. He pushed it open gingerly.

He was wellnigh exhausted, however, and his shreds of caution had vanished. Consoling himself with the thought that nothing could be worse than his present predicament, he climbed painfully up the wooden steps. After the first landing there was a light and the stairs were carpeted, and he came at last to a full stop before a handsome linenfold oak door. A small brass plate bore the simple legend, '*Mr Albert Campion. The Goods Dept.*'

There was also a very fine Florentine knocker, which, however, he did not have occasion to use, for the door opened and an entirely unexpected figure appeared in the opening.

A tall thin young man with a pale inoffensive face, and vague eyes behind enormous horn-rimmed spectacles smiled out at him with engaging friendliness. He was carefully, not to say fastidiously, dressed in evening clothes, but the correctness of his appearance was somewhat marred by the fact that in his hand he held a string to which was attached a child's balloon of a particularly vituperant pink.

He seemed to become aware of this incongruous attachment as soon as he saw his visitor, for he made several unsuccessful attempts to hide it behind his back. He held out his hand.

'Doctor Livingstone, I presume?' he said in a well-bred, slightly high-pitched voice.

Considerably startled, Gyrth put out his hand. 'I don't know who you are,' he began, 'but I'm Val Gyrth and I'm looking for a man who calls himself Albert Campion.'

'That's all right,' said the stranger releasing the balloon, which floated up to the ceiling, with the air of one giving up a tiresome problem. 'None genuine without my face on the wrapper. This is me – my door – my balloon. Please come in and have a drink. You're rather late – I was afraid you weren't coming,' he went on, escorting his visitor across a narrow hall into a small but exceedingly comfortable sitting-room, furnished and decorated in a curious and original fashion. There were several odd trophies on the walls, and above the mantelpiece, between a Rosenberg drypoint and what looked like a page from an original 'Dance of Death', was a particularly curious group composed of a knuckle-duster surmounted by a Scotland Yard Rogues' Gallery portrait of a well-known character, neatly framed and affectionately autographed. A large key of a singular pattern completed the tableau.

Val Gyrth sank down into the easy chair his host set for him. This peculiar end to his night's adventure, which in itself had been astonishing enough, had left him momentarily stupefied. He accepted the brandy-and-soda which the pale young man thrust into his hands and began to sip it without question.

It was at this point that Mr Campion appeared to notice the cut on his visitor's forehead. His concern was immediate.

'So you had a spot of trouble getting here?' he said. 'I do hope they didn't play rough.'

Val put down his glass, and sitting forward in his chair looked up into his host's face.

'Look here,' he said, 'I haven't the least idea who you are, and this night's business seems like a fairy tale. I find an envelope addressed to me, open, in the middle of Ebury Square. Out of crazy curiosity I follow it up. At Kemp's eating-house in Clerkenwell I find a letter waiting for me from you, with two pounds in it and an extraordinary invitation card. I get in a taxi to come here and the man tries to shanghai me. I scramble out of that mess with considerable damage to myself, and more to the driver, and when I get here I find you apparently quite *au fait* with my affairs and fooling about with a balloon. I may be mad – I don't know.'

Mr Campion looked hurt. 'I'm sorry about the balloon,' he said. 'I'd just come back from a gala at the Athenaeum, when Lugg phoned to say you were coming. He's out tonight, so I had to let you in myself. I don't see that you can grumble about that. The taxi sounds bad. That's why you were late, I suppose?'

'That's all right,' said Val, who was still ruffled. 'But it must be obvious to you that I want an explanation, and you know very well that you owe me one.'

It was then that Mr Campion stepped sideways so that the light from the reading-lamp on the table behind him shone directly upon his visitor's face. Then he cleared his throat and spoke with a curious deliberation quite different from his previous manner.

'*I see you take the long road, Mr Gyrth,*' he said quietly.

Val raised his eyes questioningly to his host's face. It was the second time that night that the simple remark had been made to him, and each time there had been this same curious underlying question in the words.

He stared at his host blankly, but the pale young man's slightly vacuous face wore no expression whatsoever, and his eyes were obscured behind the heavy spectacles. He did not stir, but stood there clearly awaiting a reply, and in that instant the younger man caught a glimpse of waters running too deep for him to fathom.

Chapter 3

The Fairy Tale

Val Gyrth rose to his feet.

'The man at Kemp's said that to me,' he said. 'I don't know what it means – since it's obvious that it must mean something. What do you expect me to say?'

Mr Campion's manner changed instantly. He became affable and charming. 'Do sit down,' he said. 'I owe you an apology. Only, you see, I'm not the only person who's interested in you – I shall have to explain my interest, by the way. But if my rival firm got hold of you first –'

'Well?' said Val.

'Well,' said Mr Campion, 'you might have understood about the Long Road. However, now that we can talk, suppose I unbosom myself – unless you'd like to try a blob of iodine on that scalp of yours?'

Val hesitated, and his host took his arm. 'A spot of warm water and some nice lint out of my Militia Red Cross Outfit will settle that for you,' he said. 'No one can be really absorbed by a good story if he's got gore trickling into his eyes. Come on.'

After ten minutes' first-aid in the bathroom they returned once more to the study, and Mr Campion refilled his guest's glass. 'In the first place,' he said, 'I think you ought to see this page out of last week's *Society Illustrated*. It concerns you in a way.'

He walked across the room, and unlocking a drawer in a Queen Anne bureau, returned almost immediately with a copy of the well-known weekly. He brushed over the pages and folded the magazine at a large full-page portrait of a rather foolish-looking woman of fifty odd, clad in a modern adaptation of a medieval gown, and holding in her clasped hand a chalice of arresting design. A clever photographer had succeeded in directing the eye of the beholder away from the imperfections of the sitter by focusing his attention upon the astoundingly beautiful object she held.

About eighteen inches high, it was massive in design, and consisted of a polished gold cup upon a jewelled pedestal. Beneath the portrait there were a few lines of letterpress.

A Lovely Priestess [ran the headline, and underneath]
Lady Pethwick, who before her marriage to the late Sir Lionel Pethwick was, of course, Miss Diana Gyrth, is the sister of Col. Sir Percival Gyrth, Bt, owner of the historic 'Tower' at Sanctuary in Suffolk, and keeper of the ageless Gyrth Chalice. Lady Pethwick is here seen with the precious relic, which is said to date from before the Conquest. She is also the proud possessor of the honorary title of 'Maid of the Cuppe'. The Gyrths hold the custody of the Chalice as a sacred family charge. This is the first time it has ever been photographed. Our readers may remember that it is of the Gyrth Tower that the famous story of the Secret Room is told.

Val Gyrth took the paper with casual curiosity, but the moment he caught sight of the photograph he sprang to his feet and stood towering in Mr Campion's small room, his face crimson and his intensely blue eyes narrowed and appalled. As he tried to read the inscription his hand shook so violently that he was forced to set the paper on the table and decipher it from there. When he had finished he straightened himself and faced his host. A new dignity seemed to have enveloped him in spite of his ragged clothes and generally unkempt appearance.

'Of course,' he said gravely, 'I quite understand. You're doing this for my father. I ought to go home.'

Mr Campion regarded his visitor with mild surprise.

'I'm glad you feel like that,' he said. 'But I'm not assisting your father, and I had no idea you'd feel so strongly about this piece of bad taste.'

Val snorted. 'Bad taste?' he said. 'Of course, you're a stranger, and you'll appreciate how difficult it is for me to explain how we' – he hesitated – 'regard the Chalice.' He lowered his voice upon the last word instinctively.

Mr Campion coughed. 'Look here,' he said at last, 'if you could unbend a little towards me I think I could interest you extremely. For Heaven's sake sit down and be a bit human.'

The young man smiled and dropped back into his chair, and just for a moment his youth was apparent in his face.

'Sorry,' he said, 'but I don't know who you are. Forgive me for harping on this,' he added awkwardly, 'but it does make it difficult, you know. You see, we never mention the Chalice at home. It's one of these tremendously important things one never talks about. The photograph knocked me off my balance. My father must be crazy, or –' He sat up, a sudden gleam of apprehension coming into his eyes. 'Is he all right?'

The pale young man nodded. 'Perfectly, I believe,' he said. 'That photograph was evidently taken and given to the Press without his knowledge. I expect there's been some trouble about it.'

'I bet there has.' Val spoke grimly. 'Of course, you would hardly understand, but this is sacrilege.' A flush spread over his face which Mr Campion realized was shame.

Gyrth sat huddled in his chair, the open paper on his knee. Mr Campion sighed, and perching himself upon the edge of the table began to speak.

'Look here,' he said, 'I'm going to give you a lesson in economics, and then I'm going to tell you a fairy tale. All I ask you to do is to listen to me. I think it will be worth your while.'

Val nodded. 'I don't know who you are,' he said, 'but fire away.'

Mr Campion grinned. 'Hear my piece, and you shall have my birth certificate afterwards if you want it. Sit back, and I'll go into details.'

Val leant back in his chair obediently and Mr Campion bent forward, a slightly more intelligent expression than usual upon his affable, ineffectual face.

'I don't know if you're one of these merchants who study psychology and economics and whatnot,' he began, 'but if you are you must have noticed that there comes a point when, if you're only wealthy enough, nothing else matters except what you happen to want at the moment. I mean you're above trifles like law and order and who's going to win the Boat Race.' He hesitated. Val seemed to understand. Mr Campion continued.

'Well,' he said, 'about fifty years ago half a dozen of the wealthiest men in the world – two Britons, an American, two Spaniards and a Frenchman – made this interesting discovery with regard to the collection of *objets d'art*. They each had different hobbies, fortunately, and they all had the divine mania.'

Once again he paused. 'This is where the lesson ends and the fairy story begins. Once upon a time six gentlemen found that they could buy almost anything they wanted for their various collections, of which they were very fond. Then one of them, who was a greedy fellow, started wanting things that couldn't be bought, things so valuable that eminent philanthropists had given them to museums. Also national relics of great historical value. Do you follow me?'

Gyrth nodded. 'I don't see where it's leading,' he said, 'but I'm listening.'

'The first man,' continued Mr Campion, 'whom we will call Ethel because that was obviously not his name, said to himself: "Ethel, you would like that portrait of Marie Antoinette which is in the Louvre, but it is not for sale, and if you tried to buy it very likely there would be a war, and you would not be so rich as you are now. There is only one way, therefore, of getting this beautiful picture." So he said to his servant George, who was a genius but a bad lot, I regret to say: "What do you think, George?" And George thought it could be stolen if sufficient money was forthcoming, as he knew just the man who was famous for his clever thieving. And that,' went on Mr Campion, his slightly absurd voice rising in his enthusiasm, 'is how it all began.'

Gyrth sat up. 'You don't expect me to take this seriously, do you?' he said.

'Listen,' said his host sharply, 'that's all I'm asking you. When Ethel had got the picture, and the police of four countries were looking everywhere for it except in Ethel's private collection at his country house, where they didn't go because he was an Important Person, Evelyn, a friend of his who was as wealthy as he was, and a keen collector of ceramics, came to Ethel's house, and Ethel could not resist the temptation of showing him the picture. Well, Evelyn was more than impressed. "How did you get it?" he said. "If you can get your picture of Marie Antoinette, why should I not obtain the Ming vase which is in the British Museum, because I am as rich as you?"

'"Well," said Ethel, "as you are a friend of mine and will not blackmail me, because you are too honourable for that, I will introduce you to my valet George, who might arrange it for you." And he did. And George did arrange it, only this time he went to another thief who was at the top of his class for stealing vases. Then Evelyn was very pleased and could not help telling his friend Cecil, who was a king in a small way and a collector of jewels in a large way. And of course, in the end they went to George and the thing happened all over again.

'After fifty years,' said Campion slowly, 'quite a lot of people who were very rich had employed George and George's successor, with the result that there is today quite a number of wealthy Ethels and Cecils and Evelyns. They are hardly a society, but perhaps they could be called a ring – the most powerful and the most wealthy ring in the world. You see, they are hardly criminals,' he went on, 'in the accepted sense. It is George, and George's friends, who meet the trouble when there is any, and they also pocket all the money.

'Besides, they never touch anything that can be bought in the open market. They are untouchable, the Ethels and the Cecils, because (a) they are very important people, and (b) nobody but George and George's successor ever knows where the treasures go. That is the strength of the whole thing. Now do you see what I mean?'

As his voice died away the silence in the little room became oppressive. In spite of the lightness of his words he had managed to convey a sense of reality into his story. Gyrth stared at him.

'Is this true?' he said. 'It's extraordinary if it is. Almost as extraordinary as the rest of the things that have happened to me tonight. But I don't see how it concerns me.'

'I'm coming to that,' said Mr Campion patiently. 'But first of all I want you to get it into your head that my little fairy story has one thing only to mitigate its obvious absurdity – it happens to be perfectly true. Didn't the "Mona Lisa" disappear on one occasion, turning up after a bit in most fishy circumstances? If you think back, several priceless, unpurchasable treasures have vanished from time to time; all things, you will observe, without any marketable value on account of their fame.'

'I suppose some of the original members of – of this "ring" died?' said Gyrth, carried away in spite of himself by the piquancy of the story.

'Ah,' said Mr Campion, 'I was coming to that too. During the last fifty years the percentage of millionaires has gone up considerably. This little circle of wealthy collectors has grown. Just after the War the membership numbered about twenty, men of all races and colours, and the organization which had been so successful for a small number got a bit swamped. It was at this point that one of the members, an organizing genius, a man whose name is famous over three continents, by the way, took the thing in hand and set down four or five main maxims: pulled the thing together, and put it on a business basis, in fact. So that the society, or whatever you like to call it – it has no name that I know of – is now practically omnipotent in its own sphere.'

He paused, allowing his words to sink in, and rising to his feet paced slowly up and down the room.

'I don't know the names of half the members,' he said. 'I can't tell you the names of those I do know. But when I say that neither

Scotland Yard, the Central Office, nor the Sûreté will admit a fact that is continually cropping up under their noses, you'll probably see that Ethel and his friends are pretty important people. Why, if the thing was exposed there'd be a scandal which would upset at least a couple of thrones and jeopardize the governments of four or five powers.'

Gyrth set his glass down on a small book-table beside him. 'It's a hell of a tale,' he said, 'but I think I believe you.'

The pale young man shot him a grateful smile. 'I'm so glad,' he said. 'It makes the rest of our conversation possible.'

Val frowned. 'I don't see *how* they did it,' he said, ignoring Campion's last remark. 'The George in your fairy story: how did he set about it?'

Campion shrugged his shoulders. 'That was easy enough,' he said. 'It was so simple. That's where the original gentleman's gentleman was so clever. That's what's made the business what it is today. He simply set himself up as a "fence", and let it be known in the right quarter he would pay a fabulous sum for the article indicated. I dare say it sounds rather like a "Pre-Raffleite" Brotherhood to you,' he added cheerfully. 'But you must take Uncle Albert's word for it. They pay their money and they take their choice.'

Gyrth sighed. 'It's extraordinary,' he said. 'But where do I come in? I'm not a famous crook,' he added, laughing. 'I'm afraid I couldn't pinch anything for you.'

Mr Campion shook his head. 'You've got me all wrong,' he said. 'I do *not* belong to the firm. Don't you see why I've got you here?'

Val looked at him blankly for a moment, and then a wave of understanding passed over his face and he looked at Campion with eyes that were frankly horrified.

'Good heavens!' he said, 'the Chalice!'

Mr Campion slipped off the table. 'Yes,' he said gravely, 'it's the Chalice.'

'But that's impossible!' A moment's reflection had convinced Val of the absurdity of any such suggestion. 'I won't discuss it,' he went on. 'Hang it all! You're a stranger. You don't know – you can't know the absurdity of a story like this.'

'My dear chump,' said Campion patiently, 'you can't protect anything unless you accept the reality of its danger. I've spent the last two weeks trying to find you because I happen to know for a fact that unless you do something the Gyrth Chalice will be in the private collection of a particularly illustrious Mohammedan within six months from today.'

For a moment the boy was speechless. Then he laughed. 'My dear sir,' he said, 'you're mad.'

Mr Campion was hurt. 'Have it your own way,' he said. 'But who do you suppose went to the length of trying to kidnap you in a taxi? Why do you imagine there are at least four gentlemen at present watching my front door? You'll probably see them if you care to look.'

The young man was still incredulous, but considerably startled. All the vagueness had for a moment vanished from his host's manner. Mr Campion was alert, eager, almost intelligent.

Val shook his head.

'You're not serious,' he said.

Campion took off his spectacles and looked his visitor straight in the eyes.

'Now, listen, Val Gyrth,' he said. 'You've got to believe me. I'm not nearly so ignorant of the position that the Gyrth Chalice holds in your family, *and in the country*, as you imagine. By warning you I am placing myself at direct variance with one of the most powerful organizations in the world. By offering you my assistance I am endangering my life.' He paused, but went on again immediately after.

'Would you like me to tell you of the ceremony connected with the Chalice? Of the visits of the King's Chamberlain every ten years which have taken place regularly ever since the Restoration? Or of the deed by which your entire family possessions are forfeit to the Crown should the Chalice be lost? There's a great deal more I could tell you. According to your family custom you come of age on your twenty-fifth birthday, when there is a ceremony in the East Wing of the Tower. You'll have to go to Sanctuary for that.'

Val took a deep breath. The last barriers of his prejudice were down. There was something in his host's sudden change from the inane to the fervent which was extraordinarily convincing.

Mr Campion, who was pacing rapidly up and down the room, now turned.

'However you look at it, I think you and your family are in for a pretty parroty time. That's why I looked you up. "Ethel" and his friends are after the Chalice. And they'll get it unless we do something.'

Val was silent for some minutes, surveying his host with critical eyes. His colour had heightened, and the heavy muscles at the side of his jaw beneath his stubbly beard were knotted.

'The swine!' he said suddenly. 'Of course, if this comes off it'll mean the end of us. As you know so much you must realize that this relic is the reason for our existence. We're one of the oldest families in England. Yet we take no part in politics or anything else much, simply devoting ourselves to the preservation of the Chalice.'

He stopped dead and glanced at his host, a sudden suggestion of suspicion in his eye.

'Why are you interesting yourself in this affair?' he demanded.

Mr Campion hesitated. 'It's rather difficult to explain,' he said. 'I am – or rather I was – a sort of universal uncle, a policeman's friend and master-crook's factotum. What it really boiled down to, I suppose, is that I used to undertake other people's adventures for them at a small fee. If necessary I can give you references from Scotland Yard, unofficial, of course, or from almost any other authority you might care to mention. But last year my precious uncle, His Grace the Bishop of Devizes, the only one of the family who's ever appreciated me, by the way, died and left me the savings of an episcopal lifetime. Having become a capitalist, I couldn't very well go on with my fourpence-an-hour business, so that I've been forced to look for suitable causes to which I could donate a small portion of my brains and beauty. That's one reason.

'Secondly, if you'll respect my confidence, I have a slightly personal interest in the matter. I've been practically chucked out by my family. In fact most of it is under the impression that I went to the Colonies ten years ago . . .'

Gyrth stopped him. 'When you took off your spectacles a moment ago,' he said, 'you reminded me of . . .'

Mr Campion's pale face flushed. 'Shall we leave it at that?' he suggested.

A wave of understanding passed over the boy's face. He poured himself out another drink.

'I hope you don't mind,' he said, 'but you've treated me to a series of shocks and opened a bit of a chasm beneath my feet. You're a bit hard to swallow, you know, especially after the way you hooked me in here. How did you do it?'

'Conjuring,' said Mr Campion simply and unsatisfactorily. 'It's all done with mirrors. As a matter of fact,' he went on, becoming suddenly grave, 'I've been looking for you for a fortnight. And when I spotted you I couldn't approach you, because "George's" friends were interested in you as well, and I didn't want to put my head in a hornet's nest. You see, they know me rather better than I know them.'

'I was followed?' said Val. 'What on earth for?'

'Well, they wanted to get hold of you, and so did I,' said Mr Campion. 'If a friend of mine had tapped you on the shoulder and led you into a pub, one of "George's" friends would have come too. You had to come to me of your own volition, or apparently so. That explains why my people had to drop a score of envelopes under your nose before you'd rise to the bait. Lugg's been spending his evenings at Kemp's for the last fortnight. He's my man, by the way.

'You see,' he added apologetically, 'I had to get you to go down to Clerkenwell first just to make sure they hadn't already approached you. I fancy they wanted to see you in slightly more desperate straits before they came forward with their proposition.' He paused and looked at his visitor. 'Do you follow me?' he said.

'I'm trying to,' said Gyrth valiantly. 'But I don't see why they should want to get hold of me. Here am I, completely penniless. I'm no use to anyone. I can't even get a job.'

'That,' said the pale young man gravely, 'is where we come to a personal and difficult matter. You are – estranged from your father?'

Val nodded, and the obstinate lines round his mouth hardened. 'That's true,' he said.

Mr Campion bent forward to attend to the fire. 'My dear young sir,' he said, 'as I told you, the practice of these collectors is to employ the most suitable agent for the job on hand. And although it might be perfectly obvious to anyone who knew you that the chance of buying your services was about as likely as my taking up barbola work, the dark horse who's taken on this job obviously hasn't realized this. Some people think a starving man will sell anything.'

Val exploded wrathfully. The young man waited until the paroxysm was over and then spoke mildly.

'Quite,' he said. 'Still, that explains it, doesn't it?'

Val nodded. 'And the "long road"?' he said.

'A form of salutation between "George's" friends.'

Val sighed. 'It's incredible,' he said. 'I'll put myself in your hands if I may. What are we going to do? Call in the police?'

Campion dropped into a chair beside his kinsman. 'I wish we could,' he said. 'But you see our difficulty there. If we call in the police when nothing has been stolen they won't be very sympathetic, and they won't hang about indefinitely. Once the treasure has been stolen it will pass almost immediately into the hands of people who are untouchable. It wouldn't be fair do's for the policemen. I have worked for Scotland Yard in my time. One of my best friends is a big Yard man. He'll do all he can to help us, but you see the difficulties of the situation.'

Val passed a hand over his bandaged forehead. 'What happens next?' he said.

Mr Campion reflected. 'You have to patch things up with your father,' he said quietly. 'I suppose you've realized that?'

The boy smiled faintly. 'It's funny how a single piece of information can make the thing that was worth starving for this morning seem small,' he said. 'I knew I should have to go down to Sanctuary in July. I'm twenty-five on the second. But I meant to come away again. I don't know how we're going to put this to Father. And yet,' he added, a sudden blank expression coming into his face, 'if this is true, what can we do? We can't fight a ring like this for ever. It's incredible; they're too strong.'

'There,' said Mr Campion, 'is the point which resolves the whole question into a neat "what should A do?" problem. We've got just one chance, old bird, otherwise the project would not be worth fighting and we should not have met. The rules of this acquisitive society of friends are few, but they are strict. Roughly, what they amount to is this: all members' commissions – they have to be for things definitely unpurchasable, of course – are treated with equal deference, the best agent is chosen for the job, unlimited money is supplied, and there the work of "George" and "Ethel" ends until the treasure is obtained.' He paused and looked steadily at the young man before him. 'However – and this is our one loophole – should the expert whom they have chosen meet his death in the execution of his duty – I mean, should the owner of the treasure in question kill him to save it – then they leave well alone and look out for someone else's family album.'

'If he's caught –?' began Val dubiously.

Mr Campion shrugged his shoulders. 'If he's caught he takes the consequences. Who on earth would believe him if he squealed? No, in that case the society lets him take his punishment and employs someone else. That's quite understandable. It's only if their own personal employee gets put out that they get cold feet. Not that the men they employ mind bloodshed,' he added hastily. 'The small fry – burglars, thugs, and homely little forgers – may die like flies.

"George" and "Ethel" don't have anything to do with that. It's if their own agent gets knocked on the head that they consider that the matter is at an end, so to speak.' He was silent.

'Who is the agent employed to get the Chalice?' said Gyrth abruptly.

Mr Campion's pale eyes behind his heavy spectacles grew troubled. 'That's the difficulty,' he said. 'I don't know. So you see what a mess we're in.'

Gyrth rose to his feet and stood looking at Campion in slow horror.

'What you are saying is, in effect, then,' he said, 'if we want to protect the one thing that's really precious to me and my family, the one thing that must come before everything else with me, we must find out the man employed by this society, and murder him?'

Mr Campion surveyed his visitor with the utmost gravity.

'Shall we say "dispose of him"?' he suggested gently.

Chapter 4

Brush with the County

'The last time I come past 'ere,' said Mr Lugg sepulchrally, from the back of the car, 'it was in a police van. I remember the time because I was in for three months hard. The joke was on the Beak, though. I was the wrong man as it 'appened, and that alibi was worth something, I can tell yer.'

Campion, at the wheel, spoke without turning. 'I wish you'd shut up, Lugg,' he said. 'We may be going to a house where they have real servants. You'll have to behave.'

'Servants?' said Mr Lugg indignantly. 'I'm the gent's gent of this outfit, let me tell yer, and I'm not taking any lip. Mr Gyrth knows 'oo I am. I told 'im I'd been a cut-throat when I shaved 'im this morning.'

Val, seated beside Campion in the front, chuckled. 'Lugg and Branch, my pater's old butler, ought to get on very well together,' he said. 'Branch had a wild youth, I believe, although of course his family have looked after us for years.'

''Is other name ain't Roger, by any chanst?' Mr Lugg's voice betrayed a mild interest. 'A little thin bloke with a 'ooked nose – talked with a 'orrible provincial accent?'

'That's right.' Val turned round in his seat, amused surprise on his face. 'Do you know him?'

Lugg sniffed and nodded. 'The Prince of Parkhurst, we used to call 'im, I remember,' he said, and dismissed the subject of conversation.

Val turned to Campion. 'You are a fantastic pair,' he said.

'Not at all,' said the pale young man at the wheel. 'Since we learned to speak French we can take our place in any company without embarrassment. They ought to quote Lugg's testimonials. I know he wrote 'em.'

Val laughed, and the talk languished for a minute or so. They were speeding down the main Colchester road, some thirty-six hours after Gyrth had stumbled into Mr Campion's flat off Piccadilly. Reluctantly he had allowed himself to be equipped and valeted by his host and the invaluable Lugg, and he looked a very different person from the footsore and unkempt figure he had then appeared. After his first interview with Campion he had put himself unreservedly into that extraordinary young man's hands.

Their departure from London had not been without its thrills. He had been smuggled out of the flat down a service lift into an exclusive restaurant facing into Regent Street, and thence had been spirited away in the Bentley at a reckless speed. He could not doubt that, unless his host proved to be a particularly convincing lunatic, there was genuine danger to be faced.

Mr Campion's mild voice cut in upon his thoughts.

'Without appearing unduly curious,' he ventured, 'I should like to know if you anticipate any serious difficulty in getting all friendly with your parent. It seems to me an important point just now.'

The boy shook his head. 'I don't think so,' he said. 'It has really been my own pigheadedness that has kept me from going back ever since –' He broke off, seeming unwilling to finish the sentence.

Mr Campion opened his mouth, doubtless to make some tactful reply, when he was forestalled by the irrepressible Lugg.

'If it's anything about a woman, you can tell 'im. 'E's been disappointed 'imself,' he observed lugubriously.

Mr Campion sat immovable, his face a complete blank. They were passing through one of the many small country towns on the road, and he swung the car to the side before an elaborately restored old Tudor inn.

'The inner Campion protests,' he said. 'We must eat. You go and lose yourself, Lugg.'

'All right,' said Mr Lugg. He was very much aware of his *gaffe*, and had therefore adopted a certain defiance. 'Whilst you're messing about with "the Motorist's Lunch" – seven and a kick and coffee extra – I'll go and get something to eat in the bar. It's mugs like you wot changes "The Blue Boar" into "Ye Olde Stuck Pigge for Dainty Teas".'

He lumbered out of the car, opening the door for Campion but not troubling to stand and hold it. His employer looked after him with contempt.

'Buffoon,' he said. 'That's the trouble with Lugg. He's always got the courage of his previous convictions. He used to be quite one of the most promising burglars, you know. We'll go in and see what the good brewery firm has to offer.'

Val followed the slender, slightly ineffectual figure down the two steps into the cool brick-floored dining-room, which a well-meaning if not particularly erudite management had rendered a little more Jacobean than the Jacobeans. The heavily carved oak beams which supported the ceiling had been varnished to an ebony blackness and the open fireplace at the end of the room was a mass of rusty spits and dogs, in a profusion which would have astonished their original owners.

'That spot looks good for browsing,' said Mr Campion, indicating a table in an alcove some distance from the other patrons.

As Val seated himself he glanced round him a little apprehensively. He was not anxious to encounter any old acquaintances. Mr Campion looked about also, though for a different reason. But the few people who were still lunching were for the most part cheerful, bovine persons more interested in *The East Anglian* and their food than in their neighbours.

Mr Campion frowned. 'If only I knew,' he said, 'who they'll choose to do their dirty work.'

Val bent forward. 'Any fishy character in the vicinity ought to come in for a certain amount of suspicion,' he murmured. 'The natives don't get much beyond poaching.'

The pale young man at his side did not smile. 'I know,' he said. 'That makes it worse. I flatter myself that our grasping friends will do me the honour of picking on a stranger to do their homework for them. I'm afraid it may even be amateur talent, and that's usually illogical, so you never know where you are. I say, Val,' he went on, dropping his voice, 'to put a personal question, is your Aunt Diana – er – Caesar's wife, what? I mean you don't think they could approach her with flattery and guile?'

Val frowned. 'My Aunt Diana,' he said softly, 'treats herself like a sort of vestal virgin. She's lived at the Cup House – that's on the estate, you know – ever since Uncle Lionel died, and since Father was a widower she rather took it upon herself to boss the show a bit. Penny has a dreadful time with her, I believe.'

'Penny?' inquired Mr Campion.

'My sister Penelope,' Val explained. 'One of the best.'

Mr Campion made a mental note of it. 'To return to your aunt,' he said, 'I'm sorry to keep harping on this, but is she – er – batty?'

Val grinned. 'Not certifiable,' he said. 'But she's a silly, slightly conceited woman who imagines she's got a heart; and she's made copy out of that "Maid of the Cup" business. Until her time that part of the ceremonial had been allowed to die down a bit. She looked it up in the records and insisted on her rights. She's a strong-minded person, and Father puts up with her, I think, to keep her quiet.'

Mr Campion looked dubious. 'This "Maid of the Cup" palaver,' he said. 'What is it exactly? I've never heard of it.'

The young man reflected. 'Oh, it's quite simple,' he said at last. 'Apparently in medieval times, when the menfolk were away fighting, the eldest daughter of the house was supposed to remain unmarried and to shut herself up in the Cup House and attend to the relic. Naturally this practice fell into abeyance when times got more peaceful, and that part of the affair had been obsolete until Aunt Diana hunted it all up as soon as she became a widow. She set herself up with the title complete. Father was annoyed, of course, but you can't stop a woman like that.'

'No-o,' said Mr Campion. 'Any other peculiarities?'

'Well, she's bitten by the quasi-mystical cum "noo-art" bug, or used to be before I went away,' Val went on casually. 'Wears funny clothes and wanders about at night communing with the stars and disturbing the game. Quite harmless, but rather silly. I should think that if anyone put a fishy suggestion up to her she'd scream the place down and leave it at that.'

A decrepit waiter brought them the inevitable cold roast beef and pickles of the late luncher, and shuffled away again.

Val seemed inclined to make further confidences. 'I don't expect trouble with Father,' he said. 'You know why I walked out, don't you?'

Mr Campion looked even more vague than usual. 'No?' he said. 'You got into a row at Cambridge, didn't you?'

'I got married at Cambridge,' said Val bitterly. 'The usual tale, you know. She was awfully attractive – a Varsity hanger-on. There's a good lot of 'em, I suppose. I phoned the news to Dad. He got angry and halved my allowance, so –' he shrugged his shoulders, 'she went off – back to Cambridge.'

He paused a little, and added awkwardly: 'You don't mind my telling you all this, do you? But now you're in it I feel I ought to tell you everything. Well, I came back to Sanctuary, and Hepplewhite, Dad's solicitor, was fixing up the necessary legal separation guff when I had a letter from her. She was ill, and in an awful state in London. Dad was bitter, but I went up and looked after her by selling up my flat and one thing and another, until she died. There was a filthy row at the time and I never went back. Hepplewhite tried to get hold of me several times for the old boy, but I wouldn't see him. Rather a hopeless sort of tale, I'm afraid, but you can see how it happened. Women always seem to muck things up,' he added a trifle self-consciously.

Mr Campion considered. 'Oh, I don't know,' he said, and then was silent.

They had been so engrossed in their conversation that they had not noticed a certain commotion at the far end of the room as a woman entered and saluted one or two acquaintances as she passed to her table. It was only when her high strident voice had drowned the subdued conversation in the room that the young men in the secluded corner observed her.

She was of a type not uncommon among the 'landed gentry', but mercifully rare elsewhere. Superbly self-possessed, she was slightly masculine in appearance, with square flat shoulders and narrow lips. Her hair was cut short under her mannish felt, her suit was perfectly tailored and the collar of her blouse fitted tightly at her throat.

She managed to enter the room noisily and sat down so that her face was towards them. It was a handsome face, but one to which the epithet of 'beautiful' would have seemed absurd. She was pale, with a strong prominent nose and hard closely-set blue-grey eyes. She hurled a miscellaneous collection of gloves, scarves, and papers into the chair in front of her and called loudly to the waiter.

It was evident that she was a personage, and that vague sense of uneasiness which invariably steals upon a room full of people when a celebrity is present was apparent in the stolid dining-room. Val averted his face hastily.

'Oh, Lord!' he said.

Mr Campion raised his eyebrows. 'Who is the rude lady?' he inquired casually.

Val lowered his voice. 'Mrs Dick Shannon,' he muttered. 'Surely you've heard of her? She's got a racing stable on Heronhoe Heath. One of these damn women-with-a-personality. She knows me, too. Could you wriggle in front of me, old man? She's got an eye like a hawk.'

Mr Campion did his best, but as they rose to go, their path to the door led them directly past her table. His protégé was quick, but he was not quick enough.

'Val Gyrth!' The name was bellowed through the room until Mrs

Dick Shannon's victim felt as though the entire township must have heard it. The woman caught the boy's coat-sleeve and jerked him backward with a wrist like flexed steel.

'So you're back, eh? I didn't know you'd made friends with your father again.' This piece of intimate information was also shouted. 'When did this happen?' She ignored Mr Campion with the studied rudeness which is the hall-mark of her type. He hovered for some moments ineffectually, and then drifted out into the corridor to settle the score.

Left unprotected, Val faced his captor and strove to make his excuses. He was quite aware that every ear in the room was strained to catch his reply. Gyrth was a name to conjure with in that part of the country.

Mrs Dick seemed both aware and contemptuous of her audience. 'I've just come down from the Tower,' she said. 'I'm trying to make your father sell me two yearlings. What does he want with race-horses? I told him he hadn't got the sense to train properly; and that man he's got is a fool. I saw your aunt, too,' she went on, not waiting for any comment from him. 'She gets sillier every day.'

Val gulped and murmured a few incoherent words of farewell. Mrs Dick gripped his hand and shook it vigorously.

'Well, good-bye. I shall see you again. You can tell your father I'm going to have those yearlings if I have to steal them. He's not capable of training 'em.'

The boy smiled politely and a little nervously, and turned away.

'I heard your wife was dead – so sorry,' bawled Mrs Dick for the world to hear. Val fled.

His forehead was glistening with sweat when he came up with Campion on the broad doorstep of the inn.

'Let's get away from here,' he said. 'I loathe that woman.'

'"I did but see her passing by." The rest of the song does not apply,' said Mr Campion. 'That's her car, I suppose.' He indicated a superb red and white Frazer Nash. 'Hallo, here comes Lugg, looking like a man with a mission.'

At that moment Mr Lugg appeared from the doorway of the four-ale bar. His lugubrious face was almost animated.

''Op in,' he said huskily as he came up with them. 'I got something to tell yer. While you've bin playing the gent, I've bin noticin'.'

It was not until they were once more packed into the Bentley that he unburdened himself. As they shot out of the town he leant forward from the back seat and breathed heavily into Mr Campion's ear.

''Oo d'yer think I saw in the bar?' he mumbled.

'Some low friend of yours, no doubt,' said his master, skilfully avoiding a trade van which cut in front of an approaching lorry.

'I should say!' said Lugg heavily. 'It was little Natty Johnson, one of the filthiest, dirtiest, lousiest little race-gang toughs I've ever taken off me 'at to.'

Mr Campion pricked up his ears. 'The Cleaver Gang?' he said. 'Was he with anyone?'

'That's what I'm coming to,' said Lugg reproachfully. 'You're always 'urrying on, you are. 'E was talking to a funny chap with a beard. An arty bloke. I tell yer wot – 'e reminded me of that Bloomsbury lot 'oo came to the flat and sat on the floor and sent me out for kippers and Chianti. They were talkin' nineteen to the dozen, sittin' up by theirselves in the window. I 'ad a bit o' wool in one ear or I'd 'ave 'eard all they was saying.

''Owever, that's not the reely interestin' part. Where we come in is this. The artist chap, and some more like 'im, is staying at the Tower, Sanctuary. I know, because the barman told me when I was laughin' at 'em. Friends of Lady Pethwick's, they are, 'e said, as if that explained 'em.'

Mr Campion's pale eyes flickered behind his spectacles.

'That's interesting,' he said. 'And this man –'

'Yes,' cut in Mr Lugg, ''e was talkin' confidential with Natty Johnson. I know first-class dicks 'oo'd arrest 'im fer that.'

Chapter 5
Penny: For Your Thoughts

The village of Sanctuary lay in that part of Suffolk which the railway has ignored and the motorists have not yet discovered. Moreover, the steep-sided valley of which it consisted, with the squat Norman church on one eminence and the Tower on the other, did not lie on the direct route to anywhere, so that no one turned down the narrow cherry-lined lane which was its southern approach unless they had actual business in the village. The place itself was one of those staggering pieces of beauty that made Morland paint in spite of all the noggins of rum in the world.

A little stream ran across the road dividing the two hills; while the cottages, the majority pure Elizabethan, sprawled up each side of the road like sheep asleep in a meadow. It is true that the smithy kept a petrol store housed in a decrepit engine boiler obtained from Heaven knows what dumping ground, but even that had a rustic quality. It was a fairy-tale village peopled by yokels who, if they did not wear the traditional white smocks so beloved of film producers, at least climbed the rough steps to the church on a Sunday morning in top hats of unquestionable antiquity.

The Three Drummers stood crazily with its left side a good two feet lower down the northern hill than its right side. It was of brown unrestored oak and yellow plaster, with latticed windows and a red tiled roof. It had three entrances, the main one to the corridor on the level of the road, the bar parlour up four steps upon the left, and the four-ale down two steps on the right.

It was at about five o'clock, when the whole village was basking in a quiet yellow light, that the Bentley drew up outside the Three Drummers and deposited Val Gyrth and Campion at the centre door. Lugg took the car across the road to the smithy 'garage', and the two young men stepped into the cool, sweet-smelling passage. Val had turned up his coat collar.

'I don't want to be spotted just yet,' he murmured, 'and I'd like a chat with Penny before I see the Governor. If I can get hold of Mrs Bullock, she'll fix everything.'

He tiptoed down the passage and put his head round the door of the kitchen at the far end.

'Bully!' he called softly.

There was a smothered scream and a clatter of pans on a stone floor. The next moment the good lady of the house appeared, a big florid woman in a gaily patterned cotton dress and a large blue apron. Her sleeves were rolled above her plump elbows and her brown hair was flying. She was radiant. She caught the boy by the arm and quite obviously only just prevented herself from embracing him vigorously.

'You've made it up,' she said. 'I knew you would – your birthday coming and all.'

She had a deep resonant voice with very little trace of accent in spite of her excitement.

'Won't you come into the bar and show yourself? – sir,' she added as an afterthought.

Val shook his head. 'I say, Bully,' he said, 'things aren't quite settled yet. Could you give my friend Mr Campion here a room and find us somewhere we can talk? I'd like a note taken up to Penny if possible. How is everyone at the Tower? Do you know?'

Mrs Bullock, who had sensed the urgency of his request, was wise enough to ask no questions. She had been the faithful friend and confidante of the children at the Tower ever since her early days as cook at that establishment, and their affairs were as always one of her chief concerns.

She led her visitors upstairs to a magnificent old bedroom with a small sitting-room leading out of it.

'You write your note, sir, and I'll bring you up something,' she said, throwing open the window to let in the scented evening air. 'You were asking about the folk, Mr Val. Your father's well, but worried looking. And Penny – she's lovely. Oh, I can see your mother in her – same eyes, same walk, same everything.'

'And Aunt?' said Val curiously.

Mrs Bullock snorted. 'You'll hear about your aunt soon enough,' she said. 'Having herself photographed with the Thing.' She dropped her eyes on the last word as though she experienced some embarrassment in referring to the Chalice.

'I've heard about that,' said Val quietly. 'Otherwise – she's all right?'

'Right enough, save that she fills the whole place with a pack of crazy no-goods – strutting about in funny clothes like actors and actresses. Your Ma'll turn in her grave, if she hasn't done that already.'

'The artists?' Val suggested.

'Artists? They ain't artists,' said Mrs Bullock explosively. 'I know artists. I've 'ad 'em staying here. Quiet tidy little fellows – fussy about their victuals. I don't know what your aunt's got hold of – Bolsheviks, I shouldn't wonder. You'll find paper and pen over there, Mr Val.' And with a rustle of skirts she bustled out of the room.

Val sat down at the square table in the centre of the smaller room and scribbled a few words.

'*Dear Penny,*' he wrote, '*I am up here at "The Drummers". Can you come down for a minute? Love, Val.*'

He folded the paper, thrust it in an envelope and went to the top of the oak cupboard staircase. Mrs Bullock's tousled head appeared round the door at the foot.

'Throw it down,' she whispered, 'and I'll send young George around with it.'

Val went back to Campion. 'I say,' he said, 'what about Lugg? He won't talk, will he?'

Mr Campion seemed amused. 'Not on your life,' he said. 'Lugg's down in the four-ale with his ears flapping, drinking in local wit and beer.'

Val crossed to the window and looked out over the inn garden, a mass of tangled rambler roses and vivid delphiniums stretching down amid high old red walls to the tiny stream which trickled through the village.

'It seems impossible,' he said slowly. 'Up in your flat the story sounded incredible enough, but down here with everything exactly as it always was, so quiet and peaceful and miles away from anywhere, it's just absurd. By jove, I'm glad to get back.'

Mr Campion did not speak, and at that moment the door opened and Mrs Bullock returned with a tray on which were two tankards, bread and butter, and a great plate of water-cress.

'It's home-brew,' she said confidentially. 'I only keep it for ourselves. The stuff the company sends down isn't what it used to be. You can taste the Government's hand in it, I say. I'll send Miss Penny up the moment she comes.'

She laid a fat red hand on Val's shoulder as she passed him, an ineffably caressing gesture, and went out, closing the door behind her.

'Here's to the fatted calf,' said Mr Campion, lifting his tankard. 'There's something so Olde English about you, Val, that I expect a chorus of rustic maidens with garlands and a neat portable maypole to arrive any moment. Stap me, Sir Percy! Another noggin!'

Val suddenly turned upon his companion, a shadow of suspicion in his eyes. 'Look here, Campion,' he said, 'this isn't some silly theatrical stunt to get me back into the bosom of the family, is it? You're not employed by Hepplewhite, are you?'

Mr Campion looked hurt. 'Oh, no,' he said. 'I'm my own master now. No more selling my soul to commerce – not while Uncle's money lasts, anyhow. I'm one of these capitalistic toots. Only one in five has it.'

Val grinned. 'Sorry,' he said. 'But thinking it over in cold blood, I suppose you know that the Chalice is in the Cup House chapel, and that is burglar-proof. No ordinary thief could possibly touch it.'

'No ordinary thief would want to,' said Mr Campion pointedly. 'You seem to have forgotten your fun in the taxicab. I suppose you know you bashed that chap up pretty permanently, and he didn't even mention to the hospital authorities that he had a fare on board? If someone doesn't try to murder one of us every two days you seem to think there's nothing up. Drink up your beer like a good boy, and old Uncle Al will find a nice crook for you to beat up. All I'm worrying about is if they've already got busy while we're hanging about. I say, I wish your sister would come. The Tower isn't far away, is it?'

'It's just up at the top of the hill,' said Val. 'You can't see it because of the trees. Hold on a moment – I think this is she.'

There was a chatter of feminine voices on the staircase. Campion walked over to the bedroom.

'I'll stay here till the touching reunion is over,' he said.

'Don't be a fool,' said Val testily. He got no further, for the door opened, and not one but two young women came in, with Mrs Bullock hovering in the background.

At first glance it was easy to pick out Val's sister. Penelope Gyrth was tall like her brother, with the same clear-cut features, the same very blue eyes. Her hair, which was even more yellow than Val's, was bound round her ears in long thick braids. She was hatless, and her white frock was sprinkled with a scarlet pattern. She grinned at her brother, revealing suddenly how extremely young she was.

'Hallo, old dear,' she said, and crossing the room slipped her arm through his.

A more unemotional greeting it would have been difficult to imagine, but her delight was obvious. It radiated from her eyes and from her smile.

Val kissed her, and then looked inquiringly at her companion. Penny explained.

'This is Beth,' she said. 'We were coming down to the post office when young George met us with your note, so I brought her along. Beth, this is my brother, and Val, this is Beth Cairey. Oh, of course, you haven't heard about the Caireys, have you?'

The girl who now came forward was very different from her companion. She was *petite* and vivacious, with jet-black hair sleeked down from a centre parting to a knot at the nape of her neck. Her brown eyes were round and full of laughter, and there was about her an air of suppressed delight that was well-nigh irresistible. She was a few years older than the youthful Penny, who looked scarcely out of her teens.

Mr Campion was introduced, and there was a momentary awkward pause. A quick comprehending glance passed between him and the elder girl, a silent flicker of recognition, but neither spoke. Penny sensed the general embarrassment and came to the rescue, chattering on breathlessly with youthful exuberance.

'I forgot you didn't know Beth,' she said. 'She came just after you left. She and her people have taken Tye Hall. They're American, you know. It's glorious having neighbours again – or it would be if Aunt Di hadn't behaved so disgustingly. My dear, if Beth and I hadn't conducted ourselves like respectable human beings there'd be a feud.'

Beth laughed. 'Lady Pethwick doesn't like strangers,' she said, revealing a soft unexpectedly deep voice with just a trace of a wholly delightful New England accent.

Penny was plainly ill at ease. It was evident that she was trying to behave as she fancied her brother would prefer, deliberately forcing herself to take his unexpected return as a matter of course.

Campion watched her curiously, his pale eyes alight with interest behind his huge spectacles. In spite of her gaiety and the brilliance of her complexion there were distinct traces of strain in the faint lines about her eyes and in the nervous twisting of her hands.

Val understood his sister's restraint and was grateful for it. He turned to Beth and stood smiling at her.

'Aunt Di has always been rather difficult,' he said. 'I hope Father has made up for any stupidity on her part.'

The two girls exchanged glances.

'Father,' said Penny, 'is sulky about something. You know what a narrow-minded old darling he is. I believe he's grousing about the Professor – that's Beth's father – letting the Gypsies camp in Fox Hollow. It's rather near the wood, you know. It would be just like him to get broody about it in secret and feel injured without attempting to explain.'

Beth chuckled. 'The Gypsies are Mother's fault,' she said. 'She thinks they're so picturesque. But four of her leghorns vanished this morning, so I shouldn't wonder if your Dad's grievance would be sent about its business fairly soon.'

Val glanced from one to the other of the two girls.

'Look here,' he said after a pause, 'is everything all right?'

His sister blushed scarlet, the colour mounting up her throat and disappearing into the roots of her hair. Beth looked uncomfortable. Penny hesitated.

'Val, you're extraordinary,' she said. 'You seem to smell things out like an old pointer. It doesn't matter talking in front of Beth, because she's been the only person that I could talk to down here and she knows everything. There's something awfully queer going on at home.'

Mr Campion had effaced himself. He sat at the table now with an expression of complete inanity on his pale face. Val was visibly startled. This confirmation of his fears was entirely unexpected.

'What's up?' he demanded.

Penny's next remark was hardly reassuring.

'Well, it's the Chalice,' she said. There was reluctance in her tone as though she were loth to name the relic. 'Of course, I may be just ultra-sensitive, and I don't know why I'm bothering you with all this the moment you arrive, but I've been awfully worried about it. You remember the Cup House chapel has been a sacred place ever since we were kids – I mean it's not a place where we'd take strangers except on the fixed day, is it? Well, just lately Aunt Diana seems to have gone completely mad. She was always indiscreet on the subject, of course, but now – well –' she took a deep breath and regarded her brother almost fearfully – 'she was photographed with it. I suppose that's what brought you home. Father nearly had apoplexy, but she just bullied him.'

As Val did not respond, she continued.

'That's not the worst, though. When she was in London last she developed a whole crowd of the most revolting people – a sort of semi-artistic new religion group. They've turned her into a kind of High Priestess and they go about chanting and doing funny exercises in sandals and long white night-gowns. Men, too. It's disgusting. She lets them in to see the Chalice. And one man's making a perfectly filthy drawing of her holding it.'

Val was visibly shocked. 'And Father?' he said.

Penny shrugged her shoulders. 'You can't get anything out of Father,' she said. 'Since you went he's sort of curled up in his shell and he's more morose than ever. There's something worrying him. He has most of his meals in his room. We hardly ever see him. And, Val' – she lowered her voice – 'there was a light in the East Wing last night.'

The boy raised his eyebrows in silent question, and she nodded.

Val picked up his coat.

'Look here,' he said, 'I'll come back with you if you can smuggle me into the house without encountering the visitors.' He turned to Campion. 'You'll be all right here, won't you?' he said. 'I'll come down and fetch you in the morning. We'd better stick to our original arrangement.'

Mr Campion nodded vigorously.

'I must get Lugg into training for polite society,' he said cheerfully.

He saw Penny throw a glance of by no means unfriendly curiosity in his direction as he waved the three a farewell from the top of the stairs.

Left to himself he closed the door carefully, and sitting down at the table, he removed his spectacles and extracted two very significant objects from his suitcase, a small but wicked-looking rubber truncheon and an extremely serviceable Colt revolver. From his hip-pocket he produced an exactly similar gun, save in the single remarkable fact that it was constructed to project nothing more dangerous than water. He considered the two weapons gravely.

Finally he sighed and put his toy in the case: the revolver he slipped into his hip-pocket.

Chapter 6

The Storm Breaks

''Ere, wot d'you think you're doing?'

Mr Lugg's scandalized face appeared round the corner of the door.

'Mind your own business,' said Campion without looking up. 'And, by the way, call me "sir".'

'You've bin knighted, I suppose?' observed Mr Lugg, oozing into the room and shutting the door behind him. 'I'm glad that chap's gone. I'm sick o' nobs. As soon as I caught a bosso of 'im and 'is 'arem going up that street I come up to see what the 'ell you was up to – sir.'

Mr Campion resumed his spectacles. 'You're a disgrace,' he said. 'You've got to make the "valet" grade somehow before tomorrow morning. I don't know if you realize it, but you're a social handicap.'

'Now then, no 'iding be'ind 'igh school talk,' said Mr Lugg, putting a heavy hand on the table. 'Show us what you've got in yer pocket.'

Mr Campion felt in his hip-pocket and produced the revolver obediently.

'I thought so.' Mr Lugg examined the Colt carefully and handed it back to his master with evident contempt. 'You know we're up against something. You're as jumpy as a cat. Well, I'm prepared too, in me own way.' He thrust his hand in his own pocket and drew out a life-preserver with a well-worn handle. 'You don't catch me carryin' a gun. I'm not goin' to swing for any challenge cup that ever was – but then I'm not one of the gentry. And I don't know wot you think you're up to swankin' about the cash your uncle left you. I know it paid your tailor's bill, but only up to nineteen twenty-eight, remember. You'll land us both in regular jobs workin' for a livin' if you're so soft-'earted that you take on dangerous berths for charity.'

He was silent for a moment, and then he bent forward. His entire manner had changed and there was unusual seriousness in his little black eyes.

'Sir,' he said, with deep earnestness, 'let's 'op it.'

'My dear fellow,' said Mr Campion with affable idiocy, 'I have buttered my bun and now I must lie on it. And you, my beautiful, will stand meekly by. It is difficult, I admit. Gyrth's a delightful chap, but he doesn't know what we're up against yet. After all, you can't expect him to grasp the significance of the *Société Anonyme* all at once. You're sure that was Natty Johnson?'

'Wot d'you take me for – a private dick?' said Mr Lugg with contempt. 'Of course I saw 'im. As little and as ugly as life. I don't like it.'

He glanced about him almost nervously and came a step nearer. 'There's something unnatural about this business,' he breathed. 'I was listenin' down in the bar just now and an old bloke come out with a 'orrible yarn. D'you know they've got a blinkin' two-'eaded monster up at that place?'

'Where?' said Mr Campion, considerably taken aback.

'Up at the Tower – where we've got to do the pretty. I'm not going to be mixed with the supernatural, I warn yer.'

Campion regarded his faithful servitor with interest. 'I like your "fanny",' he said. 'But they've been pulling your leg.'

'All right, clever,' said Mr Lugg, nettled. 'But it's a fac', as it 'appens. They've got a secret room in the east wing containin' some filfy family secret. There's a winder but there's no door, and when the son o' the house is twenty-five 'is father takes 'im in and shows 'im the 'orror, and 'e's never the same again. Like the king that ate the winkles. That's why they leave comin' of age till the boy is old enough to stand the shock.' He paused dramatically, and added by way of confirmation: 'The bloke 'oo was telling me was a bit tight, and the others was tryin' to shut 'im up. You could see it was the truth – they was so scared. It's bound to be a monster – somethin' you 'ave to feed with a pump.'

'Lugg, sit down.'

The words were rapped out in a way quite foreign to Mr Campion's usual manner. Considerably surprised, the big man obeyed him.

'Now, look here,' said his employer, grimly, 'you've got to forget that, Lugg. Since you know so much you may as well hear the truth. The Gyrths are a family who were going strong about the time that yours were leaping about from twig to twig. And there is, in the east wing of the Tower, I believe, a room which has no visible entrance. The story about the son of the house being initiated into the secret on his twenty-fifth birthday is all quite sound. It's a semi-religious ceremony of the family. But get this into your head. It's nothing to do with us. Whatever the Gyrths' secret, it's no one's affair but their own, and if you so much as refer to it, even to one of the lowest of the servants, you'll have made an irreparable bloomer, and I won't have you within ten miles of me again.'

'Right you are, Guv'nor. Right you are.' Mr Lugg was apologetic and a little nervous. 'I'm glad you told me, though,' he added. 'It fair put the wind up me. There's one or two things, though, that ain't nice 'ere. F'rinstance, when I was comin' acrost out of the garage, a woman put 'er 'ead out the door o' that one-eyed shop next door. She didn't arf give me a turn; she was bald – not just a bit gone on top, yer know, but quite 'airless. I asked about 'er, and they come out with a yarn about witchcraft and 'aunting and cursin' like a set o' 'eathens. There's too much 'anky-panky about this place. I don't believe in it, but I don't like it. They got a 'aunted wood 'ere, and a set o' gippos livin' in a 'ollow. Let's go 'ome.'

Mr Campion regarded his aide owlishly.

'Well, you have been having fun in your quiet way,' he said. 'You're sure your loquacious friend wasn't a Cook's Guide selling you Rural England by any chance? How much beer did it take you to collect that lot?'

'You'll see when I put in my bill for expenses,' said Mr Lugg unabashed. 'What do we do tonight? 'Ave a mike round or stay 'ere?'

'We keep well out of sight,' said Mr Campion. 'I've bought you a book of *Etiquette for Upper Servants*. It wouldn't hurt you to study it. You stay up here and do your homework.'

'Sauce!' grumbled Mr Lugg. 'I'll go and unpack yer bag. Oh, well, a quiet beginning usually means a quick finish. I'll 'ave a monument put up to you at the 'ead of the grave. A life-size image of yerself dressed as an angel – 'orn-rimmed spectacles done in gold.'

He lumbered off. Mr Campion stood at the window and looked over the shadowy garden, still scented in the dusk. There was nothing more lovely, nothing more redolent of peace and kindliness. Far out across the farther fields a nightingale had begun to sing, mimicking all the bird chatter of the sunshine. From the bar beneath his feet scraps of the strident Suffolk dialect floated up to him, mingled with occasional gusts of husky laughter.

Yet Mr Campion was not soothed. His pale eyes were troubled behind his spectacles, and once or twice he shivered. He felt himself hampered at every step. Forces were moving which he had no power to stay, forces all the more terrible because they were unknown to him, enemies which he could not recognize.

The picture of Val and the two girls standing smiling in the bright old-fashioned room sickened him. There was, as Lugg said, something unnatural about the whole business, something more than ordinary danger: and the three young people had been so very young, so very ignorant and charming. His mind wandered to the secret room, but he put the subject from him testily. It could not have any significance in the present business or he would surely have been told.

Presently he closed the window and crossed to the table, where the best dinner that Mrs Bullock could conjure was set waiting for him. He ate absently, pausing every now and then to listen intently to the gentle noises of the countryside.

But it was not until early the following morning, as he lay upon a home-cured feather bed beneath an old crocheted quilt of weird and wonderful design, that the storm broke.

He was awakened by a furious tattoo on his door and raised himself upon his elbow to find Mrs Bullock, pink and horror-stricken.

'Oh, sir,' she said, 'as Mr Val's friend, I think you ought to go up to the Tower at once. It's Lady Pethwick, sir, Mr Val's aunt. They brought her in this morning, sir – stone dead.'

Chapter 7

Death in the House

The Tower at Sanctuary managed to be beautiful in spite of itself. It stood at the top of the hill almost hidden in great clumps of oak and cedar trees with half a mile of park surrounding it in all directions. It was a mass of survivals, consisting of excellent examples of almost every period in English architecture.

Its centre was Tudor with a Georgian front; the west wing was Queen Anne; but the oldest part, and by far the most important, was the east wing, from which the house got its name. This was a great pile of old Saxon stone and Roman brick, circular in shape, rising up to a turreted tower a good sixty feet above the rest of the building. The enormously thick walls were decorated with a much later stone tracery near the top, and were studded with little windows, behind one of which, it was whispered, lay the room to which there was no door.

In spite of the odd conglomeration of periods, there was something peculiarly attractive and even majestic in the old pile. To start with, its size was prodigious, even for a country mansion. Every age had enlarged it.

The slight signs of neglect which a sudden rise in the cost of labour combined with a strangling land tax had induced upon the lawns and gardens had succeeded only in mellowing and softening the pretentiousness of the estate, and in the haze of the morning it looked kindly and inviting in spite of the fact that the doctor's venerable motor-car stood outside the square doorway and the blinds were drawn in all the front windows.

Val and Penny were standing by the window in a big shabby room at the back of the west wing. It had been their nursery when they were children, and had been regarded by them ever since as their own special domain. There were still old toys in the wide cupboards behind the yellow-white panelling, and the plain heavy furniture was battered and homely.

The view from the window, half obscured by the leaves of an

enormous oak, led the eye down the steep green hill-side to where a white road meandered away and lost itself among the fields which stretched as far as the horizon.

The scene was incredibly lovely, but the young people were not particularly impressed. Penny was very pale. She seemed to have grown several years older since the night before. Her plain white frock enhanced the pallor of her face, and her eyes seemed to have become wider and more deep in colour. Val, too, was considerably shaken.

'Look here,' he said, 'I've sent word down for Campion to come up as we arranged before. It was just Aunt's heart, of course, but it's awkward happening like this. I thought she was disgustingly full of beans at dinner last night.' He pulled himself up. 'I know I ought not to talk about her like this,' he said apologetically, 'still, it's silly to pretend that we liked her.'

He was silent for a moment, and then went on gloomily, 'The village will be seething with it, of course. Being picked up in the Pharisees' Clearing like that. What on earth did she want to go wandering about at night for?'

Penny shuddered and suddenly covered her face with her hands.

'Oh, Val,' she said, 'did you see her? I was the first to go down into the hall this morning when Will and his son brought her in on a hurdle. That look on her face – I shall never forget it. She saw something dreadful, Val. She died of fright.'

The boy put his arm round her and shook her almost roughly.

'Don't think of it,' he said. 'She'd got a bad heart and she died, that's all. It's nothing to do with – with the other thing.'

But there was no conviction in his tone and the girl was not comforted, realizing that he spoke as much to reassure himself as to soothe her.

Their nerves were so taut that a tap on the door made them both start violently. It opened immediately to admit old Doctor Cobden, the man who had brought them both into the world, and whose word had been the ultimate court of appeal ever since they could remember.

He was a large, benign old gentleman with closely cropped white hair and immense white eyebrows and he was dressed in an unconventional rough tweed suit fitting snugly to his rotund form.

He advanced across the room, hand outstretched, exuding a faint aroma of iodoform as he came.

'Val, my boy, I'm glad to see you,' he said. 'You couldn't have come back at a better time. Your father and the estate have needed you very much lately, but never so much as now.' He turned to Penny and patted her hand gently as it lay in his own. 'Pull yourself together, my dear,' he said. 'It's been a shock, I know, but there's nothing to be afraid of. I'm glad I found you two alone. I wanted to have a chat. Your father, good man, is not much assistance in an emergency.'

He spoke briskly and with a forthrightness that they had learned to respect. Val shot him a glance under his eyelashes.

'There'll have to be an inquest, I suppose, sir?' he said.

Doctor Cobden took out a pair of pince-nez and rubbed them contemplatively with an immense white handkerchief.

'Why no, Val. I don't think that'll be necessary, as it happens,' he said. 'I'm the coroner of this district, don't you know. And whereas I should perhaps have felt it was my duty to inquire into your aunt's death if I hadn't been in attendance on her quite so often lately, I really don't see any need to go into it all again.' He paused and regarded them solemnly. 'There was always a danger, of course. Any severe shock might have aggravated this aortic regurgitation, don't you know, but she was a nervy creature, poor soul, and I never saw any reason to frighten her.'

'But, Doctor, something did frighten her. Her face —' Penny could not restrain the outburst. The old man's mottled face took on a slightly deeper tone of red.

'My dear,' he said, 'death is often ugly. I'm sorry you should have had to see your aunt. Of course,' he went on hastily as he saw the doubt in their eyes, 'she must have *had* a shock, don't you know. Probably saw an owl or trod on a rabbit. I warned her against this stupid wandering about at night. Your aunt was a very peculiar woman.'

He coughed. 'Sometimes,' he added, 'I thought her a very silly woman. All this semi-mystical nonsense was very dangerous in her condition. And that's where I come to the business I wanted to discuss with you. I don't want your father bothered. I've persuaded him to take things easily. It's been a great shock to him. He's in his own rooms and I don't want him disturbed. Now, Val, I want all this crowd of your aunt's friends out of the house before tomorrow.' He paused, and his little bright eyes met the boy's inquiringly. 'I don't know how many there are,' he said, 'or who they are. Some – ah – some Bohemian set, I understand they've been getting on your father's nerves. I don't know what your aunt was doing filling the place with dozens of strangers.'

Penny looked a little surprised.

'There's only seven visitors, and they're at the Cup House now,' she said. 'We don't see much of them. Aunt used to keep them to herself.'

'Oh, I see.' The doctor looked considerably relieved. 'I understood from your father that there was an army of lunatics encamped somewhere. Oh, well, it won't be so difficult. I don't suppose they'll want to stay, don't you know.'

The old man had brightened visibly. Clearly a weight was off his mind. 'There's just one other thing,' he went on rather more slowly than usual, evidently choosing his words with deliberation. 'With regard to the funeral, I should – ah – get it over quietly, don't you know. As little fuss as possible. I don't think there's any necessity to fill the house with visitors. No last looks or any morbid rubbish of that sort. I'm sorry to speak frankly,' he went on, directing his remarks to Val, 'but it's your father we've got to think of. It's getting near your twenty-fifth birthday, you know, my boy, and that is a very trying time for both you and your father.' He paused to let his words sink in, and then added practically: 'There's no near relative that you'll offend, is there?'

Penny considered. 'There's Uncle Lionel's brothers,' she said dubiously.

'Oh, no need to worry about them. Write to them and leave it at that.' The doctor dismissed the family of the late Sir Lionel Pethwick with a wave of his hand.

Penny laid her hand upon his arm affectionately.

'You dear,' she said. 'You're trying to hush it all up for us.'

'My dear child!' The old man appeared scandalized. 'I've never heard such nonsense. There's nothing to hush up. A perfectly normal death. I'm merely considering your father, as I keep on telling you. You young people are too eager to listen to the superstitious chatter of the country folk. There's no such thing as a look of horror on a dead face. It's death itself that is horrifying. A case of a sudden end like this is always shocking. I'll make you up a sedative, Penny. One of the men can come down for it. Take it three times a day, and go to bed early.

'I'll speak to Robertson too, Val, as I go through Sudbury. You can leave everything to him. I should fix the funeral for Wednesday. Without appearing callous, the sooner you get these things over the better. You're modern young people. I'm sure you'll understand me. Now I'll go,' he added, turning briskly towards the door. 'Don't trouble to come down with me. I want to have a word with Branch on my way out. I believe that old rascal is more capable than the whole lot of you. Good-bye. I shall drop in tomorrow. Good-bye, Penny, my dear.'

He closed the door firmly behind him and they heard him padding off down the parquetted corridor. Penny turned to her brother, her eyes wide and scared.

'Val, he suspects something,' she said. 'All this quiet funeral business – it's so unlike him. Don't you remember, Mother used to say that he was as proud at a funeral as if he felt he was directly responsible for the whole thing? He doesn't like the look of it. Poor Aunt Di, she was a thorn in the flesh, but I never dreamed it would all end so quickly and horribly as this. I'd give anything to be able to hear her explain her psychic reaction to sunset over Monaco again.'

Val was troubled. 'Do you mean you think it wasn't heart failure?' he said.

'Oh, nonsense,' said Penny. 'Of course it was. But I think the doctor feels, as I did, that she must have seen something terrible. There *is* something terrible down in Pharisees' Clearing. There's something round here that we don't understand – I've known it for a long time. I –'

A gentle knocking silenced her, and they both turned to see a pale ineffectual face, half-hidden by enormous glasses, peering in at them from the doorway.

'Enter Suspicious Character,' said Mr Campion, introducing the rest of himself into the room. 'By the way, I met an irate old gentleman downstairs who told me there was a goods train at 6.15 from Hadleigh. I hope that wasn't your father, chicks.' He paused, and added awkwardly, 'I heard a rumour in the village that something rather terrible had happened.'

Val stepped forward to meet him. 'Look here, Campion,' he said, 'it's all infernally mysterious and it is terrible. Aunt Di was brought in by two yokels. They found her in a clearing in the woods quite near here. She was dead, and they insist that she had an expression of absolute horror on her face, but of course we know that's impossible. That was the doctor you saw just now. He's giving a certificate, but I can't help feeling he wouldn't be so sanguine if he didn't know the family so well. Father has shut himself up in the library and the doc says we're to clear Aunt's crowd out as soon as we can.'

He paused for breath.

'An expression of horror?' said Mr Campion. 'This is where we get out of our depth. I'm terribly sorry this has happened, Gyrth. How do you stand with your father?'

'Oh, that's all right.' The boy spoke hastily. 'I ought to have come home before. I had my own affairs too much on the brain. I think the old boy was worrying about me. Anyhow, he's very grateful to you. He wanted to send for you last night. I had to hint who you were – you don't mind that, do you? He seems to understand the situation perfectly. Frankly, I was amazed by his readiness to accept the whole story.'

Campion did not answer, but smiled affably at the boy. Val seemed relieved.

'Now I'd better go round and politely turf out that Bohemian crowd,' he said. 'I don't suppose you want to interview them, Campion?'

The young man with the pleasant vacuous face shook his head.

'No,' he said, 'I think it would be better if we did not become acquainted, as it were. There's only one thing. Branch, I suppose, will superintend the luggage?'

'Why, yes, I suppose so.' Val was almost impatient.

'Good,' said Campion. 'See that he does. By the way, he and Lugg were having an Old Boys' Reunion in the hall when I came up.' He turned to the girl. 'I say, while your brother's speeding the parting guests, I wonder if I could ask you to take me down to the clearing where they found Lady Pethwick?'

She shot him a glance of surprise, but his expression was mild and foolish as ever. 'Of course I will,' she said.

'Perhaps we could go by some back way that may exist?' Mr Campion persisted. 'I don't want my bad taste to be apparent.'

Val glanced at his sister and hesitated. 'We don't know the exact spot,' he said awkwardly.

'Naturally,' said Campion, and followed his guide out of the room. They went down a shallow Elizabethan staircase, along a wide stone-flagged passage, and came out of a side door into a flower garden. As Mr Campion stepped out blinking into the sunshine, the girl laid a hand upon his arm.

'Look,' she said, 'you can see the Cup House from here.'

Her companion followed the direction of her eyes and saw a curious rectangular building which had been completely hidden from the front of the house by the enormous eastern wing.

It was situated in a little courtyard of its own, and consisted of what appeared to be two storeys built of flint cobbles reinforced with oak, the lower floor being clearly the Chapel of the Cup, while the upper section had several windows indicating a suite of rooms.

Mr Campion regarded the structure, the sun glinting on his spectacles.

'Your aunt's artistic friends are upstairs, I suppose?' he said.

'Oh, yes,' said Penny hastily. 'The chapel is always kept locked.'

Mr Campion hesitated. 'There's no doubt,' he ventured, 'that the relic is safe at the moment?'

The girl stared at him in astonishment. 'Of course it is,' she said. 'I'm afraid all this talk of painting my aunt with the Chalice has given you a wrong impression. There were always two of the servants there at the time – Branch and someone else – and the relic was returned to its place and the doors locked after each sitting. There are three rooms up there over the chapel,' she went on, 'the Maid of the Cup's private apartments in the old days. Aunt had the big room as a sort of studio, but the two small ones are the bedrooms of the two men who have charge of this garden and the chapel building. There's an outside staircase to the first storey.'

'Oh,' said Mr Campion.

They walked down the broad grass path towards a small gate at the end of the garden. For some time there was silence, and then the girl spoke abruptly.

'Mr Campion,' she said, 'I made Val tell me about everything last night – I mean about the danger to the Chalice. You'll have to let me help. You'll find me quite as useful as he. For one thing,' she added, dropping her voice, 'I haven't got the shadow of The Room hanging over me. Besides,' she went on with a wry little smile, 'I'm the Maid of the Cup now, you know. I've got a right to come into this and you can count on me.'

Mr Campion's reply was unexpected. 'I shall hold you to that,' he said. 'Now I think we'd better hurry.'

They went through the garden gate and across the broad meadow on the other side. Here it was semi-parkland with a great bank of trees upon their left, and presently they entered a small iron gate in the hedge surrounding the wood and struck a footpath leading down into the heart of the greenery.

'Pharisees' Clearing,' said Penny, 'is just through here. It's really a strip of grass which separates our wood from the other coppice which is the Tye Hall property where Beth lives.'

'Ah,' said Mr Campion. 'And where is Fox Hollow?'

She shot him a quick glance. 'You remembered that? It's higher up on the other side of their woodlands. Dad really had cause for a grievance, you see, only Professor Cairey himself doesn't shoot, so you can't expect him to understand. And anyhow, he only wants asking. Dad's so silly that way.'

'Professor?' said Campion thoughtfully. 'What does he profess?'

'Archaeology,' said Penny promptly. 'But you don't think –?'

'My dear girl,' said Mr Campion, 'I can't see the wood for trees. "And in the night imagining some fear, how easy doth a bush appear a bear." You see,' he added with sudden seriousness, 'if your aunt met her death by someone's design, I'm not only out of my depth, but I might just as well have left my water-wings at home.' He paused and looked about him. 'I suppose this is a happy hunting ground for poachers?'

Penny shook her head. 'I don't think there's a man, woman or child in the whole of Sanctuary who'd come within a mile of Pharisees' Clearing after dark,' she said. She hesitated for some seconds as if debating whether to go on. 'I get on very well with the country folk,' she added suddenly, 'and naturally I hear a good deal of local chatter. They believe that this wood and the clearing are haunted – not by a ghost, but by something much worse than that. No one's ever seen it that I know of, but you know what country people are.'

'I thought the breed had died out,' said her companion. 'Gone are the dimpled milkmaids and the ancient gaffers of my youth. You can't even see them on the pictures.'

Penny smiled faintly. 'We're very much behind the times here,' she said. 'We've even got a local witch – poor old Mrs Munsey. She lives with her son in a little henhouse of a place some distance away from the village. They're both half-wits, you know, really, poor things. But there's a world of prejudice against them, and they're both so bad-tempered you can't do anything for them. Sammy Munsey is the village idiot, I suppose, but the old woman is a venomous old party. And that's why –' she hesitated, 'you'll probably think I'm a fool for mentioning this, but she put a curse on Aunt Di at the last full moon, and it was full moon again last night.'

She reddened and glanced furtively at her companion, whose pleasant vacant face conveyed nothing but polite interest. She looked absurdly modern in her smart white crêpe de Chine jumper suit, her bare brown arms hanging limply at her sides, and it was certainly odd to hear her speak of such an archaic practice as witchcraft as though she half believed in it.

'Now I've said it, it sounds stupid,' she remarked. 'After all, it may not even be true. It's only gossip.'

Campion regarded her quizzically. 'Did Mrs Munsey ever curse anybody with such startling success before?' he said. 'How did she build up her business, so to speak?'

The girl shrugged her shoulders. 'I don't really know,' she said, 'except that there's a list of witches burnt in 1624 still in the Lady Chapel of the church – this village managed to escape Cromwell, you know – and every other name on the sheet is Munsey. It's partly that, and then – the poor old creature is perfectly bald. In the winter it's all right, she wears a bonnet of sorts, but in hot weather she goes about uncovered. Aunt Di was always trying to be kind to her, but she had an officious way and she annoyed the old biddy somehow. Do you think I'm mad?'

'My dear young lady,' said her companion judicially, 'there are lots of rum professions. There's nothing unusual about witchcraft. I used to be a bit of a wizard myself, and I once tried to change a particularly loathsome old gentleman into a seal on a voyage to Oslo. Certainly the vulgar creature fell overboard, and they only succeeded in hauling up a small walrus, but I was never sure whether I had done it or not. They had the same moustaches, but that was all. I've often wondered if I was successful. I went in for wireless accessories after that.'

Penny regarded him with astonishment, but he seemed to be perfectly serious. They were half-way through the wood by this time. The place was a fairyland of cool green arcades with moss underfoot, and a tiny stream meandering along among the tree roots.

She pointed to a patch of sunlight at the far end of the path. 'That's the entrance to Pharisees' Clearing,' she said. 'Pharisee means "fairy", you know.'

Mr Campion nodded. 'Be careful how you talk about fairies in a wood,' he said. 'They're apt to think it disrespectful.'

They walked on, and came at last to the edge of the clearing. It was a tiny valley, walled in by high trees on each side, and possessing, even at that hour of the morning, a slightly sinister aspect.

The grey-green grass was sparse, and there were large stones scattered about; a bare unlovely place, all the more uninviting after the beauty of the wood.

The girl paused and shivered. 'It was here,' she said quietly. 'As far as I could gather from Will Tiffin, Aunt was lying quite close to this gateway – staring up with that awful look on her face.'

Campion did not move, but stood regarding the scene, his pale face even more vacuous than usual. The girl took a deep breath.

'Mr Campion,' she said, 'I've got to tell you something. I've kept quiet about it so far, but I think if I don't tell someone I shall go mad.'

She was speaking impulsively, the quick colour rising in her cheeks.

'Will Tiffin told me early this morning, and I made him swear not to breathe it to another soul. When he found her she was lying here on her back, not twisted or dishevelled as she would have been if she had lain where she had fallen, but stiff and straight, with her hands folded and her eyes closed. Don't you see –' her voice quivered and sank to a whisper – 'Will said it looked as if she had been laid out as a corpse.'

Chapter 8

The Professional Touch

'You'd be doing me a service, Mr Lugg, if you'd refrain from referring to me as No. 705. Sir Percival did my father the honour of forgetting my little lapse twenty-five years ago.'

Mr Branch, a small dignified person in black tie and jacket, paused and regarded his shady old friend with something like appeal in his eyes.

'No good thinkin' o' that,' he added, dropping his official voice and speaking with his natural Suffolk inflection.

Mr Lugg, himself resplendent in black cloth, sniffed contemptuously. ''Ave it yer own way,' he said. 'Anyway, you nipped that lot out o' the satchel as if you still knew a thing or two.'

He jerked his head towards a pile of water-colours and pencil sketches lying face downwards upon a bureau top. The two men were in one of the smaller bedrooms in the front of the mansion, at present in disuse.

The little man fidgeted nervously.

'I shan't be happy till they're out of the house,' he said. 'It's not my regular job to do the packing. The housekeeper would smell a rat immediately if any fuss was made.'

'There won't be no fuss. 'Ow many more times 'ave I got to tell yer?' Mr Lugg was irritated. 'Mr Gyrth and my young bloke said they'd take full responsibility. Livin' down 'ere on the fat of the land 'as made you flabby, my son.'

Mr Branch glanced under his eyelashes at the big man opposite him.

'Your Mr Campion,' he said. 'I shouldn't be at all surprised if 'is real name didn't begin with a K. And figuring it all out, 'is Christian name ought to be Rudolph.'

Mr Lugg's large mouth fell open. ''Ow d'yer make that out?' he demanded.

His friend wagged his head knowingly. 'A confidential family servant in a big 'ouse gets to know things by a sort of instinct,' he observed. 'Family likenesses – family manners – little tricks of 'abit, and so on.'

Unwillingly, Mr Lugg was impressed. 'Lumme!' he said. ''Ow did you get a line on 'is nibs?'

'About an hour ago,' said Branch precisely, 'I went into Mr Campion's bedroom to see if the maids had done their work. Quite by chance,' he went on studiously, 'I caught sight of 'is pyjamas. Light purple stripe – silk – come from Dodds. That didn't tell me much. But then I noticed a bit of flannel, sewed in by the firm, across the shoulder-blades. Now that's a silly idea, a woman's idea. Also I fancy I could lay me finger on the only woman 'oo could ever make Dodds do it. Then, a thing like that comes from 'abit – lifelong 'abit. It wouldn't be a wife. It'd 'ave to be a mother to fix it on a chap so's it 'ud last 'im all 'is life. I started thinkin' and remembered where I'd seen it before. Then of course I knew. The gilded bit of aristocracy 'oo comes down 'ere sometimes is just the chap to 'ave a little brother like your young bloke.'

He paused and Mr Lugg was mortified.

'Branch,' he said, 'who d'you make me out to be – Doctor Watson?'

It was evident that the butler did not follow him, and Lugg laughed. 'You're smart, but you've got no education,' he said complacently. 'What's the point of all this knowledge of yours? What d'you use it for – graft?'

Branch was shocked, and said so. Afterwards he deigned to explain. 'In the days when 'er Ladyship was alive and we used to entertain,' he said, 'it was as well to keep an eye on who was in the 'ouse. Oh, I was very useful to 'er Ladyship. She quite come to depend on me. First morning at breakfast when they come in, she'd raise 'er eyebrows at me, ever so faint, if there was any doubt, and if I knoo they was OK, I'd nod.'

'Yes?' said Lugg, fascinated by this sidelight into High Life. 'And if you wasn't satisfied?'

'Then I'd ignore 'er,' said Branch majestically.

Mr Lugg whistled. ''Ard lines on a bloke with ragged pants,' he observed.

'Oh no, you don't foller me.' Branch was vehement. 'Why, there's one pair of underpants that's been into this 'ouse reg'lar for the last fourteen years. Darned by the Duchess 'erself, bless 'er! I can tell it anywhere – it's a funny cross-stitch what she learnt in France in the fifties. You see it on all 'er family's washin'. It's as good as a crest.' He shook his head. 'No, this 'ere knowledge of mine comes by instinc'. I can't explain it.'

'Well, since you're so clever, what about this lot that's just off?' said Lugg, anxious to see if the remarkable attribute could be turned to practical account. 'Anything nobby in the way of darns there?'

Branch was contemptuous.

'Fakes!' he said. 'Low fakes, that's what they were. Nice new outfits bought for the occasion. "Something to show the servants,"' he mimicked in a horribly refined voice. 'Not every pair of legs that's covered by Burlington Arcade first kicked up in Berkeley Square, you can take it from me.'

Mr Lugg, piqued by this exhibition of talent, was stung to retort.

'Well, anyway, 'ere's your watch back,' he said, handing over a large gold turnip, and gathering up a sheaf of drawings he strode out of the room.

He padded softly down the corridor and tapped upon a door on his left. Penny's voice bade him enter, and he went in to find himself in a small sitting-room elaborately decorated in the dusty crimson and gold of the later Georges.

Mr Campion and the daughter of the house were standing beside the window, well hidden from the outside by heavy damask curtains. The young man, who had turned round as Lugg entered, raised his eyebrows inquiringly.

'I've got the doings, sir,' Lugg murmured huskily, the faded splendours of the old mansion combined with Penelope's beauty producing a certain respect in his tone. 'Just like what you thought.'

'Good,' said Mr Campion. 'Hold hard for a moment, Lugg. I'm watching our young host and your friend Branch, who I see has just come out to him, packing the intelligentsia into a couple of cars.'

'Ho.' Mr Lugg advanced on tiptoe and stood breathing heavily over his master's shoulder. They could just see a group of weirdly dressed people surrounding a venerable Daimler and a still more ancient Panhard, both belonging to the house, which were stationed outside the front door.

Lugg nudged his master. 'That's the chap I saw with Natty,' he rumbled. 'That seedy looking bloke with the ginger beard. It was 'is traps that this lot come out of.' He tapped the pile of papers in his hand.

'Do you recognize any of the others?' Mr Campion spoke softly.

Mr Lugg was silent for some moments. Then he sniffed regretfully.

'Can't say I do,' he said. 'They look genuine to me. They've got that "Gawd-made-us-and-this-is-'ow-'e-likes us" look.'

Penny touched Mr Campion's arm.

'Albert,' she said, 'do you recognize that man with the ginger beard?'

Mr Campion turned away from the window and advanced towards the table in the centre of the room.

'Rather,' he said. 'An old employee of mine. That's why I'm so glad he didn't see me. His trade name before he took up art and grew a beard was Arthur Earle. He's a jeweller's copyist, and one of the best on the shady side of the line.' He turned to Penny and grinned. 'When Lady Ermyntrude gives her dancing partner the old Earl's jewelled toodle-oo clock to keep the wolf from the door, the old Earl is awakened every morning by a careful copy of our Arthur's making. Likewise Lady Maud's ruby dog collar and the necklace Sir George gave little Eva on her twenty-first. They're all copies of the originals made by our Arthur. Arthur, in fact, is one of the lads who make Society what it is today.' He took the pile of papers from Lugg. 'This, I fancy, is some of his handiwork. Now we'll see.'

There had been a sound of wheels in the drive, and Val came in almost immediately afterwards.

'Well, they've gone,' he said. 'Hullo, what have you got there?'

Mr Campion was busy spreading out the drawings. 'A spot of Noo-Art,' he said. 'When they discover they've lost this lot they'll realize we're not completely in the dark, but we can't help that.'

The brother and sister bent forward eagerly. There were about a dozen drawings in all, each purporting to be a portrait of Lady Pethwick. In each drawing the Chalice figured. In fact the Chalice was the only subject which the artist had attempted to treat with any realism, whilst the drawings of the lady were ultra-modern, to say the best of them.

Mr Campion chuckled. 'There's not much about the treasure that our friend missed,' he said. 'It's a miracle your aunt didn't spot what he was up to. Look, here's the Chalice from the right side, from the left, from the top – see, he's even jotted down the measurements here. And I should fancy he had a pretty good idea of the weight. That's what I call thoroughness.'

Val looked at him questioningly. 'I don't quite see the idea,' he said.

'My dear old bird,' said Mr Campion, 'our Arthur was a conscientious workman in spite of his murky reputation. He must have been a bit of an actor, too, by the way, to deceive your aunt like that. These are plans' – he waved his hand to the drawings on the table – 'working diagrams, in fact. I should say that, given the materials, our Arthur could turn you out a very good copy of the Chalice from these.'

'But if they could make a copy that would deceive us, why not let his Mohammedan client have it?' said Val testily.

Mr Campion was shocked. 'My dear fellow, have you no respect for a collector's feelings?' he said. 'Arthur couldn't make anything that would deceive an expert.'

'So they were going to exchange it?' It was Penny who spoke, her eyes blazing with anger and her cheeks flushed. 'To give them plenty of time to get the real thing out of the country before we spotted anything. Pigs! Oh, the insufferable farmyard pigs! Pigs in the French sense! Why don't we wire down to the station and get the man arrested?'

'I shouldn't do that,' said Mr Campion. 'We've spiked his guns pretty effectively anyhow. And after all, I don't see what we could charge him with. He might retort that we'd pinched his drawings, which would be awkward. Lugg's record would come out and we'd all be in the soup. Besides,' he went on gravely, 'Arthur is very small fry – just about as small as Natty Johnson, in fact. That's what's worrying me,' he added with unusual violence. 'The place is swarming with minnows, but there's not a trout in the stream. And the big man is the only one who's any good to us at all. I wish I knew what your aunt saw last night.'

He gathered up the drawings and tore them neatly across and across. 'Now you can go and play bonfires, Lugg,' he said, handing him the pieces.

It was growing dark in the room, and at any moment the dinner gong might sound.

The little party was disturbed by the sudden entrance of Branch, who came in without ceremony, his usual composure completely gone.

'Mr Val, sir,' he burst out, 'would you step across the passage? There's a stranger peering in through the chapel window.'

With a smothered exclamation Val started after the butler into the spare bedroom on the opposite side of the corridor, followed by the entire company. The window afforded a perfect view of the Cup House.

'There!' said Branch, pointing down towards the old flint building. It was almost dusk, but the watchers could easily make out the figure of a man balanced upon a pile of loose stones peering in through one of the narrow lattice windows of the chapel. He was hidden by a yew hedge from the lower windows of the house, and apparently thought himself completely secluded. He had a torch in his hand with which he was trying to penetrate the darkness inside the building.

As they watched him, fascinated, the hastily improvised pedestal on which the intruder stood collapsed beneath his weight, and he stumbled to the ground with a rattle of stones. He picked himself up hastily and shot a single startled glance up at the house.

Even at that distance the features were dimly visible, revealing a handsome little man of sixty odd, with a sharp white vandyke beard and a long nose.

The next moment he was off, streaking through the flower garden like a shadow.

Penny gasped, and she and the butler exchanged glances. When at last she spoke, her voice trembled violently.

'Why, Branch,' she said, 'that – that looked very like Professor Gardner Cairey.'

Branch coughed. 'Begging your pardon, miss,' he said, 'that *was* him.'

Chapter 9
The Indelicate Creature

If the extreme unpopularity of Lady Pethwick produced in her immediate household an emotion more akin to quiet shock than overwhelming grief at her death, the village of Sanctuary seethed with excitement at the news of it, and the most extravagant gossip was rife.

Mr Campion wandered about the vicinity in a quiet, ineffectual fashion, his eyes vague and foolish behind his spectacles, but his ears alert. He learnt within a very short space of time, and on very good authority in every case, that Lady Pethwick had been (a) murdered by Gypsies; (b) confronted by the Devil, who had thereupon spirited her away at the direct instigation of Mrs Munsey, and (c) according to the more prosaic wiseacres, had died in the normal way from drink, drugs, or sheer bad temper.

Even the rational Mrs Bullock held no belief in the doctor's verdict.

On the afternoon of the funeral he absented himself, and spent that day and part of the night pursuing and finally interviewing his old friends Jacob Benwell and his mother, Mrs Sarah, mère and compère of the Benwell Gypsy tribe, who had seen fit for obvious reasons to remove from Fox Hollow on the morning on which Lady Pethwick was found in Pharisees' Clearing.

It was early afternoon of the following day, after a luncheon at which Sir Percival did not appear, that Mr Campion was standing at the nursery window regarding the flower garden attentively when Lugg came to him, an expression of mild outrage upon his ponderous face.

'A party 'as just come visitin',' he remarked. 'Tourists on 'orseback. Day after the funeral – get me? Not quite the article, I thought.'

This announcement was followed almost immediately by the entrance of Penny. Her eyes were dark and angry.

'Albert,' she said, 'have you ever heard such cheek? Mrs Dick Shannon has just arrived with two complete strangers. She has the nerve to say that she has come to pay a call of condolence, and incidentally, if you please, to show her two beastly friends the Chalice.

We open the chapel to visitors on Thursday as a rule – it's part of the Royal Charter – but this is a bit stiff, isn't it?'

She paused for breath.

'Mrs Dick Shannon?' said Mr Campion. 'Ah, yes, I remember. The megaphonic marvel. Where is she now? I suppose your father is doing the honours?'

'Father can't stand her,' said Penny. 'She's trying to make him sell her some horses – that's the real reason why she's come. Look here, you'd better come downstairs and support us. Father likes you. If you could get rid of them he might offer you my hand in marriage or put you up for his club. Anyway, come on.'

She went out of the room and Campion followed. Almost immediately Mrs Dick's penetrating voice met them from the hall below.

'Well, of course, drink's better than lunacy in a family, as I told the mother.'

The phrase met them as they descended the stairs.

Penny snorted. 'I bet she's talking about one of our relatives,' she whispered. 'It's her idea of making conversation.'

Mrs Dick, backed by her two friends, who to do them justice looked considerably embarrassed, was standing with her feet planted far apart in the centre of the huge lounge-hall. All three were in riding kit, Mrs Dick looking particularly smart in a black habit.

Once again Mr Campion was conscious of the faint atmosphere of importance which her dashing personality seemed to exude.

Colonel Sir Percival Gyrth, supported by his son, stood listening to the lady. He was a sturdy old man of the true Brass Hat species, but there was about him a suggestion that some private worry had undermined his normal good-tempered simple character. At the moment he was quite obviously annoyed. His plump hands were folded behind his back, and his eyes, blue and twinkling like his children's, had a distinctly unfriendly gleam. He was a by no means unhandsome man, with curling iron-grey hair, and a heavy-featured clean-shaven face. He glanced up hopefully as Campion entered.

'Ah,' he said, 'let me present you. Mrs Shannon, this is a young friend of Val's. Mr Campion – Mr Albert Campion.'

Mrs Dick's cold glance wandered leisurely over the young man before her. Had she spoken, her contempt could not have been more apparent. Finally she honoured him with a slight but frigid bow. Then she turned to her companions.

'Major King and Mr Horace Putnam,' she said, and then quite patently dismissed all of them as negligible.

Major King proved to be a large, florid and unhappy-looking person, slightly horsey in appearance and clearly not at his ease. Mr Putnam, on the other hand, was a small man with little bright eyes and a shrewd, wrinkled face. He too was clearly a stranger to his surroundings, but was not letting the fact worry him.

'Well?' Mrs Dick whipped the company together with the single word. 'Now, Penny Gyrth, if you'll take us over the museum, we'll go. I'm afraid the horses may be getting bored. You still maintain your complete unreasonableness about those two yearlings, Colonel?'

It said a great deal for Sir Percival's upbringing that his tone when he replied was as charming as ever.

'My dear lady, I don't want to sell. And just at the moment,' he added simply, 'I'm afraid I don't feel much like business of any sort.'

'Oh, of course. Poor Diana.' Mrs Dick was not in the least abashed. 'I always think it best to face things,' she went on, bellowing the words like a bad loudspeaker. 'Mawkishness never did anyone any good. The only wonder to my mind is that it didn't happen years ago. Cobden's such an old fool. I wouldn't let him vet me for chilblains.'

By this time the entire Gyrth family were smarting. Only their inborn politeness saved Mrs Dick and her protégés from an untimely and undignified exit. Mr Campion stood by smiling foolishly as though the lady had irresistible charm for him.

Mrs Dick moved towards the door. 'Come on,' she said. 'I'm not very interested in these things myself, but Mr Putnam is amused by all this ancient rubbish.'

Penny hung back. 'The Chalice is veiled,' she said. 'It always is, for ten days after a –' The word 'death' died on her lips as Mrs Dick interrupted her.

'Then unveil it, my dear,' she said. 'Now come along, all of you – we can't keep the horses waiting. How you've let this place go down since your wife's time, Colonel! Poor Helen, she always believed in making a good show.'

Impelled by the very force of her vigorous personality, the little company followed her. At least three of the party were bristling at her outrageous monologue, but she was superbly oblivious of any effect she might create. It was this quality which had earned her the unique position in the county which she undoubtedly occupied. Everybody knew her, nobody liked her, and most people were a little afraid of her.

Her astounding success with any species of horseflesh earned her a grudging admiration. Nobody snubbed her because the tongue capable of it had not yet been born. Her rudeness and studied discourtesy were a byword for some fifty square miles, yet she came and went where she pleased because the only way of stopping her would have been to hurl her bodily from one's front door, no mean feat in itself, and this method had not yet occurred to the conservative minds of her principal victims.

Outside on the gravel path there was still a very marked reluctance on the part of the members of the household to continue towards the Cup House, but at last the Colonel, realizing that there was no help for it, decided to get the matter over as soon as possible. Branch was dispatched for the keys and the little procession wandered round the east wing, through a small gate at the side, and came out into the flower garden. Mrs Dick still held forth, maintaining a running commentary calculated to jade the strongest of nerves.

'A very poor show of roses, Colonel. But then roses are like horses, you know. If you don't understand 'em, better leave 'em alone.'

She stood aside as Branch advanced to unlock the heavy oak and iron door of the chapel. The lock was ancient and prodigiously stiff, so that the little butler experienced considerable difficulty in inserting the great key, and there was a momentary pause as he struggled to turn it.

Before Val could step forward to assist the old man, Mrs Dick had intervened. She thrust Branch out of her way like a cobweb, and with a single twist of her fingers shot the catch back. Major King laughed nervously.

'You're strong in the wrist,' he observed.

She shot him a single withering glance. 'You can't be flabby in my profession,' she said.

The unpleasant Mr Putnam laughed. 'That's one for you, Major,' he said. 'I was watching Mrs Shannon dealing with Bitter Aloes this morning. That mare will beat you,' he added, turning to the lady. 'She's got a devil in her. I thought she was going to kill you. A bad woman and a vicious mare, they're both incorrigible. Lose 'em or shoot 'em, it's the only way.'

He turned to the rest of the party, who were unimpressed.

'There was Bitter Aloes rearing up, pawing with her front feet like a prizefighter,' he said, 'and Mrs Shannon hanging on to the halter rope, laying about with a whip like a ring-master. She got the brute down in the end. I never saw such a sight.'

It was with this conversation that the unwelcome visitors came into the ancient and sacred Chapel of the Cup.

It was a low room whose slightly vaulted ceiling was supported by immensely thick brick and stone columns, and was lit only by narrow, diamond-paned windows set at irregular intervals in the walls, so that the light was always dim even on the brightest day. The floor was paved with flat tombstones on which were several very fine brasses. It was entirely unfurnished save for a small stone altar at the far end of the chamber, the slab of which was covered with a crimson cloth held in place by two heavy brass candlesticks.

Let into the wall, directly above the centre of the altar, was a stout iron grille over a cavity in the actual stone, which was rather ingeniously lit by a slanting shaft open to the air many feet above, and sealed by a thick sheet of glass inserted at some later period than the building of the chapel.

At the moment the interior of the orifice was filled by a pyramid of embroidered black velvet.

Colonel Gyrth explained.

'Immediately a death occurs in the family,' he murmured, 'the Chalice is veiled. This covering was put on here three days ago. It is the custom,' he added, 'not to disturb it for at least ten days.' He hesitated pointedly.

Mrs Dick stood her ground. 'I suppose the grille opens with another key,' she said. 'What a business you make of it! Is there a burglar alarm concealed in the roof?'

Quite patently it had dawned upon the Colonel that the only way to get rid of his unwelcome visitors was to show them the Chalice and have done with it. He was a peace-loving man, and realizing that Mrs Dick would not shy at a scene, he had no option but to comply with her wishes. He took the smaller key which Branch handed him, and bending across the altar carefully unlocked the grille, which swung open like a door. With reverent hands he lifted the black covering.

Mr Campion, whose imagination ran always to the comic, was reminded irresistibly of a conjuring trick. A moment later his mental metaphor was unexpectedly made absolute.

There was a smothered exclamation from the Colonel and a little scream from Penny. The removal of the black cloth had revealed nothing more than a couple of bricks taken from the loose pedestal of one of the columns.

Of the Chalice there was no sign whatever.

Mrs Dick was the only person who did not realize immediately that some calamity had occurred.

'Not my idea of humour.' Her stentorian voice reverberated through the cool, dark chapel. 'Sheer bad taste.'

But Val stared at Mr Campion, and his father stared at Branch, and there was nothing but complete stupefaction and horror written on all their faces.

It was Colonel Gyrth who pulled himself together and provided the second shock within five minutes.

'Of course,' he said, 'I had quite forgotten. I'm afraid you'll be disappointed today, Mr Putnam. The Chalice is being cleaned. Some other time.'

With remarkable composure he smiled and turned away, murmuring to Val as he passed him: 'For God's sake get these people out of the house, my boy, and then come into the library, all of you.'

Chapter 10
Two Angry Ladies

Colonel Sir Percival Gyrth walked up and down the hearthrug in his library, while his two children, with Mr Campion and Branch, stood looking at him rather helplessly.

'Thank God that woman's gone.' The old man passed his hand across his forehead. 'I don't know if my explanation satisfied her. I hope so, or we'll have the whole country buzzing with it within twenty-four hours.'

Val stared at his father. 'Then it really has gone?'

'Of course it has.' There was no misunderstanding the consternation in the Colonel's voice. 'Vanished into thin air. I veiled it myself on Sunday evening, just after you said that busybody Cairey was fooling about in the courtyard. It was perfectly safe then. I brought the keys back and put them in my desk. Branch, you and I, I suppose, are the only people who knew where they were kept.'

Branch's expression was pathetic, and his employer reassured him. 'Don't worry, man. I'm not accusing anybody. It's ridiculous. The thing can't have gone.'

For a moment no one spoke. The suddenness of the loss seemed to have stunned them.

'Hadn't I better send someone for the police, sir? Or perhaps you'd rather I phoned?' It was Branch who made the suggestion.

Sir Percival hesitated. 'I don't think so, thank you, Branch,' he said. 'Anyway, not yet. You see,' he went on, turning to the others, 'to make a loss like this public entails very serious consequences. We are really the guardians of the Chalice for the Crown. I want the chapel locked as usual, Branch, and no mention of the loss to be made known to the staff, as yet.'

'But what shall we do?' said Val breathlessly. 'We can't sit down and wait for it to reappear.'

His father looked at him curiously. 'Perhaps not, my boy,' he said. 'But there's one point which must have occurred to all of you. The

Chalice is both large and heavy, and no stranger has left the house since I locked it up myself. No one except ourselves could possibly have had access to it, and we are all very particularly concerned in keeping it here.'

'According to that argument,' said Val bluntly, 'it can't have gone. And if so, where is it? Can't you send for the Chief Constable? He used to be a friend of yours.'

His father hesitated. 'I could, of course,' he said, 'though I don't see what he could do except spread the alarm and question all the servants – search the house, probably, and make a lot of fuss. No, we must find this thing ourselves.'

There was an astonishing air of finality in his tone which was not lost upon the others.

'I'm not calling in the police,' he said, 'not yet, at any rate. And I must particularly ask you not to mention this loss to anyone. I'm convinced,' he went on as they gasped at him, 'that the relic is still in the house. Now I should like to be left alone.'

They went out, all of them, except Val, who lingered, and when the door had closed behind the others he went over to the old man, who had seated himself at his desk.

'Look here, Dad,' he said, 'if you've hidden the Cup for some reason or other, for Heaven's sake let me in on it. I'm all on edge about this business, and frankly I feel I've got a right to know.'

'For Heaven's sake, boy, don't be a fool.' The older man's voice was almost unrecognizable, and the face he lifted towards his son was grey and haggard. 'This is one of the most serious, most terrifying things I have ever experienced in my whole lifetime,' he went on, his voice indubitably sincere. 'All the more so because, as it happens, we are so situated that at the moment it is impossible for me to call in the police.'

He looked the boy steadily in the eyes. 'You come of age in a week. If your birthday were today perhaps I should find this easier to explain.'

Early the following morning Mr Campion walked down the broad staircase, through the lounge-hall, and out into the sunlight. There seemed no reason for him to be particularly cheerful. So far his activities at Sanctuary seemed to have met with anything rather than conspicuous success. Lady Pethwick had died mysteriously within eight hours of his arrival, and now the main object of his visit had disappeared from almost directly beneath his nose.

Yet he sat down on one of the ornamental stone seats which flanked the porch and beamed upon a smiling world.

Presently, as his ears detected the sound for which he was listening, he began to stroll in a leisurely fashion down the drive. He was still sauntering along the middle of the broad path when the squawk of a motor-horn several times repeated made him turn to find Penny, in her little red two-seater sports car, looking at him reprovingly. She had had to stop to avoid running him over. He smiled at her foolishly from behind his spectacles.

'Where are you going to, my pretty maid?' he said. 'Would you like to give a poor traveller a lift?'

The girl did not look particularly pleased at the suggestion.

'As a matter of fact,' she said, 'I'm running up to Town to see my dressmaker. I'll give you a lift to the village if you like.'

'I'm going to London too,' said Mr Campion, climbing in. 'It's a long way from here, isn't it?' he went on with apparent imbecility. 'I knew I'd never walk it.'

Penny stared at him, her cheeks flushing. 'Surely you can't go off and leave the Tower unprotected,' she said, and there was a note of amusement in her voice.

'Never laugh at a great man,' said Mr Campion. 'Remember what happened to the vulgar little girls who threw stones at Elisha. I can imagine few worse deaths than being eaten by a bear,' he added conversationally.

The girl was silent for a moment. She was clearly considerably put out by the young man's unexpected appearance.

'Look here,' she said at last, 'I'm taking Beth with me, if you really want to know. I'm meeting her at the end of the lane.'

Mr Campion beamed. 'That's all right,' he said. 'I shan't mind being squashed. Don't let me force myself on you,' he went on. 'I shouldn't dream of doing that, but I've got to get to London somehow, and Lugg told me I couldn't use the Bentley.'

The girl looked at him incredulously. 'What is that man Lugg?' she said.

Her companion adjusted his spectacles. 'It depends how you mean,' he said. 'A species, definitely human, I should say, oh yes, without a doubt. Status – none. Past – filthy. Occupation – my valet.'

Penny laughed. 'I wondered if he were your keeper,' she suggested.

'Tut, tut,' said Mr Campion, mildly offended. 'I hope I'm going to enjoy my trip. I don't want to be "got at" in a parroty fashion all the way up. Ah, there's your little friend waiting for us. Would you like me to sit in the dickey?'

'No!' said Penny, so vehemently that he almost jumped. She bit her lip as though annoyed with herself and added more quietly, 'Sit where you are. Beth can squeeze in.'

She brought the car to a standstill against the side of the road where Beth Cairey, smart and coolly attractive in navy and white, stood waiting. She seemed surprised to see Mr Campion and her greeting was subdued.

'This appalling creature has insisted on our giving him a lift,' said Penny. 'I do hope you won't be squashed in front here.'

Mr Campion made way for her between himself and the driver.

'I couldn't very well refuse him,' Penny added apologetically to Beth. 'We shall have to put up with him.'

Mr Campion continued to look ineffably pleased with himself. 'What a good job there's no more for the Skylark, isn't it?' he remarked as she shut the door on the tightly packed little party. 'I love riding in other people's motor-cars. Such a saving of petrol, for one thing.'

'Silly and rather vulgar,' said Penny, and Mr Campion was silent.

'I suppose I can eat my sandwiches and drink my ginger beer so long as I don't throw the bottle on the road?' he said meekly after they had progressed a couple of miles without speaking. 'I've got a few oranges I could pass round too if you like.'

Penny did not deign to reply, although Beth looked upon him more kindly. Unabashed, Mr Campion continued.

'I've got a rattle to swing in the big towns,' he said. 'And a couple of funny noses for you two to wear. If we had some balloons we could tie them on the bonnet.'

Penny laughed grudgingly. 'Albert, you're an idiot,' she said. 'What do you think you're doing here, anyhow? Where are you going to in London?'

'To buy a ribbon for my straw hat,' said Mr Campion promptly. 'The thing I've got now my Aunt knitted. It's not quite the article, as Lugg would say.'

Penny slowed down. 'You're just being offensive,' she said. 'I've a good mind to make you get out and walk.'

Mr Campion looked apprehensive. 'You'd regret it all your life,' he said warningly. 'The best part of my performance is to come. Wait till you've heard me recite – wait till I've done my clog dance – wait till the clouds roll by.'

'I should turn him out,' said Beth stolidly. 'We've come a long way, it would do him good to walk back.'

They were, it happened, in one of the narrow cross-country lanes through which Penny was threading in her descent upon the main Colchester motor-way, some distance from a house of any kind, and the road was deserted.

'Don't turn me out,' pleaded Mr Campion. 'I knew a man once who turned such a respectable person out of his car after giving him a lift for a long way just like you and for the same reason, all because he'd taken a sudden dislike to him. And when he got home he found that his suitcase, which had been in the back of the car, was missing. Suppose that happened to you? You wouldn't like that, would you?'

Penny stopped the car, engine and all. Both girls were scarlet, but it was Penny who tried to rescue what was obviously an awkward situation.

'How silly of me,' she said. 'You'll have to get out and start her up. The self-starter isn't functioning.'

Mr Campion moved obediently to get out, and in doing so contrived to kneel up on the seat and grasp one end of the large suitcase which protruded from the open dickey. His next movement was so swift that neither of the two girls realized what was happening until he had leapt clear of the car and stood beaming in the road, the suitcase in his arms. In fact Penny had already trodden on the self-starter and the car was in motion before she was conscious of her loss.

Mr Campion put the suitcase on the bank and sat down on it. Penny stopped the car, and she and Beth descended and came down the road towards him. She was white with anger, and there was a gleam of defiance in Beth's brown eyes that was positively dangerous.

'Mr Campion,' said Penny, 'will you please put that case back in the car at once? Naturally, I can't offer you a lift any farther, and if ever you have the impudence to appear at the Tower again I'll have you thrown out.'

Mr Campion looked dejected, but he still retained his seat. 'Don't be unreasonable,' he begged. 'You're making me go all melodramatic and slightly silly.'

The two girls stared at him fascinated. He was juggling with a revolver which he had taken from his hip-pocket.

Penny was now thoroughly alarmed. 'What do you think you're

doing?' she demanded. 'You can't behave like this. Another car may come along at any moment. Then where will you be?'

'Then where will *you* be?' said Mr Campion pointedly.

With his free hand he slipped open the catches of the suitcase. There was a smothered scream from Beth.

'Please – please leave it alone,' she whispered.

Mr Campion shook his head. 'Sorry,' he said. 'Dooty is dooty, miss. Hullo! Is that a car?'

The inexperienced ladies were deceived by the old trick. They turned eagerly, and in the momentary respite Mr Campion whipped open the suitcase and exposed a large bundle wrapped lightly in a travelling rug.

Beth would have sprung at him, but Penny restrained her. 'It's no good,' she said, 'we're sunk.'

And they stood sullenly in the road with pink cheeks and bright eyes regarding him steadily as he unwrapped and produced to their gaze the eighteen inches of shining glory that was called the Gyrth Chalice.

Chapter 11

Mr Campion Subscribes

For some moments Mr Campion stood at the side of the glittering flint road with the bank of green behind him, and the shadows of the beech leaves making a pattern on his face and clothes. The Chalice lay in his arms, dazzling in the sunshine.

Penny and Beth stood looking at him. They were both crimson, both furious and a little afraid. Penny was fully aware of the enormity of the situation. It was Campion who spoke first.

'As amateurs,' he said judicially, 'you two only serve to show what a lot of undiscovered talent there is knocking about.'

He re-wrapped the Chalice and put it back into the suitcase.

All this time there was an ominous silence from Penny, and glancing at her he was afraid for one horrible moment that she was on the verge of tears.

'Look here,' he said, smiling at her from behind his spectacles, 'I know you think I've butted into this rather unwarrantably, but consider my position. In this affair I occupy the same sort of role as the Genie of the Lamp. Wherever the Chalice is I am liable to turn up at any moment.'

Penny's expression did not change for some seconds, and then, to his relief, a faint smile appeared at the corners of her mouth.

'How on earth did you know?' she said.

Mr Campion sighed with relief.

'The process of elimination,' said he oracularly as he picked up the suitcase and trudged back to the car with it, 'combined with a modicum of common sense, will always assist us to arrive at the correct conclusion with the maximum of possible accuracy and the minimum of hard labour. Which being translated means: I guessed it.' He lifted the case into the dickey once more, and held the door open for Penny and her companion.

She hung back. 'That's not fair,' she said. 'Suppose you explain?'

Mr Campion shrugged his shoulders. 'Well, it wasn't very difficult, was it?' he said. 'In the first place it was obvious that the chapel had not been burgled. Ergo, someone had opened the door with the key. Ergo, it must have been you, because the only other two people who could possibly have known where it was were your father and Branch, and they, if I may say so, are both a bit conservative on the subject of the Chalice.'

Penny bit her lip and climbed into the driving seat. 'Anyway,' she said, 'I'm the "Maid of the Cup".'

'Quite,' said Mr Campion. 'Hence your very natural feeling of responsibility.' He hesitated and looked at her owlishly. 'I bet I could tell you what you were going to do with it.'

'Well?' She looked at him defiantly.

Mr Campion laid his hand on that part of the suitcase which projected from the dickey. 'You were going to put this in Chancery Lane Safe Deposit,' he said.

Penny gasped at him, and there was a little smothered squeak from Beth. Mr Campion went on.

'You had relied on the ten days' veiling of the Chalice to keep its loss a secret, and I have no doubt you intended to confess the whole matter to Val and your father before they had any real cause for worry. Unfortunately, Mrs Shannon upset the apple-cart and you had to get busy right away. And that's why I was waiting for you this morning. Now shall we go on?'

Penny sat staring at him in bewilderment. 'It's not fair of you to look so idiotic,' she said involuntarily. 'People get led astray. I suppose you won't even be particularly bucked to know that you've guessed right?'

The young man with the simple face and gentle ineffectual manner looked uncomfortable.

'All this praise makes me unhappy,' he said. 'I must admit I wasn't sure until I was in the car this morning that you had the treasure in the suitcase. It was only when you were so anxious for me not to sit beside it that I knew that the rat I saw floating in the air was a *bona fide* rose to nip in the bud.'

Penny drew a deep breath. 'Well,' she said, 'I suppose we turn back.'

Mr Campion laid a hand on the driving wheel.

'Please,' he said pleadingly, with something faintly reminiscent of seriousness on his face, 'please listen to me for a little longer. You two have got to be friends with me. We're all in the soup together. Consider the facts. Here we are, sitting in the middle of a public highway with a highly incriminating piece of antiquity in the back of the car. That's bad to start with. Then – and this is much more worthy of note – if I was bright enough to spot what you were up to, what about our nosy friends who are out for crime anyhow?'

'You mean you think they might actually come down on us on the way?' said Penny apprehensively. This aspect of the case had clearly never occurred to her. 'And yet,' she added, a flash of suspicion showing in her blue eyes, 'it's perfectly ridiculous. How is any outside person to know that the Chalice isn't still in the Cup House? Only Father, Val, Branch, you and I know it's gone.'

'You forget,' said Mr Campion gently. 'You had visitors yesterday, and the unpleasant Mr Putnam, who is making use of your retiring little friend Mrs Shannon, had a face vaguely familiar to me.'

Penny's eyes flickered. 'That revolting little man?' she said. 'Is he the – the big fellow you were talking about? You know, when you said the stream was full of minnows and there were no big fish about.'

Mr Campion regarded her gravely. 'I'm afraid not,' he said. 'But he's certainly in the dab class. I fancy his real name is Matthew Sanderson. That's why I kept so quiet; I was afraid he might spot me. I don't think he did, but he certainly noticed that the Chalice had disappeared. Hang it all, he couldn't very well miss it. Anyhow, if he is the man I think he is, then I'm open to bet that he's not twenty miles away from here now.'

Penny looked at him helplessly. 'I've been a fool,' she said. 'We'll go back at once.'

Campion hesitated. 'Wait a minute,' he said, and glanced at Beth. 'I don't know if we ought to drag Miss Cairey into all this –'

An expression of determination appeared upon the elder girl's face, and her lips were set in a firm hard line.

'I'm in this with Penny,' she said.

To her surprise he nodded gravely. 'I told Val you'd be game,' he said. 'He should be waiting for us at a little pub called "The Case is Altered" just outside Coggeshall.'

'Val?' Penny was startled. 'What does he know about it?'

'Just about as much as I do,' said Mr Campion, considering. 'While you were shouting your travelling arrangements over the phone in the hall last night, he and I were discussing fat stock prices and whatnot in the smoking-room. I told him what I thought, and I persuaded him to let you carry on the good work and smuggle the thing out of the house for us.'

'Then you think it's a good idea – the safe deposit?' said Beth anxiously. 'I told Penny I was sure that was the only certain way of keeping it safe.'

Mr Campion did not answer her immediately. He had resumed his place in the car and sat regarding the dashboard thoughtfully as though he were making up his mind how much to say.

'Well, hardly, to begin with,' he ventured finally. 'Although perhaps it may come to that in the end. In the meantime I wondered if we couldn't beat our friend Arthur Earle at his own game. There's an old firm in the city – or rather the last remaining member of an old firm – who'd turn us out a first-rate copy of the Chalice, and somehow I'd rather be playing hide-and-seek with that than with the real one. I fancy we shall have to show a bait, you see, to catch the big fish.'

'Just one thing,' said Penny. 'What about Father? Does he know anything? I seem to have made a pretty prize fool of myself.'

Mr Campion looked if possible more vague than ever. 'Your father, I regret to say,' he murmured, and Penny was convinced that he was lying, 'I thought it best to keep in the dark. You left your own excuses. Val no doubt left mine and his own. But,' he went on gravely, 'that is hardly the most important point to be considered at the moment. What we have to arrange now is the safe conveyance of the Chalice to London.'

Penny swung the car up the narrow white road.

'I don't know if I'm going to agree with all this,' she said warningly, 'but I'd like to see Val. Of course, you're not really serious about this attack on the road, are you?'

Mr Campion regarded her solemnly. 'The chivalry of the road,' he said, 'is not what it was when I used to drive my four-in-hand to Richmond, don't you know. Natty Johnson is no Duval, but he might make a very fine Abbershaw, and old Putnam Sanderson can level a first-class blunderbuss. On the whole, I should think we were certainly in for fun of some sort.'

'But if this is true,' said Beth indignantly, 'why are we going on? How do you know we shan't be held up before we get to Coggeshall?'

'Deduction, dear lady,' explained Mr Campion obligingly. 'There are two roads from Sanctuary to Coggeshall. You might have taken either. After Coggeshall you must go straight to Kelvedon, and thence by main road. I fancy they'll be patrolling the main road looking for us.'

In spite of herself Penny was impressed. 'Well, you're thorough, anyway,' she said grudgingly.

'And clean,' said Mr Campion. 'In my last place the lady said no home was complete without one of these – hygienic, colourful, and only ten cents down. Get Campion-conscious today. Of course,' he went on, 'I suppose we could attempt to make a detour, but considering all things I think that the telephone wires are probably busy, and at the same time I'm rather anxious to catch a glimpse of our friends in action. I think the quicker we push on the better.'

Penny nodded. 'All right,' she said without resentment. 'We leave it to you.'

The Case is Altered was a small and unpretentious red brick building standing back from the road and fronted by a square gravel yard. Mr Campion descended, and cautiously taking the suitcase from the dickey, preceded the ladies into the bar parlour, an unlovely apartment principally ornamented by large oleographs of '*The Empty Chair*', '*The Death of Nelson*', and '*The Monarch of the Glen*', and furnished with vast quantities of floral china, bamboo furniture, and a pot of paper roses. The atmosphere was flavoured with new oilcloth and stale beer, and the motif was sedate preservation.

Val was standing on the hearthrug when they entered, a slightly amused expression on his face. Penny reddened when she saw him, and walking towards him raised her face defiantly to his.

'Well?' she said.

He kissed her.

'Honesty is the best policy, my girl,' he said. 'Have some ginger beer?'

Penny caught her brother's arm. 'Val, do you realize,' she said, 'here we are, miles from home, with the – the *Thing* actually in a portmanteau. I feel as if we might be struck by a thunderbolt for impudence.'

Val put his arm round her shoulders. 'Leave it to Albert,' he said. 'He spotted your little game. He seems to have one of his own.'

They turned to Campion inquiringly and he grinned. 'Well, look here,' he said, 'if you don't want to play darts or try the local beer or otherwise disport yourselves, I think the sooner we get on the better. What I suggest is that we split up. Penny, you and I will take the precious suitcase in the two-seater. Val and Miss Cairey will follow close behind to come to our assistance if necessary. Have you got enough petrol?' Penny looked at him in surprise. 'I think so,' she said, but as he hesitated she added, laughing, 'I'll go and see if you like.'

Mr Campion looked more foolish than before. 'Twice armed is he who speeds with an excuse, but thrice is he whose car is full of juice,' he remarked absently.

Penny went out, leaving the door open, and was just about to return after satisfying herself that all was well, when the young man came out of the doorway bearing the suitcase.

'We'll get on, if you don't mind,' he said. 'Val's just squaring up with the good lady of the establishment. They'll follow immediately.'

Penny glanced about her. 'Where is the other car?' she demanded.

There was a Ford trade van standing beside the bar entrance, but no sign of a private car.

'Round at the back,' said Campion glibly. 'There's a petrol pump there.'

He dropped the suitcase carefully into the back of the car and sprang in beside the girl. 'Now let's drive like fun,' he said happily. 'How about letting me have the wheel? I've got testimonials from every magistrate in the county.'

Somewhat reluctantly the girl gave up her place, but Mr Campion's driving soon resigned her to the change. He drove with the apparent omnipotence of the born motorist, and all the time he chattered happily in an inconsequential fashion that gave her no time to consider anyone or anything but himself.

'I love cars,' he said ecstatically. 'I knew a man once – he was a relation of mine as a matter of fact – who had one of the earliest of the breed. I believe it was a roller-skate to start with, but he kept on improving it and it got on wonderfully. About 1904 it was going really strong. It had gadgets all over it then: finally I believe he overdid the thing, but when I knew it you could light a cigarette from almost any pipe under the bonnet, and my relation made tea in the radiator as well as installing a sort of mechanical picnic-basket between the two back wheels. Then one day it died in Trafalgar Square and so –' he finished oracularly – 'the first coffee-stall was born. Phoenix-fashion, you know. But perhaps you're not liking this?' he ventured, regarding her anxiously. 'After all, I have been a bit trying this morning, haven't I?'

Penny smiled faintly at him.

'I don't really dislike you,' she said. 'No, go on. Some people drive better when they're talking, I think, don't you?'

'That's not how a young lady should talk,' said Mr Campion

reprovingly. 'It's the manners of the modern girl I deplore most. When I was a young man – years before I went to India, don't you know, to see about the Mutiny – women were women. Egad, yes. How they blushed when I passed.'

Penny shot a sidelong glance in his direction. He was pale and foolish-looking as ever, and seemed to be in deadly earnest.

'Are you trying to amuse me or are you just getting it out of your system?' she said.

'Emancipated, that's what you are,' said Mr Campion, suddenly dropping the Anglo-Indian drawl he had adopted for the last part of his homily. 'Emancipated and proud of yourself. Stap my crinoline, Amelia, if you don't think you're a better man than I am!'

Penny laughed. 'You're all right, really,' she said. 'When does the fun begin?'

'Any time from now on,' said Mr Campion gaily, as he swung the little car into the main road. Penny glanced nervously over her shoulder.

'There's no sign of the others yet,' she said.

Her companion looked faintly perturbed.

'Can't help that,' he said.

It was now about half-past eleven o'clock, and although a Friday morning, the road was not as crowded as it would become later in the day. Mr Campion drove fiercely, overtaking everything that presented itself. On the long straight strip outside Witham he once more broke into his peculiar brand of one-sided conversation.

'Then there's poetry,' he said. 'Here is today's beautiful thought:

> There was an ex-mayor in a garden
> A-playing upon a bombardon,
> His tunes were flat, crude,
> Broad, uncivic, rude,
> And –

'I don't like the look of that car which has just passed us. It's an old Staff Benz, isn't it? Sit still, and whatever you do don't try and hit anybody. If you lose your head it doesn't matter, but don't try to hit out.'

On the last word he jammed on the brakes and brought the car to a standstill only just in time, as the old German staff car, heavy as a lorry and fast as a racer, swerved violently across the road in front of them and came to a full stop diagonally across their path so that they were hemmed in by the angle. The whole thing was so neatly timed that there was no escape. It was only by brilliant driving that Mr Campion had succeeded in pulling up at all.

What took place immediately afterwards happened with the speed and precision of a well-planned smash-and-grab raid. Hardly were the two cars stationary before five men had slipped out of the Benz, the driver alone remaining in his seat, and the sports car was surrounded. The raiding party swarmed over the little car. There was no outward show of violence, and it was only when Penny glanced up into the face of the man who had stationed himself on the running-board at her side that she fully realized that the newcomers were definitely hostile.

She shot a sidelong terrified glance at Mr Campion, and saw that the man upon his side had laid a hand in an apparently friendly fashion on the back of his neck, the only untoward feature of the gesture being that in the hand was a revolver.

A third man leaned negligently against the bonnet, his hand in the pocket of his coat, while a fourth, with remarkable coolness, stood by the back of the Benz to signal that all was well to any passing motorist who might stop, suspecting a smash.

They were all heavy, flashily dressed specimens of the type only too well known to the racecourse bookmaker.

Penny opened her mouth. She was vaguely conscious of other cars on the road. The man at her side gripped her arm.

'Hold your tongue, miss,' he said softly. 'No yelping. Now then, where is it?'

Penny glanced at Albert. He was sitting very still, his expression a complete blank.

'No – no,' he said, in a slightly high-pitched voice, 'I do not wish to subscribe. I am not a music lover. Go and play outside the next house.'

The stranger's hand still rested caressingly on the back of his neck.

'Now then, no acting "crackers",' he said. 'Where is it?'

'You should take glycerine for your voice and peppermints for your breath, my friend,' continued Mr Campion querulously. 'Don't bellow at me. I'm not deaf.'

His interlocutor summoned the man who leant so negligently against the bonnet. 'There's nothing in the front of the car,' he said. 'Have a squint into the dickey.'

'No!' Penny could not repress a little cry of horror.

The man with the gun, who seemed to be in charge of the

proceedings, grinned. 'Thank you kindly, miss,' he said sarcastically. 'A girl and a loony. It's like stealing a bottle from a baby.'

'There's only my lunch in there,' said Mr Campion, but Penny noticed that his voice betrayed nothing but nervousness.

'Is that so?' The third man lifted out the suitcase. 'This is it,' he said. 'It weighs a ton. The rest of the car is empty, anyhow.'

Too terror-stricken to speak, Penny glanced wildly up the road only to see a Rolls-Royce and a van being waved on by their persecutors.

''Ere, these locks 'ave been bunged up,' said a voice behind her. 'Give us yer knife.'

The man with the gun glanced down the road, apprehensively it seemed to Penny. 'Stick it in the bus,' he said. 'There's nothing else here, anyhow. Now then, boys, scarpa!'

His four satellites were back in the Benz with the precious suitcase within ten seconds. The driver swung the car back with a roar, and the man with the gun gave up his position and leapt for it as it passed. They had chosen a moment when the coast was clear, and the whole astounding episode was over in a space of time a little under five minutes.

Mr Campion freed his brakes and started the engine, but instead of turning and following the retreating raiders as Penny had half hoped, half feared he would, he sent the car careering down the road towards London, and the speedometer finger crept round the dial like a stop watch.

It was not until they reached Witham and crawled through the narrow street that Mr Campion permitted himself a glance at his companion. Before then the car had occupied his whole attention. To his horror she was in tears. For the first time that day his nerve failed him.

Chapter 12
Holding the Baby

'*And he never stopped once to beg pardon*,' said Mr Campion, as he swung the sports car neatly into the big yard at the back of the Huguenots' Arms at Witham and brought it to a stop within a yard of the pump.

Penny hastily dabbed away her tears. 'What on earth are you talking about?'

'Poetry,' said Mr Campion. 'The highest within me. Soul juice, in fact. It's the last line of the Neo-Georgian sonnet I was declaiming to you when the rude gentleman with the acquisitive instinct stopped us. Don't you remember – about the civic person in the garden? I'd better recite the whole thing to you.'

Penny put out her hand appealingly. 'Don't,' she said. 'It's awfully good of you to try to cheer me up, but you can't realize, as a stranger, what this means. That suitcase contained the one thing that matters most in the world. I'm afraid I've lost my nerve completely. We must get to the police.'

Mr Campion sat perfectly still, regarding her with owlish solemnity.

'You're the first person I've met to feel so sensibly about a couple of bottles of bitter,' he said. 'I had no idea you'd get het-up like this.'

Penny stared at him, the truth slowly dawning upon her.

'Albert,' she said, 'you –'

He laid a hand upon her arm. 'Don't spoil the fun,' he said. 'Look.'

Even as he spoke there came the roar of an engine from outside and a trade van jolted slowly into the yard. The cab was facing them, and a gasp of mingled amusement and relief escaped Penny.

Val sat at the steering wheel, a peaked cup pulled well down over his eyes and a cheap yellow mackintosh buttoned tightly up to his throat. He had a strap buckled across one shoulder which suggested admirably the presence of a leather cash satchel. A pencil behind his ear finished the ensemble. The metamorphosis was perfect. Anyone would have been deceived.

The *chef-d'œuvre* of the outfit, however, was Beth. She had pushed her smart beret on to the back of her head, reddened her lips until they looked sticky, plastered a kiss-curl in the middle of her forehead, and had removed the jacket of her three-piece suit so that she was in a blouse and skirt. She was smiling complacently, her big dark eyes dancing with amusement. And in her arms, clasped tightly against her breast, was a precious bundle swaddled in white shawls with a lace veil over the upper part.

'There,' said Mr Campion. 'All done with a few common chalks. Our young Harry taking his missus and the kid for a trip during business hours. "Domesticity versus Efficiency", or "All His Own Work".'

Penny chuckled. 'You're wonderful,' she said. 'And the baby, of course –?'

'Is worth his weight in gold. Let's leave it at that,' said Mr Campion. 'Now, since this trip seems to have degenerated into a pub-crawl, suppose we go into the private room which Val I hope has booked on the phone and we'll shuffle and cut again.'

Ten minutes later, in a small and stuffy room on the first floor of the old road house, Mr Campion made his apologies to Penny.

'I've behaved like a common or garden toot,' he said with real penitence in his eyes. 'But you see, there wasn't time to go into full explanations at Coggeshall – and then you might not have agreed. And I did so want to get a squint at Uncle Beastly's boy friends in action. I didn't think there'd be any real danger, and there wasn't, you know. Will you forgive me?'

Penny sat down in a rickety wicker arm-chair. 'That's all right,' she said weakly. 'What happens next?'

Beth, who was standing before the mirror over the fireplace rearranging her make-up, turned to her friend.

'When we passed you, and the man who was holding you up signed to us to go on, I thought I'd die,' she said.

'If this had been a real baby I'd have squeezed the life out of it. They didn't suspect us for a moment, though, and later on, when you passed us again, we knew it was all right.'

Penny passed a hand over her forehead. 'Who worked it all out?' she said. 'I suppose you had the shawls and stuff with you, Val?'

Her brother nodded. 'When you went out to see if there was enough petrol we swapped the – the contents of the suitcase for a couple of quart bottles of bitter, and then I explained to Beth. She's been wonderful.'

He cast an admiring glance at the little dark-haired girl. Beth changed the subject.

'Did you find out what you wanted to know about the gangsters, Mr Campion?' she said. 'I mean – did you recognize any of them?'

'Yes and no, as they say in legal circles,' said Mr Campion. 'The unsavoury little object who leant on our bonnet, Penny, was our Natty Johnson, an old thorn in Lugg's flesh. Two others were "whizz boys" – pick-pockets or sneak-thieves, you know – and the gentleman who did the talking and tickled my neck with a gun muzzle is "Fingers" Hawkins, an old associate of "Putnam" Sanderson. All sound reliable workmen whose services can be obtained for a moderate fee. The driver I was unable to see, although his was a nice professional piece of work. They're now probably swigging the beer and playing "who says the rudest word". That's why we needn't fear reprisals at the moment. They've got no personal animosity, if you get me. They'll wait for instructions before they do anything else. It doesn't tell us much, unfortunately.'

Val lounged forward. 'Now I suppose we send these two kids home?' he said.

'A remark that might have been better put,' said Mr Campion mildly. 'What I was hoping we could persuade our two young female friends to do is to catch the twelve-thirty to Hadleigh from the station opposite, while we sally forth to the city in their car with their treasure.' He looked from one to the other of the two girls dubiously. 'I suppose you're going to be furious?' he inquired.

Penny looked disappointed, but Beth chuckled. 'I'll say they've got a nerve,' she said. 'Still, I guess we'll have to let them have their own way. This is strong man's work.' She imitated Val's somewhat unctuous delivery, and the boy laughed.

'She's been getting at me all the way along,' he said. 'You wait till this thing's over and I'll show you the lighter side of country life.'

Beth smiled. 'It's had its moments already,' she said, and placed the shawl-wrapped bundle in his arms.

'How about the van?' said Penny.

'That's all right,' said Val. 'I arranged with the man to leave it. It belongs to Mudds', of Ipswich. Now, suppose we get along?'

He insisted that he would accompany the girls to the station opposite, while Mr Campion got out the car and invested in another suitcase.

'When will you be back?' inquired Penny in the doorway.

'Tomorrow, if all goes well.' Campion spoke lightly. 'In the meantime rely on Lugg, my other ego. I don't think there's a chance of any trouble, but should the worst happen he's as good as a police force and about as beautiful. He's going to the nation when I die. Tell him not to wear my socks, by the way. Also my pullover in the School colours. I have spies everywhere.'

She laughed and went out. Mr Campion looked after her reflectively. 'Such a nice girl,' he observed to the world at large. 'Why in Heaven's name couldn't Marlowe Lobbett have waited a bit and picked on her instead of Biddy?'

He and Val were on the road again within twenty minutes. The younger man seemed much more cheerful than before.

'Do you know,' he confided after a long period of silence, 'there's something quite different about that girl, Beth. She's got a sort of charm. I've hated women for so long,' he went on diffidently, 'that it's marvellous to find one who breaks down your prejudices. In spite of your being such a funny bird you must know what I mean.'

'You forget I am wedded to my art,' said Mr Campion with great solemnity. 'Since I took up woodcraft women have had no place in my life.'

'I mean seriously,' said Val, a little nettled.

A slightly weary expression entered Mr Campion's pale eyes behind his enormous spectacles. 'Seriously, my dear old bird,' he said, 'Ophelia married Macbeth in my Hamlet. Now, for Heaven's sake get your mind on the business in hand.'

Val leant back in the car. 'You drive magnificently,' he said. 'I'm not sure if it's her voice or her eyes that are most attractive – which would you say?' he added irrelevantly.

Mr Campion did not reply immediately, and the little car sped on towards the city.

'We'll go straight there if you don't mind.' It was almost an hour later when he spoke again as he turned the car deviously through Aldgate and made for that ancient and slightly gloomy section of the city which is called Poultry.

Val sat forward.

'Not at all – good idea,' he said. 'Although, I say, Campion, you're sure it's safe?'

Mr Campion shrugged his shoulders. 'Melchizadek's safe enough,' he said. 'Patronized by all the best people since the first George, don't you know. And as silent as the grave. An old friend of mine, too. But, of course, I don't suppose he's bullet-proof if it comes to that. Still, I'd like his opinion on the chances of getting an undetectable copy made. Frankly, Val, how far back does this Chalice date?'

The younger man hesitated. 'It's hard to say, really,' he said at length. 'It's pre-Conquest, anyhow.'

Mr Campion all but stopped the car, and the face he turned towards his passenger was blank with astonishment. 'Look here,' he said, 'you don't mean to say this thing we've got in the suitcase is a thousand years old, do you?'

'My dear fellow, of course it is.' Val was a little hurt. 'You know the legends about it as well as I do.'

Mr Campion was silent, and the other went on. 'Why the amazement?' he demanded.

'Nothing,' said his companion. 'The idea suddenly struck me all of a heap, that's all. Here have we been playing "body in the bag" with it all the morning and its importance suddenly came home to me. Here we are, by the way.'

He turned the car dexterously into a narrow blind alley and pulled up outside a small old-fashioned shop, or rather a building with a shop window which had been half covered over with gold and black paint so that it resembled one of the many wholesale businesses with which the neighbourhood abounded. The heavy door with its shining brass trimmings stood ajar, and Mr Campion dismounted, and lifting out the new suitcase walked into the building, Val following him.

A small brass plate with the name 'I. Melchizedek' engraved upon it was fixed directly beneath the old-fashioned bell-pull. Val noticed that there was no sign of any other business in the building. He followed Campion into a large outer office with a flimsy wooden barrier across it. It all seemed very quiet and deserted, and save for two or three small showcases containing beautifully worked replicas of obscure medals and diplomatic jewellery there was no indication of the business of the firm.

Immediately upon their arrival a slight, suave young man rose from behind a roll-top desk set in the far corner behind the barrier and came towards them. Mr Campion took a card from his pocket and handed it to him.

'Will you ask Mr Melchizedek if he can spare me a few moments?' he asked.

The young man took the card and repeated the name aloud.

'Mr Christopher Twelvetrees.'

'Hullo,' said Val, 'you've made –'

To his astonishment Mr Campion signalled to him to be quiet and nodded to the clerk. 'That's all right,' he said. 'Mr Melchizadek knows me.'

As the young man disappeared Campion turned an apologetic face to his friend. 'I ought to have warned you about my many *noms de guerre*,' he said. 'It's just so that my best friends can't tell me. You won't forget, will you? I'm Christopher Twelvetrees until we get outside.'

Considerably bewildered, Val had only just time to nod in silent acquiescence when the door of the inner office through which the clerk had disappeared re-opened to admit one of the most striking-looking old men he had ever seen.

Mr Israel Melchizadek was that miracle of good breeding, the refined and intellectual Jew. Looking at him one was irresistibly reminded of the fact that his ancestors had ancestors who had conversed with Jehovah. He was nearing seventy years of age, a tall, lean old fellow with a firm delicate face of what might well have been polished ivory. He was clean-shaven and his white hair was cut close to his head. He came forward with outstretched hand.

'Mr Twelvetrees,' he said, 'I am pleased to see you.'

His voice had a luxurious quality which heightened the peculiar Oriental note of his whole personality. Campion shook hands and introduced Val.

The boy was conscious of little shrewd black eyes peering into his face, summing him up with unerring judgement. In spite of himself he was impressed. Mr Melchizadek glanced at the suitcase.

'If you'll come into my office, Mr Twelvetrees,' he said, 'we can speak without being overheard or interrupted.'

He led the way through the second doorway down a short corridor, and ushered them into a small luxurious room which served as a perfect frame for his remarkable personality.

The floor was covered with an ancient Persian rug, while the walls were hung with fine paintings; a David, a Zoffany, and, over the mantel, the head of a very beautiful woman by de Laszlo.

An immense table desk took up most of the room, and after setting chairs for his clients Mr Melchizadek sat down behind it.

'Now, Mr Twelvetrees,' he said, 'what can I do for you?' He hesitated. 'You wish me to make a copy, perhaps? Perhaps of a certain very famous chalice?'

Mr Campion raised his eyebrows.

'Taking the long road, sir?' he inquired affably.

The old man shook his head and for a moment his thin lips parted in a smile.

'No, my friend,' he said. 'I have too many clients to follow any road but my own.'

Campion sighed. 'Thank Heaven for that,' he said. 'Well, of course, you're right. I see you appreciate the gravity of the situation. What we've got here is nothing more nor less than the Gyrth Chalice.'

He picked up the suitcase and laid it reverently upon the desk. The old man rose and came forward.

'I have never seen it,' he said, 'although of course its history – or rather its legend – is quite well known to me. Really, this is going to be a most delightful experience for me, Mr Gyrth,' he added, glancing at Val. 'In the last two hundred years we have been privileged to handle many treasures, but even so this is a memorable occasion.'

'Over a thousand years old,' said Mr Campion profoundly, and, Val thought, a little foolishly, as if he were particularly anxious to impress the date on the old man's mind. 'Over a thousand years.'

He carefully unlocked the suitcase, and having first removed the motor rug, produced the Chalice, still in its wrapping of shawls.

Mr Melchizadek was surprised and even a little shocked, it seemed to Val, by this unconventional covering. However, he said nothing until Mr Campion took off the last shawl and placed the golden cup in his hands.

The picture was one that Val never forgot. The tall, austere old man appraising the magnificent workmanship with long delicate fingers. He turned the relic over and over, peering at it through a small jeweller's glass; glancing beneath it, inside it, and finally setting it down upon the desk, and turning to his visitors. He seemed a little puzzled, ill at ease.

'Mr Twelvetrees,' he said slowly, 'we are old friends, you and I.'

Mr Campion met his eyes.

'Mr Gyrth here, and I,' he said with apparent irrelevancy, 'can swear to you that that is the Gyrth Chalice. What can you tell us about it?'

For the first time Val sensed that something was wrong, and rising from his chair came to stand beside the others.

Mr Melchizadek picked up the Chalice again.

'This is a beautiful piece,' he said. 'The workmanship is magnificent, and the design is almost a replica of the one in the church of San Michele at Vecchia. But it is not medieval. I am not sure, but I believe that if you will allow me to look up our records, I can tell you the exact date when it was made.'

An inarticulate cry escaped Val, and he opened his mouth to speak angrily. Mr Campion restrained him.

'Hang on a bit, old bird,' he murmured. 'This thing's getting more complicated every minute. I fancy we're on the eve of a discovery.'

The silence which followed was broken by Mr Melchizadek's quiet voice.' I would rather you did not take my word for it, Mr Twelvetrees,' he said. 'I should like a second opinion myself. I am an old man, and remarkable freaks of period do occur. I wonder, therefore, if you would allow me to introduce a friend of mine into this discussion? Quite by chance I have in the next room one of the most famous experts on this subject in the world. He was calling on me when you arrived, and did me the honour to wait until I should be disengaged. What do you say?' He turned from Campion to Val. The boy was scarlet and frankly bewildered. Mr Melchizadek coughed.

'You can rely upon his discretion as you would upon mine,' he murmured.

'Oh, certainly,' said Val hurriedly, and Campion nodded to the old expert, who went silently out of the room.

Val turned to Campion. 'This is madness,' he said huskily. 'It –'

Mr Campion laid a hand upon his shoulder. 'Hold on,' he said, 'let them do the talking. I believe I'm getting this thing straight at last.'

He had no time for further confidences as Mr Melchizadek reappeared, and behind him came a slight, agile little man, with a high forehead and a pointed vandyke beard. His appearance was familiar to both of them, and they had recognized him even before Mr Melchizadek's opening words.

'This, gentlemen, is Professor Gardner Cairey, a great American authority. Professor Cairey, allow me to present to you Mr Gyrth and Mr Christopher Twelvetrees.'

Chapter 13

'I. Melchizadek Fecit'

There was a considerable pause after the introductions. Professor Cairey stood looking at the two young men, a slightly dubious expression in his eyes, and Val, for the first time, took good stock of him.

He was a little dapper old man, with the same delightful air of suppressed enjoyment that was so noticeable in his daughter. His face was keen and clever without being disconcertingly shrewd, and there was a friendliness about him which impressed the two immediately.

He was the first to speak, revealing a quiet, pleasant voice, with a definite transatlantic intonation which somehow underlined his appreciation of the oddity of the situation. He smiled at Mr Melchizadek.

'This is a whale of a problem,' he said. 'Luck has caught me out. I'm not on speaking terms with Mr Gyrth's folk, and I owe him an apology, anyway.'

Then he laughed, and instantly the tension relaxed. Val would have spoken had not Campion rested a hand on his arm, and Professor Cairey continued.

'I've been what my daughter would call a Kibitzer,' he said. 'In fact, I even went so far as to trespass in your garden a day or two back, Mr Gyrth. I didn't think I was seen, but in case I was perhaps I'd better explain.'

Val could not be restrained. 'I'm afraid we did see you, Professor,' he said. 'You were looking into the chapel.'

The old man grimaced. 'I was,' he said. 'I was half-way through my new book, *The Effect of the Commonwealth on East Anglian Ecclesiastical Decoration*, and I don't mind telling you I was hoping – well, to get some assistance from you folk. But I got myself in wrong with your Pa somehow, and I was as far off from the inside of your chapel as I should have been if I'd stayed at home in Westport, NJ.' He hesitated and glanced at them with bright, laughing eyes. 'I stuck it as long as I could,' he went on, 'and then the other night, before I heard of your trouble, I felt I'd attempt to have a look and finish my chapter if it meant being chased by a gardener's boy.'

Val reddened. 'I haven't been at home,' he said. 'And, of course, I'm afraid my poor aunt made things rather difficult. I'd be delighted to take you over the place any time. As a matter of fact,' he added transparently, 'I came up to Town part of the way with your daughter.'

Mr Campion, who had been silent so far during the interview, regarded the Professor with eyes that laughed behind his spectacles.

'Professor Cairey,' he said, 'you're the author of *Superstition before Cotton Mather*, aren't you?'

Professor Cairey positively blushed. 'That's so, Mr Twelvetrees,' he said, laying particular stress on the name. 'I didn't think anyone on this side took any stock of it.'

Val had the uncomfortable impression that these two were getting at one another with a certain playfulness which he did not understand.

Mr Campion's manner then became almost reverential. 'I owe you an apology, sir,' he said. 'I don't mind telling you we thought you were a bird of a very different feather. In fact,' he added with alarming frankness, 'we thought you were out after the Chalice.'

Mr Melchizadek looked horrified and muttered a word of protest. The professor soothed him with a smile.

'So I was,' he said, 'in a way.' He turned to Val and explained himself. 'Of course, I've long been familiar with the history of your great treasure, Mr Gyrth. It's one of the seven wonders of the world, in my estimation. I was naturally anxious to get a glimpse of it if I could. I had heard that there was one day in the week when it was displayed to the public, and I'd have availed myself of that, only, as I say, the Cup was hidden behind bars in a bad light and there was this mite of trouble between your aunt and Mrs Cairey, and while I was hoping that the little contretemps would blow over, your poor aunt met her death, and naturally I could hardly come visiting.'

Val, who seemed to have fallen completely under the spell of the old man's charming personality, would have launched out into a stream of incoherent apologies for what he knew instinctively was some appalling piece of bad manners from the late Lady Pethwick, when Mr Melchizadek's suave gentle voice forestalled him.

'I think,' he ventured, 'that if you would allow Professor Cairey to examine the Chalice on the table he could give an opinion of interest to all of us.'

'By all means.' Mr Campion stepped aside from the desk and revealed the Cup. The Professor pounced upon it with enthusiasm. He took it up, turned it over, and tested the metal with his thumb.

'I'll take the loan of your glass, Melchizadek,' he said. 'This is a lovely thing.'

They stood watching him, fascinated. His short capable fingers moved caressingly over the ornate surface. He appraised it almost movement for movement as Mr Melchizadek had done. Finally he set it down.

'What do you want to know about it?' he said.

'What is it?' said Mr Campion quickly, before Val could get a word in.

The Professor considered. 'It's a church chalice,' he said. 'The design is Renaissance. But the workmanship I should say is of much later date. It's about a hundred and fifty years old.'

Val looked at Campion dumbly, and Mr Melchizadek took the treasure.

'I thought so,' he said. 'If you will permit me, Mr Gyrth, I think I could prove this to you. I didn't like to suggest it before in case I was mistaken.'

He took a small slender-bladed knife from a drawer, and after studying the jewelled bosses round the pedestal of the cup through his lens for some minutes, finally began to prise gently round the base of one of them. Suddenly an exclamation of gratification escaped him, and putting down the instrument he unscrewed the jewel and its setting and laid it carefully on the desk. As the others crowded round him he pointed to the tiny smooth surface that was exposed.

There, only just decipherable, was the simple inscription, engraved upon the metal:

I. Melchizadek fecit
1772

'My great-grandfather,' said Mr Melchizadek simply, 'the founder of this firm. He invariably signed every piece that he made, although at times it was necessary for him to do so where it would not be seen by the casual observer.'

'But,' said Val, refusing to be silenced any longer, 'don't you see what this means? This is what has passed for the last – well, for my own and my father's lifetime – as the Gyrth Chalice.'

For a moment the Professor seemed as stupefied as Val. Then a light of understanding crept into his eyes. He crossed over to Mr Campion.

'Mr Twelvetrees,' he murmured, 'I'd like to have a word with you and Mr Gyrth in private. Maybe there's somewhere where we could go and talk.'

Mr Campion regarded him shrewdly from behind his heavy spectacles. 'I was hoping that myself,' he said.

Meanwhile Val, still inarticulate and bewildered, was standing staring at the handiwork of the Melchizadek great-grandparent as if he had never seen it before. Professor Cairey took the situation in hand. He bade farewell to the old Jew, with whom he seemed to be on intimate terms, the Chalice was repacked in the suitcase, and ten minutes later all three of them were squeezed into the two-seater worming their way from the City to the West End.

It did just occur to Val that this acceptance of Professor Cairey was a little sudden, to say the least of it. But the Professor was so obviously bona fide, and his disposition so kindly, that he himself was prepared to trust him to any lengths within ten minutes of their first meeting. However, Mr Campion had never struck him as being the possessor of a particularly trusting spirit, and he was surprised.

Before they had reached Piccadilly Campion had re-introduced himself with charming naïveté, and by the time they mounted the stairs to the flat they were talking like comparatively old friends.

Val, who had been considerably astonished by the open way in which Campion had approached the place, now glanced across at him as he set a chair for their visitor.

'Last time I came here,' he remarked, 'I understood from you that I was liable to be plugged at any moment if I went outside the door. Why no excitement now?'

'Now,' said Mr Campion, 'the damage is done, as far as they're concerned. It must be obvious by this time to everyone interested that you and I are on the job together. To put a bullet through you would be only wanton destructiveness. The good news has been brought from Aix to Ghent, as it were. Your father knows there's danger, Scotland Yard knows, every 'tec in the country may be on the job. "George's" minions may be watching outside, but I doubt it.'

Professor Cairey, who had been listening to this conversation, his round brown eyes alert with interest and his hands folded across his waist, now spoke quietly.

'I haven't been able to help gathering what the trouble is,' he remarked.

Val shrugged his shoulders. 'After Mr Melchizadek's discoveries,' he said slowly, 'the trouble becomes absurd. In fact, the whole thing is a tragic fiasco,' he added bitterly.

The Professor and Campion exchanged glances. It was the old man who spoke, however.

'I shouldn't waste your time thinking that, son,' he said. 'See here,' he added, turning to Campion, 'I'll say you'd better confess to Mr Gyrth right now, and then perhaps we can get going.'

Val looked quickly at Campion who came forward modestly.

'The situation is a delicate one,' he murmured. 'However, perhaps you're right and now is the time to get things sorted out. The truth is, Val, I had my doubts about the Chalice the moment I saw the photograph of it. Before I looked you up, therefore, I paid a visit to my old friend Professor Cairey, the greatest living expert on the subject, who, I discovered, was staying next door to the ancestral home. This is not the coincidence it sounds, you see. The Professor has confessed why he rented the next place to yours. He couldn't tell me for certain from the photographs, although he had very grave doubts.' He paused, and the American nodded. Campion continued:

'Since there was a little friction between your aunt and her neighbours, I couldn't very well introduce the Professor into the bosom of the family right away. I regret to say, therefore, that I called on him, and begged him to meet me up at Melchizadek's. You see, I knew it would take more than one expert opinion to convince you that the Chalice wasn't all it set itself up to be.' He paused and stood looking hesitantly at the younger man. 'I'm awfully sorry,' he said apologetically. 'You see, I was going to persuade you to bring it up to be copied, and then the girls pinched it so obligingly for us.'

Val sank down in a chair and covered his face with his hands. 'It's beyond me,' he said. 'It seems to be the end of everything.'

The Professor leant forward in his chair, and the expression upon his wise, humorous face was very kindly.

'See here,' he said, 'I don't want to upset any family arrangement whereby you're told certain things at a certain age. Also I appreciate the delicacy of the matter I'm presuming to discuss. But, if you'll permit me, I'd like to tell you certain facts that occur to me as they might to anyone who looked at this matter from the outside without being hampered by a lifelong association with one idea.'

He paused, and Val, looking up, listened to him intently.

'If you ask me,' went on the Professor, 'I'd say that that very lovely piece which you have in the case there, and which has been in your chapel for the last hundred and fifty odd years, is what might be called a "mock chalice". You see,' he continued, warming up to his subject, 'most ancient ideas were simple, obvious notions; uncomplicated methods of preserving the safety of a treasure. Now in my opinion that "mock chalice", as we'll call it, is the last of many such – probably all different in design. The real Chalice has always been kept in the background – hidden out of sight – while the show-piece took its place to appease sightseers and thieves and so forth.'

Val took a deep breath. 'I follow you,' he said, a glimmer of hope appearing in his eyes. 'You mean that the real Chalice is too valuable to be on show?'

'Absolutely – when there were marauders like your great patriot Cromwell about.' The Professor spoke with the hint of a chuckle in his voice. 'There are two or three examples of this happening before. I've made a study of this sort of thing, you know. In fact,' he added, 'I could probably tell you more about the history of your own Chalice than anyone in the world outside your own family. For instance, in the time of Richard the Second it was said to have been stolen, and again just after the Restoration. But the Gyrths' lands were never forfeited to the Crown as they would certainly have been had the real Chalice been stolen. Queen Anne granted another charter, ratifying, so to speak, your family's possession of the genuine thing.'

He paused at the boy's surprise, and Campion grinned.

'The Professor's a true son of his country – he knows more about ours than we do,' he remarked.

Val sat back in his chair. 'Look here,' he said, 'if this is the "mock chalice", as you call it, why can't we let these infernal thieves, whoever they are, have it, and say no more about it?'

Mr Campion shook his head. 'That's no good,' he said. 'In the first place they'd spot it from the thing itself, just as we have; and in the second place, unless this forfeiting business of lands and whatnot was at any rate discussed, they'd know they hadn't got the real thing and they wouldn't be happy until they had. Infernally tenacious beggars, "Ethel" and "George". No, our original scheme is the only one. We've got to find the big fish and hook him.'

'You see, Mr Gyrth,' the Professor put in slowly, 'everything that I have told you this morning would be perfectly obvious to an intelligent thief. I imagine the people you have to deal with are men of taste and discrimination. Once they had handled this Chalice themselves they'd be bound to come to the same conclusion as I have. Unfortunately it has been described by several ancient writers. Modern delinquents have much more opportunity of finding out historical facts than their medieval counterparts.'

'My dear old bird,' said Mr Campion, 'don't look so funereal. They don't know this yet, rest assured of that. There are probably only five people in the world at present aware of the existence of the second Chalice, and in order to preserve the secret of the real one we must hang on to the "mock chalice" like a pair of bull pups.'

'Yes, I see that.' Val spoke slowly. 'But where is the real Chalice – buried somewhere?'

The Professor cleared his throat. 'As an outsider,' he began, 'I hardly like to put forward the suggestion, but it seems perfectly obvious to me – allowing for the medieval mind – that that point will be made quite clear to you on your twenty-fifth birthday.'

Val started violently. '*The Room!*' he said. 'Of course.'

For a moment he was lost in wonderment. Then his expression changed and there was something that was almost fear in his eyes.

'But that's not all,' he said huskily. It was evident that the subject so long taboo had rankled in his mind, for he spoke with eagerness, almost with relief, at being able at last to speak his pent-up suspicions.

'The room in the east wing,' he said solemnly, 'contains something terrible. Do you know, Campion, I may be crazy, but I can't help feeling that it's no ordinary museum exhibit. All my life my father has been overshadowed by something. I mean,' he went on, struggling vainly to express himself, 'he has something on his mind – something that's almost too big for it. And my grandfather was the same. This is not a subject that's ever spoken of, and I've never mentioned it before to a soul, but there *is* something there, and it's something awe-inspiring.'

There was a short silence after he had spoken, and the Professor rose to his feet. 'I don't think there's any doubt,' he said quietly, 'that the real Chalice, which is made of English red gold, and is probably little bigger than a man's cupped hand, has a very terrible and effective guardian.'

Chapter 14

Fifty-seven Varieties

'All these things are ordained, as the old lady said at the Church Congress,' observed Mr Campion. 'Everything comes to an end, and we're certainly getting a bit forrader. We shall have another expert opinion in a moment or so. My friend Inspector Stanislaus Oates is a most delightful cove. He'll turn up all bright and unofficial and tell us the betting odds.'

He sank down in an arm-chair opposite Val and lit a cigarette. His friend stirred uneasily.

'We *are* having a day with the experts, aren't we?' he said. 'I say, I like the Professor. Why did you keep him up your sleeve so long?'

Mr Campion spread out his hands. 'Just low cunning,' he said. 'A foolish desire to impress. Also, you must remember, I didn't know you very well. You might not have been the sort of young person for him to associate with. Besides that, Mrs Cairey – a most charming old dear, by the way – and your aunt were playing the old feminine game of spit-scratch-and-run among the tea-cups. Sans "purr" seems to have been your aunt's motto.'

Val frowned. 'Aunt Di,' he said, 'was what Uncle Lionel's brother Adolphe used to call a freak of Nature. I remember him saying to me: "Val, my boy, you never get a woman who is a complete fool. Many men achieve that distinction, but never a woman. The exception which proves that rule is your Aunt Diana." He didn't like her. I wonder what she said to Mrs Cairey. Something offensive, I'll bet.'

'Something about the "Pilgrim Fathers being Non-conformists, anyhow", I should think,' said Mr Campion judicially, as he adjusted his glasses. 'Hullo,' he added, pricking up his ears, 'footsteps on the stairs. "And that, if I mistake not, Watson, is our client." He's early. As a rule they don't let him out till half-past six.'

He did not trouble to rise, but shouted cheerfully: 'Enter the Byng Boy! Lift the latch and come in.'

A long silence followed this invitation. Mr Campion shouted again.

'Come right in. All friends here. Leave your handcuffs on the hook provided by the management.'

There was a footstep in the passage outside, and the next moment the door of the room in which they sat was pushed cautiously open, and a small white face topped by a battered trilby hat peered through the opening. Mr Campion sprang to his feet.

'Ernie Walker!' he said. 'Shoo! Shoo! Scat! We've got a policeman coming up here.'

The pale unlovely face split into a leer. 'That's all right,' he said. 'I'm out on tick. All me papers signed up proper. I got something to tell yer. Something to make yer sit up.'

Mr Campion sat down again. 'Come in,' he said. 'Shut the door carefully behind you. Stand up straight, and wipe the egg off your upper lip.'

The leer broadened. 'I can grow a moustache if I like, can't I?' said Mr Walker without malice. He edged into the room, revealing a lank, drooping figure clad in dingy tweeds grown stiff with motor-grease. He came towards Campion with a slow self-conscious swagger.

'I can do you a bit o' good, I can,' he said. 'But it'll cost yer a fiver.'

'Just what they say in Harley Street, only not so frankly,' said Mr Campion cheerfully. 'What are you offering me? Pills? Or do you want to put me up for your club?'

Ernie Walker jerked his thumb towards Val. 'What about 'im?' he demanded.

'That's all right. He's the Lord Harry,' said Campion. 'No one of importance. Carry on. What's the tale?'

'I said a fiver,' said Ernie, removing his hat, out of deference, Val felt, to the title his friend had so suddenly bestowed upon him.

'You'll never get a job on the knocker like that,' said Mr Campion reprovingly. 'Get on with your fanny.'

Ernie winked at Val. 'Knows all the words, don't 'e?' he said. 'If 'e was as bright as 'e thinks 'e is 'e'd 'ave spotted me this morning.'

Mr Campion looked up. 'Good Lord! You drove the Benz,' he said. 'You'll get your papers "all torn up proper" if you don't look out.'

'Steady on – steady on. I wasn't doin' nothin'. Drivin' a party for an outin' – that's wot I was up to.' Ernie's expression was one of outraged innocence. 'And if you don't want to know anything, you needn't. I'm treatin' yer like a friend and yer start gettin' nasty.' He put on his hat.

'No need to replace the divot,' said Mr Campion mildly. 'You were hired for the job, I suppose?'

'That's right,' said Ernie. 'And I thought you might pay a fiver to find out who hired me.'

Mr Campion sighed. 'If you've come all this way to tell me that Matthew Sanderson doesn't like me,' he said, 'you're a bigger fool than I am, Gunga Din.'

'If it comes to callin' names,' said Mr Walker with heat, as he struggled to repress his disappointment, 'I know me piece as well as anybody.'

Campion raised a hand warningly. 'Hush,' he said, indicating Val. 'Remember the Aristocracy. Is that all you have to offer?'

'No, it ain't. Certainly Matt Sanderson engaged me, but he's working for another feller. While I was tuning up the car I kept me ears open and I 'eard 'im talkin' about the big feller. You never know when a spot of information may be useful, I says to meself.'

Mr Campion's eyes flickered behind his big spectacles. 'Now you're becoming mildly interesting,' he said.

'It's five quid,' said Ernie. 'Five quid for the name o' the bloke Sanderson was workin' for.'

Mr Campion felt for his note-case. 'It's this cheap fiction you read,' he grumbled. 'This thinking in terms of fivers. Your dad would come across for half a crown.' He held up five notes like a poker hand.

'Now,' he said, 'out with it.'

Ernie became affable. 'You're a gent,' he said, 'that's what you are. One of the nobs. Well, I 'eard Sanderson say to a pal of 'is – a stranger to the game – "I shall 'ave to answer to The Daisy for this." That was when we was drinkin' up the beer you left in the bag. Mind yer – I didn't know it was you until I saw yer in the car. You 'ad the laugh of 'em all right. They was wild.'

'The Daisy,' said Mr Campion. 'Are you sure?'

'That was the name. I remember it becos Alf Ridgway, the chap they used to call The Daisy, was strung up two years ago. At Manchester, that was.'

'Oh,' said Mr Campion, and passed over the notes. 'How's the car business?'

'As good as ever it was.' Mr Walker spoke with enthusiasm. 'I sold a lovely repaint in Norwood last week. My brother pinched it up at Newcastle. Brought it down to the garage and we faked it up lovely – registration book and everything. I was the mug, though. The dirty little tick I sold it to – a respectable 'ouseholder, too – passed a couple o' dud notes off on me. Dishonest, that's what people are half the time.'

'Hush,' said Mr Campion, 'here comes Stanislaus.'

Ernie pocketed the notes hastily and turned expectantly towards the doorway. A moment later Inspector Stanislaus Oates appeared. He was a tall, greyish man, inclined to run to fat at the stomach, but nowhere else.

'Hullo,' he said, 'do you always leave the front door open?' Then, catching sight of Ernie, he added with apparent irrelevancy: 'O – my – aunt!'

'I'm just off, sir.' Indeed, Ernie was already moving towards the door. 'I come up 'ere visitin'. Same as you, I 'ope,' he added, cocking an eye slyly at his host.

Campion chuckled. 'Shut the door behind you,' he said pointedly. 'And remember always to look at the watermark.'

'What's that?' said Inspector Oates suspiciously. But already the door had closed behind the fleeting figure of the car thief, and they were alone.

Campion introduced Val, and poured the detective a whisky-and-soda. The man from Scotland Yard lounged back in his chair.

'What are you doing with that little rat?' he demanded, waving his hand in the direction of the door through which Mr Ernest Walker had so lately disappeared. He turned to Val apologetically: 'Whenever I come up to see this man,' he said, 'I find someone on our books having a drink in the kitchen or sunning himself on the mat. Even his man is an unreformed character.'

'Steady,' said Mr Campion. 'The name of Lugg is sacred. I'm awfully glad you've turned up, old bird,' he went on. 'You're just the man I want. Do you by any chance know of a wealthy, influential man-about-the-underworld called "The Daisy"?'

'Hanged in Manchester the twenty-seventh of November, 1928,' said the man from Scotland Yard promptly. 'Filthy case. Body cut in pieces, and what-not. I remember that execution. It was raining.'

'Wrong,' said Mr Campion. 'Guess again. I mean a much more superior person. Although,' he added despondently, 'it's a hundred to one on his being an amateur.'

'There are fifty-seven varieties of Daisy that I know of,' said Mr Oates. 'If you use it as a nickname. But they're small fry – very small fry, all of 'em. What exactly are you up to now? Or is it a State Secret again?'

He laughed, and Val began to like this quiet, homely man with the twinkling grey eyes.

'Well, I'm taking the short road, as a matter of fact,' said Mr Campion, and added, as his visitor looked puzzled, 'as opposed to the long one, if you get my meaning.'

The Inspector was very silent for some moments. Then he sighed and set down his glass. 'You have my sympathy,' he said. 'If you go playing with fire, my lad, you'll get burnt one of these days. What help do you expect from me?'

'Don't you worry,' said Mr Campion, ignoring the last question. 'I shall live to be present at my godson's twenty-first. Nineteen years hence, isn't it? How is His Nibs?'

For the first time the Inspector's face became animated. 'Splendid,' he said. 'Takes the Mickey Mouse you sent him to bed with him every night. I say, you understand I'm here utterly unofficially,' he went on hurriedly. 'Although if you haven't already lost whatever you're looking after why not put it in our hands absolutely, and leave it at that?' He paused. 'The trouble with you,' he added judicially, 'is that you're so infernally keen on your job. You'll get yourself into trouble.'

Mr Campion rose to his feet. 'Look here, Stanislaus,' he said, 'you know as well as I do that in ninety-nine cases out of a hundred the police are the only people in the world to protect a man and his property. But the hundredth time, when publicity is fatal, and the only way out is a drastic spot of eradication, then the private individual has to get busy on his own account. What I want to talk to you about, however, is this. You see that suitcase over there?' He pointed to the new fibre suitcase resting upon a side table. 'That,' he said, 'has got to be protected for the next few days. What it contains is of comparatively small intrinsic value, but the agents of our friends of the long road are after it. And once they get hold of it a very great State treasure will be in jeopardy. Do you follow me?'

The Inspector considered. 'Speaking officially,' he said, 'I should say: "My dear sir, put it in a bank, or a safe deposit, or the cloakroom of a railway station – or give it to me and I'll take it to the Yard".'

'Quite,' said Mr Campion. 'But speaking as yourself, personally, to an old friend who's in this thing up to the hilt, then what?'

'Then I'd sit on it,' said the Inspector shortly. 'I wouldn't take it outside this door. This is about the safest place in London. You're over a prominent police station. I'd have a Bobby on the doorstep, a couple in old Rodriguez's cookshop, and a plain-clothes man on the roof. You can hire police protection, you know.'

'Fine,' said Mr Campion. 'How do you feel about that, Val? You stay up here with the suitcase with a small police force all round you, while I go down to Sanctuary and make an intensive effort to get a line on The Daisy?'

Val nodded. 'I'll do anything you like,' he said. 'I'm completely in your hands. There's one thing, though. You've only got four days. Next Wednesday is the second.'

'That's so,' said Mr Campion. 'Well, four days, then. Can you fix up the bodyguard, Stanislaus?'

'Sure.' The Inspector picked up the telephone, and after ten minutes' intensive instruction set it down again. 'There you are,' he said. 'Endless official forms saved you. It'll cost you a bit. Money no object, I suppose, though? By the way,' he added, 'hasn't an order come through to give you unofficially any assistance for which you may ask?'

Campion shot him a warning glance and he turned off the remark hastily. 'I probably dreamt it,' he said. He looked at Val curiously, but the boy had not noticed the incident.

'That's settled, then,' said Mr Campion. 'I'll wait till you're all fixed up, and go back to Sanctuary tomorrow morning. You'll find everything you want here, Val. I suppose it'll be all right with your pater?'

Val grinned. 'Oh, Lord, yes,' he said. 'He seems to have taken you for granted since the first time he heard of you, which is rather odd, but still – the whole thing's incomprehensible. I've ceased to marvel.'

The Inspector rose and stood beside his friend. 'Take care,' he said. 'Four days isn't long to nail down a chosen expert of *Les Inconnus* and write full-stop after his name. And besides,' he added with unmistakable gravity, 'I should hate to see you hanged.'

Mr Campion held out his hand. 'A sentiment which does you credit, kind sir,' he said. But there was a new solemnity beneath the lightness of his words, and the pale eyes behind the horn-rimmed spectacles were hard and determined.

Chapter 15

Pharisees' Clearing

When Mr Campion sailed down the drive of the Tower at about ten o'clock the next morning, Penny met him some time before he reached the garage. She came running across the sunlit lawn towards him, her yellow hair flopping in heavy braids against her cheeks.

Campion stopped the car and she sprang on to the running-board. He noticed immediately a certain hint of excitement in her manner, and her first words were not reassuring.

'I'm so glad you've come,' she said. 'Something terrible has happened to Lugg.'

Mr Campion took off his spectacles as though to see her better.

'You're joking,' he said hopefully.

'Of course I'm not.' Penny's blue eyes were dark and reproachful. 'Lugg's in bed in a sort of fit. I haven't called the doctor yet, as you said on the phone last night that you'd be down early.'

Mr Campion was still looking at her in incredulous amazement. 'What do you mean? A sort of fit?' he said. 'Apoplexy or something?'

Penny looked uncomfortable and seemed to be debating how much to say. Eventually she took a deep breath and plunged into the story.

'It happened about dawn,' she said. 'I woke up hearing a sort of dreadful howling beneath my window. I looked out, and there was Lugg outside on the lawn. He was jumping about like a maniac and bellowing the place down. I was just going down myself when Branch, whose room is over mine, you know, scuttled out and fetched him in. No one could do anything with him. He was gibbering and raving, and very puffed.' She paused. 'It may seem absurd to say so, but it looked to me like hysterics.'

Mr Campion replaced his glasses. 'What an extraordinary story,' he said. 'I suppose he hadn't found the key to the wine cellars, by any chance?'

'Oh, no, it wasn't anything like that.' Penny spoke with unusual gravity. 'Don't you see what happened? He'd been down to Pharisees' Clearing. He saw what Aunt Di saw.'

Her words seemed to sink into Mr Campion's brain slowly. He sat motionless in the car in the middle of the drive staring in front of him.

'My hat,' he said at last. 'That's a step in the right direction, if you like. I only meant to keep the old terror occupied. I had no idea there'd be any serious fun toward.'

He started the car and crawled slowly forward, the girl beside him.

'Albert,' she said severely, 'you didn't tell him to go down there at night, did you? Because, if so, you're directly responsible for this. You didn't believe me when I told you there was something fearful there. You seem to forget that it killed Aunt Di.'

Mr Campion looked hurt. 'Your Aunt Diana and my friend Magersfontein Lugg are rather different propositions,' he said. 'I only told him to improve the shining hour by finding out what it was down there. I'll go and see him at once. What does Branch say about it?'

'Branch is very discreet,' murmured Penny. 'Look here, you'd better leave the car here and go straight up.'

Mr Campion raced up the narrow staircase at the back of the house which led to the servants' quarters, the expression of hurt astonishment still on his face. He found Branch on guard outside Mr Lugg's door. The little old man seemed very shaken and his delight at seeing Campion was almost pitiful.

'Oh, sir,' he said, 'I'm so glad you've come. It's all I can do to keep 'im quiet. If 'e shouts much louder we shan't 'ave a servant left in the 'ouse by tonight.'

'What happened?' said Mr Campion, his hand on the door knob.

'I doubt not 'e went down to Pharisees' Clearing, sir.' The Suffolk accent was very apparent in the old man's voice, and his gravity was profound. Mr Campion opened the door and went in.

The room was darkened, and there was a muffled wail from a bed in the far corner. He walked across the room, pulled up the blind, and let a flood of sunshine into the apartment. Then he turned to face the cowering object who peered at him wildly from beneath the bed quilt.

'Now, what the hell?' said Mr Campion.

Mr Lugg pulled himself together. The sight of his master seemed to revive those sparks of truculence still left in his nature. 'I've resigned,' he said at length.

'I should hope so,' said Campion bitterly. 'The sooner you clear out and stop disgracing me the better I shall like it.'

Mr Lugg sat up in bed. 'Gawd, I 'ave 'ad a night,' he said weakly. 'I nearly lost me reason for yer, and this is 'ow yer treat me.'

'Nonsense,' said Campion. 'I go and leave you in a respectable household, and you bellow the place down in the middle of the night and generally carry on like an hysterical calf elephant.'

The bright sunlight combined with the uncompromising attitude of his employer began to act like a tonic upon the shaken Lugg.

'I tell yer what, mate,' he said solemnly, 'I lost me nerve. And so 'ud you if you'd seen what I seen. Lumme, what a sight!'

Mr Campion remained contemptuous. 'A couple of owls hooted at you, I suppose,' he observed. 'And you came back and screamed the place down.'

'A couple o' blood-curdling owls,' said Mr Lugg solemnly. 'And some more. I'll tell you what. You spend the night in that wood and I'll take you to Colney 'Atch in the morning. That thing killed Lady Pethwick, the sight of it, that's what it did. And she wasn't no weakling, let me tell yer. She was a strong-minded woman. A weak-minded one would 'ave burst.'

In spite of his picturesque remarks there was an underlying note of deadly seriousness in Mr Lugg's husky voice, and his little black eyes were frankly terror-stricken. Secretly Mr Campion was shocked. He and Lugg had been through many terrifying experiences together, and he knew that as far as concrete dangers were concerned his aide's nerves were of iron.

'Just what are you driving at?' he said, with more friendliness than before. 'A white lady with her head under her arm tried to get off with you, I suppose?'

Mr Lugg glanced about him fearfully.

'No jokin' with the supernatural,' he said. 'You may laugh now, but you won't later on. What I saw down in that wood last night was a monster. And what's more, it's the monster that chap in the pub was tellin' me about. The one they keep in the secret room.'

'Shut up,' said Campion. 'You're wrong there. I told you to forget that.'

'All right, clever,' said Mr Lugg sulkily. 'But what I saw wasn't of this world, I can tell you that much. For Gawd's sake come off yer perch and listen to this seriously or I'll think I've gone off me onion.'

Such an appeal from the independent, cocksure Lugg was too much for Campion. He softened visibly.

'Let's have it,' he suggested. 'Animal, vegetable, or mineral?'

Mr Lugg opened his mouth to speak, and shut it again, his eyes bulging, as he attempted to recall the scene of his adventure.

'I'm blowed if I know,' he said at last. 'You see, I was sittin' out in the clearing, like you said, smoking me pipe and wishin' it wasn't so quiet like, when I 'eard a sort of song – not church music, you know, but the sort of song an animal might sing, if you take me. I sat up, a bit rattled naturally. And then, standin' in the patch of light where the moon nipped in through the trees, I see it.' He paused dramatically. 'As filfy a sight as ever I clapped eyes on in all me born days. A great thin thing with little short legs and 'orns on its 'ead. It come towards me, and I didn't stay, but I tell yer what – I smelt it. Putrid, it was, like somethink dead. I lost me 'ead completely and come up to the 'ouse at forty miles an hour yelping like a puppy dawg. I expec' I made a bit of a fool of meself,' he added regretfully. 'But it 'ud put anyone into a ruddy funk, that would.'

Mr Campion perched himself on the edge of the bedrail. Lugg was glad to see that his animosity had given place to interest.

'Horns?' he said. 'Was it a sort of animal?'

'No ordin'ry animal,' said Lugg with decision. 'I'll tell yer what, though,' he conceded, 'it was like a ten-foot 'igh goat walkin' on its 'ind legs.'

'This has an ancient and fishlike smell,' said Mr Campion. 'Are you sure it wasn't a goat?'

'You're trying to make me out a fool. I tell you this thing was about nine foot 'igh and it 'ad 'uman 'ands – because I saw 'em. Standin' out black against the sky.'

Mr Campion rose to his feet. 'Lugg, you win,' he said. 'I apologize. Now get up. And remember, whatever you do, don't breathe a word of this to the other servants. And if they know you saw a ghost, well, it was nothing to do with the room, see? Don't you breathe a word about that. By the way, I met a friend of yours in Town. Ernie Walker.'

'Don't you 'ave nothin' to do with 'im.' The last vestige of Mr Lugg's hysteria disappeared. 'No soul above 'is work – that's the sort of bloke Ernie is. A dirty little shark 'oo'd squeal on 'is Ma for a packet o' damp fags.'

Mr Campion grinned. 'It seems as if you can't see a ghost in the place without my getting into bad company in your absence, doesn't it?' he said affably. 'Now get up and pretend you've had a bilious attack.'

'Oi, that's not quite the article,' said Mr Lugg shocked. ''Eart attack, if you don't mind. I 'ave my feelings, same as you do.'

Campion went out and stood for a moment on the landing, the

inane expression upon his face more strongly marked than ever. He went to Sir Percival's sanctum on the first floor, and remained there for twenty minutes or so. When he came out again he was more thoughtful than ever. He was about to set off downstairs when a figure which had been curled up on the windowsill at the far end of the corridor unfolded itself and Penny came towards him.

'Well?' she said. 'I hope you're convinced about Lugg now.'

To her astonishment Mr Campion linked her arm through his.

'You are now, my dear Madam, about to become my Doctor Watson,' he said. 'You will ask the inane questions, and I shall answer them with all that scintillating and superior wisdom which makes me such a favourite at all my clubs. They used to laugh when I got up to speak. Now they gag me. But do I care? No, I speak my mind. I like a plain man, a straightforward man, a man who calls a spade a pail.'

'Stop showing off,' said Penny placidly, as they emerged into the garden. 'What are you going to do?'

Mr Campion stopped and regarded her seriously. 'Look here,' he said, 'you haven't quarrelled with Beth or anything?'

'Of course not. Why? I was on the phone to her last night. She naturally wanted to know all about Val staying in Town. They seem to have got on astoundingly well together, you know.'

'Quite old friends, in fact,' said Mr Campion. 'I noticed that yesterday. Oh, I'm not so bat-eyed as you think. A youthful heart still beats beneath my nice new chest-protector and the locket containing the old school cap. No, I only asked about Beth because we are now going to visit her father, who is a very distinguished person in spite of the fact that he is a friend of mine. I ought to have told you that before, but there you are.'

'Be serious,' the girl begged. 'You seem to forget that I don't know as much about things as you do.'

'We're going to see Professor Cairey,' continued Mr Campion. 'Not charioted by Bacchus and his pards but via the footpath. You see,' he went on as they set off across the lawn, 'you're getting a big girl now, and you may be useful. The situation is roughly this. I've got three days before Val's birthday. Three days in which to spot the cause of the trouble and settle up with him. The only line I've got on the gent in question is that his pet name is "The Daisy".'

Penny looked dubious. 'It's hardly possible, is it?' she said.

Mr Campion did not answer her, but proceeded equably. 'It's perfectly obvious to me,' he continued, 'and probably to you, my dear

Watson, that there's something fishy in Pharisees' Clearing – something very fishy if Lugg is to be believed. I have a hunch that if we can lay that ghost we'll get a line on The Daisy.'

'But,' said Penny, 'if The Daisy, as you call him, is responsible for the ghost and Aunt Di was frightened intentionally, why should the creature go on haunting?'

'That,' observed Mr Campion, 'is the point under consideration. Of course Lugg may have gone batty and imagined the whole thing.'

Penny shot a quick glance at him. 'You don't believe that,' she said. Mr Campion met her gaze.

'You,' he said, 'believe it's something supernatural.'

The girl started violently and the colour came into her face.

'Oh,' she burst out suddenly, 'if you only knew as much about the country folk as I do, if you'd been brought up with them, listened to their stories and heard their beliefs, you wouldn't be so supercilious about things that aren't, well, quite right things. Of course,' she went on after a pause, 'I'm not saying anything definite. I don't know. But ever since Aunt Di's death more and more Gypsies have been pouring into the district. They say there's a small army of them on the heath.'

Mr Campion raised his eyebrows. 'Good old Mrs Sarah,' he said. 'Always do all you can for the Benwell tribe, Penny; the finest chals and churls in the world.'

Penny was mystified. 'You seem to know something about everything,' she said. 'Why are we going to see the Professor?'

'Because,' said Mr Campion, 'if our bogle in Pharisees' Clearing is a genuine local phenomenon you can bet your boots Professor Cairey knows all there is to know about it. Besides that, when dealing with the supernatural there's nothing quite so comforting as the scientific mind and a scientific explanation.'

They found the Professor at work in a green canvas shelter in the garden of his attractive Tudor house, whose colour-washed walls and rusty tiled roof rose up in the midst of a tangle of flowers. The old man rose to meet them with genuine welcome in his face.

'This is delightful. You've come to lunch, I hope? Mrs Cairey is somewhere in the house and Beth with her.'

Penny hesitated awkwardly, and it was Mr Campion who broached the all-important matter in hand.

'Professor,' he said, 'I'm in trouble again. We've come to you for help.'

'Why, sure.' The Professor's enthusiasm was indubitable. 'Judge

Lobbett, one of my greatest friends, owes his life to this young man,' he added, turning to Penny. 'Now what can I do for you two?'

'Have you ever heard of the ghost in Pharisees' Clearing?' said Penny, unable to control her curiosity any longer.

The Professor looked from one to the other of them, a curious expression in his round, dark eyes.

'Well,' he said hesitantly, 'I don't know what you'll think of me, but I've got a sort of idea that I've a photograph of it. Come into the library.'

Chapter 16

Phenomenon

In the depths of the Professor's study, a cool old-fashioned room with stamped plaster walls striped with unstained oak beams, Penny and Mr Campion listened to an extraordinary story.

'I don't want you to get me wrong,' said the Professor, as he knelt down before an exquisite old lowboy and unlocked the bottom drawer. 'I admit I've been poking my nose into other people's business and I've been trespassing. Way over across the water we don't mind if we do set our feet in a neighbour's back garden,' he added slyly.

Penny looked profoundly uncomfortable. 'Don't tease us about that, Professor,' she said pleadingly. 'That was just an unfortunate accident. Aunt Di made it awkward all round, and Father was silly about the Gypsies.'

The Professor paused with his hand on the drawer handle.

'You don't say it was that?' he said. 'Well, your father had one up on me that time. I've lost half a dozen pedigree hens to those darn hobos. I sent them off my land yesterday morning when I saw they were back again.'

Penny hardly heard him. 'The – the ghost,' she said. 'Is it a real one?'

The Professor looked at her curiously and did not answer directly. 'You'll see,' he said. 'As I was saying, I've been trespassing. I heard this yarn of a ghost long before your poor aunt passed over, and naturally I was interested. You see, I'm something of an authority on medieval witchcraft and magic – it's my hobby, you know – and there were certain peculiarities about the tales I heard that got me interested. I sat up waiting in your father's wood for several nights and I can't say I saw anything. Still, I had a gun with me and maybe that had something to do with it.'

He paused and looked at Penny searchingly. 'You probably know these stories better than I do,' he said.

She nodded. 'I've heard several things,' she admitted. 'But the photograph –?'

'I was coming to that,' said the Professor. 'I don't know if you know it, but there's a way that folks have for setting a trap to photograph animals at night. It's a dandy little arrangement whereby the animal jerks a string stretched across its path, that releases a flashlight and snaps open the camera lens. I set a thing like this two or three nights, and finally, about a fortnight back, I got a result. Now I'll show you.'

He rose to his feet carrying a big envelope. While they watched him he raised the flap and produced a large shiny reproduction.

'I had it enlarged,' he said. 'It's not good – I warn you it's not good, but it gives you an idea.'

Mr Campion and Penny bent forward eagerly. As in all flashlight photographs taken in the open at night, only a certain portion of the plate bore a clear picture, and the snapshot conveyed largely an impression of tangled leaves and branches shown up in vivid black and white. But on the edge of the circle of light, and largely obscured by the shadows, was something that was obviously a figure turned in flight.

It was horned and very tall. That was all that was clear. The rest was mostly hidden by the undergrowth and the exaggerated shadows thrown by the foliage. In the ordinary way the photograph might have been dismissed as a freak plate, an odd arrangement of light and shadow, but in view of the Professor's story and Lugg's horrific description it took on a startling significance. Seen in this light, every blur and shadow on the figure that might have passed as accidental took on a horrible suggestion of unnamable detail.

Campion looked at the Professor.

'Have you got a nice satisfying explanation for all this?' he said.

Professor Cairey's reply was guarded. 'There is a possible explanation,' he said, 'and if it's the right one it'll be one of the most interesting examples of medieval survival I've ever heard of. Naturally I haven't cared to bring this matter up, nor to go trespassing lately. You'll appreciate that the situation was a little delicate.'

'Well,' said Mr Campion, straightening his back, 'first catch your ghost. A cheery night's work for our little Albert.'

The Professor's face flushed with enthusiasm. 'I'm with you,' he said. 'I've been itching to do just that for the last month.'

There was something boyish in the old man's heartiness which Penny hardly shared. 'Look here,' she said quietly, 'if you really mean to go wandering about in Pharisees' Clearing tonight I think I can put you on to the man to help you. Young Peck. He works for you, doesn't he, Professor? He and his father know more about the countryside than all the rest of Sanctuary put together.'

Professor Cairey beamed.

'I was just about to suggest him myself,' he said. 'As a matter of fact, old Peck has been my chief source of information in this affair. A fine old chap,' he added, turning to Mr Campion. 'It took me three weeks to find out what he was talking about, but we get on famously now. He has a cottage on the edge of my willow plantation, and he spends all his days sitting in the sun "harkening in", as he calls it. His son's put him up a radio. See here,' he went on, 'if you'll stay to lunch we'll go down there afterwards and get the youngster on the job.'

'Oh, we can't force ourselves on you like this,' Penny protested. But the luncheon gong silenced her and the Professor bore them off in triumph to the dining-room.

Mrs Cairey, a gracious little woman with grey eyes and white shingled hair, received the unexpected addition to her luncheon table with charming equanimity. Whatever her quarrel with Lady Peth-wick had been, she did not allow its shadow to be visited upon the young people. Mr Campion appeared to be an old favourite of hers, and Penny was a friend of Beth's. By her pleasant personality the meal was made a jolly one, in spite of the sinister business which lay in the background of the minds of at least three of the party.

'I'm real glad Albert is no longer a secret,' said she as they settled themselves at the fine Georgian table in the graceful flower-filled room. 'Beth and I kept our promise to you,' she went on, smiling at the young man. 'Not a word about us knowing you has passed our lips. I thought this was a quiet old-fashioned county. I never dreamed I'd have so much mystery going on around me.'

The Professor grinned. 'Mother likes her mysteries kept in the kitchen,' he said.

His wife's still beautiful face flushed. 'Will I never hear the end of this teasing, Papa?' she said. 'He's making game of me,' she added, turning to the visitors, 'because when I came over here and saw this house I was so charmed with the old brick oven and the pumps and the eighteenth-century brew-house that I just made up my mind I wouldn't have the electric plant we planned, but I'd set up housekeep-ing as they did in the old days, and I'd bake and brew and I'd make Devonshire cream in the right old-fashioned way.' She paused and spread out her hands expressively. 'I had six girls in the kitchen before I'd finished, and not one of them could I get to do the necessary chores.'

The Professor chuckled. 'We bought a brewing licence down at the Post Office,' he said. 'But do you think one of the lads on the farm would drink the home-made stuff? Not on your life. They'd rather have their fourpence to go to the pub with.'

'It was the refrigerator that did it,' said Beth.

Little Mrs Cairey laughed. 'How you manage to exist without ice I don't know,' she said to Penny. 'I stuck it out for a long time, just so Papa wouldn't get the laugh on me. Then one day Beth and I went into Colchester and got just what we wanted – all worked by paraffin. Half the village came to see it, and the tales we heard about illnesses that could only be cured by an ice cube you wouldn't believe.'

Penny grinned. 'They're terrible,' she said. 'For goodness' sake don't let yourself in for too much fairy godmothering. You see,' she went on, 'all the little villages round here are really estates that have got too big and too expensive for the Squires to take care of. Death duties at ten shillings in the pound have rather spoilt the feudal system. But the people still expect to be looked after. If they live on your land they consider themselves part of the family.'

'You can get very fond of them, though,' said Mrs Cairey placidly. 'Although they like their "largesse", as they call it.'

The meal passed, and as they rose and went out on to the lawn Penny felt as though a peaceful interlude in a world of painful excitement had passed.

The Professor had a word with Campion in private under the pretence of showing him a magnificent rambler.

'I guess we ought to keep the ladies out of this,' he said.

Mr Campion nodded. 'Emphatically,' he agreed. 'But I don't know about Penny. She's a strong-minded young woman, and, as I take it, an old friend of the worthy gentleman we're just about to visit. I don't think she'll want to come ghost hunting, but her influence with the Pecks may be useful.'

The Professor hesitated. 'If it's what I think it is,' he said, 'it's no business for a woman. Still, as you say, Miss Gyrth may be a deal of help just at first. If you'll excuse me I'll have a word with Mother.'

Five minutes later the remarkable old gentleman had succeeded in allaying both the fears and the curiosity of the feminine part of his establishment, and the three walked down the shady gravel path of his flower garden and through a tiny wicket gate into a broad green meadow beyond, which was a belt of marshy land where a clump of slender willows shook their grey leaves in the sunlight.

They were unusually silent for the best part of the way, but just before they entered the clearing Penny could contain her fears no longer.

'Professor,' she said, 'you know something. Tell me, you don't think this – this phenomenon, I suppose you'd call it – is definitely supernatural?'

The old man did not answer her immediately.

'My dear young lady,' he said at last, 'if it turns out to be what I think it is, it's much more unpleasant than any ghost.'

He offered no further explanation and she did not like to question him, but his words left a chill upon her, and the underlying horror which seems always to lurk somewhere beneath the flamboyant loveliness of a lonely English countryside in the height of summer, a presence of that mysterious dread, which the ancients called panic, had become startlingly apparent.

Peck's cottage was one of those picturesque, insanitary thatched lath-and-plaster dwellings which stir admiration and envy in the hearts of all those who do not have to live in them. The thatch was moss-covered, and the whole building almost obscured by the high grass and overgrown bushes with which it was surrounded. A weed-grown brick path led up to the front door which stood open, revealing an old man in a battered felt hat seated on a low wooden chair beside an atrocious loud-speaker, which was at this moment murmuring a nasal reproduction of the advertising gramophone music from Radio Paris.

The old man cocked an eye at their approach, and rising with evident regret, switched off the instrument. Mr Peck senior was by no means an unhandsome old man, with a skin like red sandstone and a rugged toothless face, on the lower promontory of which he had raised a very fine tuft of bristly white hair. He was dressed in an odd assortment of garments, chiefly conspicuous among which were a pair of well-patched white canvas trousers and a red and green knitted waistcoat, obviously designed for a much larger man. His knuckles were swollen with rheumatism, and the backs of his hands were almost as furry as bears' paws.

'Old Man 'Possum,' said Mr Campion, *sotto voce*.

'Be quiet,' said Penny reprovingly, and went forward to greet her friend. He touched his hat to her solemnly. 'Mornin', miss,' he said.

'Good morning,' replied Penny politely but inaccurately. 'Is your son anywhere about?'

Mr Peck glanced over his shoulder. 'Perce!' he bellowed. 'Gentry be 'ere.'

'I'm now comin',' a voice replied from the depths of the cottage, and the next moment a tall, loose-limbed young countryman appeared from an inner doorway. He was in shirt-sleeves and waist-coat, and was collarless. Smiling and unembarrassed, he indicated the seats in the cottage porch.

'If you don't mind settin' there, sirs,' he said, 'I'll get Miss Penny a chair.'

They sat down, and instantly the little gathering took on the air of a conspiracy. Young Perce hovered behind his father's chair, his quick brown eyes watching their visitors, waiting for them to come to the object of their call.

'My j'ints be bad,' Mr Peck senior put forward as an opening gambit.

'I'll send you down some of cook's liniment,' Penny offered.

'Huh,' said Mr Peck, without pleasure or reproach.

'Don't take no notice on 'im,' said Percy, reddening for his father's delinquencies. ''E's as right as ever 'e was, ain't yer, Father?'

'No I ain't,' returned his father uncompromisingly, and added irrelevantly, 'I 'ear that were a quiet buryin'. Yer aunt was pison to some on us. Still, I 'ont speak ill o' the dead.'

A violent kick at the back of his chair almost upset him, and he sat quiet, mumbling, his lips together. His two subjects of conversation having been turned down, he was inclined to let people speak for themselves.

The formalities of the call being over, it was Penny who broached the all-important matter in hand.

'Percy,' she said, 'I want you to take Mr Campion and Professor Cairey down to Pharisees' Clearing tonight. They think there's – there's an animal there that wants snaring. Do you understand? You wouldn't be afraid, would you?'

'No, miss. I shouldn't be scared.' The boy spoke readily enough, but a shadow had passed over his face.

His father grunted. 'That ain't no animal, miss,' he said. 'That's a spirit, like I told Master Cairey.'

His tone was so matter-of-fact that Mr Campion shot an inquiring glance at him. The Professor spoke hastily.

'Of course, we won't want any tales told about this, Peck, you understand?'

The boy laughed. 'Us don't talk, sir,' he said. 'Was you thinkin' of trappin' that, now, or do you want to shoot ut?'

'Oh, trap it certainly,' said the Professor firmly.

Penny looked up.

'Percy,' she said, 'do you remember when Val and I were kids we helped you and young Finch to catch an old ram that had gone wild down in Happy Valley?'

'That was with a stack net, warn't ut?' The idea evidently appealed to Mr Peck junior. 'Yes, us could do that. Allowin' that's real,' he added, practically.

'You 'on't catch nothin',' observed his father, accepting a fill of tobacco gratefully from the Professor's pouch. 'That's a spirit. You'll drop a net, and that'll go right through ut, like that was water. You can make fules of yourselves ef you like: that ain't nothin' to me. Oi won't hurt.'

'Look here,' said Mr Campion, breaking into the conversation for the first time. 'Is the ghost in Pharisees' Clearing a new affair or has it been going on for some time?'

The elder Peck considered. 'There's allus been summat strange down there,' he said. 'It ain't been reg'lar. Off and on, as you might say. I mind when I was a boy the whole village were quaggly about ut. Then that died down. Then about five years agoo someone seen un, and there ain't no one been there of a night time sence. I reckon that's a spirit.'

Penny looked at the younger man. 'What do you think about it?' she said.

'I don't know, miss.' The boy was puzzled. 'I never rightly thought on ut. That never interfered with me. But I never were there at night. That's a mystery, that's what that is. Still,' he added cheerfully, 'I ain't afraid of ut. I fixed up that wireless for the old 'un and if I can rule that I can rule any ghost. Seems like that's magic,' he observed naïvely, indicating the mass of crazy looking machinery behind the old man's chair.

The Professor rose. 'Then you'll be down at Tye Hall at about eleven-thirty, with a stack net?' he said.

Mr Peck junior touched an imaginary hat. 'I will, sir.'

'I 'on't,' said his father complacently. 'I'll be harkening to a band then from Germany; they don't be so set on the Sabbath as we are 'ere, the 'eathens. And if you're wise,' he added with sudden vigour, 'you'll stay in yer beds, same as I do. There be more goes on at night than us thinks on. You stay out of ut, miss. That ain't no wild sheep down in Pharisees. And whatever comes on ut,' he concluded solemnly, 'it won't be no good.'

'I'll be there,' said his son, escorting them down the path. As they turned into the field the strains of the Soldiers' Chorus came floating to them across the tangled garden.

Chapter 17
The Stack Net

'If that owl cries again I shall have hysterics,' said Beth nervously.

There were all four of them, the two girls, Professor Cairey and Mr Campion, seated in the candle-lit library at Tye Hall, waiting for half-past eleven and the arrival of young Perce with his stack net. Mrs Cairey had retired, but nothing the Professor or Mr Campion could say would persuade the two girls to follow her example.

Earlier in the evening Campion had been pleasantly fatuous, but now, as the actual moment approached, even he seemed to have become sobered by the eeriness of the occasion. The Professor was the virtual leader of the party. His boyish enthusiasm of earlier in the day had given place to a brisk, commanding mood, and he prepared for the expedition in a business-like manner.

'Torch, travelling rug, and a hip flask,' he said, setting them on the table. 'I shouldn't take a gun in case you're tempted to loose off. I wish you two girls would go to bed and keep out of it.'

'Nonsense,' said Beth stoutly. 'We're going to hold the fort for you. Whether you see a ghost or not you'll be glad of something hot when you come in.'

Mr Campion, who had been standing in the window, turned. 'We shall have a little moon,' he said. 'I wish I knew what you were getting at, Professor. Am I to expect a wailing manacled figure, or are chains distinctly *passé*?'

The Professor shook his head. 'I'm not going to make guesses,' he said, 'in case my hunch is absolutely wrong. However, the girls will be all right up here. There won't be any clutching hands or spooks blowing out the candles. It's extraordinary how these old houses do creak at night, though,' he observed involuntarily.

Beth perched herself on the arm of Penny's chair. 'We shall hold each other's hands till you come back,' she said. 'It's hot tonight, isn't it?'

As soon as she had spoken, the oppressive warmth of the night seemed to become almost unbearable. It was a breathless evening, and the garden outside was uncannily silent, so that when an owl screamed it sounded almost as if the terrifying noise were in the room.

Long awkward silences fell on the company as they waited, and even the most casual sentence seemed jerky and nervous.

A sharp tap on the window startled them violently, and it was only when a husky Suffolk voice outside remarked confidentially: 'I be 'ere, sir,' that they realized that the party was complete.

Next moment Mr Peck junior's head and shoulders appeared in the open half of the casement. He looked a little *distrait* himself, and his grin was inclined to be sheepish. He had paid special attention to his coiffure in honour of going ghost hunting with the gentry, with the result that his brown curling locks were brushed up to a stupendous quiff on the top of his head, which gave him the startling appearance of having his hair standing on end with fright.

'I see a light, so I come 'ere, sir,' he said. 'Not wishin' to startle the maids, like. Am I right for time?'

It was evident that he was endeavouring to appear as calm as though the trip were the most usual one in the world. The Professor hastily gathered his things together.

'We'll go out by the side door,' he said to Campion. 'Wait there a minute, will you, Peck? We'll come round to you.'

'Good luck,' said Penny.

Mr Campion followed the alert and still youthful Professor out into the stone-flagged corridor and down to the half-glass garden door. They stepped out on to a soft lawn and the Professor led the way round to the side of the house, where young Peck's gaunt figure stood silhouetted against the window. As they approached, something stirred in the darkness at their feet.

''Tis Neb, sir,' said Peck in reply to the Professor's muttered exclamation. 'My owd dog. I reckoned I'd bring 'un with me. For company, like. He'll be as quiet as a meece, won't you, boy?' The last words were addressed to the dog, as he stooped and patted a shape that was rapidly becoming visible as their eyes grew accustomed to the darkness. Neb turned out to be a large, lank creature with a huge head, no tail, and ears like a calf. He moved like a shadow behind his master, being trained with that astonishing excellence that is often regarded with suspicion in those parts of the country where men preserve game.

'Have you got the net?' said Mr Campion as they crossed the grass and made for the footpath to the coppice.

''Ere it be, sir. 'Tis a piece of an old 'un. I reckoned we couldn't manage a whole heavy 'un.' He half-turned, showing a large and heavy roll of stout interlaced cords which he carried slung over his shoulder. 'I brought a hurricane with me, too,' he added, turning to the Professor, 'but I didn't light 'un by the house.'

'You can leave that,' said the Professor. 'I've got a torch.'

Mr Peck clung to his lantern.

'I reckon I'll keep that, if you don't mind, sir,' he said.

As they went through the darkness, the heavy silence closed in upon them, broken only by the rustle of their own feet in the grass.

Presently young Peck detailed his idea of their procedure.

'Since you left the trappin' of ut to me, sirs,' he ventured, 'I thought maybe you'd like to know how I be settin' out. I reckoned I'd find a good tree with a branch stickin' out on ut, and I'd set on that with the net, and when the thing come beneath then I'd drop that over ut.'

The simplicity of this plan seemed to fill the young man with pride and delight. Mr Campion and the Professor were hardly so struck by it.

'Suppose it doesn't come under your tree?' said Mr Campion.

But the younger Peck was prepared for this emergency. 'I doubt not that will, sir,' he said. He paused, and after a moment or two of consideration volunteered an enlightening remark. 'That chases people, sir. I was talking to the old 'un, tea-time. 'E told I that, and I thought ut out that if I was up the tree, sir, you could sort of lead that under I. Of course,' he went on cheerfully, 'us can't tell if that'll be there, can us?'

Mr Campion chuckled. 'I see,' he said. 'We're the bait and the poor fish too.'

Mr Peck shook with silent mirth at this sally. 'That's so, sir,' he whispered. 'Now, if you don't mind, us'll keep quiet. I'll go first, if you please.'

He slipped in front of them, treading silently as a cat, and behind him the great mongrel picked his way furtively. For some time they plodded on in silence. Mr Campion had removed his spectacles, a habit of his when action was indicated. The heat had become almost unbearable. There was only a waning moon visible, although the stars shone brightly enough.

The belt of trees which they were rapidly approaching was ink black and curiously uninviting, and the little Belgian owls with which that part of the country is infested hooted dismally from time to time.

They followed the path and entered the Professor's wood, which corresponded to the larger one belonging to the Tower on the opposite side of the clearing, and through which Penny had conducted Mr Campion on the morning of Lady Pethwick's death only a week before.

Young Peck straightened himself and pushed on doggedly as the branches over his head rendered his path almost completely black. Suddenly Neb began to snuffle, his great head bowed to his master's heels. Presently he stopped dead and emitted a suppressed whinnying sound which brought the youth to a standstill.

'What is ut, boy?' whispered Peck. The dog turned silently from the path and disappeared into the darkness, to return a moment or so later with something hanging from his jaw. The youth squatted down on his heels and lit a match. The tiny flare showed the great yellow dog with a young rabbit in his mouth. The animal was quite dead, a piece of wire drawn tightly round its neck.

Peck took it from the dog and the Professor produced his torch.

'Ah,' whispered the boy contemptuously as he threw the rabbit down. 'There's someone about don't fear no ghosts. That ain't been snared above a 'alf-hour.'

He rose to his feet, and with the dog walking obediently behind him set off once more into the silent depths of the wood. The path was one left by woodcutters in the winter, and led directly through the scrub into open space beyond.

Pharisees' Clearing was uncanny enough in the day-time, but at night it was frankly awe-inspiring. The narrow stony strip between the woods was ghostly in the starlight, and here, hemmed in between the long line of trees, the air was suffocating.

The Professor nudged Mr Campion's arm. 'Almost too good to be true,' he murmured.

Campion nodded. 'So much for background,' he whispered. 'This is the place and the hour all right. When does the performance begin?'

But if Campion could be light-hearted, Mr Peck was certainly not in the same mood. As they halted in the shadows on the edge of the clearing his voice came to them husky and alarmed.

'Reckon this is the place. You draw that under 'ere and I'll catch un,' he murmured, indicating the oak beneath which they stood. Then he disappeared like a shadow into the blackness, and they heard the soft scrape of his rubber shoes on the bole of the tree. He climbed like a monkey, no mean feat in the darkness with two stone of ropes tied round him, and they heard him grunt softly as he pulled himself up. A few moments later a whisper came from just above their heads.

'I'll rest 'ere time that comes.'

'Where's the dog?' said the Professor softly.

'That's at the foot of the tree. That won't move.'

Mr Peck seemed to have made his arrangements complete.

'What does A do now?' murmured Mr Campion.

There were faint, almost indetectable sounds all round them in the wood, minute rustlings like stifled breathings in the dark. Neither was insensible to the eeriness of the moment, but each man had his own particular interest in the matter.

'I think,' the Professor whispered, 'that if you'll work round the left side I'll go round the right. I got my photograph from the point where the Colonel's woodpath reaches the clearing. If we all three wait at equal distances round the oval, our quarry can't very well escape us, if it appears at all.'

'I wish I'd brought my twig of rowan,' said Mr Campion with apparent feeling, as he set off in the direction indicated. He moved along the side of the wood, keeping well in the shadow of the overhanging trees. Apart from the breath-taking moment when he disturbed a hare at his very feet, there were no thrills until he reached a spot about thirty yards, or so he judged, from the entrance to the Tower Wood. Here he sat down in the long grass and waited.

From the absolute silence in the clearing he guessed that the Professor had reached his point of vantage somewhere across the faintly lit stretch opposite him. The thought that there were three men and a dog watching anxiously for something unknown to appear among those loose stones and sparse clumps of coarse grass in front of him made the scene slightly more terrifying. He hunched his knees to his chin and composed himself for a long wait. He had not underestimated his vigil.

The minutes passed slowly. Once or twice a sleepy squawk sounded from the wood behind him, and, as his ears became attuned to the quietness, somewhere far away in the Tower garden a nightjar repeated its uncouth cry like an old-fashioned policeman's rattle.

And then, for the first time, Mr Campion became conscious that someone was moving clumsily in the depths of the wood behind him. He turned his head and listened intently. There was certainly nothing supernatural about this. The movements were those of a man, or some animal quite as heavy. For a minute or so he was puzzled, but a single sound reassured him, the sharp metallic click of a spring trap being set.

He listened to the rustling going farther and farther away, with occasional pauses as other traps were set. Someone evidently paid very little respect to the horror which had killed Lady Pethwick and driven Lugg into hysterics.

Once again all was silent. The illuminated hands on his watch showed half-past twelve. He sighed and settled down once more. His face in the darkness still wore his habitual expression of affable fatuity. His eyes were half-closed.

'Angels and ministers of grace defend me, I hope,' he remarked under his breath, and turned up his coat to obscure the whiteness of his collar.

The oppressive warmth of the night was giving place to the first cool breath of dawn when his senses, which had gradually become drowsy, were startled into tingling life by one of the most terrible sounds he had ever heard. It was not very loud, but its quality made up for any deficiency on that score.

It was a noise that could only be described as a gentle howling, coming swiftly through the trees, and he was reminded unpleasantly of Mr Lugg's description, 'the sort of song an animal might sing'. Not even among native races, of whom he had some little experience, had he ever heard anything quite so blood-curdling. Quite the most terrifying point about the noise was that the sound was rhythmic. It rose and fell on a definite beat, and the pitch was high and quavering.

The sound came nearer and nearer, and quite suddenly he saw the figure.

It had advanced not from the Colonel's path, as they had expected, but from the narrow opening at the northern end of the clearing, and now stood silhouetted against the lightening sky.

Mr Campion rose to his feet, only vaguely aware of his numbed and aching limbs. The creature, whatever it was, certainly had points of elemental horror about it. It was immensely tall, as Lugg had said, and almost inconceivably thin. Long caprious horns crowned its head, and its body showed grotesque and misshapen.

It advanced down the clearing, still wailing, and Campion caught a clearer glimpse of the front of it as it came nearer.

He felt suddenly sick, and his scalp tingled.

Almost at the same moment the creature came to windward of him, and he was aware of the aroma of putrefaction, strong and unclean in his nostrils.

He darted out of his hiding-place. The figure halted and turned towards him. As it did so he caught sight of a single dead eye, blank and revolting.

Mr Campion stood his ground, and the figure came nearer. From somewhere beyond it Peck's dog had begun to howl piteously. Mr Campion gave way cautiously, edging round towards the sound, allowing the apparition to gain a little upon him as he did so. Every time it came a step forward he retreated, leading it unerringly towards the trap.

Suddenly it made a rush at him, and he turned and ran for the opening, his long thin figure a picture of terror in the night. The horned thing padded after him.

He passed the whimpering dog, and for a giddy moment the creature seemed almost upon him. There was a rustle above his head and something seemed to hover for an instant in the air like a great bat. Then the weighty stack net dropped over his pursuer and a terrible half human howl went shattering through the leaves.

'Call off the dog!' shouted the Professor as he came running up. 'For God's sake call off the dog!'

Chapter 18

Survival

As he levelled his torch, the Professor's hand shook violently.

The dog, after its first frenzied attack, crouched cowering by the tree trunk, while Mr Campion bent over the struggling mass in the heavy net.

The almost blinding beam of light after the intense darkness seemed paradoxically to add to the confusion. The creature, whatever it was, had ceased to struggle and lay motionless in the net, shapeless and hairy under the tangle of ropes.

The fact that the 'ghost' actually lay captured at their feet brought home to both men how slender their hopes of success had been the previous evening. Yet there it lay, still incomprehensible, a grotesque and reeking mass.

Peck dropped to the ground from his branch, and they caught a glimpse of his face, pale, and glistening with great beads of sweat.

'Lumme,' he kept whispering to himself pathetically. 'Lumme.'

The Professor bent over the net, and when he spoke there was more excitement than horror in his tone.

'I knew it,' he said. 'I'm right. This is one of the most remarkable survivals I've ever heard of. Do you know what we've got here?'

'A woman,' said Mr Campion.

'A witch,' said the Professor. 'Look out – gently now. I'm afraid she has collapsed.'

Very carefully he began to lift off the net. Young Peck, fighting his terror with what was, in the circumstances, real heroism, set about lighting the hurricane with hands that trembled uncontrollably.

Mr Campion and the Professor gently removed the tangle of cords. The figure on the ground did not move.

'Lands sakes! I hope the shock hasn't killed her!' There was real concern in the Professor's voice. 'Bring that lantern over here, will you, Peck? That's fine. Now hold this torch.'

And then, as the light fell uninterruptedly upon their captive, the horror of Pharisees' Clearing lay exposed.

In many respects it differed from the conventional ghost, but chiefly it did so in the fact that none of its horror was lost when it was clearly seen.

The figure was that of a woman, old, and scarcely clad at all save for great uncured strips of goatskin draped upon her gaunt yellow form. Her headdress was composed of the animal's skull to which the hair still clung, and her face was hidden by a mask of fur, slits having been cut for the eye-holes. Her bony arms appeared to have been smeared with blood and the effect was unspeakable.

The Professor bent down and removed the headdress, picking it up gingerly by the horns. Mr Campion turned away for a moment, sickened. When he looked again a fresh shock awaited him. The woman's head lay exposed, and above her closed eyes her forehead seemed to stretch back unendingly. She was perfectly bald.

Young Peck's voice, husky with relief, answered the question in both their minds.

' 'Tis owd Missus Munsey,' he said. 'The old 'un said she were a witch, but I never took no heed on ut. Lumme, who'd 'a' thought ut? I never believed them tales.'

The Professor produced his travelling rug. 'Since we know who it is, it makes it much simpler,' he said. 'Where does she live? Alone, I suppose?'

'She lives with 'er son, sir – Sammy,' put in Mr Peck, whose courage was reviving apace at the discovery that the 'spirit' had human substance. ' 'E's a natural. They ain't neither on 'em right.'

'Can you lead us to the cottage?' said Campion. 'Is it far? We shall have to carry this woman.'

'No, that ain't no distance. One thing, that's some way from any other house.'

The Professor in the meantime had succeeded in disengaging the old woman from her grisly trappings and had wrapped her in the rug.

'It occurs to me,' he said, 'that if we could get this poor thing to her house before we attempt to revive her it may be better for all concerned. The discovery of herself still out here surrounded by her regalia – and us – might send her raving.'

Young Peck, who had stolen off some moments before, now reappeared with a light wooden hurdle, part of the boundary fence between the two estates. 'I thought I seen this,' he observed. 'Now, if you're ready, sirs, our best way is to set 'er on 'ere and cut through the clearin'. It ain't above a 'alf mile.'

They lifted the repellent figure on to the rough stretcher and set out.

Since the first outburst no one had spoken. This extraordinary finish to an extraordinary expedition had silenced them for the time being. Peck took the head of the procession. The hurricane clanked at his side, throwing a fitful distorted light on his path. His dog ran behind him, beneath the hurdle, and the Professor and Campion brought up the rear, stumbling along on the uneven ground.

For some time the Professor seemed lost in thought, but as the track led them up through the northern exit from the clearing he glanced at Campion.

'Do you get it?' he said.

'Vaguely,' said Campion. 'I shouldn't believe it if I hadn't seen it.'

'I suspected it all along,' the older man confided. 'The goat horns, and those yarns of the curious chantings put the idea in my head at once. It's an interesting case. There hasn't been one approaching it for fifty years that I know of. It's an example of a blind spot. Modern civilization goes on all over the country – all over the world – and yet here and there you come across a patch that hasn't been altered for three hundred years. This woman's a lunatic, of course,' he added hastily, as he became aware of Peck's large red ears strained back to catch every word. 'But there's no doubt at all in my mind that she's descended from a regular line of practising witches. Some of their beliefs have been handed down to her. That costume of hers, for instance, was authentic, and a chant like that is described by several experts. She's a throw-back. Probably she realizes what she's doing only in a dim, instinctive sort of fashion. It's most interesting – most interesting.'

'Yes, but *why*?' said Campion, who was more rattled than he cared to admit. 'Had she any motive? Did anyone put her up to it?'

The Professor considered. 'We must find that out,' he said. 'I should say, since her nocturnal trips were so frequent, she must have had some very powerful reason. But doubtless that will emerge. Of course,' he went on almost hopefully, 'this may have gone on for years. Her mother may have done the same sort of thing. You'd be astonished to discover what a lot of witchcraft has been practised in this country, and my own, in the last three hundred years. It wasn't so long ago that the authorities stopped burning 'em. A couple of years before I was born, D. D. Home was expelled from Rome as a sorcerer. A lot of it survives to this day in one superstition or another. You come across extraordinary stories of this sort in the police court reports in local newspapers.'

'Still, this is a bit unusual, isn't it?' said Mr Campion, indicating the shrouded figure on the hurdle they carried.

'Oh, this?' said the Professor. 'I'd say so. This is a survival of one of the early forms of witchcraft, but, after all, if you find these country folk sitting on three hundred year old chairs and using Elizabethan horn spoons to mix their puddings, why shouldn't you find them – very, very rarely, I admit – practising the black rites of three or four centuries back? We'll learn a lot more when we get her home, no doubt.'

'I hate to be unfeeling,' said Mr Campion, straightening his back and changing his grip on the hurdle, 'but I certainly wish the good lady had provided herself with a broomstick.'

'We're now there,' observed Peck, joining naturally in the conversation. 'That's just over this rise.'

Five minutes' plodding brought them to the top of the field. It was now nearing dawn, and in the east the sky was almost white. The light from the hurricane lantern was beginning to yellow.

The old woman's cottage was faintly visible, therefore. It was a mere shed of a building, quite obviously an out-house belonging to a cottage that had long since collapsed. As they came nearer they could make out the heterogeneous collection of boards, mud and tarred sheeting of which it was composed. It was surrounded by a patch of earth trodden bare, upon which several lean fowls nestled uneasily. Some six feet from the door young Peck turned.

'Reckon us 'ad better set un down 'ere, sir,' he suggested, 'while us find out if Sammy's t'home. Will you wait 'ere?'

He set his end of the hurdle down gratefully, and they followed suit, easing their strained backs. Mr Peck, lantern in hand, advanced towards the crazy door, his dog at his heels. He tapped upon it softly, and receiving no answer, opened it and entered.

Almost immediately there was a terrified twittering sound from within, and a figure fled out of the doorway and disappeared into the shadows round the back of the hut. The incident was so unexpected that it jolted the nerves of the two who waited almost more than any of the foregoing adventures of the night.

'Gee! what was that?' said the Professor huskily.

He was answered by Peck, who appeared a little shamefacedly in the doorway. 'That's Sammy,' he said. 'That didn't 'alf give I a turn. Shall us carry 'er in? 'Tis a wonderfully dirty place.'

Between them they lifted the hurdle once more and bore it into the dwelling. Peck hung the lantern from a hook in the roof and it shed its uncertain light on one of the most squalid of all human habitations.

A poverty-stricken collection of furniture was strewn about the low-ceilinged room. There was a bed in one corner, and a door leading into another apartment revealed a second couch. A fireplace in which there were still the relics of a fire was built in the outer wall on the left of the door, and the floor was strewn with debris.

The Professor looked about him with distaste. 'I'll say this shouldn't be allowed,' he said. 'Though it's hard to interfere always, I know. If you'll help me, Campion, I'll put her on the couch here.'

They lifted the ragged old creature, still in the rug, and set her down on the tousled bed.

'Whose land is this?' he inquired.

'That don't rightly belong to anyone, sir,' volunteered Peck. ''Tis a bit o'waste, as you might call ut. They've lived 'ere years, she and 'er mother afore 'er. There ain't nobody 'ereabouts as can do anything with 'er.'

The Professor produced his flask, and pouring a little brandy into the cupped top, forced it between the old woman's lips. She stirred uneasily and mumbled a few unintelligible words.

'Take care, sir. I doubt not she'll curse you.' Peck could not repress the warning.

The Professor grinned. 'I doubt not,' he said.

'It was at this point that a shadow appeared in the doorway, and they were conscious of a white, frightened face with a straggling growth of beard on its chin peering in at them.

'Come in,' said Mr Campion in a quiet, matter-of-fact voice. 'Your mother fainted in the wood.'

Sammy Munsey came into the room shyly, moving from side to side like a timid animal. Finally he paused beneath the light, revealing himself to be an undersized, attenuated figure clad in ragged mis-shapen garments. He stood smiling foolishly, swinging his arms.

Suddenly a thought seemed to occur to him, and he whimpered: 'You seen 'er – you seen 'er in the wood. Don't you touch me. I won't 'ave 'em after me. I ain't done nothin'.'

He exhausted himself by this outburst, and Mr Peck, who had been poking about the cabin, suddenly came forward with a pair of scarcely cold hares in his hand. Sammy snatched them from him and put them behind his back like a child, and he stood there quivering with fear and a species of temper.

'Snared,' said Mr Peck with righteous indignation. 'That's why they don't do no work,' he added, turning to the Professor. 'It's been a miracle down in the village how they lived.'

Sammy looked round for some means of escape, but his path to the doorway was blocked by his accuser. He swore vehemently for some moments, and then as though he realized his helplessness, he turned wildly to the figure on the bed.

'Mother, they've found us!' he shouted, shaking the old creature. 'They've found us out!'

The old woman opened her eyes, pale, and watery, with bloodshot rims.

'I'll curse 'em,' she murmured with sudden venom. 'They don't none of 'em dare come near me.' She turned her head and caught sight of the Professor, and raising herself upon an elbow she let out such a stream of filthy abuse that in spite of his interest he was quite obviously shocked. As he did not fly before her, however, her mood changed.

'Leave I alone,' she wailed. 'I ain't hurt ye. I ain't done nothin'. I 'on't hurt ye, if ye go.'

It was Sammy who cut in upon her wailings, and his fear was piteous. 'They've found us out,' he repeated. 'They've found us out.'

The words seemed to sink into the old creature's mind only after some moments. She began to moan to herself.

'I couldn't 'elp ut.'

It dawned upon Mr Campion that she was by no means the mental case that her son was. There was a glimmer of intelligence in the old red-rimmed eyes. As they rolled round they seemed to take in the situation pretty completely.

'Did you frighten people out of Pharisees' Clearing so that your son could poach in the wood?' he said.

She looked at him shrewdly. 'You 'on't take un away if I tell ye?'

'I won't touch him,' said Mr Campion. 'I only want to know why you dressed up like that.'

The guileless expression upon his face seemed to lull the old creature's suspicions, for her voice grew quieter. ''E ain't right,' she said. ''E couldn't catch nothing if 'e was interfered with. 'E don't know 'ow to take care of 'isself. 'E warn't afraid of I. But the others – I scared 'em.' She laughed, sucking the breath in noisily between her gums.

The Professor bent over her. 'Who taught you to do this?' he said.

She seemed to scent a challenge in his remark, for she snarled at him. 'I larnt ut when I were young. I know more'n you think. Where be my robe?'

The Professor started. 'If you mean your goatskins, they're in the wood.'

The old woman attempted to stumble out of bed. 'I must get they,' she insisted. 'There be power in they – more than you know on.'

'Soon,' promised Mr Campion. 'Soon. Lie down now, till you're stronger.'

Mrs Munsey lay back obediently, but her glance roved suspiciously about the room, and her mouth moved without words.

Mr Campion bent forward again. 'Why did you set upon Lady Pethwick?' he said. 'She wouldn't have stopped anyone poaching.'

The old woman sat bolt upright, making a fearsome picture with her bald head and her toothless gums bared like an animal's.

'I di'n't,' she said huskily.

'Then perhaps it was Sammy?' suggested Mr Campion quietly.

Mrs Munsey's red-rimmed eyes became positively venomous. She rose up in her bed and stood there, towering above them, clutching the rug about her attenuated form.

'I curse ye,' she said with concentrated hatred in her voice which was uncommonly disconcerting. 'I curse ye be a right line, a crooked line, a simple and a broken. By flame, by wind, by water, by a mass, by rain, and by clay. By a flying thing, by a creeping thing, by a sarpint. By an eye, by a hand, by a foot, by a crown, by a crost, by a sword and by a scourge I curse ye. *Haade, Mikaded, Rakeben, Rika, Rita lica, Tasarith, Modeca, Rabert, Tuth, Tumch.*'

As the last word left her lips she sank down upon the bed again, where she lay breathing heavily.

The Professor, who had listened to this wealth of archaic invective with unabashed delight, took a small notebook from his pocket and scribbled down a few words.

Mr Campion, who had received the full brunt of the lady's ill-wishes, stood his ground. Now that she was proving herself strong enough for the interview he felt more at ease.

'You frightened Lady Pethwick to death,' he said, speaking with slow, careful deliberation as though he were talking to a child. 'Afterwards, when you saw what you had done, you folded her hands and closed her eyes. Why did you do it? If it was an accident, tell us.'

Sammy, who had been listening to this harangue with his mouth hanging open, now spoke in a misguided effort to exonerate his mother from what he realized vaguely was a serious charge.

'She hid from the gentry afore Daisy told 'er about 'er Ladyship. Afore then she only chased the country folk.'

'Don' you listen to un!' screamed his mother, dancing up and down on the bed in her fury. ' 'E don't know nothin'. 'E's lyin' to 'ee.'

But Mr Campion had heard quite enough to interest him.

'Who's Daisy?' he demanded, repressing every shade of interest in his voice. 'Now, Sammy?'

'You can't blame Daisy!' shouted Mrs Munsey. 'She didn't mean for her to die. She said for to frighten 'er, so's maybe she'd take to 'er bed for a day or two. She ain't done nothin'.'

'Who *is* Daisy?' persisted Mr Campion. His pale eyes were hard, and for once there was no vacuity in his face.

'You can't blame Daisy.' Mrs Munsey repeated the words vehemently. 'I made the image on 'er Ladyship, I named ut, and I burnt ut.'

She made this startling announcement without pride or remorse, and the Professor caught his breath.

'Was it a clay image or a wax image?' he said involuntarily.

'It was mud,' said Mrs Munsey sulkily.

Mr Campion did not hear this part of the conversation: his mind was entirely taken up with Sammy. Once again he repeated his question.

The half-wit would not look at him, but bending his head, he mumbled a few almost unintelligible words.

'That's Miss Daisy she means,' he said. 'My Father worked for 'er one time when 'e was alive.'

It was Peck who came forward and supplied the final startling piece of information.

'Excuse me, sir,' he said. 'That's Mrs Daisy 'e means. Mrs Daisy Shannon, as keeps the 'orses. 'Er they call Mrs Dick.'

'Damn!' said Mr Campion, for once taken aback.

Chapter 19
'What Should A Do?'

'I'd say that's one of the most remarkable experiences of my life,' remarked the Professor to Mr Campion, as they walked back over the fields together from Mrs Munsey's cottage to the Tye Hall. 'Of course, it mustn't come out,' he went on. 'I understand that all right. There'd be endless complications. But I shall cite you as a witness if ever I write a book of reminiscences. I suppose that boy Peck will hold his tongue?'

Mr Campion seemed to drag his thoughts back from some vague and foolish calculation. 'Eh?' he said, recalling the old man's last words to his mind with a conscious effort. 'Oh, Lord, yes, he'll be as silent as the grave. In the first place, I don't think he believes it happened. Besides,' he added as his eye caught the top of the Tower rising above the trees in the distance, 'they're used to keeping secrets round here. Old Mr Peck may hear something, but no one else.'

They walked on in silence for some moments. It was now full dawn and the air was fresh and cool, and the heavy dew made the myriads of tiny cobwebs with which the grass was covered stand out in delicate tracery.

'A genuine case,' the Professor repeated. 'Did you hear what she said about her robe, and the image she'd made? The notion of making a clay figure of an enemy and breaking or maiming it to ensure that the same evils fall on the human is one of the oldest ideas in the world, an authentic traditional practice. And that curse she put upon you, Campion. Pure traditional magic. Each symbol, the right line and the "sarpint" and so on – each represents a different evil spirit. I shall set that down if I can when I get in.'

Mr Campion shrugged his shoulders. 'You might counteract it with a suitable blessing while you're about it,' he said. 'I hope to goodness it doesn't come off. If it does, I'm for a parroty time, as far as I remember. And just at the moment I need the angels on my side.'

The Professor shot him a sly glance. 'That remarkable accusation against a lady called Shannon,' he said. 'You're not taking that seriously, are you?'

The pale young man at his side vouchsafed no reply. His face was as expressionless as ever, and he seemed if anything a little tired. The Professor shook his head.

'A woman like Mrs Munsey might say anything,' he said, and went on thoughtfully: 'You can see just how it happened. There they were, friendless and practically destitute, and the boy not wise enough to go trapping satisfactorily unless he was completely undisturbed. Then his mother thinks out in that twisted, tortuous brain of hers how best she can help him, and there comes to her the memory of what her mother had taught her when she was a girl – all the old beliefs, the peculiar power of the goat. The strange half-forgotten shibboleths come crowding back into her mind, and instinctively she turns it to her own use. It wasn't the keepers she had to fear, you see. I don't preserve, so there was no man patrolling my wood. It was the other poachers. Every man's hand was against Sammy. This isn't the first or last country community that has no sympathy with the weak-minded.' He laughed shortly. 'It's a real primitive story, illustrating, probably, one of the earliest reasons for witchcraft – the terrorization of the weak by the strong. Most interesting.'

'What'll happen to them?' said Mr Campion.

'I've been thinking that out.' The Professor's face was very kindly. 'The parson down here is a very decent old man. His name's Pembroke. He and I get on very well together. He's a scholar, but a man who hasn't let the teachings of the spirit blind him to a knowledge of the world. I'll see him about these two. Maybe something can be done for them. They want looking after, and they must be looked after. Lands sakes! If Mother had seen that woman it might have scared her out of her wits. I guessed more or less what was coming, but it gave me a turn.'

'A turn?' said Mr Campion. 'I was dizzy before we'd finished. Poor old Lugg! One more shock like that and he'll sign the pledge. I wonder why Mrs Munsey took so much trouble to rearrange Lady Pethwick's body?'

'Instinct again,' said the Professor. 'That old woman scarcely thinks. She works by instinct and superstition. There's an old belief that if you leave the dead with their eyes wide open they watch you ever after.'

They had reached the lattice gate at the end of the garden by this time. 'We'll keep most of this story to ourselves,' he remarked.

'Of course,' Mr Campion agreed. 'I'll collect Penny and go back to the Tower.'

There was a fire in the library when they went in, and a scratch meal appeared upon the table. Beth and Penny were burning with excitement, but their hollow eyes and pale cheeks betrayed that their vigil had not been without its terrors. Beth kissed her father.

'Golly, I'm glad you're back,' she said. 'When it got so late Penny and I were afraid the ghost had decamped with you. Did you find anything?'

The Professor contented himself with a very brief outline of the story.

'It was simply an old woman wandering around trying to frighten folks so her son could do a bit of poaching,' he said, accepting the coffee she handed to him with gratitude. 'Nothing to get alarmed about.'

'Mrs Munsey?' said Penny quickly.

The Professor raised his eyebrows. 'What gives you that idea?' he murmured.

'It sounded like her,' said Penny cryptically.

'It sounds rather flat to me,' remarked Beth, a tinge of disappointment in her voice. 'If you'd seen the things that we've *imagined* sitting up here alone you'd have a different tale to tell.'

Mr Campion rose to his feet. 'I think, Penny,' he observed, 'you and I had better get back to the Tower. To come to lunch and stay till breakfast next morning is not quite the article. Lugg will be shocked. His book of etiquette considers over-long calls definitely low.'

Penny agreed readily. 'I'll come at once,' she said, and in spite of the Professor's protestations they gently insisted on returning.

The Professor shook Campion's hand in the hall. 'You can leave all this to me,' he murmured. 'I'll see to it.'

As they passed out of the garden Penny turned to Mr Campion suspiciously. 'Now,' she said, 'out with it. What really did happen?'

'Undue curiosity in females should be curbed on all occasions as the evidences of it are invariably distressing to the really well-bred,' said Mr Campion morosely. 'That's in the etiquette book, too. Page four. It's illustrated.'

'How dare you behave like this,' said the girl with sudden spirit, 'when you both came in looking as though you'd been through hell fire together? Mrs Munsey, was it? Did she go for Aunt Di of her own volition, or did someone put her up to it?'

Mr Campion eyed her speculatively. 'It wasn't nice,' he said. 'Even Peck's dog was shocked. It was frightened to death and kept howling about the place like an old lady at a wake. The Professor was strong and silent, of course, but Mrs Munsey's sartorial efforts blanched even his cheek. We took her to her residence, whereupon she told my fortune, in a rather pessimistic vein, I thought. Then we shook hands all round and came home. There you are, there's the whole story, hot from the horse's mouth.'

'All right,' said Penny, 'I'll find out all the details. You needn't worry.'

'I bet you will,' said Campion with contempt. 'Beth will worm the lurid story from her poor doting father, and you two, little Annie Mile and little Addie Noid, will gloat over them together like the two little nasties you are.'

Penny was silent for some time.

'Anything about The Daisy?' she ventured at last.

Mr Campion shot a quick glance at her. 'I say,' he said. 'I forgot I'd told you about that. Look here, Penny, this is deadly serious. By the bones of my Aunt Joanna and her box, swear to me that you will never breathe a word about The Daisy to a living soul, especially not to Beth and her father. Because although Mrs Munsey gave your aunt the scare that killed her, it was The Daisy who engineered the whole thing. I don't think murder was intended, but . . . I don't know.'

There was an unusual earnestness in his face and Penny, regarding him steadily, was surprised and a little flustered to see an almost imploring expression in his eyes.

'Promise,' he repeated.

'All right,' she said ungrudgingly. 'You found out something, then?'

Campion nodded. 'It may or may not be important,' he said. 'Frankly, I hope it isn't.'

Penny did not reply, but walked along beside him, her hands clasped behind her and her yellow head bent.

'I say,' he said suddenly, 'when I had a word with your father yesterday to assure him that Val would be home for his birthday the day after tomorrow he didn't say anything about the general procedure. What usually happens on these occasions?'

Penny considered. 'It was a great day, years ago, I believe,' she said dubiously. 'The family was quite wealthy in my grandfather's time, you know. Mother used to tell us that on Father's twenty-fifth birthday they had a terrific set-out with a Church service, theatricals, a house party, and a dance for the tenants in the evening. Daddy had to keep out of the fun, though, because of the midnight ceremony of the Room, when his father and the chaplain initiated him into the secret. Of course,' she said quickly, 'we don't talk about that.'

'I see,' said Mr Campion slowly. 'I suppose they dispense with a chaplain these days?'

'Well, we haven't got a private chaplain, if that's what you mean,' she said, grinning; 'although old Mr Pembroke, the vicar here, had rooms in the east wing when Father was away at the War. That was when we were children. I think he'll dine with us on the birthday night. There won't be any other celebrations, partly because we haven't got much money, and also because of poor Aunt Di. Of course,' she went on, 'I dare say you think Father has been rather curious about this whole terrible business – the way he's kept out of it all – but you can't possibly understand about him if you don't realize that he is a man with something on his mind. I mean,' she added, dropping her voice, 'I wouldn't say this to anyone but you, but the secret absorbs him. Even when he thought the Cup was missing it didn't seem to rouse him to frenzy. You do follow me? That's why he's so odd and reserved and we see so little of him.'

She paused and looked at Campion appealingly. The young man with the pale face and absent air turned to her.

'I'm not nearly the mutt I look,' he said mildly.

A wave of understanding passed over her face. 'I believe you and father are pretty thick,' she said. 'Usually he loathes strangers. Do you know, you're quite the most remarkable person I've ever met?' She looked up at him with all the admiration of her age showing in her young face.

'No vamping me,' said Mr Campion, nervously. 'My sister – her what married the Squire – would be ashamed of you.'

'That's all right,' said Penny cheerfully. 'I haven't got any designs on you. I think Val and Beth are heading for the altar, though. Val seemed to have got over his anti-woman complex with a vengeance last time I saw him.'

'You'll be a danger,' said Mr Campion, 'in a few years' time. I'll come and sit at the back of the church when you're married and weep violently among all the old maids. I always think a picturesque figure of that sort helps a wedding so. Don't you?'

Penny was not to be diverted from the matter in hand.

'You've got something on your mind,' she said.

She linked her arm through his with charming friendliness.

'In the words of my favourite authoress: "Is it a woman, my boy?" Or aren't you used to late hours?'

To her surprise he stopped dead and faced her. 'My child,' he said with great solemnity, 'in the words of the rottenest actor I ever heard on mortal stage: *"The man who raises his hand against a woman save in the way of kindness is not worthy of the name."* Which is to say: "Don't knock the lady on the head, Daddy, or the policeman will take you away." This is the most darned awkward situation I've ever been in in my life.'

Penny laughed, not realizing the significance beneath the frivolous words. 'I should give it her,' she said, 'whoever she is. I'll stand by you.'

Mr Campion permitted himself a dubious smile.

'I wonder if you would?' he murmured.

Chapter 20

Trunk Call

''Ere, wake up, sir. Inspector Stanislaus Oates, 'imself and personal, on the phone. Now we shall 'ave a chance of seein' that lovely dressin'-gown o' yours. I've bin wondering when that was comin' out.'

Mr Lugg put his head round the door of his master's room and spoke with heavy jocularity. ''E's bin ringin' you all day,' he added, assuming a certain amount of truculence to hide his apprehension. 'There's a couple o' telegrams waitin'. But I didn't like to rouse yer. Let 'im 'ave 'is beauty sleep, that's what I said.'

Mr Campion bounded out of bed, looking oddly rakish in the afternoon light. 'Good Heavens,' he said, 'what's the time?'

'Calm yerself – calm yerself. 'Alf-past four.' Mr Lugg came forward bearing a chastely coloured silk dressing-gown. 'Pull yerself together. You remind me o' Buster Keaton when you're 'alf awake. Brush yer 'air before yer go down. There's a lady 'elp what's taken my fancy 'anging on to the phone.'

Mr Campion bound the dressing-gown girdle tightly round his willowy form and snatched up his spectacles.

'What's this about phoning all day?' he said. 'If this is true I'll sack you, Lugg.'

'I've got to keep you alive. My job depends on it,' observed his valet sententiously. 'Staying out all night ghost 'untin' ain't done you no good. You look like an 'arf warmed corpse as it is. That's right – knock me about,' he added, as Mr Campion brushed past him and pattered down the stairs to the side hall where the phone was situated.

The chubby little servant girl, evidently a captive to the charms of Mr Lugg, was clinging to the receiver, which she relinquished to Campion. She stood back and would have remained at a respectful distance, if by no means out of earshot, had not Mr Lugg waved her majestically kitchenwards.

'Hallo,' said a faint voice at the far end of the crackling wire, 'is that you? At last. I was on the point of coming to you. I'm terribly sorry, old boy, but they've got it.'

Mr Campion remained silent for some moments, but in response to a sharp query from the other end of the phone he said weakly: 'Oh, yes, I can hear you all right. What do you want – congratulations?'

'Go easy,' came the distant voice imploringly. 'It was a most ingenious stunt. You'd have been sunk yourself. About two o'clock this morning a whole pack of drunks got hauled into Bottle Street Station, and about thirty of their friends arrived at the same time. There was a terrific fight, and the man on duty on your doorstep joined in, like a mutt. In the confusion someone must have peeled up your stairs and raided the flat. I've been trying to get on to you ever since. What have you been doing? Dabbling in the dew?'

In spite of the lightness of his tone it was evident to Mr Campion that his old friend was desperately worried. 'We're doing all we can,' came the voice, 'and some more. Can you give us a line?'

'Half a minute,' said Mr Campion. 'What about young Hercules?'

'Oh, Gyrth? That's half the trouble,' whispered the distant voice. 'They knocked him on the head, of course, but the moment our man on the roof dropped through the skylight he pulled himself together and shot down after his property. Frankly, we can't find him. There was a free fight going on in the street, you see, and you know what a hopeless place it is. We've rounded up the usuals, but they don't seem to know anything. We've got a dozen or so of the rowdies too. Clever men most of 'em. Have you got anything we can go on?'

Mr Campion considered. He was now fully awake. 'Have you got a pen there?' he said. 'Listen. There's two whizz-boys, Darky Farrell and a little sheeny called Diver. They may or may not be concerned, but I've seen them in the business. Oh, you've got them, have you? Well, put them through it. Then there's Natty Johnson, of course. The only other person I can think of is Fingers Hawkins, the Riverside one. How's that?'

'A nasty little list.' The far-away voice spoke with feeling. 'Righto, leave it to us. You'll stay there, will you? I'll ring you if anything happens. We're pretty sick up here, of course. They're a hot lot; all race-gang people, I notice.'

'That had occurred to me,' said Mr Campion. 'Don't get your head bashed in for my sake. Oh, and I say, Stanislaus . . . kiss that Bobby on the door for me.'

He replaced the receiver and turned wearily away from the instrument to come face to face with his aide, the sight of whom seemed to fill him with sudden wrath.

'Now you've done it,' he said. 'If we muck this whole thing up it'll be directly due to your old-hen complex. Bah! Go and keep mushrooms!'

Mr Lugg remained unabashed.

'You've mixed us up with a nice set, 'aven't yer?' he said. 'I've known ticket o' leave men who'd blush to 'ear theirselves associated with them names you've mentioned over the phone. Fight with razors and broken bottles, they do. It's the class o' the thing I object to. No one can call me a snob – not reely – but a gent 'as to draw 'is line somewhere.'

But for once Mr Campion was not mollified by this attitude.

'Put on a bath, get out the car, find a map, and go and lose yourself,' he said, and stalked off upstairs, leaving Mr Lugg speechless and startled out of his usual gloomy truculence.

A little over an hour later Penny, seated by herself in the spacious faded drawing-room whose broad lattice-paned windows overlooked the drive, was somewhat surprised to hear the door of her father's room across the hall close softly, and to see Mr Campion in a motoring coat and hatless run down the steps from the open front door, and, climbing into his car which stood waiting for him, hurtle off down the drive at an alarming speed.

She had imagined that he would have been down shortly to take tea with her, and she was just about to put her pride in her pocket and ring for Lugg and information, when Branch appeared carrying a bulky envelope on a salver.

'Mr Campion was wishful for me to give you this, miss,' he said, and withdrew.

With her curiosity considerably piqued, Penny tore open the stout manilla and shook its contents out upon the Chesterfield beside her. To her astonishment there lay disclosed upon the faded brocade a folded sheet of paper, another envelope, and a small bag made of cheap red silk. The paper was closely written in broad distinctive writing.

Dear Penny, I have gone to pay a friendly call to show off my new suit. I may be so welcome that they won't want to part with me, so don't expect me until you see me. I leave Lugg with you as a sort of keepsake. Three meals a day, my dear, and no alcohol.

I wonder if you would mind giving him the enclosed note, which I have stuck down to show my ill-breeding. No doubt he will show it to you. But I don't want him to have it until I am safely on my journey, since he is trained to follow a car. The rather garish bag, which you will see is not made to open, contains, as far as I know, a portion of the beard of a very old friend of mine (a prophet in a small way). That is for Lugg too.

Remember your promise, which only holds good while I'm alive, of course. Don't get the wind up whatever happens. If in doubt, apply to the Professor, who is a mine of information and the best sort in the world.

Such clement weather we are having for the time of year, are we not? 'The face is but the guinea's stamp. The heart's the heart for a' that.'

Believe me, Sincerely yours, W. Shakespeare.
(Bill, to you.)

The girl sat turning the paper over on her knee until Branch re-entered with the tea-wagon. But although she was burning with curiosity, it was not until a good half-hour had elapsed that she sent for Lugg. Colonel Gyrth never took tea, and she was still alone when the door opened to admit the troubled face and portly figure of Mr Campion's other ego.

The big man had a horror of the drawing-room, which he crossed as though the floor were unsteady.

'Yes, miss?' he said suspiciously.

Penny handed him the envelope in silence. He seized upon it greedily, and, quite forgetting all Branch's training of the past few days, tore it open and began to read, holding the paper very close to his little bright eyes.

'There,' he said suddenly. 'Wot did I tell yer? Now we're for it. 'Eadstrong, that's what 'e is.'

He caught sight of Penny's face, and, remembering where he was, was about to withdraw in an abashed and elephantine fashion when she stopped him.

'I had a letter from Mr Campion too,' she said. 'He said I was to give you this.' She handed him the red silk bag, and added brazenly: 'He said you'd probably show me your letter.'

Mr Lugg hesitated at first, but finally seemed relieved at the thought of having a confidante.

'There you are,' he said ungraciously. 'That'll show yer what a caution 'e is.' He tossed the note into her lap. 'It may be a bit above yer 'ead.'

Penny unfolded the missive and began to read.

Unutterable Imbecile and Cretin. Hoping this finds you as it leaves me – in a blue funk. However, don't you worry, cleversides. Have had to resort to the Moran trick. If I am not back by tomorrow morning get somebody to take the beard of the prophet to Mrs Sarah on Heronhoe Heath. Don't have hysterics again, and if the worst comes to the worst don't forge my name to any rotten references. You'd only be found out. Leave the Open Sesame to Sarah and the Chicks. Yours, Disgusted.

Penny put the note down. 'What does it all mean?' she said.

'Ask me another,' said Mr Lugg savagely. 'Sneaked off on me, that's what 'e's done. 'E knew I'd 'ave stopped 'im if 'e didn't. This 'as torn it. I'll be readin' the Situations Vacant before I know where I am. 'E ain't even left me a reference. Lumme, we are in a mess.'

'I wish you'd explain,' said Penny, whose patience was beginning to fail her. 'What's the Moran trick, anyhow?'

'Oh, that,' said Mr Lugg. 'That was silly then. It's sooicide now. We was up against a bloke called Moran, a murderer among other things, 'oo kep' a set o' coloured thugs around 'im. What did 'Is Nibs do when we couldn't get any satisfaction from 'im but walk into 'is 'ouse as cool as you please – forcin' 'em to kidnap 'im, so's 'e could find out what they was up to. "Curiosity'll kill you, my lad," I said when I got 'im out. "A lot of satisfaction it'll be to you when you're 'arping to 'ave a pile of evidence against the bloke who's bumped you off."'

Penny sprang to her feet. 'Then he knows who it is?' she said.

'O' course 'e does,' said Mr Lugg. 'Probably known it from 'is cradle – at least, that's what 'e'll tell you. But the fac' remains that we don't know. Gorn off in a silly temper and left me out of it. If I ever get 'im back from this alive I'll 'ave 'im certified.'

The girl looked at him wildly. 'But if the Cup's safe with Val, what's he doing it for?' she wailed.

Lugg cocked a wary eye at her. 'Depend upon it, miss, there's a lot o' things neither of us 'ave been told. All we can do is to carry out 'is orders and 'ope fer the best. I'll tell yer wot, though, I'll get my lucky bean out tonight – blimey if I don't.'

Penny returned to the letter. 'Who is Mrs Sarah?' she demanded.

'The Mother Superior of a lot o' gippos,' said Mr Lugg disconsolately. 'It's either nobs or nobodies with 'im, and I loathe the sight o' both of 'em – begging yer pardon, miss.'

Penny looked up quickly. 'We'll take the token together tomorrow morning,' she said. 'Heronhoe Heath is about five miles from here across country. Mrs Shannon has her racing stables on the far side of it. We'll drive over.'

Lugg raised an eyebrow. 'Mrs Shannon? Is that the party as come snooping round 'ere the day after yer aunt died?' he said. 'Powerful voiced, and nippy like?'

'That's right,' said Penny, smiling in spite of herself.

Mr Lugg whistled. 'I 'ate women,' he said, with apparent irrelevance. 'Especially in business.'

Chapter 21

The Yellow Caravan

Heronhoe Heath, a broad strip of waste land bordered by the Ipswich road on one side and Heronhoe Creek on the other, was half covered with gaudy broom bushes when Mr Lugg and Penny bumped their way across it in the two-seater on the morning after Mr Campion's departure. The sunshine was so brilliant that a grey heat haze hung over the creek end of the heath, through which the flat red buildings of Mrs Shannon's stables were faintly discernible. There was not another house for three miles either way.

The Gypsy encampment was equally remote from the world. It lay sprawled along the northern edge of the strip like a bright bandana handkerchief spread out upon the grass by the side of a little ditch of clear water which ran through to the creek.

When they were within hailing distance of the camp the track, chewed up by many caravans' wheels, became unnegotiable. Penny pulled up. 'We'll have to walk this bit,' she said.

Mr Lugg sighed and scrambled out of the car, the girl following him. They made an odd pair.

Penny was in a white silk jumper suit and no hat, while Mr Lugg wore the conventional black suit and bowler hat of the upper servant, the respectability of which he had entirely ruined by tilting the hat over one eye, thereby achieving an air of truculent bravado which was not lessened by the straw which he held between his teeth. He grumbled in a continuous breathy undertone as he lumbered along.

'Look at 'em,' he said. 'Vagabonds. 'Ut dwellers. Lumme, you wouldn't catch me spendin' my life in a marquee.'

Penny surveyed the scene in front of her with approval. The gaily painted wagons with their high hooped canvas tops, the coloured clothes hanging out on the lines, and the dozens of little fires whose smoke curled up almost perpendicularly in the breathless air were certainly attractive. There was squalor there, too, and ugliness, but on the whole the prospect was definitely pleasing, the sunlight bringing out the colours.

What impressed the girl particularly was the number of wagons and caravans; there seemed to be quite forty of them, and she noticed that they were not settled with the numerous little odd tents and shacks around them as is usual in a big encampment, but that the whole gathering had a temporary air which was heightened by the presence of a huge old-fashioned yellow charabanc of the type used by the people of the fairs.

Although she had known the Gypsies since her childhood she had never visited them before. Their haunts had been forbidden to her, and she knew them only as brown, soft-spoken people with sales methods that would put the keenest hire-system traveller to shame.

It was with some trepidation, therefore, that she walked along by the disconsolate Lugg towards the very heart of the group. Children playing half-naked round the caravans grinned at her as she approached and shouted unintelligible remarks in shrill twittering voices. Mr Lugg went on unperturbed.

A swarthy young man leaning over the half-door of one of the vans, his magnificent arms and chest looking like polished copper against the outrageous red and white print of his shirt, took one look at Lugg and burst into a bellow of delight that summoned half the clan. Heads popped out from every conceivable opening, and just for a moment Penny was afraid that the reception was not going to be wholly friendly.

Mr Lugg stood his ground. 'Party, name o' Mrs Sarah,' he demanded in stentorian tones. 'I got a message for 'er. Private and important.'

The name had a distinctly quietening effect upon the crowd which was gathering, and the young man who had heralded their arrival opened the low door of his wagon and clattered down the steps.

'Come here,' he said, and led them across the uneven turf to the very heart of the assembly, where stood a truly magnificent caravan, decorated with a portrait of the King and Queen on one side and four dolphins surrounding a lurid representation of the Siamese Twins on the other. The brasswork in the front of this exquisitely baroque chariot was polished until it looked like gold. It formed a little balcony in front of the wagon, behind which, seated in the driver's cab, was a monstrously fat old woman, her head bound round with a green and yellow cotton scarf, while an immense print overall covered her capacious form. She was smiling, her shrewd black eyes regarding the visitors with a species of royal amusement.

Their guide made a few unintelligible remarks to her in some peculiar 'back slang' which the girl did not follow. The old woman's smile broadened.

'Come up, lady,' she said, throwing out a hand to indicate the coloured steps which led into the darkness of the wagon. As she did so the sunlight caught the rings on her hand, and the blaze of real stones dazzled in the heat.

Penny clambered up the steps and took the seat opposite the old woman, while Mr Lugg lumbered after her and perched himself gingerly on the topmost step of the ladder. The crowd still hung about inquisitively. Penny was aware of eager derisive brown faces and shrill chattering tongues making remarks she could not hope to understand.

The monstrous old lady, who appeared to be Mrs Sarah, turned upon the crowd, her smile gone. A few vitriolic sentences, at the sense of which Penny could only guess, dispersed them like naughty children. With the ease of a duchess Mrs Sarah then returned to her guests.

'Who sent you, lady?' she said in her sibilant, persuasive, 'party' voice.

Mr Lugg produced the red silk bag, which he handed to Penny, who in turn gave it to the old lady. The plump brown fingers seized upon it, and with her long blackened finger-nails Mrs Sarah jerked at the cotton which bound the topmost edge of the bag. Next moment the contents lay in her hand.

Penny regarded it with curiosity. It was an old-fashioned hair ring, made of countless tiny plaits woven together with microscopic intricacy. She held it up and laughed.

'Orlando!' she said with evident delight. 'Don't worry, lady. Sarah knows. Tomorrow,' she went on slowly. 'Yes, he said the day after. Very well. We shall be ready. Good-bye, lady.'

Penny, considerably mystified, looked startled. 'Orlando?'

Mr Lugg nudged her. 'One of 'is names,' he said sepulchrally. 'Come on. The court is adjourned.'

He was obviously right: the old woman smiled and nodded but did not seem disposed to converse any further. Penny had the impression that their hostess had received a piece of information for which she had been waiting. As the girl descended the steps, however, the affable old goddess leaned forward.

'You've got a lucky face, my dear,' she said. 'You'll get a nice husband. But you won't get Orlando.'

Considerably startled by this unexpected announcement, Penny smiled at her and started after Lugg, who was making for the little car as fast as his dignity would permit.

''E calls 'isself Orlando among the gippos,' he said. 'A funny old party, wasn't she? See 'er groinies? – Rings, I mean. Close on a thousand quid's worth there, I reckoned. All made from poor mugs like us. One of 'em told my fortune once. A journey across the water, she said. I was in Parkhurst inside of a month.'

Penny was not listening to him. 'But what does it mean?' she said. 'What's he got them to do?'

Mr Lugg made an exaggerated gesture of despair. 'They're old friends of 'is,' he said. ''E goes off with 'em sometimes. 'E don't take me – leaves me at 'ome to mind the jackdaw. That's the sort of man 'e is. You got to face these things. I can see a rough 'ouse afore we've finished.'

They had reached the car by this time, and Penny did not answer, but as she climbed into the driver's seat yet another caravan passed them heading for the camp. She glanced across the heath to where the stables lay just visible in the distance. For a moment a gleam of understanding appeared in her eyes, but she did not confide her thoughts to Lugg.

They drove home through the winding lanes to Sanctuary.

''Ere! Wot's this we're in?' said Mr Lugg, after some seventeen sharp turns. 'A blinkin' maze?'

Penny, who had grown used to his artless familiarity, smiled. 'It's a long way round by road, I know,' she said. 'It's only five miles across the fields. This road dates from the time when one had to avoid the wealthy landowners' property.'

As they passed Tye Hall Beth and the Professor were at the gate. They waved to her, and Penny pulled up and got out.

'Look here,' she said to Lugg, 'you take the car back to the Tower. I'll walk home.'

Still grumbling a little, Mr Lugg obeyed, and Penny went back along the white dusty road to where her friends were waiting.

'We're waiting for the post,' said Beth cheerfully. 'Where's your funny little friend this morning?'

'Goodness only knows,' said Penny awkwardly. 'He went off last night, leaving a note to say he was going visiting. I believe he knows something.'

The Professor, very coolly and sensibly dressed in yellow shantung and a panama hat, stroked his neat little beard with a thin brown hand. 'Is that all he said?' he inquired. 'I'll say that sounds very odd.'

'To walk out at a time like this,' said Beth. 'It's not like him.'

'I think he's up to something,' said Penny, anxious to dispel any wrong impression. 'He left Lugg and me a most extraordinary errand to do. That's where we've been. We've taken a red silk bag to an old lady who looked like that figure of Hotei in your drawing-room, Professor, all wrapped up in coloured print. She's a sort of Gypsy Queen, I suppose. There's a whole crowd of them camping on Heronhoe Heath.'

The Professor's round brown eyes widened perceptibly. 'Well, now, isn't that strange?' he said, and appeared to relapse in deep thought.

'She seemed to understand what it was all about, anyhow,' Penny went on, 'which was more than I did. And she said something about tomorrow, as if he'd made a date or something. He's an extraordinary person, you know.'

Beth opened her mouth to agree, but she was silenced by an apparition which had just appeared leaning over the field gate which split the high hedge directly opposite the Tye Hall drive. A startled exclamation escaped her, and all three of them turned and stared at the dishevelled figure which clutched the topmost bar of the gate for support.

'Val!' Beth darted across the road, the other two behind her. The young man was deathly pale. He looked ill, and as he made a move towards them he swayed drunkenly. The Professor unhooked the gate, and, hitching the boy's arm round his own shoulder, half led, half dragged him across the road and up the path to the house.

'Don't chatter to him now, girls.' The Professor spoke firmly, silencing a chorus of questions. 'He looks real bad to me. Beth, cut up to the house and get out some brandy and ice water. Penny, my dear, give me a hand with his other arm.'

'I'm all right,' said Val weakly. 'I've been doped, I think. Only just came to myself – heard you talking and staggered out. I'm a silly ass, that's what I am.'

'Hold on. Don't talk for a bit,' the Professor advised, as he led the little party into the house by the side door from the lawn. 'No, it's all right,' he said to an excited maidservant who met them. 'Don't alarm Mrs Cairey. Young Mr Gyrth has come over a bit faint, that's all.'

The girl vanished with a startled 'yessir', and the Professor turned his charge into the library, where Beth was already waiting with the brandy and water.

Val would not be silenced any longer. 'I asked for it and I got it,' he said, as he sank down gratefully into a deep saddleback. 'Gosh! I've got a head like fifty champagne suppers.'

'But what's happened?' said Penny and Beth in chorus. 'And,' added his sister as the thought suddenly burst upon her, 'where's the Cup?'

Val's clouded eyes grew hard for a moment, and he tried to struggle to his feet as the recollection returned to him. Next moment, however, he had sunk back again helplessly.

'They've got it,' he said apathetically. 'Where's Campion?'

Penny made an inarticulate noise in her throat and then sat down by the table, white and trembling.

Beth seemed more concerned about Val than any chalice, however. Beneath her kindly ministrations the boy began to recover rapidly. He looked at her gratefully.

'I'm giving you an awful lot of trouble,' he said. 'I don't know how I got in that field. I woke up and heard you talking and staggered out, and here I am.'

'Now, my boy,' said the Professor, 'what happened? Can you remember?'

Val considered. 'I was at Campion's flat,' he said. 'I sat up late, reading, with the Chalice in the suitcase actually on my lap. A damn silly place to put it, I suppose. I hadn't undressed – I didn't mean to go to bed. Early in the morning, about two or three I suppose it was, I heard a fiendish noise going on outside. I looked out of the window and saw a sort of free fight in progress round that Police station downstairs. I was wondering what was up when I heard someone in the flat behind me. He must have had a pass-key, I suppose.'

He paused reflectively as he tried to piece together the jumbled events in his mind. 'Oh well, then,' he said at last, '– curse this headache, it's blinding me – then I got a crack over the skull, but not before I'd caught a glimpse of the fellow who swatted me. I recognized him. When I was down and out,' he added awkwardly, 'I went into all sorts of low eating houses. And there was one off Berwick Street, in Soho, just by the market, you know, where I used to see a whole lot of odd fishy characters going in and out. I think they had a room at the back. Well, this chap who hit me was a man I'd seen there often. I spotted him at once. He'd got a most obvious sort of face with a curious lumpy nose.'

He stopped again and the Professor nodded comprehendingly.

'Then you were knocked out?' he suggested.

'That's right,' Val agreed. 'But I don't think I was out more than a couple of minutes at the most. I remember getting in a hell of a temper and charging downstairs; the only thing clear in my mind was that dirty little dive off Berwick Street. Outside there was still a young battle going on, and I charged through it. I think I sent a bobby flying in the process. Of course, I ought to have taken a few of them with me, but that didn't occur to me at the time. They had their hands full, anyhow.'

'And when you got to Berwick Street?' said Beth, who had listened to this recital of her hero's with wide-eyed enthusiasm.

'Well, that was about all,' said Val. 'I charged into the place like a roaring bull and asked the proprietor chap for the man I wanted. He took me into the back room, where I waited, fuming, until a great lout of a fellow came in and before I knew what had happened I got a towel full of ether or chloroform or something in my face. That's all I remember, until I found myself sitting in the hedge in the field outside here, feeling like a half resuscitated corpse.

'I say,' he added suddenly, 'what's today? I mean –?'

'You're twenty-five tomorrow,' said the Professor. 'By the look of you you've been lying in that hedge since early this morning. Thank goodness it's dry weather.'

'How did I get there?' said Val in bewilderment. 'I tell you, I was laid out in a filthy little dive off Berwick Market last night – no, it couldn't have been last night. The night before, then. I suppose they injected something. Chloroform wouldn't have kept me under all that time. Here – where's Campion? I must let him know. Although,' he added morosely, 'I suppose he's heard all about it from the police by now.'

'Albert's gone,' wailed Penny. 'And we've lost the Chalice. And yet,' she added, suddenly sitting up, 'that accounts for it. Someone was phoning Albert up all day yesterday. I was in bed at the time, but Mary told me this morning. That's why he went off. He didn't want to scare Father or me, I suppose.'

She was interrupted by the arrival of Mrs Cairey, who put her head round the door.

'Papa dear,' she said, 'the postman's here. There's that special mail you've got to pay for, and I wondered if you'd like your letters too, Penny, my dear. He'll give them to you if you come. Lands above!' she added, coming into the room, all her motherly instincts aroused, 'you do look ill, Mr Gyrth. Is there anything I can do for you?'

Penny went out with the Professor almost mechanically. Her brain was whirling with the complications of this new and apparently final development. Why on earth could no one realize that the Chalice had gone?

The postman, a scarlet-faced and perspiring East Anglian, was standing at the front door leaning gratefully on his bicycle.

'Two letters for you, miss,' he remarked, as he completed his transaction with the Professor. 'Your brother ain't 'ere by any chance, is 'e?' he added, raising a hopeful blue eye in her direction.

'He is, as a matter of fact,' said Penny, considerably startled by the coincidence of such a question.

'Ain't that lucky? The only other thing for the Tower is this parcel for 'im. If you wouldn't mind, miss –?' The man was already unbuckling the prodigious canvas bag on his carrier, and the next moment he had dumped a large and heavy parcel in her arms. 'It's lucky you got it,' he said. 'It feels like it's over the regulation weight to me. Good morning, miss.'

He touched his ridiculous hat and swung on to the bicycle.

Penny, with the parcel in her arms, walked slowly back to the study. Just as she entered the room something about the weight and size of her burden sent a curious thrill through her.

'Val,' she said breathlessly, 'open this. I think – oh, I don't know – anyhow, open it.'

There was something so imperative in her tone that the boy's interest was roused.

'What in the name of –' he began. 'Oh, it's my birthday tomorrow. It's probably something stupid from one of the relations.'

Nevertheless he accepted the knife Beth handed him and ripped up the cords, displaying a stout cardboard box of the type usually used to pack large bottles. Something of his sister's excitement seemed to be conveyed to him, for the hand that unfastened the slotted end of the carton shook violently.

Next moment he had pulled out a wad of straw packing and an exclamation escaped him. The Professor, Mrs Cairey and Beth bent forward, and very gently he drew out the long, slender golden cup that Mr Melchizadek's great grandfather had made.

'The Chalice!' said Penny, a sob in her voice. 'Oh, Val, it's all right.'

The faces of the other two women reflected her delight, but the Professor and Val exchanged glances.

'How –?' said Val breathlessly. 'This is incredible. Is there any message? Who addressed it?'

A frenzied search revealed that there was no other enclosure, and that the address was printed in block capitals. The postmark was illegible.

The Professor cleared his throat. 'I guess I can understand this,' he said, tapping the relics of the parcel. 'But how you arrived in that field this morning is completely beyond my comprehension. Who set you there, and why? It doesn't make sense.'

Penny, who had been staring at her brother during the last few minutes, suddenly stretched out her hand.

'Val!' she said. 'Your buttonhole!'

Instinctively the boy put up his hand to the lapel of his collar and an expression of astonishment came into his face as he detached a drooping wild flower bud from the slit and stared at it.

'Funny,' he said. 'I certainly don't remember putting it there. It's fairly fresh, too.'

Penny snatched it from him. 'Don't you see what it is?' she said, her voice rising. 'There's hundreds of them in that field where you woke up. It's a white campion. There's only one person on earth who would think of that.'

Chapter 22

The Three-Card Trick

Mr Campion stopped his car among the high broom bushes on Heronhoe Heath that evening and sniffed the air appreciatively. He seemed if anything a little more inane than usual, and in spite of his evident anxiety, there was something about him which conveyed that he was definitely pleased with himself.

Although he had been driving most of the day there was no trace of weariness in his tall loose-limbed figure. He locked the car, slipped the key into his pocket, and stood for a moment with his hand on the bonnet. 'The highwayman's farewell to his horse,' he remarked aloud to the empty air, and then, turning abruptly, strode off across the springy turf.

Behind him the lights of the Gypsy camp glowed in the dusk, and for a moment he hesitated, half drawn by their inviting friendliness. He turned away resolutely, however, and contented himself by hailing them with a long drawn-out whistle that might easily have come from one of the myriad seabirds on the creek. He paused to listen, the heath whispering and rustling around him. Almost immediately the cry was returned, two melodious whistles that sounded pleasantly reassuring. Mr Campion appeared satisfied and strode on his way almost jauntily.

Mrs Dick's stables were only just discernible, a dark rectangular patch in the greyness. He had miscalculated the distance a little, and the walk was longer than he had anticipated. When he reached the buildings at last he stood for a moment in the shadow of a high wall listening intently. There was no sound from within, and, convinced that his approach had not been observed, he began to work slowly round the walls, moving silently and using his torch at intervals.

The building was much as he had expected. A high red wall enclosed the whole of the establishment, forming a large rectangular block, only one side of which was skirted by the rough private track which he had been so careful to avoid in his journey from the main road.

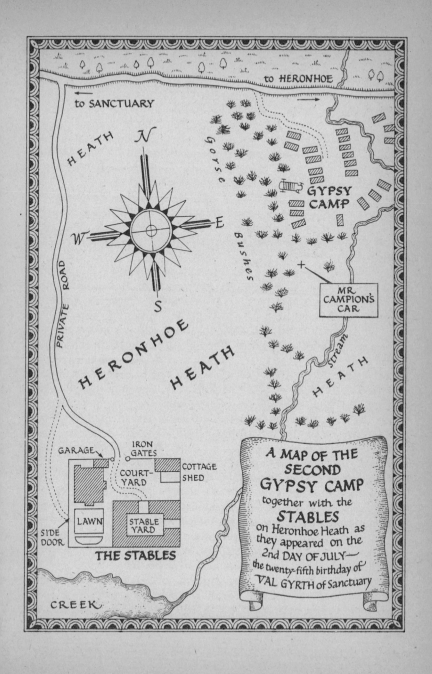

to HERONHOE

to SANCTUARY

HEATH

N

W — E

S

PRIVATE ROAD

Gorse

Bushes

GYPSY CAMP

+

MR. CAMPION'S CAR

HERONHOE HEATH

stream

HEATH

GARAGE

IRON GATES

COURT-YARD

COTTAGE SHED

LAWN

STABLE YARD

SIDE DOOR

THE STABLES

CREEK

A MAP OF THE SECOND GYPSY CAMP together with the STABLES on Heronhoe Heath as they appeared on the 2nd DAY OF JULY— the twenty-fifth birthday of VAL GYRTH of Sanctuary

The large iron gates which formed the entrance from the track were locked. Peering cautiously through them, he was relieved to find the place in darkness. The dwelling-house and garden took up the western third of the rectangle. Directly in front of him was a square court with a cottage on his left, while the stables occupied the remaining portion of the whole block. They were built on all four sides of a square, two storeys high, with big wooden gates to the courtyard and a second entrance giving on to the heath on the eastern side, at right-angles to the creek. The drive led on a gentle curve past the front door of the house to the wooden gates of the stable yard.

Alone in the darkness, Mr Campion became suddenly intensely alert. Somewhere in the house he fancied he could hear the murmur of voices. He made no attempt to enter until he had been all round the buildings, however, and by the time he had returned to the front gates once more he was considerably wiser.

The place was in appalling repair and many of the bricks had begun to fluke badly under the influence of the salt air. Mr Campion put his spectacles in his pocket, and, having chosen a suitable spot by the kitchens of the house where an overgrown creeper hung down, began to climb. It was by no means an easy ascent, for the wall was high, and it was surmounted by broken glass which the creeper only just masked. He accomplished it, however, and slid noiselessly to the ground on the other side. Once again he paused to listen, holding his breath. Still there was no noise but the continued murmur of voices somewhere on the opposite side of the house.

Having replaced his spectacles, he set off once more on his perambulation. There were no dogs nor grooms to be seen, and after careful inspection of the stable yard, the wooden doors of which stood ajar, Mr Campion was convinced that the information which he had gathered on one of his many visits that afternoon in London was substantially correct. Mrs Dick's racing stables could hardly be regarded as a going concern. Although there were boxes for twenty horses, only one of them appeared to be occupied.

The cottage by the stable gates was empty also, and evidences of decay were on all sides. Only the lawn and the courtyard were trim. The garden was a wilderness.

Very cautiously he approached the one lighted aperture in the whole establishment; two glass doors giving out on to the lawn. He had been careful to avoid the beam of light which they shed on to the lawn, but now he ventured up to it, the grass deadening his footsteps.

There was a thin net curtain over the windows, but the light inside rendered it transparent as he came nearer. In the relics of what had once been a fine room, five men and a woman were grouped round a table at which a hand of poker was in progress.

'Not a nice lot,' Mr Campion reflected as he glanced from face to face. There was Matthew Sanderson, looking more astute than ever as he dealt the cards; the horse-faced 'Major', and Fingers Hawkins, who had held him up on the road, a little ill at ease among his social superiors, but nevertheless in shirt-sleeves. Then there was a grey-headed, narrow-eyed man he did not recognize, and a little insignificant Japanese half-caste that he did, and whose presence bewildered him.

Mrs Dick dominated the group by sheer force of personality. As usual, she was strikingly smart; her black and white dress contrived to be almost theatrical in its extreme yet austere fashionableness. Her white face was twisted in a half-smile. Her hair was close-cropped like a man's, displaying her curiously lobeless ears. A heavy rope of barbaric crimson beads was coiled round her throat, and the feminine touch looked bizarre upon her angular, masculine form.

'Not staying, Major?' she said, as the red-faced man threw down his cards. 'You never have the courage to see a thing through. Sandy, I've been watching you. You're playing all you know.'

Sanderson threw down his cards. 'I wonder someone hasn't strangled you, Daisy,' he said, with more admiration than resentment in his tone.

Mrs Dick was unabashed. 'My husband tried,' she observed.

'You got him first, I suppose?' said the Major, laughing.

The woman fixed him with her peculiarly insolent stare. 'He used to say the whisky wasn't strong enough,' she said. 'I often think it was the methylated spirits we used to pep it up with that killed him.'

Sanderson turned away. 'You put the wind up me,' he said. 'The way you talk I wonder you're not afraid of the "Blacking".'

Mrs Dick laughed. 'I'd like to see any man who's got the guts to blackmail me,' she said. 'Make it five, Tony.'

'No "Blacking",' said Fingers Hawkins from the other side of the table. 'But we'll get our do's.'

'You'll get your dues and more.' Mrs Dick was inclined to be contemptuous. 'I'll make it the limit, Tony. You won't stay? Thanks. Mine.'

She threw down her hand as Mr Campion tapped on the window.

The gentle noise startled everyone save Mrs Dick, who hardly looked up from the cards she was collecting. 'Open that window, Fingers,' she murmured. 'There's something scratching on it.'

The big man went forward cautiously, and, raising the catch, jerked the half-door open, jumping smartly sideways as he did so.

Mr Campion, pale, smiling and ineffably inane, was revealed on the threshold.

'Good evening, everybody,' he said, coming into the room. 'Anybody got a good tip for the Ascot Gold Cup?'

Fingers Hawkins side-stepped behind him and passed out into the darkness. ''E's alone,' he remarked, and coming back into the room, relocked the window.

At this piece of information the spirits of the company, which had been momentarily uncertain, now became almost uproarious. Sanderson began to laugh.

'All on his own,' he said. 'Isn't that sweet and confiding? We were telling Daisy she ought to invite you for a nice quiet rest until the fun was over, and here you are.'

'Look out. P'raps there's a cartload of busies outside,' said the half-caste nervously.

Sanderson turned on him. 'Shut up, Moggie,' he said viciously. 'How many times have I told you the police aren't in this business? What d'you think they're going to get you for – being alive?'

'Well, I could understand that,' remarked Mr Campion affably. 'Still, everyone to his taste, eh, Mrs Shannon?'

Mrs Dick did not deign to look in his direction. 'What have you come here for?' she said, reshuffling the cards. 'I don't think I know you.'

'Nonsense,' said Mr Campion. 'We met at the dear Vicar's. You must remember. I was passing round the biscuits. You took two. Then we both laughed heartily.'

Mrs Dick raised her eyes and regarded him coldly. 'You seem to be even more of a fool than I took you for at first,' she said, her stentorian tones blaring at him across the card table. 'What are you doing here?'

'Calling,' said Mr Campion firmly. 'That must be obvious to the meanest intelligence.'

'Sandy,' said Mrs Shannon, 'put this creature out.'

'Not on your life.' Sanderson spoke with enthusiasm. 'Daisy underestimates you, Campion. I shall feel all the safer with you as a guest here for the next few days. Got a gun?'

'No,' said Mr Campion. 'I don't like firearms. Even pea-shooters are dangerous in my opinion.'

'No fooling. I've got mine trained on you.'

Mr Campion shrugged his shoulders and turned to Fingers.

'Do your stuff,' he said, raising his arms above his head. 'I love to see a professional at work.'

'You stow it,' said the pickpocket uneasily. Nevertheless he complied with Mr Campion's request, and stood back a moment or so later shaking his head.

Sanderson's amusement increased.

'Well, this *is* friendly,' he said. 'What d'you think you're doing? You've done some balmy things in your life, but now you've stepped clean over the edge. What's the idea?'

'You look out for 'im,' said the gentleman addressed as Moggie. ''E's as slippery as an eel. 'E's got something up his sleeve, you betcher life. Probably that great bull pup Lugg's about somewhere.'

'Write that down, sign it, send it to our head office, and we present you with a magnificent fountain pen absolutely free,' said Mr Campion. 'Every testimonial, however humble, is docketed and on view at any time.'

Mrs Dick stacked the cards up neatly and turned in her chair to survey her visitor once more. 'Why have you come here, young man?' she said. 'You're beginning to bore me.'

'Just you wait,' said Mr Campion. 'Wait till I get my personality over. I do hope you don't mind. I've been looking over your stables. There's one thing I didn't quite get. So many boxes but only 'a' horse's. I suppose the pretty creature has a different home each day, like Alice at the mad tea party.'

The woman's expression did not change, but her strong bony hands ceased to play with the cards.

'Perhaps you had better stay here for a day or two,' she said. 'Lock him up in one of the boxes, Sandy, and then for Heaven's sake stick to the game.'

'We'd better see if he *is* alone, first,' said Sanderson. 'I shan't be surprised if he is. He's conceited enough for anything.'

'If you find anyone outside he's nothing to do with me,' said Mr Campion. 'Absolutely no connection with any other firm. No; as I told you before, I'm making a perfectly normal formal call. I climbed the wall by a honeysuckle bush. Up and down, quite unaided. Moggie couldn't have done it better. Frankly,' he went on, turning towards that worthy, 'I don't see what a cat burglar is doing in this.'

'You don't have to,' cut in Sanderson quickly. 'You don't have to think about us. It's your own skin you've got to watch. Fingers, you and the Major go and have a scout round.'

'That's right,' said Mr Campion. 'And whistle all the time. Then we'll know it's you. Meantime, perhaps I could show you some card tricks?' he added, eyeing the pack on the table wistfully. 'Or I'll tell your fortune, Mrs Shannon. You've got a lucky face.'

To everyone's surprise Mrs Dick threw the pack in his direction. Mr Campion picked them up and shuffled with great solemnity.

'You cut three times towards me and wish,' he said. His pale eyes were mild and guileless, and there was an infantile expression upon his face. She cut the cards, the half-amused, half-derisive smile still twisting her small thin mouth.

Mr Campion set about arranging the cards with a portentous air. 'I see a lot of knaves about you,' he remarked cheerfully. 'One fat one,' he added, eyeing the retreating form of the 'Major'.

Sanderson laughed. 'You're a cool customer,' he said, a tinge of admiration in his voice. 'Carry on.'

'I see a great understanding,' said Mr Campion, planking down the cards one after the other. 'And a lot of trouble. Oh, dear, dear, dear! All black cards. It looks as if there's a hanging in it for somebody.'

'Shut up,' said Sanderson, stretching out a hand as if to sweep the cards off the table. 'He's playing for time, or something.'

'Hush,' said Mr Campion. 'I'm going to have my palm crossed with silver for this – I hope. Now here's a whole stack of money – I might almost say a pot of money. Ah, don't be led astray by riches, lady. Here comes the luck card. It's very close but it doesn't quite touch. There's a fair young man in between. I should watch out for him, Mrs Dick.'

He prattled on, apparently oblivious of his surroundings.

'There's an old woman and her son who'll give the game away if you don't take care – a silly old woman and a sillier son. You'll have a lot to answer for there,' he said presently, and was interrupted by the return of the two searchers.

'All the gates fast. Not a soul on the heath. He's alone,' said the Major. 'Shall we take him along now?'

'Don't interrupt,' said Mr Campion reprovingly. 'The gentleman is suffering from second sight and must not be disturbed until the fit is passed. Now, let me see.' He sat for a moment looking at the cards which he had arranged in a half circle on the table. They lay so that one broken end faced Mrs Dick and the other was beneath his hand.

'Oh, yes,' he said at last, as though a new thought had occurred to him. 'And then there's journeys.' He bent across the table and planted a single card before the woman some distance from the rest, so that the whole formation resembled a rough question mark.

'I see a far journey,' he remarked. 'Why yes, most certainly. *You take the long road.*' And then, as she stared at the table, he swept the cards carelessly aside and rose to his feet.

'The seance is ended,' he said. 'Any more for the information bureau? Sanderson, let me tell you your past.'

An explosive giggle from the 'Major' was silenced by a single savage glance from the gentleman addressed.

'You'll stop mucking about,' Sanderson said. 'Where shall I put him, Daisy? In the loft, I suppose.'

'Looks to me as though he's askin' for it a bit obvious,' said Moggie. 'What price we chuck 'im out on 'is ear?'

It was Mrs Dick who settled the discussion. 'Put him in the gate loft,' she said. 'Let him cool his heels for a couple of days.'

Sanderson grinned. 'I thought you'd see reason,' he remarked complacently. He put his hand on Campion's shoulder and jerked him towards the door. Fingers Hawkins seized his other arm, and thus, with all ignominy, was Mr Campion escorted to the stables which he had so lately examined; but although he protested the whole way, it should perhaps be recorded that on the whole he felt distinctly satisfied.

Chapter 23

'Madame, Will You Talk?'

At eight o'clock on the evening of July the second, Val Gyrth's twenty-fifth birthday, Mr Campion languished in the room over the gateway of Mrs Shannon's stableyard. It was an effective prison. The windows were barred to prevent an entry rather than an exit, but they were equally efficient in either case. The two doors which led into other first storey rooms on either side were locked. Even had he desired to escape, the process would have been difficult.

The atmosphere was suffocating under the low penthouse roof, and his couch, which consisted of a blanket thrown over a heap of straw, was not altogether comfortable. Yet he was by no means disheartened. He had had frequent visitors during the day, but so far the one person he had come to see had studiously avoided him.

While Sanderson seemed fidgety with curiosity, Mrs Dick had not yet appeared.

This was the one factor in his plans that had so far miscarried, and here he was completely in the dark. And he realized clearly that upon Mrs Dick's character everything depended.

During the day he had ascertained that there were considerably more men at the lady's command than he had encountered at the poker game, but he felt grateful at the thought of the yellow caravan across the heath.

He rose to his feet and glanced out of the window. Great dark blue streaks of cloud were beginning to creep across the golden sky in the west. A clatter in the yard sent him over to the opposite window, and he stood looking down at just such a scene as Sanderson had described to the uninterested little group in the Cup House on the day after Lady Pethwick's death.

Mrs Dick, assisted by a terrified stable-boy and the equally unhappy 'Major', was engaged in transferring her remaining pedigree mare from one box to another. They made an extraordinary picture; the woman, tall, angular and more mannish than ever in her rat-catcher riding-breeches and gaiters, and her white shirt buttoned tight to her neck and finished with a high stock tie of the same colour. Her cropped head was bare, and the evening light fell upon her pale, distorted face. The beast, a beautiful creature with a coat like black satin save for a single white stocking, was both nervous and bad-tempered. She was as heavy as a hunter and very tall, and as she moved the great muscles rippled down her shoulders like still water ruffled by the wind.

She refused the second box, and reared, pawing savagely with her forefeet. Mrs Dick, one hand gripping the bridle rein, lashed out with her whip. Again and again the mare refused, clattering over the yard till the bricks echoed. But the woman was indomitable; a dozen times she seemed to save herself by sheer skill and the single steel wrist by which she held the animal.

Mr Campion remembered the horse's name, 'Bitter Aloes'. As the words came back to him the battle outside came to a sudden end. The mare, charging savagely at her mistress, had been rewarded by a vicious punch on her velvet nose from a small but very forceful feminine fist, and as she clattered back from this unexpected attack the woman seized her opportunity and ran her back unprotesting into the box. Mrs Dick emerged a moment later, grim and triumphant, superbly conscious of her victory. She accepted the 'Major's' clumsy congratulations with a tart bellow of 'Don't be a fool,' which reached Mr Campion clearly in his prison, and once again the yard was deserted.

He remained standing by the window for some time, vaguely troubled. The presence of Moggie, the little Japanese half-caste, puzzled him. And there was the grey-headed man too. There was no telling to what particular branch of the profession he might belong.

For the rest, however, he was content to wait. If Mrs Dick had any spark of femininity in her make-up she would come to see him after the fortune-telling episode. He was a little surprised that she had not come before. The burning question of the moment, as far as he was concerned, and the sole reason for his present position, was the problem of whether Mrs Dick was alone the employee of the '*Société Anonyme*', the amateur who, with the professional assistance of Matthew Sanderson and his associates, was directly responsible for the whole adventure of the Gyrth Chalice, the employee whose death according to the rules of the society would constitute the only reason for the abandonment of the quest.

For his own sake as much as hers Mr Campion trusted fervently that this was not the case. Both he and Val had mentally shelved this aspect of the affair, concentrating doggedly on the immediate protection of the Chalice. But always this question had been lurking in the background, and now, it seemed to Campion, it clamoured for recognition.

In spite of himself he shied away from the subject and turned his thoughts towards the Tower. He imagined the sedate and rather solemn little dinner-party now in progress; Sir Percival at the head of the table with Val on his right, Penny opposite her brother, and Pembroke, the old parson, beside her. The conversation would be constrained, he felt sure, in spite of the intimate nature of the gathering. The shadow of the secret room would hang over them all relentlessly; the secret room which held the real Gyrth Chalice, and something else, that something which never seemed to leave Sir Percival's thoughts. He wondered if Val would react in the same way as his father had done, or if the sharing of the secret would lighten the burden on the old man's mind.

He was disturbed in his reflections by the sound of a motor engine in the courtyard, and, glancing out of the opposite window to that by which he had been standing, he saw Sanderson bringing out a car from the garage.

Something about this most ordinary action alarmed him unreasonably.

There was a storm blowing up, and the heat, which had been oppressive all day, was now positively unbearable. Sanderson went into the house, and Campion was able to stare at the car at his leisure. Lying over the front seat he saw a coil of very flexible rope, knotted at intervals. He was puzzled, and his pale face peering through the bars of the window wore an expression of almost childlike discomfort. There was a distinct atmosphere of preparation abroad; something was about to happen.

The sound of a key turning in a lock behind him made him spin round.

Mrs Dick stepped briskly into the room. She wore the costume in which he had seen her in the yard, and the short-handled whip was still in her hand. She stood with her back to the door, her legs slightly straddled, and regarded him insolently.

Immediately Mr Campion sensed the extreme force of her personality, for the first time, directed upon him alone. He had met forceful and unpleasant personalities before in the course of a short and somewhat chequered career, but never in a woman, and it was this fact which robbed him for the moment of his usual urbanity.

'You haven't shaved this morning,' she said suddenly. 'I like men to be clean. I don't want you in this loft any longer. Get in here, will you?'

Mr Campion looked hurt as he complied with her command, and suffered himself to be driven through a succession of similar lofts until he came to a full stop in a hay-strewn apartment which was, if anything, more hot and dusty than the one he had just left, in spite of the fact that there was a small open grating overlooking the heath in lieu of a window in the outer wall.

Mrs Dick followed him into the room and shut the door behind her.

'I want you in here because both doors bolt on the outside,' she remarked. 'Now, young man, what did you come here for?'

Mr Campion considered. 'You hurt me about not being shaved,' he said. 'None of your friends would trust me with a razor. I used to have a beard once. I called it "Impudence" – "Persuasion" out of "Cheek", you see. Rather neat, don't you think?'

Mrs Dick permitted herself one of her sour smiles.

'I've been hearing about you,' she said. 'Impudence seems to be your strong point. I'm sorry you've got yourself mixed up in this. You might have been amusing. However,' she went on, 'since you've evidently got nothing to say, it's quite obvious to me what you're doing here. Since you are a prisoner like this, it gives you an excellent excuse to explain to your employers why you've failed. I recognize that fact.'

Mr Campion grinned. 'I say,' he said, 'that's a good idea. How did you come to that startling conclusion?'

Mrs Dick remained unmoved. 'It was quite clever,' she said judicially. 'What a pity you'll never be able to use it. Sandy thinks you know much too much to get away with it. I've never paid blackmail, and I'm certainly not going to begin.'

'It must be the people you associate with,' said Mr Campion with dignity. 'My Union doesn't allow blackmail. I had no idea I was going to be a perpetual guest,' he added cheerfully. 'I do hope you won't expect me to wear an iron mask.'

Mrs Dick raised her eyebrows expressively, but she did not speak, and he went on.

'I suppose your present intention is to keep me here until you fix everything up with your London agents?'

The woman shot a penetrating glance at him. 'You know very well we haven't succeeded yet,' she said. 'You were very clever, Mr Campion, making all that fuss about your spurious Chalice. A little childish, perhaps, but quite effective. You made us waste a lot of time.'

Mr Campion's pale eyes flickered behind his spectacles. The blow had gone home.

'So you've found that out, have you?' he said. 'You've been pretty quick. Little Albert has been taking things too easily, I see. Dear, dear, dear! What are you going to do next? Have a lovely treasure hunt and give prizes? I'll come and tell you when you're getting warm.'

'I'm not amused by nonsense,' said Mrs Dick. 'In fact,' she added with devastating frankness, 'I have very little sense of humour.'

'Well, that's original, I can't say fairer than that,' said Mr Campion politely. 'May I make you a suggestion? Take the Chalice you already have. It has been in the Cup House at the Tower ever since it was made. Present it to your employers. If they cavil at it you can answer sincerely that as far as you know it is the only Gyrth Chalice in existence. I fancy that they'd pay up.'

'Now you're beginning to be genuinely amusing,' said Mrs Dick. She lit a cigarette from a yellow packet which she drew from her breeches' pocket. 'You don't seem to be very well informed. The spurious cup was sent back to the Tower the day before yesterday. I know perfectly well where the real Chalice is and I'm going to get it.'

'With Matt Sanderson, Fingers Hawkins, Natty Johnson, the Major, old Uncle Tom Moggie and all,' said Mr Campion. 'You won't get much of a look-in on the pay roll, will you? Mother, is it worth it? Father's got to have his share, you know.'

Mrs Dick stopped smoking, the cigarette hanging limply between her thin lips.

'I'm managing this,' she said. 'I was approached and the responsibility as well as the reward is entirely mine.'

Mr Campion was silent for some moments. Then he coughed, and raising his eyes to hers, he regarded her solemnly. 'If you're really responsible for this little lot,' he said gravely, 'the situation becomes exceedingly uncomfortable and difficult. In fact, to put it crudely, to end the matter satisfactorily, one or both of us will have to retire from the picture pretty effectively.'

'That,' said Mrs Dick absently, 'has already occurred to me. You won't get out of here alive, my friend.'

'Threats!' said Mr Campion, his light-heartedness returning. 'Isn't it time you hissed at me? You have an advantage over me by being dressed for the part, you know. Give me a pair of moustachios and I'll be a villain too.'

The light was gradually going, though he could still distinguish her white face across the loft, but he felt himself all the more at a disadvantage inasmuch as the finer shades of expression on it were lost to him.

'It would interest me,' she said suddenly, 'to know who employed you. The Gyrths, I suppose. How did they get wind of it in the first place? Well, I'm sorry they've wasted their money. Heaven knows they've got little enough.'

'I suppose you need money yourself,' said Campion quietly.

'Naturally. I've spent two fortunes in my time,' said Mrs Dick without boast or regret. 'That's why I've got to get hold of another. You don't think I'm going to allow a little rat like you to interfere?'

'You underestimate me,' said Mr Campion with firm politeness. 'Manly courage, intelligence and resource are my strong points.'

He raised his voice during the last words for the first time during the interview. Instantaneously there was a clatter of hoofs beneath his feet, followed by several thunderous kicks on the woodwork which shook the building.

'Bitter Aloes,' said Mrs Dick significantly. 'She's in the box beneath here. You're in good company. Keep your voice down, though . . . she's vicious with strangers.'

'Not too matey with the lady of the house,' observed Mr Campion more quietly. 'I saw you playing together in the yard like a pair of kittens. I thought she'd get you with her forefeet.'

'She killed a boy last year.' Mrs Dick's voice was brisk but expressionless. 'I was supposed to have her shot but I wangled out of it. The little beast came on her unexpectedly. I saw it happen. It wasn't a pretty death. Those forefeet of hers were like steel hammers.'

Mr Campion hunched his shoulders. 'You have a curious taste in pets,' he observed. 'Fingers Hawkins and Bitter Aloes make a very fine pair. But suppose we cut the melodrama and come back to business? In the first place – merely as a matter of curiosity, of course – how do you hope to get away with it?'

'What can prevent me?' said Mrs Dick with placid assurance. 'You seem to forget why I was invited to enter into the business at all. My position is unassailable. I can go where I like with impunity, and surround myself with as many rough customers as I like without rousing any suspicion. That's the advantage of a profession and a reputation like mine.'

'I see,' said Mr Campion. 'And this reputation of yours plus the state of your financial affairs which rendered you practically desperate, got you the contract, as we say in big business? But what I meant was, how do you expect to get clear away – go on living here, for example?'

'Why not? Mere suspicion can't upset a standing like mine. Even if the police arrested me, what possible reason could I have for stealing a gold cup? It isn't saleable, you know, and I'm not the sort of person to collect drawing-room ornaments. The police are not the people to press the question of my employers. Once I have hold of it I can do exactly as I please. The Gyrths daren't blare their loss abroad. Frankly, I don't see how the police would come into it, and ordinary county feeling has long since ceased to affect me. I assure you I've come through worse scandals than this will ever cause.'

Mr Campion was silent, and she shot him an inquisitive glance through the gloom. 'Well?' she said.

'I was thinking how clever they are, these employers of yours,' he said slowly. 'You're right. You're unassailable. In fact, there's only one danger point in your whole scheme.'

'And that?'

'Me,' said Mr Campion modestly. 'You see, I know the rules of the society as well as you do. You, I take it,' he went on quietly, 'are thinking of killing me?'

'It would be absurd of me to let you interfere with my affairs,' said Mrs Shannon. 'You might possibly have been useful to me, but as it is you're a damned little nuisance. I'm not thinking of killing you. I'm preparing to kill you.'

'So this is Suffolk,' said Mr Campion. 'Commend me to Chicago. I hate to keep raising objections, but won't you find my body about the place more than just a social nuisance? I know the police are forgiving, friendly people, but they do draw the line at a body. Perhaps you're going to bury me in the garden or throw me in the creek? Do tell.'

The woman made no reply, and he went on.

'Before you get busy, however, I must do my singing exercises. Listen to this for an E in Alt.'

He threw back his head, and the shrill bird cry that had sounded over the heath the previous evening now echoed through the little room. The grating above Mr Campion's head was open to the heath, and the sound escaped clearly to the sky beyond. Again he shouted, and the horse below clattered and kicked violently in her stable.

Mrs Dick began to laugh.

'If you've been relying on that pack of Gypsies,' she said, 'it's kindest to tell you that I had them sent off the heath this morning. You're alone. You seem to have played your cards very badly. In fact,' she added with sudden seriousness, 'you're such a damn failure that you're beginning to irritate me.'

Mr Campion's eyes were hard and anxious behind his spectacles, but his expression of charming inanity had never wavered.

'Talking of failures,' he said, 'where's your success? You're no better off than when you started. You haven't got the Chalice.'

'It's perfectly obvious where it is,' said Mrs Dick slowly. 'I was a fool not to think of it before. In that secret room in the east wing they make such a fuss about, of course. That was clear to me as soon as I found the cup in the chapel was spurious. I shall have the Chalice tonight.'

She spoke with complete assurance, a tone that dismissed any other possibility as absurd. Mr Campion stiffened.

'I see,' he said softly.

He took off his spectacles and put them in his pocket. It was growing very dark in the loft, and although he was not altogether unprepared for what followed, the suddenness of her attack caught him unawares. He saw the flash of the woman's arm in its white shirt-sleeve upraised, and the next moment the thong of her whip caught him full across the face and sent him staggering back against the wall beneath the grating.

He was vaguely aware of voices outside, but he had no time to think clearly. Mrs Dick was lashing at him with the same cool skill and deadly accuracy with which she had subdued the mare who was trampling wildly in the box beneath them. He threw up his arms to shield his face, and reeled backward as she drove him into the corner.

She came after him, feeling in the hay-strewn floor with her foot. At last she found what she sought. With a single vicious twist of her heel she shot back the iron bolt of the hay-shoot, precipitating the young man into the maelstrom of flying hoofs below.

Instinctively he threw out his hands to save himself, and his fingers caught at the edge of the trap.

For a sickening moment he swung suspended in the air. Mrs Dick, bending down to draw up the trap again, kicked his fingers from their grasp as if she were flicking a stone out of her way.

Then she drew up the door by the slack rope and slipped the bolt home.

Chapter 24
Bitter Aloes

Bitter Aloes was as frightened by the sudden intrusion into her box as was Mr Campion by his equally sudden descent. She started back, rearing and screaming, her forefeet beating wildly in the air. It was this momentary respite which saved Mr Campion's life.

Set across the corner of the stable, some four feet below the ceiling, was an old-fashioned iron hay-basket, just low enough to allow the horse to pull out mouthfuls of fodder as she desired, while saving the bulk from being fouled on the ground or in the manger.

When Mrs Dick kicked Mr Campion's fingers from their grasp, he dropped, and was actually in the low wooden manger when Bitter Aloes reared above him. Pressing himself back into a corner to save himself as much as possible from the flying hoofs, his head brushed against the bars of this hay-basket. The mare, frenzied with fear and with bad temper, rose up on her hind legs once more, pawing frantically in the gloom.

Campion leapt for the iron basket, drawing himself up into it, and at last crouched, his head and shoulders battened down beneath the rebolted trap and Bitter Aloes snapping at him not six inches below his feet. Even at that moment he could not help marvelling at the simple villainy of Mrs Dick's arrangements. A stranger found savaged to death and probably unrecognizable in a racehorse box would convey only one thing to a jury's mind, especially if the lady supplied any necessary details to show that he had entered the stable for some nefarious purpose. Twelve good Suffolk men and true would consider it a case of poetic justice.

With his head and shoulders still smarting from her whip and his body growing numb in its unnatural position, which he knew he could not hold for long, he listened intently. Bitter Aloes had quietened considerably, but he could still hear her snorting angrily and the swishing of her tail in the darkness. Outside he was vaguely aware of a bustle in the yard. Mrs Dick and her party of raiders were about to set out. He realized that she must have some very definite plan of action, and his heart failed him as he thought of the Tower completely unprotected save for Val and a handful of servants, all of whom would be taken by surprise. It would not only be robbery with violence, but robbery by a group of picked men, each a master in his own particular line. Such a party could hardly fail, since they had such a very good notion where to look for their spoil. The difficulty of tracing them once the coup was made would be unsurmountable even for Scotland Yard, since the treasure itself could never be traced.

Savage with himself as much as with the woman, Campion raised himself cautiously in his perilous cradle and tried to force the trapdoor up, against the hinge, by the whole strength of his head and shoulders. There was an ominous creak and he felt to his horror that it was the staples that supported the hay basket and not the trapdoor which were giving.

He ceased his futile efforts and crouched down once more, while Bitter Aloes, alarmed by the noise, reared again.

It was at this moment that he became aware of footsteps above his head. Someone was moving stealthily across the loft. He crouched back in the corner, fearing for an instant that Mrs Dick had returned to make sure that the mare had done her work. His alarm increased as the bolt of the trap was shot safely back and the door began to descend.

The next moment a shaft of light from an electric torch cut through the gloom and sent Bitter Aloes rearing and kicking against the outer wall of the stable. Mr Campion remained very still, racked by a thousand cramps.

The trap opened a little wider, and a soft American voice murmured:

'Say, Campion, are you there?'

The young man started so violently that the staples creaked beneath him.

'Professor Cairey!' he whispered.

'Oh, you're there, are you?' The torch was turned full on his face. 'I thought she'd got you. Hold on a minute while I let this door down. Then you can pull yourself up.'

The trapdoor descended, Mr Campion keeping his head low. A minute later, assisted by the Professor, he was dragging himself up into the loft once more. The American pulled up the trap behind him and shot the bolt.

'I'll say it was time I dropped in,' he remarked. 'What's happened to your face? Did the horse do that?'

'No, that's its mistress,' said Mr Campion bitterly. 'You've saved my life, Professor. How on earth did you land here?'

The old man rose to his feet and dusted his knees before replying. It was lighter in the loft than in the stable, and Campion could see his dapper little figure, still in his shantung suit, and the sharp triangle made by his white vandyke beard.

'Something occurred to me,' he remarked softly. 'A point I thought maybe you'd overlooked. So I just came along on a bicycle on the off-chance of finding you.' He paused. 'I figured out where you were when Penny told me she's been to see those Gypsies. I trailed around the heath until I found your car. Then I was sure. By the way, your tyres have been slashed.'

Mr Campion was still looking at him as if he could hardly believe his eyes, and the Professor's voice continued with the same gentle precision, for all the world as if he had been carrying on a most normal conversation in his own library.

'I called on the lady this afternoon,' he went on. 'Sent in my card and said I'd come about some yearlings that I thought might interest her. She sent word that she couldn't see me, and the man I saw let me out of the front door. Fortunately there was no one around. I guessed they'd keep you a prisoner, and looking at the stables I thought what a grand prison they'd make. So I nipped into an empty loose box. I've been here about two hours.' He paused, and then added quietly: 'You see, in my opinion it's vitally necessary for you to go back to the Tower tonight.'

'How did you get *here*?' said Campion, still amazed by the astounding matter-of-fact attitude of the old gentleman.

The Professor chuckled. 'I waited in a horse-box until I saw that woman fooling about with a horse. Land sakes! I thought she was going to put it in on top of me. So I nipped up a ladder on to the top floor, and I hadn't been waiting there above fifteen minutes when I heard you talking to her in here. My hearing isn't altogether what it used to be and I didn't quite make out what either of you was up to. But I heard you fall through the trap and I heard her go out. Then I had some difficulty getting the door open and it wasn't for some time that I realized where you were. The rest you know. I don't like to be disrespectful to ladies, but that woman seems an honest to God hell-cat to me.'

Mr Campion felt the weal on his face. 'I'm inclined to agree with you,' he said.

The Professor touched his arm. 'You must hurry,' he said. 'Don't worry about me. I'll get back all right. If they're going to make an attack on the genuine Chalice they'll do it tonight. That's why I came along. There's a bit of tradition that it occurred to me you might not know. I'm interested in these things; that's why it stayed in my mind. Old Peck put me wise months ago. I meant to tell you before, but what with one thing and another it slipped my mind.'

He lowered his voice still more. 'That secret room at the Tower has a window, but no apparent door, as you know. Now, on the night of the heir's twenty-fifth birthday there's a light burns in the window from sunset to cockcrow. You see,' he hurried on, ignoring Campion's smothered exclamation, 'in the old days there was always a big party on, so that every window in the house would be ablaze, but this time there isn't any party. The position of that room will be clear to anyone who cares to look from ten o'clock till dawn. Get me? That's not all, either,' he added. 'There's sure to be special preparations made to disclose the door tonight. If anyone raided the Tower now they'd find pretty clear indications of where the Room was, I'm thinking, provided they knew on what floor and in what direction to look. It may be thirty years before this opportunity occurs again. I think you ought to be on hand.'

Mr Campion was silent for some moments. 'I guessed there'd be a light, of course,' he said at last, 'but it never dawned on me it'd be on for so long. I didn't know the tradition. You're right. It's the time I've misjudged.' He hurried to the window. 'I suppose they've gone already.'

The stable-yard was deserted, but he caught a glimpse of the big car still standing before the house. 'We must get out,' he said. 'We'll go the way you came in.'

The Professor led the way down the ladder in the adjoining loft and into the empty box below. Next moment an exclamation of annoyance escaped him.

'We're bolted in,' he said. 'We shall have to nip back and get round on the top storey. If we're fixed in here we're sunk.'

'There's a window in that front room over the gate,' said Campion thoughtfully. 'I've been locked in there all day. I could get out of that, I think.'

Fortunately, the communicating doors between the two storey lofts were unlocked, and they pushed right round the square until they emerged once more into the room over the gateway. Here Mr Campion stopped dead, and the Professor, panting a little, caught up with him. From somewhere outside there had arisen a most extraordinary noise.

'Heck!' said the Professor. 'What's that?'

But Mr Campion was already at the window.

'Good old Mrs Sarah!' he said breathlessly. 'I thought that was all guff about turning them off the heath.' He caught the Professor's arm and dragged him to the window. Together they looked out over the scene below.

The sight was an extraordinary one. The remains of a lurid sunset still blazed across the heath and the wind was rising. At the moment when they first peered through the window together an immense dark object silhouetted against the sky was bearing down upon the buildings at an ever-increasing rate. As it came nearer they were just able to discern what it was. The decrepit char-a-banc which Penny had noticed in the Gypsy encampment the morning before charged upon the stables, bristling with an overload of wildly gesticulating figures.

They disappeared from the view of the watchers from the window beneath the outer wall, but the next moment a shattering crash echoed through the buildings as the iron gates were burst open. The char-a-banc swung into sight, churning off the near wheel of the Delage in its path and coming to a full stop in the gateway above which they stood. The noise was fiendish, the shrill Gypsy voices, their musical sibilance entirely vanished, mingled with the shrieking of brakes and the infuriated swearing of the members of Mrs Dick's peculiar household who came swarming out to attack the invaders.

Pandemonium broke loose. In her stable Bitter Aloes added to the increasing confusion by kicking at the woodwork in a frenzy. Innumerable figures tumbled out of the juggernaut and swarmed over the house and stables.

Mrs Dick's adherents defended themselves and their property from this unexpected attack with a savagery of their kind. The Professor, with his hands on the bars of the window and his eyes glued to the pane, whistled under his breath.

'Gee, this is the dirtiest fighting I've ever seen,' he said.

Mr Campion did not reply at once. He was wrestling with the other window whose fittings he had tentatively loosened during the day.

'They got my signal,' he said at last, between vigorous wrenches at the bars. 'I put them on to this weeks ago. I never dreamed they'd do the thing so thoroughly. When they got the signal they were to attack. If there was no signal then they were to arrive at ten. Lugg took them the sign yesterday, so they've been waiting all day. They're old enemies of this lot. Gypsies and race gangs hate each other.'

'I haven't heard any guns,' said the Professor as he watched the battle with almost boyish enthusiasm.

'They don't use guns.' Mr Campion had to raise his voice as the crashing of windows and splitting woodwork was added to the turmoil. 'They've a prejudice against them. Makes it worse if they're caught. Their own methods are quite as effective and slightly more filthy. Who's winning?'

'Hard to tell,' said the Professor. 'They all look alike to me. It's smashed up the attack on the Tower all right, I should think. I don't see Mrs Shannon anywhere.'

He broke off abruptly as a pistol shot sounded above the general uproar.

'That's Sanderson, I bet,' said Mr Campion. 'That man'll get hanged before he's finished.'

'Whoever it is,' said the Professor, 'they've got him.' He paused. 'Can you hear a car?'

'Can't hear anything through this din,' Campion grunted as he detached a bar from the window. 'Sounds like an early Christian idea of hell to me.'

'Say, Campion,' said the Professor, suddenly turning for a moment, 'there's murder going on outside. Won't your Gypsy friends have some difficulty in getting away with it?'

'More disabling than killing.' Mr Campion was edging himself through the window as he spoke. 'You don't know Gypsies, Professor. There won't be a trace of them in the morning. They'll have split up and scattered to every corner of the country by dawn. Some of them just live for fighting. This is one of their gala nights. Look here,' he added, as he prepared to lower himself out of the narrow aperture, 'your best plan is to stay here. I'll unbolt the door downstairs and let you out. If anything happens to me, you're Orlando's friend, and any Gypsy will see you clear. Don't forget, *Orlando*. I'm going after Mrs Dick. I'll never forget what you've done for me tonight, Professor.'

The old man returned to his window. 'Boy, I wouldn't miss this for a fortune,' he said. 'It's an education.'

'Going down,' sang Mr Campion, and disappeared.

He dropped into the very centre of the char-a-banc, which was at the moment an oasis amid the tumult, and groped about him for a weapon. He kicked against something hard on the floor of the vehicle, and putting his hand down came across a bottle. He bound his handkerchief round his hand and seized the glass club by the neck. Then, still keeping low, he dropped gently out of the car and slipped back the bolt of the stairway to the lofts.

'All clear, Professor,' he called softly up into the darkness. Then, stepping out gingerly once more, he was just about to work his way round to the house when he caught sight of a figure bearing down upon him, hand upraised. Campion put out his arm to ward off the blow and spoke instinctively.

'Jacob?' he said sharply.

The arm dropped to the man's side. 'Orlando?'

'Himself,' said Mr Campion, and added, drawing the Gypsy into the protecting shadow of the box: 'Where's the donah?'

'Scarpered,' said the Gypsy promptly. 'Went off in a little red motor. The finger with the gun was going with her, but we got him.'

'Scarpered?' said Mr Campion. 'Alone?'

The man shrugged his shoulders. 'I don't know. I think not; she went in a red motor that was standing by the side door when we came in. Been gone ten minutes. Took a coil of rope with her. Some of the boys started after her, I think, but she's away.'

Mr Campion's scalp tingled. Mrs Dick had nerves of iron. She had nothing to lose, and once the genuine Chalice was in her possession she was safe. Moreover, the calmness with which she had attempted to dispose of him dispelled any doubts of personal squeamishness on her part. There was nothing she might not do.

He returned to the Gypsy. 'I'm going after them,' he said, 'though Heaven knows how. I say, Jacob, there's an old finger upstairs, a great friend of Orlando's. See he gets out. Give Mrs Sarah my love. I'll see you all at Hull Fair, if not before. Round up this lot now and scarpa yourselves.'

The Gypsy nodded and disappeared silently up the stairs to carry out his instructions as far as the Professor was concerned.

Most of the fighting had by this time spread into the house whither the majority of the gang had retreated.

Mr Campion sped across the yard, which was now a mass of broken bottles, blood, and odd portions of garments, and made for the heath. It was still far from dark outside the walls. The wind was rushing great wisps of cloud across the pale sky and the stars seemed very near.

As he passed the groom's cottage a dark figure detached itself from the shadows and leapt at him. He swung his weapon which he still held and brought it down on something hard. His assailant went down. He was vaguely aware of the 'Major's' red face gaping at him from the ground, but he hurried on, one thought only clear in his mind: Mrs Dick and a coil of rope.

He stepped hopefully into the garage and looked about. To his dismay it was empty, save for the recumbent and unconscious figure of Matt Sanderson. The Delage, now completely beyond repair, and the red Fraser Nash, in which Mrs Dick was speeding towards the Tower he had no doubt, were the only vehicles it had contained. His own car, besides being some distance off across the heath, was, according to the Professor, completely out of action, and the char-a-banc in which the Gypsies had arrived would take the concerted efforts of at least a dozen men to get out of the yard. There remained the Professor's bicycle, which was hardly fast enough even could it have been found.

The problem of transport seemed insoluble, and speed mattered more than anything in the world. Even telephoning was out of the question, as he knew from experience that to cut the wires was the first care of raiding Gypsy parties. It dawned upon him that the only chance he had was to make for the camp and borrow a horse from Mrs Sarah.

He set off across the heath towards the camp at a good steady pace, taking a diagonal course towards the north-east. Almost immediately he was conscious of footsteps behind him. He stopped and turned.

A man leading a horse was coming swiftly up. Mr Campion's lank form and spectacled face were recognizable in the faint light. 'Orlando!' the man called softly.

'Who's that? Joey?' Campion recognized the voice as that belonging to Mrs Sarah's son Joey, the horse expert of the Benwell tribe. He came up.

'Jacob sent me after you. The old finger with him said you wanted to get off. I'll lend you this.' The Gypsy indicated the horse with a jerk of his head. 'Careful with her. She's all right for half an hour. She may be a bit wild after that. Lovely bit, though, ain't she?'

Mr Campion understood the insinuation perfectly. Joey, who had ever more an eye for business than for warfare, had taken the opportunity to raid Mrs Dick's stables, an act in which he had been detected by his kinsman, and straight away dispatched to Campion's assistance.

As he turned gratefully to take the bridle, forgetting for the moment the impoverished state of the lady's stables, a white stocking caught his eye. Instinctively he started back.

'Good Lord, you've got a nerve,' he said. 'This is Bitter Aloes. They keep her as a sort of executioner,' he added grimly.

'She's all right,' Joey insisted. 'Run like a lamb for half an hour. You can trust me. I've fixed her with something.'

Mr Campion glanced at the proud silky head with the ears now pricked forward, and the wild eyes comparatively mild. The mare was saddleless. It seemed madness to attempt such a ride.

The Gypsy handed him a broom-switch.

'Hurry,' he whispered. 'Turn her loose when you've done with her. I'll come after her with something in me hand that she'll follow for miles. To Sanctuary you're goin', ain't you?'

Mr Campion looked over the heath. Sanctuary was five miles as the crow flew. Even now Mrs Dick might have reached her goal. He returned to the Gypsy.

'Thank you, Joey,' he said quietly. 'Sanctuary it is,' and he vaulted lightly on to the gleaming back of Bitter Aloes.

Chapter 25

The Window

It was a light summer's night with a strong wind blowing. Strips of indigo cloud scored the pale star-strewn sky, and the air was cool after the intense heat of the day.

The heath ticked and crackled in the darkness, and the broom bushes rustled together like the swish of many skirts.

It was not a night for staying indoors: everything seemed to be abroad and the wind carried sounds for great distances, far-off sheep cries, voices, and the barking of dogs.

Most of these things were lost upon Mr Campion as he thundered across the countryside. Whatever horse-witchery Joey had practised upon Bitter Aloes, her temper had certainly subsided, but she was still very nervy and inclined to be erratic, although for the moment her innate savagery was subdued. Campion, his long thin legs wrapped round her sleek sides, trusted devoutly that for the promised half-hour, at any rate, it would remain so.

After the first breath-taking dash across the heath he forgot her vagaries and concentrated upon his goal. As he reached the road, a church clock from Heronhoe village struck eleven, and he abandoned his original intention of sticking to the road. Time was too precious. He turned the mare at the hedge which bordered one of the wide stretches of pasture-land which lay between him and the Tower. Bitter Aloes took the jump like a cat. As she rose beneath him the notion flashed into Campion's mind that she probably enjoyed the hazardous journey. Her curious twisted temperament was best pleased by danger.

He had no illusions about what he was doing. To ride a Gypsy-doctored horse over a tract of unfamiliar land in the half-darkness was more than ordinarily foolhardy. Trusting devoutly that they would not come up against any insurmountable object, and praying against wire – the recollection that this was a hunting district relieved him considerably on that score – he kept the mare's head in the direction of Sanctuary and urged her on to further efforts.

She had her moments of difficulty. A nesting partridge disturbed under her feet sent her rearing dangerously, and once when a sheep lumbered out of their path she plunged continuously for some seconds and all but unseated him.

Luck and his unerring sense of direction brought them safely over the meadows to the brow of Saddlehill, and as they galloped up the steep grassland Campion suddenly saw the end of his quest, the gaunt east wing of the Tower at Sanctuary standing up against the sky on the other side of the valley.

In the Tower, high in the topmost storey, was a lighted window. It stood out quite clearly, a little circular spot of red light in the blackness.

Although he had expected it, it startled him. It was higher than he had supposed the windows would come, and he identified it suddenly in his mind with the curious circular decoration over the centre window of the wing, an orifice which had looked like a plaque of deeply indented stone work from the ground.

As he stared at the Tower, something in the grounds attracted his attention, and he looked down to see a car's headlights turn in to the trees at the far end of the drive. Even as he looked they vanished. A panic seized him. He drove his heels gently into the mare's sides and she leapt forward quivering.

For a moment he thought he had lost control, but she quietened as the long gallop down the slope exerted her. He took her over a ditch into the lane at the foot of the hill, and they continued down the narrow road, her hoofs striking sparks from the ragged flints. The little white gate at the end of the home meadow she took almost in her stride and the steep incline hardly affected her pace: the effect of Joey's treatment was wearing off and she jerked her head angrily from time to time as though she were irritated by the reins.

Campion barely noticed her changing mood. He flung himself off her back at the end of the flower garden, and she kicked out at him as he disappeared through the gate and ran up the grass path towards the house.

There were beads of sweat on his forehead, and the expression on his pale face was no longer inane. A car had turned into the drive and had instantly switched off its lights; that was fifteen minutes ago at least, he reckoned. Even allowing for reckless driving, Mrs Dick could hardly have traversed the twelve miles of winding lane in less time than that would account for.

Therefore she was in the grounds now. He was prepared for anything. Mrs Dick's possibilities were numberless.

He glanced up at the Tower across the wide lawn. The single red eye, a significant and silent witness to the thousand rumours concerning the Gyrths' secret, glared down upon him. Behind that eye lay the Chalice, protected by something unknown, the intangible and perhaps terrible guardian upon which probably only three men living had ever looked. He had heard dozens of 'genuine explanations'; men referred to it guardedly in famous clubs, well-known books of reminiscence hinted darkly at unprintable horrors. Val himself had seemed a little afraid to consider what it might be.

He wondered how many anxious eyes were fixed on the Tower that evening. Mrs Dick's band of experts had been put out of action, certainly. But there would surely be others waiting to bear the treasure to safety. The lady herself, he fancied, would keep out of it for fear of being recognized, but would general the attack from somewhere outside.

At present all was peaceful. There were only two other lights in the whole building, both in the west wing, in the drawing-room and in the library. The servants' quarters were dark; the staff had been sent to bed early, no doubt. Campion imagined Penny alone in the drawing-room, and Val seated with his father and the old Rector in the study. And somewhere in the darkness a group of watchers, utterly without fear or scruple, eyeing, even as he, the single glaring window in the Tower.

He advanced across the lawn, keeping carefully to the deep shadow.

The uncanny silence of the garden around him filled him with apprehension. He could have sworn that there was no one moving amid the belts of trees and shrubs which surrounded the lawn. Once again he paused and stood rigid. Somewhere there had been a movement. Instinctively he glanced up. The old house stood out black against the night sky. His eyes were drawn irresistibly to the circular window. Then he started. Just above it, standing out clearly over the battlements of the east wing, there was a figure.

He waited, silent, hoping against hope that it was Val or his father, but, even as he watched, something slender, snake-like, slid down across the circle of crimson light. As he strained his eyes to make it out, the truth came slowly home to him. It was a fine flexible rope, knotted at intervals.

Instantly the question which had been rankling at the back of his mind was made blindingly clear to him. The raiders were going to make sure of the exact whereabouts of their prize before they risked an open attack. The half-caste cat burglar's part in Sanderson's scheme became obvious. He was to have been the spy, possibly even their thief, if the window were negotiable. The simplicity of it appalled him. It would be so easy. Although the Tower was about a hundred and twenty feet high, a man with nerve could make a descent to the window once its whereabouts was made clear to him. It would be dangerous, but by no means impossible, to a man of Moggie's experience.

Then he remembered that Moggie was lying in the garage with Sanderson on Heronhoe Heath. Who, then, was the climber who was about to take his place? There was an answer to this question, but his mind shrank from considering it.

He raced for the house. His first impulse was to alarm the Colonel, but as he reached the base of the east wing the intruder's means of entry was instantly apparent. One of the narrow latticed windows stood open. He climbed through it without hesitation and crept across the flagged state dining-room within to the centre hall, where a huge wooden spiral staircase, one of the showpieces of the county, reared its way up into the darkness.

He crept up the steps, the wood creaking terrifyingly beneath his weight. It was a long climb in the darkness. The stairs wound up the whole height of the Tower. At last they began to narrow and presently he felt the cool night air upon his face.

Suddenly the faint light from the open doorway above his head warned him that he was reaching the roof. He paused to listen. There was no sound in the house. All was quiet and ghostly in the gloom. He moved silently up the last half-dozen stairs, and emerged at last from the little central turret on the flat stone roof of the Tower.

For a moment he looked about him, prepared for instant attack. As far as he could see the place was deserted. Keeping his back to the wall he worked his way round the turret. Then a chill feeling of horror crept over him. He was quite alone.

A movement almost like the passing of a shadow just in front of him made him start forward, and in doing so his thigh brushed against something stretched tightly from the central flagstaff and disappeared over the edge of the battlements. He touched it with his hand. It was a rope with knots in it. In that moment he realized that the one eventuality which he had never foreseen had taken place. Whoever was undertaking the theft of the Chalice was doing it alone.

Beads of sweat stood out on his forehead. There was only one person living who would have the nerve to make such an attempt, only one person who would consider the prize worth the risk. He moved to the edge of the Tower and drew out his torch, which he had been careful not to use until now.

'Hold on,' he said firmly, 'you'd better come back.'

His voice sounded strained and theatrical to him after the silence, the words inadequate and ridiculous. He listened intently, but the reply was loud, almost as if the speaker had been standing beside him.

'I'll see you in hell first,' said Mrs Dick.

Following the rope, he bent over the parapet and switched his torch downwards. Although he had expected it, the sight sickened him. She lay against the side of the Tower like a fly on a wall, her steel hands gripping the rope which supported her as she picked her way down with easy precision. Not more than two feet below her the round window gleamed dully on to the cord as it squirmed and flopped against the stone work. In the daytime the height was sickening; at night it was impossible to see the ground, and Campion was glad of it.

He leant on the parapet looking down at her. He could see her distinctly, still in the riding costume in which she had interviewed him only that afternoon. As he stared, a thought forced itself into his mind. Mrs Dick was the employee of the society; the responsibility lay upon her shoulders alone. Should she meet with her death the danger to the Chalice would end automatically.

The rope, which alone supported her from a hundred foot drop on to the flags beneath, lay under his hand. If the cord should slip its mooring round the flagstaff . . .

He leant on the parapet and kept his eyes fixed upon her. He could find plenty of moral justification in his own mind for this execution, and he did not flinch from the fact that it would be an execution. There were passages in Mrs Dick's past that no English jury would have excused in spite of their notorious leniency towards women. He gripped the stones, his knuckles showing white in the faint light.

'Come back,' he said distinctly, turning the light full on her bent head. 'Come back before you look in that room, or I swear I'll cut this rope.'

As soon as he had spoken the meaning of his own words startled him. Once Mrs Dick, the agent for the most influential syndicate in the world, saw the prize she sought, no power on earth could save it from her. She must be prevented from reaching the window.

'I'll cut the rope,' he repeated.

She looked up at him unflinchingly, and the merciless light revealed the twisted smile on her small, hideous mouth.

'You wouldn't dare,' she said. 'You haven't the courage. Get back; I'll deal with you later.'

She descended another step deliberately.

'Come back!' Campion's voice was menacing. 'Hold tight. I'm going to draw you up.' He gripped the rope and took the strain, but she was a heavy woman, and he knew instinctively that in spite of the knots the task would be beyond him.

Mrs Dick, who had remained motionless on the rope, steadying herself for any such attempt, jeered at him openly.

'Mind your own business,' she said. 'If you must interfere, go downstairs and call a servant to help you.'

Her voice sounded a little farther away, and he knew that she was climbing down. Again he bent over the parapet. He caught sight of her feet reflecting the red glare from the window.

'Come back!' he called hoarsely. 'Come back, for God's sake!'

'Just a moment.' The words came softly to him as she deliberately lowered herself another foot, and adjusting her position, peered into the window.

There was a pause which seemed like an age. The man bending forward with his torch directed upon the hunched figure on the rope received some of the tremor which shot through her body. The red light was on her face, and he saw her shoulders twitch as she hung there, apparently fascinated by what she saw. In that moment the world seemed to have paused. It was as if the Tower and garden had held their breath.

Then from somewhere beneath him he fancied he heard a faint, almost undetectable sound. It was a sound so intangible that it did not convey anything concrete to his mind, so soft that he questioned it immediately afterwards. The effect upon Mrs Dick, however, was instantaneous.

'No!' she said distinctly, 'no!'

The last word was smothered by a shuddering intake of breath, and she swung round on the rope, hanging to the full length of her arms. Her face was turned up to the man on the Tower for an instant. He saw her lips drawn back over her teeth, her eyes wide and expressionless with fear, while a thin trickle of saliva escaped at one corner of her mouth. He bent forward.

'Hold on,' he said, not realizing that he was whispering. 'Hold on!'

But even as he looked, her limp fingers relinquished their grip, he heard the sickening hiss of the rope as it raced through her hands, and she receded with horrible slowness down, down, out of the range of his torch into the darkness below.

The body crunched as it hit the flags, and then – silence. The guardian of the Gyrth Chalice had protected its treasure.

Mr Campion, sick and trembling uncontrollably in the cold wind, reeled unsteadily to the turret and went quietly downstairs.

Chapter 26

Mr Campion's Employer

The East Suffolk Courier and Hadleigh Argus for
7 July

SAD FATALITY AT SANCTUARY

Coroner Comments on Curiosity

An inquest was held on Saturday last at the Three Drummers Inn, Sanctuary-by-Tower, before Doctor J. Cobden, Coroner for the district, on Daisy Adela Shannon (44) of Heronhoe Stables, Heronhoe, who fell from the tower in the east wing of the mansion of Colonel Sir Percival Gyrth, Bt, on the night of 2 July while a birthday party was in progress.

The body was discovered by Mr Alfred Campion, a guest at the Tower. Mr Campion, 17 Battle Street, London, W1, said that on Thursday evening he was walking across the lawn at about 11.25 p.m. when he noticed someone moving on the top of the east wing tower. He thought that it was a member of the household, and hailed them. Receiving no reply he became alarmed, a state of mind which increased when he perceived that one of the dining-room windows stood open. He ran into the house and climbed the staircase to the top landing, coming out at last upon the roof. The jury subsequently viewed the staircase, which is one of the showpieces of Suffolk.

Mr Campion, continuing, said that when he reached the roof of the Tower he found himself alone. Running downstairs again he discovered the deceased lying on the flagstones at the foot of the Tower. He immediately summoned the household.

Corroborative evidence was given by Roger Arthur Branch, butler to Sir Percival, and by the Rev. P. R. Pembroke, of The Rectory, Sanctuary, who was visiting the Tower at the time of the accident.

Dr A. H. Moore, of Sanctuary Village, said that death was due to contusion of the brain following fracture of the skull. Death was instantaneous.

Evidence of identification was given by W. W. Croxon, Veterinary Surgeon, of The Kennels, Heronhoe.

PC Henry Proudfoot deposed that he was summoned to the Tower at 11.45 p.m. on the night in question. He climbed to the top of the Tower and there discovered a length of rope (produced) attached to a flagpole on the summit.

David Cossins, of 32 Bury Road, Hadleigh, dealer, identified the rope as having been sold to the deceased on the 18th or 19th of June last. When asked if in his opinion this rope was sufficiently strong to bear the weight of a human body, witness opined that it undoubtedly was.

Sir Percival, asked by the Coroner if he could offer any explanation for deceased's presence on his estate at so late an hour, replied that he was at a total loss to account for it. He was only casually acquainted with the deceased, and she was not a guest at his son's coming-of-age party, which was necessarily an intimate affair in view of the recent bereavement in the family.

By PC Proudfoot, recalled: A red two-seater Fraser Nash motor-car, later identified by registration marks as the property of deceased, was found drawn up against some bushes in the drive later in the evening. Lights were extinguished, and it was reasonable to suppose that this was done by deceased.

Questioned, Proudfoot suggested that the deceased had attempted to lower herself on to the centre window-sill of the fourth floor of the Tower, where, according to popular superstition, some festivities took place on the occasion of a birthday in the family. Proudfoot apologized to the Court for the intrusion of common superstition and gossip, but opined that the deceased had attempted her giddy descent in the execution of a wager with some third party who had not come forward. Deceased was a well-known sporting character of the district, and had been known to enter into undertakings of this sort in the past. Witness cited the occasion of the Horse v. Automobile race in 1911, when deceased challenged Captain W. Probert, the well-known motorist, over a distance of twenty miles across country.

The Coroner told the jury that he was inclined to accept the Constable's very intelligently reasoned explanation as being as near the truth as they were likely to arrive. In her attempt to carry out this unparalleled piece of foolhardy daring in a woman of her age, the deceased had undoubtedly suffered from an attack of vertigo and so had fallen.

The Coroner added that it would be a lesson to all on the evils of undue curiosity and the undesirability of entering into foolish sporting contracts which might endanger life or limb. The Coroner said he could not express himself too strongly on the subject. He regretted, as must all those in Court, that such an unfortunate accident should have visited itself upon Colonel Sir Percival Gyrth and his family, who were already suffering from a very recent bereavement. He instructed the jury, therefore, to bring in a verdict according to the evidence. The jury returned a verdict of Accidental Death, the Foreman (Mr P. Peck, senr) remarking that they would like to second the Coroner's expressions of regret.

The funeral will take place at Heronhoe tomorrow, Tuesday. A short obituary notice appears in another column with a list of the deceased's sporting awards. It is understood that the deceased died intestate, and her property, which is in very bad repair, few of the windows being whole and many of the doors off their hinges, was in the hands of the Police when our Representative called yesterday.

'A very intelligently reasoned explanation indeed,' remarked Mr Campion, putting down the paper. 'Mark my words, Val. We shall have old Proudfoot a sergeant before we know where we are. And rightly so, as they say on the soap-box.'

He lay back in his deck-chair and put his arms behind his head. They were all four of them, Penny, Beth, Val and himself, seated beneath the trees at the far corner of the lawn on a brilliant morning some days after the events so ably recorded by the *Argus*. The adventures of the preceding weeks had left their marks on the young people, but there was a distinct hint of relief in the manner which told plainly of a tension that had relaxed.

Val had assumed a new air of responsibility during the few days since his coming of age. He seemed, as Penny remarked, to have grown up. She and Beth were frankly happy; as they lay in the comfortable chairs they looked like a couple of schoolgirls with their bare arms and long thin legs spread out to the sunlight which dappled through the leaves.

Mr Campion alone bore concrete marks of battle. His face was still scored by the weals of Mrs Dick's whip, but apart from this slightly martial disfigurement, he looked even more amiably fatuous than ever.

'They're nearly as bright about the Gypsies,' Penny observed as she took up the paper from the grass. 'Apparently "a raid was thought to have been made by van dwellers on a party of undesirables camping on Heronhoe Heath. The van dwellers have since disappeared, and some of the injured campers have been taken to the Police Infirmary." I believe you managed that, Albert. Oh, to think that it's all all right!' She sighed luxuriously. 'To look back upon it's like a welsh rarebit nightmare with you as the hero.'

'With me as the rabbit,' said Mr Campion feelingly. 'The Professor was the hero. Lugg's painting an illuminated address that we're going to present to him. It begins "Hon. Sir and Prof." and goes on with all the long words he's ever heard from the Bench. All about Depravity, Degradation, and Unparalleled Viciousness. He's turning them into the negative, of course. It'll be a stupendous document when it's finished. Perhaps the Professor will let you two have a copy of it for a wedding present.' He grinned at Val and Beth, who were quite blatantly holding hands between their deck-chairs. They smiled at each other and Mr Campion went on.

'Had it not been for the Professor, Mr "Alfred Campion" would doubtless have figured in another role, and some crueller Coroner than old Doctor Cobden would be moralizing on the dangers of putting strange animals in other people's stables. The Professor's a stout fellow, as we say in the Legion. How are the two papas today, by the way?'

'Splendid,' said Penny. 'I saw a sweet sight as I came past the library window. You know they retired to discuss deep archaeological secrets? Well, when I came past there were two armchairs drawn up by the open window, two little curls of cigar smoke, and there was Daddy deep in *The New Yorker* – a most indelicate young woman on the cover, my dears – and the Professor regaling himself with *Punch*. Too sweet.'

'Hands across the sea, in fact,' said Campion. 'I shall hear the tinkle of little silver bells in a minute.'

Beth laughed. 'The way they forgave each other for the Gypsies and your Aunt Di's *faux pas* was rather cute,' she said.

'I know,' said Penny. '"My dear sir!" "Nonsense! *My* dear sir!" "Come and shoot partridges!" "Rubbish. Come and pick my roses." All boys together. What delightful neighbours we are, are we not? Do you know, this is the first time I've felt this summer was worth living? By the way, Albert, when did you arrange everything so neatly with your fat friend, Mrs Sarah? I was trying to work it out in bed last night.'

'Irreverent hussy,' said Mr Campion, shocked. 'She'd put a spell on you for that. Then you'd know all about it. I called upon the lady in question, as a matter of fact, on the night before I came home to find Lugg so curiously indisposed. I'd previously seen her, of course, very early on in the proceedings. I guessed I might need a spot of assistance sooner or later, so I asked them to hang around. As Mr Sanderson was staying at Heronhoe, it occurred to me that the heath was very conveniently situated. I pointed this out to Mrs Sarah and she had no doubts in her mind as to where the fun would arise.'

'Then you knew about Mrs Dick?' said Val. 'From the beginning?'

'Well, yes and no,' said Mr Campion. 'I thought she might be in it, but I did so hope she wouldn't be in it alone. Mrs Munsey almost convinced me, but just before I visited Mrs Dick, I inquired about her in all the likely quarters, and after that, well it seemed desperately likely. She was head over heels in debt, and on the verge of all sorts of unkind attention from the Jockey Club Stewards. I asked my own pet turf expert about her over the phone and the Exchange cut us off long before he got into his stride. My hat! She had a nerve, though.'

Val looked at him in astonishment. 'You talk as though you admired her,' he said.

'She had a way of compelling admiration,' said Mr Campion, stroking his face thoughtfully. 'If you ask me, there weren't two hoots to choose between her and her horse. They were both vicious and both terrifying, both bad lots, but oh, boy! they both had Personality.'

Val grimaced. 'I never liked her,' he said. 'By the way, I never saw why she set Mrs Munsey on to Aunt Di. What was the point of it?'

Mr Campion considered. 'That took me off my balance at the beginning,' he admitted, 'but the local witch herself put me on to the truth. You see, Val, your aunt, silly as she was, never let the Chalice out of her sight for a second except when it was in its niche, half-hidden behind iron bars. Arthur Earle, her artist friend, probably complained to Headquarters that his hostess was a nuisance in this respect, and Mrs Dick, knowing of Mrs Munsey's peculiarities, and your aunt's propensity for wandering about at night, hit on the idea of giving her Ladyship a shock that would keep her indisposed for a day or two, during which time the disappointed artist, deprived of his sitter, might easily get permission to continue his portrait of the Chalice. You see,' he went on, 'a man like Arthur would want to weigh it and examine it really thoroughly, which he could hardly do with your aunt about. Unfortunately for all concerned, Mrs Munsey was too much for your aunt and the whole scheme came unstuck.'

Penny sighed. 'It was bad luck on Aunt Di,' she said. 'Mr Pembroke's looking after the Munseys. Did you know? They'll have to go into a home, he says, poor things.'

Val's mind still dwelt upon the mechanism of Mrs Dick's original scheme. 'I suppose,' he said bitterly, 'they set out with the idea of bribing me to swap a copy for the cup? We owe a lot to you, Campion.'

His friend did not appear to hear the last part of his remark.

'I think that was it,' Campion agreed. 'Later, the "Major" and Sanderson came to spy out the nakedness of the land themselves. I believe that the "Major" was the expert who decided that the Chalice in the Cup House was not the real one, once they got hold of it. I've never felt so sick in my life as I did when Stanislaus phoned me to tell me they'd got the copy. That was a darn clever raid of theirs. It was only sheer bad luck on Stanislaus' part that they were successful, though. If that bobby on the door had been an older hand it wouldn't have happened.'

Penny grinned at him from where she lay basking like a kitten in the heat. 'Thinking it over, Albert,' she remarked, 'it has occurred to me that you don't work up your publicity properly at all. Modesty is all very sweet and charming but it doesn't get you anywhere. According to your account of the whole thing to Daddy you haven't done anything at all worth talking about.'

Mr Campion blinked at her from behind his spectacles.

> 'Beauty is truth, truth beauty, and these three
> Hover for ever round the gorbal tree –

Ovid,' he said. 'Like Sir Isaac Newton and his fishing-rod, I cannot tell a lie.'

'Still,' said Penny, unimpressed, 'you might have put it a bit better. For instance, about Val being kidnapped. When you're asked for an explanation you simply say you called for him at a garage, and brought him back and put him in a field because you were in a hurry to get back to London to see a bookmaker. You must learn to work up your stories more. A yarn like that gets you nowhere.'

'But all quite true,' said Mr Campion mildly. 'And not really extraordinary. When Inspector Oates told me over the phone that Val had gone charging after the gentleman who had stolen his suitcase, it was perfectly obvious to me that if he had caught the thief he would have returned with him, and if he hadn't caught him, then the thieving gentleman's friends had caught Val. Therefore,' he went on, beaming at them from behind his spectacles, 'Val was the unwelcome guest of someone who was probably Mr Matthew Sanderson or one of his associates. They didn't want to keep him about the place, you see. They thought they'd got their prize, and once they had disposed of it in the right quarter, they had nothing to fear. I guessed they'd plant him somewhere and say no more about it.'

Beth's brown eyes opened wide. 'But they might have killed him,' she said.

'Hardly,' said Campion judicially. 'There is no one who is more anxious to avoid an unpleasant death in the house than your English crook. You see, in England, in nine cases out of ten, if there's a body there's a hanging. That rather cramps their style when disposing of people. Working all this out with lightning speed, what did Our

Hero do? He got out his little motor-car and went a-visiting.' He paused.

'It may have dawned on you people that all my friends are not quite the article. So, sure enough, in one of their back-yards I found our juvenile lead lying happily on a lot of old motor tyres waiting to be dropped somewhere where he could be "found wandering". I relieved the gentleman in charge of his guest, admired his wife's new frock, kissed the baby and came home. It was so abominably easy that I hadn't the face to tell you all, even if I had had time, so I left him where I thought Beth might find him and went on to see our lady friend, who was beginning to worry me.

'You were at Ernie Walker's garage, as a matter of fact, Val. He specializes in that sort of thing. It was the second place I looked. No, Penny, I regret to say that in this case I do not find myself wearing my laurel wreath with that sense of righteous satisfaction which is my wont. The Professor and the Benwells get all the credit. The way they cleared up that bunch and scarpered fills me with a sense of my own clumsiness.'

'Ah,' said Beth, 'that was the word. "Scarpa". Father was awfully interested in your Gypsy friend, who had some most extraordinary words. What does that one mean?'

'"Bunk" is the best English translation,' said Mr Campion. 'To bunk, that is – to clear off, scat, vamoose, beat it, make a getaway, hop it, or more simply, "to go". Jacob is a great lad, but Joey is the wizard. That horse was quite manageable when I rode her over, so bang goes your last illusion, Penny, of me as a second Dick Turpin. Joey must have had his eye on Bitter Aloes for days, and as soon as the opportunity offered he left the fight and slipped into her box with some filthy concoction of his own. The crooks use a hypodermic, but I fancy he has other methods.'

'I haven't got any illusions about you,' said Penny. 'I think you ought to go into a Home. When I heard someone had fallen off the Tower, I took it for granted it was you. Yes, a good comfortable Home with Lugg to dress you, and plenty of nice kind keepers who would laugh at your remarks. In the first place, I happen to know for a fact that that story about your coming into a fortune from your Uncle the Bishop is all rubbish. Lugg says he left you a hundred pounds and a couple of good books.'

Mr Campion looked uncomfortable. 'Curse Lugg,' he said. 'So much for my efforts to appear a gilded amateur. I'm sorry, Val, but this nosy little creature will have to be told. Yes, Angel-face, the poor vulgar gentleman is a Professional. I was employed, of course.'

He lay back in his chair, the sunlight glinting on his spectacles. The three young people stared at him.

'Employed?' said Val. 'Who employed you? It couldn't have been the Old Boy, because – I hate to be fearfully rude, but you must be – er – well, awfully expensive.'

'Incredibly,' said Mr Campion placidly. 'Only the highest in the land can possibly afford my services. But then, I need an immense income to support my army of spies, and my palatial offices, to say nothing of my notorious helot, Lugg.'

'He's lying,' said Penny, yawning. 'I wish you had been employed, though. You've done such a lot for us. I feel you ought to get something out of it. I'd offer you my hand if I thought I could bear you about the house. Ooh!' she added suddenly, 'look!'

Her exclamation had been occasioned by the appearance of a magnificent limousine, whose long grey body gleamed in the sunlight as it whispered expensively up the drive to the front door. Val and Penny exchanged glances.

In the car, seated behind the chauffeur, was a single slim aristocratic figure, with the unmistakable poker back of the old regime.

'There he is,' said Penny. 'That's why if you stay to lunch, Beth, you'll have to have it with Albert and me in the morning room. That's why Branch is in his show swallowtails and we've got the flag flying. Here comes the honoured guest.'

Beth leant forward in her chair. 'Is that *him*?' she said. 'No top hat? I haven't seen a good top hat since I came to England.'

'Very remiss,' said Mr Campion sternly. 'Coming down here representing the Crown without a top hat – why, the thing's absurd. Hang it, when a policeman brings a summons, which is a sort of invitation from the Crown, he wears a top hat.'

'No?' said Beth.

'No,' said Mr Campion. 'Still, the principle's the same. I don't think it's cricket to come down on a special formal occasion in an ordinary trilby that any man might wear. Look here, Val, you'd better wear yours at lunch just to show him. We keep the old flag flying, dammit.'

Beth was puzzled. 'Why don't you get lunch with this Lord whatever he is?'

'Because it's an ancient ceremony,' said Penny. 'Not the lunch –

unless cook's muffed it – but the whole business. We shall be expected to be all voile and violets at tea-time.'

'Leaving the Honourable Gentleman out of the question,' said Val, 'and returning to your last sensational announcement, Campion, in which you stated that you were not enjoying our shooting and hunting, as it were, for private but for professional reasons, may I ask, if this is so, who put you on to it, and where is your hope of reward?'

'Oh, I shall get my fourpence, don't you worry, young sir,' said Mr Campion. 'The gent who put me up to this is a real toff.' He paused. Coming across the lawn towards them, sedate, and about as graceful as a circus elephant, was Mr Lugg. As he came nearer they saw that his immense white face wore an almost reverent expression.

''Ere,' he said huskily as he approached his master, 'see oo's come? Orders are for you to nip into the 'ouse and report in the library. Lumme,' he added, 'you in flannels, too. I believe there's an 'ole comin' in the sole of them shoes.'

Mr Campion rose to his feet. 'Don't worry, Lugg,' he said. 'I shouldn't think he'd go into that.'

In the general astonishment it was Penny whose curiosity found voice.

'You?' she said. 'He wants to see you? Whatever for?'

Mr Campion turned a mildly reproachful eye in their direction. 'I thought you'd have got it a long while before now,' he said. 'He is my employer. If all goes well I shall be able to treat you to a fish-and-chip supper tonight.'

Chapter 27

There were Giants in those Days

At half-past three in the afternoon, with the strong sunlight tracing the diamond pattern of the window panes on the polished floor of the Colonel's library, lending that great austere room some of the indolent warmth of the garden, five men surrounded the heavy table desk on which the yellow length of an historical document was spead.

The great house was pleasantly silent. There were birds singing in the creeper and the droning of a bumble bee against the panes, but the thick walls successfully shut out any sounds of domestic bustle. The air was redolent with the faint mustiness of old leather-bound books, mingling delightfully with the scent of the flowers from the bed outside the windows.

The distinguished stranger, a tall, grey-headed man with cold blue eyes and a curious dry little voice, coughed formally.

'There's really no need for me to read all this through, Colonel,' he said. 'After all, we've read it through together several times before. It makes one feel old. Every reading means another decade gone.'

He sighed and shot a faint, unexpectedly shy smile at Campion and the Professor, who were standing side by side. The old American was alert and deeply interested, but his companion stood fingering his tie awkwardly, an almost imbecile smile on his mild, affable face. Val stood at his father's elbow, his young face deadly serious, a distinct hint of nervousness in his manner. The memory of his first excursion to the secret room on the night of Mrs Shannon's death was still clear in his mind. Sir Percival himself was more human than Campion or the Professor had ever seen him before. In sharing the secret of the Room with his son he seemed to have halved a burden that had been a little over-heavy for him alone.

'I think this one clause will be sufficient,' the visitor continued, placing a forefinger on a rubric at the foot of the sheet. He cleared his throat again and began to read huskily and without expression.

'"And the said representative of Her Gracious Majesty or Her Heirs shall go up into the chamber accompanied by the master and

his eldest son, providing he be of sufficient age, and they shall show
him and prove to his satisfaction that the treasure which they hold in
the stead of the Crown be whole and free from blemish, that it may be
known to Us that they have kept their loyal and sacred trust. This
shall be done by the light of day that neither use of candle or lamp
shall be needed to show the true state of the said vessel.

'"Further, We also command that in times of trouble, or such days
as the House of Gyrth may be in danger, that the master allow two
witnesses to go with them, strong men and true, sworn to keep faith
and all secrecy as to the Treasure and the manner of its keeping.

'"Given under Our Hand and Seal, this day . . ." and so on. I
think that covers the matter, Colonel.'

His quiet voice died away, and rolling up the parchment he
returned it to his host who locked it in a dispatch-box on the table.

The visitor turned to Campion and the Professor.

'Strong men and true,' he said, smiling at them. 'Of course, I
understand, strictly speaking, my dear Albert, that "such days as the
House of Gyrth may be in danger" are past. But I certainly agree with
the Colonel that in the circumstances we might stretch a point in this –
er – archaic formula. It seems the only courtesy, Professor, that we
can extend to you for your tremendous assistance in this unfortunate
and distressing affair.'

The Professor made a deprecatory gesture. 'There's nothing I
would consider a greater honour,' he said.

Mr Campion opened his mouth to speak, but thought better of it,
and was silent.

The Colonel took a small iron instrument which looked like a tiny
crowbar from his desk and led the way out of the room. They followed
him through the hall and down the long stone corridor into the seldom
used banqueting room in the east wing. They passed no one in their
journey. Branch had gathered his myrmidons in their own quarters at
the back of the west wing, while Penny and Beth remained discreetly
in the drawing room.

In the cool shadow of the great apartment the Colonel paused and
turned to them, a slightly embarrassed expression in his very blue
eyes. The visitor relieved him of an awkward duty.

'The Colonel and I,' he began, prefacing his remark with his now
familiar cough, 'feel that we should adhere to tradition in this matter.
The entrance to the – er – chamber is, and always has been, a closely
guarded secret, known only to my predecessors and the Colonel's. I

feel sure that I shall offend neither of you if I ask you to lend me your handkerchiefs and allow me to blindfold you just until we approach the treasure.'

The Professor took out a voluminous silk bandanna which proved more suitable than Mr Campion's white cambric. The blindfolding was accomplished with great solemnity.

On any other occasion such an incident might have been absurd, but there was a deadly earnestness in the precaution which no one in the group could ignore after the terrifying events of the preceding weeks. Val's hand shook as he tied the knot behind Campion's head and some of his nervousness was conveyed to the other man. After all, they were about to share a secret of no ordinary magnitude. Campion had not forgotten the expression upon Mrs Shannon's face when she had looked up for a moment after peering into the window of the grim treasure house.

The Professor, too, was unusually apprehensive. It was evident that in spite of his vast store of archaic knowledge he had no inkling of what he was to expect.

The visitor's voice came to them in the darkness. 'Val, if you'll take Campion's arm I'll look after Professor Cairey. Colonel, will you go first?'

Val linked his arm through Campion's, and he felt himself being led forward, the last of a little procession.

'Look out,' Val's voice sounded unsteadily in his ear. 'The stairs begin here.'

They ascended, and once more the wood creaked beneath his feet. They went up in silence for what seemed a long time. There were so many turns that he lost his sense of direction almost immediately. He had suffered many odd experiences in his life, but this strange halting procession was more unnerving than anything he had ever known. Curiosity is the most natural of human emotions, but there came a point in the journey when he almost wished that the mystery might remain unsolved, for him at any rate, for ever. He could hear the Professor breathing hard in front of him, and he knew that it was not the steepness of the stairs which inconvenienced the old man.

Val's pressure on his arm increased. 'Wait,' he said so softly that he was scarcely audible. Then followed a period of silence, and they went on again. The stairs had ended and they were crossing a stone floor. Then again there was a halt. The air still smelt fresh and the song of the birds sounded very near.

'Step,' whispered Val, as the procession restarted. 'Keep your head down. I shall have to come behind you.'

Mr Campion felt himself clambering up a narrow stone spiral staircase, and here the air was scarcer and there was a faint, almost intangible smell of spices. He heard the grating of iron on stone and stepped forward on to a level floor. Val was close behind him, and once again there was the grating of the iron, and then complete silence. He felt his scalp tingling. He sensed that he was in a very small space, and with them he was certain, in the instinctive fashion that one is conscious of such things, there was something else, something incredibly old, something terrible.

'Take off the bandages.'

He was never sure whether it was the Colonel or the visitor who had spoken. The voice was unrecognizable. He felt Val's icy fingers pulling at the knot behind his head. Then the cambric slipped from his eyes.

The first thing of which he was conscious as he blinked was the extraordinary crimson light in the room, and he turned instinctively to its source, the circular window with the heavy stone framework which had been sealed at some time with blood-red glass. The sunlight outside was very strong so that the tiny cell seemed full of particles of glittering red dust.

Campion turned from the window and started violently. The Gyrths' secret lay revealed.

Set immediately below the window so that the light fell directly upon it was a little stone altar, and kneeling before it, directly in front of the huddled group, was a figure in full Tourney armour.

As Campion stared, a pulse in his throat throbbing violently, the light seemed to concentrate on the figure.

It was that of a giant, and at first he thought it was but an immense suit of black armour only, fashioned for a man of legendary stature, but as his eye travelled slowly down the great gyves to the wrists, he caught sight of the human hands, gnarled, yellow, and shapeless, like knotted willow roots. Between them, resting on the slab, was the Gyrth Chalice whose history was lost behind the veils of legend.

It was a little shallow bowl of red gold, washed from the English mountain streams before the Romans came. A little shallow bowl whose beaten sides showed the marks of a long-dead goldsmith's hammer, and in whose red heart a cluster of uncut rubies lay like blood, still guarded by the first Messire Gyrth who earned for Sanctuary its name.

Campion raised his eyes slowly to the head of the figure and was relieved to find that the visor was down. The head was thrown back, the mute iron face raised to the circular window through which Mrs Dick had peered.

There was utter silence in the little cell with its ancient frescoes and dust-strewn floor of coloured flags. The door by which they had entered was hidden in the stonework. Turning again, Campion saw the great sword of the warrior hanging on the wall behind the kneeling figure, the huge hilt forming a cross behind its head.

The Professor was gazing at the Chalice with tears in his eyes, a spontaneous tribute to its beauty which he did not attempt to hide.

As Campion stared at the figure he was obsessed by the uncanny feeling that it might move at any moment, that the mummified hands might snatch the sword from the wall and the great figure tower above the impious strangers who had disturbed his vigil. It was with relief that he heard the Colonel's quiet voice.

'If you are ready, gentlemen –'

No other word was spoken. Val retied the handkerchief and once again there was the grating of metal and the procession started on its return journey. The Professor stumbled once or twice on the stairs, and Campion felt that his own knees were a little unsteady. It was not that the sight had been particularly horrible, although there had been a suggestion about the hands that was not pleasant; nor did the idea of the lonely watcher keeping eternal vigil over the treasured relic he had won fill him with repugnance. But there had been something more than mortal about this ageless giant, something uncanny which filled him with almost superstitious awe, and he was glad that Penny did not know, that she could live and laugh in a house that hid this strange piece of history within its walls, unconscious of its existence.

They were still silent when once more they stood in the daylight in the old banqueting hall. The Colonel glanced at his watch.

'We meet the ladies for tea on the lawn in fifteen minutes,' he said. 'Mrs Cairey promised me she'd come, Professor.'

The old man dusted his hands abstractedly. There were plaster and cobwebs on all their clothes. Campion carried the Professor off to his room, leaving his host to attend to the other visitor.

No word of comment had been made, not did anyone feel that any such remark was possible.

In Mr Campion's pleasant Georgian room the tension relaxed.

'Lands sakes,' said the Professor, subsiding into a little tub chair by the window. 'Lands sakes.'

Mr Campion glanced over the lawn. The white table surrounded by garden chairs was set under the trees. Branch was already half-way towards it with a tea-wagon on which glittered the best silver, and a service which had been old when Penny's grandmother was a girl. Mrs Cairey, Beth and Penny, looking cool and charming, their flowered chiffon frocks sweeping the lawn, were admiring the flower-beds in the far distance. It was a graceful, twentieth-century picture, peaceful and ineffably soothing, incredibly removed from the world they had just left. The tinkle of china came pleasantly to them as Branch began to arrange the table.

They were interrupted by the unceremonious entrance of Lugg with a tray bearing glasses, a siphon and a decanter.

'Branch sent me up with this lot,' he remarked. 'I should 'ave it. A b and s will do yer good any time o' day.'

Even the Professor, who restricted himself to one whisky-and-soda a day out of deference to his wife's principles, accepted the proffered drink gratefully. Lugg hung about, apparently seeking an opening for conversation.

'They ain't 'alf doing 'Is Nibs proud downstairs,' he said. 'I've bin 'elping that girl I took a fancy to to clean the silver all the afternoon. Old Branch didn't take 'is eyes of me the 'ole time. If 'e counted them spoons once 'e counted 'em a dozen times. I couldn't 'elp pinchin' this.' He laid a delicate pair of Georgian sugar-tongs on the dressing-table with a certain pride.

His master looked at him in disgust. 'Don't lay your filthy bone at my feet,' he said. 'What do you expect me to do with it?'

'Put it back for me,' said Mr Lugg unabashed. 'It won't look so bad if you get noticed. I've got me record to think of. There's nothing in writin' against you.'

'Go away,' said Campion. 'I'm going to sell you to a designer of children's cuddle-toys. You can pack my things after tea, by the way. We go back to Town tomorrow morning.'

'Then you've finished?' said the Professor, looking up.

Campion nodded. 'It's over,' he said. 'They'll stick to their rules, you know. Their employee is dead; that finishes it. I was talking to old poker-back downstairs. He's convinced we shall hear no more from them. The Maharajah has had his turn. They're connoisseurs more than criminals, you see. This is so definitely not one of their successes that I should think they'll turn their attention to Continental museums again for a bit.'

'I see.' The Professor was silent for some moments. Then he frowned. 'I wonder –' he began, and hesitated.

Campion seemed to understand the unspoken thought, for he turned to Lugg.

'You can go back to Audrey,' he said. 'Any more thieving, and I'll tell her about the picture of Greta Garbo you keep under your pillow.'

As the door was closed behind the disconsolate and still inquisitive Lugg, the Professor remained silent, and Campion went on.

'I couldn't understand why my precious boss downstairs hadn't told me about the second Chalice at the beginning,' he said. 'I see it now. He's a man of very conservative ideas, and after the awe-inspiring oath of secrecy I suppose he thought he had no alternative but to let me find it out for myself. That complicated things at the start, but I'm not sure it didn't make it easier for us in the long run.'

The Professor nodded absently. His mind was still dwelling upon the experience of the afternoon.

'What a lovely, lovely thing,' he said. 'I may sound a bit inhuman, but when I looked at that Chalice today, it occurred to me that probably in the last fifteen hundred years it has cost the lives of Heaven knows how many thieves and envious people, by looking at it. Campion, do you know, I thought it was worth it.'

Mr Campion did not answer. The thought in his mind was one that had rankled ever since he had stood with the others in that little painted cell, looking in at the Chalice and its guardian. What had Mrs Dick seen when she had looked in the window that had differed from their own experience? She had been no easily frightened woman, nor was hers an imaginative nature. He spoke aloud, almost without realizing it.

'What exactly did she see when she looked through that window? Why did she say "no"? Who did she say it to? Just what was it that made her let go?'

He paused. Outside on the lawn the chatter of feminine voices was coming nearer. Mr Campion was still puzzled.

'I don't understand it,' he said.

The Professor glanced up at him. 'Oh, that?' he said. 'That's quite obvious. The light was shining directly upon the figure. The head was raised to the window, if you remember.'

'Yes, but —' said Mr Campion, and was silent.

'Yes,' said the Professor thoughtfully, 'I think it's perfectly clear. On the night of the birthday, when she looked in, the visor was up. She saw his face . . . I'm afraid it may be a very shocking sight.'

'But she spoke,' said Mr Campion. 'She spoke as if she was replying to someone. And I heard something, I swear it.'

The Professor leant forward in his chair and spoke with unusual emphasis. 'My very dear boy,' he said, 'I'll say this. It doesn't do to dwell on these things.'

The gentle clangour of the gong in the hall below broke in upon the silence.